EXPLORER

ARISE 5:

Jez Cajiao

Arise :Explorer

Contents

<u>Dedication</u>

Okay everyone, well, this book is a little different as today the thanks section which is normally me thanking several people for their help, is actually going to be a dedication to a little girl.
This book is dedicated to Olivia Fuesdale as thanks to her and her parents for their kind donation to our local nursery to help raise funds for another child's needs.
Things like this, a donation with absolutely nothing expected in return and just the knowledge that you're helping improve things for another?
They give us all hope that maybe things are going to turn out alright after all.
I've included a little cameo character for Olivia in this book as well, a little devilkin girl, and I hope it'll make you smile one day.
I wanted to just say thank you, that's all!

-Jez

Arise Alpha Synopsis

Steve, a one-time thief and enforcer, is hiding on the Greek party island of Crete. He was involved in a botched bank robbery, and rather than the hundred grand plus each of the team were promised, there was a hundred grand in total.

Seeing this, and having already decided that he would run as soon as he had "his" money, Steve chose to skip the splitting of the cash, and moved straight to hiding out. With all the money.

He flew via Toronto, taking multiple flights, until he finally wound up in Crete, paying a corrupt Greek policeman for a recently deceased tourist's ID.

The next few months passed as a dream: drinking, partying, and working the bars of Crete; a new friend moved into Steve's apartment and life was good.

Right up until he decided to throw it all away, risking his life to save a pair of drowning women he'd met earlier in the day. He rode his bike off the cliffs, diving out over the treacherous rocks below, and swam down, rescuing first Marie, and then later Amanda.

Other tourists nearby had captured the whole thing on camera, and the footage went viral, helped in part when word spread that not only was he a "hero" for saving them, but that he'd been fired in turn because he was late for work.

The footage was shared, and quickly made its way to an enforcer named Kevin Sinclair, one of the organizers of the original robbery. He, in turn, hired a local ex-army, Russian enforcer named Mikhail to punish Steve, and his friends when they got in the way.

Steve, however, had already vanished.

His bike, abandoned in the sea, had begun to leak gas, and in turn the local police took his ID—including the fake—as well as his money, forcing Steve to recover his bike before he could flee the island.

In the process of attempting to raise the bike, Steve was pinned beneath it, underwater, when a hidden section of an old ship collapsed. His bike took him with it into the depths, and as he blacked out from asphyxiation, his last sight was a tentacled metallic-looking monstrosity attaching itself to his face.

Steve woke sometime later, alone, wet, and shaking with the cold. Once Steve realized where he probably was—buried deep in the bowels of an ancient shipwreck—he started to try to escape, putting the tentacled monstrosity down to asphyxia and a passing sea creature.

The superstructure was old, he realized, later finding it to be millennia more ancient than he'd first guessed. Over the course of the next several hours, Steve would find out just how old the ship—an actual long-abandoned spacecraft— would be.

The human race, he discovered, were biological weapons, ones long since discarded by our uncaring creators. In the process of escaping the ship, Steve was wounded, dying from blood loss and hypothermia; he begged for help, and his plea passed a level that a damaged, failing medical AI deemed appropriate to enable it to respond.

Arise :Explorer

He was given a choice, and with no time to examine the options, agrees to a "Support package." Unfortunately for him, the ship's supplies of anesthetic were long depleted, and the first stage of the Support package integration involved a full skeletal "strip," with everything from muscles to eyes being replaced.

When he awakened, over a day later, he was massively changed, rebuilt as a prime Biological Weapon Variant, and ready for war, with his own nanites, in addition to a nanite harvesting tool integrated into his right forearm—something that all humans, or BWVs as the system designates them, have—now unlocked.

Through the wonders of the nanotech, he was able to defeat the incoming basic security systems designed to terminate the trespasser, as the security AI attempted to kill him.

By the time Steve had escaped what he had thought was a sunken and forgotten container ship—and he now knew to be Facility 6B—he had managed to unlock both his War and Hack trees, investing points to make himself more versatile and dangerous.

Steve went back to the shore, finding the bike he'd borrowed to return to the beach was still there, and used it to return—naked—to his apartment.

On arrival, Steve climbed up onto the rear balcony and looked inside the apartment, finding his friend and houseguest, Dave, being beaten for information by the local enforcer. Torn between stepping in and saving his friend, and maintaining secrecy, he hesitated, only for Marie, the girl he'd first saved, to knock on the front door, and be captured by Mikhail.

Steve decided that he couldn't leave them to Mikhail's tender mercies and attacks, being soundly beaten, as the ex-soldier demonstrated that the training afforded to Russian special forces was significantly higher than Steve's own ex-army training was.

In a last-ditch attempt to escape and defeat Mikhail, he triggered the Assault specialization tree under War. Instantly, the tables were turned, as the inbuilt system guided him to a vicious and resounding victory. Steve ordered Marie and Dave out, and warned Sinclair, the enforcer back in England, to stay away or he'll suffer the same fate; then he killed Mikhail.

Using the Harvest function of the system embedded in his forearm, Steve stripped Mikhail of his nanites, gaining a number of attuned and usable nanites, as well as a larger number of corrupted ones, that his own systems began the process of purifying.

Dave helped Steve to burn down the apartment, concealing the damage done to the body of Mikhail, and his identity, and the two friends escaped with Marie.

Marie left them in a bar, before returning shortly with her friend Amanda, and as Steve told a much abridged and sanitized story of his adventure—keeping the nanites and ship out of it entirely—they are joined by the rest of Amanda and Marie's group.

Jonas, who led the team, recruited Steve and Dave on the promise of high wages and adventure, including the opportunity to kill criminals and murderers. Steve took the position, planning to use it as a cover to harvest more nanites and upgrade himself, while Dave took it on the grounds of a lot of money.

As a trial, Jonas sent Steve to recover his ID from the police station, and to insert a device into their network, opening it to the team, while Dave was sent to seduce a reporter who had been investigating a spate of recent murders.

Steve left the group, upgraded his Hack abilities, invested nanites recovered from Mikhail and gained access to the police systems, before he bluffed his way in, recovering the ID and money, and planting the data spike, and escaping.

Jonas and the team were surprised, but pleased at his success, and they went to observe Dave's trial. They arrived, just as Dave and the reporter were kidnapped, the group she had been tracking deciding to remove the threat.

Jonas, Steve, and Amanda followed the group into the old catacombs outside of Heraklion, splitting up when the tracks led in different directions.

Steve rushed ahead, finding a father and daughter being systematically slaughtered in a pit by *werewolves*. Steve's system identified them as an alternate "viable line" of Biological Weapon Variants.

Steve attacked the werewolves, harvesting them as he fought, and using the corrupted nanites to form tentacles of weaponized nanites, slaughtered the werewolves, as Amanda—not knowing Steve's true capabilities—ran to get backup.

By the time Jonas and Amanda returned—having rescued Dave and killed several other werewolves—Steve claimed to have killed the werewolves with the silver-edged knife Jonas had given him on arrival.

The father agreed, backing Steve, and the daughter had already lost consciousness, leaving Jonas and Amanda suspicious of Steve, but without any evidence.

Jonas suspected that Steve was a fresh "Arisen," and took him deeper into the catacombs, testing him and his abilities, and in the process, disturbed several ghouls; then he frantically escaped, his suspicions met.

Once they had joined the group outside, Jonas arranged for them to be retrieved by their shadowy employers, before having an argument with Steve and abandoning him by the side of the road, warning him that the vampires and their servants have his scent and that anywhere he ran to would only ensure more locals died.

Jonas left him, believing that it would force Steve to either admit to what he was, and they would have discovered a newly rising immortal—gaining much in their employer's eyes—or that he was a "plant" from an enemy faction.

Steve invested in his stealth abilities, hiding as the vampire and its master, Hans, arrived by the side of the road, and Hans ordered the vampire ahead. Hans then spoke to Steve, unable to locate him, but able to sense his presence.

Hans offered to teach Steve, to induct him into his new world and to answer any questions, before ostensibly leaving. Steve killed the ghouls still there, before finding Hans hadn't really left; he'd simply moved off to observe.

Again, Hans made the offer, before leaving Steve to go and rescue his former teammates and Dave.

When Steve reached the others at the retrieval site, he found one of their number—Dan, their tech specialist—dead, and the others captured, wounded, and at the vampire's mercy.

Arise :Explorer

Steve killed the remaining ghouls and the vampire, before being captured as Jonas's master—Shamal, a member of the Blessed faction—arrived.

Taking advantage of a distraction, Steve escaped, Dave helping him, and the friends parted ways, with Dave being forced to help the Blessed faction as part of Jonas's team in truth, and Steve hiding in a nearby gully overnight.

The next morning, Steve recovered the team's abandoned drone, hijacking it, and used it to guide himself around people until he reached an old friend and borrowed a motorbike, setting off for the meeting with Hans, needing more information.

Hans was as good as his word, filling Steve in on the ostensible history of the two groups. The Blessed are essentially believers in "guiding" mankind to their future, while keeping them firmly underfoot as the cattle they are.

The Awakened and Accursed, on the other hand, the faction that Hans belonged to—or paid lip service to, at least—believed that they had been cursed with immortality. Some, like Hans, simply viewed it as their right to party and enjoy life; most believed that they had been cheated of their meeting with the gods, and they will do anything to "fix" that, up to and including starting a nuclear war and killing all life.

Steve chose not to join Hans, but agreed to reach out when he had more questions. Hans, in turn, was glad to have an unaffiliated and apparently skilled new Arisen to talk to, having been pushed to the outside of his own faction by his unwillingness to aid in the genocides planned.

Hans left Steve to his own devices, while maintaining an unobtrusive watch over the younger man, and Steve returned to the nearby area of Malia, moving into a cheap apartment while he planned his next step. Before he settled, a local fight broke out, and he intervened to help two new holiday workers from being blackmailed, before leaving them to stammer their thanks.

Over the next day or so, he crafted prototype armor, designing it despite being too low in nanites to actually deploy it, then returned to the catacombs, hunting more werewolves and other creatures, before encountering two huge figures on ornate thrones guarding an entrance to a further section.

He was warned by the system that they were "Beta Level Threats" and were far beyond him, and escaped, looting several ancient artifacts as he went.

On his return to the apartment, he hid again until the sunrise, when he strolled out onto the roof terrace, half asleep to relax in the sunlight.

Realizing he's not alone, Steve silently berated himself for the stupidity, as the workers he rescued previously had been joined by several others, including an old acquaintance of his and Dave's. He also met two girls who were with the group; one realized he's the eponymous hero who saved people only days ago and vanished, and attempted to film him.

Steve remotely hacked and erased her phone, before making his excuses and leaving them to it. Once inside his room, he moved quickly, gathering up all evidence of himself, before sneaking out, believing that the group had moved on.

Unfortunately, outside he bumped into the second woman, Ingrid, a Danish archeologist. She recognized the dragon staff he carried—looted from the catacombs—and forced herself on him, demanding answers to where it was looted from.

Rather than cause a fuss where others might see, he allowed her to come with him, then gifted her the staff, asking her to leave him be. She kissed him, and for a brief moment he let himself just be a man with a beautiful woman on a sun-drenched island, rather than an immature immortal, hunted on all sides.

When Ingrid insisted on coming with him, wanting more details on the artifacts and unwilling to accept his refusal, he gave in, knowing it was a mistake, but desperate to hold onto the last vestiges of his humanity.

He took her farther across the island, helping her to arrange shipping for the dragon staff to her own museum, before taking her to dinner and arranging a room for the pair, one with twin beds.

The pair danced around each other as he attempted to use her to translate the writing on the artifacts, searching for clues as to the truth of history and "his kind." She, in turn, tried to force him to take her to the original site he'd looted the artifacts from, unaware of the infestation of lycanthropes and other creatures that still survived there.

Ingrid called in a friend, Lars, a well-respected archaeologist, to help her, and he set off, flying in.

The pair eventually gave in to mutual attraction and slept together, moving to a larger room, and made friends with the hotelier, Val. Val directed them to a second "palace" on the south side of the island that he believed Ingrid would find interesting, and where Steve would be able to find more evidence of what he was seeking.

Although the ruins were interesting, and Steve deployed his newly upgraded drone to show them the site from the air, the taverna that Steve expected to get information from—a "rescue" center for dogs injured in dog-fighting rings—instead turned out to be a cover for another group of werewolves, connected to the first.

When they attacked, and Steve revealed himself to Ingrid, she left, heartbroken and confused. Steve, hurt, decided to finish the fight, harvesting the dead and then hunting the pack leader who fled into a nearby cave.

The cave turned out to be a much larger catacomb, with a trapped creature that the ancient people of Thera and the Minoans had captured. The Reta Variant was eventually defeated, but Steve was gravely injured in the process, collapsing as soon as it was constrained again.

Ingrid, who had control of the drone, and had unknowingly taken Steve's phone in her bag, had seen the fight and the injuries he suffered. She returned, and after apologizing to him, recovered several of the bodies from the taverna. Steve, in turn, uses an unlocked ability called System Replenishment—essentially an advanced and technological version of cannibalism—to strip the dead of their genetics and biological matter to repair himself.

Over the next few hours, Ingrid explored the site; then the pair got replacement clothing—Ingrid's was ruined by the bodies she recovered and dragged to Steve—and new phones, tablets, etc.

Arise :Explorer

Eventually the pair hired a car and went to meet Lars at the airport. Ingrid, who now had a friend to help her, eventually convinced Steve to come fully clean about who and what he was, back at the hotel.

The trio returned to the site, finding the owners had returned, searching for unpaid rent, and bodies have been found. Lars started the process to buy the site and its surrounding lands, to "find" the archaeological site later and have a viable way of bringing the artifacts to the light again.

Upon return to the hotel that night, Lars and Ingrid spent the entire night arguing over translations and more, deciding that Atlantis was most likely real, and all the issues that would cause for archeologists.

Steve left the pair to sleep, and on the way to visit a local potential hidden site, came across a family who had fallen victim to people smugglers. Steve rescued the mother—who'd been taken due to her looks, when the father and two children were discarded—and he killed the majority of the smugglers.

Although the rest of the smugglers were killed, the "boss" escaped, and Steve returned the mother to her family, paying for them to stay in the hotel that he, Ingrid, and Lars were staying in.

Leaving them to recover and feeling he'd finally done something worthwhile, he went to the site he planned to visit first, and found a hidden cave system. Inside it was a woman, eons old, encased in crystal that was slowly growing and converting what was left of her body into itself.

He also discovered that the crystal was actively lethal to nanites, and that the long-dead Minoans and Therians were harvesting it, using it in creating weapons that were in turn used to fight the monsters of the ancient world.

Upon his return to the hotel, though, Steve found Hans and other Arisen waiting for him. Hans convinced him to go peacefully, as the alternative was the utter destruction of the area by another Arisen, the sadistic Athena.

Steve explained the truth of the situation, and the discovery he made, to Ingrid, Lars, and Val, injecting a laptop he recovered earlier from the people smugglers with nanites and upgrading it to help them.

Then he left, and was taken to an Arisen sub, hidden offshore. Steve was examined by the Arisen scientists and doctors, and although he managed to hide the majority of what he was—they had no clue about the ship or their technological beginnings—they did know that he was special, and they set out to find out all they can.

They chose to do so by spending the next three years torturing him over and over to death, reasoning that they were expanding their species' knowledge, and that as he can't really die, there's no long-term loss.

By the end, they found out all they could through destructive methods, and had moved to drug-induced programming as methods of control, attempting to learn ways that Steve was able to sense—albeit in a limited fashion—certain metals.

The end goal of this research was ostensibly to enable them to find and recover long-lost Arisen who were bound in metal coffins and hidden at sea. The Arisen were not above cruelty for cruelty's sake, however, and were amusing themselves with the torture.

Hans, while this was going on, had been protecting Ingrid, Val, and Lars, as well as forcing their council to intervene on Steve's behalf.

The end result was that Ingrid was permitted access to Steve, while Steve, drugged and compelled, had no clue who she was, as his "wife"—an Arisen by the name of Vitoria—amused herself by making him beg her for sex and more in front of Ingrid.

The drugs used to keep Steve pliable and confused were by necessity extremely powerful, and when a kink in the feedline stopped the drug, his mind began to clear.

Confused and faking sleep, Steve managed to force the line free, and quickly regained his wits, finding, to his dismay, that the reason he's incessantly vomiting—the only constant in his life currently—was because the Arisen had been testing the effect of force-feeding liquified humans to him.

They were unaware that it was the nanites that were responsible for his, and their, abilities, but one of the strongest of their oldest members was a cannibal, and they sought to find any connection between Steve's meteoric rise in power and that ancient.

The end result was that for months they'd been essentially feeding him on a diet of nanites, one that his own systems were frantically attempting to hold onto and assimilate.

When Vitoria and her companion brought Ingrid in to clean the room, and Steve saw her, all his memories rushed back. Knowing who she was, and who she was to him, triggered a chain reaction that unlocked his nanites.

Seeing the way that the Arisen beat Ingrid and had clearly been doing so for a while, Steve went nuclear and killed Vitoria, before being trapped in his room. The hardened walls held him for a short while, but with the nanites in his system now purified and in vast quantities, he purged his body of all contamination, before activating his armor, and creating a gravitational cannon.

Steve escaped his prison, slaughtering the guards on the way out, and all who stood between him and Ingrid, rescuing her, and declaring "open season" on all the Arisen who stand against him, before deploying wings and destroying the roof of Athena's medical wing, escaping with Ingrid in his arms.

<u>Arise Dark Crusader Synopsis</u>

Steve and Ingrid landed on the abandoned island of Skantzoura, Ingrid suffering from the cold of flight, as Steve began to learn to control his new armor. The distributed neurons of the armor's management system prevented him from removing it for several hours, and the pair explored, catching each other up on the last few years from their point of view.

Ingrid explained how she came to be at Athena's island as a servant and that Hans had been fighting to free Steve for three years, while Steve explained his new abilities, and they made a plan.

In the short-term, they needed money, clothing, and safety, and the decision was made to plunder a moored yacht for clothes and to enable them to clean up, before hitting a cash machine and finding a cheap hotel.

The first yacht was badly damaged by Steve's inexperience in flight, and they were forced to land on a second one. Ingrid made the most of the shower, before Steve unlocked the ability to "repair" others, as the system designates healing.

Upon using the skill on Ingrid, returning her—despite horrific pain—to perfect health, Steve was issued a quest, unlocking a new "tree" dedicated to the Support classes. Before the pair could fully explore the new situation, they were forced to escape as the owners' children came to check on the yacht.

Steve and Ingrid flew to a quiet nearby town on the mainland and used an old train—after raiding an ATM—to travel to Athens. Steve unlocked more of his Support tree and researched the new quest—to heal multiple people—before scaring Ingrid witless as the data download rendered him unconscious.

On arrival, Steve talked Ingrid into staying at a luxury boutique hotel, under the false identity of the "Athertons," hacking the system and ensuring that they were classed as returning guests, who have received a free upgrade to the highest levels, due to unexplained issues in the past. Issues that Steve has inserted into the hotel's systems.

The pair bluffed their way in, and were accepted, meeting James, the suite's butler, the next morning. After they spun a tale of being the victims of a robbery to him, James set about to "replace" everything they need, from clothing to toiletries and more, including electronics and underwear.

Steve and Ingrid set off the next night to begin their new plan to raise funds and get themselves out of reach of the majority of the Arisen, as Ingrid explained her plans, ones she'd spent the last three years working on.

The couple decided to convert a trawler, if they could find one, into a luxury vessel, to provide both stability and safety, as well as plenty of room. They agreed that they'd need to hire and develop staff, recruiting engineers, soldiers, researchers, and more, eventually using the team to bring some of the more desperately needed alien tech to the world.

Steve realized that in order to gain access to more "points" to spend in his upgrade trees, he needed to complete quests, and the first of those was the multiple-tier healing one recently granted to him.

That night, while Ingrid slept, Steve traveled to a local hospital, raiding several morgues on the way and stealing any viable nanites. Once there, he encountered a doctor, just before he would have stepped off the roof to his death. Steve saved him and forced the doctor to explain, discovering that a child lies dying beneath them, due to a mixture of honest mistakes and happenchance, with her best prospect of a replacement heart now lost.

Steve realized the opportunity that the situation granted, and to prevent questions, deployed his armor, now switched to a more impressive and imposing model with glowing eyes, declaring that he "will heal the child."

The night passed in a blur as he healed as many as he could, before returning to Ingrid, exhausted but ecstatic. The pair agreed that this situation gave them an opportunity to unlock trees and abilities that would be beneficial and help to make sure that they'd be safe in the future.

The first phase, however, was to get money, and both the local criminal and gambling elements would provide that easily, if not willingly.

On the way to the casino—having decided that as most casinos were rigged to ensure the "house" wins, then hacking them and flipping the tables so that they won instead was fair play—they found that the limo had additional hidden cameras, and Steve hacked them, shutting them down.

On arrival, Ingrid played on the machines, ostensibly losing money, while Steve worked on the Hack tree, moving from device to device, completing minor quests and gaining more experience with his abilities, as well as earning extra points, before the pair start to cheat.

The casino quickly banned the pair as they revel in their "luck," winning over four hundred thousand euros, and in the limo on the way back, Steve found the cameras had been reset.

Steve explained the situation to Ingrid, hacking them and shutting them down again, but in the process, found a much more paranoid security setup on the attached storage device, failing to hack it and instead triggering a program that wipes the data.

On return to the hotel, they were soon visited, at the open-air restaurant, by Yanni, a representative of one of the local mobs, an Albanian gangster who threatened Steve and Ingrid and demanded restitution…"or else."

Steve, being the gracious and subtle man that he was, hacked his phone and pointed out that Yanni's family were just as accessible to him, as he and Ingrid were to the mobster.

Yanni left, furious, and the hotel apologized for the situation, with James arranging guards for Ingrid while Steve returned to the children's wing of the hospital and resumed his healing.

Several hours later, he was interrupted by a call from Ingrid, panicked. Yanni and several of his men had broken in, killing both the guards and James the butler, and kidnapped her.

He tore his way through the nearest wall, launching himself into the air, and returned to the hotel, but too late. In a rage, he threw himself into the problem of the nanites, and found a way both to unlock the basic "healing" process of the nanites in James, and then forced his own to "fix" him, restarting the older man's heart and bringing him back to life.

Using the pattern he had seen for the encryption on the storage device the limo had been using, he retreated to a high point over the city. When he quickly identified another of the gang's vehicles, he struck, tearing the roof off and questioning the driver.

When he gets limited cooperation, he instead used the driver's body to smash the skylight on the second location he identified the encryption being used, before raiding it and slaughtering all but one of the people he found there.

The last person hid in an emergency secure vault, and Steve flipped the situation, having used local computers and found the location Ingrid was being held. He then locked the vault from the outside, and sent the location, as well as the unlocking codes, to the local branch of Interpol.

Ingrid, meanwhile, was being taken to the gang's headquarters. She met Yanni's mother, the gang kingpin, and she distracted them all, until Steve could arrive, shielding her with his wings as they fired on the pair.

Then she asked Steve, very nicely, to "hurt these people, please."

The pair escaped a few minutes later, this time with the gang's hard drives and the boss's laptop, including her bank access to over a hundred and forty million euros.

Ingrid and Steve decided that they couldn't risk returning to the hotel, not now, and instead went to a cheap "no-tell motel" and spent the night, breaking into a store on the way to dress Ingrid.

The next morning, the pair made their way to a local marina and purchased a yacht of their own, getting the seller blind drunk and getting a few lessons on how to sail as they went.

Steve bought some new clothes, realizing he's far too distinctive in the tailored suit he'd been wearing from the visit to the casino, and abandoned the suit in the bin at a marina shop.

The following morning, Steve and Ingrid made their way to a local shop, buying all the basics they think they'll need, introducing themselves to the couple who own the next yacht over, before being invited over for dinner later, along with their "uncle," who waited inside their yacht for them to return.

On entering, the pair were overjoyed to find it was James, the butler, who has tracked them down, then calmly requested an explanation, before joining them as the first member of the team.

James joined the team both for a flat fee of two million dollars a year, and, far more important to him, the healing of his son, Michael, who had a replication issue related to his nanites, mis-diagnosed as an autoimmune disorder.

James then assisted the pair in recruiting Zac and Casey, a married couple for the crew. Zac was a world-class engineer, with a somewhat murky background, and Casey, his wife, was a highly experienced and skilled steward and qualified marine geologist.

Next recruited was Jay Beraz, a highly qualified American chef, and finally Jack Cameron, recruited to the position of deckhand and general dogsbody, as well as tech support.

While James and Ingrid attempted to make contact with the doctor at the hospital, aware that he is now likely being watched by the Arisen, Steve acted as a decoy, reaching out to Hans to make contact, and carried a large boulder into the air, unbeknownst to Athena and her people, who were in a yacht below him.

When Athena interrupted the call and threatened Steve, he attacked, using the boulder as an almost orbital attack weapon, devastating her yacht and killing over half the crew aboard as it impacted.

Steve followed the boulder into the yacht, dispatching the majority of the security contingent, before fighting—and killing—Athena in single combat.

Steve stripped her of her nanites, as Hans killed the last of her security contingent, with the surviving Oracan and staff swearing allegiance to Steve.

Hans took over, agreeing to loot and raise the yacht, with it being repaired and given to Steve as a conquest, and Hans covering the costs, in exchange for half of the loot.

Steve escaped and Hans claimed to the rest of the Arisen that he was playing along with Steve to keep him close and maintain contact, while Hans instead had thrown his lot in with Steve, joining his fledgling faction.

Steve looted a safe from the sunken yacht on the way out, and returned to his own yacht, stripping the safe with the help of Ingrid and James, looting papers—both normal documents and rolled-up ones encased in wax, jewelry, bags of coins and gemstones, as well as…a desiccated body, hermetically sealed in glass.

The body was discovered to be that of Scylla, the second of Athena's daughters, kept imprisoned for centuries, according to Hans, for crossing her mother.

Steve appealed to Hans to help him set up a détente with the Arisen, basically offering to leave them alone, provided they leave him alone. Hans advised against it, pointing out that as the only one who can comprehensively and permanently kill the other Arisen, Steve was a massive threat, one that may be "resolved" with the use of nuclear weapons.

Some of the other Arisen might not want to use them, but if need be? The loss of a city to a "terrorist attack" that resulted in Steve's death would be an acceptable cost for many.

Steve agreed to keep hidden for now, and Hans filled Steve, Ingrid, and James in on more of the Arisen's ancient history, before recommending the group go off and essentially train, keeping a low profile.

Over the next few days, the remaining crew arrive, and Steve upgraded his abilities to include creation of separate artifacts, allowing him to upgrade the engines, as well as convert random matter into "null blocks," blocks of compressed high-density matter that can be used as the building blocks for almost anything.

With that done, Steve and the crew set sail for the Ambracian Gulf, a location Ingrid had identified as a potential monster nest. En route, Steve and Ingrid called her parents, having arranged a secure communication line. Steve was grilled on their relationship and condition by Ingrid's family, and over the next few days, they made several calls, getting to know one another.

Arise :Explorer

By the time the yacht landed at the Ambracian Gulf, the crew knew that there was more going on than they'd been told, but trusting James, they agreed to wait until the end of the trip for answers. Jack was left aboard ship, and the others accompanied Steve and Ingrid to the suspected infestation, finding that the local rangers were very welcoming.

At first, Steve and the others put this down to the donation they made, but as the mission went on, it became clear this was not the case.

The fens were the home to two species—beyond humanity and the "known" species—the fen nymphs were more or less friendly, although they did attack the party, both for trespassing and due to being forced to capture others for their masters, the mavka.

The second species—the mavka—were far more aggressive, a snake-like naga species with a short-range hydro-warp capability. The mavka attacked Steve, and when that went badly for them, they attempted to escape using this ability, and accidentally dragged Steve along with them to the main nest.

Steve fought and slaughtered the rest of the nest, including the queen, a massive BWV. Upon killing the remaining mavka, Steve completed his most recent quest to protect the Support class, gaining three points in the War and one in the Espionage trees. The three War points were spent, unfortunately, in surviving the injuries the mavka queen had inflicted due to her terrible acidic bite and jaws.

The three points were spent on the Armor sub-tree specifically with Biological Weapons—to understand the acidic compound better—then Atmospheric Integration and Biological Cleansing, to both provide oxygen regardless of the location, and to remove the harmful buildups of toxins.

While Steve fought and recovered, Ingrid spent time with the fen nymphs, convincing them of her potential as an ally, and when Steve returned, depositing the head—almost as big as he was—of their most feared predator, the mavka queen, the nymphs swore fealty.

One of their number, Par'a'nuit, joined the crew, bonding to three trees planted in the hot tub, and began to evolve after escorting the crew down into the underground ruins.

The locals, no longer being drugged and forced unknowingly into accepting the mavka's orders, slowly awakened and were distressed over the years of events they'd been living through. Steve and the others left, filling Jack in on the realities of life, and scaring him half to death in the process.

Upon contacting Hans, they found he was under watch by the other factions, and he recommended Steve go to Russia, specifically to the wild forested lands where other monster species still lived, hidden. Then he destroyed the phone and cut off communication for their safety.

Steve agreed, and although the others weren't happy about it, they eventually accepted that with Steve headed north and leaving enough traces along the way, that freed them up to take action to the south.

The group planned to buy an abandoned recycling plant in the Sudanese desert, one filled with radioactive and biological waste, using the converters to reduce the waste to usable null blocks, which simultaneously gave them a legal and easily verified income.

Eventually Ingrid agreed to the plan, but on the condition that Steve met her parents, properly.

James arranged for Ingrid's father, Anders, to "win" a prize: an exclusive dining experience at the most expensive and prestigious restaurant in Denmark for the entire family. Although Anders knew the truth, the rest of the family didn't, and were surprised when Steve and Ingrid arrived.

Steve admitted more to Anders than he should have, and the older man, due to his navy background and current "titan of industry" experience, signed on with them as a general manager and front man for the company.

Steve and Anders agreed that the criminal element that were prevalent in the city had no need of the wealth they'd been making, and Anders sent Steve after some of the local criminals, notably an Albanian gang focused on both people and drug smuggling.

Steve's approach, and his subsequent loss of control, both horrified and impressed Anders and the crew, as Steve slaughtered his way through the lower echelons to the top of the chain. In the process, he captured the leadership, stealing their bank accounts and draining them into the one the group was using.

Unfortunately, an innocent was killed during the mission, and Steve lost control, his rage let loose as he slaughtered the remaining gang members, before being caught on camera by a news channel's helicopter.

Steve, in a fit of rage, nearly attacked the helicopter, being stopped by Ingrid calling him and demanding he back down. Steve realized the situation he'd created, and the only available solution.

He escaped, delivering the money and laptops taken from the gang, then left, heading to Russia ahead of schedule. Ingrid was furious, and her father, who had gone to the yacht, intervened, learning the truth of Steve and his situation.

Steve allowed himself to be tracked leaving the city, and Ingrid and the others left quickly, heading back to the Med, and toward Sudan.

The next several weeks flew by, as Steve vanished into the wilds of Russia, reaching and passing Tunguska, before he encountered a wild tribe of Oracan, led by Eto, spending time with them after fighting one of their number to earn a place.

He learned the language, more or less, and traveled with a small group, thinking they were guiding him, when in reality they were taking him—as ordered—to the Erlking.

The Erlking was revealed to be one of the ancients that artificially uplifted the human race, and, when annoyed by Steve, slaughtered him in several horrific ways, after the Oracan left, returning to their tribe.

The Erlking agreed to give Steve limited help and advice, on the condition that he both heal the world, and, to prevent him taking the opportunity to gain power, he must leave it.

When Steve agreed, the location of two more of the buried facilities were shared with him: one buried on Yuzhny Island and the other sunken in Lake Tengiz, with suspected ones off the coast of Jakarta and another near Algeria south of Monaco and west of Sardinia. An additional potential site was due west of the

Pillars of Hercules in the Atlantic. Lastly, he was given a quest to help the Oracan, both saving them, and power-leveling Steve.

While leaving the details open-ended, the Erlking was also horrifically powerful enough, and unwilling enough to allow a new faction to rise and control the planet, that Steve agreed, regardless, knowing that at the least he would be able to save Ingrid and the others and leave them in a position of strength before he had to depart.

He was joined by Maribellya—or Belle, as she was more colloquially known—an elder dryad, and one of only four left in the world with her sisters: Barishka, hidden in a valley far to the south; in the middle of Africa, Annai lives hidden on an island paradise; and Jamya, the youngest, buried long ages ago in a landslide.

Steve agreed to help Belle, due to her potential to rewild the Sahara and other places, her natural growth abilities being powerful additional tools, and took her with him to search for the Oracan.

On arrival, he found that many of the clan's warriors had been killed, and fought off the werewolves, before allowing Eto and some of the other warriors to join him, tracking the werewolves back to their village.

En route, they encountered a unicorn, one of the last of its species, and Steve, attempting to tame it, was killed.

When he recovered, they continued to track the lycans, and Steve, traumatized by the ongoing deaths, had a minor breakdown. Belle helped him through it, and the lycans attacked, giving him the opportunity to take out his issues on them. After the battle, Steve admitted that although he has great advantages in battle, he was untrained in edged weapons and more, and needed help.

He traded his portion of the loot from the lycan village they destroyed for training by the Oracan, and found that, as the trainee, he was now the lowest of the low, forced to carry the litter that Belle, who had overreached in the fight, rested on.

The next of the lycan villages was more of a trial, with a much larger population, led by an alpha, with ghouls and a vampire, as well as a pair of Minotaurs. The Minotaur, Oxus, and his "calf" Xous, agreed to join Steve when Belle made him aware that Oxus was being forced to fight, under threat of Xous being eaten by the vamp.

By the end of the fight, Steve had gained the rights to the lycan camp, a formerly Oracan major village, and Eto and the rest of the clan left him, to reclaim the village.

Ronai, one of the warriors of the tribe, as well as Leo, Agnin, and Tenit, joined Steve in payment of the debt of honor owed, as well as the next morning being joined by seven more Oracan: the new ex-chief of the tribe—Kim—and his immediate family, including a daughter named Oba, and two nieces.

Steve's gift of the village to Eto had been taken to mean directly to Eto, and he had claimed the chief's role, before understanding that as chief, he'd have far more work to do.

The old chief was overjoyed, and followed Steve along instead, refusing as Eto tried to recruit him or change his mind about the chief's position.

Over the next few days, trapped in a cave by an unseasonably heavy storm, Belle spent time using her abilities to help more of the group learn English in preparation for their inevitable return to civilization.

The final village of the three was in the midst of an internal "debate" when the group found it, with the losers being noticeably dead already, and the group waited until the fight was almost over, before wading in and dealing with the survivors of the little civil war.

When the group finally reached the nearby human village—with Steve fortunately finding some pants at the last lycan village—he introduced himself and tried to make friendly contact, immediately coming under fire, as one of the small number of villagers recognized his pants as belonging to a recently vanished family member.

Once things were calmed down, the villagers turned out to not only be English, but a back-to-nature commune group of hippies and Gaia worshippers, led to the wilds and summarily abandoned by a shady figure named Oberon and his brother.

The pair had stayed long enough to avail themselves of the ladies of the group, basing their community on a "free love" model, and then moving on when they grew bored, taking all the villagers' wealth with them as they ostensibly went to "get supplies" to save the failing village.

Steve explained the realities of life to the group, including that the damage to their boat, that had necessitated the pair returning to society, was done from the inside of the boat. It also looked to have been done with a survival knife, not, as Oberon had claimed, by razor-sharp rocks in the water.

The group, now realizing the facts of their situation, agreed to help Steve, and he used the remaining points he'd gained in the Support trees to improve his construction abilities. As part of unlocking so much data, however, the download damaged Steve's brain, and he went into shock.

Over a period of several hours, Steve lost control, thrashing around and breaking much of the quarters he'd been given, before burning himself on a log kicked loose from the fire.

Steve automatically pulled up his armor to defend himself, and in doing so, activated the distributed network of neurons stored in the suit to help him deal with complex tasks. In a moment of lucidity, he upgraded the communications device at the base of his brain to store future downloads, limiting the damage done by massive amounts of data being dumped into his brain unprepared.

That helped him to survive the experience, although he was left unbalanced and confused for several days as he recovered. Belle helped him to deal with the situation, reducing his emotions to manageable levels to enable him to concentrate on the boat he needed to build to equip them to travel to a distant airport.

Once the situation had time to settle in, rather than, as Steve had hoped, the Oracan and Minotaurs settling with the hippies and staying there, the hippies joined Steve's group.

He led them all, while being considerably frustrated by their lack of common sense, to the airport, before sinking the boat to prevent questions, and hacking the local airport systems.

They found an appropriate plane being refueled, ready to be flown to Nepal and sold, and stole aboard, hiding while the pilot, a Greek named Dimi, flew them out of Russia.

Once they were clear, Steve introduced himself and eventually convinced Dimi to help them all, partly by converting some of the farm machinery in the transport section into gold bars and bribing him.

The plane was registered as having issues and the original buyers were in turn bought out by Steve, with Dimi flying them all to the Sudanese airport closest to the recycling plant, stopping several times to refuel.

Over the course of the flight, it was discovered that Dimi, a smuggler, had lost his license to fly in Europe and America due to a joke played on a stewardess when he was a commercial pilot. Steve recruited him, granting him permission to use the plane as he wants—provided Dimi pays for the fuel and stays within a certain radius—and sorted out his license with Interpol, reinstating him.

Dimi flew off to pick up his girlfriend from Germany, and Steve and the rest of the group were collected by Jay and Jack from the airport on a coach and were driven out to the now partially operational recycling plant.

Ingrid, her father Anders, and her mother Freja had taken more and more of a lead in things with the plant, and had it minimally operational. People who could be trusted had been hired, including a large number of Anders's ex-navy contacts, as well as a small cadre of engineers from Zac's past.

The German pair of tourists who Steve had rescued from the lycan fighting pit so long ago had also been recruited, Isolde and Lukas, and were traveling to join the group, as they were both under watch as a possible threat to the Arisen and themselves, and as they were gifted machinists.

Locals had been hired to do low-skilled, but massively important repair and uncovering work. Once the groups were reunited, the discovery was made that the plant, home as it was to a huge amount of biological and nuclear contaminated waste, was being monitored by a great many people.

Defunct spying devices were discovered scattered across the site, detected when Steve demonstrated who and what he truly was to a small number of the more trusted individuals.

Steve and Ingrid were reassured that the monitoring devices were "dead" but they continued to track them down, with Steve using them to level his abilities.

It was determined that Scylla's prison was cracked, and Steve, when checking for any potential issues, found new, and highly sophisticated, monitoring devices hidden in his and Ingrid's room. A trap was laid, and while waiting for the spy to retrieve their device, Scylla was allowed to regenerate, after much discussion.

She was provided food, water, and null blocks to assist, and left to regenerate, as the spy finally appears…and it was Anders.

An Anders, in addition to the one by Steve's side as they watched over the recovering Scylla. Belle confirmed that this was the real Anders with Steve, and Steve set off to chase the imposter, watching them through several cameras as they shifted, becoming Ingrid and fleeing, naked, from the building.

The creature masquerading as Ingrid ran to the local tribesmen, begging for protection as Steve launched himself from the nearby main structure, and the locals, having never seen Steve before like this, but knowing Ingrid, attacked him.

He forced his way through them, saving one of their number when she was injured by the changeling, and eventually fought and defeated it. He was then attacked by two more, this time wearing the forms of Oxus, one wielding his hammer, and they used a high explosive combined with a sensory overload device to stun Steve, before fleeing.

Steve and the others discovered that the trio had arrived recently, pretending to be washerwomen, and when Annabeth, the leader of the hippies, annoyed Ingrid, Ingrid asked for her help, for a "really important job."

Annabeth agreed, and was given the job of chief washerwoman, much to Steve's amusement. The site was searched and when it was declared as "clean," Steve decided that they could no longer wait.

The creatures admitted to working for Shamal and the Blessed faction and Steve was forced to accept that the risk was too large to continue as they were. He remembered that the most effective weapon against the Arisen was the crystal spears and blades, weapons that he'd ordered the Oracan who swore to him, and were now under Hans's protection, to gather and keep safe.

Ingrid explained the truth to the entire group, locals included, and then Steve called Dimi, ordering him to Athens, as it was faster than Dimi flying to the site's airstrip that was still being repaired and then continuing on from there.

Steve set off in search of the escaped changelings, checking the area as best he could, before he turned and headed to Athens, desperate to reach the Oracan and bring them and their weapons back to defend the recycling plant.

On arrival at Athens, Steve stole a bike to get to the yachts, not wanting to expose himself too much, and spotted Dave, his old friend, observing them. Realizing Dave was being watched, presumably by his old companions, Steve left a few gifts for him in Dave's toilet, one of the few places not covered by cameras and observation devices, then left.

Steve stole into the water and crept along the bottom to the yachts, finding a network of spy devices had been deployed. Rather than attacking, he instead invested all three of his available Hack points, upgrading his capabilities through synergistic alignment until he unlocked a new ability: Contagion.

The Contagion ability was a mixture of a Plague upgrade, spreading out across connected systems, and a Control one, giving Steve ultimate control over the technological systems he accessed. It was limited in the most basic form to a single "jump" once the indicated system was infected, "jumping" to another connected system and spreading the infection there, before settling into quiescence.

Steve attacked the detection net, taking control, before attempting to slip aboard the now refloated and undergoing repairs superyacht, one that had once belonged to Athena, and had now become Steve's by right of conquest.

The sensor net in the water, however, wasn't the only one, and as he breached the surface, an additional one, separate from the first and floating, detected him, setting off alarms that were connected to a second group of observers.

Arise :Explorer

On entry into the superyacht, Steve met and freed Athelas, the Oracan "First Warrior" and their local group leader, who admitted that they'd been captured by Shamal and Cristobel, a second Arisen who had arrived to claim the yacht.

They had managed to hide several of the crystal weapons, but the majority were stolen by the new interlopers. Steve recruited the group again, then fought and killed the guards on the pier nearby, before facing Cristobel.

In the ensuing conversation and threats, Dave managed to make contact with Steve, drawing his attention to two more yachts incoming, both in an extended firefight with each other.

Dave pointed out that the more damaged of the two was the one Jonas and the others were aboard, and begged Steve for help.

Steve attacked Cristobel, and in the course of the fight, she managed to stab him with a crystal-tipped dagger, damaging the harvest tool.

Steve was forced to use his time compression and distortion device to give himself time to react, and the vorpal blade to carve his own right arm off at the elbow, before killing Cristobel.

The infection caused by the crystal destroyed the harvest tool, and due to the nature of the lockouts the ancients set into humanity, once Steve lost it entirely—he'd been forced to strip his own nanites from the surrounding area, essentially relinquishing control over the harvest device accidentally—it could no longer be recreated.

Steve realized that to regain the harvest tool and his primary means of securing nanites, he needed to return to the facility under the ocean and recover a second one. But for the short-term, he rebuilt his lower right arm and included a nanite creation tool instead.

Steve rescued Jonas, Marie, and Amanda, and Dave rejoined him, as Steve healed Jonas, eradicating his long-term cancer in the process, and the old team—Jonas, Amanda, Marie, Dave, Paul and his wife Courtney—joined Steve.

Steve was helped by Laia, the leader of the yacht team, to contact the local mayor and warned him to draw his people back, both the navy and local forces. The mayor agreed.

Steve was contacted by Dimi, who admitted that there was a problem with the plane—an engine had failed—and Steve in turn contacted Freja, who arranged to purchase a replacement VTOL that had been embroiled in a local legal battle.

Steve ordered Dimi to change planes as fast as possible and get to the rendezvous.

The much larger group, now including the Oracan and survivors from the yachts who had sworn to follow Steve, headed for the foot of the pier, before realizing that the incoming vehicles were not, as expected, transports. Instead, they were troop transports and tanks, sent, it turned out, by Beowulf, another Arisen.

Beowulf stabbed Steve, using an advanced stealth ability to sneak up, and declared himself, making a call to Shamal and ordering his ally to lead the attack on the recycling plant.

It was Beowulf and Shamal's plan to be "forced" to come out of hiding by the situation, before swearing to the Old Ones that they'd be guided by them, keeping the other Arisen hidden, while the pair took control of the world publicly.

Beowulf admitted to Steve that he had several artifacts of his own, and in the ensuing fight, Steve killed him, contacting Dimi and rerouting him to the foot of the pier, then gathering up the team as Dimi landed nearby with their new VTOL airplane.

Steve got hold of Ingrid, explained what had happened, and found that the three changelings who had escaped him were now outside the facility, trapping the others inside and waiting for Shamal.

Steve and the others set off for the recycling facility, six hours' travel away, and en route, Steve used the nanite-filled bodies of Beowulf and Cristobel as building materials, beginning repairs and upgrades on the old VTOL, enabling them to massively decrease the time required to reach Ingrid.

Shortly after they took off, the Hellenic Air Force surrounded them, and Steve reached out to their squad leader, Flight Lieutenant Papadopoulos, taking control of his plane and giving him a demonstration of how easily he could divert or remove them, then promised to be in touch with their leaders soon, to discuss how he could help.

Between the carrot and the stick, implying that he could just as easily take over missile silos on the ground and retarget them, the Hellenic Air Force and any others nearby backed off, leaving Steve to upgrade his new plane, installing replacement engines—one at a time so that they could continue to fly while the upgrade was done—a new stealth reflective coating and a power core, as well as a rail gun.

Dimi was unsure whether he could bring himself to fire it, but his fiancée happily took it over, after they were fired upon, discovering that she actually loved heavy weaponry, and she'd just never known until then.

Steve stormed the upper floors of the recycling plant, crashing through a damaged section and killing several soldiers, as well as one of Shamal's pet Arisen, before taking their weapons and attacking the soldiers.

In the ensuing fight, Steve was seriously injured, and had his armor integrity reduced to a bare handful of percentage points, forcing him to recover additional null blocks and repair his armor into a far less secure version, essentially coating himself in solid metal.

In the assault on the next floor, fighting his way toward Scylla's cell, having realized that was where everyone had retreated to, he managed to kill two more of Shamal's Arisen. The last of them, Festus, killed Steve with his hammer as he completed the Emergency Wipe of the nanites in the dead bodies.

Steve was brought to the cell, stripped and nailed to the wall, being used as a threat to force Ingrid to open the door and let Shamal in.

Shamal tore Steve's jaw free, torturing him, before turning back to threaten Ingrid, while Steve reached out, gathering the attuned and ready nanites farther down the corridor that he'd left when he was killed, and routed them through air ducts to reach Scylla, before getting Shamal's attention and making noises.

Arise :Explorer

Shamal replaced Steve's jaw, curious to find out what Steve was trying to say, only to be told: "the enemy of my enemy is my friend."

Shamal dismissed it as bravado, only to hear it spoken again, as Scylla stepped through the previously sealed door, fully armored, and standing as Steve's ally.

Steve and Scylla fought together, Steve controlling the nanites as a weapon for Scylla, and her centuries of fighting experience along with the unpredictable nature of the nanites enabled them to win. Steve then converted Shamal into more blank nanites, using them to heal and rebuild himself over the next few days, splitting the cost between null blocks and the nanites themselves.

Several local leaders, including representatives from Europe, the UK, and North America reached out, coming to meet Steve, ostensibly to investigate the dark crusader, and at least in part to make sure that the facilities they were shipping their most hazardous waste to was actually doing something with it.

As Steve met them, half in and half out of his armor, glistening black bones on show as bubbling nanites rebuilt him before their eyes, the questions were fairly simple to field.

Mainly being around was he, and his organization, a threat, and what could they get from him.

Lastly, Dave had proposed in the midst of the battle to Amanda, fully expecting that he'd die in the fight, and wanting to go out on a high.

Unfortunately for him, he survived, and she was holding him to it.

<u>Arise Reclaimer Synopsis</u>

On recovering and after the fight for the recycling facility, Steve and the team spent the next few weeks on essential repairs, as well as integrating their new recruits into the family.

Some, such as the Oracan, were perfectly able to fit in, simply joining the existing security details and beginning to train with their new teams, used to the fluid nature of life under an Arisen.

Others, however, had more of an issue.

Scylla agreed to be bound by Steve and Ingrid's rule—"for now"—as she quickly learned that the world she had awoken in was nothing like the one she lost.

She did, however, have numerous quirks that caused issues, including being well aware that she was "born to rule" and was significantly stronger than the average breed of humanity. Local diplomats, deciding to manufacture offense at her clothing choices as a negotiating tactic, found this out…to their dismay.

When the blood was cleaned off the walls, floor, and ceiling, unsurprisingly, the surviving diplomats were considerably more willing to deal in good faith.

The surrounding countries of the Sudan—Libya and Chad—were very happy when Steve revealed his plans for the area, but Egypt refused to allow him and his team access. They went so far as to threaten the group that they would "take action" if they trespass. So, in the course of discussions, the group agreed to simply ignore the Egyptian negotiators and rules.

They were, after all, only human.

Steve and the group moved forward with their plans for the local area, including their intention to rewild the Sahara, starting with establishing a new lake nearby.

Plans were drawn up to dig down and create converters to transform the dead sand into usable materials, as well as to form a stone basin to act as the base for the new lake, with an access river running through Libya to its northern coast.

A second river would extend due west to Chad, and a smaller lake would be situated there. Water, now found to be long buried deep below the surface, would be pumped up and used to fill these huge lakes, while converters would be used to chew up the local sandy ground.

These mobile converters would leave behind massive tracks of usable land through a mixture of mass conversion and intermixing the lower levels of sand with even deeper sections of less damaged soil.

Steve and the team knew that this would be no easy feat, but if they could manage it? The potential gain for the planet would be massive.

Zac and the team of engineers worked with Steve to develop a miniature factory complex—only a handful of small systems to begin with—but they took in the null blocks gained from breaking down the waste brought to the recycling plant.

That was then fed to the converters and factory units, producing significantly upgraded solar cells, and the engineers rejoiced that they now had a method of upgrading the base overall, with the walls slowly being converted to a diamond-hard coating that would be impervious to most attacks.

Hans arrived with news from the Old Ones, and when confronted with a seemingly brainwashed Hans, Steve explained the truth of their origins.

Hans left the camp and marched into the desert, seemingly unable to accept the truth, while Scylla, already dealing with a seismic upheaval of her world from the technology of her era, accepted it easier.

When Hans didn't return, the group made plans without him, and decided that waiting to see what he would choose to do was just too dangerous.

Steve revealed the location of the crashed ship to the wider leadership group, and plans were made to reclaim it, eliminating the security AI's presence and making use of the ship itself, as well as most importantly to Steve, replacing the harvest blade and upgrading more of the group.

Secondarily and of equal importance, was that Steve suffered from mental breakdowns brought on by the massive influx of knowledge into his brain from the various classes he'd managed to unlock, and he continued to suspect that all was not right with this capability.

Steve flew ahead while Ingrid, James, Scylla, Jonas, Zac, Casey, Paul, and Courtney sailed the yacht from its berth on the Sudan. While the others would take several days to reach the ship, Steve covered most of the distance aboard the reconfigured VTOL plane, jumping out over the Med and flying the remainder of the distance on his own power.

After several hours of searching and examination, Steve hit upon the idea of using the grainy "radar" that he could generate from his tentacles to map the entire structure beneath him. Then, using a combination of this and the design and modeling facilities that he had unlocked from the various upgrades, he stripped the sand, silt, and accumulated debris of ages from the ship's image.

Using this, he found several entrances to the ship that had clearly been repaired after the crash, and more sections that were slowly being repaired, or that were in progress and were seemingly abandoned due to lack of materials.

Steve attempted a hack to gain access to the ship, only to find that the security AI was ready for him, having detected him scanning the ship.

Although Steve had easily overcome the original security systems, he quickly found that this was due to two things. First, the security AI had weathered thousands of years of inactivity and was woefully unprepared for his intrusion.

Secondly, through being able to physically breech the systems using the harvest tool and active nanites the first time around, he'd had a significant advantage.

With the loss of the harvest tool, and his subsequent wiping of the majority of his nanites to weaponized status, Steve had none of these advantages now, and the fight was much more difficult.

Steve was forced to employ both time compression capabilities, distraction in the form of the half-complete authority bequeathed to him by the Erlking, and spinning up nine sub-minds to assist.

He still barely succeeded, and upon entry into the ship, found that most of these previously unexplored sections were devastated by the long-ago crash and the march of time.

Steve received a quest to reclaim the ship. To do so, he must claim the local security stations, as well as secure those sections he had recovered against intrusion.

Over several days, the AI resurrected and repaired more and more heavily armed sentinels, as Steve fought his way across the ship.

Sections were reclaimed, and he began the process of stripping and recovering sentinels and custodians of his own. Next came converters and factory units, and the first defensive turrets were made.

As more and more sections and rooms were claimed, the security AI grew desperate and, unbeknownst to Steve, reached out to the original creators, requesting aid and authority.

A solution for the pain of data downloading was found, almost accidentally, when Steve forced one of the sub-minds he still had access to, now buried in his armor, to maintain a watch for him as he upgraded himself.

He was awoken by the sub-mind as more sentinels attacked, and the sub-mind took control of a tentacle, saving his life. After some careful consideration, Steve set this sub-mind up with more storage, and then filtered the downloading information for the Hack upgrade through that mind, creating a sub-mind with a Hack and Espionage specialty skill set.

He began setting it automated jobs, including maintaining and programming the factory units, and running the defenses.

Steve set up a remote link from the ship he was aboard to the yacht, which had now arrived overhead, and the group aboard the yacht disagreed with his intentions to secure the entire ship before they gained access.

They used the custodian Steve had sent them to upgrade their weapons and provide basic body armor.

The AI launched a counterattack, and in the process, Steve was badly injured. The combination of acids, poisons, and gamma radiation stripped the vast majority of his armor and nanites from him, and in a panic, he ordered the sub-mind to help him and to protect Ingrid.

His last thoughts before he died were of Ingrid.

The sub-mind accepted these orders, and using the remote link, continued to fight the AI to a standstill, holding the currently claimed ground, while Steve was evacuated to the ship overhead.

Steve recovered over several days, and then agreed that his time as a lone wolf was over. He returned to the ship below, now with Ingrid by his side, and with most of the crew already aboard the alien vessel.

Where Paul, Jonas, and Courtney worked hard to fight the sentinels, using their upgraded weapons and training, Zac essentially caused more problems than he solved, trying to get control of the factory systems.

When Steve arrived on site, he quickly took over and set up a second sub-mind, one housed in a factory unit that Zac could control, and at last the gifted engineer could do what he was best at.

With the sub-mind no longer hamstrung by the limited data access it could manage remotely, the tide of battle turned and the group consolidated the area.

Steve and Scylla agreed that they would loop around and secure the medical suite, while Jonas et al. would draw its attention.

The flanking attack was a dismal failure, as Scylla was killed immediately upon reentry to the ship, and the medical suite was being destroyed when Steve reached it. He died shortly after. Again.

When Steve was reawakened by his nanites, he was considerably weaker, and was being carried by a robot to be reduced to his constituent atoms in a furnace.

His body was unresponsive, and a control collar of some kind had been used on him, rendering him paralyzed. He used the small number of nanites he had access to, to form a small tentacle and damage the collar, before discovering that its construction also lent itself to a form of high-speed data access.

The tentacle carved the collar apart, and he used it to hack the robot, quickly counterattacking mere moments before he and Scylla—whose body had been recovered as well—would have been rendered down.

The security AI, realizing that it had lost control of the local area as Steve captured nearby sentinels being produced, abandoned it and fled, shutting the systems down in an attempt to prevent Steve from using them, as there was no localized power generation once that had been shut off.

Steve found that the energy generated from the conversion of higher density materials to null blocks could be siphoned away, providing power if he accepted the loss of some of the end product, and used this to kick-start the factory units around him and to repair the medical suite that had also been cut out and brought here for destruction.

When Scylla reawakened, she and Steve argued, and she struck him, before storming off. Unfortunately for Steve, by this point he was almost entirely out of nanites. Although he was more powerful than a regular human due to the changes that had been made, without the nanites to actively support him, to repair and heal him?

He was badly injured.

His last action before losing consciousness was to order the medical suite to repair him and the sentinels to protect him. As injured and desperate as the order was, it was transmitted to *all* the sentinels under his command.

Unbeknownst to him, when Scylla realized that she had caused significant damage to him, she relented and gave him a small number of her nanites through a blood transfusion.

When he reawakened, it was to the sight of Ingrid and the others, who followed the sentinels; Ingrid was berating Scylla, who fortunately refrained from stabbing her.

Steve accepted the medical suite's requests and gave it directions, regaining the harvest tool, before being stripped and repaired.

The process was horrific, as he once again was rebuilt, his upgraded skeleton and some parts being retained. But significant sections were removed and although they were reattached later, granting him his improvements again, he was reduced to a small number of nanites.

When he was finally released, he explained the process to the others, and forgave Scylla, before explaining that as Scylla had nanites still, but in far lower levels than a normal Arisen of her age, she had a choice.

She could take up residence in the medical suite, and she would have her nanites gradually unlocked, whereupon she would be upgraded and released, but the process would literally take decades. Or…

She could give up her nanites, being reduced somewhat in strength to that of a very low-level Arisen, as hardly any of them were unlocked, and the recovered nanites would be used to unlock some of the others' abilities.

Before any decision was made, the final push was made and the security AI fled into a secure fallback location, cut off from the rest of the ship. Steve and the team captured the last holdouts, but weren't granted the quest complete bonus.

Scylla suspected she was being punished for striking Steve, but accepted the removal of her nanites as it provided opportunities to upgrade Zac, Jonas, and Ingrid, who chose the paths of Support, War, and for Ingrid, the Commander class.

Where the others were determined by the design of the person, Ingrid had originally been a Support class, and would have had problems with another class being simply slapped atop her own. Due to Steve's command level access, though, and the capabilities of the Commander class, Ingrid was able to upgrade to it, unlocking group Support options.

She became the heart of the team even more, granting the abilities of silent communications, a shared command net, and being able to link to the others and highlight or project details as she unlocked more and more capabilities.

Steve, Ingrid, Jonas, and Scylla returned to the yacht with James, and headed for a nearby location that Marie, Amanda, and Dave identified as a people and drug smuggling center. Courtney, Paul, and Zac stayed below, and Casey swam down from the ship to join her husband on the alien vessel.

Steve and the small team presented themselves to the people smugglers as a target too good to let slip, and they were attacked. It didn't end well for the smugglers, and they were harvested.

Steve realized that, unfortunately, he'd been spoiled by the long years of being force-fed nanites and pureed people, as well as the constant fights against other Arisen and their attendants, as the small—in comparison—numbers of nanites harvested and then split between the team were too little.

He begrudgingly accepted that he would need to take the team to richer harvesting locations, and they attacked a nearby main base of the smugglers, freeing their victims and letting the others get more experience.

Once the enemy had been drained and the nanites shared, Steve regained access to his harvest blade, and he contacted Interpol, sharing the locations of the criminal network with one of its vice presidents, as the president of that organization was found to be corrupt.

The decision was made to spend a significant portion of the recovered nanites to have Belle flown out and then to upgrade her, and she was given, through Steve's command access, the Harvest class.

Once the team was ready, they set off to the wilds of Russia, and Steve shared as much of the quest to eliminate the Stelek as he could.

Arise :Explorer

The team were threatened and attacked when they reached the Oracan village, with Steve being forced to kill Eto, before realizing that Eto set this up deliberately.

He was unable to manage as a leader of the tribe, and due to the Oracan societal norms, couldn't step down. He'd made recent poor decisions, in sending the majority of the tribe's remaining warriors to clear out the Stelek in their ancestral home nearby, and the village was failing.

By provoking a fight with Steve, he gained the chance to do the one thing he was excellent at—fighting—and remind the tribe of who he was. Also, if he lost? He would die with honor.

When Steve killed him, he got his wish, but Steve was also left with the Oracan village, who were unable to accept him as direct leader, and yet that he couldn't simply abandon. The solution was to send Dimi back to the recycling facility, collecting the old leader of the tribe, Kim, and several others, with orders to come back, retake control over the village, and get them ready to move to the Sahara and set up a new village there.

While Dimi was doing that, one of the tribe who remembered Steve from the fighting with the lycans led the group to the nearby Stelek hive.

The Stelek were driven up from the deeper places long ago, and had in turn displaced the Oracan from their hidden city, slaughtering the majority and driving out the survivors.

Steve and his small group explored the caverns and found a preserved and ancient city that Ingrid recognized as similar to other underground locations she had studied in Turkey.

Scylla, unfortunately, recognized it as something far worse. In the course of the fighting, the group realized there were frequent sections wider than others, but beyond that, the entire supposed city was a single corridor, literally miles long.

Scylla, however, had seen this before, and she and Ingrid explained to the others what had happened, with Steve using a tentacle to verify.

The defenders of the city had been driven out, but the majority of the inhabitants hadn't. Instead, they'd closed off their living areas with great slabs of stone—emergency measures that had then turned their private quarters into tombs.

When the defenders were unable to retake the city, their families died, suffocated, starved, and dehydrated, while the insectile Stelek roamed the empty corridors, uncaring.

The group, troubled, moved on, fighting their way through successive defenders, until Steve accidentally linked his System Replenishment ability to his armor and active nanites.

The result was an abomination, as the system informed the rest of the group, ordering them to kill him and promising significant rewards if they did.

The Devourer, as Steve was identified, was named as one of the "most feared of all the legions of the ancient enemy," leading Steve down a new path of concerns as he wondered what was accurate in the information the creators had shared, and what was seemingly propaganda.

He'd been told, over and over through system messages, data leaks, and from the literal mouth of the Erlking, that humanity was an experiment that had rebelled against its creators.

That made a certain level of sense, and that once the first generation had rebelled, that the second generation was abandoned here? Well, it was short-sighted. Steve would have simply eliminated the threat personally, rather than leave it to eventually rise again, but it was understandable.

Now, though, knowing that there had once been legions of Devourers? And that whoever had interfered with the system to send that message—as it'd been different from the regular messages received from the system—viewed humanity as an ancient enemy?

It didn't fit. Either humanity was an experiment abandoned, the first generation of which had launched a full-scale war against all the galaxy seemingly, or...

Or it was once a far greater group. One that wasn't restricted to a single group of first-generation warriors, but entire legions. Ones that had been around long enough to be identified as "the ancient enemy."

Steve was left troubled, both by the revelations and by the new abilities he'd unlocked. He discovered the ability to simply burrow his way through his enemies, the coating over his still-regenerating armor literally devouring any living thing it touched and feeding him its constituent parts.

Steve and the others gained a significant number of nanites, and Steve spent more of his points, believing that even after he'd lost access to the sub-mind he'd set up before—when he'd lost access to his armor, it'd compressed down into him—he should be able to use the War tree at least.

The first of his upgrades worked well, but, buoyed up by the knowledge of his success, he invested in unlocking another ability: a nanite Tsunami conversion wave that was linked to far more than he expected at first, rendering himself catatonic. He spent most of the nanites he'd gained in the fights until now on recreating the basic version of his helmet and decompressing the Hack sub-mind into it, followed by a more basic version of a sub-mind for the Support tree as well.

Ingrid and the rest of the team, recognizing that there was nothing they could do for him, agreed to leave him behind, protected by a defensive creation of Belle's own design. Two sentinels they'd brought with them to protect the group, when and if they needed to sleep, were set up to watch over him.

When Steve regained consciousness, it was to nearby fighting and distant screams. Realizing the stupidity of his actions and the risk he had put his friends in, he joined them as they fought the Stelek queen and her guardians.

The next several hours passed quickly as Steve entered the fight as Ingrid and the others were pinned down. He used the gravity inverter to give him the gift of flight, and dropped off the sentinels to snipe at the enemy, before taking the airborne versions of the Stelek down.

The queen was killed, as were most of the hive. But at the end of the fight, they were warned by the system messages they received, and the new quest tag, that when the old queen had sensed the threat roaming the halls, she released her daughter.

With the Stelek, only a single queen could rule, and although old and weary, the queen was driven by biological demands to drive her daughter from the hive, a small number of guardians dutifully left with her.

Steve and the group harvested the dead, planning to advance and chase down the infant queen, when they received word that the sunken ship was under attack.

Returning as quickly as they could to the surface, they found that Dimi was on his way back to meet them. Already on the ragged edge from so many hours of flying, unsupported, he was barely able to keep on course, and the group made the decision to spend their nanites and points on developing their armor for flight.

A short time was spent learning to fly, aided heavily by very low-level RI—restricted intelligences—implanted into the power cores that Steve created for each of the group.

They extended their wings, and with Ingrid supporting Steve, he reached out and formed gravity bubbles around the others, helping them to fly. They were practically carried by him for great distances, before Dimi reached them, looping around and lowering the rear hatch.

The group landed aboard the plane, being practically thrown in by Steve, and they rested for a short time, with Jonas sent to assist Dimi as a second pilot.

The ship had been attacked from both ends, close to the shore, by a mixed group of lycans, werecats, and vampires, and at the other end, much deeper in the ocean, by a pair of the horrific Xi-Ma.

Two of the Xi-Ma, huge creatures that were the inspiration for the legends of giants and once the protectors of the ancient pharaohs of Egypt, had boarded the ship, aided by the security AI.

As they continued through the deeper sections of the ship, being led on a chase by sentinels that Zac had created and sent off, a small handful of enemy sentinels and custodians followed behind them, claiming sections of the ship that hadn't been fully secured.

Steve boarded the ship at the deeper point close to the Xi-Ma, but the others, not having their diving gear, nor any ability to breathe underwater, nor protection from the crushing depth, instead boarded the ship from closer to the land, reinforcing Ingrid's father Anders and the small security contingent that he'd gathered and flown in.

They took the boarding team of lycans and more from behind; the advanced weaponry and loyal sentinels that Zac had been producing made the difference in the fight.

Paul and Courtney, on the other hand, had been using their weapons and years of teamwork to slow the Xi-Ma as much as possible.

The Xi-Ma, though, were so saturated with nanites, that their wounds, including direct hits to an eyeball, simply healed over in seconds.

By the time Steve reached the fight, at around the halfway mark of the ship, Paul and Courtney had been forced back again and again, and the ship had been badly mauled by both their tridents and a high-powered energy scream attack that the Xi-Ma could unleash.

Steve, discovering that the pair were almost invulnerable due to their sheer mass of nanites, set about to steadily drain them, hacking and slashing, tearing hundreds free with each blow, but being beaten and battered in the process.

The tide of battle turned when Scylla and the team reached the fight, and heavier and specialist weapons were brought in. Ingrid's battle net ability helped to grant the combatants additional awareness of one another and the spaces around them.

Scylla managed to drive her spear through an unprotected underarm, one of the few unarmored sections of the Xi-Ma, and pierced its heart, killing one of them and sending the second into a furious counterattack.

Steve's Tsunami nanites surprise, injected earlier into one of the Xi-Ma's throats, enabled him to take control of the local muscle groups, as more and more of the nanites in the creature converted to attuned to Steve and Steve alone.

As the Xi-Ma attempted to use its energy shriek attack, Steve triggered the muscles and slammed its jaw shut, locking the lips closed, and the attack instead detonated its skull.

The death of the Xi-Ma ended the majority of the fight. The last of the secondary group, a vampire who had been hiding, attacked, thinking to use Paul as a combination of human shield and snack.

He was, however, unaware that Paul wielded both upgraded, cutting-edge weapons, and was an ex-Marine. It ended badly for the vamp.

When the battle had entirely settled down, Steve and the group took the time to dig the security AI out. Steve, now able to use his Hack ability again without fear, and having nanites to spare to form a physical bridge, directly hacked the security AI, forcing it to shift its loyalty to him, and discovered that things weren't as simple as they'd believed.

The AI had received a response when it requested help, and that was why it'd changed from the previous path of careful management of the resources it had access to, to rebuilding the factories and stripping the rest of the ship to create new sentinels.

The response came from one of the creators—not the Erlking, but one of the other two, and they'd been the one to name Steve "Devourer."

They had ordered the AI to strip the ship and make an army of sentinels, to destroy its playthings that even now ran amok.

The second of the creators was awakening, aware, and filled with hatred...hatred for the entire human race, and every single one of its offshoots.

Steve might not have gone looking for a war, but he knew instinctively he'd found one.

Arise Devourer Synopsis

Steve and the team have won the fight, but he's now started to realize just how many enemies he has—and that they're not only legion, they're also more powerful than he and his allies.

His greatest strength, however, was also his greatest weakness—the animal within.

Steve had felt it coming out many times over the last few years, and mostly it's been to his great advantage, enabling him to win despite the odds. But now, as the stakes grow higher, he's realized that he'll need that fury more than ever.

Steve admitted his fear to Anders, that he will give in to the rage that fills him, and that he may not regain control before he's made a fatal mistake, only to be stunned as Anders conceded to knowing it as well.

Anders explained his own past, and that he, too, let the beast within loose on more than one occasion. In Anders's situation, rather than a furious rage and willingness to die to win, it was a willingness to risk the lives and property of others to enable himself to climb the ranks higher.

The pair recognized that the rage and the desire they both felt were sides of the same coin: the beast within that all carry. Anders proving that mastery was possible gave Steve hope, though, and he thanked him, summoning his council together to discuss and plan their next step.

The next of the group to be "ascended" from the base stock of humanity to the next level were decided to be Corey and Joseph, the engineers, Paul and Courtney from Jonas's old team, and Oxus, the Minotaur.

Laia, formerly Athena's megayacht chief steward, was pointed out to still be suffering from issues related to her recovery, and due to the tremendous pain that engendered, there was a minor but growing concern over an addiction to medication. She was selected for ascension, as was Ronai the Oracan, his argument that he'd fight for or against Steve happily any day of the week being a valid one.

Lastly, James and Lars were selected—James so that he could essentially work even harder, and along with Lars, would be visiting extremely dangerous locations.

That the ascended could literally come back from the dead changed everything when it came to taking them to places that were dangerous, in Steve's mind.

Facility #6B and its now exposed location was dealt with next. The attack on it had been led by the Xi-Ma, with the attendant vamps, etc., supplementing it. Although it'd been carried out at the orders of another of the creators, it'd been overt enough that human witnesses had seen that something was going on.

Social media was flooded with shaky stills and camera feeds showing both them using the entrance to the ship, and Anders and his reinforcements streaming into the sea to access the ship behind them.

The decision was made that the cover story—a movie being shot in the area—wouldn't last long, and so, due to the condition of the facility, Steve decided, and convinced the others to go along with it, to destroy the ship.

The only actually intact systems, he pointed out, were those that were already under their control and were best off being moved to a secure location, or were in serious need of upgrades and repairs.

As that involved replacing them entirely with new versions, all that was left was the outer hull of the ship.

Rather than allow anyone else access to such technology, even broken as it was, Steve made the argument that converting it all to null blocks was a faster and entirely reasonable way to deal with it. They agreed to leave the shell of the ship there, and to build a supposed rocky outcropping around the small sections that Zac wanted to keep.

The resultant image was simply that another section of the ship was destroyed on impact, leaving part of the rocky seabed exposed.

Everything else was to be stripped out by massive constructors, ones that would then transport the null blocks, etc., to a heavily damaged oil tanker that Freja will have sailed into position over the ship.

That oil tanker—the *Pacific Princess*—was badly damaged by eco-terrorists earlier in the year, and had been languishing at anchor nearby as the parent company tried to offload it. Laia was picked to take over its management—and along with Joseph aboard it, and Zac and the others helping remotely—to convert the oil tanker into a floating dockyard.

The megayacht, formerly owned by Athena, was to be sailed to meet up with the oil tanker, and Zac had been given a week to oversee—with Joseph and Laia's help—its conversion into a heavily armed and armored new form.

While they're doing that, Steve and his team—Ingrid, Jonas, Scylla, and Belle—planned to assault the Xi-Ma's home, intending to try to take down the creator before it recovered from its hibernation fully.

Before that, though, the team spend their accrued nanites and points, mainly investing in new armor for them all. And as part of the process, Steve and Ingrid discovered that it was possible to "cheat" the system.

Essentially, if two people were linked together, one of those people could spend double the points and unlock an additional section of their skill tree.

If it would cost an engineer a single point to unlock the basic construction systems, then they could instead spend two and unlock it for another as well. Although that was a waste for one engineer, the other would get an artificial boost to unlock higher tech, as they only needed to spend their points on unlocking data further down the line.

Steve unlocked upgrades to his biological weapons facility and RIs, regretting that because it required an enormous amount of programming before it'd be viable. War tree upgrades were unlocked as well, first in Unarmed and then in Force, increasing the force he could deliver on impact. Finally, two more were invested in unlocking the mk4 gravity gradient cannon, or GGC as he christened it.

That left two more points to save, knowing that he needed a minimum of four points to unlock the ability to join the biological weapons systems with the GGC.

When that was done? He'd become an unholy terror to his enemies. More so than he already was. For now, though, those points were kept as a reserve, in case he desperately needed something further down the line.

When that was done, Steve headed to Heraklion—arranging to meet Hans to discuss the Elder situation after this—and searched for the local governmental officials. Most of the local Greek infrastructure, unfortunately, was so byzantine and complicated that he eventually gave up, storming out of the local offices to find a coffee shop, calling Ingrid and getting her to help remotely as he searched the area, tracking down the local leadership.

While doing so, he became aware of a team shadowing him; he judged them to be local security, essentially tracking him for the Greek government. He decided to ignore them until he'd completed his current mission: warning the Greeks to stay well clear of the sunken ship until he was done with it, and getting the oil tanker moving.

He eventually found that, despite the posted details, the local secretary general, the de facto ruler of Crete, was not currently away at an all-important conference.

He was instead busily railing his secretary in the very building where Steve had first gone looking for him. Steve kicked the door in and threatened the man, making it clear that if he did as he was told, he'd live, and even cured his lung cancer in the process. He ordered that everyone be kept clear of the sunken ship's location until he was done, on pain of death, and that "one of his servants" would be in touch to sort out the oil tanker.

That was as far as he got before being attacked by an unknown Arisen.

This one, rather than the local security, who were almost laughably ineffectual thanks to his nanites' armor, used first a regular assault rifle to get his attention, and then switched to a much more powerful and advanced weapon.

Steve was shot and injured, and the figure held up a tube, making sure he saw it, before vanishing. Before he could recover the tube and chase them, he was attacked by three more Arisen, although of lesser power.

Steve killed two of the team of three, draining them and making it clear to the dying third member that they would never rise again. The third, terrified, explained that they were sent as a warning by the Elders.

Steve had asked for a month, and they had agreed, but Steve never specified the calendar in use. The Elders and their group, being many thousands of years old, used a base twenty-nine-day month, and Steve had expected them to understand he meant a thirty-one-day month.

A common, and understandable mistake to make, perhaps, but in agreeing to the timescale, and then not attending, he was marked as an Oathbreaker, and this, an assault that would have killed any other Arisen outright, was the first warning.

Steve stripped the nanites from the two dead, and most of the nanites from the third member as an example, then dumped the body, taking the message cylinder and leaving to meet up with Hans.

Steve received a new quest to learn to split his focus, enabling a more efficient control over his Hack or Support systems, and chose the Support path, before losing the connection, leaving him in a foul mood when he reached Hans.

On arrival, Hans was furious over what he saw as Steve's failures, but over the course of the discussion, he returned to Steve's side, and agreed to go to the recycling plant, to protect the rest of the group while Steve completed one last mission, before heading to the Elders.

Steve led his team to the location he'd last seen the Xi-Ma, and after a long trek through the underground caverns and catacombs, he found that the area had been sealed off.

The blocks used were too large for him and his team to break through or move, and he was forced to accept what that meant.

Steve and the team arranged for converters to be set up in the passage, chewing through the blocks, to create a weapons emplacement, planning for whatever could be on the far aside, before reaching out to the recycling plant. Unfortunately, the first thing they found out was that Hans, in an attempt to be helpful, had invited his own sponsor, Petros, to the recycling plant to assist.

Petros admitted on the call to Steve that he had ulterior motives, mainly that he wanted help to find and recover his own sponsor, whose body had been "locked" away and disposed of in the ocean long ago.

Steve and the team, not sure they could rely on Hans, let alone this unknown Petros, were forced to separate, with Ingrid and the rest of the team going to the plant, while Jonas and Steve—flown by Dimi—instead headed off to the Elders' base in the mountains of Tibet.

On arrival, Steve and Jonas were separated from Dimi, who was escorted to a special accommodation area for humans. Their guide, Matthias, took them to the valley, passing through miles-long hangars and airfields, demonstrating that without the permission they had granted Steve and the others to land, there would be no chance they could have survived to assault the sheltered location.

More heavily armed fighters and drones were seen, ready for flight, many times more than either Steve or Jonas had ever seen before. Hints were dropped that this was only one such facility, and that the valley was nigh on impregnable.

Shortly after arrival, Steve found that not only did he have no signal—having planned to share the view from the apartment he and Jonas were assigned with Ingrid—but after a few tests, he figured out that the signals were being actively suppressed.

Spending the last two points he'd been planning to save, Steve unlocked Escape and Illusion, enabling him to create a life-size simulacrum of himself, positioning it on the couch and, with Jonas's help, making it look like he was simply being grumpy and not talking, when instead he used his Conceal ability to sneak out and explore.

Finding a local human's home after a short while, Steve hacked a baby monitor, quietly pleased that the community here didn't make everything "in house" and instead brought in supplies, including that device, which gave him unfettered access to the local network, after a little work.

Arise :Explorer

Returning to Jonas, he contacted Ingrid, being reassured that the recycling center and their people were safe, for the time being, before resting.

The next day, Matthias offered to show them around the valley, enabling them to meet the local people and to study in the "lesser" libraries. After a confrontation, Steve forced the guide's hand, and when he made to leave the valley, Matthias agreed to contact his superiors.

Instead of spending several more days being forced to wait, as the Elders made their position as the more powerful of the two groups clear, Steve and Jonas were fast-tracked through to the Great Refuge, and on the way, were told more of the true history of the world, as seen by the Elders and their servants.

After Matthias realized he wouldn't be permitted to learn any of Steve's secrets, he stormed off in a mood, leaving Steve and Jonas in the car with the driver of their car, who in turn subjected Steve to one of the most vicious auditory assaults known to man…J-Pop.

Steve and Jonas were greeted at the entrance to the Great Refuge by Timurlan, a much higher-placed guide. He explained that the Elders—those the outside world simply call the Old Ones—were working on something and would summon Steve and Jonas later.

It was explained that no slight was intended, it was simply that they were busy. Instead, the pair were led to the lower-grade artifacts, the guide expecting to overawe them with the ancient and unidentifiable artifacts of the deep past.

The first of the intact artifacts was identified as a gravitational construction device, and when Steve—after agreeing to share the information he had—explained the information he had on it, it changed the dynamic.

Steve and Jonas, after explaining the grim reality of the world to their guide, continued to explore, examining the grade-five to grade-two artifacts, being diverted and prevented from access to the grade-one level.

They were told that the grading system was based partly on use and response, and that something that was still usable, or had been in recent history, was classed as a higher grade than something that was not.

Eventually, Steve and Jonas were brought before the Elders themselves, and a battle of wills commenced as they tried to read him, and he in turn examined them.

A truce was agreed, and through a device installed in the hall of the Elders—the Nordicassian Linkage—they and Steve joined mentally. For the next several hours, they each read the other's memories, seeing the truth of each other's experiences and knowing beyond all reasonable doubt that they could trust one another.

A deal was brokered: Steve would use the medical suites to unlock the nanites of the Elders, and only the Elders, for now, but they would give twenty percent of their nanites to Steve in exchange, to ascend his own people.

The remaining eighty percent, just as Scylla's had been, would be stripped from the Elders and retained in the medical suites. They would then be available for the medical suites to use to bring back the long-dead Arisen who were destroyed.

Astorian, the Speaker, was strangely unhappy about the deal, but the others were ecstatic. The negotiations were fortunately a lot quicker and easier than expected, thanks to the device that allowed mind-to-mind linking, eliminating the usual bargaining positions.

Steve was given basic access to the rest of the refuge, and proceeded to search out the old power systems—including tracking down hidden weapons emplacements—aided by Ingrid, who now had remote access, via Steve, into the system.

After significant exploration and mapping out of the local surviving technical systems, Steve had Ingrid confirm with Hans and Petros that the Elders had spread the word that they were officially off-limits to anyone who doesn't want to defy the Elders.

In the end, Ingrid, Scylla, Belle, and Oxus set off from the recycling facility—Dimi returning to collect them—and they were bringing some custodians with them to assist in the reworking needed.

Steve found the security RI for the facility, and assumed control of #4A, discovering in the process that this facility was the original production site for the various strains of humanity.

Although it was heavily damaged, it still had massive potential, especially as a base for the Arisen. Steve decided to push toward a full alliance with them, while also maintaining control over the facility until such a time as he felt comfortable relinquishing it, just in case.

As part of gaining control, Steve found the training facilities that humanity and its various sub-races were designed to use. Although they were trashed from long ages of inactivity, they were also innovative and could be easily reproduced.

Steve made a report to the Elders, making them aware that the facility that they'd lived in for millennia was in fact far larger than they knew, and that behind certain sections of walls lay entirely unexplored—by them—areas.

These sections were heavily damaged, and where most were lost to the gradual onslaught of nature and time, some were still intact, and could be repaired.

The power facilities were found to have originally been geothermal, with the power plant having been a short-term measure to keep the facility running while geothermal and solar systems were put in place.

The geo systems, unfortunately, had long since failed and become heavily irradiated, marking those entire sections of the facility as unusable.

Steve made the decision, and recommended to the Elders, that the best method of moving forward was to build an entirely new power plant, and use that to provide power for the short-term, then create a series of smaller factories, including one that would create custodians.

Artorian spotted the flaw in this plan, in that the custodians and any new systems that Steve developed here, in the heart of the Elders' seat of power, would be controllable by Steve alone, and insisted on a local control facility being created as the first step.

Unfortunately, Artorian convinced the Elders that was the priority, and that any custodians that Steve's companions brought must also be slaved to that control facility before they were allowed into the valley.

Steve argued, but eventually agreed that he could understand their perspective, and consented to create a full control system before Ingrid and the others arrived.

The main problem with this was that it required Steve to use up most of the attuned nanites he had to create the required systems.

Steve and Jonas spent the next several hours working in the bowels of the ancient refuge, repairing systems where possible and building a small factory unit, as well as a controller system to enable the Elders to use the factory.

Steve was nearly finished with this, when he was interrupted by a draconid demanding he present himself to explain something that was unclear. Annoyed, Steve forced himself to comply, and when he was eventually brought to Artorian, deep in the hidden forest at the heart of the refuge, he was attacked.

Artorian, it turned out, was well aware that the return of the Elders to mobility and action would essentially remove the need for his role, and his own power would be massively reduced.

Rather than accept this, he planned to kill Steve and the Elders, and frame him as an assassin—twisting the narrative to prove that the outside world could not be trusted—and ruling in the Elders' place while they recover. Then he planned to "discover" that Steve's abilities meant that the Elders would not recover, at which point, he would already be ruling, leaving no reason for further dissent.

Steve fought the draconids, and Artorian, seeming to see his plan failing, fled, ordering the guards to defend the Elders, as he hides with them.

Steve gave chase, killing many of the draconids and some of the local guards in the fight, before he broke into the Elders' chambers. Artorian laughed that Steve, in his mad rampage to catch him, had provided all the evidence the twisted Speaker would ever need.

Artorian executed three of the Elders, murdering them as they lay trapped within their frozen forms.

Steve and he fought, only for Artorian to show that he'd truly planned for all contingencies: not only was he wearing an armored artifact, but he stunned Steve with cleverly placed projectors that were part of the original security system of the refuge.

Steve collapsed in agony, his nanites shutting down and crumbling under the security system's onslaught.

Cybele, the leader of the Elders, managed to force her body into action, bones shattering as she did, and lasted long enough to distract Artorian, before being gravely wounded.

At the same time, the other Elders used their telekinesis to break one of the three projectors, giving Steve a chance to counterattack.

Steve fought Artorian. Part of the way through the fight, Cybele, dying, offered him her nanites, and he drained some of the blood on the floor, before finally defeating Artorian, and against the Elders' demands, killed him.

Jonas and the guards broke in as he drained the corpse of Artorian, covered in blood, and Jonas barely managed to keep the guards from attacking Steve on the spot.

They broke the body free of Steve, and one of the guards used the linkage to speak with the surviving Elders.

They learned that Artorian was the traitor, and that Steve, now drunk on the nanites, had defended them.

Steve recovered, and accessed the linkage, expecting to be feted as a hero by the surviving Elders, only to find that even in this, Artorian had a backup plan.

Knowing that should his rebellion fail, he'd beg for death—and if it worked, he might need more scapegoats—he'd linked explosives to his suit. When he died, the defenses that the Elders had painstakingly built around the valley were robbed of power, and four of the leaders of the Blessed faction, with their forces, landed, attacking and trying to take the Great Refuge.

Artorian had gambled that should his rebellion fail, it was better that the valley fall as well, likely giving him a chance to escape.

Steve and Jonas took some of the defenders of the valley and defended the entrance, with Ingrid, Scylla, and the others arriving as the battle turned, enabling them to kill Zeus and his companions.

The Elders who were killed were inserted into the medical capsules; they were stripped of most of their nanites, and were ascended instead. Anders and Freja were also ascended, one by one.

Over the next several days, the Elders summoned the leaders of both the Blessed and the Accursed factions, as well as eliminating many of the more rabid of their supporters, showing that they were in fact always watching and ready to take action.

Both factions sent a single representative, concerned that they might be feeding that representative into the meat grinder, but in an attempt to broker peace, and a possible alliance with a now resurgent group of Elders...

Only to find that Steve and the rest of his "faction," now named as Gaia's Vengeance, had already formed such an alliance.

The factions attempted to cause issues, to drive a wedge between Steve and the Elders, only to run afoul of the Elders' mind-reading device, the Nordicassian Linkage.

Both factions attempted to manipulate Steve, finding that he holds them both in equal contempt. The representative for the Accursed, Coara, in league with one of the creators, released a nanite bioweapon upon the slowly recovering corpse of Artorian.

Artorian transformed, ripping his way free, reduced to a mindless beast, interested only in feeding, spreading the nanites' infection, and reaching a hidden device below the refuge.

While the creature that had been Artorian freed himself, Coara attempted to eliminate the Elders, only to find that Cybele, now very much awake, aware, and ready for a fight after Artorian's betrayal, took poorly to the attempt.

Steve and Ingrid were awoken by the mental screams and terror of Freja, caught unsuspecting in the corridors by the creature. As they head to her in panic, she was brutally torn limb from limb, and fed upon.

Steve and Ingrid chased the creature that had been Artorian, while Anders, broken by the death of his wife, and Belle, recovered some of her corpse.

The refuge was prepared for such an eventuality, nanite experiments having run amok before in the deep past. Unfortunately, millennia of degradation and cascading failures rendered the local solutions useless, and Steve had to order the custodians to cleanse the area.

They fell back on an automated routine, constructing specialist equipment and heading to follow the trail of death and destruction. Their nanite suppressors would destroy any nanites in the infected areas, rendering them unable to reconstitute their hosts, including Freja.

Steve ordered Belle to get herself, Anders, and a single fragment of Freja free of the infected area, explaining that it must have absolutely no trace of the infected nanites in the bloody mess, or else Freja would be lost forever.

Belle and Anders managed to escape the cleansing area and secured Freja inside a medical suite, but the limited remaining mass meant that she required a full rebuild from scratch.

While this was happening, Steve, Ingrid, and several others hunted down the corrupted creature that Artorian had become, exploring several buried sections of the facility as they went, and finally defeated it, securing an experimental gravity drive that had been hidden as well.

The Blessed faction were locked away, while the Elders attempted to figure out what happened and purge the remaining traitors in their ranks, the last of Artorian's servants having been involved in the last-ditch coup attempt.

By the time the Blessed were permitted access to their communications again, they found that one of their most secretive facilities was under attack, and as it had happened when they were being held incommunicado, Daversa, their leader, jumped to the conclusion this was some deep plot and refused to explain what was being held there, while simultaneously accusing Steve et al. of using the situation to somehow enrich himself.

Steve, realizing what the attack signifies after questioning the Blessed representative, was furious, the hours lost while what was now clearly a diversion made only worse by Daversa's refusal to explain anything.

Steve and Ingrid had already launched two satellites to try to track the rogue creator, and these were diverted to check out the attack site, while Steve and his people, joined by Cybele and Sanneth, another Elder, gathered their forces and set off.

The site, the island of Yuzhny in northern Russia, was a site that Steve was made aware of by the Erlking, as possibly holding materials that he could use to leave Earth, once his repair and rewilding efforts were complete.

Because of the multiple desperate calls on his time, Steve hadn't started to search the island yet, nor the other sites he suspected held similar troves of artifacts or damaged and abandoned ships.

The rogue creator, however, had launched a full-on assault of the area, eliminating the Blessed's encampment, which was, in turn, being used to try to eliminate the current inhabitants of the ship.

This third species had been there since time immemorial, and when the Blessed found it, they had battled to a standstill. Had the survivors of the Blessed team not retreated with verifiable artifacts, they would most likely have simply bombarded the site with bunker-busting munitions and moved on. But when artifacts were discovered? The potential gain was too great.

The creator's forces attacked the Blessed fortification from the rear, eliminating most of the defenders and driving off the survivors, before pushing ahead and boarding the buried facility, one that was later revealed to be a hidden ship.

The Xi-Ma—forced by their hulking size to crawl through the passages of the ship's hull, and unable to use their most powerful weapons for fear of damaging the ship—were slowed in their assault by sheer numbers.

The delay meant that Steve and his forces arrived in time to assault the Xi-Ma and the other forces of the creator from behind, although many of their own people were badly injured and killed in the fight. They eventually entered the ship, eliminated the remaining enemy forces, and confronted the creator: Varnock.

Varnock the Defiler, leader of the three who were banished here on Earth eons ago for the crime of unleashing humanity on the stars, unleashed the full fury of her presence on the group, forcing them to their knees.

Inbuilt into their nanites were kill codes, contingency plans that attempt to take over and shut down Steve and the others, only to be shut down a split second later, as counter commands were issued, by an unknown third party, the UC.

The UC declared that Varnock the Defiler was stripped of all authority, and named a bounty on her head. In the confusion, as their nanites battled internally and as Varnock regarded them all with disdain and hatred, Steve scented her nanites.

Unlike the forms of others, Varnock and others of her ilk consisted of nanites: nanites in their hundreds of millions restructured to form them in their entirety.

That sheer density, the unrelenting sense of the insane sheer mass of nanites within his reach, drove the Devourer into wakefulness. Knowing that this was a battle he needed every edge for, instead of fighting with it, Steve reveled in it and released the beast inside.

The Devourer rose, the most primal aspects of who and what Steve was coming to the fore; while the others cowered, confused, he attacked.

The fight was short and brutal. The field of confusion and hero-worship that was projected by Varnock faltered as she fought, and the others quickly took the opportunity to join the fight.

Varnock—after the fight turned against her and Steve's form morphed, his jaws extending as he began to feed on her—shifted, and a much less impressive form burst free of the main body.

In her pain and panic, she reverted to an earlier form, a vestigial one of her species, and as she ran…she ran headfirst into Sanneth's boot.

Kicked backward, she screamed in outrage, furious that one of her lowly creations dared to attack her, only to meet one of the weapons that the Elders had brought, this time wielded by Ingrid, who in righteous anger over what happened to her mother, killed one of the creators of her species.

Recovering from the battle, Steve and Ingrid, identified as the leaders of the raid, were given notifications from the UC, or United Confederation, identifying that not only were they "out there" still, and apparently paying close attention, but they were also well aware that the Ændari Council were as well.

Steve and Ingrid were informed that the Ændari had demanded their heads for killing a member of their race, and the only reason that the UC wasn't sharing what appeared to be clear knowledge of the location of Earth was that they, too, had an interest in the Devourer and his companions.

Hints were dropped that they wished to recruit them, and a demand was issued: either Steve and his party present themselves at a set of galactic coordinates in five solar cycles, or the limited protections that Steve—and Earth—currently enjoyed would be revoked.

The final communication from the UC brought even more confusion, as they advised that they'd now remove the security lockouts on the vessel, making it clear that unlike the rest of the ships and facilities scattered across Earth, this ship, that the companions were currently inside of, wasn't in fact an Ændari one.

<u>Prologue</u>

It'd been a long fight, Field Commander Aaronis Balthazar admitted to himself, collapsing into the chair and sighing with relief. The door to his quarters was carefully closed already, hiding any sign of weakness from his soldiers.

"I'm getting too old for this," he whispered. His helmet retracted as a filthy hand rose to rub at the bridge of his nose. Opening his eyes at the gritty sensation, he squinted at his fingers, seeing the dried blood that coated them, and tried muzzily to remember when the hell he'd gotten that on there.

He'd retracted his gauntlet to rub at his face, so he'd still been wearing them then…

He shook his head, letting out a second, deeper sigh.

It had to have happened in the gully behind the second mountain pass. He and his squad had been hit by a power suppression field, a strong one, and there'd been long seconds where their armor had flexed and failed.

He'd been intending on a cleanse anyway. Hell, the thought of standing under the sonic fields and feeling every inch of filth and the stench of battle being stripped away?

It'd been something he had been looking forward to regardless. But now?

He grunted, pulling himself upright, and ignored the slightly canted deck beneath his feet, the distant smell of burned plastic and the brimstone that had made it aboard the ship despite the scrubbers and filters.

As he stood, his baseline armor retracted, sinking back into his skin. The slithering feeling of the builders flowed from sight to store themselves inside his body. He sighed again as more and more filth fell free.

"Arturo," Aaronis datavised to the ship's AI.

"Greetings, Commander. How many I serve?" the ship's AI responded.

"My quarters need a level-two cleanse, and order a ship-wide one immediately." He damn well knew that after so many long years at war, none of his soldiers had any excuse to not order a personal cleanse, just in case one of them had brought a parasite or infection aboard. But relying on what he *knew* others should do, instead of doing it himself and making damn sure of it…

Well, that was what a lesser man did.

Take responsibility for your actions, stand tall, and let the galaxy throw whatever they might at you. A soldier of the UC would never fail.

"Yes, Commander… Warning! Incoming alert," came the datavise from Arturo.

Arronis cursed internally, looking longingly at the cubicle that was even now mushrooming up out of the floor and wall, ready to bathe him in its sonic fields.

Aaronis accepted the link that popped up, frowning. The United Confederation's standard protocols shunted all notifications for soldiers in the field to the nearest AI to hold until requested, preventing distractions and increasing combat effectiveness. So for the AI to override that most basic of protocols?

Well, whatever this was, it was important.

Aaronis stood stock-still, frozen as the scene played out before him. Long seconds passed at the end of the compressed video burst, before he played it again, and again.

Finally, sitting and staring into the distance, with his mind racing, he realized the universe had just been flipped on its head.

It *could* be bad…hell, as a soldier, you accepted that any change, especially one that came to you from the damn politicos and not your own leadership…well, that was almost *certainly* bad.

On the other hand…if even a fraction of what he'd just seen had been true?

"Arturo," he whispered, his voice weak, before clearing his throat and trying again. "Arturo, summon the first fist."

"Affirmative, Commander. First Fist Leshan is en route to your quarters. Do you want refreshments?" Arturo responded aloud as well.

"No." Aaronis grunted, before glancing at the floor, where the scattered dried blood, mud, and worse lay, then down at his hands and the tattered one-piece he wore beneath his armor. "Where is…?" he started, then sighed as the entry code chimed on his door.

Clearly he didn't have time to change before greeting the first fist.

"Enter!" he called. The datavised order to the door's controller went out at almost the same second as he invited the tall woman who stood outside to step in.

She did so, coming to attention, fist clapping to heart, as the door—again, at Aaronis's order—closed behind her.

"Lord Commander," she greeted, ducking her head in reverence.

"At ease, Leshan." He waved at her; the closed door behind her cut off the need for any formality between the two old friends.

"What's up?" she asked. The ram-rod stiff posture released as she took the second chair in the small warship's quarters, at Aaronis's weary, nodded invitation.

"Got some news from the UC," he said, attaching his approval to the files and authorizing her access to them, before sending them across with a practiced flick of the fingers.

It was an affectation, the physical gesture on top of the mental command, and one that he rarely slipped and allowed himself. But the flicker of her eyes to his hand, and then away, let him know she'd caught it.

Instead of berating himself as he normally would, showing such a thing after hundreds of years of datavising and knowing that it betrayed just how rattled and nervous he had to be to do that…instead, he just watched her.

Leshan had come up through the ranks with him. When he'd been diverted into the officer corps, and then covert squads, she'd been directed down the squad leadership route. She led her soldiers with determination and devotion, a feat that engendered her almost slavish worship in the lower ranks.

When Leshan said something was dangerous, you knew it was damn near lethal, but you also knew that she'd be right there with you. As the first fist, she led the troops themselves, where mere officers like himself made do, making requests of their betters.

Leshan was tall, although all the gene-enhanced soldiers were, and solidly built, much more inclined to muscle and stamina builds than many of her breed were—closer, in fact, to his own design.

She wore almost no expression, but after the long years fighting by her side, he could read a thousand words from a single quirk of an eyebrow, or flex of a lip.

Now, as she worked through the file, not a single movement broke free.

She was either worried, very worried indeed, or…

"Is it true?" she asked him bluntly, and his stomach knotted.

"I think it is," he replied softly. "By the Searing Void, I damn well hope so."

That last bit slipped out, and he almost cursed, until he saw the minute flex in the corner of her lips.

It didn't do to come out and admit you were a believer. Not in the assault brigades, not in enemy territory, and certainly not when in command of anything. But she'd known him long enough to know by now, regardless.

"So…are we going?" she asked, and he let out the last of his concerns in a great sigh.

"We are." He sent her the final section of the missive from higher.

Remember, Commander Balthazar, discretion is a requirement of this post. You have five solar cycles of the targeted world before they are due at the coordinates attached.

Be wary: these weapons are from inside the quarantine zone, and the data suggests they are both highly aggressive and may have access to pre-plague, _uncorrupted_ technology.

They _must_ be convinced to join the UC, but failing that, neutrality is acceptable. However, should they show any intention of joining the Ændari, they must be eliminated.

We exist in a confirmed state of cease-fire, but the UC Council, and especially the assault brigades, know very well how little that confirmation is worth.

Should the Ændari gain access to the location of the Forgeworld? They would not hesitate to claim it, unleashing a second scourge upon the galaxy.

We trust you, Commander. Make us proud.

"We're actually doing it," Leshan whispered, shaking her head, her cropped ashen-blonde hair as filthy as his own, and the disbelief in her eyes plain to see. "And if the negotiations don't go well?"

"We'll make sure they do."

"Don't announce it," she said quickly. "By the Void, you can't dangle this before the troops and then risk having it taken away…"

"I won't, but we need to finish this." He gestured at one wall, where a real-time depiction of the fight against the smuggler's forces showed even now.

"We've got two squads holding the line, with a third hammering down the leakers. We can't just pull back and leave them here like that. They'll escape into the night, and it'll take another damn decade to find them again."

"I'll take care of it," the first fist declared abruptly, standing. Her baseline armor flowed out, rebuilding and coating her in a form more familiar to him than her actual flesh and blood was. "I'll take my elites, and we'll finish this by morning."

"Requisition whatever you need." He nodded and came to his feet as well, his own armor flowing out to reform. "I'll take care of the ship. By the standard clock, we've got six days to reach the rendezvous point. It'll be tight, but we can do it."

"Then…it's time," she whispered, and a genuine smile slipped free, lighting her face.

"It is." He smiled back at his old friend, before nodding to her. "We're going *home.*"

Chapter One

"What the absolute fuck do you mean 'no,' you twat?" I glared at Zac. "I mean 'no.' Shit, boss man, it's not complicated. You asked me to do something; I told you no." Zac shrugged, utterly unrepentant as we stared at each other in the dimly lit corridor.

"Zac…" I growled, trying to stay calm.

"No, boss, seriously, just listen, all right?" he snapped back, and I glowered at him, but did so. "You want a megayacht. You want me to rebuild an alien spaceship from the dawn of fuckin' time, yup, no worries.

"You want me to create giant goddamn terraforming tanks that can chew up the desert and lay damn green grass behind them? Can do. Dig mile-deep trenches and draw up a river from under the Sahara? Right on it." He pointed out, waving one hand as he went on.

"Seriously, every time I turn around, you have another damn impossible request. An' I know this is my fault, or some of it is anyway, because I'm so damn amazin' that I've got you convinced I can do anythin'—literally.

"I should have told you no before, or done what that guy on *Star Trek* used to do, lyin' to the boss and sayin' it'd take longer than it really would so that when they came demandin' things faster, later, he was already ready to give in, but I *didn't.* I told you the truth, so that's on me. From now on? I'll jus' lie to you. Tell you it can't be done, then bask in the glory when I do it, but…"

"So you can do it?"

"What?" he snapped, before gritting his teeth and going on. "Fuck's sake, Steve, no. I mean I'll start lying from now on!"

"Zac," I said, stopping as the pair of us flattened ourselves against one wall, letting Oxus drag a massive bag past, huffing and grumbling under his breath at the weight and confined corridors.

"Zac," I said again. "I'm not telling you these timelines for shits and giggles, all right?"

"I know, boss, and I'm not saying no for a laugh, all right?"

"You saw the message." I glared at him. "Five solar cycles."

"Yeah, five turns of our solar system presumably, but that could just as easily be five turns of a particular planet, right? What if that planet takes a year or more to rotate? What if it's an hour and we're already late?"

"We need to be there," I growled. "The only timescale we can base this off is the one we have. They know where we are; they know we're here, so we have to go off our solar cycle. That's five days."

"Four and a half," he corrected. "You know, after the time it took—"

"For you to get here," I agreed, glaring at him. "Yeah, I know. Dimi already chewed my goddamn ear off for making him fly that 'death trap,' as he calls it."

"He's got a point, boss." Zac grinned. "It's only got one engine and the ass end was open to the clouds."

"Yeah, because you overloaded it!"

"You said bring what I thought I'd need."

"I… Fine, you know what? Go for it—explain why you can't do it."

"We don't know if the ship is even capable of taking off," he pointed out. "Sure, as near as we can tell it's intact, no random collapses and holes and shit, but that doesn't mean it'll fly. I mean, think about the helicopters and shit they've got in museums! Take one of them, give it ten years in a museum and try to fly it. I guarantee you, you'll all die in a fire, ending up as crispy fried Steve in a fuckin' metal box."

"And?"

"And I don't want to be crispy fried Zac!"

"What the hell has a helo got to do with this?"

"I mean that if you don't maintain shit, it won't work. You can't just rip the parts out and hope for the best with some new ones. Let's say you spend a week replacing the bits in that helo, right?"

"Right."

"You'll still die."

"Now hold on…"

"You'd need a thousand parts that were built by the original manufacturer, all right? Everything from rubber bungs to electricals. If you replace a single piece of electrical cabling? It'll be different from the original stuff. If it's working perfectly and the system it's connected to isn't? Electrical short, probably a thousand meters up. If it doesn't work? It's broken, can't fly." He rubbed the heel of one hand through his hair as he tried to think, trying to explain what he was getting at.

"You'd need *original* parts to integrate them all perfectly. You use modern kit? It's going to cause more issues. And those original parts? They'd have been built when the helo was still in operation. Literally, it'd be damn near impossible, unless you knew exactly what you were doing, and had months to strip out the sections and completely rebuild them from scratch to get a helo that'd been in a museum for ten years back into the air safely—and you want to do this with a spaceship that's older than dirt?"

"They do it with cars all the time," I pointed out. "Renovation shows—they rebuild them, fix them up, and—"

"And they go on the damn ground," he snarled. "A helo that pootles around on its wheels? I could do that, sure. Hell, any idiot could. *You*? Maybe not, but any other idiot could. Helos are made for flying around at ten thousand feet. They stop working? You don't just pull over and call the local car club to come tow you, all right? You plow into the ground in a fiery ball of death and screams."

"Fine, but this isn't our tech. This is shit that lasts forever, crystal-based, and—"

"And it's been buried for tens of thousands, if not millions of years." He shook his head. "Seriously, boss, as much as I want to—and believe me, I do want to— I can't just magically drag this out of the ground with one hand, wave my dick around, and make the magic fix it, all right? There's no way."

"We need to find a way then," I said softly. "Zac, I'm not fucking with you when I say the fate of the goddamn species depends on this."

"I read the message," he replied after a few seconds. "I know, and I'm not being a dick. Seriously, I just don't see how we could do this."

"All right," I muttered, chewing on my lip as I thought frantically. "Give me alternatives."

"We go hide on a beach somewhere?" he tried, then shook his head. "It's not an option, I know, but fuck me, it's tempting."

"It is," I agreed. "A real alternative, though, please."

"Well, that mental bitch was determined to get this place, right? And she attacked us to make sure we were too busy to stop her?"

"Yeah?"

"So, if it was going to take her weeks or months to dig this place out and then rebuild it, why was she in such a rush?"

"Because she was a psychopath?" I muttered, before nodding. "Fair point, though…"

"Hey, didn't the message say something about unlocking the ship?" he asked, and I nodded.

"It did, but she damaged the core."

"The what?"

"Come with me," I ordered, turning abruptly and heading aft, counting the stairwells and trying to remember the one I needed, before leading Zac up to the next floor.

The corridors were dimly lit, as there were nowhere near enough lights for everywhere that needed them, so they'd been restricted to the most important areas, while we waited on more being flown in. But in the areas where we had high-powered halogen lights set up, you could see the bones that creaked underfoot.

As it was, the room I led Zac to was a mess. Bodies had been dragged free, so that was an improvement, but there were still ceremonial piles of bones everywhere, and the scars of battle, the blood, and the melted remains of the armored central core.

That was what I thought it was, anyway. The Xi-Ma had been going to town on it when I'd arrived, that mental bitch Varnock the Defiler capering around like she'd pissed on an electric fence, and the six Xi-Ma had been using their scream-beams on the object of her wrath.

When the notifications had promised to release the security lockouts on our vessel? Putting two and two together, it was obvious that she'd been pissed because she wasn't getting into the ship's command and control.

Well…it also could have been that she'd just got a real issue with her temper, and that when she found the onboard coffee machine was out of those little posh cookies she decided to fuck the entire ship up. But I was betting it was more the former than the latter.

If the ship had been locked down, and given that the ship as we'd seen on exploring it—and I'd seen a hell of a lot more since the fight ended—was so very different in design than the other Ændari facilities we'd seen?

Well, that the UC could remove those lockouts, and they were evidently in opposition to the Ændari Council was the final piece in the puzzle.

This wasn't an Ændari ship.

It belonged to whoever was fighting them. And from what we'd seen so far, the people most likely to be fighting those dickbags?

The original batch of humanity, the first Biological Weapon Variants who were unleashed upon the galaxy, and their allies.

That was why the ship's design made sense to me, why we could find things easily, why it seemed that everything was sized "right" rather than too big or too small.

Then that crazy fucker had totaled something in the center of the ship when it wouldn't obey her. They'd carved through the outer armoring, and the interior? As soon as I'd seen what was inside, I'd had a damn good idea what it was.

This was the computer core, the home of the AI that ran the ship. The crystals it'd been housed in were blackened husks, cracked and shattered.

We didn't have a goddamn AI to fly the ship.

"This is the core," I said to Zac, gesturing at the pile of shattered crystals. "As near as we can tell, this is what was left of the AI that ran the ship, and that could have given us all the answers we needed."

"So…okay." Zac rubbed his chin, looking at the remains of the ship's core and nodding to himself. "All right, boss man, what do you actually need from me?"

"Seriously?" I frowned. "We need a fucking ship, Zac. We need to get to this meeting. If we don't? We risk these UC dickheads telling the Ændari where we are. You want more of them turning up?"

"Not until we've got some really nasty weapons." He grinned. "All right then, so to be clear, what you need from me is a ship that can get you from here, to there, right? Not something you can use to conquer the galaxy, not the damn death moon or whatever—just a ship that can get you from here to there, relatively safely, and you know, more or less alive."

"And fast," I said firmly. "We're gonna need to be damn fast."

"Fast. And you're gonna want some weapons, right?" He glanced at me, and I nodded. "Boss, remember the way the quests work, all right? We're gonna need a load of points to unlock shit here, so you need to say this right."

"Ah…" I took a deep breath, my mind whirling. "Zac, I need you, as the chief engineer—and your team—I need you to fix the ship and…"

"Make you a new ship," he corrected.

"A new…why the hell would that be better?"

"For a start, it'd not be buried under a fuckin' mountain and we can test the parts as we make them…unless you want to trust that things are just gonna hold together?"

"I… Good point." I sighed. "Okay, so make me a new ship, Zac. As the chief engineer, with your team, I need you to make a new ship, one that's heavily armed, armored, and fast as…a very fast thing," I finished lamely.

"Good enough." He grunted. "Got the quest, and I'll add to it the bits I need as I get the rest of the team onboard. Now, this is gonna take a few days. There's no choice there, okay?"

"We need—"

"To be there in four and a half days," he finished for me, nodding. "Gotcha. But if it's like four days' flight from here, you need to accept that it's not going to happen. I'll do what I can, okay? I'll work magic or whatever, and I'll need to pull people from…well, from everywhere. I'll need high-tech people, like three more than I've got now. A couple of guys I used to work with, they'll need ascending and bringing on."

He looked at me, and I struggled with it—not the cost; we had the nanites in insane numbers right now—but bringing in and ascending people I didn't know. Then I nodded.

I didn't have a choice, realistically. I could agree and we had a chance, or refuse and we were fucked. It wasn't a hard choice.

"Do it," I agreed, getting a quick grin from him.

"Okay, so a few last details. First, this ship is gonna be smaller than this one, a lot smaller, okay? Like we're living on top of each other. And we take a small crew."

"How small?"

"The smaller the better," he said. "Everyone who's on the ship needs to be there for a reason—that's the rule, anyway. But this ship is gonna be small if we want it made fast. We can build a better one in the future, but this one is gonna be fast and strong. It's a warship, so get used to the fact we're all gonna be eating tinned beans and bumping into each other."

"Storage space." I nodded. "We'll need more for the crew than anything else, damn."

"Even like, a week's worth of food needs a lot of space. And no offense, but we're gonna need to take at least a month's worth, then water, spare parts—" He broke off, nodding to himself and muttering under his breath. "Or not. Factory units and null coins…that'll work. Nice."

"How long to build it?" I asked bluntly.

"Depends."

"On?"

"How attached are you to the megayacht?"

"Not very. Why?"

"Because I'm scrapping it." He grinned. "The yacht has everything we need, literally, and it's nearly finished. Sure, I'll have to rip the damn hull apart *again*. I'll have to redesign it as well, strengthen the frame an' shit, but it's already designed to be a self-sufficient system on the ocean. I could tear that landing pad for the VTOL off the back, add some wings and clamp the engines to them and it'll not take long to make it airtight again. From there? I've already got good engineering spaces, storage—hell, the crew quarters and more can stay as they are, just armor the hull up."

He was nodding to himself now, gesturing at the air and seemingly drawing on something only he could see. An immediate sense of relief washed over me at Zac's permanent can-do attitude, and the knowledge that this bit of the nightmare was already in hand, and by someone much smarter than me, thankfully.

"I'll leave you to it then," I suggested, sliding away.

I made it almost all the way to the nearest bulkhead, separating this room from the next, when the engineer ruined my goddamn good mood.

"One thing, boss…" he called. "I can make you the engines, and I'll be there making damn sure they don't blow up—probably—but one thing I can't do?"

"Yeah?"

"I can't figure out those coordinates, nor how to fly the fucking ship. We need a working ship's AI." With that bombshell, he turned his back on me, looking down at the toasty remains of the AI, and shook his head. "This one's fucked!"

"Yeah," I growled. "Yeah, leave it with me."

Twenty minutes later, I'd given in and reached out to Ingrid through the systems to find out where the hell she was. Twice I'd heard her voice and been convinced she was in the next room, only to either have missed each other by a hair's breadth or to find that the ancient ship just seemed to carry echoes for fun.

She was ahead of me, it turned out, having enlisted Corey's help—one of Zac's engineers and a supposed whiz with data systems. He'd come with Zac, and he'd vanished as soon as I'd started talking to the head engineer, apparently deciding that if the bosses were talking, that gave him free rein with the rest of the ship.

Typical engineer, really. I was just damn glad he'd not blown us all up yet.

"Sure it'll work?" Ingrid was asking him.

"Nope, not at all," he replied cheerfully. "I *think* it'll work. It's based on the same systems we used, just a much more advanced version. They're logic gates, so they're running on a Boolean function and—"

"And I think I need to rescue you from this conversation." I shook my head as I walked up to Ingrid, reaching out and putting one hand on the small of her back, getting a smile from her, before she went back to it.

"There's four, right? And, Or, Not, and Nand?" she asked him, making me frown at the made-up word.

"There's seven," he corrected, opening his mouth, presumably planning to explain them all, then catching the look on my face. "But maybe they could wait?"

"Yeah, until I'm not around," I agreed, looking at Ingrid. "You understand that crap?"

"It's not complicated." She smiled. "It sounds like it, that's all. The Boolean logic base sounds complex, but it's simple enough…and you understand it as well, or you'd not be able to hack things as well as you do. It's just that you don't understand the terms and explanations for it."

"Sure," I agreed noncommittally. "So, what's going on here?"

"We're looking for the backup core," she said with a gesture at the wall.

"What?"

"The core," she explained, jerking her head back in the direction of the remains of the AI core. "That one's pretty messed up. I'm guessing it's unusable?"

"I think so." I explained what we'd come up with, getting her up to date.

"That makes sense," Corey agreed, pointing to the main doors that we were standing near. "These are the heaviest and most secure doors you've found, then?"

"They are," Ingrid agreed. "We've searched the ship, and there were three sections that were locked away and the doors were still sealed. There might still be a few more, hidden somewhere, but if there are, they're buried under the bones and the idols or whatever the renat were making."

"And you think there might be a secondary core here?" I asked, excited.

"I think it's logical." She stepped closer to me, leaning against me, and we studied the doors, staring up at their massive solidity. "I mean, the rest of the ship seems to have been built on similar logic to our own so far, and while we'd want a backup, we don't know if they believed that if this was destroyed it meant that the ship was already broken beyond repair."

"What else could it be?" I glanced from her to Corey as he answered for us all.

"Generally, on a warship, you'd have the bridge, a secondary CIC, the armory, engineering, and I guess, for a spaceship, maybe environmental?" He shook his head. "I mean, there's a lot of other things, like living quarters, storage, the mess hall…that kinda thing…but nowhere else that makes sense to have a giant door like this."

It was a fair point as well. This was an insanely large door: an air lock, or so it seemed, squared off, with a massive keypad on one side—long dead, of course—and a recess in the wall on the far side of the corridor where the door was presumably to stay when it was open.

Reaching out into the ether, using the engineering knowledge, and the Hack and Espionage tricks I knew, I searched for a signal, anything at all, but found nothing.

There was an utter lack of any power here, not even the faintest flicker of it from the ship. I shook my head.

"Well, we could try cutting our way through…" I suggested.

"Or we could not," Ingrid replied. "Corey, did you bring a power source?"

"Yeah, it's upstairs," he said, before grinning at me. "Gonna need a hand to get it down, though… You up for that, boss?"

"Yeah, yeah," I grumbled. "You want to get Cybele just in case?"

Ingrid smiled, nodding. "She's our ally, and it's right that we include her," she agreed, before squeezing my hand and letting go. "You get the generator, I'll get to work on gathering the others. Who knows, we might get lucky!"

Spoiler alert.

We didn't get fucking lucky.

I didn't, anyway. Jonas and Scylla? They were like goddamn teenagers, so I didn't put it past them to have found an out of the way corner and got their end away. But by the time we finally got power hooked up to the door, and we used a solid few thousand nanites to restructure the locking mechanism, we found that we'd struck out.

The room on the far side of the massive door was of little value to me…beyond a little academic and greedy bastard instincts, anyway.

What it was, though, was utterly priceless to Ingrid, and she burst into tears within seconds of us opening the door.

The room beyond was squared off, with dozens of small recesses in the walls, each with a clear glass—or I was willing to bet artificial sapphire—covering. It meant that we could see the items contained in the cubby holes perfectly, and no doubt, in better days, there'd have been lighting and probably mood music or something in here.

It wasn't a computer core we'd found—it was a trophy room.

One wall held a dozen sculptures, with what looked like four missing. All were made from what appeared to be diamond and obsidian, great sheets of the stuff with geometric patterning on them, looping around the outside, and the dignified face of an alien in the middle, seemingly held deep within, in some kind of suspended animation.

Looking at it from the sides, and with a bit more care taken, you could see that they were indeed carvings, but they were so lifelike that, at first, they looked as if they'd blink and wake up if you made a loud noise.

Under each was a plaque, spidery symbols that made no sense to us, possibly declaring what and who the figure had been—or the breakfast cereal box that the ship's captain had gotten them out of, for all I knew.

We searched the room, finding treasures, primitive—and not so primitive— weapons, armor, and more. Hermetically sealed canisters were stacked in special holders, and I could feel Ingrid fighting with the need to examine everything.

"Behave yourself, grave robber," I whispered to her.

"I'm a professional grave robber, I'll have you know," she replied distractedly. "I can't wait to share this with Far and…and Mor."

"You will," I assured her, wrapping my arms around her and pulling her in close, kissing the top of her head and holding her as I felt the sadness, the fear, and the hope over her mother's condition fill her.

We'd checked in as soon as the fight was won, and Anders—her "Far," as her father was called in Denmark; her mother, "Mor"—had filled us in.

She was recovering—or her body was, at any rate…no word yet on her mind, her personality, or anything else—but her body was steadily regrowing in the medical suite.

If we were lucky, tomorrow, or maybe the day after, she'd awaken, and we'd all be able to relax, a little at least. Until then, we just had to hope.

It was ridiculous, all things considered, as I'd died hundreds of times by now, and I always came back. But still, until she was there, and Ingrid had held her, she'd not be able to believe it.

"These are ancient indeed," Cybele whispered, shaking her head at the artifacts. "They look like… I've seen something like these, once, long ago." The look on her face was hard, giving as little as possible away, and Ingrid, being Ingrid, stepped in close, whispering something to her.

As we set off searching, more and more of the story came out, and Cybele admitted that it was something her father had. It was one of the artifacts that had been stored in pride of place in her family's compound, and that, like so many others, had been lost when the humans of that time attacked the Arisen.

It was interesting, though, considering that there were some missing ones, making it possible that this was where that had come from—though, try as we might, none of us could figure out any reason for it to have made its way to her father's hands.

The rest of the doors that we found in the ship over the next six hours brought more of the same—not trophy rooms, but certainly disappointment.

We found the armory, which held stands for equipment and armor, machinery that looked to have been used to maintain whatever was kept in here…and nothing else.

Next was a room which sort of resembled a full-on bridge, with massive panels that ran floor to ceiling, presumably some kind of viewscreens, and a dozen seats, but not one of them had so much as a drinks holder, never mind a computer, so we had to guess that everything was done through nanite connections.

A fourth room that we found, right after giving up, was a bit more interesting, though, considering that it again proved the similarity of the way we seemed to think with the builders.

It was a brig.

One that was designed to hold creatures that were clearly dangerous as fuck, considering the level of restraints, the sheer number of manacles, and what had to have been weapons emplacements set up around the room—all pointed at presumably the central section where their "guest" would have been kept.

I say presumably, because like the armory, the assumed weapons emplacements had all been stripped out, leaving only connectors and swivel mounts.

"Someone went through here with a fine-tooth comb," Jonas muttered, shifting one of the mounts on its gimbaled frame. "I mean, check this out. The damn thing is still usable—the frame, I mean. It moves easily, not so much as the faintest of grinding, and yet it has to have been millennia since the damn thing was oiled."

"Oiled?" I asked at the incongruity of the thought that, with all the high tech, they had been using oil, and he nodded.

"Yeah, right here, where the joint matches the frame…it's oiled."

"Let's see that." Corey grunted, moving over and peering at the arm, before shaking his head. "It's not oil." He lifted his fingers free, rubbing them together and sniffing them.

"Yeah, well, whatever alien shit they make their lube out of." The big Texan shrugged. "I didn't think they'd be using the same shit that we'd get from the 7-11, you know…"

"No, you don't get it," Corey said, still staring at his fingers. "Check the others."

We did. All of us moved to the nearest mount and checked them, only to find similar things.

"It's not oil," Corey repeated. "And it's not been put into the frame to lubricate it." He pointed to marks on the floor. "Anyone followed these?"

"No…?" I said, confused. "I mean, there's nothing on the ship now besides us and…there's nothing on here, right?"

I looked at the others, even as Ingrid sent a group-wide message, and we all pulled our armor up and into position.

Possible enemy infiltration! Be on your guard. Something else may be here…

Chapter Two

It took us five hours more to search the rest of the ship, and by that point I was getting more and more annoyed by the interruption, not to mention by the goddamn waste of the most valuable resource we had—*time*—when finally, we found it.

There was a small hatch almost totally hidden under the ship, surrounded by dozens of the weird renat tribal shrine things, that in turn led out into a cave system, and after another ten minutes of tracking, to an passage that ended in a massive underground lake.

One that, when we checked it, was salty with the taste of the sea.

"They beat us to it." Jonas voiced the thoughts most of us were having already.

"Who?" Cybele glanced over at him, and then me, seeing I was nodding my agreement.

"The Blessed," I guessed, glaring at the water and wondering just how far ahead they'd made it.

"Unlikely," Sanneth interjected, shaking his head. "The Blessed faction would have, and very happily, given the choice, but if they had ready access to the underside of the ship, why would they have maintained a garrison above?"

"I… Good point," I muttered. "The Accursed?"

"Unlikely again," Cybele agreed, nodding to Sanneth. "If either of the factions had access to the ship in this manner, they would have used it as a staging ground at the very least. The renat seem to be no more amphibious than we are, and the Arisen could have simply retreated into the water with scuba gear, returned to their ships between assaults, and we would have been none the wiser."

"There would have been no need to maintain secrecy on the upper levels, when they could just sail a sub directly to this point," Sanneth pointed out. "And if, for whatever reason, they couldn't—narrow passages or more—they could have used underwater demolitions or engineering methods to reach this passage."

"And…" Ingrid spoke up, frowning as she turned to look back in the direction of the ship. "And there's no sign of the renat here."

"What?" Jonas frowned.

"The renat," she repeated. "There's a load of their shrines around the exit to the caves, but once you step out? We've not seen a single bone or corpse. The sheer number of shrines around the hatch was unusual. I'm betting that if we examine them properly, we'll find that they mark a forbidden territory, or…"

"Or?" I prompted.

"Or something they respected," she finished in a rush. "Think about it. Someone cleaned the ship out of everything that we need, or that Varnock needed. Every weapon is gone, the ship was powered down—or we think it is; Zac's still trying to figure out the engines—but this ship had landed here. Sometime long enough ago for the mountains to have swallowed it. And yet someone came more recently and stripped everything out."

"That raises another point," Cybele agreed. "A third party."

"Oh, for fuck's sake, another one!" Jonas muttered, getting a glare from Cybele that shut him up as she went on.

"The assault, the stealing of precious antiquities from under the nose of the renat," she clarified. "These tracks…they are old, but not ancient. They were recent enough to leave valid imprints, and neither time nor the passage of creatures has removed them. See here?"

She crouched, and Scylla went with her. The rest of us stood around awkwardly, peering over their shoulders at the scuffed marks on the ground.

We'd been hurrying along the rocky passage, myself and at least half of the others ready for a fight, fully expecting to find another group of assholes trying to steal from us, probably Arisen.

Instead, as Scylla pointed out several more prints that had survived the passage of our group, and Cybele went on, I started to get a bad feeling in the pit of my stomach.

"They're armored," I said slowly. "You're sure they're not more of our prints?"

"No," Scylla agreed with Cybele and Sanneth. "Our prints are fresh. Note the hard edges of the outline, the steeper sides and the fresh infill. The older prints are likely months, if not years old, but no more."

"They're fuzzier," Ingrid said, getting a long-suffering look from Scylla, who clearly felt that "fuzzy" wasn't the correct way to be talking about the serious business of tracking.

"Exactly." Cybele smiled at Ingrid. "Fuzzy. Well, it's accurate enough. As Scylla has pointed out, the tracks are crumbling around the edges. Dust, sand, the passage of myriad tiny creatures…all have served to wear away at the edges of the older prints, leaving them softer and less defined, where our more recent ones stand clear."

"So what does this mean?" I asked, annoyed and turning to look out over the wine-dark water that gently lapped against the shore of the underground grotto.

"It means that someone with armor, similar to your own, retrieved the weapons and who knows what else from the ship in the recent past." Sanneth stepped up to stand by my side, staring out.

"Someone the renat not only didn't fight, but either fled from or welcomed, if I'm right about the shrines," Ingrid added. "Someone who came from the sea and returned to it."

"That doesn't leave us many options, or hints," I muttered.

"It can't be the Arisen." Cybele stood smoothly and moved up to the shoreline, crouching there and dipping a finger in, then tasting it and nodding to herself.

"Why not?" Jonas asked. "Believe me, some of those assholes wouldn't tell their mother good morning, never mind if they found a stash like this..."

"Opportunity and capability," Cybele said. "It comes down to who had the capability and the opportunity. First of all, limited numbers knew that anything was even here. We ourselves thought it a punishment outpost. I mean not to sound immodest, but if our spies were unaware, I doubt many others could have uncovered the truth."

"And look at the way the renat responded to Varnock," Sanneth added. "They weren't welcoming her with open arms. They attacked her just as much as they did the Blessed faction members. The Xi-Ma carved themselves a path to this point. Had the renat worshiped her the way you're suggesting they did with whoever the thief is? She could have simply walked up and done whatever she needed."

"So, the renat attacked whoever they saw—the Xi-Ma, the Blessed, the flying fucks that she had, and Varnock herself. Sounds xenophobic as fuck, but yeah, understandable. This is their home and everyone keeps streaming in, trying to rob them—I'd be the same. Pass the shotgun," I agreed.

"Except that instead of guarding against this path into their home, they built massive shrines and let anyone who comes in leave again," Ingrid suggested.

"We don't know that," Jonas pointed out. "For all we know, they killed their way through the lower ship, and the renat are just good about cleaning their shit up."

"It's possible, but unlikely." Ingrid shook her head. "The shrines are massively important to the renat. They make them from the bones of their ancestors, I'm thinking. The sheer number and design, not to mention the way they're literally everywhere? It suggests a species that reveres their past, that wants to keep them close. Most species don't treat their dead the way we do. The lycans certainly don't.

"They just leave them, expecting they'll either get back up soon or they won't. Minotaurs leave them where they fall, believing that it's a sacrilege to move them. Oracans burn and bury their dead like humans. The Stelek are a hive mind and don't seem to see the difference beyond that one form is still useful and the other is food."

Ingrid broke off, looking around at the curious looks on our faces, and sighed.

"It's the archaeologist in me," she explained. "I studied a great many of our ancestors' beliefs, and sure, a lot of the information we have has disproved their rites and so on. Most of them have to have come from interactions with the Arisen. Think about the pharaohs—everything about their first lives was geared toward their future in the next life. They believed they would die, and that the greater their tomb, and their possessions, the greater they'd be in the next life.

"They believed they'd be resurrected, and Lars and I are convinced that's from direct evidence in the past of that happening. We know that the Xi-Ma were, at one point, guardians for the original pharaohs. We don't know what happened to them, but there are legends of the pharaohs sailing across rivers and being transported beyond the stars, or into the underworld to be judged by an all-powerful god that would decide their fate. Most likely, someone back in antiquity saw something very similar to the Arisen, the pharaohs literally coming back to life and…" She faltered, looking around, as the reality of the conversation she was having dawned on her.

"You were there," she said after enduring a few seconds of amused silence, sighing at the way Sanneth and Cybele were watching her and smiling gently. "Dammit, you were there."

"Not in what you know as Egypt now—well, not for a lot of it—but yes, we passed through. And some of the factions did move there, as we discussed. So did some of our kind in the deep past. Some of our numbers created the precursor to the Egyptian mythology that you know, although much of it was less…interesting than it is now."

"Oh?"

"Our kind tended toward simple messages in the beginning," Sanneth said. "Do this, or you're dead."

"That's inaccurate." Cybele sighed. "We tried to be better at first. We tried to teach. Then, when humanity proved they were incapable of the longer-term vision, we pared things down. Those who moved to the south and into the African plains, they started out simple, then built atop it. Some of them, however, *yes*…they were prone to theatrics."

"And there you have it, folks." Jonas laughed. "Theatrics. The long-term explanation for all of humanity's god complexes: a bunch of immortals acting up on a global stage."

"Ingrid." I interrupted her gently as she went to open her mouth, ready to ask more questions of the two Elders. "You were saying that the bone shrines meant something?"

"Yes…" She sighed, shaking her head and clearly with a mind full of questions. "While not all the species we've come across have myths or beliefs that we know of, the renat clearly believe in something, and buried beneath a forest—where they could easily get access to lumber or space to dispose of their dead—they instead covered the inside of the ship in thousands of years of their ancestors.

"They clearly used the bones for some form of religious purpose, and while they might have had contact in the deep past with some Arisen or another species that led them to this, we'll never know. What we do know is that there were a lot less of the shrines in other areas. If they wanted to hide the hatch? They could have made a single shrine, layered the bones over and over. They could have carved stone, like they did at the entrance to the ship, and blocked it off.

"Instead, they surrounded the entrance with shrines. The size and sheer number of them, as well as the fact they were carefully made to be clear of the entrance, and not in the way? It suggests they worshipped it, or were afraid of it."

"The entrance to the underworld?" I suggested.

"They already live underground and appear to have no fear of the dark." She shook her head. "If it was the underworld, as we think of it, they would be more likely to have disposed of bodies by putting them above ground, 'out' from their world. If they needed the bones? They might have still left the flesh. But even if the hatch was believed to be somewhere the spirits passed through, vanishing into the depths? For the intruder to access the ship through there and to move back and forth, stripping the armory and other sections?"

"You'd be expecting a frantic fight to defend against it, rather than leaving them to do it," Jonas suggested, getting nods from most of us.

"So we're left with no fucking clue, basically?" I growled. "Someone comes from the ocean, they steal everything that's not nailed down, the renat worship them—or at least they don't attack them on sight. Which is pretty much worship as near as I can tell with these assholes. And, when they've finished nicking it all, they bugger off into the sea again."

"I'd not say we don't have any clue," Ingrid said softly. "We know of one group that could have theoretically come for the artifacts, and that would know both where they were, and where the ship was."

"Who?" I frowned.

"The people who landed it."

There was silence for long seconds, before Jonas finally broke it.

"That's a fair point," he said. "We know that the ship refused that crazy bitch, so she wiped its core out. She clearly knew about the ship, or found out about it, and believed that it'd be her ticket out of here, that all she needed was us distracted long enough for her to get here and take over, then she'd be able to fuck us up."

"She could have used the bioweapon, the one she used on Artorian, to infect someone in a hidden location in our valley, and done it at a point where it would have caused maximum damage before we found it," Cybele agreed. "Instead, it was somewhere that would cause us to lock down the area and go on the defensive, but with very little chance of success."

"He was supposed to take out that grav drive thing," I pointed out.

"And if he'd succeeded, it is likely that we'd all be dead. But if that was the overall intended target? She could have simply assumed control of the site by walking in. Without your innate nature attacking her, it is likely that she'd have been able to at least distract us all long enough to kill the majority. Should she have marched the Xi-Ma in? In a wave? As galling as it is to admit it, had she done that when we were already facing the coup, they would have won, and probably easily," Sanneth said sourly.

"So, Varnock found out about, or knew about the ship, and came right for it, risking everything, when a safer bet by far would have been a direct assault on us in the valley. Instead, she hauled ass to get here, then went mental when she found she couldn't get it to work for her?" I asked.

"Basically," Jonas agreed.

"So someone—not the dickhead creators, and most likely human, or one of our ancestors, we think—and a member of the UC, or they'd not be able to try to unlock the ship for us to use. So they landed the ship here, then fucked off into the sea?" I went on.

"And which group are we aware of, that fit the timescales even slightly, and were heavily involved in the sea?" Ingrid suggested, and I glared at her.

"I know I'm not the brightest," I said, "but come on, you don't need to lead me by the nose like this. I'll say it, though. *Atlantis.*"

"Exactly." Ingrid smiled. "You have no idea how upset Lars is going to be over this."

"I don't understand," Cybele said, and I held up a hand, as Ingrid explained Lars's history, as an archaeologist, of being constantly pestered by questions on Atlantis.

He *hated* it with a passion, first because it took away from the serious business of being an archaeologist as he saw it, and then later because if it was true, and it'd really existed, then all the fringe nutcases on the outside of the mainstream "known" truths—many of whom could also be found spouting about aliens until red in the face, and being allergic to soap or deodorant—were actually right.

That was the worst part for him, and gods I was looking forward to seeing his face when he had to admit to it.

"You all go on." I nodded to the passage that led back. "I did some upgrades to my armor awhile back, and I can survive down there easily." I gestured to the dark waters lapping near our feet.

"You're going to check it out?" Jonas asked. "I'll come with you."

"No point," I said firmly. "First of all, you don't have the upgrades for atmospheric cleansing unlocked, do you?"

"No…"

"So you'll be able to breathe for a few minutes longer than a regular human…up to half an hour I think you could last, depending on the upgrades you've got and the armor. But beyond that? It also means that in fifteen minutes, give or take, you'd need to turn back anyway."

"Better than you going alone," he pointed out.

"Sure, if there was any threat down there." I shrugged. "Cybele, Scylla, how recent do you think those prints were made?"

"Months at the very least," Cybele said firmly, and Scylla nodded in agreement. "Most are likely years old."

"I doubt anything's waiting down there. I just want to have a look around and make sure, that's all. See if there's any traces of anything that might lead us on. The only thing we've got so far is that some fucker in the sea nicked our shit. Could be that water dude from the movies for all we know."

"At least he's handsome!" Ingrid smiled, before stepping in close. We both banished our helmets and kissed, pausing for a long second, nose to nose, as we stared into each other's eyes. "No starting fights, no getting lost, and no being eaten by sea monsters, okay?"

"Yes, ma'am." I smiled.

"And I expect to see you back here in an hour. No longer."

"Maybe two." I hedged. "The passage might be longer than I'm expecting."

"Two hours, and if you're not back by then, I'm coming in after you."

"You've not got…"

"I just bought the upgrade." She stared at me. "We probably all need it, considering where we're going, so don't make me wait."

"Yes, boss." I kissed her once more, then stepped back and nodded to the others, before turning on my heel and striding out into the water.

They were quiet behind me as I went, the only sound the sloshing of the water around my ankles, then working its way up to my thighs. I hesitated for a split second, my stride slowing slightly as it reached my balls. Stupid, I know—I always did it, no matter the warmth of the water. If I was walking out into the water, there was always that shock of colder water reaching your nether region.

Here?

I was wearing a goddamn armored suit. If I felt the water getting in there? I had a hell of a lot more problems than the damn temperature. But still, on instinct, I hesitated. That, right then, as my step hitched, and I then tried to speed up, to cover that momentary lapse, was when my foot hit the hidden rock.

I tripped, twisted, and staggered, then tried to pretend I was diving, and that I'd not tripped at all, throwing myself forward.

As the world above was lost, the darkness that had already been battling with my upgraded eyes and my suit's night vision capabilities was now replaced by swirling water, disturbed sand, and the general miasma of an undersea cave system.

Everything was green and grey, the sand almost black as I struck out for deeper water. The gentle slope of the decline reached a cutoff a dozen meters ahead, and I kicked and pulled at the water…before smiling and pulling my arms in close, activating the gravity inversion capability.

Instantly, the sand and general sediment I was stirring up shifted and I shot forward. "Down" now simply showed as "ahead," as if I were diving headfirst into the depths, rather than swimming in a generally downward angle.

I started to feel good about myself, allowing another smile as I spotted sections ahead that might have indicated figures had dragged something through here…when Jonas pinged me.

I opened it in the corner of my vision, then cursed.

It was me, on repeat, along with a soundtrack from a circus clown, tripping and basically throwing myself into the water.

He'd added a clown's red nose onto my armor as well, the bastard.

I'd get him back for that, I silently vowed, moving on and reaching the drop-off, before hesitating at the edge.

There, ahead of me, and vanishing into the depths, preserved by the goddamn cold waters, were ancient stairs that led down and down.

They were carved from the side of the cliff. Here and there, the stairs had been colonized by growths of something like coral, but I'd never known such a thing to exist in extremely cold water.

I set off, floating over the edge and descending. The silence of the undersea world grew louder and louder, until my world was filled by the sound of my own breathing and heartbeat.

I stared ahead, starting to see the occasional motion. Now and then, barely able to be seen, were flashes of tiny movement. Fishes raced about, darting in and out of the growing structures, and I watched, entranced, as I sank deeper, picking up speed.

There was no light here, nothing that I understood life to need, certainly fuck all warmth, like I'd seen the weird life at the bottom of the ocean, where it was totally black, surviving around the heat vents instead.

No, here there was nothing but the cold, the dark, and what I'd have assumed was death.

Instead, there were occasional pockets of fish now, possibly hundreds, moving here and there. The deeper I went, more of them turned up. As I reached the sandy bottom, dozens of stone steps down, where the carved steps gave way to what had assumedly been a lower sea level and the rock returned to its unbothered surface, there were finally signs of something having been here.

I arched the gravity well around, almost not having to think about it now, and I tracked out the rough shape of whatever had been here, mapping it by the depressions in the sand and the broken coral growths.

Whatever it was, it'd been a good size.

That was it, or as near as I could tell, drawing it in my mind, then sending the image to Ingrid and the others, along with the location. It'd been perhaps thirty meters across at the widest point, and forty long, from the tip to the tail.

It'd also taken off and settled down with almost no trace. The sand had been shoved back as it landed and took off, but nowhere were the signs I was used to— the blasting of propellers, the jets of compressed water, or who knew what else.

It looked like a gravity field had been deployed, something high tech enough that the ship simply lifted up and out, and settled gently when needed.

Three long landing struts had deployed, and then it was off, and a thin trail of disturbed sand marked its passage before it petered out.

I followed it for a handful of minutes, passing out from a deep cave and into the ocean quicker than I expected, before losing it as the clearance grew.

I searched for a few more minutes, then gave up, returning to the surface and launching myself into the air. The crisp, clear water fell free as I twisted around, rising into the early morning sunlight.

I arched around, heading back in toward the hidden valley, noting the locations as I went, making sure we could easily find the entrance again. We damn well needed to install sensors down there, at the very least.

I sent a quick message to Zac, getting a disgruntled image of a middle finger, before it changed into a smiling professional face and a "will do, boss" reply.

Clearly, he'd either changed his mind about giving me the finger or, much more likely, he was playing games.

Fuck it. That was the joy of working with almost any Aussie, never mind engineering prodigy ones: the respect was slightly less than they gave their friends, and that, in turn, was less than they gave their worst enemy.

A short while later, I was sitting with the rest of the management team, as we had them there: Cybele, Sanneth, Ingrid, and me, with Zac pointedly being too busy to join us for *"another waste of my fucking time meeting where all I'll get is more work."*

"So," I started, shrugging after bringing them up to date on my little side adventure. "Now what?"

"We need to find where those coordinates lead to," Ingrid said. "It's unlikely that the UC and the Ændari use the same coordinates, but if they do, what are the chances of finding another intact AI in one of the other wrecks, and then being able to dig it out, and get it to accept your authority?"

She looked at me, and I shook my head. "It's unlikely," I agreed. "I've tried remoting back to the system that runs the refuge. Either it doesn't understand the question, or it's not saying, but there's nothing there I can get."

"You said it was designed to be a solid refuge for the creators to work on their experiments and likely a fallback position," Cybele pointed out. "Would there be a reason to give a limited sentience, in a building, essentially, star navigation data?"

"Not really," I grumbled. "Figured it was worth a try, though."

"Of a certainty, but still. Looking to the future, I suggest we repurpose those satellites and begin scouring the depths," Cybele said. "Ingrid, you said that you have records that speak of Atlantis being beyond the 'Pillars of Hercules,' correct?"

"Yes... Oh my gods, did you know Atlantis?" Ingrid asked Cybele suddenly, sitting forward, her eyes opening wide.

"No." Cybele smiled, taking the sting from the words. "The legends of Atlantis were known to us as well, though. But over the years, despite many attempts to find anything more than rumor and legend, we found nothing more than ancient, unpopulated ruins."

"Nothing at all?" Ingrid deflated, sat back again and crossed her arms sadly, before her eyes widened. "Wait...ruins? You *found* Atlantis already?"

"Well..." Cybele looked at Sanneth. "Would you like to explain?" she asked him.

"The myth of Atlantis was one that we were familiar with, and one that we chased most assiduously for long centuries," Sanneth said. "That there was a landmass to the south, in the Atlantic Ocean, is possible, but not in the way that people seem to believe now. If it existed at all, it was significantly smaller than most believe. The images that we saw for a long time as humans chased the myth showed Atlantis as almost the size of Africa..."

"That's one of the reasons it was disproved," Ingrid agreed, nodding. "We know that Pangea was the most recent supercontinent in Earth's history, and looking at the general shapes of the islands, the continents and more, there's just no room. Africa fits into the Americas too smoothly. The gaps that are available, if you look at it like a puzzle, are far too small to account for a missing continent, unless you look to Zealandia of course. Although, again, that would quickly be discounted due to the extreme age difference, not to mention distance."

"Exactly." Sanneth smiled at Ingrid, clearly enjoying her dedication to her craft. "There is, however, according to detailed scans of Antarctica, a significant section of that landmass that doesn't fit with anything else. It was uncovered almost a year ago, and while slightly smaller than the United Kingdom in size, the section that is missing? It would match some of the descriptions of Atlantis." He broke off, looking over at Cybele for permission before going on.

"The layout is clearly different from Plato's version, but with good reason. The manuscript he learned of Atlantis from was ancient even in his day, and that was over two thousand years ago…more a copy of a copy than anything else. But, the Azores are the most likely suspect for Atlantis that we have ever found."

"The Azores?" I frowned. "I've heard of them, but I don't really…"

"They're a small island chain governed by Portugal," Ingrid filled me in, glancing at me and moving on as quickly as she could. "But there's little in the way of any ruins on the islands, and I've never heard of them being seriously connected to the Atlantean myths."

"That's because the myths you know reference a huge island, one that was submerged in a day and a night of terrible violence, supposedly sunk by Poseidon in a fit of wrath over its people daring to raise their hands to Athens," Cybele explained with an amused smile.

"Exactly," Ingrid agreed.

"Well, that's where the story grows more interesting," Sanneth interjected laconically. "Remember that Athens was founded in around five hundred BC, if we're using your modern calendar, yes?"

We all nodded, and he went on.

"Now, the legend is that Athens was always there, first as a small seaport and a town, then as a city, and that it's simply the modern city, despite its multiple variations. That city was founded around that time, and that's more or less correct from what we remember, but as 'serious' Atlantis investigators know, the island itself was lost to the waves some nine thousand years before that date.

"That puts it at around eleven thousand years ago, and Athens, well, she started to really get going at around three thousand BC. That puts us out by around six and a half thousand years."

"That's part of the reason Atlantis was dismissed as an allegorical legend," Ingrid agreed.

"Well, that's the point. The legend that Plato references was, as you say, allegorical: 'don't mess with Athens, and pay your taxes.' The tales that he had access to, however, that he changed, to use as a lesson to his disciples, were based on much older records."

"Was it you?" I asked suddenly. The details of these people being around at the relevant point made me blurt it out, before I realized that if it was, and they were talking about finding it, then I'd just made myself look like a right idiot. "Shit, no, of course it wasn't…" I mumbled.

Sanneth scratched his chin, shaking his head as he went on. "Well, that's not that foolish a question, actually. Realistically, we had several ships in the four to three thousand BC range that could have been the start of a number of these legends of an advanced shipbuilding nation. And had we not, at that point, already heard tales of Atlantis, I'd have dismissed those legends as an obvious crossover as well. Remember that we were sailing the ocean by this point in ships not too dissimilar to those humans wouldn't discover for another two thousand years."

"You'd have been easily mixed up with that." Ingrid nodded, smiling at me. "And the claims of the trading empire of Atlantis?"

"Most likely us again," Sanneth agreed. "Our ships, and those of the early Arisen factions, were far more advanced than humanity's vessels, as well as far larger. We were exploring the oceans, mapping the world, when papyrus was the most popular building material."

"Papyrus?" I frowned. "Isn't that like, paper?"

"Essentially, yes." Sanneth grinned. "It was hilarious to watch our enemies trying to board us in those vessels. More often than not, we'd simply sail on by and leave them to drown, no effort needed on our part."

"They'd drown?" I asked, even more confused. "They made it that far out from shore on a boat made of paper?"

"Most sailors in those days couldn't swim," he added. "They believed that if their gods destroyed their boats, then it was better to die quickly, as they'd lose their position in their society. Remember these boats represented months and sometimes years of painstaking work, often by entire families. When they sank and failed on the first sailing? Hilarious."

"I don't see what's so funny about it," Ingrid replied coolly.

"You wouldn't," Sanneth agreed with a smile. "But that's because you're thinking of it with your current sensibilities. Remember that most of these were pirates, known for murder, rape, and pillaging. Imagine, just for a minute, that the very worst atrocities that the Vikings would visit on Europe some thousands of years later would be laughed off in comparison, then think about the situation with those details held in your mind.

"When these people caught one of us? They knew we were immortal, so they'd delight in torturing, murdering, and raping us. We'd be sold as slaves, *renewable* ones. Ones that could indeed be worked into a grave, then put back to work again. That's the kind of people we faced. Sailing past them and laughing as their little boats capsized?

"By the level of modern humor and sensibilities? Utterly reprehensible. By that of those days? It'd not even pass comment in a gathering. I understand your feelings, Ingrid, but believe me, if you were to find yourself magically transported to those days, you would not like the reception you'd receive."

"Remember Hans?" I whispered to Ingrid, and she hesitated before nodding.

Hans had told us once about a home for the incurably insane amongst "our kind" and how for a while they'd accepted some of the insane of humanity as well. That had rapidly been curtailed after incidents like the one where Hans had convinced a mortal madman that he was Icarus reborn.

Then he'd fired him out of a circus cannon they'd had shipped in specifically for the "fun."

Considering that not only had there been no safety net, and it'd been over the side of a mountain cliff, with "wings" they'd encouraged the madman to make out of string and paper?

It'd ended predictably for the mortal, and Hans had been exceedingly annoyed when he and his friends were then banned from "playing" with the inmates.

Arise :Explorer

Essentially, he'd argued, by the time I reached his current age of around four hundred, I'd view the world much as he did: not so much in black and white, but instead as entirely grey, with it split down lines of amusing and annoying primarily, rather than good and bad.

Ingrid and I disagreed with him, of course, but in the silence of the night, when Ingrid lay sleeping, it was the thought that I was already closer to that point than she'd ever be that kept me awake.

Regardless, the look on her face told me that she understood and agreed with my thought; namely that the Arisen, especially ones who were older by an order of magnitude, would always see the world differently.

Sanneth, for all that we got on a lot better now than we had, was still thousands of years old. And the shit that he'd lived through? Well. He tended to think of humanity as a bunch of not quite bright dogs. Golden retrievers, for example.

You liked having them around, and you were sad if you had to have them put down—for bothering the sheep, for example, especially if you were in Wales—then you did it, and you moved on.

If they caught an infection, you tried to deal with it, but if it was more hassle than it was worth, you culled the herd to prevent it spreading out of control. After all, if you let them breed uncontrolled, then pretty soon they'd be back to their old numbers again.

The worst part was that I could see that as well, and I knew Ingrid didn't.

Mind you, I'd been a sociopath, bank robber, and a killer on the run long before I'd been ascended; she'd been an archaeologist and tourist. There were bound to be some differences in the way we viewed the world.

Chapter Three

"So, we got distracted?" I prompted Sanneth, and he nodded, gathering his thoughts before going on. The annoying bastard was clearly amused by the mumbled conversation Ingrid and I had been having through looks and nods more than anything else as well.

"Yes, well. The continent of Antarctica. As I said, if you examine it more carefully—and using the latest scans it's a lot easier, thanks to global warming—you'll note that there's a scalloped-out section. It's almost three hundred miles wide, east to west, and a little over two hundred miles north to south. It's roughly an oval, and one that—again, very roughly—matches the continental uplift that's centered over the Azores.

"Before I explain why I believe it to be the Azores, I may as well explain why the records you are likely to have access to are inaccurate. So. Your main references to Atlantis were the stories of Plato, correct? The original manuscript that Plato got his description from was supposedly from Solon.

"Solon was Plato's uncle, and he managed to commission a translation of the document from an Egyptian text. That text, when I eventually recovered it—after a *lot* of research—was a translation of a much older version. That text was, in turn, written in a dialect of Kerma. In Plato's defense, he was actually reading a fragment that had already been translated and copied at least three times, and poorly at that, so much of his version was inconsistent. Also, the Kerma version was most likely translated from the original language that was spoken on the islands when we visited."

He held his hand up, smiling as Ingrid opened her mouth to ask a question.

"If I may guess at your next question, yes, I know the Azores are currently Portuguese in nationality and language. When the Portuguese claimed the islands, some six hundred years ago as near as I can remember, their sailors claimed there were no native inhabitants to be found there.

"By that point, that may well have been true. I do remember they had a few fairly localized and virulent plagues on the islands. A lot of us took to avoiding them entirely, but I remember the natives there could speak a bastardized version of Kerma. Suggesting that there was at least regular contact at that point. Frankly, it caused me no end of issues to learn that language, when I visited those islands in my search for Atlantis, around the fifth century BC."

"You were there?" she asked, eyes wide, her fingers twitching convulsively as, if I knew her at all, I guessed she was making mental notes.

"I was. I was studying the legends, determined to prove once and for all that there was no such place. I'd been searching for some time, because we know that there were other Arisen before ourselves, and although their stories were lost, thanks to the purge by humanity and the terrible devastation they wrought, we were determined to find more of our kind."

"We searched for literally thousands of years," Cybele said sadly. "*Thousands* of years, as the eldest among us sank into immobility, as more and more of the world that we'd lost faded from us, and we lost those ancients, burying them, then burning them, trying to set them free of the prisons of flesh they were trapped within."

"Best we leave that subject," Sanneth said after a long look at Cybele. "Enough to say that the past had been lost, and that's why we were searching for Atlantis, hoping to find distant kin. When I visited the Azores, I found an island people, advanced seafarers certainly. There were also many unusual ruins that were apparently demolished over the intervening centuries, but it was their *legends* that captivated me.

"The original description of Atlantis was of a mountain in the middle of an island larger than Asia and Libya combined. Let's see, how did that description go? 'The mountain was split, and from that point the people of Atlas came, for it was originally called the Island of Atlas and only translated as Atlantis, for he who was supposedly its king, named it after himself.'

"Those people carved great channels—moats and canals, they'd be called in more modern times—but channels that allowed their ships access to the interior of the island. That, at least, was right. Where that fool Plato gets it wrong is that not only was the island not so huge as all that, it was nothing like he described.

"People wasted hundreds of years searching for the damn place, and in reality, it was simply sunk into the sea through a particularly violent set of volcanic eruptions that left only the tips of the mountains showing. People have searched the islands, looking for anything that resembled his words, not knowing that any word that old fool couldn't understand, his pride wouldn't allow him to admit to.

"The central island had a mountain, yes, it certainly did, but the descriptions that I read, and that were confirmed by other scholars of the time, referenced a mighty fire mountain—a volcano—that lay on the eastern side. It was the mountain that was supposedly beloved of Poseidon and his lover, the mother of the twins who would become the island's rulers.

"In reality, I've no idea where the legends of Poseidon and those demigods came from. They were referenced in older texts, and by older names, but I forget them now. They were supposedly immortal, though, and the repeated references to another group of immortals was part of the reason we started searching. Simply put, we suspected they were like us." He paused, gathering his thoughts, and Cybele spoke.

"Sanneth, the condensed version, please. We don't have time for this."

He glared at her, before taking a deep breath and going on. "Condensed, yes, well…there's a lot of information to get across, my princess, but very well. We've established now why I believe Plato's account and the original versions, including the descriptions of the ringed islands and so on, were at best an exaggeration. Now, let's explain where the details match.

"First of all, sections of the island chain were more accessible before the sea levels rose. Looking at them now, you won't match anything that seems familiar from the descriptions, but that's due mainly to the passage of thousands of years, and the fact that the original translations were done so poorly.

"Next, the eastern edge of the island in the records that we've translated correctly had a volcano, and the overall shape was indeed an oval, more or less, certainly described as longer east to west than north to south, and this matches the Azores almost perfectly.

"The volcano in the east loomed over the 'Plains of Ammeth,' according to the records. They were supposedly the bounty that enabled the natives there to develop a seagoing empire. There was a massive basin, one with a freshwater lake at its heart. The sides of the basin were heavily irrigated, and stepped, in the eastern style. We have several drawings of terraces that would not only make most of the land available to grow food, but would in turn allow rainwater to flow down, through the earth.

"The soil was known to be volcanic, enabling rapid growth and bountiful harvests, and the outer edge of the island was most likely a crater impact point from some time in Earth's past. It was described as having a wall atop a cliff that ran its length, pausing only at the mouth of the harbor.

"That harbor, in turn, was heavily fortified and led into the freshwater lake, through what the descriptions suggest were an ingenious series of locks."

"Locks?" I asked, and he nodded animatedly.

"Have you ever seen a canal? When they need to go up or down a level, a lock is used. Simply pour the water from one end into the next, a simple engineering design, and yet revolutionary. It enabled the Atlanteans to dig a passage from the central lake all the way to the sea, and yet the freshwater remained uncontaminated." He paused, looking around before he went on.

"Again, this is circumstantial evidence, not definitive, but had you seen the ruins on the islands that I did, you would have been able to clearly assign them to similar uses.

"Moving onto the circular design of the island referenced in many of the legends…if instead of huge rivers that rotated around the central axis, we consider the lakes and canals, then we can see how a nation of shipbuilders would have been able to easily access and leave the island, while still maintaining both control and secrecy.

"The islands that are now known as the Azores are most likely the resting place of the mythical Atlantis, but we, as the Arisen, encountered no unequivocal proof of the supposedly advanced civilization's existence. No survivors, no artifacts, no evidence that couldn't be explained away.

"When I searched—and believe me, I searched with the intention of proving that there was no such place—I eventually came to the conclusion that, in fact, it had most likely once existed. The sheer amount of corroboration, the discovery of the ruins, the records, the…*well*. If Atlantis as we believe it to be did exist, then it was in the Azores as I said, and it was lost, most likely through a volcanic eruption of such significant magnitude that it sank the entire surrounding area.

"There was significant evidence that myths of our past and the Atlantean myths were mixed together. That, as well as the inaccuracies in translation, suggested to me that although Atlantis, or whatever was the basis for those myths, *did* exist, it was lost before we sailed those seas, and as such it was either a much earlier version of our own civilization, or an entirely separate one."

He paused, glancing around the table. "This is what I believe. The evidence I have seen with my own eyes and the records we have access to point to this, but we cannot know for sure. We have limited time, and this is the best advice I can offer."

"Well, there were a few details that we can confirm as well…" Ingrid said slowly. "First of all, some of the Minoan records and the artifacts…they showed a landmass with rivers and lakes in the Atlantic Ocean. It was farther north, and larger, but that could be attributed to cartographical mistakes."

"The mapmakers of antiquity tended to make their own homes much larger and more impressive than reality dictated." Cybele smiled. "It was amusing to see England and her Isles larger than France, for example."

"That's because we were better than the damn French," I said, before grinning.

"It's sounding more and more like Arisen helped in the long-term design of the island at that time—irrigation, massive community projects, and so on," Ingrid agreed. "Do you…do you have those scrolls still?" She asked that last in a rush, her innate "need" to see such reference materials coming out.

"The original scrolls are long since dust…" Sanneth said sadly, waiting until she sagged with disappointment, before smiling gently. "But we made meticulous copies. And as with all such records, every three centuries, they are reproduced by the librarians."

"When all of this is over, would you like to see them, my dear?" Cybele asked archly. "I'm sure we can come to an arrangement. Perhaps you'd like to apprentice with the librarians for, oh, say a century, collecting and examining the records we hold? You'd be able to ask us, and get answers to the questions that have infuriated your kind for millennia, and we'd get another dedicated historian to sort that mess out. You'd be surprised how few of our people are actually interested in maintaining such things…"

"No," I said firmly, reaching out and taking Ingrid's hand in my own.

"But…" She groaned, turning to look at me, her eyes huge and desperate. "Steve…"

"We've got a galaxy to explore, entire civilizations to meet, and probably start wars and have all sorts of fun with. Until that's sorted, no, you can't go play in the library." I said it with a wink, clearly tongue in cheek. If that was seriously what she wanted to do, I'd never stand in her way, but the offer they'd just made? It was like offering a meth addict a pipe and an unlimited supply. The look on Cybele's face let me know that she damn well knew that as well.

"So, no offense, Sanneth, and I know this shit is interesting as hell to you guys, but what the fuck does any of this have to do with Atlantis, and more importantly, if it was totaled thousands of years ago, what does that have to do with us now? Did they sprout gills and swim all this way to nick our damn gear?"

"Steve, as ever, you both annoy and amuse me." Sanneth sighed. "Your lack of interest in the past and the secrets it holds horrifies me, even now, knowing that most likely there are secrets here that we can link to others and guess more accurately at the past than ever before, and you're bored by it all."

"And I amuse you as well," I pointed out.

"You do," he agreed laconically. "Can you also balance a treat on your nose? My dog can, and frankly, he amuses me in much the same way you do."

"Well, woof, woof." I sighed. "I'd be upset, but you know, I'm not being insulted by anyone who matters to me, so…"

"Steve." Ingrid said my name in a warning tone, the drawing out of the *e* and the frown she gave me being replicated almost perfectly at the same time by Cybele as she said Sanneth's name in warning.

"Sorry," I muttered.

"My apologies," Sanneth offered. "I forget that to you, this is all new, Steve, and while the lovely Ingrid shares my passion about the past, and the secrets it holds, you do not. Very well. As my princess requested, this is merely a condensed version.

"This was accepted by us as likely the source of the myths, and a possible precursor civilization to ourselves, but one that would have been left to be explored at our leisure, and only when the world was calmer. Only, that is, if not for the current evidence and situation."

"And…?" I asked as he paused.

"And that would have been the end of it," Ingrid said softly, looking over at me. "If not for your meeting with the Erlking."

"Ah shit," I muttered. If the creators were involved, it meant that a little thing like a volcano and the entire island being written off didn't mean anything was final at all.

"Quite," Sanneth said with a thin smile. "Steve, when we first met and you shared some of your experiences through the orb—the linkage, I suppose I should call it—you let slip that you were aware of another of the creators, and that you suspected them to be involved with Atlantis. Considering all that has been discovered of late, I think this is where you explain your part in the story."

I stared at him for a few seconds, gathering my thoughts, then nodded and began.

"All right, so you know what I said about the Erlking, and what a dick he was. Well, he said there were three of them. He never used a name, not that I remember anyway. The Oracan named him the Erlking, and so did Belle and the others… Shit, you think she'd be able to help with this?" I suggested hopefully to Ingrid.

"I'll tie her into the command net conversation," Ingrid offered, gesturing for me to go on, and that she'd bring Belle up to speed.

"Thanks." I smiled at her. "Okay, so…the Erlking is a real military-grade wanker, killed me a few times just for not showing 'the proper humility,' if you can believe that?" I looked around the group for support.

"You did insult him," Ingrid pointed out.

"Yes, you accused the Erlking of, and I quote, 'cry-wanking himself off and complaining that it wasn't his fault.'"

That was Belle's first contribution to the conversation, and as Ingrid repeated it aloud, I paused as Sanneth puzzled through the terms, before figuring out its meaning and bursting into laughter.

"Steve…I think that perhaps in the future, another of us should be in charge of diplomatic relations?" Cybele suggested, trying to hide a slight smile.

"I can be diplomatic," I muttered.

"No, you can't," Belle corrected. *"After you recovered from the Erlking killing you, your first words were to call it a 'wanker' and telling it that it was a 'shitty excuse for a god' that had traumatized your entire species through its incompetence."*

"Ingrid, perhaps you or I should lead on negotiations in the future?" Cybele suggested, and Ingrid nodded firmly.

"I'll keep mine under control if you keep yours as well?" she suggested, getting a smile and a nod from the elder princess. "Then that's settled."

"Hey now—" I started.

"Do you *want* to do the negotiating?" Ingrid asked me seriously.

"Well, no, but—"

"So don't complain, dear." She patted my hand. "Now, you were going to explain what the Erlking told you?"

"Right." I sighed. "Okay then, the Erlking said that there were three of them here, all right? They were all involved in the council's project to create us as weapons, and they were all punished when the first generation went off the rails and essentially kicked the fuck out of the cosmos.

"The Erlking said that they were ordered to leave their ships and everything else, to walk away and to start a new life here. It was punishment. The Erlking basically took it as it was intended, I guess. It lived with the creatures it'd helped create, and just, I don't know, chilled out?"

"The Erlking established what would be referenced later by your sacred texts as the Garden of Eden," Belle explained. *"It provided refuge to many species, turning them out when they grew strong enough or angered it, but attempting to teach the various species to live in harmony with each other. We, the greater dryads, I mean, were apparently its most successful experiment."*

"Cool. Well, that's the path the Erlking took. It also did some forging and grew the valley into this seriously nice area—like wild, but nice with it…not too much of any one plant, everything living in harmony as Belle says. It warned me, though, that before it'd unlock any further systems for me, I'd need to prove myself to it, and to the others here.

"I managed to upset it enough that it declared it never wanted to see me again for some reason. It gave me that authority anyway, but the way that it did it, it was damaged, so I guess that's not something we can replicate. In the conversation, though, it explained that the remaining two were under the land and the sea, respectively.

"The one under the land, I'm guessing was Varnock, as he said she was continuing the experiments that had gotten them banned. He also told me to stay the fuck away from her." I scratched at my chin as I thought, both about needing a shave and trying to remember the details of a single conversation months ago.

"And the last of them?" Sanneth prompted.

"He said something like 'she shapeshifted and went into the sea,'" I mused.

"The other took a new form and sank beneath the waves, taking their home with them long ago. They were angered by the arrogance of their followers and sought to punish their blasphemy when they attempted to reach too high. Should you encounter them, I recommend humility." Belle repeated the exact words for us all, and I grunted in shock.

"How the hell did you do that?" I asked.

"It is a gift of my kind," she explained. *"I was there when you had this conversation, and as such, I can repeat it."*

"Repeat it all for us please, Belle, from start to finish," Ingrid ordered, and I winced, as she began.

It took awhile, and several times, listening to Belle pretending to be me and saying certain things which I was sure were an exaggeration, I wanted to stop her, but by the end, yeah, we were all convinced.

"So, it sounds like the third of the creators made Atlantis, and then sunk it in a fit of rage," Ingrid suggested.

"It certainly does," Cybele agreed. "Add in that while the Erlking was apparently unfriendly to some degree, and certainly unsociable with humans, he had no problem with dryads nor any other races that visited him."

"That implies that Varnock's hatred of our kind may have been simply her own. This third shadowy figure may not be hostile to us at all," Sanneth added in.

"If anything, they seem to have taught those they allowed to live near them, and although it's not certain that it's them, someone who has an affinity with water both knew about this ship, and raided it. I think, absent better intelligence, that they are likely to be our best choice," Cybele finished.

"Great," I agreed. "So, we've got like four days, probably less, considering we need to damn well fly across the galaxy maybe, and there's time needed for things like installation—oh, and building a fucking starship. Any clue where we start?"

"Where else?" Sanneth said with a smile. "I think it's time to head to the Azores."

Chapter Four

I t wasn't that easy, of course.

We didn't all point dramatically to the ceiling and shout "To the Azores!" then race off.

—Enter cutscene of the group splitting up, me and Ingrid relaxing in luxury on some random private plane, before boinking like crazy all the way—

No, it took a few hours to get things sorted out, mainly making sure that we weren't needed here, checking on the others, and realizing that the insane numbers of nanites we had access to in the various corpses meant that we had no choice but to use the Emergency Wipe option.

Between the vast number of the Xi-Ma's nanites—around seven or eight million a body, and there were apparently twenty of them—then the nanites we'd gotten from Varnock...

Then add in the bodies of her other monsters, and the corpses of the renat?

The numbers were staggering, and I was still moving like I'd spent a weekend earning extra cash starring in dubious "art" movies.

I couldn't store those kinds of numbers, not even slightly, though I knew that there had to be a way that I could, or we'd never grow in power like the Ændari had.

I was bloated to buggery, and I was wiping them, forming blocks of attuned nanites, then moving on. The room we'd fought Varnock in was filled with compressed blocks of solid attuned nanites now. The worst thing was, to keep from them essentially failing and falling apart, when I killed her and they'd started to...I don't know, fission or whatever, like they were breaking down...I'd had to wipe and attune them to *me.*

That meant that for anyone else to use them?

We needed to wipe them again, taking what had been over a billion, to half that, and then they'd need to half that again by the time the nanites were ready to be used by anyone else, if Belle used an Emergency Wipe as well.

Overall, we were focusing on simply forming solid and cohesive, stable blocks for now, ones that others could attune later.

That was a hell of a job, and not one that we could do anywhere else, but leaving Belle behind meant that the job would take twice as long as if we were both doing it.

Unfortunately, there wasn't another option.

The end result was that we were expecting to harvest around six hundred million nanites from this entire mission, split between ourselves and the Elders. That gave us around three hundred million to each group, and as much as we wanted it—and in all honesty, I *really* wanted it—it meant our team couldn't just keep our portion.

Three hundred million nanites meant that we could raise hundreds of our people. And not just that—we could use some of those nanites to give them access to the things they needed, like armor for Freja and Anders, or indeed anyone who'd be going outside our little refuge.

It meant that we could set up the hospital we'd been talking about, and power level some doctors, using the nanites that we gave them in place of medicines, to heal hundreds.

Where I'd spent days frantically trying to beg, borrow, and steal—well, I'd killed criminals and stole from corpses, but the phrase was too good not to use— to get enough nanites to heal those children in the hospital in Athens?

Now I could do it practically endlessly.

I could go from one end of that hospital to the other inside of a day, and because the system wanted me to level in numbers, like heal five kids, then ten, then twenty-five or whatever?

It meant that we could have a real healer, someone who was power leveled to fuck in the Support tree, in short order.

They could do quest after quest after quest!

Hell, because it was in the Support tree—we had healers under the Repair section, because the system viewed us as disposable weapons—we could even send out engineers! They could cheat the system and get free points, over and over, that they could in turn invest in the sections that we needed!

All of that meant that by the time we'd gotten the first few things in order, and I'd found and booted Dimi out of his camp bed and forced him into the plane again, demanding he take us to the Azores, more hours were lost.

By the time we landed there, literally halfway around the world and a handful of hours later, it was late morning, and my God, I loved the sight that greeted me.

Although less than I did the sight of Ingrid, admittedly.

The main airfield that we landed at, just outside the regional capital of Ponta Delgada, was like a more beautiful England.

That didn't sound hard to find, all things considered, but the thing that I'd always loved about my home was the greenery.

No matter where you went, the entire United Kingdom was bustling with life. Now, some might say that was because it was massively overpopulated— compared to virtually everywhere else that wasn't in Asia—or because our national export might as well be rats—either the kind with four legs and a tail or our politicians—but for me it was because it rained for fun.

Arise :Explorer

Seriously, in the north of England, and pretty much the rest of the UK that wasn't the south, rain could be our primary product. In the depths of summer, now and then, we saw the sun, and occasionally in winter we saw some snow, or hail or whatever. But thanks to the various streams in the ocean that encircled our dreary little mist-wreathed island, what we saw without fail, pretty much on a daily basis, was rain.

The temperature rarely got too high, and it almost never got too low. Instead, it just sat at a steady drizzle. And as much as we all complained about it, we loved it really.

Literally, the grass was green, the trees were too, generally, and it was damn rare that you found anywhere that things weren't growing.

Or admittedly, being washed away.

When I went to the Middle East, the Mediterranean, or especially the Sahara and places like that, that was what I missed the most.

On Yuzhny Island, there'd been greenery, but it was mostly of the evergreen variety, with almost no grass, thanks to how goddamn cold it was there in northern Russia.

Here?

It was a tiny set of islands in the middle of the Atlantic Ocean, not far from the equator, and it was sodding *beautiful*. The air was filled with the scent of recent rain, and as I stomped down the steps, striding out onto the tarmac, I drew a deep lungful and just felt *better*.

"I hoped for sun…" Ingrid whispered, stepping up by my side and leaning in as I wrapped one arm around her shoulders, kissing the top of her head.

"It'll come," I assured her, looking around and seeing the small group that were even now hurrying across the intervening space, coming to try to find out who the hell we were.

"So, which persona shall we try?" I asked the little group brightly, seeing the amused look on Sanneth's face, as he stepped up to my shoulder.

The others spread out around us, Jonas and Scylla as always taking up flanking positions. Belle and Oxus—thankfully—had stayed behind on the buried ship to harvest more nanites. Ingrid was on my right and Sanneth on the left, and Dimi…well, Dimi was already closing the gangway behind us.

He'd been grumbling about being "forced to fly around the world twice before breakfast" again, and I guessed he was going back to bed.

Or out for lunch.

"I think the polite one," Ingrid said clearly, looking up at me. "No scaring people with the angel."

"Angel?" Sanneth asked, then he smiled. "Ah, the angel of vengeance armor you have been using in public, I presume? Yes, very appropriate…use that."

"Angel it is then!" I smiled, just as Ingrid cursed and tried to stop me.

"Said NOT the angel!" She was growling as I lifted my arm from around her shoulders and strode forward.

The tarmac was glossy grey and black, and the airport terminal had its lights on, the sky grey with the promise of more rain. Standing puddles of water dotted the surface here and there, giving the futuristic plane we'd arrived on even more of an ethereal image.

That was only added to as I strode forward, rolling my shoulders slightly, before summoning my armor.

It flowed up; pinpricks scattered across the surface of my skin as thousands of tiny holes, almost infinitesimally small, opened and the nanites that were stored within, beneath my skin and in the literal hearts of my bones, rippled out.

It was almost a release, the tiny flare of pain so common that I'd long since stopped noticing it, as the black and shimmering red mass streamed out from under my clothes, pouring across my body and transforming me.

I was impressive as I stood, I knew, over seven feet in height, solidly, perhaps too heavily muscled, and if I said so myself, pretty goddamn good-looking. I'd certainly give any Greek statues a run for their money. As part of the original "upgrade" I'd gotten when I first ascended, I'd had all the minor issues fixed: slight variations from my genetic ideal, things like a twist in my right pinky, random scars, all that shit.

Now I was a hell of a sight, and that was dressed normally, as I was when they started toward us, in basically a singlet that covered me from the neck down. Add on the armor flowing out like liquid to cover me, pouring up to layer over my face, my eyes starting to glow with an unholy fire as I strode out from beneath the shadow of the plane?

Yeah.

They stopped dead. Several backed up; one fell to their knees, making various religious gestures. Only one continued forward, seemingly unaware that the others had stopped.

He realized his mistake about halfway between his friends and me, and by that point he clearly knew he was too far gone to just back up, so kept coming.

"W-welcome…sir?" he squeaked, staring up, and I couldn't help but smile at him.

He was a little over five and a half feet in height. The top of his head maybe came to mid-chest on me, with thinning black hair that was plastered down by a combination of the recent rain and some hair product.

He was basically styling a really blatant comb-over, and clearly had no clue that anyone over five and a half feet could see it.

Poor dude made me feel sorry for him.

"You have my thanks." I nodded. "Mine companions and I have need of this location as we explore thine islands. Thou hast no objections, I trust?"

"Ah…" He was struggling, both with the fact that he was speaking what was clearly not his native tongue, and that I was apparently a demi-god, a complete fabrication, or an angel of vengeance, depending on which news article you read.

Now I'd turned up here, on his island, armored to buggery, aboard a plane that looked more like a stingray on steroids, and knowing Dimi…he'd probably told them something ridiculous when he asked for permission to land.

"You were aware of our arrival?" I asked after a few seconds of his lips flapping and no sound coming out.

"You…you just appeared!" he babbled, and internally, I swore.

Arise :Explorer

Our stealth setup was insane. In less than a week, the plane that had been top of the line and probably so secretive that it was marked "slit your wrists on seeing" had been claimed as a spoil of war, and we'd then upgraded it further.

The Arisen liked having the coolest toys anyway, and this thing probably didn't show on any radar that any national system had access to, so as I looked back and up at it, spotting Dimi as he ducked out of sight in the cockpit, I just knew the fucker hadn't asked for landing permission.

Hell, no wonder they'd all come marching across to see what was going on. With all the mist and rain here, we'd probably just floated out of the gloom and set down.

We were lucky nobody had fired on us.

"I see." I sighed. "Mine servants shall be reprimanded. I will require an audience with your rulers, and they shall in turn explain all thou needest learn."

"Our rulers…?" He took a deep breath, forcing a smile, holding up a hand in a "wait one second" gesture and speaking into a radio in a rapid-fire burst of Portuguese.

I reached out, linking to the local internet easily enough, barely even noticing as the Hack sub-mind went active and cleared out the frankly laughable protection.

As soon as I was in, I linked to several natural language AIs, a translation program, and then back, feeding his words into it, and focusing.

The language was a mess at first, as more and more of my sub-mind came online. The Hack sub-mind wasn't really designed for this, but, looking at it from another perspective, languages were simply puzzles.

I'd gotten most of the language caught up when Sanneth evidently grew bored and strode out from where the others were waiting, and started to speak, apparently in ancient Kermic.

His own words were so archaic the translation failed entirely, not even coming close, as the little man gaped at him.

"The language has evolved since then," I pointed out to him dryly.

"This is what they spoke when last I visited these islands," he said.

"And that was…?" I prompted, grinning as I saw the little man was listening.

"Around twenty-seven hundred years ago." He shrugged. "Give or take a century. I decided it would be worth a try."

"Wh…what?" The official gasped, and I sighed, turning back to him.

"Mine companion last visited your isles some time ago," I said simply. "We do not age as you mortals do. Now, we have business here, and we require access to the islands, a place to safely store our vessel, and a meeting with your rulers…"

"An' some food an' drinks!" Jonas said loudly, walking up, and I glared at him. "Hey, ah'm just saying we could all do with some food, boss."

"Perhaps I should handle the locals?" Ingrid suggested, walking up to join us. Her armor gleamed as a fresh band of rain started to pelt the tarmac.

I looked from her to Scylla, then to the others, and I nodded. Ingrid was far better at this shit than I was, and Sanneth, who I'd expected to be brilliant at this, had totally derailed the little progress I'd made with his casual attempt at speaking a language that had apparently been extinct for at least a thousand years.

"Excellent," I said, trying to keep the image going. "We will begin exploring the island. Join us when you can."

Ingrid nodded, and I said nothing as she stepped between us, facing the small man and speaking to him in fluent Portuguese. Scylla moved to stand with her by unspoken agreement.

In seconds, they were chattering away, and I cut the input to the language program I'd almost got working. If I didn't need it, it was one less issue for me to fuck about with.

Best of all, the rest of us, bar Sanneth, could fly, so we simply unfurled our wings, practically making the little guy shit himself, as I spoke quietly to Sanneth.

"I'll handle the flight, that alright with you?" I asked.

"I trust it will not require me sitting on your back?" he responded dryly.

"Oh no, princess carry all the way," I assured him, before snorting as he stared at me in confusion.

"I am no princess, Steve—"

I reached out to him, folding a bubble of gravity around him and lifting him as we launched ourselves into the air.

As we took off—Sanneth, Jonas, and I—I think we all secretly enjoyed the look of shock and confusion on the faces of the staff who had come to stand around the glass in the airport, and certainly the way that the group on the tarmac flinched and ducked.

We'd done some research on the flight on the way over, picking out several locations to check out, and we currently had one of the satellites adjusting its orbit to take up geo-sync overhead.

The pair we'd deployed mere days ago were equipped with scanners that could penetrate the ground a short distance, but they should have far less issues with the ocean. I had hopes that scanning for the specific technological structures that were used in most of the creator's equipment, or certain metals for example, would give us a place to start.

Regardless, though, we had several areas that we could examine and that would make a decent jumping-off point.

The Lagoa do Fogo, or the Lake of Fire, was a crater that was all that was left of the volcano that had stood here. Sanneth was convinced that this was the one that had once been referenced as being the seat of Poseidon and a holy place in all the manuscripts he'd seen.

There were several other smaller volcanoes as well, but much of the overall shape of the "original" island was lost.

We'd managed to get some images of the seabed around here, not many, but some, and using them, and with what we'd figured out about the original shape of the islands, we'd drawn a few conclusions.

First of all, if one of the creators had indeed set up here, and was possibly still about, and was anywhere near as hostile to humanity as Varnock was? Well, there was no way that the ships that had brought colonists and more here would have been allowed to gain a foothold.

That she'd apparently left them to live here, provided nothing disturbed her? That gave us some hope.

Of course, it didn't mean that she'd tolerate anyone encroaching into her territory, though. And even if she was relatively benign—as far as the creators went—she'd apparently already sank the islands once when she was pissed about something.

That meant she'd probably not have any issues doing the same with boats or whatever if they annoyed her as well.

That gave us a starting point. Our search of the local databases showed three areas where there were both a larger than average number of disappearances and a lot of unexplained shit.

If you looked at the islands overall, there'd been an absolute shitload of shipwrecks over the years. Mainly that was because out in the middle of the damn Atlantic as it was, it had some wild weather, and it'd been a stopping point for ships for basically forever.

That made perfect sense to me. After all, if you were sailing from one continent to the other, and there was a chance to stop off for a few days and restock during the voyage? Or somewhere to seek shelter from the worst of the storms, and to carry out repairs?

You'd be mad not to take it.

The little details, though? They didn't add up.

The Azores were a beautiful location, and they were a perfect tourist destination. They alternated between heavy rains and lush greenery, and beautiful sunshine, picturesque buildings, and friendly people.

They should be making the absolute most of that, becoming a massive hub for tourism, especially for diving on the wrecks. And as a playground for the rich and shameless? It'd be perfect.

Hell, they could make a tax haven of the islands—more than Portugal already was—and they'd be able to turn the entire economy into an insanely profitable one.

Knowing this, and that the Portuguese government wasn't exactly adverse to tax-free and mass money-making schemes, that entire swathes of these sunken wrecks and significant sections of the islands were entirely off-limits to tourists? That made no sense.

Tourists weren't permitted to explore certain areas around the calderas. It wasn't phrased that way, of course; it was things like "Due to the narrow and old roads, only locally certified vehicles, driven by drivers with permits, may drive on 'x' roads."

It all made sense, until you took a careful look at the islands from above. Entire sections were utterly wild, with what looked to be suspiciously regular shapes hidden beneath the wilderness.

You'd also see much better roads around the rest of the islands and then little shitty ones that were far too narrow in other areas.

Places where it'd be easy to expand that road out. Hell, make a car park and a deli or whatever, but nobody had.

Sure, it was easily explained away as an effort to preserve the natural beauty of the islands. That was what I'd probably have seen if I wasn't such a suspicious bastard. But as soon as I started digging? I found a dozen other projects for things like that, that were given joyful approval.

In certain areas, though…*nothing*—no building was permitted at all. Although the population wasn't exactly cramped, they were also far more concentrated in set areas.

These were little details, inconsequential even, but when enough little details started adding up, they started to look like something else entirely.

The Blue Lagoon, or the Lagoa Azul, as it was named locally, was a site that was dedicated to tourism, little villages of tourist housing that could be rented for short- or long-term visits, all well designed, popular, and firmly located the hell away from the area we were interested in.

It was like the island had been split into no-go areas. And the sea?

If you compared the sheer number of shipwrecks, there were more than expected, but it was understandable for the location. Sure.

What wasn't…were the ship *disappearances.*

Off the west coast of the main island, and tracking out over what would have been central Atlantis, moving to the middle of the plateau, ships had vanished regularly.

They were marked as lost over all the Atlantic, but a little careful digging showed that they all lost contact around the same area, and although they were reported as lost further into their voyages, the last places they were seen were all noticeably similar when I did a little hacking and compared logs on the flight over.

We'd be heading out to there soon, but for now, while Ingrid did a little digging with the locals, questioning them and making it clear that we fucking knew shit was going on, and they knew that we weren't "human," Jonas, Sanneth, and I were exploring the mountains.

"I still say we should have gone for lunch first, boss," Jonas called to me. He'd said it aloud; Sanneth, still not being fully ascended, wasn't able to use the same neural link, but he nodded as well, agreeing that the meal would have been welcome.

"I could murder a steak, yeah," I called back. The three of us flashed through the cloud cover, erupting into bright sunlight a scant few minutes after leaving the ground. "Let's wrap this shit up fast. Hopefully we can negotiate with them, rather than fight."

"It'd be a relief," Jonas agreed quickly, angling in closer and gliding. My gravitational manipulation kept the three of us aloft as much as anything he was doing. "We're not exactly geared up for this going south, boss."

"South?" Sanneth asked.

"When the shit hits the fan!" Jonas tried again. "When Steve fucks up the negotiations and it becomes a fight, I mean."

"Ah, yes, this is likely."

"Fuck you both very much." I grunted. "Ingrid's handling the locals, and…"

"And that means she doesn't expect us to find anything up here, doesn't it?" Jonas asked.

"Probably," I muttered, before raising my voice again. "Seriously, though, is it more likely that we'll find what we need in the ocean? Sure. There's whole sections of the island that are no-go areas, though, and they're damn subtle about it. While she gets us smoothed into place with the locals, we can check this out, then we eat and make a decision on the next step."

"Which will be?" Sanneth asked.

"I guess we'll try to negotiate with the creator, then when it all falls apart, we'll fly the rest of the team in, and whatever forces you can spare, and we fight the fuckers."

"And this is why I chose to join you, Steve." Sanneth sighed. "If there is an option that does not result in a war, we need to take it. Thanks to the actions of our enemies, we are already in a poor situation. We need time to recover, and to repair, not to mention make the most of the new upgrades you have given us access to."

It was an argument we'd had on the flight and before it as well. For some reason, the others seemed to think I was some kind of blunt instrument, incapable of subtlety.

I'd be annoyed, but it was too damn accurate for that.

<u>Chapter Five</u>

The island tour was an absolute bust.

Well, ninety-nine percent a bust.

I did see some really nice places that I wanted to take Ingrid, and a few villas that I'd damn well love to buy if I could. Living here, hell, spending a few days here, chilling out and soaking up the sun, then getting to watch absolutely thunderous downpours?

I could be happy here. There were some damn nice restaurants as well. But even when the satellite was distantly able to observe the area of the island we were over, it found absolutely bugger all that was useful to us.

Each of the buildings that were buried in the area surrounding Lagoa do Fogo was a ruin. Besides being able to tell from on high that they were likely all abandoned around the same time, and they were most definitely made *after* the volcano had collapsed into the caldera that eventually became the lagoon, there was nothing useful.

At first, I'd wondered whether they were all made previously, and it might have been the ruins of the original Atlantean buildings…and I was told very clearly by Sanneth that I was an idiot.

Although some buildings would last that long—indeed, some were even still about…some place in Turkey he named that I couldn't even pronounce was a great example, apparently—the vast majority wouldn't. And sure as shit, if there was a big enough explosion that it ripped a volcano a new asshole to such a degree it collapsed into its own caldera, then there was no chance of a building surviving.

Fair enough.

We met Ingrid and Scylla at a little hilltop restaurant on the far side of the island a few hours later, with the sun setting, and the entire group tired, starving, and ratty about the time we'd lost.

Ingrid had managed to confirm that the island's rulers did indeed know of the Arisen, and they were very happy to keep their mouths shut and stay out of the way, as well as clearing up any "issues" at the airport. But when she questioned them about the various little stitched-up projects, and the way that certain areas were left alone?

It was clear this was something they'd always done, rather than a recent thing.

Arise :Explorer

Certain farming families were viewed as untouchable because they fed a full third of their harvest to "the gods," although how and why wasn't really clear.

It was apparently part of some "pagan traditions" that they weren't happy to talk about. She'd pressed hard to get answers, but it boiled down to the food being put on the shore in small reed baskets and allowed to float out with the tide as an offering to the "Lady of Miracles."

They'd all sink, and that was that.

They'd been told a few times to stop doing such stupid shit by outsiders, and that they were wasting their harvest. When one of the farmer's sons, a few years back and something of a modernist, had taken over one of the family farms, he put a stop to it.

Almost immediately after the offering was missed, there'd been a terrible storm that winter that lasted days, and at the same time almost the entire fishing fleet was sunk.

Added to that, for weeks since the harvest offering, all the usual fish—the blue marlin, the tuna, and dorado—were all scared off by something in the depths. Pots that were sunk were almost universally lost, or they came back up torn apart and empty.

The locals took the hint, made the farmer an offer he couldn't refuse—involving a metal spike and his remains being used to bait the fishing pots—and then made a much larger offering than normal as an apology.

Almost overnight, the storms cleared and the fish returned.

Most of it, Ingrid was sure, was a coincidence. The storm's timing certainly would have been, but the fish being driven away and the damage to the pots could be real.

Either way, though, the locals believed that there was life below the waves, and that under absolutely no circumstances should they fuck with it.

It wasn't a "we must worship them" Innsmouth situation. Oh no, it was much more of a "don't make eye contact and under no circumstances draw their attention" kinda thing.

It wasn't hard, once Ingrid started pushing, to learn that there were regular sightings of creatures in the ocean to the west, roughly where we were looking, and that the government made a concerted effort to keep people well clear of there.

In the past, it was easier to lie and say the ships just left and boom, all good; wherever it sank, it wasn't here and we don't give a shit, kinda thing. These days, when a ship went down and there were no survivors, or worse, when there were some who saw *things*…?

There were so many more details to be attended to.

Luckily, the various nations were used to dealing with the Arisen at the higher levels, so they assumed this was them fucking around, and they helped to cover it up as best they could as a matter of course.

Now, as the five of us sat eating, literally enjoying a veritable half a cow each for Scylla, Sanneth, and me, and enormous blue fin tuna steaks for Ingrid and Jonas, we talked about the next step as the evening rains hammered the metal roof overhead, making it hard to hear one another.

It didn't matter, though. Mainly, we all demolished the food, with the look on Sanneth's face being the best bit of it for everyone.

When he'd lost the ability to move, his long eons of life having contributed to an insane amount of corrupted nanites building up in his body, he'd also lost the ability, and the need, to eat.

His nanites had been able to process the atmosphere into energy, and although it'd not been a good quality of life, he'd not died.

He had, however, taken literally years to get used to the fact that he could no longer eat.

His body had been maintained at its peak, so his entire digestive tract was ready and raring to go, and it was totally empty. That meant that he and the other Elders had been essentially starving forever.

They'd started small when they regained the ability to eat, by Kemet's recommendation, and had been eating a basic and bland nutrient paste.

Sanneth had decided that enough was enough, though, and on top of the sheer joy of any "real" food, he was introduced to modern condiments for the first time.

Mayonnaise was a hit, as was ketchup. HP Brown sauce? Yeah, he liked that, but the big winner was *barbecue*. He absolutely loved that, smothering his food in it, much to all our amusement, before finally meeting the wonderful mess of chilies that Jonas had ordered.

Whatever the hell it was, it was strong. I'd tried it, and after a few mouthfuls, left it well alone. Scylla smelled it and refused it point-blank. Ingrid loved it, but she was crazy at times, and she and Jonas convinced Sanneth to try it.

Then, between urgent runs to the washroom for Sanneth—which we all found hilarious—we made a plan for the next stage.

The ocean almost exactly due west of the island we were on was most likely the home of whatever was here, and before we could do any real exploring, we'd need to sort some things out.

First and foremost was that despite the best will in the world, this was the fucking Atlantic Ocean: it was going to be damn cold and dark down there.

As much as the movies liked to bullshit that the bottom of the ocean was all floating lights and more, it wasn't.

It was colder than a witch's tit and twice as dark as her heart.

We needed a ship as a central point at least for Sanneth to wait aboard, and although the others had unlocked their atmospheric systems—after Ingrid apparently made sure they all did it—so they could survive underwater for extended periods like me, it was still going to be a right ballache.

We agreed to hire a ship, and then we'd take turns resting on it for a few hours.

The area we'd need to cover was realistically around six hundred square miles, and none of us liked the idea of spreading out far enough that we could cover all of it quicker.

Most of us had seen *Jaws*, and we definitely knew there was something out there fucking with ships.

Unfortunately, that left us with two problems.

First, the locals *knew* that there were things that sank ships if you went screwing around in the wrong areas, and most of the time, those people on said ships were never seen again.

That meant that there wasn't a cat in hell's chance of us chartering a boat, or hiring one. We had to *buy* it, and at a price that should have covered a damn luxury yacht, instead of the piece of shit ex-fishing trawler we ended up with.

The second issue was that because of both the local time—the sun was now fully down—and the limited time we had to get everything done, we weren't getting any sleep tonight.

We had about six hundred square miles, possibly less—but knowing my luck, probably more—of monster- and dickhead-infested ocean to search.

Great.

By the time midnight had come and gone, Ingrid, Scylla, and Sanneth were steadily chugging out of the harbor aboard a ship that belched smoke, hadn't been cleaned nor apparently maintained since the conquistadors passed through, and reeked of dead fish.

I was damn glad to already be beneath the waves with Jonas.

We'd flown out ahead of the others, diving at the agreed upon start of the run, and, because we had so little time to screw around…I was sending heavy gravity waves out.

We'd worked it out while waiting for Sanneth as he suffered in the toilet, but basically, we needed to be prepared to search each and every inch if need be.

Realistically, though, that wasn't our best chance of success, or even meeting anything.

The best chance wasn't swimming the ocean and searching for the fuckers: it was drawing them to us.

To do that, we decided on the radar-like pulses that I'd been learning to use to map things—just, instead of using the weak version, I needed to go all out.

It was the same kind of theory that subs and more mapped the ocean floor with: sending out a pulse, usually sound, and then marking up the response. Sound was great for this kinda thing, and was the standard method, but NASA had apparently been experimenting with mapping through minute fluctuations in the gravity field and had found a shitload more accuracy in surveys.

For me, it was a lot easier.

I literally got Corey, one of Zac's assistants, to cobble together a version that accepted the signals I was relaying to read the seabed. I'd have loved to simply unlock a more appropriate version, and hell, I had no doubt that one would exist in the byzantine myriad of upgrades I could select, but for the first time in ages, I was out of points, and having technical issues to boot.

I didn't have a single quest, and that freaked me out, because when I went looking? Checking for the quests that I'd had before?

They were *all* gone.

Like the one about learning to hack my way through interconnected Wi-Fi systems, or the gradually increasing ones about healing people?

Hacking complex encoding and gaining points, and all the various system quests I'd had were gone. And when I tried to use my system to identify a bloody fish that zipped past?

Nada.

That was starting to concern me. I'd been able to start quests for other people, encouraged by Zac, so the system was still registering me, more or less, but I'd lost access to all the "in progress" ones.

We'd only found this out a few hours ago, and I'd tried all the usual shit to get them back, hoping at first that it was some kind of a system reset, and that if that was the case, I could instead start from scratch.

Hack one thing, get a point. Hack five, then ten…essentially power level myself again from the beginning.

But nope. I could hack things, and I'd done it quickly to a few things as a tester, but there were no corresponding quests offered, and that was making me shit myself.

I'd had to draft in Corey, and a bit of jiggery-pokery later—and not the kind I liked—I was barreling through the ocean, with Jonas shadowing me above and slightly behind, hiding in my wake, as I sent out powerful pulses.

These were in turn interpreted, and the result relayed to the satellite, where, after Corey was finished, it was redirected to Ingrid to share, sending them back to Sanneth on the ship.

At first, I found little—a few interesting shapes, crevices, and collapsed sections of rock—but that was all. The water was shallow enough here that sunlight got through to help things grow, like coral and the various sub-sea species, and yet it was deep enough that you weren't seeing the bottom without specialist equipment.

I experimented, broadcasting waves powerful enough to send the fish into a panicked frenzy, snapping and biting at each other, racing in all directions and literally causing the sand to shiver.

Then I sent out waves that were barely felt, adjusting them over and over, trying to find the ideal mixture to cut through the silt and sand to reveal the bedrock, and yet not kill off the wildlife.

It took a few attempts, but I managed it, grinning as I started to pick up a far more detailed picture of the seabed.

The satellite was fully focusing now. Something about the angle it had been at before meant that scanning the ocean was much harder than the land. It was steadily tracking back and forth high overhead as well, its sweeps uncovering more and more.

I was at the southernmost tip of the area we wanted to search, and it was at the northernmost, and we searched as fast as we could.

Steadily, images started to resolve for us all, collated by Ingrid in the command link, and using a tablet that she'd gotten from somewhere to show Sanneth.

The images we found, though?

They were magnificent.

Arise :Explorer

The first of them was a ship, long lost to the depths, with various marine life and the frame melting through rust and worse. I didn't fully understand why some did and some didn't, but the one thing that was clear was that it was a wreck.

It was old, at least fifty years, probably a lot older, with styling that suggested the turn of the century.

Massive boilers and steam towers had once kept the ship knifing through the waves. The signs of missing sections on the decks suggested that wood had stood there once.

I could imagine passengers striding back and forth—women with gleaming white parasols and men smoking cigars and proclaiming bloody stupid things—right up until something took a strip out of the hull.

It ran from nearly the tip of the bow to the stern, and it'd apparently opened the entire ship's starboard side like a can opener.

That it'd been over in an instant was obvious. The escape vessels were clear for all to see, two to a side on what was left of the ship's deck. Three were still in place, slumped into the deck now, the mounts that were there to swing them out over the side collapsed along with the rest.

The fourth boat was a short distance away, having clearly come loose in the spiral of death to the bottom, shattered into a million pieces. The ship looked as though it'd been going so fast it'd tried to cork-screw itself into the seabed. And at some point, just to add insult to injury, a boiler looked to have exploded as well.

That was a single ship, on the far northern end of the area we were searching, and maybe fifty miles from land.

By the time that Ingrid reached our position an hour later?

I'd scanned sixteen similar wrecks, with the satellite picking up another twelve.

That'd be horrific enough, but even worse were the traces we'd found below the ships.

That this was once Atlantis was far from a certainty at the minute, but what was clear was that once it'd certainly been above the ocean, and that tens of thousands must have died when it sank.

We'd found the wall that was supposed to have surrounded the island. Sanneth was overjoyed that it was exactly as described, until we saw the ruins that surrounded it.

It'd been a crater wall, presumably a caldera or impact point that had been built upon, the rough edges smoothed, encased in stone and built up.

They'd have been a wonder of engineering, truly a wonder of the ancient world on sheer scale alone, but the damage? It was beyond horrific. It looked as if an angry god had smashed the entire island into the sea.

At first, I thought it'd been a meteor impact, but the buildings?

We found them in their hundreds, rolling back in clearly defined streets, now long since choked by silt and sand, shattered and buried where only crustaceans roamed.

They were small, not as high as modern flats and apartments or whatever, and certainly not skyscrapers. The majority looked to be two- or three-story buildings.

They were rent asunder by whatever had happened, but not destroyed. An orbital impact would have levelled the place; this looked as if it'd been hammered with a giant someone's fists, then pushed under, like a god had been intent on drowning a rival.

I passed over shattered domes, the darkness within filled with muck and crawling silent creatures.

The more we found? The worse it became.

Entire sections of the city were partly intact, although devastated by time, while others were literally cratered.

As I passed over them, I wondered about the force used. The way it'd been restricted, it genuinely looked like an angry giant had done it.

That led me down the path of the gods as we knew them, and the way we'd assumed they were all based on those dickhead immortals.

Was it possible they weren't?

Could there have been a god that existed, and had done this? Or was it an example of one of us, a horrifically powerful one, perhaps using the gravity manipulation abilities I had?

I shook the thoughts free, finding I'd been blankly staring at an ancient statue of a man in armor, and forced myself on.

There were strings of pots, presumably for lobsters, crabs, or whatever, and they'd been lost, crisscrossing each other—dozens here, hundreds there—caught on the remains of buildings that had been colonized by the creeping ocean life.

Fish flitted here and there, and over it all were the wrecks. Scarcely a pass was completed without finding a lost ship, and the force that they'd been impacted with was almost universal.

Some were clearly more "honest" victims, simply being sunk by the elements. The ships looked more or less intact, or in one case, actually snapped in half by what must have been a rogue wave, according to Sanneth.

The majority, though, had been gutted—sections ripped apart like they were nothing. And what was the most terrifying was the apparent disinterest after that.

If this was a hidden Arisen base of some kind, leading back millennia, then I could have understood it, and not just because they were dicks, generally.

The Arisen would have happily looted ships of everything that they wanted, with absolutely no compunction about recovering the sailors and passengers.

If it'd been them, though, I'd have expected to see the ships being looted afterward.

One of the ships had already gotten Ingrid fixated, as it'd apparently been sunk with an absolute fuckload of gold aboard.

She wasn't fussed on the gold so much as the stories the artifacts would tell us of the past. But a slight calibration to the sensors aboard the satellite had stripped away that interest almost entirely.

We'd not been searching for gold—we had enough, after all—and were looking primarily for the various exotics that were common in the alien constructions of the ships.

There'd been such a concentration of gold on that single ship, though, that Ingrid had realized what the other traces had to be, and made a slight alteration.

Arise :Explorer

Now?

The city veritably *glowed.*

The gold, silver, platinum, and onyx that had been revealed showed that whatever happened to the city, it'd happened all at once, because there sure as shit wasn't time for people to take their valuables with them, if this was any example of it.

Jonas and I were passing above a section of street, when we realized what was down there probably had more gold in it than the heart of fucking London. We slowed, staring and entranced by the overlaid images.

Literal sections of several buildings glowed with piled treasures, making us think that they were storerooms, or treasuries, until Sanneth spoke up.

"Atlantis was known for its treasuries…but to see that it was true…"

"What?" Jonas frowned. "You're telling me that's all real? It's not a screw-up on the scanners?"

"No. I mean, yes, it's probably real," Sanneth replied, staring in shock. "One of the legends of Atlantis said that they had so much wealth that they used gold to sheathe the bottoms of their ships against the sea…"

"That's just fucking stupid," I muttered. "They'd sink, right?"

"It was intended as an example of their wealth, not reality," Sanneth snapped. "Most likely, they simply had access to lands where gold was less valuable and used that to build their economy. If they truly were the master mariners of the past, they may well have had contact with the Incas and Mayans, trading with them for gold, jade, and onyx."

"Either way, we just stopped needing to worry about bills, boss." Jonas sounded amused. "Is this a good time to bring up that I always wanted a condo in LA?"

"Buy two." I snorted. "Seriously, people, is anyone else getting freaked out by the shit we're seeing, but more worried about what we're not seeing?"

"You mean whatever carved the bottom of those boats out?" Ingrid asked, and I nodded, forgetting she couldn't see me.

"Crap, yeah," I added.

"I think whatever does this, has to be big," Scylla said into the silence. "The marks indicate strength and speed, making it unlikely to be a natural predator, considering the lack of a second attack and the scarcity of large prey in the area."

"I agree," Ingrid said. "There's nothing big enough to keep an alpha predator in the area. And if it was moving around, I think it'd have been seen before now."

"A megalodon?" Jonas suggested dubiously. "I've seen movies about them lately and…"

"And they're ridiculous," Scylla replied flatly. "You made me watch two of them before I could drag you into our bed to escape it. First, those are giant sharks. Although such a creature could still exist, it is unlikely. From my own investigations—"

She broke off, apparently getting a look from Ingrid and Sanneth, and explained that she'd been curious, and so had used the web to look it up.

She was getting used to modern life at an almost insane rate, and I grinned as I sent waves thrumming through the water in all directions.

"As I was saying," Scylla started again. "The megalodon was a shark, and such a creature would have no reason to attack vessels like this. If it did so anyway, driven mad, starving or somehow goaded into it, the damage would be different. I have fought sharks. Their attacks leave distinct markings, injuries, and damage. None of this fits a shark."

"Well said," Sanneth agreed. "Add to that, most likely it's a single creature, and something native to these waters. If it was a migratory species, it'd have been far more likely to be discovered before now, and yet, as you say, there's a significant lack of large prey species in the area. It would starve."

"If it's attacking the ships here, what's keeping it from taking out all the others?" Jonas asked suddenly. "I mean, I can understand the whole 'let's punish the locals' if they stopped the offerings and something down here was receiving them. But if that was the Arisen, they'd have simply swam up and taken what they wanted. They'd not care to wait. And when the offerings stopped? They'd have come to shore and made examples of a few people."

"And by 'the others,' you mean the ships?" Sanneth queried, getting a nod. "It is uncertain. Clearly something is roaming these waters, and yet—"

"Contact!" I barked, having been listening with half an ear as I watched in all directions as best I could.

The gravity waves were being sent out as they were, modulating frequencies and strengths, for literally two reasons.

First? We were mapping, searching the undersea world, and we needed to know what worked. Some crevasses would be missed by a weaker pulse that covered the area, and a stronger, more specific one had to, by its nature, be more focused.

The other reason, though, was that with as little time as we had for this shit?

We were fishing.

Chapter Six

Whatever it was that was coming for us, Ingrid and Scylla moved almost as soon as the word was out of my mouth, diving over the side and into the air. Their flight capability enabled them to get out of the danger zone much more rapidly than Sanneth, the only one of us without access to armor and more.

The little fishing boat almost tipped over, he threw the rudder that hard to port as he hammered the engines. The single prop carved a white wake behind him as he sped away, cursing his lack of appropriate upgrades.

While they were doing that, Jonas and I were doing the opposite, turning and heading straight at the incoming contact. I was in the lead and slightly deeper, sending the pulses out steadily, washing them over it.

Jonas maintained his position above and slightly behind me, watching my back, ready to counterattack if it attacked us.

As the images built up a picture, though, as more and more of it was revealed, I started to get concerned.

First of all, it wasn't an animal. Not a fishy thingy, or fuck knew what the term was, because I was far too worried to care right then.

Its carapace was armored, and although it "swam," its tail swishing from side to side, and what I was guessing were its arms tucked into its sides, it was also using some kind of undersea propulsion.

The water around it was almost slipping out of its way, and there was a solid wake left behind that felt—I was still seeing all of this through gravity manipulation, after all—like the water was being compressed and it was riding the wave.

Secondly?

The armor was far too thick and well designed to be natural.

I was trying to scan it, as best I could at this distance, and the responses suggested it was almost solid.

It didn't show up as a shell atop a crab or whatever. Instead, it seemed far more heavily built. Like tank armor that covered something, and that the inside was almost as dense as the outside.

The more I saw of it, the more concerned I got.

"It's a fucking machine!" I swore at almost the same time that Jonas spoke.

"Uh, boss? Maybe we need to reconsider this…"

The first thing I saw through the soupy darkness of the Atlantic Ocean were its eyes, gleaming a malevolent red, as it swam straight at me.

The rest of the massive bulk slid out of the darkness, and I got a sense of scale, which had been lacking before, and it absolutely *terrified* me.

This thing had more mass than a goddamn supercarrier, and it was probably as long as one as well.

I reached out, frantically trying to find any kind of a control signal on it, a guidance method, *anything*…but I was coming up empty.

The head was small, glowing eyes resolving as it closed with me. What had been two enormous eyes became clear as a cluster of smaller ones—an entire collection of tiny red dots that were set close together—shifted slowly.

The face was…it *wasn't* a damn face. That was it, and part of the reason I was so sure it was a machine. The lights looked to be various sensors, and although the "head" was there, and clearly articulated, shifting as it tried to follow me, there was no mouth, nowhere for it to shovel the insane number of calories something that size would need.

I shoved "down" hard with my gravity abilities, both on the water between me and it, and on the damn thing's head, shoving it into an unexpected decline that allowed me to flip over its head as the massive monstrosity flashed past beneath me…and kept on going.

It was huge.

Jonas was already headed up, flashing through the water and making for the surface, intending on getting out of the line of fire, when the tail finally appeared. I got a good look at it, as the "beast" arched down deeper and twisted behind some towers.

Then the slipstream hit me. The wake, or whatever the damn nautical phrase was, sucked me back down and sent me spinning. I shoved back from it with a great roar, the world spiraling out of control.

"Steve?" Ingrid's voice rang in my ears as I frantically tried to level out, to make sense of the spinning.

Fortunately, the inner-ear improvements and the various little changes that I'd made of late enabled me to lock onto the rear of it as it disappeared, and what I saw left no doubt my guess was right.

There were a dozen legs, all curled up, tucked into recesses, seemingly covered in the scum of ages. And all along the rear, above and below the body, and running down the tail…there were outtake jets.

I hadn't seen the intake ones, but presumably they were dotted around the front, or hell, who knew where.

What I did know was that there was no way in hell a creature could evolve to be the size of a supercarrier, develop underwater jet propulsion, and not have been fucking seen before now.

It had two larger arms that had been tucked in close to its body, but were coming out now. They ended in claws like a lobster's pincers. A spine jutted out of the top of the shell and ran down its back that looked to be razor-sharp.

Smaller ones sprang from the sides of the arms, like blades. And as I spotted them and larger ones?

I knew I'd seen their handiwork on the ships that lay wrecked all around me.

"Steve…tell me what you're seeing." Ingrid's voice rang out, and I blinked, shaking my stunned amazement away as the tip of the tail faded from view. Her frantic "knocking" on my senses made it clear that for some reason I'd not allowed her access to them as I usually did.

I swore, accepting her request and feeling her taking up residence in my mind, and sharing my vision with the others.

"It's a machine," I said definitively. "Huge, like a football field—hell, two maybe—across the shoulders. It's a machine, though: jets running along its back and underside to send it through the water, glowing red eyes…the works.

"The head is small, recessed into a section of the shoulders, but the main carapace is huge. It looks sort of like a crab, or a lobster, but not really…" I finished lamely.

"Like this?" Ingrid sent me an image that I glanced at, then returned to scanning the seas around me with a wide-angle gravity pulse.

The image I was shown was old, seriously so, apparently carved into a rock somewhere, and weathered by long ages of wind and water.

It also looked like something that had been carved from a description, not from the artist's experience. There were lines that didn't match up, sections that couldn't move, where there were clearly joints on this thing. But for all of that?

It was clearly the same creature.

"What is it?" I locked onto it as it swung around a collection of ruins, dipping down to hide. I shook my head at how goddamn cunning the thing was. It'd plunged low, trying to meld in with the wrecks and ruins of the seabed, and had slowed a lot, now drifting, moving slowly into position for a second attack run— this time from below, straight up toward me.

And when I tried to examine it, nothing opened, making me guess that it was either out of range, or not in the database maybe? Then my stomach dropped as I tried again, this time focusing on a nearby fish, and got, again, absolutely nothing.

My systems were definitely acting hinky, and that was terrifying.

"It's the leviathan," Ingrid said quickly, her voice tight and focused. "It's a sea monster of legend. Supposedly it shows in a dozen various myths of the ancient world, including the Bible. That image is from a temple in Central America, and was named as one of the demons of the underworld that escaped imprisonment somewhere deeper."

"Riiiight," I muttered, still watching it, and pinging its location for the others.

They were flying in, Ingrid and Scylla, their wings formed into massive scoops as they moved to take up station high overhead, ready to dive in, as we worked out the best way to deal with this thing.

Ingrid went on slowly, clearly researching even as she came into position, and we listened, hoping for a hint of a weakness.

"According to the legends from there, it was apparently a statue that was washed up ashore, in a great flood. There was a battle fought over it by the local tribes, who each tried to claim it for their people alone. The gods grew angry and changed it from stone to life, and it killed all it could find, before vanishing again, as they'd been proven unworthy of the god's gift." There was a slight pause as she checked something else before going on.

"Most likely, it was washed ashore in some ancient flood, possibly the one that your people carried out..." She paused, directing that at Sanneth, who was hopefully listening, but made no response. "Anyway, if it was washed ashore in some massive flood, and woke up surrounded by native tribes, I can see it killing anything it found nearby and returning to the ocean, that's for sure."

"Yeah," I agreed. "There's loads of little legs in recesses, and it looks like it was meant to do land and sea. But whatever it was built for, it's *really* pissed right now."

I meant it as well. The damn thing had slid around some big-ass columns of rock that it presumably thought could hide it, and it'd slid into position right below me, crouching and getting ready.

I was trying to figure out how to communicate with it, to try to do the whole "we mean you no harm" spiel, when it launched itself up at me, and I almost turned the water brown.

This time, the fucker cracked its arms loose of its sides. Sediment burst free as they unlocked and swung out, making it clear just how long it'd been since it had done that, and they angled wide, darting in toward me.

They were literally designed for one thing—cutting and slicing up its prey—and they were *fast*.

I was already moving, using both my gravity manipulation and my aquatic wings. The rippling pattern that flowed along them sent me flashing through water. Despite the speed and the grace, it was barely enough to keep me ahead of it.

"Little help here, people!" I called out, twisting and diving.

The leviathan flipped over, its tail beating the water and driving it after me. Jets opened along its side; the pressure shoved it ahead even faster, closing the gap as it seemingly brought additional propulsion online.

I dove for the bottom, swearing as I went. Unusual for me, I know.

Twisting, I felt the detonation as something went off behind me. My gravitational senses pinged as Jonas filled the comms with frankly disgraceful language.

"Gonna be less help than ah'd like, boss..." he forced out through gritted teeth. "Ah thought ma gun was fine to fire underwater..."

"You okay?" I asked distractedly, doubling down and going even faster as I dragged my wings in tight, focusing on using my gravity all the way, beyond a super cavitation spike forming ahead of me.

"Not really, no..." he growled.

"Get out of the water," I ordered. "You can't do any good back there."

Then I did what I really didn't want to do...and I closed my eyes.

It went against every instinct, literally.

I could barely see down here as it was, but the radar return ahead was incredibly busy and what I was seeing...there was just too much confusion.

Too many bits that made no sense: towers that had fallen but had a single section upright, or walls that were slumped inward, arches that stood in small sections, all covered in random sea growths and the detritus of the ocean, including what looked like the rib cage of a whale. And who knew what else.

I needed to reduce it as much as I could. I twisted in the water, forcing myself around from heading down like a spear, to arcing back up, and rolled to avoid the crumbling dome of a ruined building.

An arch flashed past as I dodged to the right; then, twisting again, I passed under it. The pressure of my high-speed pass ripped stones free, that in turn set loose a rolling collapse.

"Bring it close to the surface, and I will board it," Scylla said.

I grunted an affirmative, not knowing how the hell I was going to do that, but loving that she, at least, had a plan.

The monster was right behind me, and I felt the impacts of the collapsing structure as it ripped through the arch I'd just slipped around. If they did any damage to the thing, though, it wasn't apparent.

Multiple tons of solid stone fell onto its back and were utterly ignored as they rolled and slid off. A pincer flashed out, crashing through a building right behind me.

Clouds of sediment exploded from the ruins with every impact, making the water even darker. I was using gravity waves instead of vision to see, but it was getting harder considering how much floating crap interfered with the return.

I ducked even lower, literally blurring through the half-filled streets. Buildings loomed over me on either side...

And I winced as I heard the gasps from Ingrid as the big fucker smashed through another of them, trying to close on me.

She knew I was immortal; she knew I'd always come back... None of the buildings would, though, and I ground my teeth as I changed my mind and decided to do something *very* stupid, not sure whether it was for her or despite her, considering that I damn well knew I'd be getting it in the ear later.

As the leviathan twisted, aligning itself on the street below it, claws reaching and doubling down, clearly determined to catch me, I arced back up and used my gravity manipulation to jerk myself backward, coming to an almost complete halt for a split second, before going in the other direction, and *fast.*

The abrupt change of direction was as unexpected for me as it was for the fucking lobster with delusions of grandeur, considering I'd done it entirely on instinct. I triggered both my temporal manipulation and my combat systems. The predictions flashed up and blurred as they evaluated the fucker.

The claws were surrounded by images for a split second; then they vanished as the advanced sections completed their assessments. My own gravity fields rippled outward, filled with power for a second as more data was gathered.

Then I was twisting; my world flipped sideways as I found myself arcing around a grasping pincer. My vorpal and harvest blades slid out and flashed across the surface of the armor.

They carved thin lines in it, barely cutting at all. But in that moment of frantic contact, I had what I needed.

"Coming to you!" I shouted into the connection to Scylla. I twisted and dove, passing under and along its body, blades extended and carving lines of damage as it folded in on itself, desperately trying to track me.

Instead, I was scanning it, every inch I could see: searching for weaknesses, finding connections. The closer I was, the clearer they were. The sections that allowed the damn thing to flex and turn were armored, like the main shell or whatever was, but they were much thinner.

They had to be, or it'd not be able to turn worth a damn.

My blades had carved thin lines into its armor, letting me know that it wasn't invincible, merely made on an insane scale.

"The outer shell is stone," I called into the link. *"Not sure what's under it, but I can sense metals in there, and it's definitely a machine."*

"And it's pissed!" Jonas added, getting a grunt from me.

"Yeah, not sure why, but it really doesn't like us being here."

"It's guarding the area," Ingrid said. *"If it's a machine, someone probably set it to guard the area, and we're in its territory, that's all. Do you think it'll follow you?"*

"Yeah," I said, the strain in my voice clear as I passed under it. A leg barely missed me by literal inches, and slammed into the seabed.

It rolled as I pulled up, aiming for the surface and shoving hard. The cavitation bubble around me tore the water into insane flurries as I went, twisting and rolling on instinct.

"Yeah, it's definitely following me," I warned them. I sent a gravitational pulse downward, showing the creature crashing through buildings as it finished its roll; seeing I'd escaped, it launched itself back in pursuit.

It undulated, the tail being used as combination rudder and part of its style of swimming; swirling water propelled out of the jets, blasting a great section of the buried city clear of the filth of the ages.

It was closing fast, though, and as I doubled down, twisting to the right, my arms pulled in tight. My nanites transformed me into a spear-like rocket of madness…

Then the world around me vanished in a sudden bright beam of horrific power.

"Steve!" Ingrid shouted into the link.

I screamed. Pain filled my world, as heat, *terrible* heat, surged through me in an instant.

The water around the outer core and me flash-boiled. The water closer to the center of the beam simply evaporated. My armor? It reached horrific temperatures, and I lost control of the gravity I'd been using to fire myself along.

The entire world made no sense suddenly, I was in so much pain. I could feel myself spinning—*everything* was spinning—and it took a few seconds to dawn on me that it wasn't my inner ear…I actually was twisting over and over. And then I hit the water again.

Or, more accurately, it hit me.

Thousands of gallons of seawater—Tons? Pounds? Fuck knew…I certainly didn't—but an insane amount of water slammed into me, hammering me down even harder. The inrushing sea carried me along with it, driving me into the armored carapace of the creature as if I'd been fired from a cannon.

I could hear Ingrid shouting, feel her in my mind, but the pain? It was like I'd been dipped in boiling oil—literally, bathed in it—then rolled in salt as my skin peeled off.

It was horrific, and I only knew that was what it felt like because for a horrible few seconds, as I tried to make sense of everything, I was back in Athena's play palace, with her and her friends torturing me for fun.

I *knew* what it felt like to experience that, because she'd done it to me…that and worse.

I was back there, lost in agony; then a sudden fresh pain bloomed as my right arm snagged on something. My entire body pivoted around it, the arm taking the weight off my falling form as my hand was trapped in a gap that closed around it.

My bones had been long since transformed to nefindium, and as part of that transformation, there was no way that a "little" impact like this could really damage them. But it sure as shit could damage the joining tissues.

I hissed in pain, reaching out, grabbing onto something blindly and pulling, taking some of my weight with my left hand. My feet scraped across the surface of…of the behemoth's armor.

I focused finally, seeing the surface right in front of my eyes: the grey stone-like structure, the carved lines that made it up, the green, black, and grey algae that overfilled each and every crevice, scraped free by my frantic battering and who knew how many buildings the bugger had wrecked chasing me.

Now I was pinned to its side—about halfway down, under the main armor that made up most of it—and wedged into a flexion point.

Somehow, in the collapse of the water, I'd been shoved down and had landed at just the wrong point, my hand getting caught in a gap. The wrist bent and was painful, but the armor around it couldn't simply crush it.

I shifted, shaking myself, and reached out to the others as I braced myself and tried to get my hand free, hearing the relief in Ingrid's voice as she replied.

"Oh, thank the gods!" she groaned. "Steve, I was so worried!"

"What…happened?" I grunted, still trying to get my hand free as the monster swam on.

"It used some kind of a lightning attack, or fire, or…I don't know what. It vaporized a load of the water. I think it missed you…uh, yes. Of course it missed you, or you'd be a lot more hurt. Sorry. That was obvious," Ingrid apologized.

"I'm pretty fucking hurt," I muttered.

"Not like you would have been," she disagreed. "We were shoved back by the water around the blast being converted into gas, then the ocean collapsed in on the empty space that was left behind."

"Where are you?" I grunted, tugging at my hand again.

"Following you. We're about half a mile behind you, and above, flying southeast, and we're heading away from where we thought Atlantis was."

"We're heading out into the ocean?" I asked.

"I think so. What's it doing? It stopped suddenly, like it'd been hit with something…now it seems to have settled back down. What did you do?"

"I don't know. Hell, I don't think I did anything." I strained against the pinning pressure. "Fuck's sake, my hands stuck…" I felt their attention as they looked at it, and I looked around for context, showing them where I was.

"So, now what?" Jonas asked, and I grunted, still trying to free my hand.

"Steve, stop," Ingrid said suddenly.

"What?"

"It's heading in a straight line. It's going somewhere, and quickly—it's not deviating, or patrolling or whatever. I think it's been ordered home."

"Right?" I agreed, half listening and tugging at my hand again.

"If it realizes you're there, it'll go mad attacking you again. Steve, hold on, and when it gets wherever it's going, then get loose," she ordered, and I growled.

"Easy for you to say," I snapped. "If it decides to scratch an itch, I end up as roadkill."

"It's a machine." She repeated my words back to me. "It doesn't feel itches, and the way it's going, it's definitely heading somewhere, and as quickly as it can."

"You think it's headed to Atlantis?" I asked.

"I think it's heading home. Whoever used to live at Atlantis, they clearly aren't there anymore. This is our best lead, Steve."

"Dammit," I muttered, finally giving up and reaching out with my nanites.

My armor had been cooked by that blast, but it'd been more the shock of the overload than any significant damage. I still had a solid five million nanites in me, nearly all attuned now, and three million weaponized, meaning that I had plenty for a little experiment.

I reached out with my left hand, forming the nanites there into a flat pool—immensely relieved I could still do that—then pressing it to the side of the wall of armor before me.

The nanites bonded with it easily, giving me a solid connection, and I did the same with my feet. Once I was sure I was attached securely, I waited for the armor to flex nearby. The undulating motion of its swimming let me feel when it tightened around my grip and not, and I got ready to pull it out as soon as I could.

In the meantime?

I released a tentacle from my trapped right hand, filtering it out into the cracks of the armor around my fist.

The solid stone there was fracturing. Clearly unable to break my armor, it was instead breaking down, and that gave me a point to exploit.

The tentacle flattened itself down, feeding through the smaller cracks, then expanding into gaps as they appeared, sliding onward, around blocks of carved stone that seemed to be alive with power.

There were thousands, hundreds of thousands of them, and I stared in amazement as I built up a mental image, unwilling to risk using a pulse of gravity to map its internals, just in case it'd detect it.

At first, I'd thought they were round; then I'd realized that they had dozens of flat faces. I couldn't remember the name of the shape, but mentally drawing it in the comm link got me an answer quickly enough.

A polyhedron, apparently.

Arise :Explorer

The internals of the massive creation were just tens or even hundreds of thousands of these, and at first, I couldn't make sense of it, until I felt the creature shifting slightly and diving into a long, deep crevasse.

As it moved, the little ball-like things inside shifted, adjusted, and flowed into a new configuration, and it suddenly all made sense to me.

The reason it registered as solid was because the fucker *was* solid. It didn't have air pockets to cause issues when it went deep, or to form weak spots.

Instead, it could shift and twist around these thousands of balls. And the design?

I was getting sparks of recognition and inspiration from the Engineering sub-mind, and although I couldn't fully "get" the engineering principles behind the balls, or *polyhedrons*, what I was getting was that each was, in its own way, an individual power source as well as a storage device.

Something to do with the way that the design was laid out meant that these units, if the overall creature took serious damage, could act as miniature repair units, which was both cool as hell, and concerning.

Any damage we did would have to be serious. Most robots or drones? You could hit a central point, a brain or whatever, or a power core and boom, no more issue. This fucker?

It'd go down for a bit probably, but then it'd be repaired by the damn things and get back up!

It was a veritable war machine. And the more I looked at it? The less I thought this was from whoever lived here originally.

There was just no way that people who were building houses out of stone and sailing in wooden ships were also making shit like that. That meant that Ingrid was right, and although it'd come looking when we'd rang the dinner bell, it wasn't Atlantean, I'd guess.

Half an hour later? The bugger finally reached its destination, right at what had to be one of the deepest sections of the goddamn planet.

Chapter Seven

Where the Mariana Trench was supposedly the deepest spot on Earth, it was only the deepest if you counted from the surface of the sea down in a straight line.

Shortly after we'd entered this unnamed crevasse, the creature had taken a hard right, heading down a long, narrow passageway at breakneck speed, then a left through a massive arch of worked and ancient stone, before descending deeper and deeper into the blackness.

The sections that were passing by in a blur were terrifyingly close now and then, alternating between sections that had to have been formed from cooling lava and other processes that had once created enormous caves, and obviously carved reinforcement work.

Fish, few and far between, vanished in frantic blurs now, all but ignored by the massive apex hunter, while here and there creatures that glowed and sent bursts of light flooding across their bodies pressed themselves against the walls and ceiling.

I saw something that looked like a squid on steroids in a nearby offshoot cavern. A single massive eye stared at us, as it lifted off the ground in a great blast of disturbed sand, and damn, I sent an image and a warning to the others about that.

Ingrid and the others had dove into the sea by that point, not wanting to be left behind, but Sanneth had been left well and truly behind by now. He'd agreed to return to the refuge, and begin his own ascension, when it became clear the ancient fishing vessel just couldn't keep up.

He was furious at missing out on the chance of exploring the depths, but he had to admit that although the armored suit he wore was impressive, there was no way he could catch up for several hours and that would only be to the surface anyway. The sheer versatility of our own systems had left him behind some time ago.

Even if he was close enough to join us, diving now, and heading to what looked to be the deepest areas of the ocean? It was just a solid no.

Arise :Explorer

Ingrid led Scylla and Jonas—who was apparently still reforming part of his arm and hand—into the depths, their own armor flowing into more appropriate undersea versions.

The one thing they didn't have, and wouldn't dare use if they did, was any form of sonar or gravity wave.

It'd be too obvious, and it'd no doubt draw the leviathan's attention, so they were making do with their enhanced vision and the mapping I was doing my best to produce, from where I was stuck to the side of the big bugger.

It passed through cave after cave, some showing the signs of clear work, maintaining or repairing damage from some point. And the deeper we went? The more there was.

Huge columns, like battered and chewed rock towers, held a ceiling that vanished into the distance as the monster twisted a final time, then dove straight down before levelling out suddenly. Its arms flared, then slid back to rest in carved recesses. The tail jets sent a great blast of compressed water out to clear a section of the cave floor away.

I twisted, seeing a groove that was clearly a permanent resting place, or dock carved into the cave floor, and that the section I was currently hiding in? Yeah…it was intended to be pretty much flush with the rock face.

Cursing as I realized I might have waited too long, I yanked and yanked. The tentacle I'd been using to map out its internals flashed back to me, being absorbed as quickly as it could.

As soon as the majority was back inside me, I flexed what was left, feeding it into the gaps of the shattered stone around my fist, then twisted and expanded them.

It worked!

Cracks radiated outward, dozens of them, as the stone around my fist crumbled. I shoved off, swimming as hard as I could, turning the nanites that coated my armor into a great scoop and arcing it, jetting myself free of the edge of the behemoth as it lowered into its pit.

The blast of water being shoved aside in favor of the bulk that settled in helped, pushing me up and out of the way. I hit the side of the cliff nearby, scraping against the wall. A small cascade of rocks tumbled free, clattering across the carapace, but whether it was tired, uninterested, or didn't notice, I was damn glad when nothing happened in response to it.

I stared around, spotting three other sections nearby on the floor that looked similar to the one the leviathan was currently docked in. Although covered in sludge and general underwater muck, the recesses were presumably meant to have something resting in them at some point.

The only one that had appeared "clean" when we came in was this one, and the state of the others…it made me guess that they'd been unoccupied for a long-ass time.

Looking back up the way I'd come, there was a cliff leading upward, the same one that I'd scraped along literal seconds ago. Distantly above that, I could see the roof narrowing down toward the entrance we'd come in through.

From that point moving outward, the roof of the cave vanished upward, and on all sides, the walls extended away.

There were spaces for three more leviathans to be docked here, presumably for repairs, recharging, or whatever. And then, on the far side of them and vanishing downward, was another cliff edge.

The difference was that this cliff had a faint glimmer of light shining up from below to illuminate it.

Looking from that point and back up to where the others would be trying to find their way down to me, I was insanely tempted to creep past the monster and see what was making the light.

I decided against it in the end, though.

No matter how stupid I was—and I was *plenty* stupid—if that big bugger woke up, I wanted my friends there with me.

I wasn't sure we could even defeat it, but I was damn sure that if I tried alone, at the very least, whoever lived down here would be aware of us.

I didn't want to fight this thing, and then a swarm of Xi-Ma right after it if I could help it.

Flowing out from my armor, I created a wide "wing" of nanites, then gently lifted myself and set it to ripple, passing the water under and over it, arcing myself up and along the cliff, and back the way I'd come.

I watched the massive creation as I went, half expecting it to start moving, to burst into action, having spotted me, but fortunately it didn't.

Another half an hour later, slipping from cavern to cave to passage to cavern again, I finally saw the others closing in, and we shared immense relief as we were reunited.

We'd been in touch through the comm link all the way, but damn, actually seeing them emerge from the undersea gloom? It was amazing.

We moved to the far side, deliberately settling down behind a load of tumbled rocks, just in case, and I pulled Ingrid into an embrace.

"Are you okay?" I asked her at almost the same time she asked me the same.

"Of course I am!" She shook her head. "I was never in danger. You're the one who was almost cooked by that...thing!"

"Yeah, boss. That was damn close." Jonas nodded. "You think you'd have survived it?"

"A head-on hit?" I asked, and he nodded again. "No."

"Shit." He grunted.

"Then we have a worthy adversary," Scylla whispered, getting a look from Ingrid.

"What we have," Ingrid pointed out, "is an opportunity to hopefully speak with its master while not fighting, and considering the size and strength of that thing, we need to take it."

"We do," I agreed, getting a look from Scylla. "Hey, don't give me that 'disappointed in you' shit. I spent the last hour or more stuck to the bastard's side, mapping it out."

"And?" Ingrid asked.

"And I don't know if we could defeat it," I said. "It's insides are made up of tens of thousands of those balls, and they're all flexible. As near as I can tell, any damage it takes? They'll flow out like blood and rebuild it."

"If it bleeds, we can kill it." Scylla nodded to herself.

"Scylla, you remember the conversation we had about not testing ourselves against unnecessary adversaries?" Ingrid asked Scylla in a tight voice.

"I do. I also know that this creature has been the bane of the seas since long before I was born. Many of my comrades were lost to the oceans over the centuries. Perhaps this is my chance to avenge them."

"Or perhaps they found a pleasant island and lived out their lives in the sun," Ingrid said in a flat voice. "We don't know if this thing was responsible for any of their deaths, and unless you know something you're not telling us, you've never seen this before either, have you?"

"Well, no…"

"So this might have nothing to do with their deaths, or their disappearances, and there's no reason to attack it, when we need to try to develop a relationship here?"

"Well…"

"Thank you for agreeing, Scylla," Ingrid finished, in a tone that brooked no argument, as she stood and looked back the way I'd come. "I think we need to get moving. We're well into the morning now, and although the sun wasn't up here when we entered the water, it's only a matter of time."

"Then let's move," I agreed, setting off and leading the way back down to the creature.

Ingrid was, as always, graceful as hell. The flowing movements of my extended wings curled in slightly as I glanced back at her. Her own design to get through the water was more streamlined, and I couldn't help but be impressed.

I was also seriously impressed with the way she'd shut Scylla down back there. The woman was a lunatic and obsessed with honor. I'd have gone down the "let's explore first and stab the fucker later" route, trying to get Scylla on my side, and I'd have probably buggered it up.

Instead, she grumbled a little, but had fallen into line.

Jonas, when I looked over at him, was swimming alongside Scylla, clearly in a singular conversation between the pair, judging from the way they looked at each other.

He also looked well and truly messed up on the right side, his armor battered and regrowing over sections, reforming even as I watched.

"What happened to Jonas?" I asked Ingrid.

"That's the first thing you ask?" She sounded almost disappointed in me.

"We're in a cave at the bottom of the ocean, swimming toward what might be a fight with monsters from myth and legend. One of which has definitely claimed tens of thousands of lives of sailors at least. He's one of our hardest hitters with his guns, and he's clearly fucked up, so yeah. As much as I want to be asking how your day's gone, and how excited you are to be here, or what you think all this shit means, we need to be realistic."

"Okay, I understand, and yeah, that makes sense." She still sounded disappointed and a little hurt.

"I do care, believe me, but Ingrid, we need to be ready here. What happened, or should I ask him?" I pressed.

"He tried to fire his gun underwater, thinking with it being a rail gun, instead of an explosive detonation, like a regular firearm, it would work."

"And?"

"And it didn't," she said. "I don't know if it was the kind of projectile he tried to use, or the actual weapon, or the force, but the gun exploded. It shredded half his arm and made a mess of his side.

"He made that worse by trying to stay in the fight and reform the gun from his nanites instead of letting them heal him, and it slowed his repairs down. That's why he's still looking like that."

"I'd have thought he'd be healed by now…" I muttered.

"*You* would be," she stressed. "You took points in the Repair trees and you're used to healing yourself—remember that the nanites respond to you at an instinctual level. He was directing them away from the damage to repair his weapon instead."

"Has he…?"

"He's got his weapon back, and he's spent some points he had in reserve on improving the design. Apparently, it's now suitable for underwater work. It wasn't before, clearly. Unfortunately, it means he needs to build a new one as soon as possible, as evidently the version he's built is now unsuitable to use out of the water. That's what happens when you rush."

"Yeah," I agreed. "Okay, now that I know he's getting there, what do you think about…"

We talked as we swam through the caves and passages back to the still stationary leviathan, moving slower and slower as we approached its resting spot, until we peered over the side, staring down at the massive figure.

"Eurypterid." Ingrid breathed, and I looked over at her.

"What?"

"A sea scorpion." She sighed. "They must have based it off that design. The upper body is far wider, but the shape of the tail and the flexion points? The head and the way it was moving before?"

"Damn, yeah," Jonas muttered. "I saw one of those things in a museum…"

"I have not seen these creatures. Where did they catch one?" Scylla sounded confused, before Jonas started to explain the reality of modern museums and the replicas they would use.

Apparently, the ones in her day were a lot less open to the public, and a lot more "specialist private collector" in nature.

That, or the ones that the Arisen bothered with were. They'd known the people who were now referred to as the "old masters," when they were struggling bums trying to sell paintings on the street, so it kinda changed your perspective a little.

Eventually, and moving one at a time, we jumped over the edge of the cliff, swimming as gently as we could around the leviathan, and giving it as much space as possible as we crept around it.

Arise :Explorer

There were a couple of hair-raising moments when we landed. A collection of rocks shifted and caused a minor cascade nearby. Scylla hesitated, the proton lance she was still carrying—the weapon that had earned Zeus the "king of the gods" moniker from the primitive people of that time and she'd claimed—held ready.

I winced, not sure an insanely powerful cattle prod was the ideal weapon of choice for an under-frickin'-water battle. But when the leviathan slumbered on, uncaring, I breathed a sigh of relief.

Now that I was alongside the massive creation, and it thankfully wasn't trying to fucking kill us, I paused at Ingrid's gesture, agreeing when she asked for a few minutes, which wouldn't make a huge difference at this stage, and might help us later.

Despite every instinct to press on desperately, if we stepped out over the edge and this thing woke up? It was going to get messy.

Looking at it again, I could see that the entire surface was covered in some kind of runic pattern, one that Ingrid was apparently investigating.

The link to the satellite overhead was strong enough thanks to her upgrades that I could sense a steady connection to it, and as the stream continued, I started to see a mass of symbols.

She was mapping the side of the creation, at first just visually, and then…

Then she scanned it.

A jet of water pulsed out from under it; the entire thing started to move, and she quickly cut off the short-lived pulse, severing the link to the satellite overhead as well.

We all crouched down, staying as low and unthreatening as possible—even Scylla. And after a long minute in which my heart hammered in my ears?

It settled back down, the sudden feeling of oppressive danger slowly seeping away.

"*Have you been touched by madness?*" Scylla spoke for us all, hissing it into the comm link, only to be overwhelmed by the apologies that spilled out of Ingrid.

"I'm so sorry!" she whispered, clearly embarrassed. "I didn't mean to scan it!"

There were a few minutes of muttered apologies and attempts at explanations by Ingrid before we all managed to get her to be quiet and accept that we were fine. Then we waited another few minutes in silence, just in case, before we moved again.

This time, *away* from the goddamn monstrosity.

We reached the edge a few seconds later, and promptly forgot all about the overgrown sea-whatsit behind us.

The Lost City of Atlantis would have been great to find, sure, but whatever the hell this was?

It *wasn't* that.

Chapter Eight

I didn't know what I'd been expecting. A massive city? Glowing jellyfish being used as streetlights, millions of people streaming back and forth in glowing ships? Some of them wearing blatantly bad wigs that somehow never got filled by undersea creatures maybe? Weird that, considering the whole propensity for tiny creatures to find anything that looked like hair, and fuckin' hide in it…

Well, whatever I'd been expecting, what I saw below? It was more like an emergency armed camp.

A collection of lights became clearer as we floated down slowly over the side, shining on a massive creature.

And when I say massive, I mean *massive*.

It dwarfed the damn behemoth we'd just left behind.

The section that I could see from this angle as we drifted down? It was trapped in a cave; the side of the creature partially bulged out of the opening into the cavern that we were approaching, and it looked all kinds of wrong.

I couldn't decide whether it was a snake, or a dragon, or an octopus with counting issues, or…my brain just blanked on it, shuddering away from the immensity of the creature.

The impression that I was left with was teeth, scales, and muscle—masses of all of them.

It also felt…wrong.

Every instinct screamed at me to run, to get away, that nothing that large should exist, and certainly not buried down here where, if it farted, the world above would suffer earthquakes and tsunamis.

"What do we do?" Ingrid whispered into the link.

I blinked, shaking my head, the overwhelming wrongness still there, but somehow diminished by the remembrance that my friends were with me.

As I looked at the monolithic creature again, I noticed something else: massive, gleaming chains. Chains that looked to be almost entirely composed of light, surrounded by flowing lines of something, blocks that seemed to flex and twist, arcing out into the cavern and vanishing from sight.

The ground was coming up fast, and I looked away again, catching myself and landing, knees bent to take the impact.

As we'd been floating down, it'd been…well, it'd been silent, the bulging monstrosity of madness ahead overtaking most of the cavern. But the rest of the area?

The cliff face we'd just dropped down opened out into a new cavern at the base of the cliff. It'd been relatively tight as we got closer and closer to the bottom, narrowing in until it opened into a second cavern, this one smaller, but holding far more of interest.

First and foremost was the massive bulging *thing*, sure.

But the rest of the cavern? It was definitely a home.

There was a small but clearly well maintained—if ancient—collection of structures that made me think of the Mars habitation shit they kept drawing as concept stuff, then never building.

There were dim lights shining out of portholes, an air lock that had been used more times than a US presidential nominee told lies, and yet still it was standing.

It seemed impossible.

Either way, the small hab emitted a dim light from several portholes. And scattered around it were a dozen cases of equipment, all stacked neatly, with equipment clearly in the middle of being maintained, repaired, or upgraded.

That this was being done outside, at the bottom of the ocean?

Well, that kinda gave a hint as to how little the inhabitants had, despite the fact there were stacks of what looked to be null coins.

They were being churned out, oh *so* slowly, from a single factory unit that was, in turn…absorbing the remains of compressed reed baskets.

"The baskets," Ingrid said softly, as she touched down next to me, pointing at them, before flinching wildly. A dozen lights sprang to full life, bathing us in their brightness, and our armor registered multiple locks from all around the cave as weapons targeted us.

We froze. Not a single one of us moved, realizing that whatever we'd just triggered, if it opened fire? We'd be damn lucky to survive.

I spotted drones floating forward, oblong things that looked more like short ingots of metal. But the business end of the dual projectors that rose from either side of the narrow shape?

It was a trapezoid—I think, anyway—in that it was wider at the bottom than the top, and about twelve inches long. Looking at it from the end, it was maybe four inches on the bottom and three on the top, slanted sides going to the narrower upper section, and then two posts rising up from there to hold what were clearly weapons projectors.

They were focused unerringly on us all, drifting slowly as the current flowed. The airlock nearby started to clank and hiss, and then the massive thing on the far side of the chamber stirred.

That was even scarier than the multiple drones. But the weirdest part? The airlock, as it burst open, released a barrage of bubbles, the three figures that emerged from within clearly unwilling to lose the time that was needed to fully complete the cycle.

To our shock, though, besides a quick glance from two of them, we were mainly dismissed as unimportant, as they both raced to the side of the massive creature.

One of the figures reached out, placing both hands atop the quivering flesh, and bowed its head, clearly focusing, while the other made adjustments to something nearby, looking like a control pedestal or something.

The multiple lights shut off, leaving us all in utter darkness for long seconds as our eyes adjusted again. And when they did? I found the third figure that had left the airlock, floating a few meters away, with two swords held ready.

"Now what do we do?" Jonas asked.

The figure flinched, twisting to look at him.

"Can you hear me?" I asked, drawing the figure's attention.

"Or me?" Ingrid whispered, dropping her voice to see whether it was the sheer volume of the words being carried somehow through the water.

When the head turned to track her, I reached out—not physically, but with my Hack capabilities, even as I looked over the figure's armor.

It was eerily similar to Jonas's armor, if considerably more ornate, but the overall design was clearly related. As were the weapons.

I looked at the swords, seeing the shimmer in the water around the blades, and guessed that they were currently vibrating the same way my vorpal blade did. And that meant…

I felt the connection as soon as it formed: two sides of the same coin, reaching out to communicate, the access protocols and more meeting, doing a security and verification "handshake" before combining and forming a neural language link.

I felt it all as it happened, understanding at an instinctual level that the figure wasn't attempting to "hack" me. Instead, they were holding out a metaphorical hand, and in it? A neural language kernel.

I accepted it. My own systems went into "insane paranoia" level of monitoring, as details meshed and were explored, before sharing our own kernel.

In a matter of seconds, though, it was complete, and the world made even less sense than before.

"You're us," I said, shocked as I realized the truth of it. "Fuck, I mean…you're Biological Weapon Variants! We found you."

"No," came the response, the voice croaky as the figure tried to speak.

I stared in shock, opening the link so the others could hear.

"We are no longer weapons…now, we guard. We protect."

"Well, fuck me with a lit Roman candle," Jonas whispered. "We actually did it."

There were a few seconds of silence as we stared at him and he stared at us; then he shook his head and gestured to the habitation section.

"This way. We must not disturb them. The risk is too great."

With that enigmatic fuckin' statement, he turned, twisting his arms as the swords seemingly rotated sideways and vanished. Then he gestured sharply in a peculiar way—first two fingers out, third at ninety degrees, and the fourth touching the tip of his thumb.

Arise :Explorer

It meant nothing to us, but apparently it was a signal, as the floating drones spun and darted away, moving like fish dispersing when a predator appears.

We hesitated, looking at one another, then followed him, trying to make sense of the undersea world we'd found ourselves in.

He led us to the entrance of the undersea hab, pausing as he apparently realized as there were now five of us, including him, that unless we wanted to get really friendly, we couldn't all fit in the air lock. Then a little dance ensued.

Apparently, it wouldn't respond to anyone not "bound to the flame" as he'd called it, so he had to stand in the middle of the airlock, let two in, close up and let them out, then repeat for the second pair, following through to stand on the inside a minute or so later, as we stared around in shock.

The hab that we found ourselves in was…well, it was *weird*.

It looked like they'd taken something the military would issue and they'd tried to make it homey, personal even, but had almost no clue how to go about it.

Things like seashells, and carved wood here and there, and sections that looked as if they'd been melted and carved out of scrap plastic that had been floating on the ocean. Sections looked to have been replaced with stone that they'd had a go at carving then given up on. And everywhere were signs of long, *long* habitation.

Then there were actual tech items. They looked as though they'd been used to the point of wearing out, and yet instead of simply having them refurbished, having a factory unit rebuild them, they were forcing themselves to make do.

Sections of damaged tech were neatly stacked in a bin on one side, and four rows of bunk beds stood through a second, open, airlock door into what had to be the bedroom.

That was it.

There wasn't so much as a kitchen, a toilet—hell, there wasn't even a curtain that could be dragged around the edge of the beds for a bit of privacy.

Nothing.

We stood there awkwardly, as the figure strode into the middle of the room, regarding us, glancing from one to another, before sighing and retracting their armored helm.

The figure that was revealed was…*tired*.

That was the best description I could give. He was clearly old, and he carried a sense that he'd watched stars fail with less reaction than we were getting right now.

He clearly felt extremely uncomfortable, and even more so when we continued to stare at him.

He was healthy, more or less; certainly, he gave an impression of strength still, and the feeling that there was nothing we could do that could ever surprise him. Like he'd seen it all, and we were pale imitations of the last visitors he'd had but he'd put up with us, for now.

"You might as well relax," he ordered us, gesturing to the floor where a series of strange mats were set out, then sitting on one himself. "The commander is going to be out there for a while, and nothing is happening until he comes back in."

"Who are you?" Ingrid's helm flowed back to reveal her, and when he shrugged, seemingly uninterested in speaking further, we all followed suit.

Ingrid reached up, shaking her hair out of the single ponytail she'd had it in, tucked down the back of her helm. She drew her armored gauntlets back, scratching furiously at her scalp. The feeling of the helmet being gone always left an itch that was wonderful to scratch.

That shocked him—not how beautiful she was, I realized a few seconds later; simply that her hair was so long, and maybe that here, in the home of another, she was retracting her armor so easily.

I did the same—not the hair scratching thing; my hair was short enough that I could get away with it, although it really did need a trim, I realized belatedly.

No, for me, it was my steadily growing beard. As close as the helmet was, pressed literally against the skin, it always made my hairs twist weirdly along one side of my jaw.

"So much has changed," the figure whispered, and I looked at him in question. "Your…hair," he admitted after a few seconds.

I frowned, just as Scylla spoke up.

"You have none," she said.

At first, that seemed a stupid statement, but as I looked him over, I saw it as well.

There wasn't so much as an eyelash, no eyebrows, no hair of any kind, and although I wasn't going to go looking, I was betting that the rest of his body was the same.

"Of course not." He snorted.

"Why?" I asked, and he stared at me, seemingly confused.

"You will speak to the commander," he repeated.

We watched him, trying to get comfy on the mats, before dismissing our armor at Ingrid's silent suggestion. We relaxed a little, as Ingrid tried to make small talk, finding that it was almost impossible.

Asking for his name just got a glare; asking why and how they came to be there? We were clearly at risk of being stabbed. There wasn't the weather to talk about, or any kind of shared cultural heritage like sports or TV, and I had no clue whether they monitored the outside world or had no real clue it was there.

We tried a dozen lesser "getting to know you" questions and comments, before he abruptly stood.

"I must speak with the commander. You will wait here. Touch nothing."

With that, he started to walk for the door, and I scrambled to my feet. He stopped, his right and left hands held out to either side, as if a heartbeat from drawing those shimmering swords again.

"Whoa…" I lifted my hands, trying to show I was unarmed, and got another glare from him as I realized he was falling into a defensive stance on instinct. "Stop, I'm not doing anything!" I finished quickly, realizing to him, lifting your hands up in front of you and obviously empty might be a sign I wanted to wrestle, or play hide the sausage, or who knew what.

"Stand down and resume your place," he growled.

"We're running out of time." I spoke quickly. "The Ændari and the UC have a cease-fire, and we're going to breach it unless we get some data. We need it and we need it fast."

"Ændari scum," he spat, shaking his head in disgust. "Not a day goes by that they don't draw more into their petty wars. We want no part of this."

"That's fine," Ingrid said quickly. "I'm Ingrid. This is Steve, Jonas, and Scylla." She gestured to each of us in turn. "We're trying to *avert* a war, that's all. Please, speak with us, just for a minute."

"No."

With that wonderful demonstration of trust, he glared around again. "Touch nothing, or face the consequences." Then he stepped through the airlock, his helmet flowing up to cover his face, hiding him as the door closed, the sound of rushing water and evacuating air clear on the far side.

"Well, that went well," I muttered.

"We're not at war with them," Scylla pointed out. "In their culture, this may be the friendliest they get."

"Well, that's just peachy," Jonas drawled. "Another race of stuck-up assholes…just what we needed."

"They are warriors," Scylla snapped. "We are unexpected intruders from far away, who may bring risks to their mission."

"What's the mission, though…that's the question," I muttered.

"I think we'll find out when they're ready," Ingrid said softly. "Okay, we need to not be obvious about this, and certainly not disrespectful, but we should look around. See what the rest of the habitation chamber can tell us about our hosts."

"My little grave robber." I smiled at her, and she snorted, before accepting my kiss and giving me one in return.

"Play nice. And remember, Steve, these people might be the answer to our prayers or our most dangerous enemies, so you need to be patient."

"It's not exactly my strong suit—patience—so I'll let you do most of the talking," I suggested, and she nodded.

I also pointedly ignored the fervent nods from the other two as they clearly agreed that Ingrid should take the lead.

A search of the interior didn't take long, and although we didn't find much, there were some interesting things.

First and foremost, the beds.

At first glance, they were nothing special, just beds with metal frames, etc., sure. The thing was? The metal was old, exceedingly so, and tarnished, but in good repair.

The mattress, though? They reminded me of my old days in the military, where after lying on one of them you wondered whether you'd be more comfortable lying on the floor instead.

The one difference between them and the ones I'd used in my stint in the army? These looked newer.

That wasn't me taking the piss out of the army procurement and the backhanders that were commonplace; this was the simple truth. They looked like they were all a few weeks or months old, if that.

More minor details around the room were like that. Sections of the bedframe on one side were replaced with gleaming new metal, while more and more of the room looked to be insanely old, just well maintained.

There were sections of carefully carved rock used to replace panels that must have failed. And the closer I looked? Most of what I'd assumed to be the "homey" touches? They weren't.

It wasn't that they were crap—which they really were; it was that they were repairs that had been done with literally the only things that came to hand.

Stone, bone, and shells.

That got us thinking: if they'd done that, over time, then why the hell hadn't they fed the stone or whatever into the converter and made replacement parts?

The answer became obvious a few minutes later, when the commander of the little group stormed into the hab, clearly furious.

"What in the Great Souza's name are you doing here!" he snarled. "This entire planet is off-limits. We stationed markers around the damn system, so what the hell…"

"We live here," I replied, before wincing and glancing at Ingrid in apology. "Sorry, your turn."

"Thank you, Steve," she said with a half-smile, before repeating my words. "It's true, though. We do live here."

"For how long?"

"All our lives," she said. "So, you're the commander of this group?"

"Aye, Commander Yeshin Val-Aturr, Second Phalanx, ELF."

"You're an elf?" Jonas asked, before closing his mouth with a wince, and another apology to Ingrid.

"Eastern Liberation Front," Yeshin snapped. "We were part of the ELF for six hundred cycles, then were tasked here to ensure constraint was maintained on the part of the Ændari prisoners."

"Huh," I muttered, before clamping my lips shut.

"You've been here all that time?" Ingrid asked, shocked. "You were part of the original experiments?"

"Don't be ridiculous," he snarled, glaring at us. "We're fifth generation, not…" He paused, frowning before going on in a more careful voice. "When the war cooled, and the cease-fire was agreed, we and others were sent to rumored prison planets, agreeing to maintain a watch until the prisoners took the final step."

"Step?"

"Until they killed themselves," I suggested, getting a slow nod.

"That's why we're here. But you? You claim to be local inhabitants?"

"Yes," Ingrid said quickly. "We were born here."

"And yet you've got active nanites and bastardized variants of our armor. Who's your commanding officer?"

"Steve, I guess?" Ingrid said hesitantly, before taking a deep breath and straightening. "Okay, look, can you calm down, retract your armor, and sit? This is going to take some explaining…"

"Be warned, attack me at your peril," he growled. But after a few seconds, he retracted his helm to show a face covered in blue tattoos.

Arise :Explorer

A line ran down the center of his skull, with one side of his head marked in intricate patterns, the other left bare beyond a single stylized collection of dots and dashes.

The next hour was spent in slow discussion. The other two of his companions appeared for a few minutes at a time, then vanished after gathering materials and various bits and bobs from the hab, before returning outside.

By then, eventually, we'd explained who and what we were, and it was his turn.

They were, he confirmed again, part of the original "batches" of humanity released into the wild. That was only the beginning, though. They were all of the fifth generation, bred from the earlier ones, and damn were they old.

He wouldn't tell us when or where he'd been born, or when they'd arrived on Earth…only that when they came? They'd been expecting to find a wilderness inhabited by scattered tribes.

They'd landed in the far north of what would one day be called Russia. The ship was buried deliberately to form a secure base, before they got to work properly.

They'd been tasked with monitoring this world, and like several other prison planets, it had both terrifying creatures and wonderful resources.

In this case, it was the birthplace of our species, and yet…he'd been informed that there should be no more than a few hundred of us scattered across the world, with the three creators forced into hiding, working off their debt to the universe in solitary confinement.

Instead, they'd discovered one of the creators had apparently founded a city.

They'd found it as soon as they dropped from warp. The gravity drive released the twisting of space-time and deposited them at the Lagrange point, before moving into geosynchronous orbit around the world.

They'd found it, and they'd reported back and asked for permission to glass it.

The UC had refused, seeing that according to the scans they'd made, it was entirely inhabited by their distant cousins, several times removed, who were apparently trying to build a civilization.

Instead, the monitors—his group, he explained—were ordered to continue with their primary mission.

They were to watch over the prisoners, and also evaluate any of the BWV offshoots, and if it was judged that they could be useful, a full report would be made to the council.

Once it became clear that they'd apparently, somehow, managed to activate some of their nanites and achieve a higher than average concentration, as well as a city?

The mission was changed from mainly watching the prisoners and evaluating the scattered tribes, into a long-ranging "observe and wait" program, as the levels of both aggression and mental acuity that were standard among the subjects appeared to be wildly different than the released BWVs.

Notably, the wild humans who roamed the planet were aggressive, underhanded, and vicious to a level that was deemed unlikely to survive, and certainly not viable to be trained up.

They spent the next few centuries exploring the world, sneaking into the city at first. And then, when it became obvious that they were indeed humans, just Arisen, they started to visit on a regular basis.

The creator who visited and led the city was apparently attempting to maintain a code of ethics, as well as building a stable society. Although it was outside of her terms of banishment, the council decided to permit it, and instead ordered an ongoing observation protocol.

Every three centuries, the team made a full report, until eventually the day came that they were told to enact and maintain strict radio silence. They were to maintain that until a signal was sent on a reserved channel, and unless they received that, they were to remain hidden. Several of the prison worlds had been recently fought over in expansions of the old wars, and out of necessity the council had restricted knowledge of this and others, to keep it out of the hands of their enemies.

The team developed and deployed a nanite test site and contagion warning drones, before deploying them to the system limits, warning any incoming vessels that might find the system that there was an uncontrolled nanite conversion running rampant in the system, and that all intruders would be subject to summary "cleansing."

Also known as execution.

That done, and as they'd found and secured a monitoring station for each of the prisoners, they settled down and over the next few centuries, they actually began to enjoy living here.

They took partners and had homes. They interbred with the locals, and for several hundred years, they loved their lives.

The prisoners were always there, and each century the watch would be changed, with some of their team going to or leaving the monitoring station. It was confirmed that the one who would become the Erlking was apparently attempting to serve a penance as the cease-fire demanded. With Varnock the Defiler sulking in her cave, that only left one of their number to truly concern them.

Tiamak, also known as the Sculptor.

It was she who had twisted and improved on the original genes that were used to create humanity; it wasn't likely to be a coincidence that she was the patron of the only city of advanced "humans" on the planet.

Certainly not that only this variant had access to their basic nanite life extensions.

She split her time between working in seclusion and returning to the city, teaching and leading the people there.

After a few centuries of observation, it was decided that Yeshin would get closer to her, to watch and report, after nothing untoward had been found, aided by his first fist, Diamos.

Fast-forward three centuries later, and all hell had broken loose.

I managed to keep from asking questions, as he dismissed his gloves as well; he reached out to the center of the matted area, where there was a small clear patch of stone.

He pressed it, then twisted his hand, the palm flat against what was revealed to be a panel, as it rose, to show a collection of vials standing in holders.

"Take one," he ordered, taking his own and watching silently as Ingrid took four, handing the other three out and looking at her own.

"What are they?" Ingrid asked.

"Take it, or this discussion is over," he snapped, before upending his own and downing it in one. "It will have no ill effect, should you be one of us as you claim. If not…"

He glared at us, and I was struck by the feeling that as a literal elder of our kind, perhaps the eldest alive, and already fully ascended? He could probably tear his way through us all like a bullet through wet tissue paper if he wanted.

Reaching out with my senses to probe him, the data that came back? Yeah, he was the real deal. Where with others I could sense rough numbers of nanites, he just registered as…solid. Like he was a black mass in the sightless vision of the world around me, one that was somehow more "real" than the world around me, and yet, I could read nothing else.

I hesitated, then nodded, accepting that if he truly wished us ill, he could have already slaughtered us all.

The vials were thin, more like test tubes than anything you should really be drinking out of. I had a momentary flashback to the dodgy cocktails they sold in some nightclubs in these kind of vials.

That made chugging the liquid, as he did, both harder and easier.

It wasn't the first time I'd chugged a cocktail in medical-grade glassware—that was the easier part. The harder? Well, my stomach remembered the results of chugging those dodgy cocktails, and twisted almost before the liquid hit it.

When it did?

I gasped as a feeling of icy-cold serenity filled me. The entire world took on a shimmer, like even the cheapest surface was covered in diamonds, and someone was gently shining a light across it.

"What…" Scylla growled, shaking her head. "What did you give us?"

"Gleam." Yeshin snorted. "It's hard to synthesize now, but worth it in this situation. You'll find it a fun experience, should you be one of us, and a terminal one should you be of the Ændari, wearing a face."

"Wearing a face?" I mumbled, shaking my head and focusing, expecting my nanites to strip whatever this "gleam"' shit was away easily enough.

Instead, directing my nanites to it seemed to have the exact opposite experience, as the world around me exploded into light and cheerfulness.

I couldn't help but smile, as the room around me was revealed to be…wonderful!

Literally, I was amazed by the sheer artistry and skill that had been put into the room. And staring at the mat I was sitting on?

Just beautiful!

Yeshin started to talk again, and I forced myself to listen with half an ear.

He and Diamos had served the twisted creature who had a hand in creating his race, and what he'd found had astonished him.

First, she bitterly regretted the galactic war that she'd helped to spark off. And secondly? She was a scientist as a second career.

The thing that she was most of all? She was an *artist*. Her clay was flesh, and she'd spent her time on Earth since her banishment rebuilding her labs.

She'd been forced to rediscover the basic levels of her technology and learn to make things from absolute scratch. The council's edict demanding she abandon all the tech that they were given and live out her days as a local had been taken, in her mind, to mean that as long as she built it herself, she could use it.

Where the Erlking served its penance in solitude, generally looking down on the creatures it'd helped to create as a disappointment that it was forced to share the world with, and Varnock despised them, Tiamak loved them.

She'd been the one who had attempted to tweak and cure each and every weakness in our design, fixing what Varnock in her rage had broken, and her determination to create a race of superhumans had resulted in the advantages we enjoyed now. The pair watching her worked hard to move closer, eventually earning places in her personal guard.

Yeshin and Diamos spent long years anonymous, pretending to be nothing but another of her followers, until the day one of his devices, a suppression field that made him appear to her and the others much as any of the others nearby, glitched for a fraction of a second.

Tiamak had apparently seen it but hadn't reacted, later admitting that she believed he was there to assassinate her, possibly sent by Varnock. She ordered the rest of the "guards" from the room, declaring that she was retiring for contemplation, but would keep one of them nearby to assist.

She'd had no realistic need of them—they were Arisen, but they were also the lowest level of ascended BWVs, never upgraded beyond the basics. They'd been an honor guard, that was all.

Whereas she was ancient and powerful in her own right by then, and armored to boot.

She'd ordered him to accompany her, and had led him to a remote and hidden base.

Ten years they'd been living and working with her by then, and she believed that some assassin had killed one of her most loyal guards. She'd been planning to kill Yeshin in turn, and to keep her other guards "safe" from a threat that they stood no chance against.

The ensuing conflict had sunk a smaller island in the Atlantean archipelago, as well as several ships. But when Yeshin and Tiamak had managed to fight to a standstill, a sort of uneasy truce had been agreed.

Eventually she'd realized that he wasn't an assassin, and he'd not killed the guard she'd grown to rely on to take his place. Instead, it'd come out that he was that guard and he'd realized in turn that she really didn't want to fight.

That was when Diamos had arrived, and a whole new surprise came when he stripped his own shielding away, and the entire fight had nearly started again.

It took a few days, but they set out the rules to their situation, and began trying to live with the new reality.

Over the next fifty years, Tiamak and Diamos moved from an uneasy peace between prisoner and observer to devoted lovers. Then the BWV and its maker, bound by love and duty, set to work on improving and repairing the damage that Varnock, in her determination to "fix" the rebelling early versions, had broken.

Eighty years further along, and the pair were consumed with their labor, almost entirely retired from public life now. Atlantis was given over to a republic, while they left the island, spending the next two centuries travelling, researching, and essentially loving their life.

Their children—grown in a womb-tank as no joining of Ændari and BWV could ever naturally bear fruit—had stayed behind, enjoying the virtual paradise that was Atlantis.

The others sent to Earth with Yeshin had gradually moved away, enjoying life and viewing their time here as a well-deserved retirement, him included, while Diamos and Tiamak travelled, with only two of their number remaining in Atlantis as "guardians."

When they returned, they found Atlantis had fallen from grace, the republic had failed, and within ten years of their leaving, a new monarchy had risen to rule.

One of their fellow soldiers, Chae, had brutally murdered the other, Mual, using stolen Ændari technology to ensure that he could never rise again, and consuming his nanites. He'd trusted one of his own children, telling them the truth and giving them access to the secret weapons. He trusted that they would guard them for him, only to have them in turn brutally murder him.

That child had sparked off a war for control of Atlantis, and as often happened in rebellions, those who started it all ended with nothing.

The new rulers of Atlantis used the stolen technology to harvest any dissenters, and by the time Diamos and Tiamak returned?

Atlantis had gone from a shining example of what was possible, to a bloodthirsty pit of tyrants, plundering and enslaving all they encountered, sending raiding vessels to harvest slaves from the local unevolved populations, as well as murdering the "true" heirs to the throne, the pair's children.

Diamos and Tiamak disagreed on the best method to regain control and cleanse Atlantis, with him pleading with her to accept he knew war best as a BWV. She relented and agreed to wait and monitor the situation while he left to gather Yeshin and the rest of his people from their "retirement" around the world.

By the time they returned, Tiamak was raging and out of control, having used every trick she could come up with, and then more, to get Diamos to leave her alone long enough. She then resurrected hidden ancient plans for the ultimate weapon and began her transformation.

She'd made several miscalculations, though, rushing a design that wasn't entirely finished. And to cover for the shortfalls in her research, she used DNA from a captured Reta variant.

They'd been a scourge of the galaxy from an earlier species' experimentations, it was believed, and whoo-boy had it ended badly.

Yeshin broke off at seemingly a signal from somewhere, tilting his head as he appeared to be listening to something. Then he stared at us each in turn as we gaped at him, basically stoned to fuck, before he nodded, smiling tightly as he went on.

"Had you the stain of the Reta variant in you, you'd be dead from the gleam now, and an Ændari would be close to death as well. You are as you claim," he declared, relaxing for the first time.

Panels in the wall opened, and two more figures blurred into sight, lowering weapons and retracting their armor.

"Huh…?" I managed, before taking a small cube he offered each of us.

"It's an antidote," he assured us, again taking it himself, and waiting as we basically broke free of the insane drugs he'd just supplied.

"What the absolute fuck was that shit?" I forced out a few minutes later, my anger rising as I struggled to focus and stay upright.

"Gleam," he said flatly. "As I told you earlier, it's difficult to synthesize here, but worth the effort. Now, I cannot waste more time away from my role, so listen carefully. The gleam enhances memory, as well as other senses, so all that I said before now will be available with perfect recall."

I focused and was stunned to realize he was right: I could literally remember his every word from the description of Atlantis to its fall from grace.

"It will fade in time to the level of a regular memory, but for now, listen." He adjusted himself, shifting to be more comfortable as he started to speak again.

"Tiamak was out of control when we returned, raging, driven mad by pain and grief, the corpses of her and Diamos' children found at last. Instead of scaring the people of Atlantis as a 'living god' as she'd intended, forcing them to live in fear of the gods to enforce their good behavior, she destroyed the city in a terrible day and night.

"She drove the survivors from there, giving them no time to take the treasures they'd long coveted, nor the technologies that had made their life so comfortable. Instead, she fed on and harvested the vast majority of them, allowing only a scant few to flee, carried on the waves, before she in turn fled from Diamos, seeking to bury herself and create a cure."

"And did she manage it?" Ingrid asked after a short silence.

The response that Yeshin gave her, simply a glare, made it clear that Tiamak had not managed it, before he relented and went on.

"She is bound in slumber now…her lover, Diamos, bound to her, awake for eternity, entombed alongside her, watching over and regulating her. She lies out there, her body grown impossibly vast enough that, should she wake fully? Even adjusting her position would be catastrophic for your kind. The seas would rise, continents would fall, and most life on this world would be lost in the upheaval."

"So…not a good idea to wake her then." I winced.

"A very bad idea," Yeshin agreed firmly.

Chapter Nine

Yeshin had gotten up at that point, ordering us to rest and that he would "deal with us" once he'd finished calming Tiamak down from the sudden shock of our arrival.

Then he went outside and resumed his position next to the massive form, head bowed, hands planted on her scales, and apparently communing with her in some fashion, while above him, what we now realized was Diamos, hung suspended, half sunken into his lover's side.

We waited two damn hours in there, alone, before the first guy finally came back, still acting like we might explode or turn into dragons or something.

"There's not much food," he said by way of greeting. "But if you require it, then it's in there."

He'd gestured to a small cupboard, and we all looked at the food that he'd referenced, then at one another, trying to decide who was going to say it.

"Are you for goddamn real?" Jonas eventually blurted out. "That ain't food. What the hell happened to you all? It's just mush!"

"It's a mixture of single-celled proteins, amino acids, vitamins, and minerals."

"It smells like it'd be banned under the Geneva Conventions as cruel and unusual punishment," he retorted. "Seriously, *that's* what you eat?"

"I know not what this convention is, but yes. We are restricted on the various fats and proteins available to us here, and so we manage it more carefully than you may be used to."

"Don't you get food from the islands?" Ingrid asked carefully. "The ones around what used to be Atlantis?"

"The supplicants?" His brows drew down in confusion. "Of course, this is how we maintain our watch, but their offering is scarce compared to our needs."

"Your needs," I said quickly, seizing on that detail. "You've got a factory unit, you've got converters…"

"One."

"Well, you can use it to build more, right?" I suggested.

"To what end?"

"To— Fuck's sake, man, the least you could do is build a damn farm or something, right?"

"We are warriors," he replied flatly. "Dispatched here to maintain a watch over the prisoners."

"Yeah, we got that, but—" I broke off, staring at him, then shaking my head in shock. "Shit. You can't, can you?"

"What cannot we do?" another asked. The airlock door opened as they strode in. Their armor retracted to show a solidly built woman with cheeks that could have put a fashion model to shame and a glare to outdo a hawk.

"Uh, hi," I greeted her, before going on. "The converter and factory unit…you can't use them, can you?"

"Incorrect. They are working out there right now," she countered.

"Yeah…but you've got no real control, have you?" I stood and moved to the nearest porthole, staring out and searching. It took only a few seconds to find the factory unit. And when I did, it was less than three more seconds before I had remote access to it. "Interesting design for the security drones," I said distractedly.

"What?" The woman's voice turned notably colder.

"The drones…you've only got four designs unlocked on the damn factory unit, and three of them are useless underwater. That one? It's good, but wouldn't you be better with something bigger? Something that could hunt for you and bring food back?"

"We have that," she snapped. "You saw it already. And should we have not ordered its return, you'd not be so pleased with yourself."

"You mean the leviathan?" I turned away from the window. "That massive fucker that's been slaughtering innocent sailors for literally thousands of fucking years?"

There was a brief uncomfortable silence, before she spoke up again, glaring at her companion, who was cursing.

"We repurposed it, but the original orders occasionally return. We believed it was tamed, but the unleashing of the proton beam suggested otherwise. We will examine it."

"Bullshit," I said very clearly. "You're wondering how we found our way to you? I got attacked by the damn thing and held onto it all the way back here!"

"Ah." She closed her eyes, taking a deep breath and letting it out in a long, slow exhale. "That is less than ideal, and we regret it. However, this raises another issue. The commander may have additional questions for you, both regarding the unit's recent behavior, and your apparent easy access to the maker."

"Maker…you mean the factory unit?" I asked. "The little box that…"

"Yes."

"Fair enough." I grunted. "Look, no offense, but the UC ordered us to meet them ASAP, so…how long's he gonna be?"

"Asp?" the first guy asked, mangling the acronym.

"*As soon as possible.*" I spelled it out. "They gave us five days to get to a location, to prevent the cease-fire breaking down between the UC and the Ændari."

"So what are you doing here?" the woman snapped. "You should be on your way!"

"Yeah, and we'd love to, except that mad bitch Varnock trashed your ship's AI core, so we don't know where the hell we're going!"

"What?"

"They gave us galactic coordinates, but no way to communicate with them, nor anything to reference the location," Ingrid explained, stepping up to my side and laying a hand on my shoulder. "We need access to either a UC navigation system, a navigator, or a working AI."

"And now you are here." The woman shook her head. "Now it all makes sense."

"Yes, but it has become even more of a problem," the guy responded, glancing at her. "If the Ændari start searching for this world… You are the ones who killed Varnock?" He paused, and I nodded. "Excellent. She was an evil creature and the galaxy is a better place without her. However, if you killed her? The Ændari are going to want to use that as a pretext to find this place. And if they do? They would find Tiamak."

"That cannot be allowed," the woman growled.

"Agreed. So, what did the UC say in their message?" he asked, turning back to Ingrid and me.

"That's not for our ears before the commander's!" the woman snapped, heading for the door. "I'll take an extra shift, see if she'll respond to me, and let him return to deal with this."

"My companion is right." He sighed, seeming to deflate as soon as she'd left, and we were all trying not to wince at the glares they'd been giving each other. "My apologies. The desire for news, for information about the outside world? It consumes me after so long without."

"I can understand that." I grunted. "You've been stuck down here for so long that time must get meaningless."

"You have no idea," he whispered. "We all hate what Chae did, and yet, we understand it."

"Yeah…" I agreed, wincing as Ingrid shook her head, confused, while Scylla stiffened, glancing at me to see if I felt it too. Jonas didn't seem to get it either.

But the local guy saw the look we exchanged and nodded.

"It's cost us uncountable cycles down here, watching over her, and yet…if we'd stayed out there and active? Even if we'd never fought again, we'd have grown in strength to the level we could face fleets alone. Instead? Trapped down here? We've evolved, sure, but we've not been tested, and I miss the challenge."

Scylla nodded then, fervently, and I forced a smile, having thought that he was going to say something else.

"You miss the fight?" Ingrid asked him, and he shrugged.

"The contest," he corrected.

"I don't understand."

"I miss the joy of battle and the opportunity to improve, to test myself against my opponents, more than anything."

"And the bloodshed?"

"It is part of it," he said. "But it's the challenge I miss. The opportunity to grow, to stretch myself and to rise higher, to improve."

I nodded at that, and he stood, glancing out of the porthole at the factory unit I'd spotted before.

"Can you change its settings?" he asked me abruptly. "Make it useful to us?"

"Probably. I can access them from here, so the encryption wasn't good. I don't know what you want it to be able to do, though. There's no other programs in it, so all it could make is what I have access to, not whatever tech your people did."

"And the guardians?"

"The what?"

"The machines, the…"

"The drones?" I nodded. "Yeah, I can leave them on it, and just add more data to the unit. Why? And why the hell didn't you just make more of them?"

"We have had the unit only a short time," he admitted, before shaking his head. "The commander comes. He will explain."

A few minutes later, the commander, Yeshin, was back with us, and we'd finished going over the last part of the story with him, stressing that we needed an AI, a working navigation system, or a damn navigator to go with us.

He in turn glared at us, and explained that should the Ændari come looking, and find Tiamak? They'd gut the planet in a heartbeat to recover her.

"They are obsessed with improving their bodies to reach perfection—not of form, but of immortality. They believe they are the primary species, the one all lesser beings are descended from, and as such it is their duty to survive. They desire to rule over all, and we, as their wayward children, deserve any punishments they choose to inflict, should we fail to obey."

"Right." I nodded. "But let's face it, she's literally miles down here. It's not like—"

"They would find her the instant they arrived in orbit," he snapped. "Any competent sensor would map the planet in minutes, if not hours."

"Well, fuck, thanks for just adding to my wonderful day!" I growled. "So now that we're all lubed up, you might as well pound it in… Do you have a navigation system or not?"

"No."

"*Fuck*!" I hissed, barely suppressing the need to lash out, to punch a bulkhead or…

"But we can make one."

"What?" I twisted back to stare at him.

"We can make one," he repeated.

"And what will this cost us?" Ingrid stepped forward and rested a hand on my chest, gently but firmly, pressing me back as I started to speak.

"The materials required to make a working navigation system are not simple, but we could do it."

"'Could,' not 'will,' I notice," she pointed out, and he nodded.

"We spend our lives here, buried beneath the ocean, permanently on guard as we watch over Tiamak. We cannot harvest the required components ourselves. Neither can we leave her side, less we curse the world above to destruction."

"You need materials." I grunted. "Fine, we can do that."

"No," he corrected. "*You* need materials. Our needs are different."

"Explain, please," Ingrid asked.

"You say that one of our guardians has run amok again? It is a constant issue. No matter how much we attempt to stop them, they revert to their original commands on an irregular basis. And with our mission here, we can do naught but summon them to return, and only one now responds."

"Them?" Ingrid asked, and I groaned.

"There are four, besides the one that you tracked to here." He nodded. "This one? With a new memory core, we could entirely remove the old commands and simply wipe it, ensuring that it will no longer have old commands to default to, should you provide one."

"Okay…" I waited for it, knowing there was more to come.

"The maker unit you have observed outside. We recently recovered it, in the hope that it could be used to create more of the weapons platforms, the drones as you call them, to hunt down and eliminate these rogue systems, as well as to protect this location."

"You got it from your ship," I stated.

"We did," he said, apparently unconcerned that we knew.

"Fine, no stress there, but the weapons and armor that you recovered?"

"Yes?"

"We want some, as examples of—"

"No."

"Shit, man, come on!"

He shook his head. "You do not understand. We have limited stores, limited heavy metals, and little time to do anything but maintain our watch over Tiamak. The weapons and armor were recovered, as were any of the secondary systems that were judged to be expendable. They were fed to the converter to provide raw materials to build the drones."

"*Are you fucking kidding me?*" I whimpered, torn between grabbing him and screaming it into his face, and breaking down in disbelief.

"I do not joke."

"Oh my God…" Ingrid whispered, closing her eyes and resting her face in her palms.

"We needed the drones more than we needed old armor and weapons. We have evolved past any need for them, especially in our role here."

"You stupid fuck." I sighed, feeling the full ridiculousness of what they'd done. To them? The weapons and armor were indeed useless. They had their own armor and inbuilt weapons like I did, and they knew that should Tiamak ever awaken and decide to go on a rampage, her mind truly lost, then no armor they could imagine would be of use against her. She was truly the ender of worlds— or this one, at least.

They'd used what they viewed as useless materials and had turned them into something they could use.

That was great and all, but it just showed the difference between BWVs and BSVs.

The Biological Weapon Variants, like them, had literally no access to the systems that ran the factory units, and so they saw them in straightforward terms:

the converter churned out null coins to use in building the drones, and therefore, they might as well feed in the scrap they didn't need.

They probably got loads more null coins out of the armor and shit than they got out of the rotten remains of the baskets they were feeding in now.

Any Biological Support Variant who had accessed the converter or factory unit could change the settings in seconds.

"You will show the commander the respect he deserves!" the other guy snarled, and I glared at him.

"You fed advanced armors into the fucking converter, instead of the one thing you have an unlimited supply of." I growled. "Water!"

"What?"

"It's a molecular substance!" I pointed out. "You could have set it to goddamn convert indefinitely—it'd be slow but it'd keep going. Or rock, or that scrap, the baskets and shit, sure! You didn't have to give up your armor!"

"The converter does not accept just anything." Yeshin sneered.

"Yes!" I snapped at him. "Yes, it damn well does!" I turned and reached out to it, focusing and hacking the converter, then searching through the settings. It was in there, a setting to ensure maximum efficiency in production time. Basically, it was set to not allow atmospheric or liquid input so that it'd always be fed solids, as that was more efficient. All that was needed? To flip a goddamn mental switch.

"It's done."

"What is?"

"The converter!" I spun on my heel and stared at them, wondering whether they were really this stupid, or whether this was the result of thousands of years of doing the same thing over and over again.

"You can do that?" He glanced from me to the machine, where it was merrily chugging away outside.

"Easily."

"Mannet, link to the maker and confirm," he ordered one of the others, before he straightened up, fixing me with a glare. "You need our help to get you to the meeting, and we, in turn, have a need of your help. Even with the converter running now, and if we were to feed it refined metals, which we have none of on hand, it would take days to create the required memory modules. Can you unlock them?"

"They're not in the unit's memory," I forced out, my fists creaking as I clenched them.

"I suspected as much. They are not currently there, but if you were to be given a sample, could you access the maker's replicator function and copy the design?"

"Yeah...?" I guessed, frowning as I remoted into the little factory unit and accessed it, searching. "Yeah, I think so. Have you got—"

"No."

"Are you having a fucking laugh here?" I snapped.

"No." He glared at me. "You need the memory units, and that is where your needs and ours align. You need both the memory units and Diamos's memories to fill them. And us? Well, you stated that our guardian units are currently going rogue and have been terminating unauthorized targets. We need them stopped."

I nodded, then glanced at the others as they jerked, and were clearly looking at notifications.

"What's up?" I asked Ingrid.

"The quest," she murmured, still obviously reading. "It's a good reward, isn't it?"

"What quest?"

"What?" She blinked, then looked from me to Yeshin, who was staring at me as well.

"The quest," I repeated. "I didn't get one."

"You should have." Yeshin frowned, focusing in and seemingly looking at something. "What about now?"

"No?"

"Steve, when was the last time you had any notifications?" Ingrid stared at me, confused.

"The fight with Varnock, and the conversation after with the UC?"

"Share them," Yeshin ordered.

After a brief hesitation, and a little mental reassurance from Ingrid, I did.

Several minutes went by as he apparently searched and looked at something, before he spoke again.

"You need our help more than you thought," he said finally. "You've been convicted of a war crime."

"Yeah, when we killed Varnock." I shrugged. "Although she had a bounty on her head, and it wasn't even me who killed her."

"Did you do most of the fatal damage?"

"Maybe?" I guessed. "We all took a hand in it. Why?"

"The system must have locked onto your part in it, perhaps as the overall battle leader, and has convicted you of a war crime," he said simply. "Your system is locked to its last configuration, and you can no longer receive or complete quests."

"You're shitting me."

"The UC Council, should they accept your version of events and still have access to the quadrant node, can reboot your system again. Until then, you have lost access to that path."

"Fuck!"

"So, should you not meet with them on time, not only are you forever blocked from your own personal growth, but you stand an excellent chance of drawing the Ændari here and destroying your world."

"I'm not so much of an asshole that I'd not go and let the world burn," I growled.

"Then this is good." He nodded. "I simply wished to be sure. So, we have four rogue units out there currently that we can track, two different models of guardians. Both variants are significantly smaller than the one you have met already, and yet each is highly dangerous to unaugmented local life-forms."

"Right." I knew what was coming.

"You need the memory modules, and we need the units destroyed, as well as their parts to enable us to develop the local area. We cannot risk leaving Tiamak. The risk was deemed acceptable when we sent one of our number to retrieve them from the ship, and when they were gone, signals were sent that roused Tiamak from her slumber. We were barely able to calm her; we cannot risk one of us leaving again."

"So you want us to go kill these beasties and bring their corpses to you?" I asked.

"Yes."

"The quest has the option of bringing them a working memory module, or recovering one from the guardians and bringing them that along with a hundred null coins," Ingrid explained. "That's the value of the four corpses, apparently."

"Then we'll kill them, harvest the memory modules, and bring you the coins." I sighed. "There's no point in us lugging the corpses around the damn planet, unless... I don't suppose they're nearby?"

"They are spread extensively. Their command programming requires they protect the area around Atlantis and patrol against enemy incursions. The beasts of the day were considered highly dangerous, should the populace be caught unawares."

"And so now that Atlantis is gone, they're spread out, trying to find and patrol an area that no longer exists?" I grit my teeth as he nodded. "Fine." I stood, gesturing at the others. "Do we have a location for any of them?"

"Here."

I received a ping and accepted it. A map unfurled in my view, one that showed the planet and four blinking dots, three of which were currently in the deep ocean.

They flashed in a regular pattern, and when I focused on them, I got an image of something like a really pissed-off-looking giant croc motherfucker, with a spikey sharp fin down its back and a fuckload of teeth that probably gave Jaws nightmares.

They were literally spread out: one in the North Atlantic, the other two in the Pacific, one not far from Easter Island, and the other in deep, deep water practically in the middle of nowhere.

"It's a mosasaur variant," Ingrid whispered, her eyes gleaming, and I couldn't help but smile.

They were easy enough to spot, I guessed, before looking at the single flashing icon that indicated a different design or species. I laughed. "Are they programmed to hide from people?"

"Not as far as I'm aware. Why?"

"This one?" I mentally tapped on the image. "It's been hiding there for fucking years. People keep saying they've seen something, but then it's dismissed as bullshit."

"It would have no interest in your people, searching instead for threats to them in its location."

"So it probably only comes near the surface when it needs to, like if it's traced something that looked suspicious, and the rest of the time it's in its lair?"

"More likely it shuts down and buries itself in the debris at the bottom of the lake. It does not require air, after all, so unless it senses a threat, it will simply wait."

"And that makes perfect sense." I snorted. "No wonder they can never find it. They're looking for something moving, for it hunting or whatever. They've probably scanned it a dozen times and had no clue what it was!"

"And yet you recognize it?" Yeshin pressed.

"Oh, fuck yes." I snorted, sharing the details with the others, who started to laugh. Even Scylla joined in when Jonas explained it to her.

"Well, I always said I wanted to be a monster hunter," Jonas said. "So let's go fuck up Nessie!"

<u>Chapter Ten</u>

It took us an hour to get free of the little group of lunatics. We'd just started to leave when another of them arrived back at the hab, and we had to go over things quickly with them again, before finally being escorted out of the depths and to the leviathan.

Yeshin didn't come. He went straight back to try to soothe Tiamak, but the newcomer, Tarrn, did. He was by far the most cheerful of the group, and the thought of not only a little bit more in the way of luxuries, but also real food down there to join them on their eternal watch?

It was all he needed.

He took us to the leviathan and explained that the control system for it was based on a faster-than-light signal. Essentially, it was always broadcasting, but unless you knew where and when to listen, you'd stand no chance.

To my mind, because of the way he explained it, I needed to be listening a quarter of a second ahead of when I actually was, and because the access pulse was calibrated to last a tenth of a second?

It was almost impossible.

With that knowledge in place, though? We simply had to ping the same signal in the right way, and use my time dilation.

As soon as we did, I found the control signal and tried to access it, finding ten thousand plus years of overwritten coding and commands that were making an utter mess of the damn thing's mind.

"Holy shit," I whispered. "You…who did this?"

"We did," Tarrn said proudly. "We all helped."

"Well, no fucking wonder it's insane," I muttered. "You're telling it to do a thousand different things, one atop the other. Why the hell…"

A little digging, and we found that the plan had been as they explained earlier: that as it was a guardian of Atlantis, it'd guard their resting place. As well as snagging the food they'd managed to convince the islanders they should donate at some point.

They'd tried to give it orders to cover any eventuality, including things like swimmers who were too close, subs, drones, seals, playful dolphins…all of it.

Then they'd told it what was a dolphin being playful, and what was a shark being a dick, and a lot more, which was a bit excessive, but hey.

The real issue, though?

They'd all taken turns at it, adding "helpful" clarifications and added details. *Thousands* of them as they occurred to them.

As it was? If the underside of a ship was between X length and Y length, and painted red, for example, it was left alone, because they'd identified from intercepted signals that humans did that.

If it was covered in barnacles, or blue and red because the paint was peeling off one section more than another and it'd been repainted? It was a target.

No wonder the leviathan was fucked up.

I copied the insane mass of data from it, and told Tarrn to wipe everything, tell it to shut down until we came back and that we were friendly.

Then we continued up and through cave after cavern, passes, crevasses, and fuck knew what they were called, until eventually we saw the sparkle of the sun shining on the sea above.

We picked up speed then, more than ready to be out of the depths, bursting free and soaring high as quickly as we could.

Dimi was circling nearby—Ingrid had reached out to him—and as soon as he saw us, he swooped in and slowed down, lowering the boarding ramp and letting us land, one at a time.

I was the last, touching down on the foot of the ramp and catching myself on the guard rail. I turned to look out across the glittering blue of the ocean, hardly a cloud in sight, as the plane started to bank.

I stood there, the boarding ramp slowly whirring as it rose back into the plane, lifting me with it, watching until the sight was cut off, and I found myself in the belly of the plane.

It was incredibly luxurious, the inside paneled in expensive woods, painted in creams, and with paintings on the walls. Golden gleams reflected from their frames as I walked down the corridor, heading to the middle deck.

This had been Zeus's personal transport, and damn, it was still nice. We'd stripped out some of the most ostentatious crap, and we'd remodeled a lot of it so that it was no longer just a one-man—or weapon-grade wanker's—pleasure platform.

It was useful for us all now, with areas that we could actually work in, that could accommodate troops, and that could do more than just polish an idiot's ego.

That being said, it was also insanely nice, and although Zeus had been an asshole, he also had good taste. There was no need to rip the carpets out just to prove how much better we were than him, for example.

Those areas where we'd had to remove walls and so on? We'd tried to make the general areas match as much as possible.

Or Dimi had, anyway.

I'd barely made it aboard before I was getting bombarded with his requests to make sure he was ascended ASAP, and his fiancée too, and fending off his requests to take a holiday with her.

One that also included taking the plane, "for a shakedown cruise."

"Not the time for it," I told him grimly when I'd reached the cockpit, plotting out a route that'd get us back to the ship on Yuzhny, so we could pick up Belle and Oxus, then head to Scotland.

"Okay, boss, but you know, I've been doing a lot of flying of late, and I deserve—"

"I've just swam through around forty miles of caverns, deep under the ocean, where there's never been light, *ever*," I pointed out. "Next stop is picking our friends up, then Scotland for a fight, followed..."

"Sounds normal for Scotland," he muttered.

"Well, yeah, it is, except we're going to kill a part of their national identity, so the locals are gonna be even more pissed than normal," I growled. "*Then*, we're off after three mozziesaurs—"

"Mosasaurs," Ingrid corrected, coming onto the flight deck and checking a few readouts with a surprisingly knowledgeable air. "How long until we reach the island, Dimi?"

"Uh, three hours. Two if I push, but..."

"Push it," she said. "We've got no time, and we need to get back to Scotland. Get us there as quickly as possible, please."

I nodded my agreement, and she took my hand, practically dragging me from the room and back into the main areas.

"You need a shower," she told me.

"Do I smell?" I sniffed at myself, wincing. "I do."

"You do." She smiled to take the sting out of the words. "But..."

Before she could finish, I'd flooded my skin with nanites. The little buggers scoured off the top layer and absorbed it, along with anything smelly or less than fresh in a heartbeat.

Then they flowed back into my skin, smoothly, and I grinned at her. "Ta-daaa!" I said, making a "jazz hands" gesture.

"Oh," she said, surprised, then sighed. "It's for the best, I suppose. We've got a lot of work to do..."

"Wait, what?" I grunted, dismayed at what I just realized she'd been hinting at. "No! No, I definitely need a shower..."

"I... I'm getting a connection from Far," she said suddenly, the smile that had started to bloom on her face banished by a look of joint fear and hope.

"Take it," I said quickly. By the unfocused look on her face, she already had.

I guided her to a seat; then, when she showed no sign of coming out of it anytime soon, I sighed and headed to the galley, in search of food.

By the time she'd come out of it, nearly half an hour later, I had a decent meal on the go for us all, and even Dimi, now that he had a rudimentary autopilot working, joined us.

Ingrid filled us in on the changes in her mother's condition. It wasn't great news, although more of her body was being built now. Hopefully soon the "upper layer" would form, as currently her organs were still clearly visible, as were her bones.

That hadn't been the reason for the call, though. As much as Anders had hated doing it, he was calling to ask for help.

With the condition that Freja was in, she was obviously incapable of doing her job, and he wasn't doing anywhere near what he needed to be doing.

The pair—along with James and Laia—ran the business side of everything that we did. The shipping in and out of the hazardous materials, the billing, bookings, and more that were the public side were only the most basic jobs that they handled.

The main things they were doing, day-to-day, included managing Zac and the others and continuing with the improvements to the recycling plant and the surrounding area, not to mention the building of our citadel.

Some of it was already in progress, just working away merrily, not needing real supervision.

Other jobs were being picked up by others, such as Casey, Zac's wife, who'd taken some of the jobs under her wing and was helping to keep the engineers moving.

The problem was, when you took the top people out, and didn't specify "go to Bob," for example, in the short-term, and others stepped up to help as best they could?

Nobody knew for sure what was happening.

Some jobs were being entirely missed, others were in progress, but the person handling them wasn't aware of some details, and the shit would be hitting the fan sometime soon.

In other places…it already had.

Ingrid spent the next half hour giving out jobs, having us make calls, check details, and basically get an up-to-date look at everything, then input it into the command network into a section she specially created for it.

It didn't help that James was heavily involved in the starship project, and Laia with him, as she was currently working on the rebuild of the *Pacific Princess*, into the mobile construction yard that we so desperately needed.

The pair of them were insanely busy on projects that we couldn't afford to pull them from.

Unfortunately, that meant that we were down to just us, and we were kinda busy as well.

By the time we landed close to the ship, Belle and Oxus were ready. They stormed aboard, Oxus having directed "his" Minotaurs to help out by guarding the perimeter of the ship and its hallways for now.

By the time Belle arrived, passing out slabs of blank and ready nanites to each of us, I couldn't help but grin, knowing that I had literally ten million nanites there ready to be absorbed.

That was the deal we'd settled on, even though I wanted more. We now had three hundred million nanites, and as much as I wanted loads and to only take ten out of three hundred seemed crazy?

It was the right thing to do.

There were six of us: Ingrid, Belle, Scylla, and Jonas, as well as Oxus and me. That was sixty million nanites right there. Again, it didn't sound like much.

Double it, though, and it was nearly half of the total.

So we settled on what we'd killed ourselves and had already claimed, and then ten of the "slush pool."

That gave us two hundred and forty million to use for all the other projects we had, including two hundred thousand nanites per person to carry out a bunch of ascensions.

We got five people ascended per million nanite clusters, so forty million would ascend two hundred people. Although, the final numbers might change, because Minotaurs, for example, needed double doses because of their sheer size.

That left two hundred million. Although the desire was there to dip into the pool to fuel our personal upgrades, instead it was going into the project pot.

Essentially, a hundred were dedicated to the insane starship project, as Zac had it in his head that the best kind of a starship we could build, given that we had access to so much, was a *living* one.

It would evolve and grow with us, and when it needed repairs and upgrades? It'd be a hell of a better experience. This one wasn't it, not entirely; the one he was building currently would be the seed that would one day grow into the real vessel. But damn. The potential? Incredible.

I was still a fan of the simpler option, but at the end of the day, he was the expert, and our resident madman, so fuck it.

That left another hundred million for sundries, you know, like fixing the sink, improving on current machines, raising the dead, and replacing leaky windows and shit.

I pulled up my personal stat menu. The upgrade options on that, although it still worked—sort of—were blocked out as well, and I barely suppressed the urge to swear.

If that was blocked from me doing anything, and so was the main upgrade system? I was going to be losing out on so many possible goddamn points. And worst of all, it wasn't even a case of me just saving them for later!

I wasn't getting the quest unlocks, and I was effectively "full," so I couldn't store more nanites either!

Sure, I could work on doing what the others like Varnock had done, and start to replace my cells, literally, with nanites, but I'd need a fuckload more than I had currently to make a real difference.

Or, I could do like the Elders and others had been doing forever and simply impregnate myself with them.

The human body had an insane amount of space in it, all things considered, and when you started using nanites to replace parts, be that as a red blood cell transportation system, or for example your liver, you found massive surges in effectiveness.

That was one possible path to improvements for me, as really, I needed to damn well spend these nanites, or I couldn't harvest any more.

The other...?

That was something I'd been toying with for a while, and I kept it in the back of my mind as I took over some of the engineering, as well as the environmental projects.

Arise :Explorer

We landed at Loch Ness an hour or so later. The transport settled down late evening, local time, and scared the absolute crap out of a bunch of fishermen who were following the age-old traditions of their hobby.

That meant that they were ignoring the loch almost totally and getting roaring drunk with friends.

The transport was almost silent as it settled in, and it wasn't until we were on final approach that they even noticed us. Dimi, being Dimi, skimmed in over the surface of the loch at about ten meters from the lapping wavelets.

He also absolutely fucked the setup the fishermen had going, when the downdraft sent several of them flying. He also sent all the rods into the water, where some sank and one, with a freshly hooked fish, made a bid for freedom.

That meant that when we walked down the descending gangway, the locals were torn between attacking us on the spot, running away, and trying to demand payment for the lost rods and spilled booze.

I solved it by walking up to them in full armor, only my helm retracted and wings on full display, then picking the remains of the spilled whisky up and taking a long slug from the bottle.

"Goddamn, that's good," I proclaimed, and got a round of nods from them all.

I might be an angel, a demon, or an alien, come in on my ship like that, they seemed to be thinking, but if I understood good whisky, that made me almost Scottish and therefore civilized.

That, in turn, meant that although they were still willing to fight me, it was more of a general "the sun is up" thing, rather than out of hatred.

"Sorry to interrupt, lads…" I tried to keep my English accent as low as possible, and push my northern a little. "I'm here to sort Nessie out, then we'll fuck off. Who do I owe money to for the damage?"

That cut right to the heart of it.

If I was there to "sort out Nessie," then there were three possible outcomes. First, I was a nutter, and therefore best left alone. Second, I was going to pick a fight with Nessie, in which case they needed to be there and watching, both to record it for the world, and because if there was anything a Scotsman liked more than whisky and money, it was watching someone fight, or joining in themselves.

Third, if I actually didn't manage to find Nessie, they'd still have a hell of a story, time to take some photos, and some money as well.

They looked at one another, then nodded almost in unison. There were five of them, and the largest stepped forward.

"Well, ah own the loch, this bit of it, see, and the lads? They own the rest, but we could see lettin' yer park yer…" He paused, glancing up at the obviously weird and advanced flying machine, then at the armor we all wore, and struggled on bravely. "Yer thingy there. For, oh, five 'undred quid?" he suggested, looking at the others to gauge whether this was ridiculously low, too high, or about right.

"Each," another interjected.

"Obviously!" the apparent leader added quickly, stroking his beard and nodding as the others made noncommittal grumbles, waiting to see whether the outspoken ones would be zapped with ray guns or whatever.

"Aye, no worries," I agreed, nodding. "An hour?"

"Five 'undred, each, an hour?" One of them gasped, then recovered and nodded seriously when the others stared at him. "Well, ah mean, aye. That'll do."

"And what do I owe for the damage?" I grinned at the looks on their faces. "Your fishing gear, an' the whisky…call it a grand each?"

"Oh aye, that'll do," another said, nodding and smiling.

"Fair enough. Log into your banks, lads…let's get this sorted." I rubbed my hands and reached out mentally to their phones with the Hack sub-mind.

By the time they'd pulled their phones out, had logged in and brought their balances up, I was nearly done, transferring a solid five thousand pounds Sterling to each of them.

"That should see us eight hours on site." I watched as they stared at their phones, grinning. I damn well knew not one of them had any rights to be fishing right next to a sign that said "No fishing without a permit," but it kept them happy, made them less likely to call for the army or whatever, and it was a good deed. "Oh, and lads? The government is after me, trying to claim shit they've no rights to, so anyone asks what I look like? Tell them a load of shite, all right?"

That got nods. Especially as in Scotland, as the main government for the United Kingdom was down in London, and was hated by the entire rest of the country.

Scotland had set up their own devolved government a few years back, and like a lot of people, I'd had high hopes that as new starters they'd actually do shit with the people in mind first.

They had, it could be argued; it just involved buying their own people stuff with government money first. And by "their people," I meant that some people got a nice new camper van, and the neighbors got told to fuck off or they'd get a tax investigation.

Even the massive Minotaur that was Oxus got little more than stares. Knowing the locals here, if he stood his ground in a bar, they'd accept him no questions asked.

Belle, well…she was dressed, thanks to the armor she wore, but it was designed half by the ancient system's protocols, and half by an incredibly horny dryad, so it was pretty sheer.

The small group looked from him, to her, to the rest of us, then back again, before their leader reached out for the whisky bottle from me, and started to drink.

These were more my people than most: a bunch of guys who just wanted to hang out with their friends and drink whisky, while telling the authorities to go fuck themselves by deliberately setting up fishing right next to a sign.

With them all sorted, I joined the others, striding toward the water, with Ingrid pausing to look at the fishermen.

"You might want to move back from the water. This could get messy," she warned them, knowing that it was unlikely that we'd end up back here, but that all things were possible.

We'd picked Nessie up on arrival. It wasn't particularly hard, not once you knew what you were looking for, and we headed straight for the closest landing spot to her.

Arise :Explorer

She was, as many of the witnesses had claimed, and then been laughed at, a plesiosaur variant. Admittedly, she was more machine than life-form, but she had a rudimentary AI, and it was that memory module that we were looking to harvest. That meant that the head needed to be intact, at the very least.

She had been laid at rest at the bottom of the loch, covered in what had to be weeks of sediment, while fish and the various life that lived in the loch carried on with their business all around her.

As soon as we'd landed, the scanners had picked her up, and she'd started to move.

We weren't sure whether it was the scanners on the transport, the gravitational ones I was using, or something to do with the metals that were used, but she was making a beeline for us, and she wasn't coming to invite us to tea.

Chapter Eleven

We'd made it nearly to the pebbled shoreline when the guys behind us saw the first signs of her. We knew that, because the swearing and shouts that rose were suddenly panicked and frantic.

Mostly they were getting their cameras working on their phones, and getting the hell back, as our helmets sealed and we closed the distance.

"Okay, team, we don't know what to expect. Spread out and try to keep it to ranged options," Ingrid said, her voice crisp and professional as we went, and I couldn't help but smile.

She sounded a little nervous as well, but I doubted the others knew her well enough to pick up on that—besides Belle, anyway.

I was proud of her, knowing that at least some of that newfound confidence would have come from hard study on her part, at every available opportunity.

I banished it from my mind as the water swelled upward even higher, now barely a hundred meters ahead of us. The telltale bulge of something large and fast approaching from deep beneath the waves was unmissable now.

It wasn't clear to the locals at first what or who it was, but I instinctively spun up my GGC. The gravity gradient cannon flowed into reality as my nanites bulged upward. The block of ammunition already cracked free a single dart as I activated my systems and examined the target.

Or I tried to.

All I got was a series of crashes, and I guessed that was what had happened before, with the leviathan. I cursed, sighting carefully, and waiting.

As the cannon finished forming and the gravity rings shivered into life, a single neutral point was created, holding the first dart in place as the rings began to draw energy from the power core.

I could feel the drain, and the joy of combat filling me, as the "sight" at the end of the GGC finished forming and went live, providing me with a perfect image and overlaying my own vision with a crosshairs.

"Oxus, keep back and be ready. Your job is to take the head," Ingrid ordered. "Jonas, Steve, right and left. I want you to distract and harry it. Make it come in as close in as possible. We don't want to be fighting it in its element…make it come onto ours."

We nodded, moving into position, as she went on.

"Belle, you're with me. Scylla…" She paused, then just accepted reality. "You be wherever you can be most effective."

Scylla had ranged weapons, she liked guns, and she had the proton lance, so yeah that'd be damn effective. But until we knew what it was going to do, she'd do what she did best and bring the carnage.

"I think we need to encourage Belle to focus on the healing paths as well," I sent to Ingrid as the thought occurred to me. *"If she focuses exclusively on repair and harvesting, she shouldn't go too far into anything to hurt her, and then we'd have a healer as well."*

"I think we've got a pair of good tanks, between you and Oxus, Jonas is ranged, as am I, and Scylla…" Ingrid replied distractedly, clearly focusing on the fight to come.

"She's Scylla," I finished for her, sending her a mental kiss.

"Exactly." I could practically feel the eyeroll, and I smiled.

The rising swell out on the loch was joined by a second, bigger one that started farther back. I stared for a second, thinking there were two of them, until the head broke the surface, and the long neck that joined the two humps was revealed.

Shouts rose behind me, and I knew on seeing the reality of Nessie, the Scots had just gone from "they're all mad, those buggers; they can't do that" into the "ohmafuckin'godkillitw'fire" camp.

What the tabloids and sightings apparently got right was that she was a plesiosaur in layout, as mad as that was.

Where they got it wrong was thinking that meant she was alive, or naturally evolved, which was pretty reasonable, all things considered.

The monster that increased speed as it sensed the threat we posed was neither organic nor anything that nature had a hand in creating, despite Atlantis's original design template being based on one.

She was half again the "regular" size, making her body about the size of a commercial long-distance bus, with a neck that was around the ten-meter mark, and a head that was at least two meters long.

Add on the fins and the tail, and damn. Two commercial buses at least.

She also had more teeth than was reasonable under any circumstances. The mouth was about a meter long. And then, the back of the head, with all the lovely memory modules we needed to strip out and copy, was another meter on top of that.

Her jaws were wide at the base, coming to a narrow but blunt point. I knew that if this was in fact based on a real, living version? It'd have made snacks of mosasaurs and fucking megalodons.

Nessie was all kinds of impressive, and the first shot that Jonas fired from his rifle smashed into the bridge of her nose, before spanging off in a random direction. The handgun definitely needed to be replaced, he'd admitted on the flight; he'd tried to fix it again himself and now it was completely buggered.

"Don't damage the head!" Ingrid snapped at him, getting a low mutter of "I don't think I fucking can." She glared at him, and he coughed.

"Sorry, boss," he said, sounding like he meant it, as I took aim with the GGC.

"Aiming for the throat," I called out, before firing.

The GGC was a rail gun, built using alien tech and gravity instead of magnetics. But most importantly, it wasn't a rail *gun*, so much as a rail *cannon*.

The dart that was fired was a little over an inch long, metal fletching at the rear to stabilize it, with a pointed tip, and the impact with the center of the fucker's neck was far more satisfying.

Nessie reared back, twisting to the side as a hole bigger than my fist was blown in one side and out the far side of her neck. And that was when everything went wrong.

First of all, she ducked her head under the water again and picked up speed, which was surprising. And secondly? Sections along her back opened: hexagonal spaces appeared in the black and green patterning that exposed recessed canisters.

"What the hell…" I grunted, having not considered that she'd have ranged weaponry, when the head burst back out of the water, rearing up.

Her neck was spraying liquid and…

I blinked. It *wasn't* a damn liquid—it was the same polygon shapes I'd sensed inside the leviathan, flowing out of the wound!

They must have been under pressure, and sprayed out at first, the edges fragmenting and clinging to the ragged hole. Then they started twisting around and locking in, reforming, creating a sort of clot of machines, one that was rebuilding the damn thing and repairing its injury!

"Mother fu—" I growled, staring as Ingrid's voice cut through the shock.

"Fire!" she barked. "Scylla, Steve, focus fire on the neck—try to behead it! Jonas, do something damn useful! Oxus, get ready to draw its attention once it reaches the land… Belle, if it comes out, I want it slowed…"

"On it!" Belle replied cheerfully, pulling something out of her armor and raising it to her lips, as her helmet split apart to expose them. She closed her eyes and breathed out over whatever it was, clearly doing something, but I had no time to watch.

Instead, I was snapping free one of the rounds that would do maximum damage and loading it into the GGC, as the various sections spun up again.

The round I'd chosen this time wasn't a "round" by any means. It was one of the custom "joined" rounds—I really needed to name these fuckers at some point—that were essentially a loose collection of darts gathered around a larger one.

They were each connected by a monofilament thread, and although they were compressed together in the barrel, as soon as they were fired out, they'd expand into a circle.

If they hit something at just the right angle, they'd probably cut straight through it; the main dart would punch through in the center, and then the exterior ones would follow, with the monofilament cutting a bigger section free.

To make sure that the fucker didn't just keep going, though, I'd been playing with my rounds of late.

The tip was still aerodynamic in flight, but now…I'd blunted it, and the tip on the connected darts.

That meant that instead of ripping through and carrying on, the entire force of the impact was released as heat, light, and basically an explosion.

Or it would have, *if* the bastard had hit.

The head came down, mouth opening wide as it reached the shore, and it *screamed*. The air between it and us literally shook, with everything becoming blurred. My round, and the shots that Jonas had fired, detonated in the air halfway, sending fragments in all directions as we were picked up and hurled backward.

Dimi had already taken off, clearly seeing Nessie and deciding that he had an urgent appointment to get his hair dyed somewhere far away. But he was caught in the blast, twisting as he climbed; the tail spun to one side before he corrected for it.

I was literally flying through the air, crashing into a low series of bushes and tearing through, meeting a low drainage gully and falling into that with a shouted oath.

I blinked, shaking my head, and twisted. The gully had been hidden in the bushes, and was a meter deep and wide, running out of sight with a metal mesh that covered it in places. Something, or someone, had clearly removed it here.

I swore, activating my gravity manipulation and my tentacles. I flipped myself around and crashed back out, in a spray of broken plants and flying debris.

Nessie was halfway up the bank, the flippers having a flex point halfway that enabled it to move on land to a limited degree. It'd come far enough up out of the water that it'd braced itself, and the head dipped down, its eyes locking in on me, as the recessed containers in the back shifted.

They were hexagonal, and arranged in two rows of four, rolling back down the central body. Only three managed to fully deploy—a testament to the age of the systems, I guessed—but goddamn.

The canisters fired out with a solid "cha-unk" that I felt in my gut. Three of them blasted upward, with sections on all sides breaking free.

I stared up, then cursed, blinking as I realized the time I'd wasted in shock. I reached out, twisting gravity and forming a scoop, flipping as many as I could up and around, back toward the creature.

Some were too fast—landing all around me, flying past, touching down. And wherever they landed? Fire and shrapnel.

They exploded. Some were filled with tiny darts that went flying out, trailing their own razor wire, scything through trees, bushes, and into us.

I caught one almost full-on. Not knowing where the others were, or the locals, I'd formed a secondary field, shoving down and forward, feeding in from around me, thinking to protect those I loved. Instantly, I knew that whoever designed this thing, they knew war.

I was hit with two of the razor wire versions. The darts seemingly zeroed in on me and adjusted their flight to impact, flexing and sealing to my armor as the razor wire was yanked inward, dragging the box that had held it across the ground toward me.

As they activated, flooding my armor with a powerful, localized electrical pulse, another slammed into my shoulder. Then it detonated, throwing me sideways.

I hit the floor, my head reeling. My armor registered dozens of cracks and points of failure, atmospheric outgassing—unimportant considering where I was, but still—and a dozen warnings…then the electrical pulse fired again.

As that happened, though, the gravity wave I'd used to shove the other canisters back toward the monster impacted as well. Dozens of the tiny devices exploded in showers of wire, tiny shrapnel charges, electrical explosions, and more.

Nessie staggered, almost vanishing from sight as flames covered it. It frantically screamed again, forcing a fresh shield of air into place between it and us.

The flames and shrapnel were blasted back toward me. I wrapped my arms around myself, dropping to one knee instinctively, head down and protecting it as best I could. A split second later, panic rose…as did the pain.

"Ingrid!" I bellowed. My eyes searched my readout, even as my heart and head did the same, only to find that unlike me, she was already on station, and was fine.

A little bruised, a little battered, as were the others, but in popping up the way I'd done, I'd apparently made myself the focus of the monster's ire.

Now she was moving. The command link, lost for a few seconds in the stress and the raging adrenal response, now came flooding back, and I saw the battlefield as Ingrid did.

I activated my increased perception of time, and everything became clear.

As I rose from the dirt—partly aflame, bloody, and battered—my armor was already repairing itself, as Oxus roared and charged in at Nessie from the side.

Belle was crouching next to Ingrid, working on whatever she was doing, but I got an impression of annoyance, frustration at the delay, and a short timescale.

I also noticed a load of twisting vines and thorned plants that were growing a good distance back behind us all, and I guessed that the blast had blown all her seeds or whatever she'd been working on all the way back there instead.

Jonas was crouched, rifle up and firing, hitting Nessie with round after round. But they were small, more of an annoyance than anything else.

He was working one-handed though, his left holding something that… I blinked, seeing the details that were shared with the group, and grinned to myself.

"Jonas!" I bellowed, already sliding my rifle away, and forming my harvest and vorpal blades instead. "How long?"

"Thirty seconds!" he retorted. "It's a one-off, though!"

"Moving!" I replied, sending a burst of intent into the command link, letting the others know what I was doing.

"Steve, work with Oxus. Scylla, distract it—keep its attention to the left. Belle, when Steve and Oxus put it down, you pin it. Jonas, that'll be your shot."

We all sent various agreements, racing forward.

The monstrosity stomped out of the remnants of fire, shaking itself like a dog coming out of a pond. The crap that had covered its outer armoring for millennia was gone now, literally burned and blasted free, and the original form was on display.

The body, neck, and head were a dull grey, intricate carvings laid over and over in repeating patterns that ran its length, each section overlapping the one before.

When it'd been created, it must have been a thing of beauty and overt threat. Now it was a mess.

Sections were fractured; others looked as though they'd broken away eons ago, with tattered and messy plating in place of the original. More were blackened and dented than were intact, and here and there were ancient wounds, sections where something truly massive had tried to feed on it.

Dents that ran in a row suggested a maw the size of a house had bitten down, before being beaten off.

The damaged sections were clearly being fixed by the internal hexagons. Sections looked as if they'd been spot-welded or plastered over and reducing the overall flexibility were everywhere, but the one thing that it wasn't was out of the fight.

The legs, where it'd dragged itself up out of the water, had been flippers. But since I'd seen that, I'd not looked again; now, as it staggered unsteadily out of the flames, three of the four were shifted. The wide panels that made up the flat surface of the flipper were folded in, leaving the middle "strut" with a joint halfway down; now it looked more like a reinforced spider's leg.

Three of them were dragging it forward, digging into the muck and sinking a bit, then apparently finding solid enough stone and more deeper down to hold it.

The fourth leg, the back left when we faced it head-on, was stuck. It'd gotten halfway through a transformation and the panels were jammed, clicking back and forth with something lodged in the mechanism.

That gave it a staggering, lurching walk, with the head scarred and torn up from shrapnel, the eyes glowing a solid red, and the back still patterned with those canisters.

Two of the panels that covered the launchers were jammed shut, not even twitching. One clicked over and over, rocking in and out but wouldn't open all the way. Three had fired and were empty now, presumably awaiting a restock, rebuilding, or whatever. And the last two were open, with the top of the canisters on show, but they either hadn't been fired yet, or couldn't.

It drew back its head, opening its mouth and clearly about to scream again, as Jonas peppered the jaw and teeth with bullets and I searched for a weak spot.

The hexagon things were on clear display in places. The neck, where I'd blown a hole through, was a mass of them; they broke apart, shifting to repair the damaged section. Here and there, I could see systems beneath the surface moving behind cracks, but they were apparently too big to get out to fix the damage, and so were rattling back and forth, waiting for a bigger hole to appear.

I sprinted forward, hurdling burning plants as I closed on it. A massive blast of lightning, the bolt at least as thick around as my thigh, tore through the air to my left and slammed into the middle of its chest, staggering it and sending it reeling sideways.

Oxus hit it from my right, swinging a hammer almost as big as he was; the head probably weighed the same as a family car. It crashed into the top of the front leg joint, buckling part of the panels around it. Sparks flew and the leg twisted sideways, bringing the creation lurching back around and downward.

It clearly saw Oxus and lunged at him. The head came around and jaws snapped shut inches from him as he dove aside. A second blast from Scylla hit its right shoulder, knocking it backward, and I leapt, hacking at its neck.

My blades sent chunks flying and cracks radiating outward in fractal patterns. But I fell back, landing hard then slashing right and left at its lower chest.

Its back gave out a tremendous clatter, and Ingrid sent us all a panicked message.

"The coverings just blasted free! At least two more of those canisters are clear now!"

I sensed the change, as the covers clattered to the ground nearby, the canisters shifting in its back. The overall battle senses let me feel everything around me as Oxus rolled to his feet nearby, and Ingrid's plans slipped into place, clear as day, shifting by the second as the battle flowed.

"Now!" I shouted to Oxus, the gravitational fields I conjured on the spur of the moment spinning up.

I wasn't strong enough to manipulate it everywhere I needed to, so I risked it all on a single roll of the dice.

I created a bubble that shoved upward on the leg that Oxus rose beneath, his massive shoulders heaving as he grabbed onto the lower leg and lifted.

Racing to my left, I hacked down from right to left into the other leg, cutting deep enough that as the gravity field and Oxus's immense strength lifted the opposite side, the massive creation twisted.

The damaged leg I'd just hacked into tried to take most of the weight, the back leg on that side being stuck half changed and unable to bear much of it, and it collapsed.

As soon as the front leg went, the back followed. A sound like rolling thunder rang out as the body hit, metal twisting and shearing loose, and I was moving already.

I raced at the base of the neck, the closest section to me, and stabbed out with both blades, putting all my weight behind them, and feeling them crunch through the armoring.

As soon as I was inside, I felt the grating against the tips of the machines within. I tore left and right, carving as wide a hole as possible, nearly severing the tree trunk-thick neck.

While I was doing that, Oxus released the leg and was moving as well, lumbering around me and heading for the head. As he moved and I cut, vines were surging again, this time raining down as they grew at an insane rate, Belle having thrown them over us.

As they reached the ground, they burrowed in, branching, splitting and desperately growing, tearing up the earth as they spread. She'd clearly tailored them somehow, or was guiding their growth. As soon as they touched our armored forms, they twisted free.

When they found Nessie, though, they showed the power of nature, expending themselves in a glorious burst of energy, sending roots burrowing into her superstructure, fracturing armored cracks wider and clogging up the hexagons from reaching the damaged areas.

Oxus raced for the head, even as Scylla appeared by my side, bringing the proton lance around and jamming it into the neck wound I was working on. A bright pulse of lightning fired down the throat and into the chest cavity, making the entire machine judder to a halt.

It seized up, its jaws locking, and Oxus used that opportunity to grab onto it. As the lightning died away, he dug his feet in and heaved, dragging the head—with the long neck still attached—backward, trying to get it as far from the body as possible.

While we were doing this, while Ingrid directed, updating the plans and enabling us to see on all sides, boosting my gravitational capabilities and helping me to pin it with increased gravity on one side, while I stabbed and hacked with my blades...Jonas was running.

He'd finished his creation, and it was a hell of a weapon, all right.

He'd taken losing his handgun badly, especially as his rifle just didn't pack the same kind of punch, particularly when it came to fighting basically a walking tank.

So he'd used the last of his latest points to unlock explosives.

The grenade he'd formed, entirely out of his own nanites, was fucking insane. It looked more like a classic "thermal detonator" from the movies, but the internals...

I didn't have a clue how it worked, but I'd already mentally tagged that I needed some from him, preferably at least a dozen. They were small versions of thermobaric warheads.

Literally, they had a compressed core, much like the way that a diver had compressed air in their tanks, except that in this case it used some kind of technical wizardry to fit a huge amount of gas into a tiny space.

When the grenade was activated, sections all around it slid open, and the gas was released; it would ignite, at variable times.

The shorter the time between release and ignition, the greater the blast.

In this case, I got an impression of "run like your arse is on fire" from him as he hurdled the monster's back; his own tentacles flashed out to grab onto it, helping him to clear it.

He landed on the far side, triggered the grenade, then slammed it into one of the holes that had held the canisters in Nessie's back. Then a seal of nanites erupted from his hand, covering the opening, and he left it there, running like crazy.

Scylla fired another blast into the now wide-open hole into the body cavity, and I hacked at the last sections, the neck stump coming loose even as hexagons poured free.

Oxus was dragging the head as it recovered, trying to snap at him, and Jonas grabbed on at the top of the neck behind the head, huffing as he helped to carry it.

It was slow going. As soon as the neck was free, Scylla slung her proton lance over her shoulder and grabbed onto the neck as well. I sprinted around her, racing to the head a few inches behind Jonas's grip.

"Fucking move!" I shouted at them, stabbing my blades in and trying to carve the head loose now that the rest of the body was down.

"No time!" Jonas screamed. "Book it!"

"B…" That was all I got out before the torso exploded.

<u>Chapter Twelve</u>

When I could see again, the world slowly filtering back into focus in that weird way, nearby sounds coming first, then farther out and only then vision…*well*.

It turns out that fighting Nessie was possibly a bit of a big order for us, all things considered. Where I'd glibly thought we'd be able to kick the shit out of her easily enough, and then get onto the next job?

The devastation we'd left behind made it clear that wasn't an option.

The sky overhead had been striated with clouds. Streaks here and there let through the evening moonlight, but little else.

There was a section of clear sky overhead, and for at least a few hundred meters in all directions from the epicenter, the ground was scorched and bare.

The locals were a mess, burned badly, though alive—but that was only because they were out of sight, having been hiding in the gully.

If they'd been outside of it, they'd have been dead.

As it was, Ingrid was pulsing a medical emergency to me, desperately marking up the injuries she could identify on them. I forced myself to my feet, staggering before setting off running.

The entire area around us had been scoured free of everything. Even the grass was burned and blackened. The remains of our target…

Yeah, it was toast.

Most of the body was now a hollowed-out shell, blackened and twisted, and at least a hundred meters away from where it'd been when the grenade went off.

It'd sparked something else, and the interior had ended up like a firecracker: bouncing, jerking, and then jet-propelled as internals exploded. The force was directed out through the sections that had previously been reserved for the canisters.

They'd acted like rocket boosters. The body crashed through the waves and along the pebbled beach.

Which was damn lucky. Because if it'd stayed where it was originally before detonation, there was no chance the locals would have survived.

As it was, I dove into the gully, finding the small group there in a hell of a mess. Most of their hair was gone; clothing was torn and blackened; flesh was peeling or burned. Worst of all was that they had been peeking over the top, and had taken injuries to their eyes and lungs.

Thankfully, my medical capability kicked in when I tried it, highlighting that although they were in lots of pain, and their heart rates were through the roof, as well as being "slightly" irradiated…most of their actual injuries were small.

The overall mass that would need to be repaired or replaced was often less than many of the children I'd healed in the hospital.

Ten minutes later, when the last of them had stopped screaming, they were all staring at one another in horror, fear, and…stunned joy as Ingrid explained things to them, carefully.

"Whut der ya mean? Ah've noo got ma wee cancer nee more?" one of them was asking her in a heavy Glaswegian accent.

She stared at him, trying to make sense of the words, when I laughed tiredly and waved to get his attention.

"Literally, mate, you lot are as healthy as you've ever been. Believe me," I said. "I found the cancer when I was fixing your lungs. Your nan—"

"Your bodies will heal properly now." Ingrid cut me off, before I could give too much away.

"Aye?" another asked, disbelievingly. "Errr, are we all healed, like…you know, everywhere?" His eyes darted from side to side as I stared at him. Then he leaned forward, seemingly embarrassed to say it to Ingrid, who, even in full armor, was notably female.

Then he gestured downward, toward his groin, and made a "snip-snip" motion with his right hand where the others couldn't see.

"Ah…yeah. Anything that might be wrong with your body, now it's sorted," I assured him, suppressing a laugh behind a cough.

"Like ya pecker what don't peck?" another of the group called to him, elbowing one of the others and nodding for him to join in. "Mebbie yer lass will stop shaggin' tha postie noo…"

I snorted and turned from them at that point, relieved. If they were feeling okay enough to take the piss out of each other, then they were all right. I looked across the loch. Distant sirens and shouts were clearly incoming, even as the clouds finished rolling back in.

"I don't think we need to be here for the local coppers," I said idly to Ingrid, who nodded.

"Dimi is incoming. What do we do with the body?"

We both turned to look at what was left of the body laid with the shallow waves lapping around it, and the head that Oxus and Jonas were dragging through the pebbles toward us.

"We take the head," I said firmly. "Cut the neck off, and we can leave it here. The body…"

"I think we should take it as well," Ingrid said after a few seconds. "We can study the armor and see if we can replicate it. If nothing else, it keeps dangerous technology out of the hands of the British government."

"Seems like a good idea to me," I agreed. "I didn't realize you were so anti-government?"

"I'm not," she said firmly. "I'm anti-*British*-government. There's a massive difference."

"Oh?"

"You've not been keeping up with their actions of late. They're so corrupt they make a banana republic's leader look honest and upstanding." She sighed, shaking her head. "I don't know why you're so surprised—you don't trust them either."

"I'd not trust them with a boiled egg," I agreed. "But you're right, if we leave that here and the Scottish government recovers it, Westminster will go mental trying to get it, like a terrier after a bone."

"And if the Scottish government doesn't hand it over?"

"They'd probably march the army in."

"*Exactly*, against their own people." She shook her head disgustedly. "I'm sorry, Steve, I know this is your home, or a little farther south was, but it's...well..."

"It's dodgier than eating a kebab from an all-you-can-eat mystery meat place?" I suggested. "Or is it that only the dumbest of criminals end up in gangs and shit, because the smartest ones are working in government?"

That stopped her for a few seconds, and she hesitated. The pair of us walked over to help the others, as she seemed to think of how to phrase her next words.

"Steve..." she said slowly, and I turned to look at her. "Don't take this the wrong way, but that was a bit of a strange thing for you to say."

"Sorry, just stressed I guess..." I started to apologize.

"No, no, that's not what I meant." She shook her head. "It...oh gods, how to say this without..."

She took my hand and led me aside from the others, making them look over in confusion, having been expecting our help.

"This is important, so I'm going to say it anyway, but please don't be offended." She waited for my nod of bemused agreement. "Are you getting smarter?"

"I...no?" I replied, confused.

"That comment, and there's been others of late..." She banished her helmet, staring at me; I did the same, seeing her desperately searching my eyes for understanding or offense. "You were never stupid, Steve. Please don't think that I believe that. But you weren't exactly..."

"I'm not NASA material." I snorted. "It's fine, you know. I don't have to be. That's why I like smart people around me. They can sort all the shit out, and I get to break things...you know, the stuff I'm good at."

"That's just it. I think you're actually getting more intelligent, and it makes sense that you would be. You've been unlocking and investing in your mind, after all. It's just that you need to train it."

"Train..." I muttered, then shook my head. "No."

"But—"

"Ingrid, I'll do whatever you want later, but right now, anything that's not us dealing with the challenge right in front of us is too dangerous. We can fuck about with it all later. For now? We focus."

She started to say something else, then clearly thought better of it as Jonas glared at us, still dragging the head.

We jogged over. My blades made short work of the neck, leaving it in a mangled chunk on the floor that Scylla and Jonas grabbed. Oxus and I hefted the head, moving into position as Dimi came in for a landing.

As the landing gear lowered, the first of the local police made it off the nearby road, heading in our direction, the sirens blaring.

"Uh, so what do we tell them?" one of the fishermen asked, glancing from me—my helmet had now reformed, as had Ingrid's—to the police.

"Tell them I'm an intergalactic angel bounty hunter," I said.

"Are you?" he asked, mouth agape.

"No, but it'll confuse the fuck outta them." I snorted. "Seriously, anything that happens here is going to be viewed as weird as fuck by the lower levels of national security, and the highest already know who and what I am, as well as not to fuck with me. Tell them anything you want, but I'd appreciate it if you'd make out that we were a little more inhuman, and that you didn't understand us. That way they're less likely to give you grief."

"Aye, nay botha," he muttered, still staring as we manhandled the head of Scotland's most enduring mythical beast into the belly of a flying stingray.

"Oh, and you might want to get your stories straight," Ingrid pointed out to the group. "Perhaps I just wiped your memories with a wave of my hand? I'll gesture and you all fall down?"

"Aye, aye, tha works," another of the group agreed. "Get ready, lads—then the wives don't get te question us neither!"

"Oh, shite, aye—get wavin', lass," another said. "Ready?"

I could hear Ingrid snorting as she tried to stifle laughter; she waved one hand dramatically and the group half fell to the floor. It was pretty poorly done, mainly because three of them caught themselves before hitting the pebbled ground, but the police car in the lead chose that moment to find the drainage gully with its front wheels.

There was an almighty crunch and the car came to a complete stop. Others behind it screeched to a halt or drove into the back of it.

Ingrid hurried up the ramp, Dimi closing it behind her as he shouted down from the flight deck.

"You want me to do what!" he called.

"Grab that damn corpse!" I called back. The three of us struggled into the middle of the room; then, in unspoken agreement, dumped the head on the table. It promptly crushed it to the floor. All three of us stared at the broken wood, as Ingrid shouted up from below.

"What was that?"

"You can explain this," I ordered Jonas heroically, legging it in the direction of the flight deck, before Ingrid saw the state of the table.

I was fairly sure it was just old and ornate, not an archaeological treasure. But knowing my luck, it was the original Round Table of King Arthur or something.

I'd barely made it out of the room, when I heard Ingrid's sharply indrawn breath, and I definitely didn't stop.

Arise :Explorer

Dimi was seated in the middle of…well, the stingray, as that was what we kept referring to the plane as, had a weird cockpit.

The main pilot sat in the middle, screens and controls all around him, like he was sealed into a tiny room made of glass and tech, with three more stations on the flight deck ready for staff, when we finally got some people to fill those posts out.

As it was, stepping into the flight deck from behind him, I grabbed onto the back of one of the seats and swung it around, dropping into it and twisting back to face its dedicated screens.

He was at the front, with two stations on the right-hand side, one on the left, and a solid bank of what looked like server towers on the left as well. We were currently swinging around in the air. The stingray sent a powerful downdraft from the multiple engines and gravitational manipulation devices that flung dust, dirt, and debris around.

The combination of basically a low-grade "not-a-nuke-by-semantics-alone" explosion going off, and then the burning of anything nearby that could burn, meant that there was a fuckload of dust that could be swept up by the VTOL engines. And so, for the world around us, we were vanishing into a cloud.

We could see perfectly well. The systems that were in already, upgraded partially as they were, had been designed to make damn sure that assholes like Zeus didn't get a boo-boo when it was landing in all conditions, as that tended to result in possibly years of torture for the pilot.

Dimi was using all those systems, and his own madness and skill, to swing the stingray around, positioning it over the corpse, and I reached out with a gravity bubble to recover it.

It wasn't perfect—hell, it was far from it—as part of using a gravity bubble to pick something up meant that I didn't just get the remnants of the corpse.

I also got a load of pebbles, two small fish, a crab, some water…load of extras that looked frankly insane as we burst upward through the dust cloud, and into the dark sky.

"Where to?" Dimi called over his shoulder at me, as he angled us around, flying south on instinct, while he waited for confirmation.

"Home," Ingrid ordered. The door whooshed open behind me as she joined us. "The recycling plant, I mean, Dimi. We need to drop the corpse off and get the systems working on replicating the memory modules. Steve, that table…"

"Was it a relic?" I asked as Dimi adjusted the flight path, angling around and whistling innocently.

"Not everything can be sorted down into that, Steve!" she snapped. "It was at least five hundred years old, probably more and…"

The conversation went nowhere after that, and after a few minutes, we moved down into the main cabin. Things only got worse when Dimi informed us that because of the mass we were lugging below the ship, we were about as stealthy as a drunk with a takeaway stumbling in the door at four a.m.

Ingrid stormed off to our room, and I was left mentally flexing a muscle as I made sure that Nessie stayed attached to the underside of the ship.

That meant that as we lined up on the Sahara, it wasn't long before Dimi asked for permission to "boot it," as we were apparently getting a lot of attention.

First the RAF, and then European forces, were scrambling fighter jets, as well as trying to identify us. And when Dimi responded to their demands for identification with a quote from a film, telling them they couldn't handle the truth, it only got more crowded up here.

"Dimi, are the engines online?" I called up to him.

"Well, we're in the sky and I'm not screaming 'Oh my God, we're all gonna die,' so does that answer your incredibly stupid question?" he yelled back.

"Asshole." I groaned. "I mean, can we go all out? Are all the engines finished with their upgrades?"

"Well, yeah! That's why I want to test them," he shouted.

"Fine, do it!" I yelled.

"Whoop! You might want to hold onto something…" he called back, giving me absolutely no time to do so, as he hit what had to be full speed for a missile in about half a second.

Then it accelerated past that to a point I felt was totally unreasonable.

I'd deployed my claws on instinct, and even with inertial dampeners, I was still skidding backward, grabbing onto the nearest seats and clinging on for dear life. The terrified bellow of Oxus from one of the nearby rooms made it clear he'd not been ready either.

Jonas and Scylla were strapped into a pair of seats across the room, watching me as my feet lifted from the floor, only hanging onto the chair by sheer willpower and claws now, as the sound of tearing fabric filled the air.

Ingrid shouted something from our room that was clearly not a good thing, and I swore under my breath.

I just *knew* I was going to get the blame for this as well.

Dimi was the one having fun here, I reflected, as I dragged myself up and into the seat, grabbing the belts and strapping in. The inertial dampeners finally spun all the way up to counter the force we'd been "enjoying."

Dimi was laughing his fucking ass off from overhead, and yet I just knew…

"*STEVE!*" Ingrid hissed. The door into our bedroom slid open to reveal that she'd apparently been in the process of doing something with her makeup when the acceleration had hit.

She looked as if she'd been dragged through a hedge backward, with a collection of four-year-olds helping her to apply it all at the same time.

I couldn't help it—I burst out laughing, and whoo-boy was that the wrong reaction.

Twenty minutes later, Dimi was slowing us to line up on the facility, I was still getting the cold shoulder, and Jonas and Scylla were apparently having a great time watching, as I tried to explain for the third time that I had no way of knowing that the lunatic pilot was going to do that.

He'd received a talking-to from Ingrid as well, but she'd decided that him getting to clean the craft up was enough of a punishment, as Oxus wasn't a good flier, and had liberally painted the walls of his and Belle's room in a new paint scheme that would be forever known as "Terrified Minotaur Brown."

Arise :Explorer

I loved that Dimi was having to deal with that, but not so much that until it was dealt with, the entire stingray reeked.

Dimi brought us in for a smooth landing outside of the facility, with me dropping the corpse off a few dozen meters to one side, and he landed the stingray next to it.

He also notably didn't leave the flight deck until we'd disembarked. I guessed he was sulking, but that thought was banished as soon as the boarding ramp lowered.

The blast of cold air that washed over us was all we needed to remind us that we were in the Sahara again.

It was crazy that during the day you could hard-boil an egg in your pocket in the damn desert, and yet at night you'd have frost, if there was enough water for it.

It was a desert, but damn, the nights were nicer than the days here.

We strode down the steps: Oxus and I with the head, Ingrid helping us now, and with Scylla, Belle, and Jonas bringing the neck.

It took us a few minutes to make it across the airstrip toward the main building. By the time we made it, there were a dozen Oracan joining us, and a litter being constructed to carry the head.

Twenty minutes after that, I was cursing that Zac, who was the golden boy of engineering, wasn't there. He was on board the warship, still doing whatever, or maybe aboard the *Pacific Princess*, helping with its rebuilding options.

I didn't know, but it meant that the only engineers I had here were human, Corey being with Zac on the warship and Joseph on the *Princess*.

I cursed long and loud, before getting to work, extruding the vorpal blade and starting to cut.

The head, once I'd gotten it open, was fortunately pretty simple inside.

The connections were clear, and I made sure to feed samples of them, as well as the surrounding structure, into the factory units before I started with the memory modules.

They were the real prize, but if the only way to link one to whatever other systems we had required this? Well, I needed to be careful.

Cracking the remainder of the skull apart and freeing the memory units was a bit worrying, but seeing the glowing white crystals come free, intact and gently humming, it was worth taking the time.

When I was finally finished, the factory unit happily confirming the viability of the modules and beginning construction of our own versions from them, the sun was well up outside, and I was starting to get damn worried about timing.

Two hours was all that I could justify, while the factory churned out the memory units. As it did that, I caught up with jobs along with Ingrid, who'd stepped into the void left by her parents.

James had picked up a lot of the slack, as had the others, but still, as the leadership of our little band of lunatics, we needed to get updates, adjust plans, and get things moving again, and I was sent to talk to the others working in the growing forest.

The rewilding project had gotten a boost we weren't expecting, mainly because not only had our soil rejuvenation project borne fruit, it was actually producing better than we had dared hope.

Casey had arranged for samples from volcanic areas to be flown in, and the insanely rich loam of Ireland had provided more data. Additional samples from both the Amazon and the Madagascan jungles had provided the missing links.

When all four sets of samples were combined, and the converters were set to produce that, the resultant soil that I was now walking across was both incredibly right in life-giving minerals and easily reproduced.

Add in that we needed biological matter, which was liberated from the water buried deep below the sands, and pumped to the surface, and from dredging a section of the Nile where it passed through the Sudan.

The local government, knowing what we were doing, were absolutely overjoyed to take a payment of a few million dollars—most of which I suspected went directly into the back pockets of the ministers involved—to let us dredge that section up.

Casey, being Casey, was thorough as always, ensuring that a new converter was left at the bottom of the Nile for several days as her team worked.

It converted sand and silt to pure water, making sure that the stirred-up filth at the bottom didn't cause any issues, and produced more life-giving water for the locals while she was at it.

The end result was an incredibly thick and healthy soil layer that was entirely custom built to convert the surrounding area.

Add to it that to maintain the carefully designed ecosystem she was working on, Casey had taken my plans for sand traps—literally tarps that would funnel the sand sent flying in sandstorms into the converters—and she'd dramatically upgraded them.

When all that you needed was essentially time to produce anything, it seriously changed the building you could make.

She'd used a form of artificial sapphire to create sheets, using them to make insanely strong, light, and well-anchored polytunnels.

The soil was spread thickly beneath it, and then seeds disseminated, liberally watered with the microbe and bacterially rich dirt lifted from the bottom of the Nile.

The final stage was already underway, as Par'a'nuit had finally finished their evolution.

The former fen nymph had been evolving for some time, and I'd frankly forgotten all about the little bugger, until I stumbled to a stop, staring at the figure who was working with Casey and Belle to coax the saplings into life.

This clearly wasn't the original nymph who had first approached us. Admittedly, "approached" was a stretch. They'd tried to capture us all to feed us to the mavka, but that wasn't the point.

There'd been a shitty situation going on, where the nymphs were being fed on by the mavka, trapped on a series of small islands that were surrounded by the malicious water creatures.

They'd been given the choice of feed their children to the mavka, or outsiders, preferably the damn humans who kept chopping their trees down.

Considering that if you chopped down a tree a nymph was bonded to, at the very least you hurt it gravely, and often it'd die as well?

The choice hadn't been one they'd liked, being pacifists by nature, but they'd done it.

I'd been attacked by the mavka, and I'd left Ingrid and our friends to basically parley with the nymphs while I went all murder hobo on the queen and her daughters.

By the time I made it back, bringing the others the head of the crazed bitch because it was huge and full of nanites I was busily stripping, the nymphs were stunned, terrified, and overjoyed all rolled into one.

Even more so when Ingrid explained that she wanted to learn from them, and in exchange she'd provide new trees, and that we wanted nothing else save information in return.

Par'a had been a member of their clan, and unusually for his species, "he" was curious about the outside world and decided to come with us.

The nymphs were sexless, developing the relevant organs when they needed them, and then discarding them when they were no longer needed. That meant that "they" was a more appropriate moniker than "he" or "she." Seeing the difficulty I was having getting my head around that, Par'a, understanding that it wasn't any kind of slight, just that it made it easier for others, declared itself to be "male" for now.

That was apparently an entirely made-up thing, though, because he'd finally finished its current evolution, and once again, like Belle, had no issues about body modesty.

Fortunately for my heart rate, unlike Belle, he'd not chosen to be female and fixated on seducing every male in a ten-mile radius to gain their seed.

Instead, Par'a was about six foot now, willowy and fine featured, with eyes like black onyx, a thin mouth and nose, elven ears, three-fingered hands, and moved with a grace that was just mesmerizing.

He was also clearly made of wood. The gentle whorls and grain that made up his skin appeared to almost glow as if freshly varnished, as he came to his feet, smiling widely and bowing to me.

"Par'a?" I strode across the black earth, the harsh daytime glare of the sun overhead reduced to a gentle warmth by some magic of the design of the growing areas.

"Lord Steve," he greeted me, his voice surprisingly high and clear.

"It's good to see you," I replied, letting out a smile of thanks as Belle shot the results of the examine ability I'd just tried to use on him across to me.

Greater Nymph	Biological Weapon Variant
A Greater Nymph is as far from the baseline variant as a BWV is from the baseline human, gaining local growth and flora alignment capabilities.	

Although rare, requiring activated nanites to reach this level, greater nymphs are highly useful guardians and tenders, a single variant capable of maintaining a significant growing area.

Capabilities:

Glamour: Greater nymphs are able to hide from almost all biological sensors when in their territory, coaxing their plants to release powerful toxins to enable them to twist the minds of the weak.

Bonded-Flow: While the greater nymph loses access to the phase-shift ability, it is compensated with the capability to flow through any bonded flora, abandoning its physical form at one point, to regrow it at another. Be warned: this is detrimental to the flora at the target location, due to the enhanced growth medium required.

Enhanced: Due to the donated genetic material of an active BWV, this greater nymph has gained access to a more powerful physical form, permitting significant bonuses to physical capabilities.

HP: 250/250	Nymph

I was starting to get really concerned about that, but at least I understood why it was happening now.

"So…what's going on?" I asked the trio, scanning the details before flicking the screen away.

"We've discovered that we can work together, with surprising results!" Belle smiled at me.

"Oh?"

"From past experience, nymphs have many of the same gifts that dryads do…those bonded to actively growing trees, anyway. They are usually considerably less powerful than even lesser dryads, though, and I confess, I was expecting this union to be much the same, and yet…"

"It's been wonderful!" Casey said quickly. "Steve, seriously, you've got no idea. Par'a can boost the health and viability of plants, essentially making them more likely to grow to reach their potential. But where they have problems is in germination."

"That is almost the opposite of a dryad, though," Belle added, beaming. "For us, we exist to…what was the word that you used…ah! To *terraform* the area with viable plants to support our BWV companions. Our focus is on creation, not tending so much, and although we have gifts in that area, they are less than the creative side. We essentially bond with a viable tree and improve that, then we move to the next."

"And Belle's tree is with the Erlking," Casey added.

"It is, and should I break that bond…the Erlking would be unhappy in the extreme, I think," she finished, shaking her head that it'd be unwise at the very least.

"But with Par'a, we don't need to!" Casey went on, as Par'a picked up the conversation and carried it.

"The changes that I have been gifted with enable me to act as tender to growing seeds, guiding and enhancing them, as well as directing the various insects that Casey has introduced into a more central location."

"Insects?" I frowned, even though I knew we needed them, then waved to Dave and Amanda as I saw them making their way over to join us.

"They're necessary," Casey clarified. "Nobody likes them, but they perform a vital function in the ecosystem. Removing them wouldn't be a good thing."

"So we guide them to a particular plant, dedicating that one to them, enabling them to breed more efficiently, while the plants around it grow unimpeded," Par'a added.

"Okay, so what's the overall plan look like?" I asked.

"Little change, except that the timescale has been moved up," Casey said. "Since Belle can essentially create a huge number of viable and strong seeds for us, giving them a kick-start to life, and then Par'a can take over, guiding them and giving them a boost from that point?"

"We suspect that we can bring a viable forest into being here, covering one square mile, in about a week," Belle finished in a rush. "It's not something that we can keep doing—it'd kill Par'a to do that regularly. He'll need at least a month between each section produced to recover, while I, well, I could use a month to 'restock' as well." She smiled, leaving us in no doubt about what she needed. As a dryad who essentially converted "seed" from her mates into literal seeds, it was going to be less in terms of "rest" and more "screwing Oxus's brains out."

"Okay, but while that's great for the overall plan, it's shit for reality," I grumbled. "Belle, we need you. Leaving you here to redo mile after mile? As much as I want to get the rewilding project up and running…"

"And that's where the others come in." Casey smiled. "Have you had a conversation with Dave, Marie, and Amanda yet?"

"No, they—" I glanced from the smile on her face to Belle. "They found them?"

"One at least." Belle nodded. "I think they've found Jamya."

"Uh…"

"My youngest sister," she clarified. "She was lost in a landslide and has been silent for long ages."

"But you know where she is?" I pushed.

"The team believe they've found her, although she'll need to be recovered and nursed back to health. Jamya may be beyond recovery, but I have hope."

"Okay, so we need a team to go after her and…" I paused, cursing at how easily I was distracted. "And as much as I damn well want that team to be us, it can't be." I sighed.

"No, I understand that," Belle assured me.

"Casey, we really need to get you ascended," I said, getting a smile in response.

"I will," she agreed. "There's just not been time, and there's always so much to do."

"Well, before we leave, we either set a plan for it, or if you're with us, it happens immediately. You're at least as busy as Zac, so being able to do more with your time is only common sense, as is having you protected."

"We'll see." She shrugged. "When we've got time, I will."

"Hey, sorry, I'm a bit slow moving around at the minute." Amanda moved over to join us, one hand on Dave's shoulder as he helped her across the uneven ground, her pregnancy now much more obvious. "I have good news, and a request."

"Oh?" I reached out and casually offered Dave a fist-bump when he let go of his fiancée and stepped up. "You all right, man?"

"Yeah." He grinned. "So, I hear you've been off playing boss man, eh?"

"He's been kicking the hell out of the leadership of the Blessed," Amanda agreed, smiling at me, before reclaiming her partner's arm.

"Yeah, I'd have done it better," Dave lied, and I shook my head at the daft bastard's antics.

"So what's up?" I asked Amanda, deliberately directing my question to her rather than Dave, who I liked, but I also trusted less than a priest in playschool.

"Well, depending on your point of view, finding Jamya, and bringing her here, is easy," she assured me.

"Oh?"

"Yeah, we just give the job to someone we don't like." An evil smile spread across her face.

"I like the sound of this already."

"Well, you remember that we—oh, and congratulations on starting a new faction, by the way…" She paused, glancing at me, as she turned, gesturing to the main tower. "Do you mind if we head back across and sit inside? I know it's not as incredibly hot here as it is outside, but it'd be great to get off my feet, and this would be easier if I show you."

"Yeah, no worries," I agreed, waving goodbye to Casey and Par'a, as Belle slipped up on Amanda's other side, taking her hand and helping her across the dirt with Dave.

"Yeah, the factions." I shrugged. "It seemed like a solution, and a way to get things moving in the right direction."

"Oh, it was," she agreed, nodding to me and smiling at Belle in thanks. "That everyone heard about it around the same time as they learned that not only had you practically salted and gutted Zeus and several of the other leaders of the Blessed faction? But that you took their entire assault force on alone?"

"We weren't alone." I shook my head. "No clue how that rumor started, but Jonas and I had ninety of the locals with us."

"Yeah." She snorted. "There it is."

"What?"

"You and Jonas, who—if people believe the rumors…and I know it's true obviously, but remember, rumors—was only recently Arisen. Then add in that us people at the bottom of the totem pole are pretty convinced that the Elders are myths, so they'll discount them."

"I thought people revered them?"

"Some do," she said. "Some of the Arisen have been to meet them, but remember that once one of us has ascended in the Blessed they basically view the rest of us as disposable chew toys. Their personal team? They might support and take with them—that was our deal, that if one of us got 'made,' then the others would be looked after. That deal is contingent on the rest of the team knowing that we need to obey them. So...

"There's less than a ten percent chance of one of us surviving the traditional ascension process rather than yours. Also, at most, the majority of the Arisen will raise up another who might become a competitor, maybe once a century, if that? Once someone is Arisen, all their old friendships with other 'low' humans are generally discarded, meaning that we're always waiting for someone to fuck with us. As a mere soldier for the Arisen, we hear rumors about the Elders, but they could be bullshit for all we know...you get that, right?"

"Yeah, okay." I nodded.

"So, you come out of the blue. You're generally used as an example of why you should never, ever fuck with the Arisen...three years of constant torture, and you're one of their kind, right?" She glanced over at me. "Then, the next thing that people are hearing is that not only did you escape, but you did it by killing everyone in that base. The only survivors are the ones who ran and hid. Everyone who faced you? Dead."

"Yeah, well, they deserved it."

"Not gonna disagree. But that included Arisen, creatures that we 'know' are literally immortal. But then you killed them. Then you vanish *again*, only to show up and kill Athena herself, then half her pet Arisen, before, *poof*, you're gone again. You pop up now and then, usually accompanied by more of the Arisen vanishing or being rendered down to kibble. Then, one of the most powerful of the Blessed, Shamal, along with Beowulf, cross you, and they and their literal armies are cut to pieces, then blended into the walls of your new house.

"Can you *imagine* how that looks to the low-level soldiers and the weakest Arisen? They're surviving on rumor more than anything, and the one thing that everyone hears is that if they fuck with you, they pull back a bloody stump with no body attached."

"Heh, well, they deserve a little worry in their lives," I told her.

"They do—*we* do—but it gets better. You're recorded picking tanks up and smashing them into pieces, you can fly, and then you ascend one of your enemies, making him into your most loyal supporter. That fresh Arisen, who'd been a nobody, just like the rest of us soldiers, who would have been squashed like a bug if he even caught his betters' eye?

"He then fights one of the eldest and most powerful of the Blessed, and kills him. *Alone.* People don't know what to believe, just that if they fuck with you, at all, they're done. But, oh wait, it gets better. Zeus and the rest of his little cabal, they attacked the *Elders*, a group I'll remind you that we at the bottom of the pile only know about through rumors.

"You and Jonas kill all four of the strongest of the Blessed faction, then most of their armies, beating them into submission, literally."

"Uh huh."

"*But wait, it gets better,*" she repeated grimly.

"Hey, he's not all that, you know…" Dave cut in, clearly not happy that his fiancée was making so much of me.

"Yes dear, don't worry, you're wonderful, great in bed and the biggest I've ever seen…is that enough massaging your ego? Can the adults keep talking?" Amanda reached out, patting the top of his head condescendingly.

"I hate you," Dave muttered.

"No you don't." She smiled. "Seriously, Dave, this is how it looks, and he needs to understand it, okay?"

"Fine," he grumbled.

"*So…*" She began again, pausing as she gathered her thoughts. "Right, so you're now being looked at by the bottom echelon, and the next few up, as basically a god. One who eats the rest of the 'gods' we all live in fear of for breakfast."

"Okay…" I agreed, and because I was such an adult, I blew Dave a kiss and waggled my eyebrows at him behind her back.

"Then the Elders, who we're only now finding out are basically what we should have been serving, instead of the arrogant dickheads we're stuck with, declare that you've got a *faction.*"

"Why's that important?" I asked.

"Because a faction implies you're growing. It implies that you're not just a gang, or a private-only group—you're a serious contender for power, and that *you're accepting new members*! Then the rumors start that you're ascending your followers? That your people *all* survive ascension?" She shook her head.

"You've got no idea how it is, Steve. This is what the lowest-level members desperately want…the chance. Then you look at the next rung up? The Arisen who are shit on by those above? They know that they've got to get stronger— that's their only chance of not being a lapdog for the rest of their existence. They've made peace with the fact that they'll be weak as fuck and abused for the next few centuries.

"Instead, one of them, your former enemy, is serving you and feeding Zeus his own thunderbolt up his ass?" She laughed. "You've got no idea how much that mental image is worth. That arrogant fuckstick being taught respect is something that could keep most of the women in all the factions warm in the depths of an artic winter!"

"Jonas did well," I agreed.

"He did." She nodded, smiling broadly. "Oh, he did, and we're getting to the best bit here, so pay attention."

"Yes, ma'am."

"So. You did all of this, *then* were recognized as having your own faction, one that is actively recruiting, that the Elders support as their ally."

"Uh huh."

"*Then,* you essentially wiped out the remaining Blessed faction leaders. There were seven in the council that ran the Blessed. There's two of them left, Daversa and Umesh. Umesh has gone to ground, while Daversa is 'discussing things' with the Elders. Everyone knows what that means, and that they're basically under your thumb. Add in that not only did the Elders publicly announce that our faction is to be left alone on pain of a fucking lot of pain, but you've got a pair of members of the *Accursed*, Hans and Petros, actively recruiting for you."

"So…" I prompted, still waiting for her to get to the point.

"*So*, we've got a shitload of prospective recruits from both factions desperate to join! They know that if they try to go back to the Blessed or the Accursed, they'll be punished at best, probably tortured, killed, then locked up and sunk, and *they're still here wanting to join*. They think it's their only chance, that the factions are collapsing, and the one that's going to come out on top is ours, joined with the Elders."

"That's great, but fuck's sake, Amanda, get to the point!" I groaned.

"That *is* the point!" She swore. "There's dozens of Arisen here waiting to talk to you. They've got their own forces, and that's literally hundreds of people in most cases, all waiting and hoping you'll accept them. This is an insane opportunity to make them do something useful for once."

"You mean…" I paused as I finally realized what she was getting at. "We could split them up, and send them off to do this shit for us?"

"Oh, thank the gods. At last he's getting it!" she called to the sky, before she rolled her eyes and then looked at me. "I was starting to think you were like Dave."

"Hey!" Dave complained, looking hurt.

"That's unfair," I said firmly.

"Thanks, man…" Dave started to say.

"I'm at least twice as intelligent as he is." I grinned at my old friend.

"And therefore half as intelligent as an average woman," Amanda finished for me. "Seriously, though, we've got hundreds of these idiots out there, camped on the far side of the facility, waiting to hear if they're going to be accepted. You must have seen them when you landed?"

"No, we were inside," I said. "I wasn't looking out over the facility."

"Then go, speak to Hans and Petros, and make some of these fuckers actually work for a living for once. It'll get you a better idea of who they are, and it'll save you doing these jobs by yourself."

"I will, thank you," I said, meaning it.

"Good. Now, if you don't mind, I really need to lie down. Damn baby is killing me, I swear." She sighed and reached out to take Dave's hand.

"And Steve…" she said, "as much as I like picking on him, I have to admit that Dave's actually really good at research. I don't know how, but he always finds what we need."

"Well done, man," I said.

"Shit, you mustn't be feeling well," Dave muttered, straightening and leading Amanda off to the side. "When you're nice to me, I know something's really wrong."

"Oh, screw off. I can be nice…" she started, and Belle and I left the pair to it, heading into the tower and down to the first lower level as they headed in the opposite direction to the lift up to their quarters

Chapter Thirteen

The meeting with Hans and Petros was a more or less painless one, if unsurprisingly annoying.

Belle and I talked idly about random things on the way, the elevator slow, but smooth, only to have the conversation washed away in the babble of overlapping voices that poured over us as the doors opened.

This first sub-level in the tower had, like all the others, been full of radioactive, biological, and contaminated waste when we'd first taken the site over.

Now it was contaminated with a far worse scourge. *Bureaucrats.*

As soon as we stepped out, we were surrounded by people. Some of them were, like us, trying to get to places and had been caught up in the hubbub.

Most, though, were sitting, standing, or sprawled on the floor, waiting for their number to be called.

"Green twelve!" someone called, and a man sprang up from the floor, grinning at the person next to him, as he pushed through the mass, holding a ticket high to show it was him.

"What the hell is all of this?" I muttered.

"I'd heard it was the most efficient method to sort people," Belle said, having to send it to me through the command link, rather than speak it, the general buzz of conversation so high.

"Yeah, what the fuck is going on?" I sighed, striding through the fifty or so people clogging up the entrance, only to find that the next room beyond, that led onto the main level, splitting to the left and right to form a ring, or straight ahead into the corridor beyond, was packed as well.

Passing through the first few people, and then trying to reach the front of the queue, I was intercepted by a guy who looked like he'd just stepped out of a court in LA.

"There's a line for a reason," he drawled, looking me up and down, clearly seeing the dirty clothes and the muck that still clung to my boots and fingers, and sneering.

"Yeah, I'm too busy for that." I shrugged.

"You're too busy?" He sighed, looking me over again. "Well, I suppose I shouldn't be surprised. If you cared, you'd have made an effort, not shown up looking like you've just been sent from the fields. Tell me, are you lost? Perhaps your master sent you to the wrong place?"

"You know what, maybe I am lost..." I agreed, nodding and smiling like an imbecile. "What do they do down here?"

"What do they..." He paused; then, evidently getting bored of the conversation, smiled widely, nudging a friend. "Why this is where you get your new jobs. I mean, you *are* here to look for work, right?"

"Oh, I think I've got plenty on my plate at the minute. I just wanted to get some details from whoever is running the place."

"You're too busy for their jobs then?"

"Definitely."

"Well then, why don't you tell them that? In fact, I think I see one of their leaders there, at the back. You should go and tell him right now that you're not here to work, and what you want. I bet he'll help you out, and you'll not have to wait in the line at all."

I turned in the direction he indicated, and nodded, spotting Hans talking to someone on the other side of a small barrier.

"You think I should just go and talk to him?" I asked.

"Definitely."

"Thanks, I think I will. What was your name again?"

"Oh, I'm Victor. Victor Bonifacio." He smiled.

"Thanks, I'll remember that," I assured him, before turning and striding forward through the mass of people. Another annoyed person, a massive man this time, glared at me and started to step in my way, clearly also not happy that I was planning to skip the line. Rather than stopping and playing nice, this time I snorted and kept going.

My armor flowed out of my skin, rippling across my clothing. A liquid pool of black shining nanites flooded me, then reformed into my imposing "dark angel" armor configuration.

The figure that had been glaring and moving to block me off couldn't move fast enough as he practically dove out of the way.

The conversations and muttering stopped dead, and all around me, people dropped to their knees in a great wave.

"Steve!" Hans greeted me, smiling and gesturing to me to come to him, even as a few of the figures nearby hurried to move the barriers for Belle and me to pass through.

I couldn't help it, though—as I followed Hans through the now silent hall, stepping into his office, I turned to close the door behind Belle, and pulled back my armor, exposing my face.

Then I winked at Victor Bonifacio, who looked sick suddenly, before I closed the door.

"It's good to see you again, my friend!" Hans declared, stepping up as I dismissed my armor and hugged the smaller man. "And you *have* to teach me that trick." He stared avidly as my armor drained away.

"I will," I assured him. "Have you been kept up to date on what's happening?"

"More or less, I think. Ah, Petros should be back in a minute. He was visiting the bathroom. He will want to meet you properly, but tell me, what are you doing here?"

We sat, Hans taking what looked to be his usual seat behind a small desk. A computer hummed gently on it, the screen turned away from the collection of seats spread around the room.

The room I saw, at a glance, was one of the old storerooms, once full of contaminated waste, now clean, if a little battered, and clearly reworked into a makeshift office.

"You know that Ingrid and I are back for a few hours?" I asked him, settling back into a plastic chair that creaked alarmingly under my weight as he nodded. "It's literally that. We've got no time, but I needed to get something built. As soon as it's done, we need to drop that off, and then we're onto the next job."

"And yet you came to see how the interviews were going?" he asked curiously. "I know we're friends, Steve, but I suspect this is more to do with my role than me perhaps?"

"It is," I admitted, feeling a bit shitty about it. Hans had struck me as a weird one from the beginning, mainly because he was so open about a lot of things, and at times, such an asshole.

Now, seeing him, and how pleased and hopeful he was that I was here to see him, it made me realize just how much his actions over the years had come down to him simply being lonely, and wanting a damn friend he could talk to as his equal.

"I thought so." He forced a smile. "So, what can I do?"

"I need your help," I said, changing what I was going to say. "Hans, we've got so many things going on all the time that I can barely keep up, and I need someone I can trust to lead the way on some of those jobs."

As I said it, I sent Ingrid a quick message, showing her what I was thinking, and getting her agreement.

"Belle here, you've met before," I said.

"We have met." He nodded to her in greeting.

"Well, Amanda and her team have found—"

"We think," Belle added.

"We think, one of Belle's sisters," I finished. "There are three of them left that we know of, spread out around the world. In order to rewild the Sahara as we'd planned, we need a greater dryad, but three would be even better."

"And Belle is too busy." He nodded, seeing the issue. "I've met Par'a. I take it that a dryad would be able to work with him to increase the planting?"

"If I was able to simply dedicate myself to the rewilding as I originally expected to," she said, "and with appropriate soils, I'd be able to convert hundreds of square miles of desert in a few short years."

"And you think that your sister, if she was found, could do this?" Hans asked, breaking off as a firm knock rang out on his door, followed by Petros stepping in. "Ah! Steve, Belle, this is Petros, my mentor."

The figure who stepped in was well dressed, a gleaming blue shirt, a smart suit, and yeah, shiny fuckin' shoes. He had olive skin—not the color of "fresh-pressed olives," as I'd once heard it described, which was fuckin' yellow after all, but Mediterranean tanned, and glowing with health. His hair was oiled, his tie perfect, his fingers manicured, the works.

There followed a few minutes of introductions, the usual polite conversation and general "how are you" shite, until I could get the conversation back on track.

"Look, it's great to meet you and all, Petros, and sorry, I'm not trying to be fuckin'… I'm not trying to be rude," I forced myself to say, still not sure about him, as I tried not to swear and went on. "I know that you and Hans have been helping here, recruiting for us, and generally working out who's a shitebag and who's here honestly, right?"

"We have," Hans agreed, as Petros sat back in his chair, clearly amused at my language.

"Well, I need people to recover the dryads, to free them and bring them back here to recuperate. I've got maybe two and a half days left before we need to meet the representatives of the United Confederation, and that's in deep space. We don't know where it is, and we don't know how long it's going to take to get there, so as much as I'd like to sort this all out with you, and get to know you both more? I don't have the time, I'm sorry." I saw the confusion on their faces and sighed.

"There's a lot to get you caught up on, and Belle can do that once I've moved onto the next job, but for now, Hans, do you have some of these assholes you think you can trust?"

"The supplicants?" He indicated the people outside the door with a jerk of his head.

"Yeah."

"We believe so."

"Good. How many do you think you can trust to do as you tell them?"

"I believe, perhaps ten Arisen, and a thousand of their servants," he said.

"Good," I said, relieved. "I need you to take them to a location that Belle and Amanda will share with you, and bring…"

"Amanda will provide the location to you, but you should only uncover the tree. Do not disturb her," Belle stressed to them both. "Jamya is likely to be exceedingly weak, and should she sense a threat, she may attack. You'll need to uncover her, then back away, leave her fresh water and wait for us to reach you for the final stage, or for her to approach you. Also…"

"Really?" I cursed, looking at Belle. "We need to be there for that?"

"If possible, we should," she said. "If Jamya awakens to humans and Arisen around her, she is likely to try to defend herself, and that may be through attacking them, or…" She smiled. "She may regress into a more primal state of being, seeking to assuage only her hunger."

"She'll eat them?" I asked; then, seeing the quirked eyebrow, I snorted. "She'll fuck them to death, right. Got it."

"Excuse me?" Petros asked, confused.

"Dryads need men to reproduce, and in exchange, they basically shift their form and use pheromones to match exactly what their prey finds most attractive. Then they'll fuck them until their hearts give out, feeding on their seed, while their bodies decompose and feed their tree."

"And that's the second option. If she should approach you, before we return, I would recommend having at least a dozen healthy males ready to respond to her, and at least twice that in females to carry them free once they've been drained. I assure you, once they've been removed from her immediate presence, they will recover. And once her most desperate needs are met, if you leave her be for a few days, you will be able to approach her with far less risk."

"I see… And she'd really do this?" Petros blinked, as if shocked. "She'd, ummm, she'd fornicate with them until the point of death?"

"Most of my mates have been enthusiastic about falling prey to me." Belle smiled. "But my current mate provides for me in glorious abundance."

"I really didn't need to know that." I shook my head. "She's fucking a literal Minotaur," I clarified for the other two. "Now, moving on, Hans. I want you to gather those fuckers up and go find Jamya. As Belle says, uncover her, but don't disturb her. Let her rest, and we'll come to you."

"And you do not trust me to help?" Petros asked curiously.

"Actually…" I hesitated, then sighed, knowing that he'd given me no reason not to trust him—yet—and we damn well needed him. "I need you to continue doing what you're doing."

"Interviewing the new supplicants?" he asked, clearly surprised.

"Yeah. Is that a problem?"

"No, I simply expected that you'd have taken the role for one you trusted more."

"Because you're essentially recruiting for the faction, and developing your own position of power?" I suggested, getting a nod. "Well, let's address that."

"Please."

"You came here wanting to prove yourself, and to help, so that you'd in turn be able to ask me to help you search for your friends who were locked away and dumped in the ocean, right?"

He nodded.

"The Elders asked me to do the same," I told him. "I agreed to help you both. I have satellites—only two right now, so don't get too excited—but we have two that are currently scanning the ocean. There will be more as soon as we can manage it, but they'll find your people, and the Elders will help us to recover and heal them as best as we can."

"Oh, thank the gods," Petros mumbled, sagging in relief. "I…I wasn't sure that you would."

"I said I would. Listen, Petros, while we've basically spoken for all of five minutes before this? I don't have a fucking choice, all right? Either I trust you, who has named his price and earned a little trust, or I put someone else in your place. Someone I don't have."

"You have humans who were your companions before?" he suggested.

"You don't want to help anymore?"

"No!" he almost shouted, before pausing, taking a deep breath and carrying on, sitting back in his chair. "No, I want to help. I simply meant that I believed without Hans here to watch over me, you might have chosen to replace me with one of your companions."

"I would have," I said. "If Hans hadn't spoken about you before. You've earned his trust, and I'm going to honor that. I have other companions who are already needed elsewhere. Most of them are going with me, and that means that anything they start to do here? They'll be leaving it behind for someone else to take over. Instead of replacing you with them to do this, then them with someone else, I'm going to trust you."

"I thank you," he said simply.

"Don't." I snorted. "Damn, Petros, you think this is a good thing? You're going to be working with all those assholes out there!"

"That is a point." He smiled. "But for now at least, I have power over them, and they know that, meaning they'll behave."

"Well, we'll be starting to awaken your nanites, along with the rest of our people soon," I told them both. "It'll take a few days to be done, so we'll need to arrange it, but when it's done, you'll have full access to your systems, I hope."

"I…confess I am curious about the change," Petros said, as Hans nodded.

"It will be an experience," Hans said softly.

"It's how I did all my tricks," I admitted. "You remember my drone?"

"Ah!" Hans nodded. "Yes, I remember that, and I thank you, Steve. Such a gift as you offer…we shall strive to be worthy of it."

"You will. And I hope I don't need to say this, but I'm going to say it anyway. If you go off the rails and abuse this power? I'll strip it from you."

"I…*we* shall prove your trust is not in vain," Petros assured me.

"Glad to hear it. Also, be warned—you'll lose a lot of your physical strength as well, but you'll regain it a lot faster the second time around. It's complicated to explain, and I'm probably not doing a great job of it right now, but believe me, it's a massive improvement. One last thing before I fuck off…"

"Yes?"

"How the hell does that work out there?" I jerked my head back in the direction of the mess of people outside.

"Ha, well, it's simple." Hans smiled. "There are three desks and ten tickets. Humans are green, Arisen are red, and those who were awaiting their ascension are yellow. The teams outside interview them all, giving out tickets as people arrive and depending on their situation. Then we give a second interview to those who are needed."

"What gets them through to you?" I asked. "I mean, are you interviewing everyone?"

"Ah, no," Hans clarified. "I interview the Arisen first, passing those who are deemed to be more or less honest and respectful to Petros, and he interviews them again, further winnowing them down from the main group.

"Those who are human or close to being ascended are only passed through to us if there is something that deserves it. Unfortunately, due to the sheer numbers involved, we can only give a general yes, maybe, or no, focusing our real attention on the Arisen."

"Why do you both interview the same people?" I asked. "Seems like you're wasting a lot of time."

"As much as we discuss things, there are simply too many details for us to share each time," Hans admitted.

"My experience of most of those we speak to is hopelessly out of date," Petros added. "I've had little contact with the rest of our kind for several centuries, so I prod and ask sensitive questions, playing word games and essentially trying to detect falsehoods, while Hans filters out those he knows to be untrustworthy."

"Falsehoods," I muttered, rubbing at the bridge of my nose as I realized what I'd forgotten. "Fucking hell, I'm an idiot."

"Oh, you don't need to call yourself that." Belle smiled at me. "There's a lot of people who'll do it for you!"

"Ha. Ha," I deadpanned. "The Nordicassian Linkage." I shook my head, looking around. "Just one of a thousand things we damn well need."

I looked at the curious faces of Hans and Petros and nodded. "You're doing great, but soon, if I can make it work, I'll arrange access to a device that will let you read their minds. It'll speed things up."

"That…that would be helpful, yes." Petros snorted. "Of course, that will mean that we need to reinterview everyone from scratch as well."

"Fuck. Uh…have I told you I appreciate you?" I tried, giving him a pained smile and a double thumbs-up.

Chapter Fourteen

I left Belle with Hans and Petros—after telling her that I didn't care how quick she was, there was no time for playing "hide the sausage" with either of them—and she took Hans to meet with Amanda, the pair of them organizing the party that would go to look for Jamya.

While they were doing that, I checked on the build line with the factory units, altered it to make damn sure I had what *I* needed—it's good to be the boss sometimes—and then I headed up to meet up with Ingrid.

"Hey, my love," I whispered into her ear, leaning down behind her and kissing her cheek.

"Hey." She sighed, sounding exhausted, as she turned and pecked me on the cheek. "You need a shave."

"What's up?" I scratched at my cheek, accepting that yeah, my designer stubble was definitely a distant memory now, and I was rocking a full-on beard again.

I needed to commit to trimming it, or shaving it all off, rather than rocking a "half-Gandalf" as it felt like right now.

"I'm trying to get everything back on track," she admitted. "Some of the things I thought weren't done? They were…just some weren't finished, people thought that others were doing part of the job, or they've been waiting for orders."

She dropped her head into her hands, letting out a groan, and I rubbed her back, between her shoulder blades as she went on.

"You remember the terraformer plan? The one with the massive diggers that will basically chew their way through everything and pave the way for the river to the sea? Well, Zac…he made some changes to the plan."

"Oh, fuck no…" I groaned.

"He made a smaller one, a sort of transporter and testbed design, one to keep people's attention as he takes everything he needs from the remains of the ship. He's loaded a factory unit onto its back, and it's been making and linking up converters. It's ten meters wide and fifty long, hollow pretty much, and it's going to lay the first pass as it works its way to us."

"Right?"

"As it goes, it's got a few custodians working inside it. It'll chew up the ground, laying the path to us, and all the ground it eats, it'll be converting into null coins."

"Okay, that sort of makes sense."

"The coins are then being split off, half into a storage section, and half into making more custodians, factory units, and converters. He said that he's programmed it to keep going until it's full, then it's to stop and the custodians make a second one. The first will start going again once it's got room, and the second will do the same, working alongside it, the pair building a third and fourth."

"The plan is that by the time it makes it here, it'll have built a solid path for the big ones to follow back, making it quicker and easier for them to do their job, and it'll have made more equipment for us, enabling us to strip out the factory units and the rest. They can then be used to make a new gigafactory, as he calls it."

"Okay, typical Zac—it's batshit and yet makes perfect sense. What's the problem?"

"The first one is in the Mediterranean Sea still, and Egypt and Libya are on the verge of war over it."

"What?" I groaned.

"Zac sent it off, telling Far where it'd be, but he didn't want it to just start plowing its way through the little villages between the sea and here, so he set it to wait near the shore, where he thought it'd not be seen."

"And?"

"And then Mor was attacked and Far was distracted and forgot all about it," she said. "Also, Zac didn't consider that the water nearer the shore is clear, and so the locals found it, yesterday apparently. The Libyan navy moved in overnight, and the Egyptian navy is trying to bully them into leaving it to them."

"And if we leave it alone, they'll come to blows sooner rather than later." I swore. "Fine. Have we got control of it?"

"We can reach out to it easily enough. Zac deployed signal repeater satellites near here and over the Med, just in case."

"Right. Want me to deal with that then?" I asked.

"How?"

"I'll start it working, and I'll call the Libyan contact, tell them it's ours and to fuck off."

"I..." She looked at me, then smiled and nodded in relief. "Actually, yes please. You deal with that, and I'll get on with the next job."

"No worries." I settled into a nearby chair, leaning back on its back legs and putting my feet on the table before me.

"Steve," Ingrid said in a warning tone.

"Is this our place?" I smiled in her direction, even as I reached out through the system. It definitely looked like only the upgrade system was borked for me at the minute, which was a massive relief.

"It is."

"Then it's half my table." I grinned. "You can not put your feet on your half if you don't want to, but I like putting mine up."

"You're such a child at times." She snorted, but with clear affection in her voice.

I continued reaching out through the systems, my mind seeming to flow across the hundreds of empty miles of desert, until I found it.

Literally half a mile off the coast, the device was currently surrounded by divers, several of whom were moving back as a frigate floated closer overhead; a pair of smaller, but heavily armed ships were moving up to try to cut her off.

I swore, seeing that they were minutes away from escalation, and I needed to move before I lost the chance.

Getting to my feet, I reached out, connecting to the nearest camera, focusing it in on me, and pulled my armor up, wings folded behind my back, eyes glowing. I linked the camera signal and microphone to the naval minister of Libya.

He'd been in the middle of a shouting match with someone else, and appeared pretty confused when his previous call was cut off. But on seeing me, he scrambled to his feet, nodding in an awkward half-bow.

"Blessed one," he greeted me, weirdly.

"You have ships around a device of mine," I said, ignoring the usual pleasantries. "I will start moving it to dig the channel to my facility in the next few minutes. Move anything that you don't want destroyed away from it."

With that, as he started to stammer, I cut the call off, knowing that the Libyan side would not be the problem.

The Egyptian minister of defense hung up on me twice. The third time, on finding that his phone wouldn't accept him prodding the end call button, he instead threw the phone out of the window.

I knew this, because when the call went through, I was using my Hack sub-mind to trace it, finding the building he was in, then flowing through the various security systems until I found the fucker.

I could see him, sitting quite happily, drinking a truly tiny cup of coffee that was blacker than the inside of a black cat at midnight.

I also found nothing in the room that could work as a speaker, unfortunately. The shitbag even looked up at the camera in the corner of the room as if he knew what I was doing, sneering.

That did it.

I had enough going on. I wasn't wasting any more time dealing with this dickhead, so I patched myself through to the nearby missile control systems, authenticated myself as the one and only correct owner, and tracked a ship that was just leaving the harbor of Port Said.

It took several minutes, but by the time I got through to it, and I made sure I could do what I wanted to, and that the "splash damage" wouldn't be too much, I had a solid plan in place.

"Steve…" Ingrid said warningly, as she apparently sensed that I was getting annoyed.

"It's all right, I'm just making a point," I assured her, locking in my control of the ship's weapons systems and activating them.

The target I'd selected was the minister of defense's office, and although he'd apparently thought to remove all the speakers so I couldn't talk to him, he'd not considered that talking might not be all I chose to do.

This fucker was happy to try to bully a smaller nation's navy, to take advantage of the situation he thought he was in, but clearly, he'd not thought any further down the line as to possible consequences.

Interestingly, in his files, when I was looking for leverage on him, I found all that I needed—and a damn good reason, at last, as to why the Egyptian contingent I'd been dealing with before were such dickheads.

They must have suspected some of my capabilities before, because when they'd been interacting with me, they'd been careful to make it look like institutional corruption, rather than specific. Now, though, as I dug a little deeper, I found all that I needed.

The minister sure as shit started to consider those consequences once the security shutters came down around his office.

They were *nice* shutters, high tech, and clearly reinforced to fuck. They slid out of the wall to roll over the doors and windows, sealing him inside, all nice and secure.

Then the alarms started to go off in the building, as the message made it through that they'd lost control over one of their ships, and its most advanced weaponry.

The missile I'd targeted on his office had to have triggered a few alerts as well, I had to think.

It was even better when he started to his feet, jabbing a chubby finger into the phone on his desk, screaming something at his staff, before running at the door and trying to open it.

It took him all of thirty seconds of panicked banging on the door to put it all together. Then he went looking for his phone, blanching as he remembered he'd thrown it out of the window.

I'd not bothered connecting to his landline.

Not out of any disapproval of the landline, just because the throwing of his phone out the window was fucking clear enough. I'd planned to make the threat clear through the speakers, only to find that they were gone, and now he was gesturing at the landline angrily, shouting something while waving at the camera.

I took that as my cue and called him.

"You think we will obey?" he spat. "You know nothing of our people. We do not bend, we do not break! By Ma'at, we shall not be forced to bend to your will!"

"Yeah... I don't give two fucks."

"What?"

"You will bend, you won't bend...that's fine. I took the time to make sure, and you issued the orders for the navy to start that fight over *my* shit. Not your government, not your president—you."

"I am the minister of defense, and I..."

"And you're in the middle of trying to carry out a coup," I added, making it clear that I knew about that too. "Stand it down, or I fucking will. Last chance."

"Fuck you and all your kind!" he screamed at the phone, holding it before his face, spittle flying. "You think to claim our treasures? You think to claim Egypt? We are closed to you! You and all your carrion-eating filthy kind!"

"My kind?" I said softly, staring at the video of him and shaking my head in wonder. "You mean the Arisen?"

"You are all filth! Souls that were refused passage to judgment!" He cursed, slipping from English into Egyptian and continuing to rant in that language now, occasionally throwing in names I vaguely recognized as ancient gods.

"You know…" I said after a few seconds to admire the sheer brass balls on the motherfucker, "I almost wish I could see what would have happened to you and your friends if you'd said that to Athena, or Zeus. Hell, Shamal or Beowulf would have ripped your entrails out of your dick slowly, no doubt."

"You are…" he continued, and I shrugged, saying one last thing before cutting the line entirely. "You might want to look out of any gaps in the north window. That'll give you the best view."

Then I set to work, leaving him ranting.

The closest of his co-conspirators were easy to assemble, as most of them were in the same building. They got a message, supposedly from him on their government-issue, highly unhackable secure phones, to gather in a central location downstairs in the same building. They also got a message telling them that what was going on upstairs was part of the plan and to ignore it.

Shmucks.

While they were gathering, I sent a full debrief on the situation to the Egyptian president, along with a list of all those involved, their texts, their plans, all that good shit, and a photo I'd found of the minister of defense and his mistress.

Apparently, he liked her dressing in his uniform and beating him.

Although I wasn't one to kink-shame, the picture was frankly fucking hilarious, so I included that as well for good measure.

Considering they were involved in a military coup, it was laughably easy to gather all but a few of them up. The only issue I had, at one point, was making sure one of them sent his wife and daughter away. He'd decided to bring them in on a tour of the base that day, showing them a general's office and dropping unsubtle hints to his wife that he'd soon be getting a "big" promotion.

Once it was all done and the innocents were cleared out? I triggered the doors downstairs and locked all the idiots in as well.

Next step was setting off a nuclear and biological contamination alarm on the base and sending out a general emergency evacuation order.

I gave them a minute, watching as the other buildings on the base suddenly boiled with running people, looking like rats fleeing a sinking ship.

Then it was simple. I reached out from the frigate I was connected to, tagging the second and third, and slaved them into my control as well—assuring Ingrid, when she asked me what I was doing, that I was "handling things" in a totally reasonable manner. Honest.

Then I targeted their Harpoon II missiles on the facility as well, disabled their kill switches, and launched three of the fuckers at once.

Once they were in the air, I made a fresh call, this time to the current Egyptian president, again cutting off his panicked call with several loyal generals.

"Who are you?" he asked me slowly, staring at the image of me that took up one wall of his admittedly luxurious office.

"You know who and what I am," I said, choosing to dismiss the silly phrasing and posturing. "I gave you a chance to benefit from my presence in the desert, and I was insulted and threatened by your representative. I've now discovered that not all of that was according to any plan of yours, but some of it? Yeah, you're an asshole who thought you could benefit from taking a hard line with me and my people.

"Most of it, though, was down to your defense minister setting things up for his own benefit. As was his play at intercepting *my* property off the coast of Libya. That's why I've forwarded the plans he made to replace you." I stood there, in full armor, waiting.

The president struggled to speak, clearly still coming to terms with the fact that he'd been only a handful of days from being ousted in a military takeover. When he finally did manage to speak, my impression of him went down even further.

"How do I know any of this is true?" he spat out. "This could all be a conspiracy you've come up with to ensure that you can control me and gain access to Egypt's treasures..."

"How do you know?" I asked, as if curious, before stepping closer to the camera pickup, zooming it in slightly so that I seemed to loom even larger. "You know because your opinion is utterly worthless to me. If I wanted you dead? You'd already be dead. If I want your treasures? I'll tear the roof off your museum and I'll take what I want. You seem confused, so I'll make this *very* clear. Your minister for defense has offended me, and in the process, I discovered he was planning to remove you and install a military dictatorship. I've stopped him. You're welcome."

An aide barged into the room, panicked, with a pair of flustered soldiers racing in behind him as he waved a phone at his boss, letting loose a rapid-fire blast of Arabic that I didn't bother trying to translate. He broke off, eyes going wide as he saw me on the wall.

The president ripped the phone from his hand and started to speak into it. His face grew whiter as he was presumably brought up to date on the condition of "his" warships and the missiles that were even now streaking through the air toward the military base.

Eventually, he seemed to grasp what was going on, and he turned back to me.

"You," he said hesitantly, terror warring with fury. "This is you."

"Yes."

"What do you think you will get from this? The hands of every nation will be turned against you... My allies will not stand for this..."

"Your allies don't give two fucks, and you damn well know it," I corrected. "Almost all nations' leaders accept that they rule by the sufferance of the Arisen."

"It will not always be so!" he snapped, shaking with what was clearly rage.

"No, no, it probably won't, but let's have a quick reality check, shall we?" I suggested. I was actually enjoying this. It wasn't often I got to bully a country. "We've got about a minute before those missiles hit their target, so you've got some time."

"Missiles…!" I heard Ingrid gasp, and then the sudden burgeoning presence of her in my mind as she dropped whatever she was doing in favor of trying to calm the situation.

"I… I…" the president whispered, shaking his head. "You know that this will solidify their hatred of you, and…"

"No," I pointed out. "No, it won't. First of all, those missiles are aimed at the minister of defense, and almost his entire leadership cadre. There are seven people left outside of the target area, all of whom I've given you the details of. Secondly, you fucking started this, you idiot."

"What?" He gasped, spinning and grabbing the phone again, rapid-fire barking into it, making sure that he wasn't the target, and that instead of wiping him out, I was killing his enemies.

I gave him thirty seconds to make sure of things, and by that time his attitude was markedly less confrontational.

"I am listening," he prompted, annoying me all over again.

"Right." I grunted. "So this is how it is. We tried to work with you, and in your greed, you tried to *fuck us over*. Your minister of defense made that even worse, deliberately encouraging your people to make unreasonable demands and made sure that we knew it was a setup, but making it look like it was down to you, not him.

"When we told them to fuck off, and started working with the Libyans instead, it weakened your position and your power base, enabling him to get his little coup on the move. Then, just because you're a fucking idiot, you authorized him to move the navy into a standoff position with the Libyans—and let's face it, calling their sea forces a navy is a fucking insult to navies.

"You outnumber them by…hell, I don't even care how much. You'd roll over them in a day if you decided to try to annex their nation. And the only reason you don't? You know it'd be a nightmare. They're all kinds of fucked up already thanks to the shit that's been going on over the last few decades, and the only things they have going for them? You're currently trying to steal.

"So, I've taken care of your little military problem—and, to be clear, that wasn't as a favor to you. I did it because when I tried to speak to that asshole, he hung up on me. This is the result."

I changed the connection to his office to display an image from the nose cone of the incoming lead missile on one side, showing the target building getting bigger and bigger. On the other side, I had a camera on the edge of the base that looked over its interior playing.

The streak of fire and light that was just identifiable on the edge of the screen quickly vanished. The missile impacted the building and punched through, driving deeper and deeper.

I'd deliberately adjusted the impact settings, making sure the missiles would hit from almost directly above, and dig down as far as possible before detonating.

That caused the main building to be pretty much the only casualty. Had it punched in from one side? The blast radius would have been spread out, especially with two more missiles hitting split seconds later.

Instead, the detonation went almost straight up. The building was ripped apart, literally flung half into the air and massive blocks of masonry and marble, steel and ceramics thrown in all directions.

The devastation was limited, though, making damn sure that the surrounding buildings, although damaged, were repairable, and the fleeing locals got minor injuries, if anything at all.

"So, now that you hopefully understand what happens when you annoy me? Let's move on. You're trying to lay claim to my possessions, and you're threatening to start a war with Libya to do it. You've got one minute to pull back all your forces in the area. You'll note that the Libyans already abandoned it."

"I... I..."

"And then you're going to help them rebuild their country, and sort their shit out, as penance for you pulling this crap," I went on. "Now the reason I know you're going to do this? Nice and simple."

Quickly searching, I pulled up the cost of the three frigates that I currently had control over.

"You spent two *billion* euros on these frigates, one of which is currently pissing me off and floating in another nation's waters. The others you have here? I have complete control over them, and..."

I trailed off, focusing, reaching out and pouring over the last stages of the security that protected the frigates' systems, absorbing them and taking control.

It was child's play to turn the ship, powering up the engines and taking it off station, headed back toward Egyptian waters, as her smaller consorts floundered, trying to get out of her way, then following like ducklings chasing their mother, squawking questions as the ships' crew panicked and screamed at each other.

"And there we go." I sighed. "Okay, so if you don't help the Libyans and bring a little fucking sanity to the area, what I'm going to do is have each of these frigates fire on each other. They'll expend all their highly fucking expensive ammunition on each other, right after every single ship they can reach in your harbor.

"Now, considering that's your primary naval base? I've got to think that they're going to do at least another few billions' worth of damage."

"You can't!" he half screamed, the fear clear as he saw that I was deadly serious.

I switched the transmission from the remains of the base to display the frigates instead, flicking from camera to camera, showing the panicking sailors as they tried to regain control of their very expensive toys.

"I will remove the entire Egyptian naval fleet from existence," I said very clearly. "I will sink everything you think protects you, and then I'll start with the land and air forces. Every single missile you have in every silo, I will expend on your own forces. I will erase your ability to make war in any form beyond sharp pointy fucking sticks. And if that's not enough to calm you down? Well, then I'll start to get angry, instead of merely annoyed, and I'll get involved *personally*."

The camera zoomed in on my armored helm, my eyes glowing with a fierce internal fire.

"I am here with a mission and have limited time," I explained coldly. "If I have to raze your lands from one border to the other, to make an example of you, to ensure that other nations understand their position? I will count it as a small cost. You hate and fear the Arisen? The nations of Earth worship and grovel for them when they make their demands. They are the power behind every throne and scepter. They manipulate your elections and they rule your corporations...*and they kneel when I enter the room.*"

I let that hang there for several long heartbeats.

"Issue the orders, pull back your forces, and I'll return control of them to you. Begin humanitarian projects and start fixing this planet instead of fucking it up, or the next time we talk, I'll make sure it's the last words you ever hear."

With that, I cut the link, relaxing, banishing my armor and turning to face Ingrid, who stared at me in horror.

"What?" I frowned at her. "You said you wanted me to deal with it. It's dealt with."

Chapter Fifteen

For some reason, Ingrid wasn't too happy with my solution. But even she had to admit that in less than ten minutes of unsubtle action, tensions in the area were markedly lowered between all nations.

Satellite images showed Egyptian forces leaving the area as fast as they could, and a little digging confirmed that as well as the orders being issued to get things rolling with humanitarian aid, and negotiations commencing with their Libyan counterparts, there was also a subtle and desperate search beginning for new control methods for the ships and missiles.

The sneaky fuckers were trying to make sure I couldn't take them over again.

That was fine, though, because as part of taking over the systems, I now had a back door into them. Although I was letting them control the ships again, I'd not relinquished control entirely.

I made a mental note that once we had an AI, or even RIs, that'd be a use for them to make sure that no other fucker had control over these systems.

For a second, I wondered about Skynet, and the possibilities that integrating an experimental AI built by a distracted idiot might bring…then I remembered that it'd not be me building it, and that given the choice between these lunatics running it, and me?

I'd pick me every day.

Ingrid had made it clear that she wasn't going to be passing any more diplomatic jobs onto me for a while for some reason, so I got back to work with the terraformer, reaching out to Libya again, and making sure they knew where it was going.

Then I drove it up the beach, out of the water, and had it chew its way through the hillside, creating a steady slope to the higher headland behind it.

The design that Zac had gone with in the end was a lot smaller than the "real" terraformers would be. It was a mere ten meters wide and fifty long, looking like a curved rectangle, moving on massive tracks like a tank. It also apparently had a limited gravity system in case it needed to make it over ditches and so on, making itself lighter, but it couldn't fly or anything mental like that.

Which, to be fair, knowing Zac, was a fuckin' relief, really.

I got it up onto the mainland, rolled across a road or two and through a few farmers' fields, making a mental note to send them some money as an apology, and lined it up on the first waypoint.

Until there, it was essentially going cross country, leaving a trail of devastation behind it. Once it hit the first waypoint, though, then it was going almost straight all the way to the recycling facility. The Libyan government had already reached out to the farmers and landowners along the route, making them offers for the land they had.

I'd been pissed about that at first, because in my eyes, that was land that the farmers were going to really regret losing. They'd be going from practically worthless land to insanely valuable literal riverfront property.

Then Ingrid pointed out that we were keeping everyone back from the water anyway, as it was ours with a section on either side reserved. Then she reminded me that the plan was that the farmers could draw water from the river to irrigate their lands, and suddenly the whole deal looked a lot better for the people than the government.

I distrusted the government instinctively, knowing the fuckers would generally be getting their beak wet somewhere, but decided that as long as they didn't fuck things up too badly, I'd accept it. If I spent the next decade working on it, I'd still never make politicians honest, and I had…*yeah*. Not that long to play.

That done, I started work on the last problem on my list.

The factory.

Zac's grand plan for the massive terraformers and more was that we'd always need factory units here, as well as converters. Even if we just made factory units that made more factory units and converters exclusively, there was no realistic way that we'd have enough inside a year for everything we needed. And even then, we'd not have enough to deal with the things our allies would need, let alone look at sorting out the planet.

Ingrid and Freja had been talking about making massive converters that could be set up in central locations for the various nations, enabling them to take the waste that society produced daily, feed it in, and then get viable resources out of the far side.

It was a great idea, and damn, it'd help sort out the mess that the planet was in as well. But reaching the point that we could do that realistically?

It was years away.

The best solution for now, and the best for us as well, was that we allowed the other nations to send us all their rubbish once they ran out of the nuclear, biological, and toxic crap they were panicking over until now.

Eventually, though, supplying them was part of the plan.

The factory as it was, though? It was…lacking.

Zac had great plans for it, and the others had done what they could, but some utter bastard kept yanking Zac off to work on another project. He never got to really finish any of them for some reason, so I guessed fixing this part of the plan was up to me.

The factory unit was about a quarter done, as I walked out to look it over. Or, at least, this stage of it was.

The plan had shifted slightly from the ones I'd been involved in. When I'd started to look it over, Ingrid had shot me a plan that Zac had given to Anders and James, and they'd apparently passed it to her.

That it had helpful little notes on it like *"Don't let that bastard Steve fuck with this"* and *"Don't change this, I'll fuckin' know"* from Zac was fun as well.

As it was, the smaller factory units I was used to dealing with had been used to produce the parts for a much larger one. Where normally they might be the size of a large suitcase, and the bigger ones in the facility had been around the size of a small truck, the units here had produced parts that could be linked together to create a unit I could stand in.

It was about the size of a Challenger main battle tank, or would be by the time it was assembled, and looking at it, it was going to be awesome.

The issue was that it needed to be completed. There were custodians about, and even a few of the big construction spiderbots that the mad bastard had created. Again, there was a lack of management, because for some reason Freja and Anders had been needed with me at the Great Refuge.

Ignoring that there was a common factor in everyone getting taken off their jobs before they could finish them, I decided that rather than pulling the custodians and spiders off their current jobs to help me fix the factory, I'd sort it out myself.

The parts were simple enough, thankfully. My Engineering sub-mind identified them and the required layout in minutes. From there? I reached out to Jonas and Scylla, and got a little muscle involved, then Oxus, then a few of the Oracan, and then almost before I knew it, I had fifty people working.

That was mainly because even with the best will in the world, holding some of the sections in place needed serious strength. So by the time Ingrid came down, the memory modules being loaded into the stingray, along with the null coins for the loonies under the sea…she just laughed.

It took another half an hour, but the final sections were locked into place. Within seconds, the spiderbots were clanking into sight, carrying parts for the converters needed to feed it.

They had that up and running, and a conveyor belt from it into the factory in a matter of minutes. And by the time we took off? The first of the second-generation spiderbots was rolling out of the new factory.

"What's the next step?" I asked Ingrid, looking out of the window as we lifted off into the early afternoon light.

"For what?" she asked distractedly.

"For the factory, for us, for…oh, you know."

"The factory is making a dozen constructor bots. Once they're done, it starts on the parts for the gigafactory."

"How big is that thing going to be?" I frowned.

"About the size of a large, detached house. It'll be able to make the terraformers, though as complicated as they are, they'll take around a week each to build."

"Coolio." I grunted. "And for us?"

"We're flying to meet Yeshin and the others, drop the memory module off and get it working, along with null coins. Then we'll start hunting down the last three rogue guardians… But you know this…what's going on?"

"Where's Zac up to with the ship?" I asked instead of answering.

"The ship…" She paused, then sighed and went on. "We're not going to make it."

I looked at her, knowing that as much as we desperately needed this not to be the case, it was a fucking starship that we were attempting to botch together. No matter how skilled the engineer, or how gifted and motivated they were, the time just wasn't enough.

"He thinks he can get it ready—it'll be able to fly, at least. And once there's a solid memory core in there, we should be able to download an RI from one of the custodians or something into it to operate the data." She shook her head.

"That side isn't the problem. It'll fly. It's graceless and barely holding together, and it'll probably be leaking atmosphere like a sieve, but we can survive in our armor if need be. The problem is that to get there in time, if it's anywhere outside of the system, we'd need a gravity drive, and the one we have access to…"

"Which one?"

"The one in the ship."

"What about the one in the Great Refuge?"

"That…the one that we found after Mor—" She shook her head. "Zac looked at the details we have for it. It's powerful, much more so than the one in the warship, but it's untested."

"So's the rest of the ship."

"It is, well, it's untested in *space*."

"Our spaceship is a yacht that's already been sunk once," I pointed out. "I'm not exactly celebrating that our first time in space is going to be something stuck together with spit, glue, hopes and dreams."

She smiled. "Americans made it to the moon with less."

"Americans think they should all be allowed as many guns as they can carry, and looking at Jay and Paul as perfect examples, I'd not trust most of them with a plastic paper clip. They're crazy."

"And we're not?"

"Point."

"So… Zac considered the grav drive, but he's more concerned that due to the size and power needs, it's more likely to rip free of the ship than get us there. The older ship's version is smaller. Yes, it's integrated into the hull, but we could cut it out and have it installed in about seven hours, that's the timescale, and that'd be if we fly the ship there."

"It's ready to fly?"

"It will be in four hours." She reached out and took my hand, squeezing it gently. "I'm worried, Steve."

"I don't blame you." I squeezed her back. "I'm scared shitless."

"Zac said he could get the smaller grav drive out of the warship, but there'd be no time for tests of any kind. And depending on the location we're supposed to meet at? He doesn't think the drive will be able to do it."

"Why not?"

"It's time, literally," she explained. "It's been laid there for thousands of years. I don't get it, but he said that it's basically solid-state, and so the timescale isn't that important. What matters is that the grav drive was entirely powered down, which, from what he's been able to figure out, means it can only be powered up again, over several months…"

"*Months!*" I grunted in shock.

"Don't panic," she said quickly. "The nature of the gravity drive means it's always available, apparently, and this is something that can literally create tears in the fabric of the universe, flinging something across the galaxy. To do that, though, you need the drive to accumulate…something. It's powered up slowly, allowing it to draw in branes…I think."

"Brains?" I frowned.

"No, branes…" She repeated the same goddamn word as I stared at her. "Uh! Look, I'm not the one who should try to explain this—Zac could barely explain it. It's some kind of multi-dimensional string theory that explains why gravity is weak, that's all I know."

"Gravity isn't weak," I said. The months of "playing" with the gravity manipulation ability and the various systems I'd designed and used meant that I damn well knew that, if nothing else.

"Well, no, not really, but the way he explained it? It…actually, no, you know what? Let him explain. We've got about an hour until we get to the drop-off point. Call him."

I did, the relief when she'd not have to explain "brain" theory to me clear. Zac seemed to have been expecting the call, as I settled back, closing my eyes and bringing up the command link, reaching out and linking up to him.

"*Don't you give me any shit.*" Those were his first words. "*Seriously, boss, I've not slept in three days, I'm on the ragged fuckin' edge, and I've not had a beer, a blowy, or a burger in too fuckin' long.*"

"*And hello to you too.*" I sighed. "*Zac, look—*"

"*I can't do it.*" He cut me off. "*Seriously, boss, if you're calling me now, it's because you want to try to convince me I can work some kind of magic, right? You want me to somehow turn time back and make there be enough hours between now and when we need to be wherever. It can't be done. Seriously, unless the meeting is like on the dark side of the fuckin' moon or something, somewhere we could have nicked a 'SpaceY' rocket and just flew to already? It ain't happenin'.*"

"*Why not?*"

"*Seriously?*"

"*Zac, you said you might be able to do it—not you could…you might. You've taken a broken yacht and made it so that it's basically a spaceship, in what, two fucking days? Explain what's stopping you doing it.*"

"*Okay, look.*" He sighed. "*The ship itself? A yacht is designed to keep the water out, and the stuff inside dry and safe. It was a megayacht anyway—all I've done is add better engines, some better controls and power systems, then strengthened and sealed it a bit more. It's not that bad…*" At that point, professional pride reared its head, and he hesitated.

"Okay, I mean, yeah, taking a broken boat and fixing it up to fly into space? None of those posh gits at NASA could have done it, in ten years with a million, billion in gold, but that's not the point. I'm an engineer—I can do anything."

"Got that," I agreed, nodding.

"So I can get the ship into space, all right? It's not pretty, and yeah, no matter how much I'm trying, there's gonna be some leaks. Nothing I can do about that. Also, it's not gonna be tested. Like, to test it? I need to either dump it in the ocean, and then if it sinks it'll take days that we don't have to fix it, or we need to take it to space to test it—again, not something we've got time to do."

"Okay, so it'll be a trial by fire. Either it works or we die."

"Well, we've all got armor, or something like it," he corrected. *"We can seal ourselves in as best as we can and limp home if it goes wrong. Probably."*

"So?"

"So the problem's the drive," he admitted. *"I had to leave it to last because the goddamn systems that it needs to be connected to needed to be built from scratch, all right? Now I'm looking at them, and where I thought the gravity drive could be ripped out and plugged in? That's where the problems come in."*

"Go on."

"The gravity drive works by plucking the branes that run between planes of reality."

"What?"

"Fuck, how did I get this job?" he muttered. *"All right, look at the world— everything we see…the universe, time, space, all that shite, right? That's this reality. That's it. There's more than one. There's a fuckload of them apparently, according to the theory that I think closest fits the grav drive.*

"There's branes, not fuckin' brains like the ones you're missing either. Branes. Like…" He paused, trying to think of a better analogy. *"Think of a filter, all right? Like you're cleaning an engine out. You pour the oil through a filter, and it catches a load of rubbish, yeah?"*

"Okay…"

"Now that filter, that's a brane. All you see around us? That's caught in the filter. It's kept here." He gestured enthusiastically. *"Think of it like oil on the top of the water. It's all on this side, but it can't go further. Now, think about those branes. There's a handful of them…some theories like five, others eleven. I like seven, but that's because I just like seven, so fuck it.*

"So there's seven different filters, and they all catch different things. One of the few things that can pass through the branes, and keeps going, is gravity. What a grav drive does is open a hole with a burst of energy that drills down to a point in the lower branes; then, when the energy runs out, the filter pops you back out, all right? It doesn't destroy you. It's just got no space for you there, so it sort of pushes you back up to the point you should be at.

"We can predict how far it'll get you by picking the amount of energy put into the hole we drill, and then as we rise back out of it, we adjust course slightly…a little push here, a bubble there."

"Okay, seems mental, but so does the rest of my life. So what's the problem?"

"The problem is capacity. First, we need to learn to use the damn drive. Secondly, we need to power it up, and that's a slow process, seriously. We rush it, it's likely to accidentally trigger and we could end up on the far side of the galaxy with a broken drive. Third? We've got the basics on how to use the drive that's in the warship, and I mean the basics. They're all there in the system linked to how to repair and build one, but they're the idiot's guide, nothing more!"

"And the one under the Great Refuge?" I asked.

"Don't even think about it," he warned me. *"I mean it."*

"Why not?"

"It's a prototype," he snapped. *"There's records of their attempts to make more powerful and more advanced grav drives—they blew up star systems when they went wrong."*

"Uh huh," I agreed. *"And the systems that were destroyed, were they this end or the far end?"*

"What?"

"If we trigger it here, and it goes wrong, is it…" I paused, trying to think of the name of our system; it wasn't like it was ever needed in conversation normally.

"Sol system." Zac sighed.

"Right! So is it Sol that goes boom, or the other end?"

"The other end," he said. *"It's something to do with the release of energy not being stabilized."*

"So, if this one that's a prototype is really working as they claimed, that they'd figured it out and basically it was left there because they were exiled and they weren't going to share it…"

"Yeah?"

"Then even if it goes wrong, Earth is all right?"

"Probably, but the other end won't be!"

"What if we pick a place between stars, on the way to wherever we need to go?"

"Between the stars?"

"Yeah, I mean, there's nothing there, right?"

"You're an idiot."

"I get that a lot, Zac, but why this time?" I struggled to keep my temper.

"Dude, boss man, seriously?" he asked, clearly picking up on my annoyance. *"Asteroids, comets, all the shite that we see zipping around the system? It's come from out there, in the deep dark. For all we know, it's packed with shite!"*

"Is it likely to be packed with life?*"*

"Well, no…"

"So it could be a load of dead rocks."

"Yeah, that's almost certainly what's there. But popping up between the rocks isn't going to end well!"

"Will we smash into them?"

"Well, probably not, no?" he said. *"It'd be like when something pops up in the bath—all the water pushes things out of the way, but then they come back!"*

"And we'll move," I suggested. *"Zac, look, if the UC doesn't find us there, they're not going to protect us. What they'll do is say they're staying out of it, all*

right? No protecting Earth. They've been keeping us hidden all this time, giving us a chance to grow, but the Ændari, if they find that mental bitch who turned herself into a giant sea dragon or whatever? They'll wake her, at the least. That's gonna destroy the world, probably reduce the surviving population down to double digits, all right? Then the plagues that'd come from all the bodies...the starvation..."

"We'd be fucked," he said. *"I know that, boss, but..."*

"We don't know how far we need to go, so if the other drive is more powerful, we need to risk it," I said. *"You said that the problem with the drives is energy, and that the branes were an issue?"*

"The drive needs to be powered up in stages," he said. *"If we try to power it all the way to like full, or even half, it'll tear itself apart. You need to power it fully over months, which means short-distance hops at first."*

"Right, and they'd have known that, wouldn't they? They said they'd unlock the warship for us to use, but never thought about checking to make sure it was flight capable. They had to have known it'd be powered down, though, so they must have picked somewhere we could reach."

"I hope so, boss. Look, my vote, for what it's worth? Powering up the more powerful engine is likely to get us there easier than the other one, sure, but if we have no details on how to fucking use it? We power it up to ten percent for the first week or so. If we can get it working at that level, then we could power it to one percent and do a bunch of small jumps around the local systems to calibrate it."

"So why not..."

"Because the first jump either works or we all die," he snapped. *"If it fucks up? We want to be as far from here as possible when the energy outburst comes. That means the first jump is gonna be at the full ten percent we can manage. Then, if we fuckin' live, we can do little learning jumps, bouncing around and making sure we know what we're doing, right?"*

"Okay...?"

"But we don't have the time to do that," he said. *"We'd need to be leaving like now, or better yet, a few days ago. If instead we wait, get things in place, test the systems and make sure they're watertight, then go? We'll have maybe, at best, a day before we need to be there. We know that the jumps are near instantaneous in local space, but the farther out you go, the more time dilation becomes an issue. We jump across a serious distance? It'd feel like an eye blink to us, and our sun might have died out a thousand years ago."*

"How the fuck do they work out timescales then? How do they know how long five days, or revolutions or whatever, is?"

"No clue." Zac shrugged. *"I can think of a couple of ways you might be able to do it, but they'd all be based on a universal time constant. And how it'd be worked here? No idea. We'd have to travel to a central point, and get specific materials that would decay at a set rate, relative to the—"*

"And that's enough of that shit." I shook my head. *"Sorry, dude, I know you find this stuff interesting, but not me."*

"Well, ah, screw it, man. You're the boss. What do we do then?" he asked.

"We…" I hesitated, then reached out, pulling Ingrid into the conversation, then added Anders, who sent us a burst of "not now" and left instantly.

"What…?" I asked Ingrid, blinking my eyes open, only to see unshed tears in her eyes.

"It's Mor," she whispered, also leaving the command link. "She's waking up."

"Already?" I cursed. "Fuck, we should be there. We should—"

"I'll go," she said quickly. "You go to Yeshin and the others. It'll take you an hour to get down there at least, and it's another hour nearly to get to the drop-off. We'll get going straight to the refuge."

"But—"

"Zac will be finished with the ship in about four hours…finished enough that he can fly it, anyway. It won't be pretty, but get him to come for you, then you go and get the drive."

"That's the point." I sighed. "The drive…Zac wants to—"

"Steve." She stopped me dead, her fingers pressed to my lips. "I'm going to link to Far so I can see Mor as soon as I can, to see if she's…her or not. At the end of the day, this is why companies have CEOs and countries have one person in charge. Make a decision, and stick to it. You've gotten us this far. We trust your instincts."

With that, she was settling back and closing her eyes again, and I was suddenly alone, back to making the decisions.

"Okay then." I lay back and slipped into the command net, sensing that Ingrid had granted me access to her expanded capabilities in a massive demonstration of trust. I started reaching out, signaling to people that they needed to get ready, and that I'd be speaking to them all in a minute.

"Zac, shit's changed on us again, so what I need you to do is—"

The scream that cut me off went on a lot longer than I felt was reasonable.

Chapter Sixteen

The swim back down to the depths to meet Yeshin and his people was fairly boring up to the halfway point. Jonas, Scylla, and I carried everything down, along with another converter for them, as well as a factory unit that had all our current designs, including food.

That was a serious upgrade, I knew. The concept had always been there, but when Jonas explained to me that he'd just gotten the factory unit to scan the food that Jay had made for the day, as a last-minute "I wonder if this works"?

It was going to be a game changer.

There were a dozen dishes that had been made for late-night snacks, cold meats for those who would be working in the fields, and a load of breakfast and supper foods ready for the changing shifts, as well as every raw ingredient we had.

Logically, there was no reason that it shouldn't work. Food was generally a lot easier to produce, and more needed than anything else.

That had sparked a debate about what we should be doing with the tech we had all over again. Scylla was of the opinion that people who were starving were responsible for themselves, as they should move, or take the food they needed from others.

Jonas was arguing that we should set up distribution hubs that could hand out wheat and more, and make sure that people had enough food.

I agreed with both sides, as much as I didn't like it.

First, if we had the food and the means to provide it, then we damn well should be helping people who were less fortunate. We needed to set up those hubs and start feeding people.

Secondly, there was a portion of humanity that I'd dealt with over the years who, if we gave them everything they needed? They'd just take it. It wouldn't be a case of this seeing them through shitty times: some people would simply take and take, and not bother to contribute.

It was a small percentage, admittedly, no matter what the right-wing assholes liked to pretend. But some people, if they were given the chance to do nothing but consume, would genuinely do that.

The thing was, though, I didn't have the right to decide that they should be refused that chance.

I'd added to the list of jobs for our people, and part of that was setting up those distribution hubs, ones with the fundamental staples of life: food, water, and basic shelter.

They were to be set up and provided for people. As much as I was an asshole, if I could help it, no little kid would be going hungry.

I'd just made that declaration, and started things moving in that direction—further delaying other projects on our side, like the citadel or whatever we were going to call it—when the leviathan came swimming out of the darkness ahead, and I damn well nearly turned the water brown.

Fortunately, it flashed straight past us, arcing slightly to the left and ignoring us beyond that.

I started to use my gravity senses again after that, though.

By the time we reached the bottom of the trenches and passages, leaving the last of the outside world behind to enter the last cavern, we found Yeshin waiting for us.

"You have the memory modules?" he asked abruptly.

"Yeah, hi, Yeshin, great to see you too," I shot back. "The swim? No, it's just a few solid hours, and Nessie? She's dead. Oh no, we've not slept for days, but it's okay, we're tough like that. We'll rest once we've saved everyone!"

"Good."

"'Good,'" I repeated flatly.

"Yes, it is good that you have accomplished as much as you have. However, there are still three rogue guardians out there, and—"

"And we'll deal with them later." I cut him off. "We've brought you their value and more in null coins, as well as a factory unit and another converter."

"That is welcome, but our agreement was—"

"Yeshin, if I stay here and hunt those fuckers right now, I won't make it to the meeting on time. What will the UC do?"

"We do not know," he admitted. "There are several likely outcomes."

"Go for it..."

"First, they will wait, reporting back that you have not arrived."

"Uh huh, and then what?"

"Most likely they will declare you have not fulfilled your end of the agreement and will withdraw their protection."

"Exactly. If we're a bit late, they might let us off and hang around to see if we make it. Or they might show up, and if we're not there, they fuck off instantly," I said. "We just don't know. If they share the location with the Ændari Council? Give it a week at most, and they'll be here. Not 'here' in terms of the planet—I mean fucking *here*. You said that if they find her, and they will, then it's all over."

"And so you come seeking a change to our arrangement."

"No, actually." I smiled at him. "I didn't get access to the quest, so I don't have the exact wording in front of me, but I'm fairly sure it didn't specify a timescale, just that we had to kill all four, and provide the memory modules to you, along with blanks to copy. You also didn't specify that it was me who needed to kill them, right?"

"You seek to send others in your stead?"

"Yeah, basically," I said. "I'll send some of my team after them, have them kill the damn things, and they'll get to keep the corpses as well. One is dead. The blank memory units are here, their value in null coins is here, and we've even brought you the converter and second factory unit so that you can finally get a little luxury in your lives again."

"And the factory is programmed with food," Jonas added as Yeshin looked to be wavering.

"Food?"

"You did know it could produce food, right?" I pretended we'd always known that.

"Only the blandest of foods." He grunted. "Ingestible nutrition pastes…"

"Jonas?" I asked.

"Tested it myself on a burger. Couldn't tell the difference between the one it printed and Jay's own."

"You guys are in for a treat," I promised Yeshin, who sighed, then gestured that we were to follow him.

He'd met us at the bottom of the passage that led into their cavern, and we'd set the modules and everything else on the seafloor when we landed.

Now we had to move them by hand, he informed us, as the fewer possible disturbances to Tiamak the better.

I'd used gravitational manipulation to get it all down here, with the others mainly providing adjustments, and we all groaned at the sheer mass we needed to lug by hand.

The memory module was first, set up in the air-locked chamber where a handful of their precious tech devices had been installed already.

They were to provide the basic configuration, with the navigator, Diamos, providing the more complex overlays. Apparently, as a qualified and specialist navigator, he was used to being plugged into the ship, and although he'd reference the data that ship stored, it was his capabilities and his connection that the ship used to get wherever it was going.

We were hoping that as James had taken the Command path, just like Ingrid had, he'd be able to substitute for that. But as with the rest of the damn mission, this was going to be a botch-and-pray situation.

It took two hours to set up the baseline capabilities into the memory modules, as well as making sure that the system was stable and that it'd work with us, as this wasn't something we could try twice.

Yeshin was willing to distract Diamos once, to upload all that he knew to the modules, layering what he felt was needed into the spaces it held.

Once that was done, though, he'd not be disturbed again.

While the base systems were installing and being tweaked, though, that meant that Jonas, Scylla, and I got to lug the mass of stuff we'd brought with us into places around the cavern.

Once that was done, I assigned command privileges to Yeshin and his people on the factory and converter units, then finally started the basics to printing.

I thought of them as the basics, anyway.

A few minor luxuries, food that wasn't literal paste, seats that weren't fucked, and a series of parts that could be connected together to form much bigger living quarters for them all.

The biggest thing for them were heaters.

I'd noticed it before, that it was cold down there…not like "Oh my God, we're all going to die" levels of cold, thanks to the enhancements we had. But still, it was in the minus temps, and although we could survive it, it sure as shit wasn't comfortable.

The converters provided a little extra power, as they worked, and connecting them up to the hab chambers meant that they got that overflow of power. Then a simple space heater, little more than the kind of thing we'd have used in an office back home, and they were staring at it like I'd dumped luxuries they'd never dreamt of on their doorstep.

Diamos, when I was taken to him, along with the memory modules—they didn't dare waste the time to try to remove him and take him to the hab, if it was even possible—was in a hell of a state.

He'd been there for thousands of years, held in her embrace, the pair of them growing into one.

He was half subsumed into the wall of flesh that made up a fraction of Tiamak, with one of the group permanently dedicated to keeping him from being drawn deeper. I winced, seeing them working the edges of her flesh where they bonded to him, separating them like a chef removing the skin of a salmon from a steak.

It was insane. Literally, they were dedicated to cutting the flesh away at a speed that almost blurred, and they'd do this for an entire day at a time, before their replacement took over.

They didn't cut deeper, as the pair had suffered when they tried in the past. Although Yeshin had said that they "chose" not to risk things by removing him, looking at it, I honestly didn't see how it would have been possible.

As near as I could tell, they literally were bonded together, now—their nervous systems, flesh…all of it.

It was even freakier as his eyes flickered open at our arrival, because as he was, he looked like he should have been dead.

His armor was retracted, and yet he showed no signs of being uncomfortable. If anything, he looked like he was the most relaxed of all of us.

He half stood, half laid in the wall of her form. Where her side towered upward, vanishing behind the rock, he lay there, stuck a few feet up from the ground. It was as if he'd stepped back into Jell-O or something, and it was slowly eating its way up his exposed skin, flowing to cover him.

That was where they worked to keep him free, running their blades along the outside, trimming away the pseudopods that attempted to cover him and draw him deeper.

The back of his skull was lost, melded into her flesh, as were his hands and feet…and his crotch, which Yeshin had explained as a simple acceptance of reality.

Literally, with him being bonded to her like this, he no longer needed to worry about waste, it being taken from him by her internal connections.

As we approached, though, his eyes flickered open. At seeing the others, he blinked slowly, before focusing on us.

His eyes were weird, split into three separate irises—no clue why. They were joined in the eyeball but seemed to flow and shift as he looked from one of us to the next, before a slim, segmented nanite cable flowed up from just over his right temple.

It flashed forward, latching onto the memory module, even as the massive wall of flesh shivered slightly.

Yeshin and the others dropped everything, moving into position, hands pressed flat against Tiamak as they worked to calm her.

Clouds of silt floated free of the edges around the wall as a greater shiver ran through her flesh. The little group redoubled their efforts, as Diamos kept his strange eyes locked on mine.

Long seconds passed, and I could feel *something* at the edge of my mind. I opened myself to it, inviting him to link with me, to communicate, and yet there was nothing.

I sensed something there. The connection between him and the memory module was live, and linking to that, I could feel the data being written in, but there was…there was nothing of him that I could sense.

Minutes passed until abruptly he disconnected from the module. The small cable flashed back through the water to him, and his eyes closed immediately. Almost instantly, so did the shivering of Tiamak. Though the others remained pressed to her side for a few more minutes, Yeshin eventually stepped free and ordered half of the others to do so as well.

They did it slowly, each disconnecting separately, showing they'd done this an unfathomable number of times over the millennia, tempting her back to her rest, while others stayed, working hard.

"It is done," Yeshin told me, gesturing to the stack. "Take it and leave."

"Uh…thank you," I said slowly. "Is he okay?"

"He's gone," he said flatly, before shaking his head and sagging. "He's been gone a long time. All that's left… He was the greatest of the fist."

"The fist?"

"A unit of BWVs in the UC." It was the woman, and I realized again that she'd never introduced herself. I started to ask for her name, and she spoke on, ignoring me. "Diamos was the first fist. First in the fist below its commander. He led us, while the commander guided us all."

"Right," I muttered. "He was your sarge."

"Call it what you will," Yeshin said. "Regardless, your intrusion will leave Tiamak disturbed and on the edge of awakening for cycles to come. The leviathan is reset. That should give us a few years before it attacks anything again. It will return with the food given by the supplicants, and we will have a replacement module for it. See you do not leave the others to roam too long."

With that, he basically told us to fuck off, and the others left us, not one of them interested in talking to us.

That was fine by me, though. Gathering up the others, I headed for the surface with our new navigation system.

The swim wasn't as exciting as the one down had been. We had neither the wonderful, if terrifying experience of seeing the leviathan again, nor the fear that something might go wrong with the setup.

They'd accepted my compromise, as I'd hoped they would, and Cybele, when I'd explained what the guardians were, had been happy to take that quest on.

I didn't know whether my people would get the rewards, but it got the problem dealt with, and saved us some time.

That was the one thing there was never enough of. And by the time we reached the surface, we found that once again, we were waiting.

Well, we didn't just float around, our thumbs up our asses. I used my gravity manipulation to get us all aloft, and then we reformed our wings, taking turns to carry the navigation system, while I had an argument with Zac.

"The hell do you think!" he was roaring at someone when I finally managed to get him to connect. "Fuck's sake!"

"Zac…" I growled.

"Oh, for fuck's… Right, look, boss, we're on our way, all right? You wanted a spaceship built in a few goddamn days, okay? You know how hard that is to do?"

"I know you, Zac…you did it."

"Yeah, yeah, you're right, I did! I built it, now I'm trying to keep the fucker together while people are shooting at us, while James is literally learning to control the damn thing, and missiles are flying past us, and planes are buzzing us, and *did I mention we're being fucking shot at, you wanker!*"

"Zac," I said tightly. "Lock onto us and come get us. I'll take care of the rest."

"Yeah, you fucking better. You know that crazy bastard Courtney's on the roof? She's shooting modern fighter jets down *with a goddamn sniper rifle!* That's impossible. I *know* it's impossible, but she keeps goddamn doing it!"

"And what's Paul doing?" I asked distractedly, fearing the worst as I started to make connections from satellite to satellite.

"He's shaking his dick at them!" he howled. "Literally! He's on the roof, no pants on, and he's helicoptering his knob at them as they fly past!"

"Well, at least they'll die laughing," I muttered. "Right, I'm online. Get ready."

"Ready for what, you pommy bastard? You—"

I cut the connection.

I'd made it across literally thousands of miles, rerouting through half a dozen different satellites, and taking remote possession of a Spanish missile control platform, using it as the central point for my counterattack.

As I did that, I connected to our base at the recycling center, flashing through a dozen systems until I popped up on the computer that Petros was working on.

He had his tongue stuck out and held between his teeth as he fumbled his way through using the machine, and he nearly bit through it when I flashed up before him.

I barked out orders, then cut the connection, hoping he'd be able to do something, but knowing that really, it was up to me here and now.

Some of what Zac had said was insanely right, I had to admit. The ship was flying and being buzzed constantly by fighters. What looked to be half a carrier battlegroup was chasing it. And there, when I zoomed right in, were Paul and Court on the roof of the damn thing.

Courtney was firing fast enough it could pass for a full auto, despite it apparently being a modified sniper rifle as Zac had said.

And yeah, Paul had dropped his pants, the fucking lunatic.

The first stop was the ship that was in the middle of it all: a supercarrier that was moving very carefully, clearly encountering some shallow drafts and trying to avoid them.

Well, that was a relief.

The Hack sub-mind took an annoyingly long seventeen seconds to break into the military encryption it was using, then I barely got a tendril inside before they switched the link off, clearly having heard about this trick from the Egyptians.

It was too late, though, as I was in.

I connected to it, scanning the readings on the inside of the system. I set Tsunami loose into the main hub, flooding the ship with my own systems, rippling through firewalls, as the crew attempted to disconnect launchers.

I got enough control to do what I needed to, though. While they were frantically trying to stop me taking over its weapons systems, I instead went for the engines, activating the props on one side to full, and reversing the other.

The ship lurched to port. The forward anchor ripped free and plunged to the bottom of the sea, catching and swinging the ship around, before driving it into a submerged reef.

That was enough for me. I didn't want to kill them, but they were trying to kill my people, and if they managed to damage the ship, we were all fucked.

I saw a pair of missiles explode as they neared our ship. A blur took them out as Zac apparently got something online at last.

While he did that, and Courtney drove off the fighters, I started on the next ship in line. This time, I just released Contagion into their systems and moved on, the slowly replicating takeover of their systems hidden until it reached critical mass.

The advantage of using Contagion for this was that it spawned a copy, one that inserted itself into the nearest joined system. In this case, that was a small gunboat. Although there was a lot less that I could do with its systems, I could still kill its power, shutting everything down.

I leapt from system to system as Zac screamed at me to "Fuckin' do something," splitting off copies as I took more and more over: controlling missiles, anti-aircraft systems, CIWS. The world blurred for me as I kept going, Jonas and Scylla moving in to take turns. One started to carry the nav system, and the other essentially moved in behind me, guiding me with a gentle tap of their wings when I got too distracted, veering off course or starting to drift downward.

As soon as all the battlegroup were infected, I triggered the Contagion and Tsunami together, shutting half of the ships down. The other half twisted in the water, weapons locking onto one another instead of our ship.

I could have been killing the engines, the communications or their offensive systems, but the disadvantage of Contagion, as always, was that it worked slowly through the network, gobbling up section by section as the chance presented itself.

If the engine's management system on a ship was on the far side of the network, it took forever to reach it.

Over and over, I claimed wastewater management systems, media libraries, disciplinary files, and more.

Where I could, though, I shut their systems down with as little damage as possible.

When the ship was hit by a missile, though, and was nearly smashed from the skies, the gloves came off.

It was a German ship that had launched it. The joint task force that was flooding the Med and trying to cut off our people's escape had four frigates providing its heart, and although Zac had managed to cut down the others, one made it through.

The Exocet missile detonated just off the bow. A lucky hit from the single defensive system Zac had working had caught it, but too close.

Paul and Courtney barely held on, only managing it in the end thanks to the inhuman upgrade to BWVs they'd received. Zac and several others of the crew were thrown around the interior, slammed into bulkheads, and the ship started to roll. One side billowed smoke and orange, red, and yellow flames.

"STEVE!" Zac screamed, frantically trying to bring the ship around and stop her plowing into the ground, as I went nuclear.

Paul was yelling into the net as well, frantically trying to reach Courtney as she slowly slid farther and farther from him, closer and closer to falling over the side and hundreds of meters to the water far below.

The entire American task force that had been shut down by me over the last few minutes roared to life; targeting clusters locked onto the offending ship and launched over and over again.

Each ship emptied its magazines. Missile after missile flared to life, roaring into the sky and arcing around, heading inward toward the joint task group run by the NATO alliance.

Their masters knew who really ruled here, and I'd almost given up on finding them. Searches spammed into the various nets, then abandoned to either succeed or fail, as I battled over and over with the automated systems, before finally, wonderfully, the entire task force turned hard to port.

"STEVE!" came the scream again.

A wingtip smacked into the back of my head, making me blink and check my height, my course, my—

"STEVE, YOU FUCKING LUNATIC! STOP!" It was Jonas.

Arise :Explorer

Jonas landed on my back, smacking the back of my head and shouting into the command link. "THEY'RE TRYING TO SURRENDER!"

Chapter Seventeen

The NATO meeting had apparently been derailed entirely as a multitude of the Arisen trying to join our faction went to work "proving themselves" as Petros had ordered them to do.

They'd started pulling strings, making grisly threats and basically calling in all the favors they'd spent years building.

The result was that every single member of the NATO alliance was basically bombarded from all sides. Everything the Arisen had on them—from blackmail, sexual histories and bribes, promises of favors, outright threats, and everything in between—was used, and the great and powerful of the Western world crumbled like a child's sandcastle in the path of a tsunami.

I had to divert the missiles to prevent them taking half the fleet out. Some of them were close enough to use against each other, twisting them into each other's paths, taking several out in fiery explosions. But many were simply too well spaced, or too close to something that would be easily broken.

Like Europe.

In those situations, the missiles twisted on their course and locked onto a patch of uninhabited rock just off the north coast of Morrocco called Isla de Alboran.

I'd had literally three seconds to confirm it was uninhabited. As the first missiles hit, I finally got the results back from the search I'd loaded in, finding out that it was in fact a Spanish military post.

I'd scanned it from goddamn orbit, and it'd registered as a few dozen seabirds and basically that was it. Sod's law, two seconds later, I found reports that there were buried bunkers and more, finding that there may have been a few people on the island after all.

Cursing, I hoped that if there were many on the island, they'd been deep inside the tunnels. But considering the options were to do that or hit their original target?

It wasn't exactly a hard decision to make.

For a split second, I'd also considered doing like they did in the movies and plow the missiles into the sea.

The issue with that in the real world was that hitting the water at speed and from high up wasn't much different from hitting concrete. Most of the missiles would explode, sending masses of shrapnel, flaming debris, and more in all directions, massively wiping out the sea life. They'd end up damaging shipping or possibly even ricocheting off in new directions, sinking and not going off, triggering later and taking out ships, or have them hit land or sea that was in use.

I accepted that as the cost of saving my people.

Then I made it very clear to Petros that he was to take point on this, and make goddamn sure the leaders of NATO explained themselves, and didn't blame anyone else.

That was patently impossible, of course, but it gave him something useful to do, and it got the politicians off my back.

Zac had managed to keep the ship in the air even with the damage it'd taken, before turning it around and setting a course for the Great Refuge. We'd landed on it, then managed to get everyone inside.

That bit wasn't so hard, thanks to the goddamn hole in one of the main panels, but it certainly made an impression on the fleet that we then flew back over.

I'd basically ripped their internal systems apart in my frenzy to shut them down, and now almost the entire fleet was looking like a lot of dead ducks.

The sailors were all right, though, and they were out on the deck in their hundreds watching.

The ship, the yacht, the...? Dammit. We needed to come up with a goddamn name for it, but whatever we called it, the thing was a mess.

As Zac had said he would, he'd used the original base of the megayacht to make the ship triangular, although a long-ass one, wide in the middle and a flat backside.

Then we'd said it needed to be stealthy as all hell, even as a yacht, and powerful. So, he'd armored it up. He'd encased the outside in radar-deflecting paneling, then installed weapons hardpoints, upgrading the power systems, and essentially making it a wonder of technology.

Then, because there wasn't much going on, and Zac was basically a lazy bugger who needed to be kept busy...

We'd decided that we now needed to make it into a spaceship.

He'd worked a miracle with it, to be fair, smoothing a few sections out and essentially increasing some of the armoring, then he'd armored up the top layer.

Taking away little things like a railing and a deck to walk around on, or to sunbathe, and the goddamn pool that had been in the middle of the upper deck— seriously, you're on a seagoing yacht, you're surrounded by fuckin' water, and you put a pool in? No. Just... no.

I got the idea behind a whirlpool or something. That was for sexy time, no matter what bullshit people claimed. But a goddamn pool? A real *big-ass* Olympic-size swimming pool? Madness.

Anyway, the pool was gone, and in place of it was a section that was carved out and ready for the grav drive to be installed, then additional armoring to be layered over the top, sealing the ship up.

It was the lack of that armoring that had nearly killed everyone.

Entire sections of the ship were exposed to the air, or would be soon to vacuum. They were sealed away from the "secure" areas, but as Zac had said, he couldn't do everything, not in the time he had.

There were two stubby wings that extended from the rear, flaring out to hold the in-atmosphere engines, and the ion pulse engine was attached to the rear of the ship.

The grav drive would go into the middle of the ship, as it was going to be the thing that meant we either got home again or didn't. As it didn't need to be external, it'd be insane to risk it to random rocks and crap.

As it was, almost a full third of the ship was unarmored, and when the anti-aircraft missiles had gone off nearby, detonating and firing out masses of fléchettes in an attempt to shred it, it'd caused a huge amount of damage.

I made the situation very clear to Petros, once I was inside the ship, which was that we were on the verge of the planet being invaded and all life here destroyed, if we didn't get to the meeting on time and make nice—and right now, the ship we needed to do that in was a flying colander.

A *barely* flying colander.

He agreed to make the point very clear to the leaders of NATO and whoever had started the whole thing off, and I left it to him to do that. I knew damn well, having seen the sheer amount of damage that ran through the ship, the injuries that our crew had taken and more? If I was to do it myself, only abject groveling and blood in the place of apologies would be accepted.

They'd not only nearly killed my friends, but they'd almost removed any chance for the species to survive at the same time.

I was furious. I desperately wanted to fucking slaughter someone and bathe in their blood, and I damn well knew that most of the people involved had done what they saw as the right thing.

Sure, there'd no doubt been some asshole at the top of the food chain who'd panicked, or who had seen a chance for personal gain, and everyone else had been stuck carrying out the orders that they thought were to defend their families.

That meant that if I went along to the meetings with these fuckers, and one of them tried to bluff or bully their way through it? I was likely to murder them, publicly, and I really shouldn't do that.

Instead, Zac, Corey—who he'd drafted onto the ship—and I were frantically working to fix anything and everything we could. Jonas and Scylla were working with Corey to get the nav system installed. James was literally plugged into the ship and was keeping us going.

Casey was with us as well. She was currently working on the lower deck, performing a dozen integration tests that Zac hadn't had time to do yet. And I had no clue why, but that mad bastard Jay was even on board. Apparently, he'd ended up leaving some of his staff in charge back in the Sudan, and had been overseeing the food for the staff on the *Pacific Princess* refit.

Then, when the shit hit the fan, he'd dumped his chef tools into a bag and had boarded the ship with a huge handgun to help out.

He'd not been party to most of the conversations about where and what we were doing for a while—not because we didn't trust him, but...well, he ran the kitchens.

Not to say that good food wasn't important, it was insanely important, but the fucker was running the kitchens while we were dealing with interstellar politics and deep-sea guardians from fuckin' Atlantis.

So, he'd been out of the loop on where the ship was going, and what it was going to be doing. He'd just done what he always did, and had stepped up to help out.

Now that meant that he was lending a hand in the best way he could, considering we had no need for food at the minute, and was cleaning the masses of shrapnel, discarded ammunition, and general crap from the ship.

The next several hours as James limped us along, across the Mediterranean, over Turkey, then through the airspace of a lot of countries ending in "stan," were painful ones.

One of the systems that had been installed and tested—and was now a wonderful mess of shattered crispy fragments—was responsible for most of the damage to the ship, and of course, it was one of those really unimportant ones.

It was "just" the atmospheric systems.

Zac had been planning to unveil that he'd managed to get it done after all, and he'd even managed to have it pressurized—or it'd been in the process of doing that when something shredded the oxygen cylinder.

It was an emergency backup of the backup, considering a converter could literally make more air if we needed it, but this was him trying to make sure we were covered by installing it anyway. Then it'd exploded and taken out the entire system.

The area around it had been blown outward, and that had caused the ship to buck like a two a.m. drunken hookup, nearly throwing Courtney off the side.

It was a miracle that she'd managed to hang on at all. But she'd lost her rifle in the process, and she was clearly ready to commit murder as she stalked the length of the ship, cursing anyone and everyone.

Five hours in total it took us from when we boarded the ship, despite the actual top speed being far higher. But that meant that by the time we finally landed at the Great Refuge, they were ready for us.

Freja was alive, and as much as we automatically believed that when you wake from a coma or some kind of serious injury you should be exhausted and worn out, as she'd been literally regrown from a fragment…she was anything but.

Instead, she was ruling the roost. The remaining Elders had all started the ascension process, and those who were up and running, and Cybele, had agreed to do anything they could to help.

Freja and Anders were making the most of this, as was Ingrid, although I noticed the three all stayed remarkably close together.

They'd gotten a team, and the grav drive was already making its way through the bowels of the old refuge, ready to reach the ship, while others raced about doing whatever we needed as quickly as possible.

Somehow Zac had found the time to get us a medical facility aboard the ship as well, with a tube already in position. Zac had looted it from Facility #6B, just in case.

Almost as soon as we'd landed, the ship was practically swarmed by helpers, and that included people carrying everything that Ingrid had decided we needed.

Fortunately, she'd not gone quite as overboard as she had when we'd gone to Russia and she'd basically packed the kitchen sink. What she'd done instead was arrange a fuckload of high-tech scrap to be loaded aboard, ready to be broken down in the converters into usable null coins.

Two of the custodians we'd brought to the valley were requisitioned for the ship, and the larger-scale spiderbots that were in the valley already were all waiting as well. The damaged armoring sections were torn free, and the systems that were fucked were just ripped out.

Over a hundred people raced at the ship with everything from grinders to portable laser cutters, welding torches and buckets—literally—of nanites.

Two hours was all we had, and we made the absolute most of it.

James had stayed connected to the ship, and as soon as the nav system was plugged in, and Corey made sure he could access it, he'd dived right in.

He soon found that the information was off—a little, anyway.

Some of the systems didn't match what we had already, others were out of alignment, but with the galactic coordinates home systems to use as reference, the rest could be figured out.

That meant that when the drive was carried about, the massive spiderbots lowering it into place, as Zac and his team worked to connect it all, I was working alongside them.

I'd basically stopped long enough to kiss Ingrid, to hold her mother and tell her how goddamn relieved I was to see her, and to get a hug from Anders—which, again, was weird, considering my family dynamics, but was also kinda nice.

Then I'd been ordered back into the bowels of the ship, and back to work.

The drive was powered, tested, and then the next thing I knew was Ingrid kicking the bottom of my boot.

I was on my back, half under the drive at that point, testing connections and replacing ones that were failing from my own nanites stores.

That was what I'd found to be the quickest way of doing it, when I was surprised by the sudden pain. I kept working, thinking someone just stood on my foot, passing by and hadn't seen me under it, when she kicked me again.

"What?" I snapped.

"Get out here!" She sighed. "Seriously, Steve, it's taken me ten minutes to get down to you, and we've got no time for this."

"What?" I grunted, confused to buggery as I inched my way back out from under the drive.

I was even more confused to find that the ship was shaking as I made it out.

"We're moving?" I asked her blankly.

"You shut down your link," she accused me. "None of us could find you, and you almost gave me a heart attack!"

"I was…" I gestured behind me as I clambered to my feet, feeling the ache of being in a stupid position for too long as I twisted my back, filling the air with a series of pops and clicks. "What did I miss?"

"The meeting," she said flatly. "We knew you were alive, and Zac said that someone was in here fixing things, so we decided not to disturb you."

"Okay, so what was the meeting?" I asked, a little annoyed that they'd had one without me, but also really thankful that, well, they'd had the meeting without me.

"We're on our way," she said.

"Where?"

"To the rendezvous." A sudden smile broke out, and she seemed to relax for the first time in days. "Steve, we're only eight hours out from where we need to be!"

"They…it's that close?" My mind whirled.

"No, it's four systems over, at the edge of an exclusion zone, but we're going to make it!"

"It was that close all along?" I tried to get my head around it.

"It's not close, not if you think of the distances involved," she assured me. "But in galactic terms, it's close enough that we'll be outside of the exclusion zone and therefore they can meet us."

"I… Fuck, now I wish I was in the meeting. This makes no sense to me," I muttered.

"Okay, let's go back." She smiled, resting her hands on my forearms and squeezing gently. "So, James managed to integrate the navigation system. It's out of date, and a lot of the details are missing—like a *lot* of them—but there's enough to be able to plot out what we think is the correct location.

"Using that, we can jump out of our solar system and into the next nearest. We don't have very good scanners, so we're limited in the jumps we can make, but we can jump just a short distance, search the area, and then jump again."

"And it'll take eight hours to get to the contact point?" I asked.

"It's the grav drive," she explained. "It's crazily powerful technology, but it has a flaw. As powerful as it is, it needs a lot of power if it's too close to a gravity point."

"Like a planet?"

"Exactly," she agreed. "It means we either need to jump directly to the Lagrange point and then fly in from there, which will take most of the time we will be travelling, or we need to be able to power it up a lot more to overcome the gravity ripples that it'd cause otherwise."

"And the Lagrange point is…?" I asked, confused.

"It's, oh gods, I don't know if I can fully explain it. It's like a safe zone? It's where the gravitational pull of Earth and the sun, as an example, equal each other out.

"Think of it as a point that there's no gravity. It's not halfway between Earth and the sun, because the sun is so much more massive than Earth, but if they were both the same size and density they would be."

"Okay, so a gravitational null zone between two points." I nodded. "Makes sense. I deal with gravity all the time, so what's the issue?"

"Ah, okay…well, when we jump into a system, the gravity drive opens a rift that we slip through, and when we pop out of the other side, the local gravity field changes the angle, speed, and condition of the vessel as we appear."

"So if we're too close to a world, we might get compressed to the size of a pea and fired out in a random direction away from the gravity zone, unless we've got a hell of a lot of power to even out the local field," I guessed.

"Steve, you're definitely getting smarter," Ingrid said after a few seconds of staring at me. "I'm sorry, and you know that I love you, so this isn't me being belittling, but when we first met, you'd have never understood that. And now, with the most basic details explained by me, someone who doesn't fully understand it? You grasped it in seconds. James had to explain it three different ways to get some of the group to get that."

"I deal with gravity a lot," I explained again and shrugged. "Right, so we're picking a location in the system, then figuring out the nearest area to the Lagrange points and where we want to be? Then we jump to that?"

"Essentially, yes." Ingrid sighed. "That's the plan anyway."

"What about the sensors?" I asked.

"The ones we have are a little better than Earth's, but that's all," she admitted. "None of the engineers have any points left, and nobody invested in that line so we have only the most basic designs, as well as no time to invest in earning more."

"Shite."

"Exactly." She smiled.

"So…okay, so we're moving, and we can make it on time?" I asked her again.

"We can, if we can get the gravity drive to work out okay."

"And if not?"

"Well, you know better than me, but there's a chance that the rift collapses and we're converted into pure energy, then spat out into regular space."

"So, not a good thing then," I quipped, before sighing and scrubbing at my face. "Okay, so now what?"

"We talked, and considering the options, I made the call to just go," she said. "Mor and Far stayed behind. They're getting Dimi to take them back to the Sudan. The family is being flown in, those who weren't there already."

"I didn't even see any of them when we were there," I muttered. "Hell, we were there for…"

"We were working and trying to get everything on track to save the planet and the species," she assured me. "I saw my sister, and I explained everything. Believe me, she's desperate to see our parents, but beyond that she's okay. Oh, and she's terrified that she's never going to see us again, so we need to return soon."

"Okay, but we took off?"

"We did." She nodded, before pausing. "You don't mind that I made that call without discussing it, do you?"

"No," I said hurriedly. "God no, sorry, no. What I mean is I didn't even notice, fuck's sake."

"You were connecting an alien gravity drive to a spaceship, with half of the ship either on fire, damaged, or still under construction. I can forgive you for being distracted." She smiled. "So, yes, though, we took off. Most of the old crew stayed on, and by crew I mean that Zac and Casey are onboard as engineering and general steward duties. James is the pilot. Jonas, Scylla, Paul, Courtney, and Oxus are our security team, along with you of course. Jay wrangled his way aboard the ship when Zac was leaving, and considering we would need food at some point…also, he was desperate to be the first interstellar chef…he's aboard too. Then there's Belle and me. That's it."

"That all of us?" I asked, a little surprised.

"It is. There was that Scotsman Macleod, as well…he and Kat were with us in the assault on the ship?"

"Yeah, I remember him."

"Well, he wanted to come as well. He said something about not trusting the fate of the galaxy to a sassenach…" She paused, grinning as I winced at that. Every instinct in me rebelled against being lumped in by a Scotsman as "just another Englishman" before she went on. "But considering the team we already had with us, there wasn't much need for another member of the security team. If anything, we're ridiculously short of any kind of scientific personnel, especially for this to be the first modern starship populated by free humans to leave the solar system."

"You want to swing past NASA and grab someone at random?" I suggested, half joking.

"Honestly, I feel like we should," she said after a brief pause. "Well, not that we *should*, I mean, we'd have to ascend them for a start, and then we'd need to teach them how to do…well, everything, I guess. Then they'd be pestering us all the time to check out things, when we're needing to do things for the mission and ignore all that, and—"

I laughed, kissing her to stop her runaway mind, and hugging her close. "I love you."

"Thank you, I think?" she replied. "I mean, I love you too, but why are you laughing? These are perfectly reasonable concerns…"

"Of course they are," I agreed, trying to stifle my amusement. "Seriously, though, can you imagine it? We just zip over to NASA central or Cape whatsit or wherever, then land, still probably trailing smoke and having clearly been attacked, then rock out and shout that we want a volunteer to explore the cosmos?"

"Ah…" She winced.

"Or were you just planning that we grab the first person we see and abduct them?" I suggested, loving the mental image. "I mean, we'd need to make sure we don't get the delivery dude who's just there to drop off the local coffee shop order or whatever, but I suppose they'd be happy still. We'd just need to hold back on the anal probing."

"The *what?*" She snorted, the comment having made its way through the mass of imagery.

"Anal probing. That's what all the Americans get when they're abducted, right? You never noticed that it's not as common in Europe? When Americans get abducted and taken into space, they're all 'gotta tell the world about the aliens fingerin' ma bum.'" I said the last in a terrible redneck impression.

"Oh gods, I never noticed that!" She gasped, covering her mouth and laughing. "It's true! Every program, they'll go on about that, and yet when it happens in Europe…"

"There's no anal." I nodded, then waggled my hand left and right. "Well, none in the alien abductions anyway…"

"Hush." She shook her head. "Seriously, though, why is that?"

"Repressed." I sighed. "All those poor Americans who are so repressed they think that if you've got a healthy sex life, you're insane."

"And the anal?"

"Probably so relieved that nothing they do is going to be believed that they're grabbing the poor aliens," I suggested, grinning. "You know, here's poor Zorg, diplomat for his race, here to make peaceful contact, and the first American he meets sexually assaults him, screaming about bum-fun."

"And then they leave as fast as they can and never come back." She sighed. "It makes sense, really. I wonder if there's a culture out there warning aliens about visiting…"

"If so, that'd explain a lot as well. It'd mean only the alien perverts come here now."

We both looked at each other and grinned, imagining a world where that was real, instead of the damn lunatic mess that we knew was the cosmos so far.

"Are you done?" She nodded back to the drive. "There's a lot more to…"

"Dammit, no. Sorry, I'll be about another ten minutes." I groaned. "I'll go as quick as I can, but you…"

"But you can't rush this," she agreed. "It's fine. We're currently hovering in the atmosphere. Zac's doing tests on the ship, says we'll be entering 'real' space in about half an hour."

"I'll be there," I assured her, getting one last kiss, before dropping back down on the floor and sliding myself under the drive.

I'd have loved to use my gravity ability, simply make myself weightless and slide in and out instead of crawling, but I couldn't help but feel creating gravity disturbances around a machine designed to do that on a grand scale would be a mistake.

<u>Chapter Eighteen</u>

It took me nearly twenty minutes in the end, and the final connection was made by tentacle at a bloody stupid angle around a corner and down under the bracing.

Eventually, though, as I dragged myself out from under it, I was done, and I could actually breathe a little. I'd forgotten how much I didn't like enclosed spaces until I'd had to wedge myself into one again.

Looking around the ship, as I set off walking, I finally took the time to do what I'd not before now, and pay a little attention to the details.

The ship had obviously been rebuilt, considering the heavy armor plating overhead certainly didn't match with the individual ornate tiling around the walls of the former swimming pool. Where the door led out into the passage from there, the décor changed again. Turning right, I had to assume were "working" areas of the ship, being all grey metal, with the pipework looking more like something I'd seen when serving in the army.

I'd only been on a single warship, and it was for a short time when we were being cross-loaded and the helo was being refueled, but damn, the navy lived and worked in almost no space, compared to the size of their warships.

That was true here as well, where walking along at just over seven feet, I was seriously at risk of getting a crick in my neck. As soon as I left that passage and entered the main command deck?

It was massively different.

The wheelhouse, or bridge or whatever they called it, was at least twice the size that I'd seen on my last "visit" to the megayacht. The front of the room was sloped, starting at about five feet from the ground to angle backward toward the rear, topping out at about fifteen feet, with two rows of stations at the back.

The pilot's position at the front was taken, with James on his back in a small, enclosed acceleration couch. His eyes were shut and he appeared fast asleep.

Behind him, the room extended out in an arc, with half a dozen more stations in various stages of completion.

Behind James's apparent napping station, there were three rows of seats, two abreast with screens attached to the armrest, looking like a cross between airline seats and a pilot's chair in a fighter.

They definitely didn't look comfortable, but they were functional, with the same bands that enclosed and restrained James currently peeking out from the edges.

I nodded to myself, realizing that made sense. The acceleration couch that James was currently lying in had been clear to me as soon as I'd seen it, despite me having never seen one before. It was from the engineering data I had, a logical system that was best in place for a pilot to ensure that even if the gravity failed or something happened, they were locked in place and could respond.

The seats down the middle? They were for whoever needed to be up here, with one for the ship's commander, clearly. That seat had controls on the arms, but only a few. This was a testbed, after all. There was no real need for the captain or commander or whatever to press buttons when they could reach out to the ship's systems mentally.

Overall, the bridge looked fairly cool, but it was also a mess. Zac was nowhere in sight, but the others were, with Jonas and Paul arguing over data connections for what looked to be curved monitors to be attached to the seats on movable arms.

It looked as if they'd raided a computer warehouse and had stolen everything they could, with readily identifiable packaging strewn around the room.

"The hell would I know?" Jonas was snarling. "It's a damn cable—stick it in the screen, and the other end into the ship!"

"It doesn't match!" Paul growled back, shaking the cable at his boss. "See this? It's square, or mostly…flat on one side anyway. That hole? It's not!"

"Just jam it in!" Jonas snapped.

"It doesn't work like that!" Paul roared. "If I ram it in, it'll never do the job! It needs to be the right fit!"

"That's what she said!" I added happily, unable to help myself.

"Oh, for fuck's sake, now the idiot's here." Paul swore, throwing his arms up.

"Well hello to you too," I replied, not taking any offense.

"Oh shit," Paul muttered when he twisted around and saw me. "Uh, sorry, boss. Usually when someone says shit like that, it's Dave."

"Yeah, I couldn't help it," I admitted. "So, what's the problem?"

"This…" He waved the cable at me.

I moved over, checking the end and the connection, then nodded and pulled the other end of the cable up, checking that one…then extruding a blade and hacking one end off.

I formed a blob of nanites over the end, stuck it into the back of the screen and ordered it to join the cable and the screen, before nodding in satisfaction at how easy it was.

"What the hell was that?" He glared at me.

"Nanites. You just need to—"

"You mean use *my* nanites to fix that wanker Zac's fuck-up?" he asked after a few seconds, shaking his head. "We're low on them, and I need these fuckers."

"More than you think we need to be able to see where we're going?" I asked.

"I…ah, dammit."

"Exactly." I reached out, easily making contact with Ingrid, who was in the engineering section with Zac, looping him in as the pair were checking on some of the secondary systems. "What's happening?" I asked her.

"We're making sure it's all good," she said. "Zac found a leak. It's sorted now, but we were losing air. I asked Jonas and Paul to set up the monitors on the bridge…"

"I'm here now," I said. "They're fighting with connections."

"The HDMI and so on?" Zac asked, and I nodded, despite him being unable to see me. "Tell them there's two boxes of damn cables, just find the right ones!"

"And don't let them waste their nanites on botching together a fix," Ingrid said quickly. "We need them, and there's plenty of cables if they just bother to look."

"Of course," I agreed quickly. "I'll sort it out."

"I'll be up there in a few minutes," Ingrid said as I disconnected, turning and glancing around the room.

By now, Paul had moved onto another pile of monitors, and clearly being a tidy worker, he was basically ripping the boxes apart in his hands, tearing the polystyrene into sections and tossing them about.

I got it; he was glorying in how much stronger he was now than ever before, but fuck me.

Tiny bits of polystyrene were floating around, torn bits of cardboard everywhere, including…a manual—literally an instruction manual, tossed over a shoulder—that was now draped across James's face.

I sighed, plucking that off him, and getting a mental "thank you" sent over, as I turned and regarded the room.

Paul and Jonas, between them, had turned the room into a bomb site in the last few minutes. Shredded packaging was mainly confined to Paul's side, but the boxes tossed aside on Jonas's made it clear he wasn't thinking either.

"Guys," I said firmly. "If Ingrid, Courtney, or Scylla walk in here right now? We're all getting the blame for this mess." And it was true. I knew that instinctively, despite the fact that I'd had nothing to do with it. Being this close to a mess and male meant I was getting the blame as well.

"Ah… I'll be right back…" Paul muttered, seeming to see the mess he'd made for the first time. "Just gonna hit the head and—"

"Stop right there, goddammit, Paul!" Jonas roared as Paul raced for the nearest door. "Every damn time!"

"What?" I asked, stunned at how fast the bugger had vanished.

"I'm gonna kill him," Jonas started, heading for the exit, just as I heard the approaching sound of footsteps from another direction.

"Oh, hell no!"

The words were barely out of my mouth as three things happened at once. First, Jonas made it out of the door and vanished. Second, Courtney and Ingrid arrived. And third, a random blast of air tore through the bridge from somewhere deeper in the ship as a seal gave way.

That meant that not only was I alone in the middle of a sudden absolute mess, but the shredded cardboard, instruction manuals, and polystyrene were raining down across the bridge as the ladies entered.

"Fuck," I muttered. The looks on Ingrid and Courtney's faces were almost identical as they latched onto the only target in the room, considering that James was interfaced with the ship…and was currently wearing another manual again. "This isn't what it looks like," I tried to explain, before cursing as I got a burst of laughter sent to me from both Jonas and Paul.

I'd been set up! I realized it just as the ladies started to harangue me, while picking up the mess and complaining that I should know better.

"I'm going to kill you both," I sent to the laughing pair, who were no doubt hiding out of sight somewhere, watching through some ship's systems.

"Payback's a bitch," was all I got from Paul, and I cursed again, not even knowing what I'd done this time around, but knowing damn well that they'd started something.

The next few minutes as Zac worked on fixing the faulty seal deeper in the ship were a mix of me tidying, the ladies listening to me cursing Paul and Jonas, and then finally, as all the boxes were tidied up…the pair reentering the room as if nothing had happened.

"Where were you two?" Ingrid asked them suspiciously.

"We went for a drink," Jonas said.

"The head," Paul said at the same time. The pair hesitated, then exchanged a long look.

"The head," Jonas agreed.

"A drink," Paul corrected.

"And now we see the truth." Courtney sighed. "Okay, you deal with that one, I'll deal with my idiot." With that, she grabbed Paul by the ear, twisted, and dragged him to the side to apparently have a word.

Ingrid looked at me, then Jonas, and shook her head. "You two sort this out. Jonas, you're too old, and I thought too responsible to be doing something so childish. And Steve? Next time, *explain.*"

"I—" I shook my head as another blast of air burst loose from deeper in the ship, hurrying to deal with that as I reflected on the fact that I *had* tried to explain it, and they'd both ignored it.

"Sorry, boss," Jonas muttered as I passed him.

"No you're not, you dick," I replied, but I couldn't help but smile. I jogged down the passage, following the roar of escaping air as a sudden lightness made it clear that James was lowering the ship again into the atmosphere.

Half an hour later, and I was in the engineering section, behind our quarters apparently—which was a little weird, considering I'd be in my bedroom on the other side of the wall I was currently leaning against, and Zac's office was this close to it—but regardless…

Zac, Casey, and I watched a marker on the wall, and as it stayed steady for a seeming eternity as the clock counted down…we breathed a sigh of relief.

We'd finally gotten all the leaks, and now there was no noticeable outgassing.

The systems we had meant that we'd be able to create more air if we needed it, but leaving the atmosphere without knowing for sure that we were secure was just stupid on so many different levels.

"You're going in the tub," Zac said flatly, turning to look at Casey, who sighed and rolled her eyes.

"Seriously, I can wait, honey," she tried, as he stood, dragging her to her feet.

"The damn ship's secure, we're on our way, and there's no end of shite that can go wrong out here. If you die as you are, you're gone, that's it. Get you in the tub an' fixed up? You'll get over it."

"Steve…" she started. "Honestly, I don't need to…"

"You do," I said firmly. "Ingrid agreed with you coming on the condition that you ascended. If you don't want to do that now? We need to go back and drop you off."

"I don't want to waste the ascension, or the nanites," she admitted. "Do I want it? Of course I do. But I'm no engineer, and I'm no soldier, so…"

"So you take Support and see what you end up with," I said. "The system matches you. Support doesn't mean just engineering. When I unlocked the 'real' system, there were literally millions of options there. There's got to be something that seems appropriate to you. And if there isn't? At least we can resurrect you."

"An' I'm not losing you," Zac said. "I love you, an' you agreed to this, so get your pretty little ass in there."

She smiled at him, nodded to me, then headed to the medical suite a few rooms down, before Zac paused by my side, eyeing me.

"You want to ask Ingrid to come and set her up?" he suggested. "You know, considering she's my wife and she's going to be naked in there and all?"

"Crap. Yes, sorry." I facepalmed, having not even thought about it. "I'll send her."

I turned, heading back along the passage, passing several closed doors, including the one to our quarters, and a stairway to the next level down.

The babble of voices that rose from there told me that Paul, Courtney, Belle, and Oxus were down there at least. Making it to the bridge, I found that Scylla must have been as well, considering that besides Ingrid in the command chair and James in the pilot's couch, only Jonas was left, staring wide-eyed at the sight of Earth below us, slowly rotating in all its blue, green, and brown glory.

"It's beautiful, isn't it," Ingrid said softly as I moved to join her, standing and staring out over the silent world so far below.

"You are," I agreed, kissing her and taking her in my arms, before shifting back to stare out across the world below.

Ingrid hurried to the medical suite as soon as I explained the situation. Despite not really needing to be there physically, she went for moral support for Casey, and half an hour later as the final tests were completed, she returned.

Then, for the first time in recorded human history, an Earth-built starship turned from the Earth, heading for the nearest Lagrange point and deep space.

The first gravity jump was a hell of an experience, there was no doubt. We'd agreed that we needed to leave it all down to James—he was the pilot, after all—but as he'd powered the jump, gravity around the ship twisting to form a tunnel, I'd felt such echoes as I couldn't believe.

The jump—as that was the best way to describe it, we'd decided, warp and so on just feeling wrong—was almost instantaneous. Almost.

It was a weird experience. I'd triggered my time compression and accelerated senses as we did it, reaching out to see the space around us with my gravity senses, and what I'd seen had left me amazed.

An actual tunnel formed, starting with gravity like a blank, flat sheet before us, hanging there in space. Then it dimpled, dipping deeper in the center, before seeming to fall away before us, sucking us into the sudden vortex.

Walls formed in the tunnel on either side as time seemed to freeze. Our ship dove beyond its reach, entering a bubble of twisted space that sank, then was buoyed back up as the energy invested into the drive ran out.

It was like a bubble under the sea then: flashing back out, seeming almost random in the way it slipped left and right, heading for the surface.

As it went, though, I felt…I felt others out there. Things that moved, senses that brushed against the bubble, and I couldn't decide what they were.

I knew I should be terrified, as I sensed massive forms that slid past us. Some of them were clearly organic. And the fact that there was anything that could naturally generate gravity fields, let alone be big enough to fucking be felt through the slipstream like this?

It should have terrified me. Instead, I gloried in it.

The minds that I sensed distantly didn't feel antagonistic; they didn't feel aggressive or threatening. They felt like…they felt curious and almost bemused, like a whale in the ocean as a minnow flashed past an eye.

It noticed us; it saw that we were there, and it knew that it could inhale and end us…but it chose not to. It had no reason to—it simply existed.

I had no better way to explain it beyond that, but as we rose, the sensations that I felt out there were incredible.

As we burst back into normal space? For a few seconds as the gravity field around us dissipated, I could feel *everything:* The planets. The star we orbited. Asteroids. Meteors. And even weird resonances here and there.

It faded away in literal seconds, but damn, I knew what it felt like to be a god for that short period.

I also felt the way that nearby things, such as small rocks and random debris, dust, and, well, space shite, was shoved aside by the bubble, meaning that we appeared in a safe patch of space.

"We made it!" Ingrid cried, and all around us—from deeper in the ship to James slumped, seemingly unaware—people celebrated.

"The first time we've left the system," Jonas whispered, shaking his head slowly, tears clear in his eyes as we all stared at the red dwarf of Proxima Centauri. "The first humans to make it out of the damn system without being carried."

"We used their tech," I said softly.

"We stole their fucking tech," he corrected. "Those Ændari took our ancestors out by force, they conscripted them, and now we're free."

"That we are, my friend," I said, as the others came up onto the bridge, staring out in wonder at the system that was revealed before us.

There were three planets that we'd managed to pick up already. According to the nav system data we'd gained from Diamos, there were at least two more worlds here, but they were all small, dull and lifeless.

I wanted to explore. Damn, I wanted to do a flyby around the system or something, to find out what those resonances were at least, but I forced myself to sit back.

I was in the command chair, Ingrid having insisted, and I spoke loudly to everyone as they stared out at the tiny star in the distance.

"Okay, everyone, back to your positions, please."

"But—"

I didn't even bother to pay attention to the plea, knowing that we were all feeling the same way.

"We can't," I said. "James, check the local area, and as far out as you can sense. Make sure the readings we have are correct, then plot the next jump. We've got a chance to be on time here, and that's something we nearly lost. Let's not waste it."

There was some grumbling, but they all knew what had to be done. Although a few people snagged seats on the bridge, the rest moved back to their quarters or the secure areas below.

The next few jumps were small—gathering data, making damn sure that what we thought we were sensing out there was real—and then another full system jump, leaving Proxima behind.

This time, rather than a jump where we seemed to barely enter the bubble, popping out at the next closest Lagrange point a heartbeat later, we went deeper, heading for the next star.

The joy of the navigational system became clear as we jumped from system to system, seeming to leap back and forth as we built up a picture of the local area.

James had tried to explain it to Ingrid and me, and although we both understood different parts of the explanation, neither of us understood it all.

For me, terms like "precession" and "Parallax" meant nothing, and for Ingrid, the gravitational brane pattern meant even less.

James, in selecting the Navigational option and investing every point he'd apparently been hoarding in that, was learning at an insane rate. He'd selected Engineering as his first option, using it to accrue a load of "easy" points from the simple starter quests, but each one he'd spent had been in stellar navigation, piloting, and systems integration.

When he'd made it out of the system, with him flying the ship, he'd gained a handful of points as a bonus, and then from there, he'd invested even more as he accepted quests to "explore the local area."

He'd jumped us to the bare minimum needed to get the quest completed and to be able to unlock more advanced sensors and integration capabilities.

Then he'd input their design into the factory unit we had in the belly of the ship, with Zac working feverishly to rebuild the ship with each system he unlocked.

We hit Barnard's Star; then Wolf 359 and Gliese 65; then Ross 154, followed by 248; Ran and then 61 Cygni, before we stopped, unable to put it off any longer.

We'd found that the main issue was the distance. The farther out we needed to jump, the more risk there was of something going seriously wrong. Not only were there a number of systems in the navigation data that were blank, but also an equal number of systems that had any data. And among the systems with actual data, the data was frequently wrong.

That might not mean much when it comes to certain things, but a minor detail was that if we were to enter the system too close to a major gravitational source, and with the systems still essentially powering up, we'd end up emerging as various forms of energy.

Basically, we'd enter as people and exit as hard radiation, and that was going to ruin my goddamn day.

That meant that we needed to jump, recharge the drive, jump again, and again, and again, each time repeating the process and scanning the system as best we could, making damn sure that what we thought was there, was right.

Each time we emerged and found a planet or a moon where it shouldn't be, we realized all over again just how lucky we were to be alive.

We'd done it around small jumps because it got us data, and it unlocked James's points and skills, getting him better at his job, but also, it helped me.

I was finding that the sensing of the system we were jumping into was as much art as it was science. Although I didn't understand a freaky amount of the shite that was being referenced by James, I did know what I was feeling.

After about the fifth jump, I reached out to him, unable to put the feelings into words, and instead shared what I was sensing.

He did the same, reaching out and laying his—and the ship's—records over mine. They highlighted a load of shared details, and we were both missing sections as well.

The next few jumps grew more and more accurate, factoring in the readings we got, and then in the end, running the ship's sensors through me, with Ingrid tying James and me together to share it all at a subliminal level.

That was enough, we decided, making a final jump out at the edge of the system, where the interstellar medium and the solar system balanced each other out.

It was a last test, to make sure we were ready for the big jump, and it was nearly our undoing. We came out into what *had* to be an uncharted asteroid belt.

"What the hell!" I cried, eyes flashing open a split second before we emerged, the tunnel collapsing as we did.

James felt the field shivering around us as well, and frantically triggered a second jump, desperately trying to dive us out.

The ship was hit from all sides—booms echoing, explosive outgassing making those of us without armor equipped wince.

All throughout the ship, the emergency bulkheads slammed shut, trying to prevent a total loss. I frantically stared, reaching out with my capabilities and finding them woefully weak compared to the strength I'd need.

"STOP!" James ordered me.

The desperate order, the need, overrode me as I'd started trying to form a gravity field around us, shoving back at the incoming masses.

I hesitated, then collapsed the field I'd been forming, trusting him, but reaching out blindly, grabbing Ingrid's hand and squeezing it tight…as the drive triggered and we dove back into the brane.

Arise :Explorer

A heartbeat, two at most—my time compression was still spinning up—and then we were out. Space around us exploded in violence as sections of massive asteroids, down to fragmentary space dust and pulverized who-knew-what was flung outward in all directions.

"What the hell just happened!?" I shouted, reaching out to the ship. I pulled up a mass of errors, of failures, warnings, possible brownouts in the damn power systems, and worst of all, the warnings that an absolute fuckload of targeting sensors and weapons systems were locked in on us, as a warship off our starboard bow opened fire.

Chapter Nineteen

"We are so fucked."

It was a few minutes later. The firing had ceased, but those were the first words out of my mouth as we stared out at the warship that hung in the cold of space ahead of us.

"Don't get paranoid," Ingrid said softly, but her tone told me she felt exactly the same as I did. And the fact that our ship was in a wild roll that brought their ship into view every few seconds really wasn't helping.

"Just because they're all out to get you doesn't mean you're paranoid," I muttered, before shaking my head. "Gods, I wish we'd had the chance to get the damn coffee machine set up."

"Me too," James called from the piloting couch, and I nodded. He was "awake" now, having given up on trying to stop the spin as Zac worked on fixes.

Unlike the first dozen or so jumps, where they'd been terrifying, then exciting, then growing steadily more boring, this one, into a settled system, was done with an absolutely packed bridge.

When we'd finally arrived at the rendezvous coordinates—twenty minutes ahead of what we thought was the agreed time—we nearly shit ourselves over the massive, battered warship waiting for us.

What made it worse, from both sides' point of view, was that our emergency jump from the edge of the system meant that as the hole opened, not only had we dove down it, panicked, streaming atmo and having taken a hell of a lot of damage, but the gravity "bubble" had included everything that was in too close to us.

That'd included a fuckload of rock and debris. And then, with the return to normal space?

Instead of "sucking in" as the gravity field did on entering the brane, it pushed out. That'd basically fired the equivalent of a giant shotgun loaded with fragments of asteroids in all directions.

One of those directions being filled with a UC warship, that had been waiting for us to arrive.

Spoiler alert: They weren't happy.

Their warship, their leader would later explain, was already ready to defend itself, unsure whether we were genuinely coming to make peaceful contact, or whether it was all a trick. Then they'd detected something incoming, emerging far too close to them, before they were bombarded by asteroids, rocks, and dust.

They'd opened fire, scouring their immediate area clean, before hesitating. The commander spotted that instead of attacking them and using the debris as a distraction or cover, our ship was rolling furiously, at least two sections were heavily damaged, outgassing and adding to a roll that had been started by an impact.

The warship they'd been expecting?

They'd been told to expect one of their own class—ancient, but hopefully intact, and possibly even possessing tech that'd been lost since the fall.

Instead, a ship that was roughly the same size as one of their assault landing craft had exploded out of a jump, sending rock, atmosphere, and devastation in all directions.

They'd almost opened fire on us instinctively, and then again when they registered the wildly fluctuating energy levels from our drive.

By the time one of our rear engines exploded?

They'd made their decision.

Tractor beams lashed out and locked onto us. The immediate roll arrested, and a laser carved the remaining engine free in a terrifying display of accuracy. Once it was released from the hull, the tractor beam dragged us clear, and the ship moved back before blowing the remaining engine into tiny pieces.

We received a message then, one that we had to work to translate, as it was being sent in what my armor identified as a variant of Ændari, and it wasn't exactly a reassuring one.

Unknown vessel, stand down.

You have entered a confirmed quarantine zone. Prepare for boarding and identity confirmation.

That was it. Not so much as a "Hi, welcome to the galaxy" or a "Sorry we carved up your ship like a fucking Christmas turkey."

It really boiled my piss.

That, and that I was who I was, was why Ingrid was seriously unhappy about me being in the air lock first, waiting for the interstellar wankers to make their entrance.

We were kept at a distance, held in the tractor beam or whatever it was, pinned in space, while a single figure leapt free of the warship. Correctional jets burped as they landed on the ship's hull, then stomped across it, the *clank, clank* of presumably magnetic boots keeping them attached after landing.

They used the air lock, thankfully. Admittedly, there wasn't much air left in the goddamn ship now, but there were a few sections that were still sealed. One of which was notably where Casey, due to her lack of any armor yet, was being kept safe, as she'd only emerged from the medical facility twenty minutes ago.

Beyond that, most of the ship was now in vacuum, and I was damn glad the air lock worked, all things considered.

I was waiting inside, my own armor pulled up. Although I had my blades and gravity gradient cannon retracted, I was a hairsbreadth from whipping them out.

Instead, as the air lock clanked and whooshed, the tiny amount of air left in it being sucked clear, I got ready.

The air was stored in tanks, ones that dutifully held it until the outer hatch was closed and sealed; then it released, attempting to equalize the pressure again, before I eventually smacked the override and released the door.

The pressure inside was so fucked and fluid, the ship trying to replace the air and the damage sucking it free, that the system would never match up.

As the door opened, the figure that stepped forward was terrifying in both their size, and the sheer lethality and overt threat they exuded.

I was tall, at over seven foot, but this fucker? Nine at least, maybe more, and they had to be almost as wide as they were tall. They wore what had to be powered armor that was covered in scratches. But for all of that? They looked absolutely lethal. There was a massive rifle strapped to their back, a dagger on their chest in a quick release rig, a short, stubby handgun on either hip, then dozens of smaller weapons secreted across their armor.

There were small orbs, spiked things, cubes that were clearly kept close to hand, but no clue what they were for. The armor had a backpack that extended up and out behind the shoulders, directional nozzles used to guide them as they jetted across, and everywhere there was evidence of this being a working, and heavily used, suit of armor.

It was massive. I kept using that term even to myself, but there wasn't a better one to describe it. The shoulders were topped with huge pauldrons that came halfway down their arms. The elbows were heavily articulated, the gauntlets studded with spikes, and the fingers clearly flexible even as they were encased in metal.

The arms, the legs—hell, everywhere that was under the bigger slabs of metal—was still armored, just with a smaller section. And below that?

Judging from the glimpses I got as they strode forward, between the fingers and at the articulation points, there was something like high-tech bulletproof fabric under that.

The suit had clear sections where it looked to open and close. And the chest? They wore a breastplate that had to be supported on servos or something, because it had to weigh as much as a goddamn car.

The head was encased in a helmet. A stylized beast's head caught in mid-snarl was etched into it, and the eyes that glowed a dull red just topped it off.

There'd clearly been a recent attempt to touch the armor up, with both shoulders repainted to show some kind of unit insignia. But beyond that? Looking at the state of the figure, I knew one thing beyond any doubt.

This was a soldier. This was someone who battled day in and day out, no matter that there was a supposed cease-fire in place.

"Welcome to our ship." I reached out with my Hack sub-mind, not really sure how to do this, but knowing damn well that the chances of a conversation in vacuum were slim if they didn't understand what I was doing.

The sub-mind reached out, offering a digital link, and an open one at that, while sitting ready to defend me if they tried to attack through it.

Fortunately, after nearly giving me a heart attack when they jerked to a halt, the figure cocked their head to one side, before a transmission came through to our ship from the other one again.

Unknown trespasser. Identify yourself and declare your intentions.

I paused as Ingrid had a brief conversation with the ship, before being told by her to try again, pushing my identity out at the message, as well as the intention behind the data link.

There were a few seconds, where I guessed that the figure before me was discussing it with their chain of command, before finally, a link was established. With a wall of static, a barrage of meaningless words poured down the link.

"Well, fuck," I muttered, focusing on their words, on the translation systems I'd already developed, and the data we had from the BWVs we'd met under the sea.

I gestured for them to keep talking as they fell silent, introducing myself again, and getting nothing understandable from them. As the seconds passed in a blur, the soldier, seeming to understand what was happening, continued to talk.

At first it was a meaningless gabble of words, but as it lengthened to minutes, understandable words slid free.

They were few and far between, but as more time passed, they grew clearer.

"Are you okay?" Ingrid asked, and I nodded, not wanting to break the flow and knowing that she'd be able to see what I was doing.

We were connected in the command link, and I mentally cursed that it didn't seem compatible with the soldier before me, as it had been with the BWVs under the sea.

Instead, I was stuck using fragments of their language that we'd gained from speaking to them, then the various ancient languages of Earth, and the language of the scum-sucking pig-fuckers the Ændari.

Why the hell the language their ship reached out with was so different I had no clue. It was like speaking to someone over the radio in English, meeting them face-to-face and finding out that they only spoke Swahili.

It took fifteen minutes, but eventually we had a basic kernel, and using that, my sub-mind stripped their words, then started assembling a new language for me.

"You hear?" I asked. The mass of random words coming from them shut off immediately.

"I hear," came the response.

"You...fuck...uh, you stand under—" I stopped, then tried again. "You understand me?"

"Understand. Identify."

"I..." I hesitated. Clearly, fuckin' "Steve" wasn't going to mean anything to them, but I knew what had before. "I Devourer," I said softly, watching them.

"Prove."

"Prove it?" I bit my lip. Then, shrugging, I released the curbs I kept on my armor normally. The red-black sheen, like sentient oil, flooded to the surface of my armor.

It took a bare second, but the difference, as it flowed forth, was insane.

The soldier took two steps back, then dropped to one knee, fists pressed to their chest, head bowed, and stayed there, silent.

"Uh…hello?" I tried, getting no response. After a few seconds, I took a knee before them as well, before pulling the Devourer back into my armor. That seemed to make the difference, as they raised their head then. I stared back at them, trying to figure out what the hell I was supposed to do now.

"Ask them for their identity," Ingrid suggested, and I stifled a curse. It was a bloody obvious step.

"Identify?" I asked, and they cocked their head, paused, then straightened.

"Leshan, First Fist… Assault …" There were a few unknown words in there, presumably something to do with rank, but the "first fist" bit? That was the same designation as Diamos.

"First fist?" I pointed to them, getting a strange look at my finger. I cursed and dropped my hand, realizing that for all I knew, I just propositioned them, or declared war.

"First Fist Leshan," they repeated, tapping their chest with the first and second fingers of each hand.

"Devourer." I imitated the gesture. "Steve."

"Steeeve."

"Steve."

"Stiv."

"Ste-v-uh."

"Steve. Devourer?"

"Steve." I tapped myself, then flooded the Devourer free to coat my armor. "Devourer."

"Identify…" they said again, but this time they tapped the ship's hull, sounding worried, and if possible, sad.

"Ship," I said. "Our ship."

"More Devourer?"

"Ingrid, come through, please."

It only took a few seconds. She'd been waiting nearby, ready to fight if need be, and she strode out, holding her hands to either side.

At her appearance, the soldier's attitude changed, growing markedly more animated, and I realized why after a few seconds of them speaking too fast for either of us to understand.

All we'd gotten was something about an officer, a demand for identity, and some query about the status of the ship, and the…the warship!

The reason they'd acted differently, though? That took a few minutes to figure out. Ingrid and the others, as I led the soldier deeper into the ship, showing them where the others were waiting, and even James, where he laid encased in the pilot's couch, his own armor covering his face and the sections that were outside of its protection—all of them had one thing in common.

They'd all unlocked and augmented the system-provided armor.

I'd not done that.

I'd been too new to it, and in having the entire system unlocked to draw from? I'd designed my own armor. It'd been basic as fuck, compared to the starter armor the others had, but the advantages were that I'd been able to play with it and make whatever I'd needed at the time.

Now, though…now it was marking another difference between me and the others for this First Fist Leshan. They'd all turned up wearing something that was clearly identifiable; the armor was adjusted from the original versions, for most of my usual team anyway, but James, Paul, Courtney, and Oxus wore the basic version.

Another good thing that came of showing Leshan around the ship was that they met Oxus, who, in his armor wasn't much smaller than they were but was markedly inhuman, the horns and hooves clear even when wearing it.

Ingrid stepped up to Leshan and started to speak quickly. The soldier responded slowly, shifting unconsciously to put their back to a wall, and made sure they had the entire room in sight at all times.

I bet it was unconscious, anyway, because I knew it was something that I'd done from my first few deployments. And as I'd ended up fighting as much as I did these days? It was entirely on instinct.

Fighting as much as this soldier looked to have been, I had to think that it'd be ingrained to a level that they'd never notice it.

Leshan asked to be shown all of the ship, and when we came across Zac?

Even I got a shock.

Zac's armor was, like everything he had, a custom design. It was something that was just a weird mess in so many ways, and *damn*. It was half and half: the original nanite armor, and overlaying that, something closer to the power armor that the soldier wore.

He also had six goddamn arms, and he was sealing a section at the same time that another arm removed a section of replacement plating from a goddamn miniature factory unit he'd strapped to his back.

Leshan stopped dead, watching the fucking lunatic as he laid the new strip in place, a welding arm sliding around and flooding the passage in light as he sealed the section into place.

Another arm reached down, plucking a section of the discarded old metal free of the floor and sliding it into the top of the unit, making it clear that he had a tiny converter stashed in there as well as it began to be cannibalized.

All of us watched him for a minute, as Ingrid attempted to explain things to Leshan. Several minutes passed before Leshan stiffened, holding a hand out to stop her, then turned to face me and spoke again.

By now, between Ingrid and me, her command software, and the language data we had, communication was rapidly becoming easier.

"I have been ordered to return to my commander and report," the soldier said. "We ask that you remain here. Command will contact you." With that, they knelt again, then stood and headed straight to the exit.

We followed along, not trusting them, but also, not really sure what the hell else we should do.

As soon as they were gone, though, Zac marched through the areas they'd been in, scanning carefully.

"Checking to see if they left anything behind," he grunted when questioned, and I nodded, leaving him to it. The rest of us moved to the bridge, checking the available systems and making sure that as soon as Zac was back, we could repressurize it.

Ten minutes passed and he was there, declaring that Leshan had apparently left nothing behind at all, not even dirt, so at least they'd not left a bomb or spying devices that we could detect. That spurred a brief argument over whether we'd even be able to detect them, before I stiffened. A fresh connection linked to the ship, before requesting and establishing a direct link to me.

The connection was clear, and as I scanned it with my sub-mind, it appeared both visual and audio. I made sure that I was in the command link, with Ingrid controlling most of it, then nestled myself in the middle of the regular communication link, creating a kind of pocket that was open from the point of view of the others, but appearing private between me and the caller, who would hopefully have no clue they were there.

"Devourer." The figure that appeared in my mind greeted me, and I smiled as soon as I saw them.

They were human.

"I am," I said, not really sure what the hell else to say, projecting an image of me in the command chair of the bridge, matching the image of him, where he sat in a huge throne-like command chair.

At first glance, it looked weird, like he was a kid sitting in his dad's chair. Then I realized it was sized to accommodate him in armor.

"I am Field Commander Aaronis Balthazar. Eleventh Assault Brigade, Fifth Wing."

"I'm Steve," I said simply. "Devourer."

"You certainly need no further rank." He nodded thoughtfully. "Please, Devourer…Steve, if I offend, I am unsure of your customs. Do you accept this explanation?"

"I do," I agreed, thinking it was a fucking good place to start a conversation, saying that basically if you fucked anyone off, it was unintentional. "I am equally unaware of your customs. We agree to show each other…uh…patience?" It wasn't the right word, but it was as good as I could think of for now.

"We agree." He smiled a tight-lipped smile. "Now, your vessel…on arrival, it appeared to be on the verge of detonation. We removed the remaining engine, not to prevent your escape, but to protect our vessel. Do you accept this explanation?"

"I do," I said slowly. "Do you accept that we had no intention of causing you or your ship any harm when we jumped in?"

"Jumped…" He paused, then nodded. "We call it 'warp'. The asteroids and debris? Yes. We accept that if you have access to the technology seen aboard your ship, you are likely to have been able to conceive of a better assault, had that been your intention."

"Well, that's a good start. So, now what then? You accept that we're not assholes, and you agree we didn't try to start shit with you. You asked us to meet you here, in five goddamn days, which we managed, so…your move, I guess."

"Our…move…?" He frowned. "You wish to know of our intentions toward you?"

"Yeah."

"This is less simple."

"Story of my fuckin' life," I muttered. "So what's the problem?"

"First, we were given very specific details of what we were to expect, and why. While you match some of those details, we cannot deviate on something this important. We've received confirmation and rendezvous coordinates for the quadrant's Forgeship, and I request that you accompany us to a formal meeting aboard it."

"Well, gee, I don't know," I replied, pretending to think about it. "You know, I was planning on exploring the galaxy with our amazing ship, but you've asked us so nicely…"

He paused, then allowed a ghost of a smile to cross his lips, before settling back in the seat. "This is an attempt at humor?" he guessed.

"Well, my partner tells me I should try to get on with people more." I shrugged. "You know, rather than just killing them."

"Both are valuable talents." He shrugged. "Do you have needs?"

"You have no idea."

"Speak them, and if we can assist, we will." He seemed to mean it.

Zac spoke up in the command link. *"Mass, dude…just a fuckload of mass…but I'd not say no to a sample of their armor and weapons as well."*

"Well, we can repair our ship, according to my chief engineer…" I left out that he was also the only engineer I had aboard. "But we're low on mass, thanks to all the damage. If you've got anything we could use?"

"High atomic mass?" he asked, and I nodded after being prompted by Zac. "Yes."

"Do you have harvesting capabilities?"

"We can make it work," I said, guessing at his meaning.

"This quadrant's Forgeship is moving to meet us, but we have…possibly seven hours before we must leave, providing us with an opportunity to assist each other, and perhaps build a base of trust.

"Your vessel is…unlikely to be capable of independent flight. I recommend we dock you on our ship and stop off on a harvestable moon on the way. Is this acceptable?"

"Yeah, man, sounds good," I agreed readily, trying to hide just how relieved I was that they weren't declaring war on us for setting off a stone-filled shotgun at them.

"Be aware, the most valuable and local target will be infested by the corrupt. Is this an issue?"

"It's full of politicians?"

"I am unsure as to your meaning."

"Doesn't matter." I forced a smile, internally cursing as Ingrid told me off for the throwaway comment as well. "What do you mean by the corrupt?"

"Corrupt?" he asked again, tilting his head to one side. "You do not have this?"

"Oh, we have corrupt people," I assured him. "But I don't know what you mean by corrupted, not in this context. You mean people who take for themselves, who are infected with something, or…"

"Yes."

"Yes?"

"Yes to all."

"So…scavengers? Looters?" I suggested. After a few seconds, a vision appeared to one side. It appeared slowly, the commander watching me carefully, clearly wanting to make sure that I knew this was a projection or a hologram or whatever, not something actually joining us.

A wire form outline came first: a destroyed section of bulkhead, an air lock close by, the door twisted and shattered, lunar dust deep in drifts in the corners and craters nearby, making it clear that the wreck had been here for long ages.

Then came more details, highlighted disturbances that I guessed were motion trackers going off. A handful of seconds later, the first figure staggered out of the darkness, and I felt the others watching with me stiffening.

"What the hell is that?" I asked, stunned.

"The corrupt," Aaronis declared flatly, and damn, I could see why.

The figure was encased in what looked to be pretty ancient armor, obviously high tech in nature, an armored space suit of sorts—kind of halfway between the nanite-based systems we had now, and the old NASA traditional white suits with the massive helmets.

They had what looked to be connection points for ammo or weapons, an empty sheathe on one hip, and obvious armor plating. Looking it over, they were obviously ex-soldiers, and they were also, clearly, beyond any doubt, dead.

The body that staggered through the doorway was battered to all hell: holes torn in the suit that looked to have passed straight through; one gauntlet was entirely missing, showing a three-fingered hand that was desiccated and broken, the fingers jerking like an electrical input had been hooked up.

The real decider for me, though, was the head. The front of the head was sealed into a dome-like helmet. What had been glass or similar was shattered and whatever atmosphere the user was used to had been long since lost.

The skull was slumped to the side, half of the bone exposed and an empty eye socket hollow, the skin long since boiled away in the vacuum of space.

The other half, though, was encased in what looked to be a fluid mess of nanites, black and oily as I was used to, but moving in ways that were entirely alien.

A single ruby-red glowing eye was in the center—what I guessed had been a cybernetic eye at some point, subsumed into the boiling mass.

As soon as it fixed on whoever was exploring the wreck, it froze, staring. For a long count of three, nothing moved, until the explorer started to slowly back away.

Arise :Explorer

The movement was all it took: the corrupted figure went from frozen immobility to an all-out rabid sprint in seconds, as the explorer spun and started to run.

Words were panted out, panic clear in their voice as they presumably pleaded for help. I didn't know; it was an entirely different language, but the fear and horror were real.

It was even worse as they raced through the outer sections of the wreck, and someone responded.

Whatever was said, the explorer started to scream into their comms, as other voices broke in, arguing or shouting in pain and fear.

In seconds, the comm link was full of yelling, panicked voices, and the figure we rode brought their left arm up, showing a much more modern version of that same armoring.

On the back of the left forearm were a screen and a dozen large buttons. Three-fingered hands frantically jabbed at the buttons. The screen flashed details and options, as they jabbered and babbled in fear.

It flashed red, then green, then red again. The fingers smacked the screen in frustration, then started again, the figure taking a corner around a section of rounded passage that was half submerged in the dust.

The light was hard here, I'd noticed, the shadows black pits; the sections that were in the light were fully lit like a summer's day, and it was Zac who pointed out that it was the lack of any atmosphere that caused it.

"Nothing to refract the light..." he muttered in our private command link, but before he could say anything else, Scylla spoke up as well.

"From the right, at the corner of his eye."

I looked, having missed it, but as the figure looked up from the gauntlet again, their breath hissing as they tried to hurry and tap out commands at the same time…I saw something racing to intercept.

It wasn't the same figure as before. This one was much bigger and was missing more than half its suit, looking like it'd been built for someone smaller, and then ripped free of, the creature within made up from a mixture of beast and machine.

The nanites were clear, holding more and more of the mass together as it scuttled across the top of a shattered passage.

The stars above it gleamed cold and distant as the explorer finally saw something. Not the creature that closed on it—oh no, it was much worse.

Rising from a crater ahead, the dust-covered wall having hidden it until now, was a ship.

It was a mess, clearly cobbled together out of dozens of sections, presumably repaired again and again, as more parts became available. It was a monstrosity of a ship, graceless in every way, save that it was leaving the surface, born aloft on a dozen pillars of flame.

Screams filled the comms then, no longer just the panic of being chased, nor the pain of fighting and being consumed.

Now there was the sure and certain knowledge that the figures on the surface were being abandoned in every voice, and what that meant for their futures.

Before the explorer could finish whatever they were tapping out on the screen, they were hit from one side, hurtling through the void and into a section of the hull.

They crashed through it, bouncing off another and flying on to impact a last section, the reduced gravity of the moon making itself clear.

They slid down the hull, impacting the ground and sending up a small plume of dust. The figure lay there for a brief time, stunned, shaking and presumably in shock, before a moving shadow caught their attention.

It was long and clearly artificial. The stark white dust that the figure lay in was steadily eclipsed by hard lines as it moved, building speed.

The explorer looked up slowly, before throwing their arms up and letting loose a panicked scream. The hull over them collapsed, sliding sideways and crashing down atop them, cutting off the light and pinning them beneath the mass.

"This is the end of the usable section of the transmission," Aaronis said. "Though there are several more minutes left in the logs, they were pinned in place, trapped, but, they believed, they were out of reach of the corrupt, as several tried to reach them under the hull, but were unable to."

"I guess it doesn't end well?"

"A smaller variant drags itself free of its suit, abandoning several limbs to reach them. The end is quick, but knowing that their companions abandoned them, the remaining segment of the transmission was sent on an all-frequencies emergency broadcast. It included the identity of the ship, its home port, and the many piracies the crew carried out, clearly a last-ditch attempt to punish their comrades."

"Did they get caught?" I asked.

"The pirates?"

"Yeah."

"They did. They, in turn, led us to a group of smugglers who had been ferrying stolen and recovered technologies to the Ændari and others. We were in the middle of cleaning up that little mess when we were re-tasked to meet with you."

I hesitated, watching his face as he said that, unsure why it'd been added. "Should I be apologizing?" I asked after a few seconds. "You were hunting smugglers, and you got pulled off that job?"

"No." He shook his head. "I meant no offense, Devourer. Meeting you has a much greater priority than hunting smugglers. I apologize. However, the location that is most likely to have heavy metals and high atomic value components that you can repurpose is the moon that these recordings came from.

"They are several months old, but the corrupt will be unaffected by the passage of time. And we are frequently re-tasked rather than being deployed on clearance missions, even if we had the teams to spare."

"But you want us to go?" I asked.

"I simply present the option to harvest your needed materials on this world. It is a known corrupted infection point, and must be cleansed at some point. I suggest that if we harvest there now, you will have the opportunity to gain materials, while we will provide cover. Reducing the number of corrupt that are capable of infecting others is always a necessary task," he replied. "I mean no offense,

Devourer. I know not your capabilities, nor if our involvement in eliminating the corrupt is offensive to you. We offer our assistance, and transportation to the location."

"I think he means that he thinks you could take care of them easily, and he's worried if he puts a team out to screen while we harvest the materials we need, we'll be offended by that. Also, I'm betting he's wanting to see you do something with your armor, something that confirms to him what you are." Ingrid clarified to me

"Aaronis, I'll just say it, all right? I'm hard to offend. If you think you might have upset me, but you're not sure? You haven't. Use that as a rule of thumb."

"I see…"

"If there's any fucking doubt? I'm not offended," I clarified. "When I'm pissed about something, I'm very clear."

"Right."

"I'm really not explaining this very well," I muttered. "Ingrid, can you join us?"

A second later, Ingrid appeared, and a second after that, making it clear that Aaronis had some of his team watching just as I had, a big woman joined the conversation on his side.

"This is Ingrid," I introduced her. "My partner."

"This is Leshan, my first fist." He introduced the woman.

I nodded, having had no clue that the huge, armored soldier who had stomped around our ship had been a heavily muscled woman. Mind you, it could have been a sentient pot of custard in there for all I'd known.

"First Fist," I greeted her, and the others all smiled and nodded, depending on their preference.

"Commander Aaronis Balthazar, First Fist Leshan…" Ingrid started. "You were looking for confirmation as to our capabilities and intentions regarding your people, should we land on this moon and harvest it for materials, is that correct?"

"Yes, Partner Ingrid," Aaronis said approvingly.

"Ah, I'm Steve's partner…perhaps, 'mate' might be better? Lover?" she tried, and the pair frowned.

"Ingrid was my lover and friend first, becoming a life partner, and then a Command variant," I interjected, trying to explain, only to stop when they both jerked at that.

"We do not mean to offend your sensibilities," Ingrid said slowly. "Are physical relations between yourselves a matter of open record or private shame?"

"Neither," Aaronis grunted, as even Leshan's lips quirked for a second before flattening again. "Our personal physical and emotional entanglements, be they permanent pair or group bonding, or simple amusement, are not something we discuss."

"This is taboo?"

"Tah-boo…" Aaronis muttered, then shook his head as whatever translation system was working helped to smooth the meaning out. "Forbidden? No. It is simply not something that is considered of import beyond those in the situation. For the sake of clarity, Leshan and I are not bonded in that way."

"We are warriors first, and have served together to protect the UC for many centuries," she added.

"Work wife." I smiled. "We have a saying in our culture, that you'd be a 'work wife.' Not a relationship in a physical or emotional way, but a friendship that had grown from long, professional interactions. You are closer than the others around you, and act in the other's best interests whenever you can."

"Yes. This is accurate."

"Ingrid is my partner," I explained. "Both in a private, physical and emotional sense, and we work to lead our people together."

"You and she are the leaders?"

"We are two of a group of four," Ingrid said. "My parents are the other two."

"They are with you?"

"No, they're back at our base, protecting our people," she said.

"You hold power because of familial connections?" Leshan asked curiously, and I laughed as Ingrid tried to explain that no, we weren't a monarchy; it'd just happened like that.

That started another explanation, and after a few seconds, I held up both hands. "We can talk about all this once we've got things sorted out. For now, no, we'd not be offended if you provide security on the ground as we harvest mass, and we'd not hold you responsible if anything gets through to us."

I said it as clear-cut as I could, getting a nod from Aaronis.

"Then we shall dock you and make haste to the quarantine site. I suggest you prepare any weapons you feel you will need." That ended the conversation, as they stood, bowed, then disconnected before we could do anything like return the gesture.

A few minutes later, we were docked to the side of their ship. The event was pretty anticlimactic, unfortunately, as was the trip to the moon.

We were literally dragged in close by tractor beams, then something slid out, attaching to our vessel and pulling us against their hull. There were a series of clicks and booms as we impacted, but beyond a little staggering and a fresh warning of a new leak, that was it.

Silence filled the cabin, and we all looked at one another, while Zac raced off to find the new leak and plug it.

"Now what then?" Paul asked. "I mean, seriously, that fucker was impressive in all that armor, but we don't know if they can actually fight or anything."

"Oh, I think they can fight." I snorted.

"Maybe. And they didn't seem bothered about the zombie monster shits, but do we trust them?" he asked again.

This time, Courtney nodded as the others shifted uneasily.

"Trust them?" I shook my head. "I trust us, and that's it."

"But we came out here for a reason. We need to show them a little trust, and they've done nothing to show us they're not potential allies, so we'll be polite, and we'll learn from them, okay?" Ingrid said firmly.

"Yeah," I agreed. "They're taking us somewhere that we can basically grab a fuckload of mass apparently, and there's ruined starships there, so that's a possible source of tech that we just don't have…"

"And freaky monsters," Paul pointed out, before being glared at by Jonas.

"Yes, and freaky monsters," I agreed. "But they didn't seem particularly concerned about them, and they offered to act as security. This is too good a chance to see what's out there and maybe grab some shit, as well as seeing their soldiers in action and getting a look at their weapons and tactics without being on the receiving end."

"But we'll be armed and ready to take care of our people, right, boss?" Jonas said.

"Oh yeah, we're going down there loaded out as if the others don't exist," I clarified. "They'll be watching us as much as we are watching them, so we need to put on a good show, but not too good, all right? Keep some shit in reserve if we can, but go all out if we have to."

"So what's the plan?"

"This is a low-gravity moon from the recording, so we need a small team that can pretend to have been in zero-g before, at the least. Sorry, Scylla, but that counts you out. Have you even seen a movie set in space yet?"

"I…" She paused, then shook her head. "Not that I remember."

"Then you stay onboard for now," I ordered. "We limit it to one team outside and one in, ready to help if need be. Jonas, you and Paul, Zac, and me for now. Courtney, Scylla, Oxus, Belle, and Ingrid in the second team—" I broke off, then sighed.

"Fuck, it looks like it's practically boys versus girls now. Okay, quick explanation, though I'm not doing this shit every time, all right?" I snapped. "Jonas and Paul are with me because the three of us have had conversations about fighting in zero-g and I know they've watched a load of movies about it. We're all going to make mistakes, but at least they have some idea about the shit we need to do to walk and so on. Zac? We need the goddamn engineer to decide what we can take and what is scrap.

"Courtney is in team two, because as much as I know she's probably watched the same movies and she's been in the same conversations, she's also a lot brighter than Paul—"

"Hey!" Paul complained.

"And we need a sniper ready to take anything down if we have to retreat," I finished. "If you're in the trenches with us, or inside the ship or whatever, you're not covering our retreat. Scylla? You're a lethal badass, and if these people decide with half of us out that they want to attack the ship? They'll have to come inside the ship, and into melee range. That's where you're the best of us.

"Oxus is pure power, and no offense, big man, but you're not exactly graceful. Moving in space is likely to need a lot of practice for you, and again, movies. There's a lot of background information that you just don't have yet.

"Belle? There's nothing out there you can grow or affect with your skills, and if we need healing, you're gonna need to get access to our bodies. We can't open our suits out there, so you might as well be here." I turned to Ingrid last.

"Ingrid? You're in charge. If they take me out, you need to get the others the fuck out of here. In that mess we saw on the recording, it's likely to be short-range fighting, and that's what Jonas, Paul, and I are good at."

"And James?" she asked, clearly not liking my logic, but unable to argue with it.

"He's our only pilot," I said, thinking that was bloody obvious.

"He is, but you were ignoring him, Jay, and Casey," Ingrid sent to me separately. *"Best to at least mention why you're dismissing them."*

"Also, and no offense, Casey, but you're not a fighter…that's why I wasn't including you, Jay, or James in that list. He's our only pilot and without you and Jay—"

I broke off, trying to think about how to phrase it.

"You'd have nobody to cook and clean?" Casey asked calmly, making me wince.

"You do more than that…"

"I do." She laughed. "Honestly, it's okay. We understand. We're literally the support team, and we're all finding our places. Thanks for thinking of us, though."

I nodded, barely keeping from admitting it as Ingrid sent me another message.

"Don't you dare tell them you forgot."

"It was you prompting me…" I shot back.

"And they don't need to know that."

More might have been said, but that was when we all received a brief transmission from the warship, and we all hurried to the nearest screen.

Transitioning in 3, 2, 1… Gravitational transition complete. Setting course for target.

That was literally it: the warship slid into the gravitational branes smooth as silk, before sliding back out seemingly almost before the back of the damn ship could have gotten in.

Literally, it was an eye blink—a flash of light and the galaxy had changed. Staring out at the brightly burning distant stars, we couldn't help but grab onto things as the ship altered course. The bright lights whirled and tilted, then seemed to return to utter stillness.

"So, are we going or not?" Paul asked after a few seconds.

"Paul, you can't believe what you see in movies," Casey explained. "If we're going fast enough, you can see the stars moving. We're not going home to anyone you're ever going to know."

"What?"

"Ever heard of the laws of relativity?"

"That's about Arkansas, right? Something to do with marrying your cousin?"

"Yeah." Casey winced. "Something like that… I don't think I can explain it to you, though."

"Don't worry about it. Loads of people think they know stuff, but they can't explain it properly. It doesn't mean you're dumb that you can't explain it, just that, you know…" He shrugged, looking at Casey as if she were the one with the issue in the group.

"Paul?" Courtney said into the heavy silence.

"Yeah?"

"The adults are talking, hun. Hush."

More silence, as Paul tried to make sense of what was going on, and I spoke up, partly to break the silence, and partly because I'd just figured out what was so weird about that jump.

"There was nothing in the branes," I said, making the others look at me weird. "Dammit. Okay, as we went into the gravity branes, the jump space, or whatever you want to call it, right?" I looked around, making sure they were all listening.

"When we just jumped, there was nothing else in there."

"Right?" Jonas agreed.

"No, I mean…argh, fuck's sake. James?" I appealed to the pilot.

"There were masses in the gravity field when we passed through it on our own," James explained. "They appeared to be in motion, but when we entered the jump with this warship attached, it was empty and silent. I couldn't sense anything nearby."

"Could it be because you weren't controlling the ship?" Ingrid asked.

"It could," he agreed. "But it felt more like—" He broke off, considering, and I spoke up.

"We slid in and out like we'd been lubed up."

"Yes…" James agreed slowly, clearly not liking the description. "We definitely seemed to encounter less friction. It may be because their drive is fully powered, and so we simply felt nothing, or it may be a difference in technology. Our drive was developed tens of thousands of years ago, after all."

"That's another point," Jonas said quickly, gesturing out at the warship we were attached to. The hull took up half the vision on the screen. "That ship? It matches the style and mock-ups of the warship that's buried back on Earth. It's big, and sure, it's impressive, but fuck me, you don't just get to a point and stop innovating, do you? I mean, it's not the pinnacle of all possible ships, is it? You'd expect a few changes at least."

"Maybe this was to make us feel at home?" Ingrid suggested, but in a tone that said she probably didn't believe it either.

The next half an hour or so was filled with general discussion as we all tried to make sense of what was going on.

"Okay, it all seems a bit mental, I think—" I started, before being cut off.

Approaching orbital insertion. Prepare for landing.

They were fast, I'd give them that.

"We won't know anything without asking the right questions and watching everything around us, so let's see what we can learn," Ingrid said as the universe twisted and turned around us again.

The angle we were coming in meant that we saw basically nothing until it was almost too late, the moon right below us as we came in for a landing strapped to the side of the warship.

Three seconds before the ship shuddered, some kind of landing gear taking the vessel's weight as we came to a stop, was the only chance we got to see anything besides random stars.

"What the fuck is *that!*" I gasped, staring out at the massive, shattered structure that obscured half the sky.

<u>Chapter Twenty</u>

"How the hell did that thing ever fly?" Jonas muttered as we trooped out onto the side of the hull, hesitating as we got a clear look at the devastated wreck before us.

The sight was even more mind-blowing as the four of us stepped from the air lock out into the low-gravity moonlet, stopping to stare up, dumbfounded, at the remains of the massive structure that seemed to take up half the goddamn moon.

"How the hell did they crash it, you mean? Was Court driving?" Paul added.

"I'll get you for that." Courtney's voice snapped through the command link, and Paul flinched, before forcing a nervous laugh, while Jonas, Zac, and I subtly stepped away from the ex-marine in case his wife came after him.

"Zac, that link ready?" I asked, getting a grunt from him, then a thumbs-up.

I reached out to the small box he'd cobbled together, patching through that to our ship, and from there, our ship patched to the UC vessel, then finally to Leshan.

I didn't know why the ships could integrate so easily, and Leshan could with the ship, but not with us. Zac had said he thought it had to be a closed loop, presumably for security, but the engineering golden boy hadn't taken long to figure out a workaround.

I felt the request sliding out to us, and I reached out in return, enabling the link and tying First Fist Leshan into a communication link again, Zac having worked some kind of technological wizardry to patch us with their systems.

"My forces are deploying to surround the ship now, Devourer. Have you identified a target site?" she asked.

As I looked back out over the giant vessel's graveyard, I couldn't articulate the words, simply staring at the side of the massive ruin.

It was a ship, once. That much was clear. The engines could be seen in the distance, thoroughly trashed, as were the sides of the vessel that we lay in shadow of.

"Uh... Zac?" I asked after a second, glancing at him and figuring he'd know what he needed best as my eyes were drawn back to the devastation.

"There." Zac pointed to and pinged a section of damaged metal that looked to have fallen free in the impact.

I nodded absently, looking from left to right. The skeleton of the ship literally covered miles, with what I guessed had to be the remains of in-atmosphere engines, the size of skyscrapers, laid broken in distant craters.

There were cracks in the moon's surface, where parts had speared deep. Other bits looked to have melted, the heat and energy of the impact having presumably been horrific.

Then there were the remains of possibly hundreds of decks, broken sections bleached to grey by the constant radiation of the sun, making it impossible to imagine how something so huge could have been made.

I had a sudden image of someone taking an island, like one of those I'd spent so long on in the Mediterranean, then making the fucker fly. That was the kind of size I was seeing here, and that was mind-blowing.

"With your permission, Devourer, my team will lead," Leshan said, her people already moving.

"Go for it," I agreed absently, wanting to see more of their forces, and having little goddamn clue what we needed to do here really.

They obviously viewed me being a Devourer as a big deal, but they were also making it clear that although they were being polite, they were moving out.

"What happened here?" I moved up to the edge of our ship and leapt free, falling to the ground twenty meters or so below and shifting gravity to guide the others down smoothly as I did.

"The ship, or the looters?" she asked, and I hesitated.

"Both?"

"The vessel was identified as part of the Altimeran enslavement fleet. It was destroyed in a battle near here several centuries ago. This ship looks to have drifted in space until it was caught by the nearby gas giant's gravity field and pulled in, possibly dragged into an unlucky intercept by the moon's gravity field."

"So…it was just left to drift after the battle?" I frowned.

"There were no other life signs identified beyond the Altimerans, and the ship was deemed too damaged to be repaired. They sacrificed their slaves to ensure they couldn't be recovered, so the engines and any communication capabilities were destroyed, and the slavers were left to rot."

"And then they crashed into this moon?"

"It appears so," she replied uncaringly. "I mean no offense, Devourer, but we are aware of corrupted in the area. I must focus on the safety of yourselves and my unit. Please, contact me should you have further questions or needs."

With that, she cut the link, making it clear that "questions and needs" didn't include idle curiosity.

"I can take a hint," I muttered, as we turned to watch and follow the soldiers who were ringing and escorting us.

That they held the Altimerans in contempt was clear in the way Leshan had spoken about them. But even if that wasn't obvious, that they were slavers and had literally killed their slaves rather than risk them being rescued? Assholes.

Looking up at their ship, though, I had to admit they'd been industrious shits. The damn thing was the size of a city, at least a mile deep with levels, judging from the bits I could see internally in damaged sections in the distance, and at least six miles across, maybe more.

Hell, without anything I could really use for reference, it might be ten times that size. Looking down from the wreckage to the space around the ship as figures stormed forward, taking up station, I had to admit that Leshan and her team were equally impressive, though they were heavily armed, and I mean *heavily*. One of them carried something like the kind of chain gun I'd only ever seen on TV being attached to warships to shoot down incoming missiles.

They carried it attached and slung under one arm, as well as a massive box on their back that was presumably ammunition. Again, I was struck by a sense of something being not quite right with things.

They all wore the same cool as fuck and massive power armor, and they were carrying utterly insane levels of weapons, but…

The BWVs I'd met under the ocean? They'd viewed the armor they had access to as a waste of their time. Hell, it'd been so meaningless that they'd scrapped it, but they also knew that there was a risk of the Ændari finding them. They seemed to believe that if that happened, then they'd deal with it, even though the "sleeping god of the sea" awakening would obviously destroy the world.

They'd acted as though they'd evolved past needing the armor, and therefore it was useless. It wasn't that they didn't need it today—more like the armor was only part of their strength, and that they didn't need it anymore.

The response from Leshan when she'd seen us all in our armor showed that she had seen something similar before. But her response wasn't that we were using antiquated tech—it was more shock that we had it at all.

Judging from the way the other soldiers kept turning to check on, and lingering on us, they weren't looking down on us either.

It just didn't make sense.

We'd clearly landed somewhere different than the recording we'd seen. I squinted, then zoomed in, using both my enhanced vision and the suit's capabilities, until I reached out to Leshan with a question.

"Is that a ship?" I pinged the location, and got barely a pause before she replied.

"A looter," she guessed. "It looks to have been here awhile." She paused, looking at me, then went on. "It's most likely rigged to detonate should any but its master attempt entry. I would recommend avoiding it."

"Damn," I muttered, having thought about all the stuff that we could gain from the ship, as soon as I'd seen it. Hell, at the very least, we could strip its parts out for spares. And at best? It had to have tech that we could copy and integrate, if not just outright tear out and use.

"You wish to attempt entry?" she asked, making it clear it was an option, but not a happy one.

"You don't think it's worth trying?" I asked.

"No," she replied. "This is a forbidden zone. Any ship found inside it without authorization from the UC is to be eliminated and their ship towed into the star's gravitational pull. Nobody honest would ever be here…" She glanced at me, then went on. "Well, not without a very compelling reason."

"And us needing random mass is that?" I asked skeptically.

"Of course not."

"So…why are we here?"

"You are a Devourer," she said, as if that answered everything.

"Yeah…"

"You are in no danger from the likes of the corrupt. Neither are we."

"Right…" I agreed after a few awkward seconds. "And they'd rig their ships to blow because…?"

"Because anyone bar themselves who attempted to access it would be, at best, intending on rendering it unusable, taking the ship or stealing data from its core. Most likely, they would wait for the owner to return and then kill them as well. Should it be a UC team that found them, they could expect us to put them to the question, before executing them, and we would be the most merciful they would encounter out here."

"Ah. Friendly neighborhood then," I quipped.

"Do you wish to attempt entry?" she asked me again.

"I would have happily taken it," I admitted. "If we could have attached our ship to it, I'd have stripped it of all the mass we need, not to mention learning about the local area."

"It's a smuggler's vessel. It is unlikely to be worth the effort," she said. "We have attempted to strip their memory cores many times, but the resulting data is usually corrupted. Our orders now are to destroy them whenever they are identified, to remove the temptation from others to carry out such actions."

"Looting?"

"Looting, piracy, smuggling, slaving…" She sighed. "There are many in the galaxy who seek to turn a profit through those who are weaker. We fight against this."

"Okay."

I cut the connection, getting an even stronger feeling of something "wrong" than anything else, and resolving to see whether the rest of my team were getting this as well.

"What's up?" Ingrid asked me on singular engagement mode.

"This doesn't seem right," I said instead, sending it into the command link. *"They want to help us, but they're acting like we're VIPs, and their tech is all kinds of wrong. They should be light-years ahead of us. Instead, they're flying around in exactly the same shit as they were thousands of years ago. They want the data on the abandoned ships, but if they get too close, they'll blow up? Why not hack them?"*

"Too much doesn't make sense," Jonas agreed. *"Seriously, boss, I think we need to—"*

"Contact!" came the call, as several of the soldiers opened fire at once.

"Later!" I snapped into our command link. The four of us fell in close together, guns raised to watch as a section of shattered rock nearby was torn apart in a blur of sparking fire.

I frowned, not knowing what they were aiming at, until I suddenly realized what I'd been feeling all the way since we landed on the moon, and that I'd not felt overly from Leshan and the soldiers.

Nanites.

I *could* feel them. They were activated—Leshan's, I mean, and the soldiers who were close enough—but there wasn't anywhere near as many as there should be.

I could feel a fuckload of corrupted nanites around us, though, and especially boiling up toward the hole that had just been blasted into the ground.

Not *ground*, I suddenly realized.

A hole blasted into the surface of the ship! We were walking on another section of hull!

"Leshan!" I barked, connecting to her and explaining quickly through the link, a sense of shock coming from her at the sudden burst of data, before she politely replied, making it clear that what she meant was "Well yeah, duh" about the surface we were walking across being part of the ship.

Then came the shock that I could sense the corrupt, and the sheer numbers that were here.

She hesitated only a split second, before ordering her people to fall back to form up around us.

As soon as the barrage of fire the first guy had been laying down on the hole ceased, more of the broken figures tore their way free.

In almost less time than it took to count them, a dozen were out. Then twenty, thirty, fifty....

They just kept coming, and as I focused, I could sense more and more below us, desperate to reach us, desperate to reach...

"Our nanites," I whispered to myself. "We're active in a way the others aren't!" I barked it into the general link, forgetting that Leshan was in it still. "Form up, people. We've got incoming, and they're focusing on us!"

Leshan barked orders in her own command system, judging from the sudden movements those around us made. But what grabbed everyone's attention was the boiling mass of figures that just kept coming.

"Devourer," Leshan said suddenly, switching back to us. "Hold your position and take no action without declaring it first."

"What?" I asked, not sure I'd heard right.

"Command, we have a level-three corrupt swarm congregating beneath us," she said, letting me hear this as she reached out to her commander.

"Confirmed, First Fist. Do you require assistance?" Aaronis's voice came back.

"Negative. Beginning extermination."

She wasn't kidding, either.

The swarm that had burst free of the ground a hundred or so meters away had been closing frantically on our position; I could sense more directly below us. But the rest of the soldiers with her finally opened fire, and *damn*.

The figures that had been racing toward us were clearly long dead. Some had been formed into weird amalgamations of several bodies, shapes that were all arms and legs. Some were huge, presumably formed from the "slave races," considering that they were of such different shapes.

They didn't all come from underground, either. A figure that made me think of a troll lumbered into sight from around a torn section of wall. It was the size of a Xi-Ma but without the stunning musculature, instead clad in flexible stone-like armor that had to weigh literal tons.

Each step it took crushed its companions and broke their bodies, but neither they nor it seemed to care. The creatures running on either side of the crushed ones didn't even glance in their direction or try to dodge.

They came in a great wave, and one and all, they were torn apart.

The soldiers with Leshan were clad in the same armor, literally. The only difference was the helmet that she wore had a face on it, and her huge pauldrons were colored.

Beyond that, and the individual weapons, they were identical, and they were *terrifying*. The soldiers' chain guns cut through the corrupted like they were paper. Bullets glowed cherry-red and white-hot as they punched through body after body.

Others had handguns that I'd have struggled to lift outside of my own armor—a half meter of boxy metal with great curved magazines extending down and forward—matched by swords in their other hands.

They stood like statues, their guns blazing. Shots tore their targets apart, and over and over, the corrupt raced forward.

A single bullet hitting them, though? That was all it took.

Bodies staggered as the slug passed through them; then they'd keep coming, making it a step, two, then three. But as I watched, I noted that the soldiers never shot the same ones twice.

A handful of steps, if that, the corrupt made it, before collapsing as their nanites lost cohesion.

More and more were falling as I stared, stunned by the sheer level of devastation unleashed by these power armor-suited figures.

In maybe ten seconds, the ground before us for hundreds of meters had been covered in a mass of zombie-like motherfuckers, and in roughly the same time again, it was instead washed in black, fragmenting nanites.

"What the absolute fuck are you doing?" I gasped, horrified by the sheer waste.

"Devourer?" Leshan asked me, confused. "They are corrupt."

"What about attuning them?"

"Attuning?"

"Holy shit, now it makes sense," I whispered, staring wide-eyed at the dissolving corpses that blanketed the floor, even as more raced out of the darkness below. "You—"

"*Don't!*" Ingrid sent me, and I barely stopped myself. "*We don't know enough, not yet. If we tell them the truth, what happens?*"

"*And what happens if we can't actually use these nanites?*" Zac added. "*I mean, they're fucked, right? What if they can't be attuned?*"

"*That's...that's a point. Can we capture one? Or a sample of the nanites?*" Ingrid asked, and I hesitated, before speaking up.

"Leshan, do you have anything that can hold one of these? So that it's not a threat?"

"To question it?" she asked, confused. "Devourer, they are long dead. They cannot—"

"No. To examine it."

"We have records on their corruption. The commander may be able to request access from higher to permit you to examine them," she suggested doubtfully.

"I need to do it myself," I said.

For a few seconds, she clearly warred with common sense and the ingrained response to do as a Devourer ordered. Then deference won out.

"Fist Seven, capture a sample for the Devourer. Soldiers, provide cover fire," she ordered.

A soldier stepped forward as the others nearby slightly shifted their aim, clearing a path for a single creature.

It was smaller than the rest, clearly carefully chosen, and looked to be all limbs, a small central mass that was barely large enough to attach the rest to.

It raced across the dusty stone and metal, almost falling repeatedly, like an over-excited puppy, constantly on the verge of collapse.

The soldier stuck his handgun to his hip, then turned the sword sideways and did something.

It began to glow, a bright-blue light shining, before he smacked it down hard atop his target.

The creature had skipped to the side, seemingly viewing him as an obstacle, nothing more, and trying to get around him and to us. But it was too slow and too uncoordinated to avoid the blow. When it hit, there was a brief burst of static in the line, then the creature was tumbling, spasming, and clearly knocked senseless.

I watched as the lines of fire continued to rip out. Shots passed the soldier at seemingly insane closeness, but he just casually picked the stunned corrupt up, and carried it directly back down his safe path.

As soon as he was out of the way, the others picked up their pace, making sure the gap was closed, firing in a hellishly exact barrage. Leshan stepped closer to me, presumably handing command over to another as she drew a blade of her own that glowed.

"Devourer, we need to move. Whatever is causing the swarm to fixate on you, they're also burrowing up from underneath us. If we stay here, they'll break through soon to attack you directly," she told me earnestly, watching the stunned body that was being brought closer.

I nodded, listening but searching the creature being carried over with almost all my attention.

"Devourer. We need to move now," she repeated, sounding concerned.

"How far do we need to move?" I asked. "And can they fly?"

"Some can. Most can't," she said. "They're fixated on us, though, and the moon holds a significantly greater infestation than we first suspected. This harvesting mission is now deemed an unreasonable risk. We need to return to the ship."

"We need the mass, and I need to examine this," I said just as firmly. "How do they infect others?"

"An injection of their core matter." She shifted from one foot to the other, watching the surrounding figures as she went on. "Through bite, insertion, or spore dissemination, depending on the location and originally infested species."

"Interesting."

"Devourer, with my apologies, we need to move," she repeated, glancing over her shoulder at the insane mass closing on us. "I cannot guarantee your safety here and…"

I glanced around, then highlighted a nearby structure for Zac, getting an "Aye it'll do, I guess" from him. I reached out, still primarily fixated on the creature that the soldier had brought to me, and, using the much-reduced gravity of the moon, I triggered a gravity bubble. I grabbed a large chunk of ruined metal nearby, dragging it into the air and gesturing in the direction of the ship with my other hand.

"We can fall back then," I said, annoyed. "I don't know if we can get enough from this, but…"

"I can make do," Zac assured me, and I nodded.

"Well, let's get out of here then." I reached out to take the creature from the soldier, having him hand it over calmly, but take up station on my other side. I also noticed that he did that with the blade glowing blue again and clearly at the ready as I tried to examine it, before sighing and getting Zac to do it and pass the details to me.

Corrupted Variant	Corrupt
A failed nanite blockchain extension that has degenerated into a self-replicating mass. This corrupted form exists only to absorb and reboot.	
Corrupt	Corrupt

That was fairly clear, and yet so uninformative it was ridiculous.

"It's a failed nanite extension," I said to the group, aware that Leshan was still in it, but deciding to use that fact as a sudden burst of inspiration came to me.

"Can it be used?" Ingrid asked carefully.

"I don't know," I admitted. "I could test it with an emergency cleanse, or…"

"Or?"

"Or I could Tsunami it," I said slowly. "Their only function is to spread their current configuration to others. I could inject it with a dormant Tsunami, then we release it, let it infect the others and see if they can be used that way."

"Is it safe?" Ingrid asked.

"For us? Yeah." I shrugged. "We can take off and just dump it behind. It'll start working as soon as it recovers."

"And any other tests?" Zac asked. "I mean, if you do that, we won't know for ages, right?"

"Point," I said. "I'll grab a second one and I'll devour this."

"Steve, no!" Ingrid sent it on singular to me, but it was already too late.

"Don't panic, I'm faking it," I sent to her, along with a burst of the plan that had come to me as I was examining the creature.

The Tsunami was a real possibility to clear areas like this, and so was the system that we'd already seen deployed by the custodians to clear the infected nanites in the refuge. That had to be how the soldiers were taking them down, I guessed, having seen a familiar radiance to their bullets, a vibrational frequency that reminded me of the projectors the custodians had used.

Remembering that had made me think of this plan, knowing that worst-case scenario, I could always cheat and chuck a bunch of them down later to fix it if my test went badly wrong.

With that in mind, I let the Devourer flood my hand, reaching into the stirring figure…and I injected a handful of nanites into its chest, driving a spike into the middle and unleashing Tsunami, along with a set of *very* specific orders.

Then I pretended to be annoyed, cursing as I threw the corpse backward and it started to shake.

The body seemed to collapse in seconds, shattering into dust, cascading from my hand. I made a point of staring after it and shaking my head, feeling self-conscious about my poor acting, but fuck it.

"What the hell are you doing?" Ingrid sent to me.

"Play along and tell me off, I'll explain later," I sent to her.

"What happened?" Jonas asked, at the same time as Ingrid started berating me in the comm link for my stupid risk-taking, and Zac tried to step forward and examine the crumbling mass.

"It's the Devourer armor," I explained. "The nanites must be incompatible—" I broke off, before ostensibly shaking my head. "All right, everyone, we learned enough for now. We're out of here!"

Leshan and the rest of their soldiers didn't need to be told twice, falling in around us and laying down withering fields of fire as I cut off questions and complaints from the others as we hurried back.

Behind us, hopefully unnoticed, in the mass of crumbling nanites, was the kernel I'd just created and dropped. As the soldiers stomped backward, their withering fire scything through the desperately onrushing mass, I ordered it to stay down, to remain dormant for now, just in case.

Then I felt the crash and a searing "wrongness" in the world as the weapons on the warship let loose into the onrushing creatures. There was a sense of pressure, which was insane being on a moonlet, and entire packs of the oncoming enemy vanished in an eye blink, making me pause in amazement.

"Impressive and terrifying what ship-borne weapons can do to personnel, isn't it," Leshan said to me dryly. "Still, there's a great deal more coming, so if we could hurry along, please, sir?"

I turned, searching. Dozens more of the soldiers were arrayed in squads all around the massive warship, covering sections as the ship's weapons carved great lines through the oncoming enemies.

"Devourer. I request you return to our vessel immediately," came Aaronis's voice suddenly. "While we are in no danger of being eliminated by the onrushing mass, enough of them will damage the ship and delay our rendezvous."

"You're not at risk?" I asked.

"We are not." He snorted. "I mean no offense, Devourer, but considering your own effect on the one that you interacted with, I believe you can understand why? Few of your kind roam the expanse, but those who do? You can turn the tide of wars with good reason. One of your fellows made an adjustment to our armor template, instilling an immunity to such creations. Our ship, however, is granted no such protection, so please hurry."

With that, he closed the connection, and I cursed. I glanced back at the multi-ton mass of metal that was floating serenely through the extremely thin atmosphere of the blasted moon.

I hesitated only a brief second before speaking into the command link. *"Everyone back to the ship. Fly."* I deployed my wings, drawing stunned looks from the soldiers around us as we leapt into the air.

As soon as we left the ground, the effect that we'd been having, the frantic need that was driving the mass of corrupt to flood the area, seemed to lessen. It was clear by the way that those that could no longer see us changed.

The front rows, already racing forward and sensing us, continued. They ran without caring for their fellows. The giant troll-like fuckers crushed more under foot as three more, then four, stomped into view.

As they did, though, the rest started to drift. Farther back, more and more were turning, distracted by something, and although they apparently were too mindless to feel fear or pain, they were also mindless enough to get lost.

As more and more raced full-pelt into gulleys and gaps between structures, trying to find their way around them to the fresh meat in nice tinfoil before them, others followed.

The ship opened fire again. Point defense lasers and turrets slid from side to side, burning through thousands at a time.

Creatures long dead and denied their rest, their corpses bullied into a horrific semblance of life, were reduced to greasy smoke, which in turn collapsed as the lasers' heat stripped the thin atmosphere even further.

We landed on our own ship easily. The soldiers fell back in organized groups, leapfrogging each other, taking up position, then covering their companions as more and more repeated the motion. In a bare handful of minutes, it was all over.

Reaching out mentally, I guided the mass of metal sideways, bringing it in closer…until the warship activated a tractor beam and took over.

I relaxed; the strain had been more than I was used to, to hold something so large for so long. But in seconds, it was nestled tight by our ship, and Zac stomped across it, his own boots apparently magnetic as well.

The last of the soldiers stepped in closer beneath the warship, lines descending that attached to their suits. Then we all felt the shift and the sudden heaviness as we were lifting. The engines sent great blasts of fire and overpressure across the surface, charring and eliminating the hundreds of creatures that were left.

As soon as the ship was off the ground, I felt the gravity manipulation kick in, realizing that they had to have deliberately used the engines to clear a space and to make sure there was nothing aboard.

Stepping inside the airlock with the others, I allowed myself a little smile, reaching out and feeling my little gift to the airless moon, as it neared the edge of my range.

I triggered the brief set of orders I'd had time to load into it, feeling the shift as it began burrowing into the ship that lay beneath it. As the outer door sealed, the inner clanking as it adjusted to the pressure and tested the seals, I nodded to myself. Glad that, for once, we had a damn backup plan.

Chapter Twenty-One

The next few hours were both boring and exciting, alternating in bursts. We went from seeing everything that had happened outside, and examining the records that Aaronis gave us access to regarding the moon, to putting up with Zac. He was complaining about how hard it was to redesign a goddamn engine and its attendant parts.

He kept whining on and on, something about the entire ship dipping in and out of gravitational branes, and that we were clamped to the side of another vessel.

Apparently, the minor gravity fluctuations meant that any kind of calibration of the remaining, integrated, and much smaller engine couldn't be carried out. Although we could have done this if we were on a planet, or even inside the warship in a repair dock, being secured to the side of it through some combination of magnetics, gravitonics, and fuckknewwhatitics meant that was a no-go.

In the end, we accepted Aaronis's gracious offer, and damn well filed out of the ship, stomped across the warship's hull, and into the nearest air lock.

We'd waited a little while, as Zac needed time to scrap his current project and work on a pair of suits that would provide basic protection for both Casey and James. While he did that, I talked them through attuning their share of their nanites—we'd taken a literal pot of them from the Great Refuge that still held about sixty million units even after all of Zac's panicked uses of them on the test flights, so they got a decent dosing—and the eventual unlocking and assigning of their armor.

They were jobs that needed doing, but stepping into the warship was a weird experience.

The ship that was buried on Yuzhny Island was the same in many ways. Hell, it looked to literally be the exact model—like they had a factory somewhere that was set to churn out the same version again and again.

Unlike the ship that was buried in the north of Russia, though, this one was a working vessel, and it was full of signs of hard use. That one? It was almost pristine in comparison.

Literally, when the BWVs who had left that ship—I supposed I needed to find out what the hell they called themselves, besides that they were members of the UC—they'd closed it up carefully.

They'd done the maintenance required to make sure that if they needed to get it back up and running, they could do so, and they'd also done all the things you'd do when closing a house up for winter or whatever.

They'd cleaned it all down, making sure that everything was put away, bulkheads were sealed…the whole thing.

At some point, those mental bastards, the renat, had found their way in, and when the BWVs had returned to do whatever, they'd clearly left enough of an impression on them that they thought they were gods.

Then the Blessed had found the place and they'd been fighting over it, followed by that bitch Varnock making it ground zero for a new war with the Xi-Ma.

The renat had spent hundreds of years, if not thousands, redecorating with a skull and bone motif, one that covered the entire insides of the damn ship, focusing heavily over any form of tech. And that ship, even with all of that?

It was less battered than this one.

This looked like what happened when you took something pristine straight off the production line, then gave it to a bunch of marines for a weekend.

I don't mean that the ship had been lost, broken, or made pregnant—which was what usually happened when marines were left alone with anything, up to and including an anvil in a locked room. But still.

Everywhere we looked, there were signs of extreme wear.

Sections of the hull had been replaced with new paneling; then that had been damaged and fresh patches were laid over the top of those.

Walls had clearly been painted at some point. The drab utilitarian grey-blue that had probably been the original color—and that reminded me of travelling on any naval military vessel ever—was still visible here and there, but shit, it was battered.

There were stacked boxes that looked to have been hurriedly moved to one side as we entered the ship. And as soon as we exited the airlock, a team of soldiers, drawn up on either side of us, clapped fists to chest, before lowering their heads in a snap movement that looked heavily rehearsed.

Standing ready before me was the man I'd met on the link already, Field Commander Aaronis Balthazar, and by his side was Leshan.

Aaronis was a bear of a man, and Leshan was only slightly less huge out of her armor. Where he made me think of Russian stock— large hands, broad shoulders, his hair so much salt-and-pepper that although it might have been ginger or even brown once, you'd have no way to tell how long ago—she was more "strolling tiger" than bear.

The pair moved with a smooth grace that was almost unnerving, every movement looking like it was a hairsbreadth from lethal commitment.

It took a few seconds as we made the introductions—we'd brought everyone across but had hidden one of the custodians aboard the ship just in case—but it eventually clicked what it was.

It was a flow to their movements that was somewhat wrong, in my eyes, because they rested their arms, and stood slightly "weird."

It was the armor.

They unconsciously left their arms at the rest position that they'd fall into naturally if they were carrying a rifle and with the extra mass around their limbs of armor.

Add to that the movements as they did move? It was like when you watched a master martial artist perform a demonstration.

Every movement was smooth and refined. There was no wasted effort. And the sheer perfection of their movements made me feel slow, clumsy, and lumbering in comparison.

I could see that the others as we walked deeper into the ship felt the same way, even if they'd not yet realized why.

Ingrid, of course, took the lead, as I tried to get a handle on what was wrong here. They just seemed so goddamn happy to see us. I might be paranoid, but I sure as shit wasn't used to anyone being that happy to see me.

"Thank you for your invitation," she said with a smile, and Aaronis nodded, a tight-lipped smile clear.

"Please, refreshments have been provided, and a place to rest as we travel," he offered. "We are a military vessel, and on deployment, so luxuries are scarce, but all wished to contribute."

"Thank you?" I replied, not sure on the "contribute" part.

The airlock we'd entered through had led into a large open space, one that we recognized in our ship on Earth as having been filled with renat huts and similar places. It'd made it difficult to see what it was originally used for, but looking it over here, I had to guess a combination storage area and gathering point.

The ceiling was high, easily four meters, and the room had to be a hundred or so wide, by at least thirty deep. That we marched between soldiers drawn up for half of that distance, in rows three deep, made it clear they were an honor guard of some kind.

Ingrid and I—and the others, but it'd come down to Ingrid and me in the end, with James advising—had decided that sharing as little as possible was the best way to go here.

I didn't like it, but until we knew where we stood, this was the safest way.

Aaronis led us from the first room, into a corridor, then down that and up to the next level. All the way, the scratched, battered, and oft-repaired nature of the ship was made clear.

I wasn't sure whether this was an attempt to show us that they were always in the fight, so basically "don't fuck with us" or whether they were leading us a way that was designed to hide the main damage, and this was simply the least damaged route?

Hell, it might have been that they didn't even consider how scuffed, battered, and broken the ship looked.

"So, what can you tell me of your people?" I asked Aaronis as we walked, and he glanced at me, before taking a deep breath.

"You mean of our history, our culture, or something else?"

"Yes," I said, before shooting him a smile. "Honestly, we'd like to know all of it. My group is diverse, as we weren't sure what to expect, so anything and everything is of interest."

"Perhaps the past would be a good place to start, and your current situation with the Ændari?" Ingrid pointed out.

"That, again, is complex, and when we were tasked to meet you, we were given strict guidelines, so many details will have to be omitted," he said apologetically. "But I can explain the basics, certainly."

The next room we entered was one we were more familiar with, considering we'd used it on the ship for exactly this use as well. It was literally a large meeting room, a wide table with identical, individual seats.

Curving up from the ground, they flowed as if they'd been grown out of steel, and yet were surprisingly comfortable, as well as almost impossible to move until you learned the trick.

Holding onto the back, you squeezed, then moved them smoothly but slowly. If you tried to make a sudden movement? They locked in place. Try to push them back without gripping the correct area, on either side of the seat or the seat back?

You weren't going anywhere. They locked to the deck magnetically. And when Zac had examined them, he'd mentioned a form of molecular bonding that was just insane.

That our hosts led us into the room with these chairs could be a test. Not sure exactly what they were looking for, still, we demonstrated that we had access to and were familiar with the tech, as they waited for us to sit, then joined us.

The table was set with a load of food, none of which we recognized, and when I glanced at Aaronis in question, he smiled.

"Meals from the home worlds of the crew," he said proudly. "They each wanted to contribute."

"Thank you," Ingrid said again, forcing a smile.

I glanced at her; I knew she was feeling the same unsettled, frankly freaked out, feeling I was.

"So, do you regularly eat like this?" I gestured at the food before us. "The ship's converters make life a lot easier."

"The converters…" He hesitated, before shaking his head. "They are limited to certain meals, unfortunately. Yours are different then?"

He was fishing, just as much as I was, I guessed.

"They're limited," I agreed. "Much of what we'd like to access was lost."

"You lost access to it?" he asked slowly, settling back and lowering the fork he'd just picked up, looking as if he'd been sucker punched in the gut. "All of the designs?"

"Which designs?"

"Which designs do you have access to?" he shot back, watching me.

"Oh, you know, some." The rest of the table was silent as we talked. The others waited and watched, as both Aaronis and I tried to pretend we were more suited to this shit than we were.

"Perhaps a different starting point?" Ingrid suggested. "Commander Balthazar, you were given certain information you could share with us, I'd expect?"

"I was given recommendations of areas to avoid," he admitted. "The current political and militaristic situations chief amongst them."

"So, was the past discussed?"

"In part," he said.

I glanced from one to the other, reaching out and spearing what looked like a chicken skewer, minus the skewer. The mystery meat was pale as hell, lumpy and sealed together, but more importantly, it was dripping a red sauce that was either a really thick Chinese style glaze, or…

"May we ask what you were advised?"

"Fuck it," I muttered, drawing their eyes back to me as I bit down, having noticed that everyone was waiting for someone else to start eating.

"What do you think?" Leshan asked me after a few seconds as I chewed carefully.

"It's different," I said diplomatically. "The sauce?"

"Lanatai."

"And that is?"

"A form of spice," Leshan said slowly, clearly wanting to smile, but trying to be professional.

"Tastes a bit like a sweet chili dip," I told the others, taking another bite and watching her as she glanced from me to the group, waiting.

"Oh my fucking God…" Zac groaned, after a single bite, fanning at his mouth.

"Oh man, now that's *nice*!" Paul declared, grabbing another, as Zac, who apparently had absolutely no tolerance for spicy food, desperately searched for a drink.

Leshan looked at me and nodded slightly toward one of the jugs of liquid as Zac frantically poured a glass from the other. I poured a drink from the one she'd indicated, sipping at it, and found it was even spicier than the food.

She poured herself one and drank it down in one.

"Paul," I offered, having tasted it and finding that although it was harsh, it was harsh like good rum, with a complex aftertaste.

"Damn," he whispered. "I don't know where you got this one from, but I want to go."

"It's from my home." Leshan nodded to him in respect as he took another gulp. "But perhaps slow down on it. It is difficult to make, and rare."

"Shit, so it's expensive." He winced. "Uh, sorry."

"No, I chose to share it here, so please, do enjoy it. I wanted others to have a chance to share it, that's all," she clarified.

"Boss, do we have anything in ours like this?" Paul asked, as Jay tried it, before smiling.

"Oh, ah think ah can provide something ya'll will like," he assured us.

"Jay is our chef." I introduced him. "If you like barbecue, he's a king of the slow-roasted brisket."

"I'm sure that is wonderful," Aaronis responded diplomatically. "However, I suggest we limit the conversation to such matters as this." He gestured to the table before us. "I am no diplomat, and the details you wish will be shared on the Forgeship soon enough."

"What's a Forgeship?" Zac asked, still trying to put out the burning of his tongue. "Damn, that's hot!"

251

"A Forgeship?" Aaronis said slowly, glancing at Leshan. "The Forgeships are ancient, but given that we are approaching one now, I think their existence is obvious enough that we can discuss them."

"They are the hearts of the UC," Leshan agreed. "Mighty fleets protect each, and they in turn build the fleets, providing the required tools of war that keep our people safe."

"So they're like mobile shipyards?" Zac asked. "Giant ships that make other ships?"

"Essentially," Aaronis said after a few seconds. "Though it is an oversimplification. The Forgeships once consumed entire asteroids, and are still the backbone of the UC. There are legends of greater vessels, but as an example, should you wish to walk across the surface of a Forgeship, moving at a normal walking speed, it would take you around sixty of your solar cycles to return to the same point."

"Holy shit," I muttered. "So they're big, all right."

"And this ship was produced in one?" Ingrid asked suddenly.

"Yes," Aaronis admitted warily.

"Was it produced intact?"

"I do not understand."

"I mean, was it produced all in one go, with all the technology in place?" she clarified. "The guns, the engines, the bedding, everything?"

"It was."

"And it was produced using a factory unit, one that converts raw materials into literally a fully stocked ship, but you've been forced into patching and repairing this ship, as it is?"

"Yes." He hesitated, then shook his head. "Forgive me, Ingrid, I cannot answer more. Clearly you are seeking some knowledge, but my instructions are to discuss as little of import as possible with you, and to render a report when we are on our approach. As such, I ask that we limit our conversation to mundane matters. Perhaps you could tell us of your home world?"

"Certainly." She smiled. "If you tell us of yours?"

The next hour or more, until Aaronis left, leaving us with Leshan as we neared the rendezvous, was spent talking about the most mundane details we could. Everything from discussing the water and temperature of our worlds to the numbers and population centers or tech levels was done carefully.

When Leshan in turn left us to it, the ship apparently docking, and we were asked to remain in the conference room, I couldn't help but breathe a sigh of relief.

"Fuck me, that was painful," I whispered. "Seriously, what the fuck?"

"They want details on who and what we are, and so do we," Ingrid said simply.

"Yeah, but they're giving us nothing," I pointed out. "If they distrust us that much, why let us aboard? Hell, why even speak to us?"

"They wish to know if we are a threat, potential allies, or neutral parties," Scylla said, getting a nod from Jonas.

"So why invite us in?" Paul asked. "I mean, they could have just left us aboard our ship. I'd not have had to put pants on."

"Believe me," James said dryly. "One of the rules of returning to that ship is that you must wear pants in any and all social situations."

"But…"

"Please, God," Courtney said quickly. "I approve of this rule."

"Hey! You're naked more than I am!" Paul complained.

"Really?" Zac asked, perking up as he looked over at the toned and well-muscled soldier…and then began apologizing frantically as Casey apparently grabbed something under the table and squeezed.

"Social means outside of your room or where anyone else might see you, Paul, and pants are *not* optional." Ingrid sighed. "I swear, it's like looking after a child."

"We've got kids in the family, our Gunnar is generally better behaved," Courtney assured her. "So, what's the game plan?"

"We back Ingrid and Steve up, and learn all we can," James said. "In the meantime, if you are at all unsure if you should say something, take a lesson from our hosts. Simply explain that you are unsure what is appropriate to share, and as such direct all questions to Ingrid."

"Not Steve?" Zac asked.

Silence reigned for several seconds as everyone looked at me before James spoke.

"As I said, direct questions to *Ingrid*."

"I hate you all," I muttered.

We cleared the table, by which I mean we ate practically everything up to and including the cutlery and the plates, then sat about, relaxing as we waited.

Several times, I was tempted to reach out, arguing with myself as I went from "it's common sense; be prepared just in case" and "don't fucking antagonize the super soldiers," and in the end, I behaved.

It was damn hard, though.

Eventually, just as I was debating asking them where the hell the nearest toilet was, and whether we needed an escort to use it—I was guessing that they needed to have them, after all; there were some in the ship we had, but they were in individual quarters only—when Aaronis returned.

"We're here," he said, and I cursed. The goddamn warship hadn't made a single sound we could hear as it landed.

Chapter Twenty-Two

We got to our feet quickly, with Jay being pretty unsubtle as he tried to hide his "doggy bag" of samples that he was apparently going to be feeding to his factory unit aboard our ship.

We were all as smartly dressed as we were going to get, though, so we trooped out to follow Aaronis as he led us through the ship.

"Are you going with us?" I asked him, and the grizzled soldier hesitated, before shaking his head.

"I do not know," he admitted. "I was ordered to deliver you to the council representatives, but I am unsure I will be permitted to enter the chamber, nor take part in the discussions."

"Why not?" Ingrid asked.

"I am a simple field commander." He shrugged. "I am not involved in politics beyond the sharp end."

"Yeah, I'd rather be on the front lines as well," I said. "I'm not good with the careful phrases and so on."

"A soldier's place is where we are sent," he agreed. "Either way, it was our honor to have hosted you aboard our ship, and to have shared our food."

I looked at him, seeing that he genuinely meant that, and I couldn't help but ask why.

"Because regardless of the outcome of your meeting, at worst, you are another offshoot of our past, and at best…"

"At best?" I prompted when he fell silent.

"Are you really from the Forgeworld?" he asked suddenly, the sharply indrawn breath from Leshan as we approached the air lock ahead clear.

"I don't know what that is."

"The home, the place we came from, all of our kind." His voice dropped to barely above a whisper. "They said you killed Varnock the Defiler. Is it true?"

"We all did. Hell, Ingrid actually made the final blow."

"But they were exiled," he said quickly. "They were trapped on the Forgeworld, supposedly to punish them for creating us all and using us for their own twisted desires."

"What, like, fuck buddies?" I asked, stunned. "Seriously, I didn't get that vibe from her at all. I mean—"

"Steve!" Ingrid cut me off. "I think Aaronis means that they were taught that Varnock and the others created us without the Ændari Council's approval."

"Exactly…" Aaronis glanced at her. "You say that in a way that suggests that they did approve?"

"From what we know, we were all created to be her race's tools of conquest," Ingrid said softly. "And yes, our world was where the tests were first carried out, as near as we can tell."

"So it has been found at last," he whispered. "And so close…"

"How the hell was it ever lost?" I shook my head. "I mean, it's not like it takes a long time to travel between stars…"

"Quarantine zones," he said quickly, slowing slightly as we neared the exit. "We didn't discuss this, but…the corrupt? Any system that is found to house a significant number of them is quarantined, the surrounding systems restricted. They've been known to spread like wildfire. And as much as they are little threat to us in our armor, should they reach a population center, they've been known to spread in exponential curves, causing the loss of billions."

"Entire worlds were reduced to glass," Leshan agreed. "So when the corrupt show up, the systems they're in are quarantined, and the surrounding ones as well, until a full cleansing can be carried out."

"But if the infection is too deep?" Aaronis finished. "If too many worlds are lost to it, then the area is restricted. Set for a full cleansing in the future, when it is 'economically viable.'" He practically spat out that last bit.

"Until then, any ship that is caught accessing the systems are viewed as contaminated, and are banned from any UC facility. Should they attempt to enter a UC system, or even one of the independents? It'll be fired on, as I explained before."

"There are independent worlds?" Ingrid latched onto that before I could, and he nodded.

"Around half of the UC military comes from the independent worlds. 'Serve and gain citizenship' and all that," Leshan added.

"Steve, a little advice?" Aaronis said quietly. "Not all the council will seek to aid you. Some may look to take care of their own 'need' first, even ahead of those of the UC, and perhaps…those who should greet you most assiduously may yet try to gain the most."

"It's time," Leshan said quickly.

Aaronis straightened, looking at me meaningfully.

"Thanks," I whispered, then nodded as the airlock entrance cycled, the inner door opening for us. Leshan and two of her soldiers accompanied Aaronis and the rest of us. But as soon as we stepped outside, the massive outer air lock cycling open, it was clear that we weren't in Kansas anymore.

The hangar that we sat inside of made the warship we'd just exited look like a pea in a drum. It was hundreds of meters high, thousands of meters of space to the right and the left, and parked at regular intervals, gleaming and seemingly ready, were warships identical to the one we'd just left.

Arise :Explorer

The looks on Leshan's and Aaronis's faces at seeing those ships there, gleaming and unmarred by battle, while their own ship looked so beaten up, was priceless.

They were stunned, and clearly hadn't been expecting to see them, giving us another little tidbit to file away, as a hint of jealousy reared its head on seeing them.

The reception committee waiting for us was made up of three distinct races, and humans were the smallest of them, as well as appearing to be physically the weakest.

Aaronis marched up and saluted, index and middle fingertips pressed over his heart, and he bowed his head.

"Honored Council members, I am Field Commander Aaronis Balthazar. Eleventh Assault Brigade, Fifth Wing. Thus has my duty been fulfilled."

"Thank you, Field Commander," one of the central figures said with a slight growl, ducking its head in reply. "The Assault Brigades, as always, serve the UC with honor."

It sounded ritualistic, but as far as I was concerned, it was a minor detail. The really important one? The guy speaking—or girl; I mean, I had no way to tell—was a saurian and they were freaking huge.

They were easily four meters at the shoulders, bipedal with a slight forward lean, offset by the long tail that flicked behind them. The speaker wore little; a cloak of flowing purple silk that ran from the shoulders, with a narrow band of spikes, like antlers protruding from its back, getting shorter and shorter as they rose from behind its shoulder blades to flow around to jut forward from above the temples.

He was heavily muscled, with tech embedded in a sort of shoulder harness that the cloak was attached to, almost like he was wearing a backpack, then decided to install a good desktop's worth of tech into the straps.

That they wore something that looked more like a thong than anything else for modesty was also a little alarming.

I felt overdressed and wondered instinctively whether I was going to end up walking around in budgie smugglers in council meetings.

The saurian had a low jaw that jutted forward, exposed, sharp teeth, and recessed black, marble-like eyes beneath heavy brows.

Topping off the impression that the speaker was a warrior, or at least dangerous as fuck, was that they wore a glove on their right hand that was covered in blades, and their left hand was kept free.

It reached up and pressed the fingers of the non-weapon-wielding hand to its chest and bowed its head to Aaronis, before rising and focusing on me.

I'd noticed as we approached that there were three of these creatures. On the far side were three humans, who looked almost childlike in comparison, and between them were four of another, taller race of beings that floated just off the ground.

The floaters moved gently and gracefully, as if they were underwater. Four tentacles in place of legs, and three arms, spaced equidistantly around the body were weird enough, but the weirdest thing was the *head*.

They had three faces, literally. Their faces stuck out, spaced equally around the head, and as they watched us approach, they spun gently, a different head coming to the fore to watch.

The humans?

They were the weirdest of all.

Where the soldiers like Aaronis and Leshan were huge and clearly augmented, like I and my people were, these humans looked stunted, as though they'd started growing, then just…gave it up.

Where the saurian were huge and well-muscled, projecting an air of competent danger, and the floaters were, well, *weird* but looked to be interested, the humans were dressed to impress. All reds and golds, silver hues and gemstones.

"Be welcome, Steve of the Devourers." The lead saurian bowed its head lower than it had for Aaronis, making the point of stooping so that its own head was lower than mine. "I am Shanah, First of the Triumvirate of Saa aboard the Forgeship *Hephaestus*."

"I am Clicqo," the next in line said, floating forward. "I lead the Delegates of Orm aboard the Forgeship *Hephaestus*."

I nodded to the blue floating creature.

"I am the Lord Emberalis, High Seat of the House of Paendrag, Guide of the Eastern Marches, He Who Grants Succor, Wolven Bane, Emissary Potentate for the Worlds of Hemora…" The human who had stepped forward hadn't stopped where he was. Instead, he'd subtly edged in front of the others, and was reeling off title after title, clearly intent on going on for several minutes until Shanah let loose a cough that sounded like a growl, hurrying the smallest figure along.

"I lead the Right Arm of Man aboard the Forgeship *Hephaestus*," he finished sourly, only stepping back when he realized he was getting glares from literally everyone else in their group.

"Thank you all for your greeting," I said in as polite and respectful a tone as I could manage, instantly disliking the guy, but not really knowing why. "And my thanks to Field Commander Aaronis Balthazar, and the Eleventh Assault Brigade for their kind guidance and assistance after our own craft suffered damage. This is Ingrid, my co-leader."

I'd deliberately avoided adding anything else. For a few seconds, as Emberalis had been going on, I'd been tempted to claim to be an emperor or something just to fuck with him, before deciding that less was more, and the title of Devourer was clearly impressive as fuck to these people already.

"Well done, Commander Balthazar," Emberalis said before anyone else could add anything. "I believe your ship has patrols to continue along?"

"I noted on our arrival that you had many such vessels as the commander's?" I gestured to the rows of parked ships vanishing into the distance.

"We do. This is one of the greatest of the Forgeships," Emberalis said proudly.

"Excellent. Their ship was damaged when we made contact," I said, speaking entirely on instinct. "I was concerned that they might be punished for my own mistakes. I assume that it won't be a problem to provide them with a new ship then?"

"Your ship was damaged?" Shanah rumbled, glancing at Aaronis. "Are your crew intact?"

"My crew are fine, though thank you for your concern, Shanah of the Triumvirate of Saa. The damage was—"

"The damage was not your fault," Ingrid said quickly, cutting him off and picking up the conversation. "A minor issue caused by us being forced to rush to this meeting surely wouldn't be held against him?"

I noted the way that Ingrid smiled at the other two, before bowing her head to Shanah.

"Of course not," the big saurian rumbled. "As you noted, there are several of that model of warship available in this area. I believe not all of these have been assigned a new crew yet, have they, Lord Emberalis?"

"Well, no, but the materials cost alone of a new ship—" the human started, before cutting off as Ingrid snorted.

"Oh, I'm sorry," she apologized, smiling prettily. "I assumed you were joking. The cost of a new ship of that size, well, it's simply the old ship, isn't it? With an energy penalty, certainly, but a fifth of its size being stripped from an asteroid would provide that, wouldn't it? Or don't you have access to such technologies?"

"We do!" he said quickly. "But we would be interested in discussing your own, and of course, as you were responsible for that damage being inflicted..."

"We of course would not dream of holding you responsible," Shanah rumbled.

"No, we do not," Clicqo agreed, all four of its kind spinning to show first smiling faces to us, then flowing back in perfect choreography to show a calm face again.

"Then it's settled." I smiled. "A wonderful first meeting between us all, and any debt to the commander, on our behalf, is absolved."

"It is," Emberalis agreed sourly. "Perhaps we can discuss such debts later in private, one to one."

"All things are possible," Ingrid replied. The pair of us took note of the way that the four "Delegates of Orm" shifted suddenly.

The first face that we'd seen watching us, an open and calm appearing one, was replaced with an angry one on two of them; the other two remained calm, outwardly, as they all turned to face Emberalis.

"Anyone else think the little guy isn't popular?" Jonas sent to the group.

"Hush," James sent back, but I could feel his agreement.

"Now that is dealt with, perhaps we could discuss your situation?" Shanah gestured with one arm toward a door off to one side. "We are unsure of your negotiating style. Some races prefer to do so over a shared meal, as mine do, while others find that offensive. We mean you no insult."

"None taken," I said. "I'm always ready to eat."

That was true as well. It'd been a good meal, and it was less than an hour ago, but one of the "wonders" of nanites was that although you were never really in danger of dying through starvation, as they could absorb energy when needed from the air...you were always ready to eat.

James had commented that it was down to the way our bodies processed food. They'd grown so much more efficient it was unreal, but the side effect was that you were empty a *lot* sooner.

"Excellent. Do you have dietary requirements?" Shanah asked.

"We ate aboard Aaronis's ship on our way in. All the foods served there were excellent," I said happily. "But we're omnivores, much as your own BWVs are."

"That…is not a common term in use here," Shanah said carefully, glancing at the human in their midst.

"We are usually known by the world we hail from," Emberalis added, sounding offended. "Our slave designations are *never* used."

"Then we apologize," Ingrid said quickly, shooting me a glance in warning. "It was not our intent to offend."

"I am a soldier," I said bluntly. "My partner and co-leader Ingrid is far more diplomatic than I am, but I also meant no offense."

"And none is taken," Shanah said firmly, glaring at the small human group when it looked as though they might disagree. "When a word is used in error, and then an apology is given freely and without reservation, then my people dismiss any harm that had been inflicted. Otherwise, grudges are formed, and that way leads to anger."

"I feel the same way." I agreed with the big saurian. "So, let's get food and a chat. Aaronis, are you joining us?" I turned to him.

"I think not, but thank you for the invitation, Devourer," he said, a twitch of a smile clear as he glanced from me to the council members and back. "If I am to move my entire command to a new ship, then I have much to do before I leave on my patrol. Thank you again for your kind words. It was our honor to escort you here."

"I'd like to see you again before you leave on patrol, if possible," I said, not wanting to give anyone a chance to weasel out of giving him a shiny new ship. "Perhaps a tour of your ship when you're all settled in?"

"It would be my honor," he said. With that, he and his team left, as Shanah and the others led us across the hangar and toward a nearby set of doors.

"Nearby" was a relative term, though, considering the size of the damn ship. I half expected an X-wing to drop something down an exhaust port at any minute.

The room that we were led to was smaller than I'd assumed, and although there were enough seats for us all, it was clearly going to be cramped.

Add to that, the table was multileveled to accommodate everyone, which took up even more space. The one thing it really had going for it, though, was a hell of a view.

A single wall had been replaced with what seemed to be glass, and it looked out across an indoor forest. Alien trees twisted in peculiar shapes and crystal gleamed as it reflected the light of two presumably simulated suns overhead.

Shanah pointed out the chairs that were for our party, before hesitating. "In negotiations, always there is the risk of offense, therefore we say this respectfully…perhaps, not all of your party are required?"

"Zac, want to go on a tour of the facility?" I asked him bluntly.

"Hell yes!" he agreed quickly.

"James, keep them out of trouble." I nodded in the direction of the door, wishing that I'd been able to go with them. The weird woodland below looked way more fun to explore than the damn meeting with these guys promised to be.

"And Belle? No shagging anyone."

I got a sense of an amused "Oh, all right" from Belle, and excitement from the others as Ingrid and I moved deeper into the room, taking our seats as they all left. Two of Clicqo's companions, and one each of Shanah and Emberalis's, went with them.

"Thank you," Shanah said, before huffing out an annoyed breath as Emberalis shifted a chair to sit between the saurian and us. The table was round, and Emberalis was clearly setting up an "us and them" layout, while smiling at Ingrid *waaaay* too much.

I'd not noticed it at first—well, not much—because Aaronis's people did the same, staring at Ingrid and the others of the party with longer hair, because for them, it clearly wasn't an option in their helmets.

I'd figured it was just a peculiarity of the soldier caste or whatever. The BWVs under the ocean had done the same, after all. But seeing the others here, I realized that wasn't it, or at least that wasn't all of it.

For the soldiers, the long hair was a thing. I liked it myself, so I couldn't complain, but they were much more in awe of her than consumed with lust.

The looks the human contingent were giving her, though… They weren't gazing at her with hungry "I fancy the pants off her" looks. They were more like cats eyeing a mouse, and I realized I was getting some of the same looks from them as well.

That made me pause, and I silently cursed myself. If I was picking up on things from the humans, that had to be either because they were deliberately laying those things out for me to catch, because they were just so unsubtle that even I could catch it, or…

Or I didn't know. But one thing that stood out for me was that if I was picking it up from these guys, that meant that I was probably missing all the signs the alien ones were giving off.

I made a mental note to look out for that, then cursed myself for getting fucking distracted in the middle of talks already.

"…History," Emberalis finished with a toothy smile.

"Of course, we'd be pleased to share our history," Ingrid replied after a few seconds as I clearly tried to figure out what I'd missed. "But, some of our history and yours will be different, so perhaps you could start us off. I'd love to understand more of the history of our distant cousins."

"Perhaps we should start with something more recent," Shanah suggested, seeming to smile as he steepled his fingers, leaning his elbows on the table and peering down at Ingrid and Emberalis.

"Yeah, recent sounds good," I agreed. "Let's start with the condition of the UC and the Ændari. Also, I'm really not very good at the whole verbal fencing thing, so how about you tell us where you stand, and we'll tell you where we do?"

There was a minute of silence, as I could literally feel Ingrid being torn between cursing me and laughing her ass off at the affronted look on Emberalis's face.

"We agree," Clicqo said suddenly. "We do not hide our intentions as much as other races. We find such posturing frustrating, and welcome a desire for clear communication."

"We accept," Shanah rumbled.

"Of course." Emberalis smiled toothily. "A straight and clear discussion is refreshing."

"So?" I prompted, only to be cut off as Shanah lifted one hand, looking into the distance as all the little council stiffened.

"What the…" I muttered, only to hear alarms break out, filling the air.

Symbols on the silvery walls nearby suddenly burst to life. Red flashing triangles that folded into themselves became a virulent yellow, then red again; script flowed across them in glowing 3D letters that neither of us could read.

"It appears we have a problem." Emberalis stared at us as all the locals seemed to wake at the same time. "The Ændari."

"They're dickheads," I said instinctively, "but what's the problem?"

"They have arrived here, as in 'here in the system.' Their nearest system ambassador just arrived, with a significant portion of the quadrant's battle fleet," Clicqo replied slowly. "And they demand the right to land and discuss matters of a breach of the cease-fire."

"Are you going to let them?" I asked.

"Considering they ask permission, but with a fleet drawn up behind them?" Emberalis asked. "I vote we accept their request for parley."

"We have no choice," agreed Clicqo, all four faces now showing the angry one. "Our fleet is maintaining patrol, with only a fraction of its force here. While we could hold them off, waiting on our forces returning…"

"We have no choice," agreed Shanah. "They clearly know of your arrival, and regardless of how they have come to this, they must be faced eventually." He turned to face Ingrid and me, and sighed.

"The Ændari have invoked the right to parley, claiming that a senior scientist of their race has been brutally murdered by a criminal hiding aboard this Forgeship. The terms of the cease-fire are clear, and should you be an unaffiliated third party, then this decision should be easy," Shanah admitted.

"Regardless of the 'right' of the situation, handing over one small vessel to stave off a war in which hundreds of millions would die is an obvious decision," Emberalis agreed after a pause. "However, to hand over honest people, who have done no wrong? I refuse. I claim them as my own family."

"I…what?" I asked, confused and stunned.

"I name you kin," he repeated, smiling widely. "Don't be afraid. It's simply a formality, and it doesn't lessen your own authority. It simply formalizes your position as members of my clan."

"Under your authority, I assume?" I asked carefully, feeling suddenly like we were being maneuvered into this.

"Well, certainly, as the head of my clan, that would be part of this, but is that really so terrible?" He appeared shocked. "To prevent a war, you fear submitting to my authority so much?"

"Perhaps another option would be wiser," Shanah rumbled. "After all, our original intention is still valid."

"And yet there's a battle fleet closing on the Forgeship as we speak," Emberalis said quickly. "Our options are far more limited than we wish—"

"Regardless, any opportunity to prevent war in the quadrant must be taken," Clicqo declared. "We must listen to their submission, and yet, this cannot be a coincidence that they are here, now, just as you arrive."

"So, most likely we have a spy in our midst," Shanah admitted. "Very well. Give their ambassador permission to land. And Emberalis?"

"Yes?"

"Cease this maneuvering. There is no time."

"Did I interfere with your actions in Rigel?" Emberalis asked Shanah scathingly. "No, and yet you believe—"

"My own actions in Rigel had no risk to the quadrant," Shanah snapped. "These do. Cease them, I say!"

"Perhaps these discussions would be better off held in private," Clicqo suggested carefully. "For now, with limited time, we must move quickly."

"And here it comes," I muttered.

"You chose to come to this meeting, and you knew that in doing so, by involving the UC as we have chosen to do, we would bear the majority of the risk," Shanah said clearly, watching Ingrid and me over the top of his interlaced fingers, as finally, the food was carried in. "You must have realized there would be a cost."

"Yes and no," Ingrid said softly, sitting forward and smiling at the massive saurian. "We realized that the announcement and contact meant that both the Ændari and the UC still existed. What that would mean for us and for our world? We didn't know."

"And we fucking still don't," I added, leaning forward and resting both hands on the table. "Seriously, you're all hinting that you want something, right? Well, so do we. Thing is, nobody has a clue what the cards the other has are worth, because none of us have a fucking clue what's going on!"

"What my partner means to say," Ingrid said quickly, "is that without context, neither side is fully aware of the potential we have. How long do we have before the ambassador is here?"

"About twenty of your minutes," Clicqo admitted.

"See, that's a fucking great example right there!" I snapped. "Twenty of 'our minutes'…you know what a minute is, so why the hell did you say a solar cycle in that message? What the fuck does that even mean?!"

"We are learning about you currently," the alien replied. "One of our mates has only recently asked for your references of time."

"Clicqo is the lead of their people, but each of their companions are sharing their interactions," Shanah explained, and when I looked at Ingrid in question, she nodded.

"I think anything said to one of the aliens is said to all of them, like they share a hive mind or some form of communication like our command link," she explained to me by private link, and I grunted.

"Okay, so we've got twenty minutes to sort this shit out. Who wants to go first?" I asked.

"What is it that you wish?" Shanah asked.

"We need to know who and what you all are, and what the hell is going on in this quadrant," Ingrid said quickly. "The information we have may be incorrect or out of date."

"It is almost certainly both of those things." Shanah sighed, before shaking his massive head at the food that was finally laid out before them all. "What a waste…"

"A waste?" I asked.

"The Ændari believe that feeding in front of another race is a sign of weakness, and so, if we are to speak with them soon, much of this will be left."

"Nope," I said firmly, reaching out and grasping a leg of something that looked like a chicken drumstick, if the chicken had been the size of a horse. "I'm eating, so someone else can start and we'll add in our history once you're done. Tick-tock!"

"Tick…" Clicqo muttered, before shaking its head. "A reference to time passing I suspect." It reached out to delicately lift a small dish of raw, pale flesh, and moved it closer to itself, slipping a section into a hole that opened up at the base of its throat, while continuing to speak. "As I do not need to cease eating to speak, I shall start."

<u>Chapter Twenty-Three</u>

"Our race was one of the original sapient races in this quadrant, and one of only five still to exist to this point in time, in any marked numbers. Some thousand years ago, we expanded from our world, into a galaxy that was already aflame with the wars that have raged since."

"They come from a water world," Emberalis added, gesturing with something like a pear, seemingly not hungry. "As such, and with an abundance of such chemicals being more readily available from gas giants, their world had been mostly ignored."

"It was a mistake by all sides, as we were abundantly rich in many flora and fauna, and yet—"

"Ninety percent of their home world is locked under ice, and until they reached the stars, nobody even knew they were sapient," Emberalis muttered to Ingrid, clearly trying to foster the "them and us" image more. I grunted in annoyance as Clicqo ignored the byplay, and Ingrid pretended it'd been a helpful comment, nodding.

"Once we reached the stars, beginning to explore the local system, we discovered that our timing could not have been worse," Clicqo continued. "A recent pitched battle had left much of our system contaminated with drifting wreckage and hundreds of warships, and their unexpended munitions were left to spiral into the gravitational pull of nearby worlds, one of which we inhabited.

"The crew of the exploratory craft attempted to deflect much of the incoming debris, and eventually gave their lives in that effort, all the while transmitting their findings to the world below." The alien paused, bowing their head and breaking off to speak in a low ritual tone as the others waited patiently.

After about a minute, with me getting worried about how much time they were wasting, they finally raised their head and went on.

"Those lost that day, and over the subsequent months and years to the incoming devastation, are remembered with great reverence by my people, not least because their actions convinced us to band together.

"No longer were we dissenting tribes and clans who argued over the use of our resources and world, fighting petty wars over arbitrary lines on a map. We banded together and formed the first Delegates of Orm."

"Orm is their home world, and the delegates are groups of three to eleven of their people, bound together through a linkage that enables them to share their minds and experiences. If you speak to one of the delegates, you speak to all of their bonded group," Emberalis said softly in explanation, before taking a delicate bite of his fruit.

"Just so," Clicqo agreed. "Once we had developed the Congress of Orm, our focus turned to security and protecting our people from the incidents in the stars that had so recently laid waste to our world.

"We started small, sending up fast, but poorly constructed craft, desperate to make it into orbit, to claim as much of the surviving technology as possible before it could be damaged entering our atmosphere. Much of what we found was badly damaged already, of course. But that which wasn't was quickly gathered. A small space station followed.

"Over the next several years, we expanded the station rapidly, devoting a massive amount of the production of our world to ensuring that not only was the station and our world as secure as possible, but that we were ready for the next time the invaders came."

"Which was when we met," Shanah interjected; the big saurian had been tearing bites out of a similar leg to the one I was eating. "We'd entered the system, having detected signals from a fleet lost nearby, and our vessels came looking for emergency pods."

"Unbeknownst to my people, we'd been salvaging such pods, and believing that no sapient creature could survive the conditions that the bodies were in, we'd set them free to travel to the next life," Clicqo whispered, shaking its head in sorrow.

"Our emergency pods had frozen their occupants and had been keeping them in hibernation at the time," Shanah said regretfully. "Both sides, on meeting, took offense at the first opportunity."

"We believed that the invaders had despoiled our system, and held them responsible for the deaths of hundreds of thousands, through the munitions and debris that devastated our world, and they…"

"We found that an unknown race had stripped our hibernating brethren from their pods and had then apparently burned them in some savage offering to their gods," Shanah said. "They stole our technology, and threatened the recovery vessel with it, before accidentally activating a distress beacon."

"It was one of the pods that had belonged to the Ændari we accidentally triggered, as it was they who Shanah's ancestors had warred with," Clicqo added sadly. "The activation of an enemy distress beacon only made it seem more suspicious. Both sides saw only the worst in each other, and when they began the fight, others would follow."

"At the same time, a new force, tricked by the Ændari into servitude, was being deployed in a system nearby," Emberalis explained. "The originals that you know as BWVs were lied to and controlled by their Ændari overlords, forced into fighting with others for their gain. Truly, it was a dark time."

"A dark time indeed, but one that led to the alliance of the United Confederation," Shanah said. "Time is brief, and although I would recommend

265

that learning the truth of the wars and background of the systems is valuable to understand each of the races, we cannot spend that time now. As such, the shortened version."

"Go on." I nodded, biting down on the leg again. I'd been listening, don't get me wrong, but damn the leg was good. It was tender, tasty, and all it needed was a little butter, garlic, salt, and mayo and I'd have been set for the rest of the day.

"As our two races fought, the BWVs devastated world after world. Word spread of a devastating new weapon that was being deployed by the Ændari, and a coalition was formed of smaller worlds. Although individually we were unable to fight them, together, we had a chance," Shanah declared.

"Eleven species and star systems banded together, bringing the Ændari advance to a halt. As the war escalated, a small force of the new creatures crashed on the surface of a moon, and in the subsequent battle for the system, they were left behind when the Ændari retreated.

"Once they were cut off from their controllers, however, the reality of the situation became clear, and the BWVs were offered amnesty, as well as support. They had already grown to distrust their overlords, and although they distrusted us as well, the evidence that we gave them matched their own suspicions."

"On learning that we'd been used, forced to conquer worlds against our will, our ancestors rebelled, leading the fight against their oppressors the Ændari, and freeing their brothers and sisters," Emberalis said quickly, leaning in to take over the story, twisting it to sound as positive as possible. "The next few hundred cycles were dark ones, for all the galaxy. And at the end of it, only a fraction of those who had fought so valiantly still lived."

"Hundreds of millions died in their ships," Shanah said. "Tens of billions more were lost across the worlds that were scorched from existence. The galaxy was left torn and battered, and in the end, a cease-fire was agreed. It was not a peace, there can never be a peace with the Ændari, but a cessation of hostilities was accepted."

"Much was lost in the wars, including the home worlds of many races. An agreement was reached that the Forgeships would be built, and that no genetic uplifting would ever be permitted. Knowing that they could never expunge that they were responsible for the destruction of so much, that it was their fault and their wars, the Ændari started to shift the blame onto anyone they could.

"It had been the Ændari attacking my people that had caused the battle that devastated Orm, like so many worlds. Although they couldn't hide that they had started the war, they sought to deflect it, spreading rumors, planting evidence and more of another shadowy group, one that had secretly manipulated them to create your kind.

"The Ændari blamed the entire war on a rogue element within their government, and have spent thousands of years using sympathizers to alter the records of other worlds. Varnock was one of those chosen to be sacrificed…apparently a willing member of some cabal, according to the Ændari Council. Instead of what had evidently been expected by her to be a short sentence of banishment, she and her companions were banished for all eternity."

"That came about at the end of another period of intense fighting, when the cease-fire had broken down, *again*, and the UC had gained the upper hand. It was around this time that both sides realized that the location of the Forgeworld had been lost," Emberalis added angrily.

"Forgeworld?" I asked.

"The location that the Ændari had found your kind's progenitors, and that they had uplifted you. Records had already been doctored repeatedly, from what we know, in an attempt to hide your location from the enemy. Then came the plagues and the loss of many memories and records. By this point, evidence was presented of a system killer superweapon, and your system was declared to have been one of its first confirmed tests."

"They claimed to have blown up a system, and you just accepted it?" Ingrid asked skeptically.

"You have no idea of the legends that even now exist. Many were believed to be utterly ridiculous, until they were proven to be true. That a system had been lost? This was proven to have happened dozens of times. 'New' systems were explored, claimed, and when settlers arrived, they found ancient ruins, buried cities, and most annoying of all? They found that frequently other empires had beaten them to that world."

"Why was that annoying?" I asked.

"Because that empire would then claim the world," Shanah grumbled. "The lost cities would be excavated, and although frequently little of the technology uncovered would be usable, occasionally things would be found that would grant a failing empire a sudden resurgence."

"And you just gave it up?" I asked disbelievingly. "None of you just pretended it hadn't been there and explored it quietly?"

"Some of those without honor did attempt such a thing," Shanah admitted. "But the UC is based on trust, and as such, those with honor enforced those rules, penalizing those without when the truth came out."

"I don't get this," I said. "Seriously, so much of the shit that's going on, it just doesn't make sense. Like the fleets that are out there? Or this Forgeship. Why the hell don't you just create massive fleets, and pack them out with AI? Stomp the Ændari flat with overwhelming numbers?"

"I think that's enou—" Emberalis started to say, before being talked over by Clicqo.

"Because in the course of nearly thirty thousand years of war, too much has been lost. The Forgeships are locked to set designs, ones that cannot be changed, and as they age, as more and more of these great marvels from our ancestors break down, we are left poorer and weaker in their passing."

"*Some* of the worlds are weaker," Emberalis said quickly, glaring at the floating figure. "Not all worlds are. So many have risen higher and—"

"And claiming so does not make it true," Shanah growled. "Devourer, you ask for our past and why we are where we are, ready to risk another war? Now you know. There are many details we must discuss, including the plagues that erased much of recorded history, and our eldest's memories, but we have no time. The Forgeworld was long lost, but when you exterminated that vile scum Varnock, you released a warning to her kind. One that has identified your world as being in this quadrant through the system node that carried the declaration. And as such, you ignited a desperate race to be the first to claim it."

"Claim it?" I asked flatly, stiffening in my seat and lowering the half-eaten leg. "*Claim* my home?"

"Both sides unleashed terrible weapons in the war," Clicqo explained. "Much was lost, not just in terms of technology and physical losses, but in memory. Not only were many of the secrets of technology lost, but even the memories of those things. Devices that were capable of creating entire fleets were reduced to single designs. Food replication was reset to the last printed item. Medical technologies?" It shook its head.

"Viruses were used, ones that rampaged out of control, replicating over and over, flooding the builders of those who had access to them, contaminating and flowing on. Any maker they were connected to was wiped. And should they be in the middle of a creation? Well, whatever they were working on was all that remained."

"The buffers," I muttered, having seen the systems when I'd worked with them. "When they're printing, they store the latest template in a secure buffer in case there's an issue and they lose power or whatever. It stops them starting again from scratch because the buffer knows where they're up to."

"You think the memory modules were wiped?" Ingrid asked me, and I nodded.

"Probably. Something that got out of control on both sides."

"The Ændari claimed that they lost nothing, of course, but since the plague, well..." Emberalis shrugged.

"There was a marked loss in their production facility," Shanah agreed. "Ships manufactured can still be given the data we have access to, as one of the Devourers was gracious enough to speak to the makers, instructing them to share the designs within themselves, but still..."

"Do you have access to custodians?" I asked.

"No," Emberalis said. "The last of them failed several centuries ago."

I noted the look that Shanah and Clicqo shared, and I snorted.

"Bullshit. But okay, so you've got no custodians, or at least very few and you've got only access to the designs that were in progress..." I trailed off, unable to help myself as I smiled. "Just to be clear, the Ændari got mind fucked too? That's what happened, right? Everyone's memories were wiped?"

"Essentially," Shanah admitted. "It is one of the reasons for the frantic search for any remaining technologies from the past."

"And yet you just left our solar systems alone, because of the contamination markers?" Ingrid asked. "Why? I mean, I understand why you might want to not risk things, but your soldiers are good. They could wipe out the corrupt and just move on, right? Focus in and clean those systems out? If you'd done that, you'd have found us pretty quickly."

"It's not that simple." Shanah shook his head. "If that was all that was needed? Yes, of course we could. But first of all, although officially there's a cease-fire in place, both sides know it's only a matter of time. Should we pull enough of our forces away from patrolling the front lines and being held in reserve, to do this? The Ændari would attack."

"And even if they didn't, most likely the independents would," Emberalis commented bluntly. "We're surrounded on all sides. And although it's been long eons since the war was at its hottest, the fighting is still constant. Those times that we risked everything and plunged forces into the corrupt zones, or other possible locations?

"We found nothing. No secret grand caches of technology—only more blank systems, more losses, and occasionally, more enemies for our trouble. The forces that come from our training cadres account for less than a third of our losses. Our armies dwindle as our enemies rise."

"Finally, after long centuries of desperate work, we have ships in production…newer, more advanced versions. The UC and the others involved have essentially reverse engineered much of the technology that we have. But to do so, without the construction facilities we had? We've been forced to continue to use the Forgeships and their fleets as the primary defenses while new fleets are assembled and held ready," Clicqo said, sounding unsure.

I wasn't confident either. If they had to build entire new fleets and the construction yards from scratch? I had visions of the kind of buildup that'd be needed to do that, and the mass losses whenever something went wrong as they went on in their explanation.

"The Ændari are doing the same, we know. Both sides are involved in a constant low-key, cold conflict, resulting in the sabotage of the enemy's facilities," Clicqo went on. "With raids on the independent worlds to steal their mobile shipyards or production facilities common as well."

"The only real deterrent is the soldier core, those who were once the BWVs, and yet, they are only so many," Shanah said grimly. "Those who once replaced their ranks can no longer ascend as they once did."

"Holy fuck." I grunted, turning to stare at Emberalis, as the various little hints all clicked into place. "You're broken."

"Excuse me!" He gasped, looking mortally offended. "How *dare* you!"

"Steve!" Ingrid hissed, before forcing a smile and turning to Emberalis. "Lord Emberalis, what my partner meant to say was—"

"No. I said what I meant—you're broken," I repeated, staring at the smaller man. "That's why you're small, why I can't sense your active nanites, and why you're so desperate to get Ingrid and me—hell, *all* our people under your control. And the soldiers? They're the same—they can't upgrade! How long do you live?"

"Are you hearing this?" he spluttered to the others. "He offended me at the very deepest level, and I withdraw my offer of patronage!"

"Using your own solar cycle, perhaps as many as a hundred and fifty years, though frequently significantly less. The average is, I believe, a hundred and ten," Clicqo interjected cheerfully, both faces now switched to "happy," and making it clear that they didn't particularly like Emberalis.

"Shit, no wonder you've got a Napoleon complex," I muttered.

"Steve!" Ingrid hissed.

"I am offended!"

"Yeah, you already said that," I pointed out unconcernedly. "Okay, I think I get where you're all coming from now. So, just to make things really clear, you've got access to a limited amount of data, literally just notes and shit from the past, and any kind of physical methods, like books, but nothing digital?"

"Highly limited digital archives exist, but many require gene-mapped or authorization protocols that we cannot provide for higher access. Those individuals who managed to keep separated from the rest of our infected ancestors long enough for the nanite plague to burn itself out managed to store some details, and they shared what they remembered of their history once we made contact," Shanah rumbled.

"It took many hundreds of years to erase the contamination, but by the time it was done"—Emberalis glared at me—"it was too late. None of our kind had access to those memories, and neither did any of our machines."

"Some claim that the Devourers still have access to them, as evidenced by them being able to unlock the Forgeships to share the data they had between one another, but they have refused to speak on it further," Shanah said.

"Anything else you think I should know?" I asked as an alarm went off again. "And what the hell is that?"

"The ambassador is landing," Clicqo informed me, standing. "I suggest we make our way to meet them."

"And only one last detail," Emberalis admitted, clearly still pissed but trying to force a smile. "You asked why we don't interact and cleanse the lost worlds that are full of the corrupt?"

"Yeah? Wait, there's *worlds*?" I asked, aghast. "I thought it was like moons or something."

"There are multiple worlds and star systems that were lost to them," Emberalis whispered, straightening his clothing. "You ask why they were left?"

"Yeah?"

"Emberalis…" Clicqo shook its head.

"They are our shame," he finished flatly. "Those worlds were lost to the corrupted, and some of the worse contaminations of corrupted came about because of our attempts at unlocking our memories, or curing ourselves of the plagues."

"The memory wipes." I winced. "You tried to hack the nanites, without anything to go off of?"

"And the result, we suspect, was the first of the corrupted," Clicqo admitted. "Once they started to spread, they became almost unstoppable. Those who were uninfected could not bear to kill their loved ones at first, and when they finally accepted it…"

"It was too late," I finished for them. "Fuck."

"Steve…" Ingrid said, and I glanced at her in question. "First, wipe your beard."

"Dammit." I grunted, feeling the sticky residue on my beard with my fingers, before smiling and pooling a patch of my Devourer armor in my hand, then wiping it across my mouth. As I'd hoped, anything that wasn't "me" was ingested and broken down. It was food, after all, and organic.

"That's so cheating." She sighed. "Okay, let's go before the ambassador arrives," she suggested to the rest of the room. "Or do we want to be late?"

"We would be better served by having a plan, but failing that, Devourer Steve, our information has been shared. I wish to know your intentions," Shanah rumbled formally, rising to his feet and towering over most of the room.

"I don't like the Ændari," I said. "And nothing you've said has changed that. It sounds like those dickheads caused a fuckload of problems out here, just like they did on my world, and they've learned nothing. So, yeah, my intentions are meet them, fuck them off, and get back to us talking about the future. But for now, you managed to reach out and contact me—through the system, I mean. Who did that and how?"

"We have highly limited access to the universal system through a link to the quadrant node," Shanah said. "It is possible to communicate through it, hence our contact to you. We currently hold that node, though it is at the edge of our territory."

"Currently?" I asked, getting a bad fucking feeling about that.

"Stellar drift and the power requirements for the system mean that it moves over time. Currently, it is on the edge of our borders, having been under our control for some time, but that will not be so forever. We've been forced to accept that on occasion Ændari vessels have trespassed there."

"So your hated enemy that you know created this and is fucking insane, hating you all with a passion, has access to the system that controls your very goddamn cells, and you don't think it's an important detail?"

"It would be," Shanah said, "if anyone could access the facility more than to make the most basic of data transfer requests. It has been locked down since time immemorial. Great fleets once patrolled the system, fighting over access to it, but once it became clear that no matter what we did, we could not secure it, nor access its systems beyond the most basic interactions? It became pointless."

"That doesn't explain how you used it to contact me," I said as we left the room, walking along the corridor and heading back into the hangar.

"We will explain that in a moment. However, your armor?" Clicqo said abruptly to Ingrid. "It is clearly of Ændari design, and restricted to their higher-end warriors, and our most advanced soldiers. Should you meet the Ændari representative in such, they will immediately suspect that you have access to more technology than they would wish to share. The Devourer armor, similarly, is recognizable, but it is uncertain that you are the Devourer mentioned in system release updates of late.

"I suggest you adjust your armor if you can, and quickly, to ensure that the Ændari cannot identify it, nor your race," they suggested.

Ingrid and I shared a long look, well aware that to do so, and to do it right now, was literally a demonstration of the control we had over our systems.

We hesitated as Ingrid and I meshed our minds for a few seconds, evaluating everything, reading each other's thoughts and concerns, before coming to a decision.

"We agree," Ingrid said.

I focused in, using one of the earlier templates that I'd designed for my own armor, and slid it across to her, along with a few tweaks that I'd been working into my own of late.

Ingrid seemed to shiver. A ripple started in the middle of her chest, spreading out to flood across her breastplate and pouring around her, leaving a new form in its wake as it went.

The new armor was much cruder in appearance, seeming more like a cobbled-together and patched suit, similar to the power armor that the soldiers had been wearing, but much smaller and clearly weaker.

Or it looked that way, anyway. The reality was that should it come to it, we could go one-on-one with the soldiers in our suits and probably match them at the very least. Give Oxus a few upgrades and he'd tear through them like wet tissue paper.

The change to our armor, and the ease that we did it, though…that definitely changed things for the council members, considering the looks they gave us.

As soon as it was done, we set off again, quickly reaching the end of the corridor and passing back out into the main hangar.

The team stationed as an honor guard for our arrival was there again, as were others, and every single damn one was armed to the teeth now.

"So, this node? How'd you use it to talk to us before?" I asked again.

"System designation control." Emberalis sighed. "Those of us who control a system can submit proof of that to remote facilities; control of enough of those facilities under a single group results in access to the Universal System Quadrant Node to make limited requests of the most basic kind. As joint controllers of the areas closest to that you were in when you killed Varnock, we could therefore reach out to you."

"Okay, and if you lose control of some of those remote facilities?" I asked, the beginning of a plan forming.

"Then we lose access to the system node."

"How many do you need?" I asked Emberalis, who'd been notably chewing on his lip. "To maintain access, I mean."

"Thirty."

"And you have…?"

"Thirty."

"Oh shit. And the other side have…?"

"Thirty."

"Wait, what?"

"It was part of the cease-fire agreement. They retreated to their side of the great divide, and we to ours," Shanah explained. "This way we both have access, and neither side has control. The location of the node is in one of our systems currently, Scorpio, but as nothing can alter the commands that the node runs on…"

"It doesn't matter where it is," I said. "So, nothing can control the node, or get it to let you inside?"

"Nothing we know of," Clicqo corrected helpfully.

"What?" Ingrid asked.

"Nothing we know of," the alien repeated. "It is one of the arguments that prove that the Ændari lost their memories as well. They created the system, after all—they should be able to alter it as they wish."

"And how did you all get access to it?" Ingrid asked carefully as we approached the point we'd met them before. A distant door in the side of the wall cracked open. Revealing itself to be, in fact, a massive hangar door that admitted a ship the size of a small town.

"The nanite plagues." Shanah shook his head in disgust. "Who created the first plague is not known, but our ancestors' attempts to mitigate it, while using it as an attack vector against our enemies, inflicted it upon us all. Those of our races who had no access to the systems that the BWVs had, and therefore should have survived the effects easily, had unfortunately been involved in great uplifts, as our ancestors injected us with various adjusted nanites in an attempt to even the field."

"So you're all equally vulnerable," I muttered. "Damn. Well, it sort of makes sense."

The conversation died off a little as we watched the ship as it entered the hangar, continuing dead ahead, aimed at us.

It was clearly planned as a threat, roughly triangular, with a long central spine that ran front to back and bristled with weaponry. Wings that were short and stubby almost in comparison were folded back and presumably helped with in-atmosphere flight, but who knew really.

The front of the ship came to a sharp point, sliding backward and increasing wider with the stubby wings extending behind it.

"So, before this bastard comes here and makes whatever claims they're going to make, what's the deal you're looking for?" I asked the others, making the point of looking to Shanah for a response.

"Most likely we come to agreement on sharing any technology you have access to, for a fair price and utter secrecy, and in return the UC names you as a bounty hunter. We claim that we had already authorized and registered you and your team, who are all from independent systems, and you declare that you found Varnock in space somewhere nearby."

"Utter secrecy?" I asked, and Ingrid spoke up.

"If the Ændari learn that the UC have access to more advanced technology than they do, they'll attack. If they leave it until later, they'd not stand a chance, so they'd need to attack, and straightaway, both to stop the UC gaining access to that technology and to get at it themselves."

"As you say," Clicqo agreed.

"Do you agree?" Shanah asked me. The delegates went silent as they watched Ingrid and me.

"Well?" I asked her.

"We need assurances, but yes."

"Tell them what we need," I suggested. *"I've got no clue."*

"We accept, on certain conditions," Ingrid said, as the Ændari ship finally started to slow, turning to land sideways, claiming as large a section of the hangar as possible.

"Name them," Emberalis said hungrily.

"Earth, our home, that you know as Forgeworld, is ours. You have no claim over it, and you agree to help defend it as any world of the UC. We are the leaders of the faction that claims Earth, and as such we gain a full representative status in the UC relevant to the power differential as full members on equal standing with any of you."

"And what do you bring to the table that is worth all of that? I doubt that we could do it, even if we wanted to. We'd have to spend all our political capital and more to accomplish that." He sneered. "There has been no proof yet that—"

I triggered my armor on the side that faced them. The Devourer's red-black oily surface flooded my own for a few seconds before vanishing again.

"I'll unlock your potential again," I said. "You're terrified of death, because you know that only soldiers come back to life, only they recover, and even they are trapped, reduced to using power armor that was designed for the most basic warriors, because they can't upgrade anymore."

I glanced from him to the others, and then back at Ingrid before going on.

"We'll teach your soldiers to fight as they once did, and give them access to the tools they'll need, as well as helping you to unlock a form of cruisers for the UC. You say that you have access only to warships currently, and they're expensive to build, because you only have how many 'makers' working now?"

"Two," Shanah admitted. "Out of thirty."

"How many of those that are broken are bigger than those two?"

"Almost all." He snorted. "We're reduced to warships and shuttles, that's it. The last fighter was damaged beyond repair twelve years ago."

"Well, that's all gonna change," I said, unable to keep the smile from my face as the ship touched down. "Let's fuck these off and get the ball rolling."

Chapter Twenty-Four

The Ændari were…underwhelming, frankly.

At first sight, I wanted to pounce on the fuckers and slaughter them all, they were that impregnated with nanites, but Shanah had made two things clear to me in the last seconds as they approached.

First, I was a mercenary, and a bounty hunter, supposedly. That meant I was markedly subservient to anyone there, and ostensibly, I was from the independent worlds originally, using my killing of Varnock to earn credits in the UC as a registered bounty hunter.

That gave me all the excuses I needed for anything that I did that was weird or anything that I didn't understand. There were hundreds of settled worlds out there and most of them were literally a single town or city at most.

They ranged from one that apparently had a population of three people, to others that held hundreds of millions of sapiens of dozens of different species.

The second point was that although I was there to *be* discussed, I was to keep my mouth shut as much as possible. As a bounty hunter, I was barely on the right side of the law, and should appear to be both nervous and looking to curry favor with anyone involved under normal circumstances.

Also, the Ændari apparently used bounty hunters a lot, so they'd be expecting to see some traits they recognized, despite the others running out of time to explain to me what those might be.

That gave me both bugger all that was useful, and awesome inspiration as I made some last-minute changes.

"Did you just adjust your armor to look more like Fett?" Ingrid asked me suddenly, and I grinned inside my helm, nodding subtly. *"Oh gods…"*

"He's the most iconic bounty hunter in the history of bounty hunting," I pointed out. *"It was either him or Eastwood I was going to use as inspiration, and I think shooting them on sight with an insanely large hand cannon while chewing on a cigar is probably not the right impression."*

"Members of the Rebellion," the Ændari greeted the UC representatives when they finally exited their ship, and although I felt them stiffen with offense, I fucking loved it.

"If he calls them herders or something, I'm shooting him in the face," I told Ingrid, practically bouncing in my armor in my excitement.

"Calm down!" she sent frantically, and I stiffened, realizing that my armor was adjusting to reflect my excitement, ridges flowing across my back as tentacles readied to burst forth.

"Shit, sorry." I focused on the figure before me as he continued to ensure he was a valid target for the rest of his life.

"Pathetic, really. Still, you are in possession of a criminal, one who somehow managed to make the greatest mistake its species could, in involving itself in the end of one of my kind's glorious existences—"

"No, we're not," Shanah said simply.

"As such, you'll hand it over to me now and I will… Wait, what?"

"We're not slavers," Shanah hissed. "All creatures inside the borders of the UC are free sapiens, so we're not in 'possession' of the bounty hunter."

"Urgh. Whatever." The little shit sighed. "Fine, you can call it a free thing, but I know the truth, and so does it, don't you…*Biological Weapon Variant #1137824916O3?*"

He said it with such conviction, such excitement, and such *malice,* that I nearly lopped the little fucker's head off on general principles.

I actively considered it as well, right up until I felt the love, support, and confidence that Ingrid was emanating and sending to me.

Then I focused on looking the creature up and down, as well as the pair that stood on either side of it.

They were Xi-Ma, or some variant of them—shrunken, wasted, and much weaker in appearance than the ones I was used to dealing with. But the little bastard leading them?

He was…he was much closer to the creature that escaped from Varnock's corpse toward the end of the fight than she'd looked at the beginning, put it that way.

I stared at him and said nothing, drawing the moment out and making it clear that I really didn't give a fuck.

"Well?" he said after a minute, and I snorted, amused the little bugger had cracked already.

"Well, what?" I asked, sounding bored.

"Do you deny it?" he snapped.

"Deny what?" I cocked my head to one side.

"That you were involved in the death of a glorious and esteemed—"

"Oh, no, you're wrong."

"You *lie!*"

"I did kill Varnock the Defiler, though."

"You admit to lying and—"

"You claimed I killed someone 'glorious and esteemed,'" I corrected. "I didn't. I killed Varnock the Defiler, who had a valid bounty on her head. And she begged for mercy before she died."

"Impossible!"

"What happened to you?" I asked, acting confused. "I mean, seriously, you're what, a third of the size she was? And she didn't put up much of a fight, not once we'd killed all her guards. She started begging and claiming that she knew we'd come, that she shouldn't have left the forbidden world, and promising to tell us where it was—"

"Where!" the creature hissed, going from apparently mortally offended at my referencing its size, to utterly uncaring of anything else beyond that information.

"What's it worth to you?" I asked bluntly.

"*What!*" he hissed.

"What. Is. It. Worth. To. You," I repeated slowly and clearly. "If you want to buy the location that Varnock offered me, I'll sell it, but I'm not giving you anything for free."

"I shall have it ripped from your screaming corpse! You murdered an esteemed scientist—"

"Who had a bounty on her head and had been banished to a forbidden world—by your people apparently," I repeated, speaking over him.

"That doesn't mean you're not guilty of murder!"

"Execution," Shanah said firmly. "The bounty hunter executed the bounty, as verified by the universal system acknowledging that he and others in his party executed the target correctly."

"We do not accept that claim!" the Ændari ambassador snapped. "That bounty was never accepted by the Ændari Council and—"

"But you did banish her, and the condition that should she leave the forbidden world was that she would be summarily executed," Emberalis pointed out coolly. "You banished her to a forbidden world, where, if legends are to be believed, she was involved in the creation of my own race."

"You accept that our race created yours then, *slave.*" The ambassador sneered.

I shook my head in disgust and amazement that this race ever lived long enough to make it to the stars. I looked down at the figure that stood before me, apparently on the brink of monologuing, it was that stupid and evil.

The form that Varnock had retreated down to was half the size of this one, topping out somewhere around two and a half feet tall, but we'd done massive damage to that fucker, and still that was all she could form.

This one, though? I had no clue what its excuse was, but at five feet, barely, it looked like it was being held together by malice and vicious mockery, and that was it.

It was bipedal, with a toast-rack chest, a fat potbelly and wearing golden robes that flowed down from its shoulders to float away behind it. Red streamers extended back from the shoulders, rippling as if they were caught in a breeze, and it stood like it was expecting a fashion photographer to appear and snap away at any second.

Its horns were bedecked in jewels, looking more like polished tree branches than anything else, probably well-oiled and with holes in them that allowed strings of presumably precious metals to be passed through and looped around each in patterns.

Arise :Explorer

Every movement of the ambassador's head filled the air with subtle chimes, and a pair of tiny golden square boxes trailed fragrant smoke like incense.

Its face was animalistic, closer to a deer mixed with a rat than anything else, with a maw full of stumpy, yet sharp-looking fangs, with irises that shone with a radiant inner light, set deep in gleaming black eyes.

All in all, it was a creature that should have been stepped on as soon as it crawled out of the primordial ooze, by anything that had even the slightest good taste.

"We accept that we were once enslaved by your kind, forced to fight for your greed, and now we are free!" Emberalis snapped back.

"You simply accepted then that we were your natural masters, and you worshipped us for it," the Ændari replied airily. "The crimes that your kind committed in a misguided attempt to curry favor with us? Those were all your own."

"This rehashing of ancient history does none of us any good," Clicqo stated. "Ambassador, you requested this meeting. Do you wish to adjourn to a meeting room to discuss your requests?"

"We do not require special rooms to make our words more important." The Ændari sneered again. "We—"

"But you couldn't make your request over a comm link?" I interjected. "Sounds like you don't understand what it's for—"

"Quiet!" Ingrid shot at me, and I gritted my teeth, remembering that I was supposed to be a damn mercenary here, not a leader.

"In-person discussions are required to collect our possessions," the Ændari hissed. "But very well, you wish a frank discussion? Give that one to me." It raised one hand and pointed at me, a glittering claw tip extending slowly.

"The bounty hunter is no slave to be sold, nor exchanged for favor." Shanah growled. "We have no claim to them and refuse."

"That creature admits to having murdered a member of the Ændari race. I will have its head to present to the council, or the recording of the destruction of this pathetic remnant of the wars you all squat aboard. I have an entire fleet behind me, so choose your next words carefully."

"Excuse me, Ambassador," Ingrid said suddenly, and everyone looked at her in surprise. "I mean no offense, but we do not know your name, and as such, do not know how to address you correctly."

"I thought we weren't supposed to be addressing them at all?" I sent to her.

"Well, you screwed that up, so we need to move on with plan B now."

"I am the Ændari Ambassador to Quadrant Eleven, Commissioner of…" The introduction went on for several minutes, and out of all of it, there wasn't a single name that I could pick out, just titles after titles.

"So…was there a name in there?" I asked at the end.

"Your kind are too lowly to—"

"I'm gonna call you 'Francine' then," I declared. "That good with you?"

"How *dare* you!" he gasped, clearly mortally offended.

"Great, glad you like it." I smiled.

"So, *Francine*..." Ingrid said, a clear mix of almost hysterical amusement and disbelief in her voice, as she tried to be serious. "You came here looking for something, and while you brought your fleet with you, it must have been to make a point, not in an actual desire to start a fight."

"Why do you say this?" Clicqo asked her.

"Well, I'm just a bounty hunter, admittedly," Ingrid said pointedly, "but if they declare war on you, and they're right here when they do it? You already know that we've killed one of them, and Varnock had much more impressive guards with her. So, if they were to declare war, all you have to do is put a bounty on the ambassador's head, and we'll happily kill him for you here and now."

"My fleet would attack!" Francine snarled.

"But you'd be dead," I pointed out.

"You'd all die!"

"Wanna bet?"

"You think a Forgeship defenseless?" Shanah rumbled. "Many of your ancestors made that same mistake, Ambassador. The Forgeship is still here—they are not."

"And this forgotten maker is no longer in the condition that those fleets found it in! You think we don't know that more than half the vessel is derelict?"

"You think that we don't know that your fleet is entirely made up of the most basic of your vessels? That you lost access to most of your own fleet systems after the plague?" Emberalis snapped back hotly. "We know of your spies in the Forgeship, and we decide what they report to you."

"You know nothing..." The Ændari snorted.

"We can see your fleet," Shanah said. "We know that you have only lesser vessels shepherded by two aging cruisers. The repair work done to them is poor but clear. You suspect that the Forgeship is damaged, but you have no proof, so tell me, Ambassador, who is in the weaker position currently?"

"You know nothing of the strength of my fleet." Francine snarled.

"And you know nothing that you can verify about ours," Clicqo said. "All that you know is that a bounty hunter arrived here to claim the bounty on Varnock the Defiler, and this is they."

"I will give you one chance," the ambassador said to me, turning to glare up from its highly unimpressive five-foot frame. "Surrender to me now. Come with me voluntarily and share the information you have admitted you possess, or else—"

"No," I said flatly, doing my best Fett impression, and staring down at it. "You want the information I have? You pay me for it, here and now."

"And then you come to my ship—" he countered, and I snorted.

"You already promised to rip the information from my 'screaming corpse' so, no. I would have to be an idiot to go anywhere with you. You want the information I have, and I want you to leave me alone to work. Not having to look over my shoulder as I hunt other bounties, waiting for you to turn up and try to capture me and mine."

"Give me the information, before I loose my fleet and—"

"And if you loose your fleet on the Forgeship right now, then you die." I cut him off. "Either because I receive a bounty on you right now and I kill you, or, if you're extremely lucky and win the coming fight…you seem to have forgotten that you're *aboard the damn ship with us.*"

"Honored Ambassador…" Ingrid interjected, bowing slightly. "Greatly honored representatives of the UC, we are simple bounty hunters. As my master has declared, we wish simply to be paid for the bounty we earned, then to move on with our lives. Perhaps there is a way to accomplish this without bloodshed?"

"You are surprisingly squeamish for a bounty hunter," Francine muttered, squinting at her. "Although you are more properly respectful, when it suits you."

"We are not being paid to fight, therefore we will not," Ingrid replied. "We mean no offense to either side, but this is your war, your cease-fire, and your argument. We simply wish to be paid and to move on. With that in mind, perhaps a compromise?"

"We're listening," Emberalis agreed slowly, appearing none too happy about the way the conversation was going.

"The data we have is highly valuable, to both parties, and should we provide such data to only the Ændari, and it be found to have issues of accuracy, then we lose the goodwill of the Ændari. This limits the areas we can work, do you agree?"

"You are correct." Francine grunted.

"Excellent. Well, as you are both aware, while the independent worlds do have some bounties available to us, many would at the very least require us to access Ændari and UC space, even to carry those out. The vast majority of the work that we look to carry out? This is provided by the UC directly."

"Correct," Shanah agreed, frowning.

"Therefore, we would be at the very least foolish to restrict our access to the markets, and at most, likely suicidal," Ingrid finished. "We wish to be able to work for both parties. Therefore, we are willing to reach a reasonable price to sell the data to you both."

"What is the nature of the data?" Emberalis asked slowly. "We need specifics."

"The final moments of the creature we executed the bounty on, and her statements about the location of the world she fled," Ingrid lied.

"You'll need to do the bargaining and distract them," she sent to me at the same time. *"If I'm going to forge a false memory and make it look even half decent, then I'll need the others to help as well."*

"I'll distract them," I assured her.

"The price better be worth it," I said. "That data's worth a lot to me, considering it's an untapped world."

"We will pay for exclusive access to it," Emberalis said suddenly.

I wasn't sure whether he was playing along or trying to play the game with the Ændari.

"No!" Shanah snapped. "The hunter is right. The only way this works is if both sides gain the data at once."

"The Forgeship is too slow," Emberalis snapped right back. "My own personal forces are faster, and it's the birthplace of *my* race. I will not risk the Ændari getting there first!"

"We will not share the data!" Francine snarled. "It came from our scientist!"

"Who was banished!"

"We will purchase the data directly." Clicqo spoke up suddenly. "The Right Arm of Man and the Ændari both are warlike in the extreme. Would you sell an entire planet full of possible slaves or warriors to either?"

"I'll sell the data to whoever pays me the most." I grunted. "It's a legend, and legends are worthless to me."

"Master…" Ingrid said suddenly, drawing every eye as she pretended to try to negotiate with me. "There could be untouched ships, terraforming vessels, uncorrupted makers…"

"Shoot me down," Ingrid sent to me at the same time. *"I'm planting the seeds, that's all."*

"A new ship now is worth a hundred in the future," I snapped. "Know your place."

"I apologize, my master," she replied quickly, bowing and stepping back as if dismissed and afraid of me. It provided the cover she needed to no longer be involved in speaking, as I felt the links she was tying together with James, Casey, and Zac.

All three were working with her to adjust different parts of a supposed memory of the fight, as well as to link up some of the data we'd gotten from the BWVs under the sea.

Diamos had given us incomplete star charts, but at least one of the most distant systems he'd given us had a marker for a nanite contamination zone, and that it was highly dangerous.

It was also right at the limit of the explored zone that they had travelled to at that point, hundreds of systems distant, and considering the losses in information that both sides had suffered since then, I figured it was a fair bet that they'd not been back there recently.

Ingrid was a natural at this, and James's recent experience with photo and video editing software—he'd used human AI at that point, but now made use of the upgraded security AI that we'd brought with us—meant that it all came together surprisingly quickly and cleanly.

"We will only buy the star charts if we are the only ones to have them!" Francine declared angrily.

"Excellent," Emberalis snapped. "In that case, we will buy them and we won't have to worry about you following us!"

"No!"

"You cannot sell to the Ændari!" Clicqo beseeched me. "The location of the legendary Forgeworld could change the fate of the war, and who knows what remains there. There could be evolved weapons, schematics, secrets of their original creation…"

"The highest bidder will find out." I stood as arrogantly as I could.

Arise :Explorer

A few minutes of heated arguing over who should have access to the Forgeworld was ended abruptly by Emberalis as he turned to me.

"You said that you wanted credits, presumably to buy a ship?"

"Mine took damage."

"What about a repair instead?" he countered. "Fifty thousand credits and ten thousand in repair credits."

"Don't waste my time!"

"What?"

"I already earned nearly eighty thousand in credits for the head of Varnock. You expect me to sell you her base and the source of your race's secrets for less?"

"Sixty."

"Eighty," Francine snapped. "And access to Ændari space."

"A hundred and fifty," I countered. "Full access to Ændari space *and* a marker that we're approved for high-level bounties by your office."

I was making that last one up, I had no clue if there was such a thing, but it sounded like the kind of bureaucratic bullshit that anyone who had ambassadors would come up with.

"A hundred and fifty!" Francine gasped, and the others looked on, shocked.

"Anyone got a handle on what a credit's worth yet?" I sent into the command link, getting a variety of responses around the "no clue" mark.

"Perhaps a hundred thousand credits would be possible..." Shanah said slowly. "But you wish the funds to purchase a ship?"

"A new one."

"The ships that are available to a mercenary are limited in scope and capability, by law in the UC."

"I know that," I lied.

"What if there was a way around those laws?"

"I'm listening."

"We could employ you directly by the UC as a contractor. It would preclude you accepting work for the Ændari, but between the UC and the independent worlds, you would have more than enough work."

"And the ship?"

"Insanity!" Francine hissed. "The UC barely approve of bounty hunters at all. The Ændari use your kind extensively. You know this!"

"We have recently had an older warship become available," Clicqo admitted. "That ship could be provided to you, for a significant cost, along with the necessary permissions."

"A *warship*?" I made it look like I was stunned more than anything else, though at this point it could be taken either way. For all I knew, the damn ship was worth a few hundred credits as easily as several hundred thousand.

"The warship that you already had contact with," Emberalis agreed slowly. "Her crew is being transferred off, and it was being prepared for—" He broke off, scratching his chin as if hiding whatever he was about to say. "Perhaps, and I mean *perhaps*, you could be approved to take that ship. But it would be in lieu of payment of any kind."

"Fifty thousand and the ship," I said. "Full repairs and full rights to use the ship in UC and independent space."

"Perhaps…"

"We agree," Francine hissed.

"What?"

"We will provide a warship of equal value, a captured one, and fifty thousand credits."

"And the right to access Ændari space?" I asked.

"Access is granted." He smiled thinly, and I wondered whether that look was the last thing a mouse saw when a cat cornered it.

"Access is, exit isn't," Ingrid warned me. *"If we did that, I'm betting there'd be a tracker aboard and we'd never be seen again."*

"The only way I'm intending on entering their space is to fire nukes at the fuckers, so I don't care."

"It's the principle of the thing," she sent me with a mental peck on the cheek.

"Just to make my position clear," I said slowly, staring at the Ændari. "If you try to fuck me on this deal, you'll regret it."

"Threaten me again, hunter, and the deal is off."

"The warship and ten thousand," Emberalis snapped. "If you go with them, you know you'll never get the ship. They'll have you stripped and mind raped before you're out of the system."

"Kinky," I muttered.

"I resent that accusation," Francine hissed.

"Why? Too accurate?" I asked him, grinning to myself when he spun to glare at me. "Fine. A warship from you, and thirty thousand credits…" I said to Emberalis. "*Or*, a warship from the UC and a hundred thousand from the Ændari. Credits only from you, because I'm not going anywhere under your control," I added to Francine.

"Then we refuse!" the Ændari snapped. And before Emberalis could do more than open his mouth, one of the Xi-Ma stepped forward, snarling and slapped a hand over my helm, closing its fist and dragging me forward as a shield shimmered into being behind me.

It cut me off from the UC representatives, putting me on the Ændari side of the barrier as the little bastard cackled and spoke up quickly.

"You think I care about your opinions? Possession is mine!" Francine chortled.

The UC soldiers moved smoothly, stepping up and raising their weapons, and the ambassador's ship powered its own, locking onto them in turn.

The UC ambassadors retreated behind their own barriers quickly, shouting about betrayal, and that was when Ingrid stepped into the ground that had opened up between the two groups.

She could feel me still—we were linked, after all—and she damn well knew what I was planning, and why I'd allowed the bargain-basement knockoff Xi-Ma to take me so easily.

Arise :Explorer

I moved smoothly as the massive creature dragged me. My gravity manipulation actually helped it to open the distance between me and the others, before I showed that despite the Ændari's belief...I was far from helpless.

One claw-tipped hand was wrapped around my helm, and the other had clamped onto my left shoulder, dragging me forward. As soon as I was sure I was far enough that the others would not be caught in the cross fire, and Francine had fully committed...I reversed my "lightening" of the load.

Gravity around me suddenly tripled, then tripled again. The Xi-Ma grunted in surprise, before hissing as it stumbled. The massive weight that appeared from nowhere shoved it off-balance, just as I grabbed both of its wrists.

Then I increased the gravity on it again and again.

It hissed, then screeched, trying to drag its hands free, twisting this way and that. But, unlike its larger brethren from Earth, it had neither the inherent strength nor the leverage to break free, and that was when the second surprise made itself known.

My armor shifted as the surface was flooded with the Devourer. The red-black oil spread like a malicious oil slick across the ocean, and everywhere it touched the Xi-Ma, it began to feed.

The previously arrogant creature screamed even louder, jerking frantically as its hands began to dissolve into my armor, armor that flowed out, sliding up and over its fingers.

Spikes ripped free of my chest, lunging into its unprotected form, punching through the thin material it wore, burrowing into its organs and spreading fast, consuming all that they could as my shroud flowed around me, pouring across its flesh like sentient silk.

The entire hangar went suddenly silent, apart from the screeches of the bodyguard. As it sagged to its knees, I twisted my arms suddenly, savagely, snapping its arms and dislocating its elbows.

It dragged in a long-suffering breath, ready to scream again in agony, and I released the left arm, slapping my right palm over its mouth and flooding its throat and face with Devourer nanites.

"Shhhh..." I crooned, before turning my head slowly to fix the Ændari ambassador with the emotionless gale of my helmet.

"You just tried to attack me," I said softly. "Under a flag of truce that you discarded..."

"No..." Francine whispered, clearly seeing me for the first time and recognizing that I was one of the hated and feared Devourer mutations.

"Oh *yes*," I growled. I ripped the cloak free of the Xi-Ma. The half-eaten and twitching corpse crashed to the floor behind me as I lifted into the air. My tentacles retracted from the corpse and flashed through the air to lasso around the throat, wrists, and ankles of the second Xi-Ma as it leapt forward, trying to interpose itself between me and its master.

I jerked it sideways, flipping gravity to make it light enough to do so seemingly effortlessly, even as I formed spikes inward from the loops I'd formed around the throat, wrists, and ankles. Then the Devourer spiked out again, forming fractal patterns to link up with the other spikes...and closed the loop.

The Xi-Ma lost its head, hands, and feet in a sudden burst of blood. I discarded the corpse and formed a final gravity bubble around the Ændari.

He'd barely taken a handful of steps, and suddenly he was lifted from the floor, feet frantically scrabbling, as he became weightless, then slid backward toward me.

"Do you understand now?" I asked. The bubble twisted around in midair, holding him in place before me. "You attacked me, and…"

"I'll fire!" He gasped, eyes bulging. "Harm me, and my ship will open fire!"

"So?" I glanced at the ship, and then back at him. "You know what I am now. What I took from her. You think your ship could hurt me?" I bluffed, guessing that it damn well could, but pretending that I knew different.

"The…the others!" He gasped. "They'll die!"

"So?"

"So…your companion!" he tried frantically.

"A hireling."

"A…uh…" He was panicking now.

"Bounty hunter!"

A voice called out from behind, and I turned to look at them, hovering in the air as the Ændari shook and gibbered in fear.

"What?"

"Stand down, if you please," Shanah said quickly. "The Ændari as a whole should not be judged by a mistake made by their ambassador's guards."

"Yes…yes…!" Francine gurgled frantically, trying to twist away, hovering weightless in the bubble as my tentacles slid closer to him. "A mistake!"

"A *big* mistake," I agreed ominously.

"A soldier!" He gasped. "You said you were a bounty hunter!"

"I am," I snapped. "I'm no member of the UC."

"You…you're not? But you're a…"

I could see the wheels turning behind his eyes, as he made the connections, that not only was I not a member of the UC and not a soldier—apparently—but that I was a Devourer.

If that was true and I was an independent, someone who had only gained the armor and ability through something that had happened with access to Varnock, then maybe they could repeat it. Maybe they could get access to Devourers of their own.

"Two hundred thousand!" He promised desperately. "Two hundred and all of your memories!"

"Or I could just rip your head from your shoulders…" I suggested. "And claim your ship."

"Devourer!" That was Emberalis. "Lord Devourer, I offer a ship and the fifty thousand you wanted, if you sell to me."

"And the right to hunt in UC space using a warship," Shanah agreed.

"You will start a war if you sell to just one!" Clicqo called. "Please, Devourer, bounty hunter…whatever you choose to be known as—should you do this and sell the information to one side only, the other will be forced to fire upon them. They cannot be permitted to leave the system with such knowledge."

"What do you suggest?" I called back, weighing my options and genuinely wondering whether I could hack the Ændari ship. In finding that they'd lost access to most of the tech that they should have had, I at least had to have a chance, right?

"Sell to both sides," Clicqo said firmly. "Your original request—you offered to sell to both sides, because you understood that it would put any confrontation off, for now at least. If only one side has such information? If you sold it to the Ændari, for example? The cease-fire would be broken, as we could never allow them to leave with the secret.

"Instead, sell to both sides. We will provide a warship and the right to work and use such a ship in UC space, and we swear to permit the ambassador to retreat from the system. He will take his fleet, and we will take ours. Thus is the balance preserved."

"But when we reach the Forgeworld..." Emberalis swore. "You fool! They'd have an advantage—they're faster than us!"

"You would start a fresh war! To inflict the horrors of those days on us all for a system that may be abandoned or long dead anyway!" Clicqo snapped. "If there is something there? You can take your personal forces and risk everything to find it, but my own will not leave this sector!"

"Most likely there is nothing there. Else why would Varnock have left the sector to travel here?" Shanah rumbled. "But I agree. My people will cover a third of the cost to the UC, provided that you share the data equally."

"Two hundred thousand," I growled at Francine, who blanched, his mouth dropping open in realization before he spoke.

"I...don't have it," he admitted.

"So you were going to kill me and take it after all then." I snorted.

"NO!" he frantically screeched as the tentacles flowed closer. "No, no, I wasn't... I have a hundred and eleven, that is all I have. More I would have gotten for you, but it would have had to come from the Ændari Council! That was why we needed to leave the system together."

The way he stumbled over the excuse made it clear it was bullshit, but I pretended to accept it, considering I had absolutely no intention of going anywhere with him, or giving him anything accurate anyway.

"All of that then," I snapped. "The hundred and eleven thousand credits..." I saw what had to be relief crossing his face, and it infuriated me. "And your hand and horn."

"My...hand and horn?" He blanched, not understanding.

"The UC gives me and mine official status as bounty hunters in their territory and a warship, which they were going to do anyway. From you? After you tried to capture me and no doubt torture me to death, and you didn't even have the credits you'd promised? I get the hundred and eleven thousand credits, both of these corpses..." I jerked my head in the direction of the two dead Xi-Ma. "And I get your right hand and right horn."

"I don't understand." He whined. "What do you—"

I lashed out. Two tentacles latched onto him, one wrapping around his right wrist and the second around the base of his right horn, then sealing tight.

"I take them both," I snarled. "In exchange for letting you live."

"You can't!" he whispered, stunned, jerking and trying to get free.

"Devourer…perhaps you have forgotten that in Ændari society, an individual who is…*incomplete* is shunned until they have regrown?" Clicqo suggested.

"An excellent suggestion, Devourer!" Emberalis called, suddenly maliciously cheerful. "We accept!"

"Do you agree?" I asked Francine, staring into his eyes. "Or do I kill you and offer the information to your next in command? I'm betting they'll not care that you're dead."

"I…" He stared at me. His eyes roamed my cold, emotionless helmet in horror. "You can't…"

"Oh, I *can*," I corrected. "I can and I will…because I *want* to. So, either you pay me, right now, both the credit and flesh cost, or I kill you and take my offer to your subordinate."

"*Steve… this might be too much,*" Ingrid sent me, and for a second, I listened, knowing that she knew better than me in so many ways, that she knew when to push and when to bargain.

Then I discarded it. I'd already made my deal out loud. I'd already made the offer, and I knew it was the right thing to do, and it wasn't just vengeance talking.

I puzzled through the reasoning as the silence dragged out. My instincts screamed that it was right before my head could justify it, but I saw why as it shuddered and looked away, nodding in acceptance.

"*I'll get the UC to create an account for us. They can hold the payment from the Ændari so they don't find out we've not got one,*" Ingrid sent to me. My reasoning filtered through to her as she sent it, and a grudging acceptance flowed back.

She didn't agree, but she understood, and that was enough for now.

If we let him return as he was, he'd have had no reason to go straight to the coordinates. He'd have had a damn good reason, in fact, to hang around and make sure nobody from the UC left the Forgeship, and no transmissions of that data got out. He'd have had a perfect excuse to attack: to try to shut us all up in a final battle, then to take his survivors—if he won—to claim Earth.

Now, though? Diminished in the eyes of his society—which was a stupid way of looking at it, regardless of whether they healed or not—he had no choice but to try to claim the world before anyone else. Notably, he couldn't risk summoning any other Ændari, as they'd be likely to strip him of his command.

This was all filtering through from Ingrid as much as I was making the conscious connections, and I couldn't help but sneer at how stupid it was.

As someone who had lost limbs, knowing that although they might regrow, but they might not? It was a stupid way of looking at it, in my eyes, considering that the thing that made me, *me*, wasn't a hand or a leg, an eye, or a finger.

I was me, regardless of the number of limbs or whatever. I wasn't less because I lost one. Hell, if anything, I'd learned a shitload about myself in losing my limbs. I'd had to grow, as me, not just physically, but in coming to terms with the situation and the mental damage it'd done.

I was stronger than I'd ever been, and even if my limbs wouldn't regrow, I had.

Arise :Explorer

Knowing that these stupid fuckers would think less of one of their own because of *that*, instead of the fact he'd tried to attack us under a truce, on a diplo-fucking-matic mission, and had failed?

It just made me more determined to slaughter every one of them.

Also…if I was honest, as I kinda had to be with myself at least?

I'd done it in large part because I could sense the nanites, and I damn well wanted them.

Feeding the Devourer on those two Xi-Ma had helped, genuinely it had, but knowing that this little bastard was so much stronger and more saturated than they were, and I was going to have to let him go?

That had rankled.

A little taste, though? An extra punishment for him and a boost for me?

Hell yes.

I made sure the little bastard started the transfer to the account that Ingrid arranged with the UC—it was something they'd set up for one of their spies to use to have access to funds in the independent systems, we found out later—then, as Ingrid confirmed the memory was ready, I transferred it to both the UC and the Ændari. I did it at the same time as I extended the Devourer and sliced loose the little fucker's horn and hand.

<u>Chapter Twenty-Five</u>

"It's really ours?" Zac asked me a handful of hours later, as the pair of us stood in the guts of the battered warship, staring at the grav drive that had powered this vessel across space for so many years. "The whole ship?"

"It is," I agreed for perhaps the fifth time. "The deal was binding, which that little shit Emberalis didn't seem very happy about when he realized it, but fuck it."

"Weird that we've come all this way and it's still a human who tries to screw us over," Zac muttered.

"That's humans." I snorted. "The saurian…uh, Shanah, I mean? He said that this was going to be scrapped anyway."

"So what was the problem then? I mean, if all they have to do is feed in raw material and boom, you get a new ship out of the other side?" Paul leaned against the doorframe, watching us as Zac continued to look the connections over.

"Yeah, this can be ripped out," Zac muttered to himself, apparently making mental notes as we went. "Ours is better…plug that in and we'll be a lot faster."

"The Forgeship is on its last legs." I shrugged. "They can only make warships and shuttles now, and to make the warships takes weeks of work to gather enough materials in the first place. The access routes to the converters have been blocked for years apparently, but they can't just cut the side of the ship away to expose the innards and make it easier."

"The Ændari would know just how fucked the ship is if they did that," Zac said, taking over the explanation. "And the machines they'd have to cut out? They used to work—they've just broken down over time, so they're constantly tinkering and trying to fix them."

"But I mean, they've been trying this shit for what, decades?"

"Centuries at least, and yeah, probably eons," I agreed. "But they can't agree on anything. Half of them want to keep it all because it's what they've always done, and the other half want to keep some of it at least, just so they can study it."

"And none of them can agree on what should be kept and what should be scrapped." Paul grunted. "Sounds stupid to me."

"If you look at it from the outside, it is," I said. "They've been stuck in this loop forever. To them, this shit is normal."

"So what do we do now?" He straightened and stepped away from the door. "The Ændari have fucked off, so what's next? We heading home?"

"We can't go to Earth," I said softly, having been thinking about it loads, and coming to a hard decision. "Or at least, we can't go back *yet*."

"Why not?"

"Too risky. The Ændari took the memory that Ingrid sent them, and they ran with it. But they've got to figure out sooner or later that it's bullshit, even if they do go there looking first."

"And you think they'll come back here looking for us?"

"Probably. I mean, once they figure it out, they will, but the Forgeship is moving on, continuing its patrol route, and getting more reinforcements just in case. The problem is, either we stay with them from now on, and when the Ændari come we fight them, kicking off a war, or we go, and they either tell them we've gone, or they try to sort it out then."

"And then there's just us when the Ændari come looking, right? Sounds a bit shit on us," Paul pointed out.

"Better that we kick a war off? Millions could die," I asked.

"Better that we fuck off and they don't find us," he corrected. "They never found Earth before, and we don't know any of these millions."

"Nope, they didn't," I agreed. "But they didn't have a reason to look, or any clue where it was, and there's a lot of empty space to search."

"But now they know that there's something in this quadrant," Zac grunted. "You know, boss, every time we get something sorted, like kicking the crap out of those asshole 'Blessed,' we just get deeper in the shit."

"I know," I agreed glumly. "I think we need a discussion, a proper one between us all. See if anyone else has any better ideas, before I offer mine."

"Why?" Paul asked suspiciously. "How stupid is yours?"

"Oh, it's plenty stupid," I assured him. "Dangerous too."

"Fuck's sake."

That pretty much ended that conversation, and kick-started the next, although it was a few hours later that we had it. In the meantime, we got some basic materials delivered, and access to the funds that we'd bargained for and earned through the bounty.

We also found out that a good meal was a single credit, with a crappy takeaway type of meal, the type that has less nutritional value in the meal than there was in the packaging? They were a quarter credit.

We now had a solid balance of 188,962Cr.

That was enough in the independent systems to buy the settlement rights to a small planet in the outer systems, or in most inner worlds to at least live a *very* nice life.

It wasn't enough for a ship, admittedly—not a decent new and powerful one— but hopefully it'd be enough to repair one. Although we could form a new ship from the equipment we had, the sheer scale of the ship meant it'd take us weeks just to fix the gaping holes in the hull that were left by the main guns and most of the inbuilt upgradable systems having already been removed.

That had seriously pissed me off, and Emberalis and I weren't on speaking terms since he'd told me.

But, as he'd pointed out, the ship was functional, it just wasn't pretty, and they'd promised to cover the cost of a functional warship.

As soon as approval was given to transfer the crew to the new ship, the other crews on board the Forgeship, knowing that the warship was destined to be chopped up and fed into the converters anyway, had fallen on it like goddamn locusts, stripping anything they might need as spares.

They'd not known, of course, that we were taking it, and Emberalis had forbidden the parts being returned, moving him up a few ranks on my list of people who needed a good punch in the face.

Shanah had tried to smooth things over, pointing out that they damn well knew the data was fake, and that they'd given me the ship anyway.

They wanted to bargain for fully working and unlocked tech, makers that could be used to rebuild the Forgeship and more, but unfortunately, as much as I wanted the UC on our side…we didn't have that data to give.

What we did have was access to custodians that could repair their systems. But they'd take a lot of time to do that, and realistically, the tech that we could give them, such as the makers that were more fully unlocked, or rebooting their nanites and giving them full access to the system?

That would remove any value we brought to the table.

Once the deal was done, they'd not need us any longer, and so we'd left Ingrid bargaining over those points. James had joined her, and I was with Zac and the others exploring the ship and making plans.

We'd already agreed that we'd provide them with a design for a cruiser, and that was, well…

I'd been bullshitting and bargaining on the fly, with the plan that all we'd need to do was scale up the current design. When I'd told Zac that, and that "It'll be easy, right?," he'd nearly punched me in the face.

Now we were exploring our "new" ship and I was trying not to annoy the master engineer any more than I already had.

The ship was…well, it was in far worse condition than we'd thought, and that was before the others had started stripping it. Aaronis had sent word that he'd come and give us a "proper" tour of the ship as soon as he was finished getting his people settled, and he'd promised that there were bonuses to the ship that we were likely unaware of yet.

I was hoping so, because just as the first example? The shield generator that was installed was the most basic model on the market, apparently, as they'd taken that as a backup for their new ship before they found out that we were getting the older one.

We'd only gotten this basic model thanks to Clicqo. It'd been a spare on one of their ships that was in dock, and they'd arranged for it to be delivered to us.

The reactor was fine, thankfully. It was certainly all we needed for now, but it'd need replacing and upgrading as we did the rest of the ship. The command-and-control systems were okay too, though they'd been patched more times than a hobo's underwear.

Arise :Explorer

The ship's AI—Arturo—was currently undergoing a reboot as it was changed to our control, and was apparently the standard model all the warships had. That meant that it was probably at least as advanced as the AI we'd been running in that upgraded custodian.

The control runs that ran the length of the ship were fine. The cargo bays and engines were decent; they were too big to be worth stripping out generally, and for those that would have, they needed a lot more prep to get free.

That wasn't to say that someone hadn't been trying when the ship had been hastily recommissioned, so one of the engine support struts was now being reattached by a particularly pissed-off welding team.

The auto turrets were now unarmed. Hell, the missile launchers, lasers, and the main guns were ripped out within the first twenty minutes.

What we had was a working frame that was battered to buggery, engines that were solid, if not overly powerful, a mid-range reactor and enough mass for it for at least a few months.

A decent, if unexciting AI core, and a working, solid nav system, thank fuck. Nobody had gone for that yet, probably because like the AI core, it was in the center of the ship and less likely to be buggered up in a fight.

The booster engines were used both for landing and takeoff, and when you needed a little extra maneuverability, they were okay. Five out of six worked: one was a mess and needed repairs, but that wasn't too bad. Fuel tanks weren't really a thing, fortunately, and although the ships had basic "makers," as these people called factory units, they didn't have many settings unlocked.

The food that was in them was an uninspiring slop, or the most basic raw ingredients, so Jay was sweating his ass off, lugging everything from his kitchen aboard our ship into this one. Zac's next job after the basic tour was going to be setting the makers in the galley and about the ship to produce the things we needed.

That meant that there was usually a fair amount of space in the ships that needed to be retrofitted from their original uses to serve as food storage for the soldiers.

That was something we'd be changing.

More makers being unlocked meant that we could get rid of that space entirely, either gaining more cargo areas, more crew spaces, or whatever the hell else we wanted.

Probably more guns.

The ship was huge compared to ours, and although yeah, it was a bit buggered up? That didn't mean we couldn't fix it and still come out ahead.

By the time I got Ingrid back inside the ship, Zac had updated a design he'd made back in Facility #6B with a few new bits of tech he'd unlocked since. Now a new flying drone was sweeping the ship for any kind of listening devices that might have been "accidentally" left behind.

Fortunately, we didn't find anything, but it was better to be careful.

"What's the deal?" I asked Ingrid bluntly after kissing her. The pair of us sat in the command-and-control center of the ship with James, Jonas, and Zac.

"Essentially, we're going to make small steps and reevaluate regularly." She sighed, sitting back and closing her eyes. "I hate negotiating. I spent the entire time thinking I was going to give away too much and that I'd let you all down. I really wish Far was here."

"We all do." I smiled. "And we all know you'll have done your best. At the very least, you'll have done a lot better than me!"

"You'd have threatened to stab everyone," she replied tiredly, shooting me an exhausted smile. "So, what we're giving them, for now, is access to medical technology, the tubes, and unlocking the most basic of their nanite functions. That'll correct the issues that are preventing them breeding any more soldiers and give them longevity again."

"Right..." I agreed. My stomach dropped at the thought of giving anyone access to their systems again.

"We're locking the medical facilities to soldiers, or war variants, only," she clarified, using the proper name. "But we'll unlock it so that any of them can gain it, not just those who are descended from BWVs."

"That's a lot." My words slipped out before I could help myself, and I winced as soon as they did.

"It is," she agreed, looking annoyed, before shaking her head and taking a deep breath. "It is. There wasn't much choice, though, if we want the UC to accept us, as in *us*, as the rulers of Earth and Earth as under our control..."

We both saw the wince that James gave at that, and Ingrid went on quickly.

"*We* know it's not just ours, but otherwise Emberalis was going to go straight there and start stripping the planet to find anything he could. Remember, they know where Earth is. They managed to hide that from the Ændari, but the only thing stopping them going there and searching without that concession? It was opportunity. You better believe that Emberalis would have been on his way already if we'd not gotten that in place.

"As it is, in exchange for that, Earth is now a full voting member of the UC, and we are its protectors, with our faction in full control of the Earth until a formal vote can be held by the Earth to elect its world leaders."

"When do we need to do that by?" James asked, making notes.

"We don't." She snorted. "Typical bureaucracy. They want the trappings of democracy, but not to actually put up with the risk of losing their power, so we just had to agree that we would look to do it when it's feasible."

"Coolio. Nice easy out there then. What else?" I asked.

"We also have the right to accept and place bounties, general rights on area and claimed territory, and most importantly, defense. The UC agrees that Earth is a full member, so they have to dedicate the same resources to us as they do any other capital world."

"Oh?"

"Three warships on roving duty, two assault brigades to be stationed on Earth, or in its system, under the direct command of the system governors, and only contacting its direct representatives until they're authorized to do anything else."

"Us," I said, seeing what she'd done.

"Exactly." She smiled. "Now that Earth is a member, we've got some cover for it at least. And if the Ændari attack? They'll call for help—a call that the UC military is required to answer."

"But three ships are going to be fuck all use against that fleet we saw earlier," I muttered. "What did they have? Fifty ships?"

"Thirty-eight," Ingrid corrected. "Two cruisers, one heavy transport, thirty-five lesser vessels, roughly equal to the warships in tonnage and capability."

"So three ships would last a few minutes, if that." I grunted.

"It's minutes we didn't have before," Ingrid snapped, before taking a deep breath, as I winced.

"I'm sorry," I said, at almost the same time as she did.

"I'm sorry," she whispered. "I tried for more, but…"

"You did the best you could have. If that's all we've got from the UC, it's a hell of a lot more than we had… So. We need a fleet."

"What we need is a Forgeship," Zac muttered.

"Yeah, I think they'll be pissy if we kill everyone and take this one." I snorted.

"They would," he agreed. "But you said the weird three-faced one…Clikky?"

"Clicqo."

"Yeah, them." He shrugged. "They said that their people started a war with the big dino-looking guys because they'd had a fight in the system and the wrecks were trashing their world, right?"

"Yeah?"

"So there's got to be more battlefields out there, right?" He shrugged. "Let's go find one, preferably an old one that's got the old designs and shit in there still."

"You think they'd not have thought of stripping the battlefields?" I asked him, frowning. "They must have."

"They have," Ingrid assured us. "I asked. There's hundreds of them out there. Most are broken scrap. Others are spread across multiple systems, shredding the worlds in them."

"They'd have spent millennia crashing into each other if they're in a gravity well, and would be damaged beyond recovery. Or, if not, they'd be spread across…who knows how great an area." James shook his head. "That couldn't work. At the very least, it'd take decades to find anything that was in any condition to be useful."

"True, if we were trying to recover working ships." Zac grinned evilly.

"What have you got in that twisted melon you call a head?" I grunted, frowning at him as I picked up one of the apples that someone had thoughtfully printed from our own makers, and had settled on the tabletop.

The gleaming red of the apple shone as I lightly buffed it on my chest, then bit down.

"Well, the custodians can fix things, right?" he suggested. "They don't have full access to schematics that we can pull out of them, and believe me, I've tried, but they have a seriously big engineering database in there. They share data like the nanites do—the more of them around, the smarter they are, up to a point."

"Go on."

"Well, we find one of these battlefields and the trashed ships. We make a converter and a factory unit…"

"Maker," I corrected.

"What?"

"They call them makers. We might as well get used to it, there's hundreds of worlds calling them that. If we're the only ones calling them factories, we look like lunatics."

"And if they called them something stupid?" he asked.

"Then we'd ignore them." I shrugged. "But makers work well—they make shit."

"Fine, whatever." He snorted, shaking his head and grabbing an apple of his own. "So we make some converters and *makers*, and we set some custodians away, stripping some worthless parts and making more of themselves from one wreck, okay?

"Then we set them loose on another ship, a *proper* wreck, but big, like a battleship or something. If there's enough trash for raw materials, they'll keep going until they fix it, right? They could make us a fleet of our own." He shrugged as if that solved everything.

"Yeah, great," I asked carefully. "And the crew we'd fucking need for that? Can we just print them up as well? Come on, Zac!"

"Hey, fuck you, mate." He snorted. "It's a real option, all right?"

"It's actually not a bad idea," James said slowly.

"What?" I asked, surprised.

"We build a fleet."

"Okay, now I'm interested," I admitted, shifting in my seat.

"Hey, how come when James says it, it's suddenly reasonable?" Zac complained.

"Because I think problems through, Zac, not simply pass sections off as 'not my problem,'" James replied, then smiled to take the sting out of the words. "In all seriousness, though, a fleet is exactly what we need…and I don't just mean Earth. The UC, from what we've found out, is essentially running on fumes. It's got a lot of great people, but it's gotten used to the fact that the soldiers, provided you recover their bodies, will eventually recuperate from almost any wound.

"That means that as more than ninety-nine percent of the sapiens in the UC won't come back to life, they've become highly risk averse. They simply don't see why they should risk their one life, when another could do it for them and recover."

"But if the soldiers are killed in space, they don't recover, right?" I frowned as I tried to figure this out.

"Well, that's not entirely accurate," James said carefully. "Ingrid, can you confirm this—the UC and the Ændari…they lost *all* memories?"

"From what they said, yes. There were some, like the Devourers, who didn't, but almost everyone else did. They just woke up one day with their minds wiped and had to try to put everything back together."

"Okay, well, that makes sense from the details we learned then. Because they've got active nanites, the soldiers recover, but as their memories were wiped, they simply don't remember their earlier lives and have no access to real technological marvels. They've lost the system in the way that we have it and can no longer upgrade and unlock abilities or data.

"To put it another way, they simply endure, coming back to life provided they have the energy in their cells to regenerate and for their nanites to reconstitute them, or access to mass that their nanites can use to rebuild them. There are tales of UC soldiers waking up on forgotten moons and worlds after the ship they were on was destroyed. Their corpses were damaged on reentry but over time, their systems recovered and they live again, waking on a new planet, with only the memories they've gained since the plague."

"Okay…" I nodded, imagining the sheer confusion that would bring.

"The issue is that if the enemy used a highly powered laser, gamma for example, in the battle and hit the soldier? That soldier is now dead and cannot be recovered because their nanites are lost."

"Right." I nodded. "So what's your point?"

"There are medical facilities on the Forgeship," he said. "Ingrid has agreed that we will bring them back online and unblock the soldiers' BWV systems. My point is, why stop there?"

"Go on," I encouraged him curiously.

"What if, instead of just raiding these ships and battlefields, we specifically stripped out any repairable medical facilities? We know from those on Earth that if the database survived, they can reconstitute people. If we find older shipwrecks, in theory we could remove the medical suites, install them in our ship, and provide them with fresh batches of nanites. They could bring back the literal dead, people who were stored in the system buffers for millennia."

"We get crews for the ships." I nodded. "And once we've got a decent crew who can help us aboard our ship, we can start recovering a second, and a third ship, send them off to find others…"

"Wait," Jonas said suddenly. "What's to stop these ancient soldiers, these ancient war variants, from just saying 'thanks very much' and leaving us, going straight back to the UC?"

"Nothing," Ingrid said softly. "And that's the best bit."

"What?" I asked, confused.

"If we can do that, if we can not only bring about a resurgence in the UC to the point that they could actually challenge and either eliminate or force the Ændari to back off? That brings a chance for real peace to the galaxy. More to the point, as a member world of the UC, we increase our standing *inside* it. Add in that if *we're* the ones doing all of this? We become so valuable to the UC, and especially to its actual fighting forces, that they will make damn sure Earth is protected. Imagine it; you wake up after thousands of years of drifting in space, only to find that again, just like Yeshin said, the Ændari are still causing problems.

"You find that *again*, the UC is incapable of sorting this out for more than a stalemate at best, but then you find that the people who found you? Who woke and healed you and are bringing your friends back? Not only are they from the original legendary homeworld of your kind, but they've got a plan, and they're already doing something about it. I'm not saying we poach the UC's best and brightest…" She lifted her hands in a weighing gesture and tilted them from side to side.

"But if they chose to come and serve us, as members of the UC and people who have a right to call on them instead, that wouldn't be something anyone could complain about." I nodded. "Okay, I like it, but we'd need to be quick about this…"

"When do we not?" Zac groaned. "Seriously, boss man, don't go telling me I need to make a new ship by the weekend, all right? I'll just tell you to fuck off."

"That's just crazy talk." I pretended to be affronted.

"Good…"

"We'd need it by Friday," I finished with a smile.

"Fuck. Right. Off," Zac said slowly and distinctly, giving me the finger. "Seriously, you can—"

"Zac, Steve." Ingrid chastised us both. "Play nice, the pair of you!"

"I was joking…"

"You better have been," Zac muttered.

"Probably," I added in a low voice.

"Zac, you know he's joking." Ingrid sighed.

"Glad to hear it, boss." He smiled at her.

"We *are* going to need to make some serious changes to the ship, though," she went on, smiling right back at him. "And one of those is going to be the cabins."

"Oh, for…"

"I think the ones from our original ship could be cut out and installed quite easily?" James pointed out. "We could literally make use of the fact that the hull is currently open—cut a bit more of the structure out and insert the old ship entirely, seal it into place and have the custodians seal things back over and connect it up correctly?"

"Sounds good to me," I agreed.

"Well, yeah, all right," Zac agreed after a few seconds, thinking it through and realizing that this could work and not really need any extra effort on his part. "I've seen the cabins on this tub of rust. They're crap."

"They were designed to provide everything a warrior needed." Aaronis entered the far end of the room, with Leshan close behind him. "Is there a problem with them?"

"They're crap. There's no shower, and I can't attach a sex swing anywhere," Zac said without missing a beat. "Seriously, did you buggers have like a special room for bucking or something? I'd break my back on those beds…"

"Bucking?" Aaronis frowned. "I am afraid I do not understand."

"Yeah, just ignore him." I gestured to a seat at the table. "Welcome, Aaronis, Leshan. Grab a seat—and an apple, if you want—and tell us about the ship."

"I thank you." Aaronis nodded, taking a seat and picking a red apple up, staring at it in curiosity.

"Like this," I said, before biting through the skin of mine and chewing.

"I see." The pair followed suit, biting in and being apparently surprised at the crisp and juicy innards.

We gave them a minute to enjoy the apple, the centuries of being a soldier suddenly damn obvious as they both relished any opportunity to eat.

"So, you said that the ship isn't as crap as we were worried she was?" I prompted.

"Indeed. And my thanks for your intervention on our behalf. My brigade is praising your name right now, even as they fight over the new bunks."

"It's fine," I said. "That asshole Emberalis wanted to show off, so we let him, that's all."

"Well, a replacement ship is a rare thing in my experience, so my thanks thrice over," Aaronis said again anyway. "Beyond that, you have my apologies. When a ship is slated to be destroyed, it is stripped as quickly as possible. While it's officially frowned upon, as the mass is needed to feed the makers, it's also well known that if there is an identical mass given to the ship that is to be sacrificed? Then nothing else is said.

"To that end, all ships carry a certain amount of high atomic value cargo, ready to swap out with another for those parts, or to feed its own makers."

"Okay, that could be useful," Zac admitted. "How much and where?"

"The cargo holds are…" He hesitated. "They are perhaps not the only places that cargo may have been accidentally stored…"

"What, like the corridors and shit?" I asked.

"More like there might be some little nooks and crannies where things get set to be extra safe, just in case they're needed later?" Zac asked shrewdly. "The kind of things that should probably be handed in to the government, or some officials, but that might have been put somewhere for safekeeping, and then 'forgotten'?"

"Exactly those kind of places." He nodded carefully. "A ship that serves as long as our warships do? Well, they often end up with special compartments that are designed to keep things safe in certain situations. Perhaps a special gift for someone special needs keeping safe, or a treasure that has been recovered, but that should only be handed to certain authorities…is forgotten about."

I smiled as I finally twigged to what he was saying. The ship had smuggling compartments!

"These places…would they have all been emptied?" I asked cautiously.

"Not all of them, no." Aaronis smiled. "Those that were left may have been accidentally forgotten about, and along with the atomic scrap, it could go some way to helping you with any replacement parts?"

"These replacements," James asked. "Where would you recommend we go about getting them?"

"There are numerous systems, independent ones, that specialize in shipping, be that commercial, fighting, or construction. Those systems are unlikely to be safe places, especially for someone with a lot of credits. But for a UC vessel, and more to the point, one with soldiers aboard?"

"We don't have any soldiers," I said.

"No…but perhaps if you had access to some of our armor, you could make some of your own…" he suggested carefully.

"I'm sure that if we had access to that we could manage it," I agreed, keeping my smile as small as possible.

"Then perhaps searching some of those storage areas would reveal spare armor parts, parts that should have been handed in for reclamation."

"I like it." I grunted. "Zac, you need to find these places and get that armor copied into our databases."

"On it already, boss," he assured me, standing and hesitating when Aaronis stood with him, gesturing toward the door and leading him out.

"Perhaps I could show these places to your engineer, and then I must return to my duties, before I am missed."

"Thank you," I said to Aaronis. "That's going to help a lot." He nodded and left, while Leshan stayed seated, in what was obviously a planned situation. "So…" I prompted her once Aaronis was out of earshot. "What's going on?"

"Perhaps some unimportant details are best left to lower ranks to deal with," she said blandly. "Then, should a higher-placed officer ask questions, the answers can be given with complete honesty."

"I knew I recognized a career NCO when I saw you." I snorted.

She frowned. "NCO?"

"A non-commissioned officer," I clarified. "Essentially, in our own military there are those who are groomed and raised up to lead, who are taught in special places to be able to lead battles and wars—they're the officers. But when it comes to the details, to the things that make things really work? They need NCOs to be the bridge between their plans and the shit that actually happens. Sometimes that means that the officers have to leave things in the hands of those they trust to make things work out right."

"A squad leader role." She approved. "And other times?"

"Those officers are told to go play in the corner while the real soldiers do the things they can't," I said flatly. "Clearly Aaronis isn't one of those types, but perhaps his higher officers are?"

"Perhaps," she said carefully. "Perhaps those with higher command authority are the ones you would be familiar with."

"Gotcha," I agreed, nodding. "So anything that gets said here is just us spitballing…uh, us talking about hypothetical situations. Nothing is real; it's all just possible things we might want to consider."

"Exactly." She nodded. "To that end, the commander suggested I show you a few details." She reached out and triggered the table we all sat around.

We'd seen that it had a low lip and a shiny surface, with dozens of buttons and more all the way around the outside, but we'd not had the chance to actually try everything yet.

As such, it was a bit of a surprise when it sprang to life, projecting a complex star chart over the piled apples.

"Here we are." She tapped and highlighted a star system that immediately expanded to fill the floating area. Worlds spun lazily around the central star, with a pulsing set of triangular symbols in the center, and two circles that glowed a deep and angry red at the edge of the system.

I reached out and plucked the apples out of the way, staring in wonder at the image.

"These are the fleet and Forgeship," she explained, indicating the ships, and showing the way that we could bring up data on the sensor contacts, tapping a control on the side; another screen, one that took up a third of a nearby wall, suddenly sprung to life and showed in-depth data on the ships.

"Here, though, are the issues." She indicated the two flashing red circles. "This is an Ændari Skyslayer." She tapped it, and a second image filled another wall.

"The Skyslayer class is used to track other ships. They're rare. As far as we know, there are only four still active. This one arrived shortly before the fleet left and has been hovering at the extreme edge of the system since then."

"How are they different from the regular ships?" Ingrid asked.

"A regular Ændari Skarn is of comparable size and capability as our assault warships, but the Skyslayer is designed to track all outgoing ships from a set location. They can't maintain it indefinitely, but from what we know, they lock onto the individual gravitational signature of the ship's drive. From there, they act as a relay point to share that data, and using their spy satellites, they can track a number of ships through numerous systems."

"So, basically, we jump from one system to another, and they can track us, even without following us?" I asked.

"For a number of systems, yes." She nodded. "It is not unlimited, and should there be a particular ship they are interested in, then they will usually move the Skyslayer to enable more accurate tracking."

"But it's here to make sure they can find us."

"Most likely, yes."

"Will they know which warship we have?" I asked.

"Possibly. It depends on how advanced their spy network is. As soldiers, we are judged not to need the data on countering that, generally. Most likely, they will simply track you for several jumps, along with the other ships that leave here when the Forgeship leaves.

"Then, should they need to find you again, it will be easier as they have a set of samples of your drives to track."

"Why are they called 'Skyslayers'?" James asked curiously.

"They were used extensively in the early centuries of the last war to track ships to their home worlds, and they are equipped with multiple heavy-impact drivers. They have, in addition to heavy missile banks, the ability to adjust an asteroid's course and accelerate them to impact their targets."

"They send global killers after planets." I grunted. "Fuck me…every time I think they can't get any lower…"

"What about the other marker?" Ingrid asked.

"A Skarn vessel." Leshan pulled that image up next. "The equivalent vessel to our warship, although lighter armored, and loaded with conscripted fighters in place of a dedicated crew. They generally load around three times the maximum we can, and have better shields, with rotary energy cannons as their main armament."

"So not a good idea taking them on as we are right now," I muttered.

"You would likely be destroyed before you got close enough to see them visually," she agreed. "Most likely, they are here to report if we attempt to take out the Skyslayer, as they are both faster and more maneuverable."

"So what are our options with replacing the looted parts?" I asked.

"This is the nearest viable location in the independent worlds." She pulled the map of the system back, and then flicked over a dozen systems along. "Should you be capable of jumping to here, this shipyard would be your best choice. It is dangerous, but as the commander suggested, the locals do not wish to offend the UC. Perhaps pretending to be soldiers would be in your best interest. Once landed, any of the individual shipyards would be capable of repairing and replacing enough systems that you could then defend yourself at the very least."

"Okay, what about the level of tech?" I asked.

"Explain, please."

"Tech, uh…the guns you have on the ship, for example, or the shields? Are the ones we can get there likely to be of comparable strength as the ones that have been removed?"

"Yes and no," she replied after a few seconds of thought. "The UC shields, for example, are more efficient than the independent reverse engineered options. Some independent systems have managed to create versions that are capable of higher output, for a correspondingly higher cost in energy. Or so I've heard.

"We've faced pirate vessels and found that, on occasion, their shields or other systems were more advanced than expected, making it a harder fight than it should have been."

"But you always won?" I asked.

"Of course." She snorted as if offended. "We're the UC."

"But that's why the ship looks like it does?" James questioned. "The exterior damage, it's from ongoing clashes with pirates and more?"

"It is," she admitted. "And with that in mind, there is a second option."

"Oh?"

"You came here as bounty hunters, and while as a Devourer that role is somewhat beneath you, it would provide an opportunity for both easy access to replacement systems and loot, and an ongoing source of credits for the systems that must be bought," she suggested carefully.

"We become bounty hunters for real?" I mused. "It's actually not a bad idea."

"Do we have time?" Ingrid asked me. "It's a good idea, but I don't see that we do."

"We can talk about it," I agreed. "Is there anything else, Leshan?" I asked, and she nodded.

"Two things, first and foremost… I'm saying this as a soldier, and certainly not as a first fist, whose loyalty is to the UC, you understand?"

"I do. Go on." I frowned.

"You might not be aware of your authority," she said as delicately as she could. "As a Devourer…you don't have to ask. You can tell."

"Ask who?"

"Anyone."

"I don't…" I trailed off as more and more details clicked for me. "The other Devourers, they're not involved in the day-to-day running of the UC, are they?"

"Definitely not."

"And if they were?"

"They would be issuing the orders that the UC follows," she finished, watching me carefully.

"That's why they seemed so surprised that we were negotiating." I groaned. "As a Devourer, we should have been issuing orders."

"Well, you're new to your abilities," Ingrid pointed out. "It's probably better if we negotiate where we can for now, and then when we need something…" She hesitated and sighed. "That's not going to work, is it? If we give up that authority now, we can't use it later and expect it to work."

"Probably not. For now, as long as they give us what we need, we play nice." I shook my head. "But if they're dicks, we make it clear that we were being polite in asking."

"Thank you for that, Leshan." Ingrid smiled at the first fist. "We appreciate it."

"We do." I nodded to her. "And the second thing?"

"I need to introduce you to Arturo." She smiled and cocked her head to one side as she spoke seemingly to the air. "Arturo, are you online?"

"I am, First Fist," a bland, pleasant male voice said into the silence.

"Arturo, are you aware of the recent changes in ownership of this vessel and yourself?"

"I am, First Fist."

"Arturo, I am Steve. Do you know who I am?" I asked.

"Yes, Devourer," the voice came again, bland and pleasant, without any real interest. "I have been informed that I have been recommissioned, instead of being rendered down to my constituent atoms and being reformed into a new ship. You have been identified as my new commander, along with co-leader Ingrid."

"Hello, Arturo," Ingrid called.

"Good enough." I grunted, mentally marking out that I needed to look into Arturo and make damn sure it was as it was supposed to be. "This is James. He is our pilot…" I gestured to James, who nodded.

"Welcome, Pilot James."

"Thank you, Arturo. I look forward to working together," he said politely, getting no response.

I went around the room, introducing those who were there, and describing those who weren't, giving Arturo specific commands, such as that in the condition of one of us being unable to fulfill their command duties, the next in the chain of command was authorized to take over.

That necessitated explaining our command structure, and Paul was going to be so pissed when he found out that even Jay outranked him.

"May I ask for clarification?" Leshan asked before leaving. "You rank your cook higher than your soldiers?"

"Not all my soldiers, just Paul. He's a hell of a fighter, but if we had a ship's cat, I'd put it above him in the chain of command as well."

"Ah. He is…"

"A gifted soldier," I admitted. "He's just crazy as well."

"Very well." She nodded to me and headed for the door.

That was another job dealt with, which I was glad to have ticked off. But as soon as Leshan left, Ingrid nodded and stood, offering me her hand.

"I think we need to have a talk."

I winced. No good had *ever* come of those words coming from a partner.

<u>Chapter Twenty-Six</u>

Thankfully, the conversation wasn't about children or marriage, which was a fucking relief, all things considered.

Ingrid and I had walked around the outside of the ship and into our own much, much smaller vessel, then we'd gone into our quarters. For a half second, I'd had a spark of hope that she'd actually been feeling frisky.

I was quickly disabused of that notion.

An even bigger disappointment was that Ingrid had asked enough questions of the three leaders—Shanah, Clicqo, and Emberalis—to find that I still had a serious problem.

Essentially, the council could indeed unlock and reboot my systems, allowing me access to my overall upgrades and quests again. But to do that, they needed their systems up and running, and they needed command access, then they could try to do it.

That left us with two choices. First, we accept that as a necessary cost and give them the facility to replace us, or at best, relegate us to a minor player again.

Or…

Or we went for option two, which I'd been kinda thinking we'd need to do anyway, and so, it seemed, had Ingrid.

The Universal System Quadrant Node was heavily locked down, and there was no two ways about that. It'd permit ships to dock with its outer frame, something which was apparently popular for the young, rich, or terminally stupid of the Ændari, UC, and independent worlds to do.

They'd fly to the outer frame and spend some time "communing" with the "spirits" of their ancestors.

It was bullshit, I was sure, and the information that Ingrid had managed to get was that a sort of shanty city had sprung up there, and that it was full of all the nutjobs of the various races.

Notably, the rich ones, as they were the only ones capable of space travel to there.

From how she described it, I was seriously getting concerned that it sounded like the worst of the social media "influencers" and "lifestyles of the rich and shameless" lunatics I'd seen. All the hippie-dippie "believe and the universe will reward you" absolute nutters were pretty much congregating there, trying to commune with the spirits—while doing a fuck ton of drugs—and the various criminal elements were making a killing "serving" them.

I didn't know what was putting me off more: that the Ændari apparently had a sub-class that were just as useless and mental as our own, or that no matter where you went in the galaxy, there was always going to be some asshole trying to sell me a fucking dreamcatcher. Worst of all was knowing that they'd try to be nice to me while they did it.

If they did that, I couldn't harvest them, and that was what the Ændari were *for*. I'd have to be as polite as I could, because otherwise we'd end up in some battle with the criminal underworld idiots who were, apparently, also ubiquitous across settled space.

The node itself was heavily impregnated with nanites, and they'd formed an almost indestructible surface, literally designed to hold off the UC's fleets and others in the distant past.

That meant that the surface of the docking area was made of the same stuff, and as nobody could get inside the main doors…well.

A shanty city had sprung up. Some enterprising creatures had set up a bar; then came accommodations, basic repair and food facilities…

I wasn't sure when it'd been built, but as Ingrid told me about it, she laughed that there was even a brothel set up, and that Emberalis had tried to change the subject when Clicqo had mentioned something about the "indiscriminate appetites" of certain species.

None of the locals could get inside past the docking rings and reception area, and they couldn't damage the surface, so they couldn't burrow into it.

That meant they couldn't make houses or attach things like anchor points to the walls, so every structure was built using scrap metals and stone recovered from the surrounding systems.

The "normal" Ændari would turn up every so often and screech about the "lesser races" contaminating their relics, while ignoring that some of their own were among them, and the interlopers would flee.

They'd come and sweep the place clean of any homes that had been made, often killing anyone they found in "accidental weapons discharges." But would leave their own to wander and sulk in the corners while they did it.

Then the UC would show up, and both sides would shout at each other a bit, then slope off, until the next time.

That was all very interesting when she explained it, but the real details that mattered? This was the home of the universal system in this quadrant. The one that all our nanites worked through and that we communicated with.

It controlled literally *everything*, and for long centuries, both sides had tried to get inside, to reset their abilities, to no avail.

That they continually tried showed that they still believed it was an option, and when Ingrid and I had heard about it, we decided that it made sense as well.

It had to be that the main system could be controlled from there. Otherwise, what was the point of it? And if it could be taken? It'd be a game changer.

As it was, we just damn well knew the Ændari would be going there again, and soon.

Once they got to the arse end of the galaxy and found that Ingrid had made up the memory they'd bought, along with the locational data, they were going to be gunning for us, and that left us precious little in the way of options.

They'd be coming for us, and they'd be looking for Earth. If they couldn't find us, the only other option—besides searching every other system out there until they found it—would be to examine the logs that the Universal System Quadrant Node had to have.

That would, in theory, have the locational data for every one of us, all those who accessed the system. And if they managed to actually get access?

They could probably switch our systems off as well.

The thought of being midway through a battle with the Ændari and suddenly losing control of my nanites?

It was *terrifying*.

I didn't know why they'd not done this in the past, before they lost access to the systems if it could be done, which hinted that maybe they couldn't, but not knowing?

If the Ændari beat us to it, we'd lose, I had no doubt.

As usual, though, we had both limited time and limited resources, so as I sat on the swivel chair, bolted to the ground in the middle of what had once been Athena's private bedroom aboard her megayacht, Ingrid and I started to work on a new plan.

What we needed was simply everything.

We needed a fleet, we needed an army, and we needed time. None of which we could get our hands on. So we came up with a plan that would give us at least the start on the first two.

Then, because I was a filthy pervert, I asked her whether we had time for a quick shower.

Because, you know, an opportunity missed is gone forever.

Two hours later, as we received word that the Forgeship was preparing to jump out of the system and we had to either leave, or prepare for a jump that would take us several hours in the wrong direction, Ingrid and I reentered the bridge of our new warship.

James, who was interred in his special pilot's section, half encased in cushioned and protective padding, was powering the ship up, with Jonas in the captain's chair.

He rose as we entered, looked from Ingrid's clearly still wet hair to my grin and shook his head.

"So we're working our goddamn asses off and you've been having fun?" he whispered to me as I stopped near him. "It's a disgrace is what it is."

"Perks of command, my son." I clapped him on the shoulder. "Seriously, though, we were working."

"Uh huh," he said noncommittally. "That's 'work' now, is it?"

"James, are we ready?" Ingrid asked loudly, making me jerk as a hologram of James flickered into life nearby.

"Dude, seriously?" I snapped, looking him over.

"My apologies, Steve, Ingrid. As you can clearly see, the warship has facilities to share my image," he stated with a smile. "And, you'll be pleased to know, Casey has begun construction of a coffee machine."

"Oh, thank the gods." Ingrid smiled. "Tell me there's tea as well?"

"There will be soon," he said. "The majority of the ship is now sealed, and while our vessel is still attached to the outside, that will require more complex systems to move than we have currently. The tractor system…was a casualty of the situation." He sounded annoyed.

"The gravitational system is working, as are engines, navigation, and the more basic onboard systems. The shield has finished basic integration, and test powering is proceeding well. Zac is examining the engines and believes we should be good to go soon, but asks that we either go now, and jump separate from the Forgeship, or we wait until their jump is complete."

"Now?" Jonas asked me, and I shook my head as I took a seat next to Ingrid.

"We were going to," I said. "But if we're the only ones leaving now, we'll be easy for the Ændari to track. Tell Zac to hold fire, please, James. We launch after their jump, along with the others."

"We've just spoken to the council members here, and they agreed to dispatch warships to Earth immediately after the jump as well. They'll be sent by a roundabout route to keep it as safe as possible, jumping out in the direction the other Ændari have already gone.

"They'll jump back as soon as they're outside of the Skyslayer's range and they're sure it's lost its lock on them. Then they'll head directly to Earth to take up their stations there. In the meantime, the fleet is heading to rendezvous with the Forgeship. We'll essentially launch into the fleet as it meets up, and Shanah is arranging to have the fleet break up and do a dozen jumps in all directions for a day or so.

"It should make it impossible for the Skyslayer to track us, as we'll be one amongst many, and while they might get lucky, most likely we'll be a few days ahead of them at least," Ingrid finished, glancing over the screen displayed to the left of her seat.

She'd pulled up a series of star systems, and was working through them, plotting a route from where we were to one of the independent systems that Leshan had shown us.

"James, this system has three settled worlds. One of them has a shipyard in orbit and…"

"This is the one that the first fist recommended," James said, making it flash blue. "Is this the plan then? That we head to there for repairs?"

"For now," Ingrid said. "We need to get this ship up to scratch, and as part of achieving that, we need to, at the very least, seal the outer hull and get our old vessel inside."

"While that's being done, we can make a proper plan," I added. "I've asked that Aaronis be placed in command of the Earth defense force. He's agreed to place a stealthed comm node in several systems so that we can get a real-time link back to Earth."

"Also, considering that his people, when they're not based in space, are going to be housed in the Sahara with maybe some time at the Great Refuge as well, we're at least going to be able to guarantee the safety of our people there from any attacks by the remnants of the Blessed and the Accursed."

Ingrid said it in a firm voice, making it damn clear that although she intended to make sure that while we were doing our best to protect all of Earth, she was also making sure our people were safe regardless.

"Sounds good to me," Jonas said. "I know when we left, your parents were talking about pulling in all our people, families, and so on. Is that still the plan?"

"Definitely," Ingrid said. "The desert plant is still pulling in a lot of Earth's waste, and regardless of the moral situation—that we can fix it, so we should— it's also providing us with a secure location and a huge amount of resources to convert the local area.

"If we're going to keep that as our main base on Earth, that means that in addition to the fortress that Far designed, and that we've all been adding bits to, we're going to need a shipyard and landing facilities. All those things come with a massively increased need for security, and having all our people behind that line of UC soldiers just makes sense."

"So, is this the destination as soon as we launch?" James asked. One wall of the bridge was suddenly lit by a star chart that matched the one that Ingrid had on her display.

"I think so," Ingrid said slowly, looking over the data we had on it. Another display lit suddenly, and a collage of images filled it: first the shipyard floating in space above a grey and brown world, the sun shooting rays around the edge of the planet to illuminate the station as the UC vessel that had presumably taken the images passed by.

Then there were zoomed-in shots, multiple different images of the shipyards themselves, along with data, estimates, and identification tags that were linked to the ships that could be seen.

Finally, several dozen sections of the shipyards were tagged and identified as having energy readings that suggested obscured weapons emplacements, and possibly concealed launch ports for either fighters or newly constructed ships that had been hastily hidden from view.

More images showed the dock that the UC vessel was assigned, strategic data on the likely entrance and exit points, and again, the hidden weapons emplacements that the dock had, ready to open fire on the vessel at any time.

"Friendly bunch, aren't they," I muttered as we watched a delegation come out to meet the UC soldiers, and basically give them a brief "watch yourselves; if you get in the shit, we're not coming to help you, and if you shoot the place up, we'll shoot you" speech.

"They let them dock," Jonas pointed out.

"Yeah, but is that because they wanted them to, or because they didn't want to risk the damage if they said no?" I asked.

"Most likely, if the facility is as lawless as was implied by the first fist, they literally didn't care," James replied. "I've done some reading since we got access to the basic database from Arturo. The independent systems are a mixture of entirely lawless areas and feudal states. Some are relatively benign and rule by a code or law system; others are literally pirate havens where slavery and murder are considered the rule of the day."

"And this one?" I asked grimly.

"A middle ground," James explained. "The laws in this system are exceedingly lax, but they do exist. As do security firms that are literally hired to make sure that any who do business here are protected. The lack of any real laws in regard to labor or restrictions on technology have fueled great growth, and the security forces ensure that nobody who 'matters' is killed on a regular basis.

"The upshot of this is that many of the leading research and design companies are based here. The UC can't afford to alienate them, as they have a significant input into repairing and replacing the larger ships that make up what is referred to as 'home fleet,' and yet they also use practices that the UC cannot approve of, so they're based out of here."

"Somewhere the UC has no authority beyond the strength of their weapons." I grunted. "And Leshan wanted us to come here?"

"It makes sense," Ingrid said. "What did you find out about the home fleet?"

"Little. Mainly references to it, oblique ones, suggesting that it's an open secret."

"That sounds right. Arturo, can you explain this please?" Ingrid asked.

"I may offer limited confirmations only," Arturo replied. "Due in part to the fact that as representatives of a member world of the UC, you are entitled to such information, but as your membership is in process, all levels of data have not yet been unlocked."

"Okay…" Ingrid tapped one fingernail in the edge of the table as she thought. "Arturo, the home fleet is the replacement fleet for the UC, is that right?"

"Partly."

"What is incorrect?"

"'Replacement' implies the older and therefore obsolete vessels will be retired. This is incorrect."

"Okay, so the UC are building a new fleet, one that they're loading up with all the tech they can, and that they're hiding from the Ændari."

"Correct."

"And they're keeping the older ships patrolling and fighting on the border while they do this?"

"Correct."

"Are the Ændari doing the same?"

"It is considered likely."

"Great," I muttered. "For a whole half a second, I had some hopes raised there."

"It's common sense, I guess," Ingrid said. "There's a cease-fire in place, not a peace, so both sides are rearming as fast as they can."

"Makes sense," I agreed. "So, you said they'd have new tech…this is coming from here?"

"They have the shipyards, they have the opportunities, and they have access to technology that is probably considerably more advanced than the rest of the UC."

"How?" Jonas frowned. "I mean, they're supplying it, so they have access to it."

"Ever bought a computer?" James asked him, sounding distracted as he apparently ran through some jump calculations.

"Well, yeah?"

"The latest model is usually, I believe, three to five years out of date when it launches."

"What? How's that work?" Jonas asked, confused.

"The development cycle is constant," James said. "As soon as say, a graphics card is completed, it enters heavy testing periods, that while they have been ongoing through development, now they need to be carried out again, and under more careful conditions. Errors, problems in the design, manufacturing arrangements…all need to be looked at, and all that time, the next model is being worked on by the original inventors.

"The model that is launched, finally, as the new and most up to date, 'available on the market' is already obsolete when compared to the next design that's being worked on, and this is only one component. This is a process that is being carried out dozens of times in each machine that is offered, and the cutoff for the design phase, when all of these components are 'locked in,' is often a year or more after the company got access to the 'new' graphics card. Add in their manufacturing, assembly, and shipping time?

"The new computer is usually three years out of date by the time it reaches the shelves, along with an average lifespan, commercially, of two to four years. So, if we take that experience—and that's a commercial process, not one that involves military or political involvement and approval cycles—and then we add on those two? The technology that I would expect these companies to be producing is likely five or more years ahead of the most cutting-edge technology that is being installed in the UC's main hidden fleets."

"Shit. And don't forget that no independent arms dealer in history has ever just sold to one side. You mean that both sides are rearming with the latest and greatest kit, and they're gonna have representatives here as well." Jonas groaned.

"Most likely," James finished.

"So what do we do?" Jonas asked, looking over at Ingrid and me.

"Well, unlike anything that you and your filthy mind might have been imagining, we were actually working on that before we came up here." Ingrid stared at Jonas, daring him to say anything.

I remembered exactly what we'd been doing in that shower, and coughed, nodding and forcing a frown as I looked at him too.

"Yeah, get your mind out of the gutter, ya filthy animal," I added, hoping that he'd not heard anything through the hull. We'd not exactly been quiet, after all. He just stared at us both, waiting, and Ingrid went on, apparently not feeling even slightly guilty.

I mean, neither was I, but she was generally the more innocent and honest of the two of us. Also, because I was a bastard, I sent her a mental image through a private link, a memory of a sight I'd had while we were "working" earlier.

I felt the mental prod that Ingrid sent and the slight embarrassment from that image, as well as the hopeful "later?" she sent back. I enthusiastically agreed, making a mental note to make sure the new quarters, when they were installed, were soundproofed.

"Anyway!" Ingrid said after a few long seconds of silence. "What we're going to do is dock there. Zac has access to the armor that Leshan left us, and he's going to start making some up for us all, but…"

"I like this," Jonas agreed, nodding.

"But it won't be ready in the short-term. We'll have to use our own armor at first, and you'll both play bodyguard," I explained, taking over the thread. "Oxus, Paul, and Courtney will defend the ship. You and Scylla'll defend Ingrid and me, as we go get some quotes for shipbuilding and upgrades."

"To be clear," Ingrid said. "I'll be going to negotiate with the technology suppliers, as they're more likely to be—"

"Posh dickheads," I interjected.

"Designers and corporate types," Ingrid finished, ignoring me. "While Steve and either you or Scylla will go deal with the shipyards."

"It's probably better that Scylla is taking the shipyards," Jonas said. "No offense, boss, but if you're going to be spending hours with corpo types, I'm probably better off by your side. Of the two of us…"

"You're less likely to stab first and ask questions never?" I suggested.

"I'll not tell Scylla you said that." Jonas shrugged. "But only because I like you and wouldn't want to see you get stabbed."

"But you think that taking her to a shipyard to book in for work is likely to work better?" I suggested.

"You think that she's more or less likely to get into a fight around corpo scumbags?"

"Point," I agreed with a sigh. "Ingrid, best if you take Belle as well. She can read other species, after all. Might give you an edge."

"Good idea. You should probably take Zac with you as well…"

"Dammit," I muttered.

"Well, he knows what he needs for the ship, much more than the rest of us do. The last issue is down to us," Ingrid said softly. "Who and what do we claim to be?"

"I thought we were bounty hunters?" I asked.

"We can be, but most likely, as soon as the Ændari find that they've lost us, they'll start scouring space for a group of human bounty hunters, and…" She shrugged.

"That's true, but the systems we're going to need…I mean, it's not like we can pretend to be fish people and then want air recyclers and so on, right?" I suggested.

"We've got—"

"You know what I mean." I cut her off. "I mean that in negotiations and so on, they're likely to see us, and even if we fake what we look like, as soon as we rock up in a cast-off UC warship… I mean, they said that this was a level of tech they don't let anyone get normally. The Ændari know that we're getting one, right?"

"Yes, but I'm betting that there are some out there, regardless of anything Leshan said. I mean, if pirates haven't captured one at least, they're idiots."

"Or rebuilt one." I grunted. "Yeah, I mean, if you're in UC space and a UC warship jumps near you, you're more likely to heave to or whatever, right? Rather than fight?"

"Exactly. If the pirates here haven't figured that out, I'd be surprised," Ingrid said.

"Crap," I muttered. "Arturo, are you there?" I asked the empty air.

"Affirmative, Devourer."

"Are there reports of UC warships being used by pirates?" I asked.

"Rarely," the ship's AI replied. "Those incidents are heavily punished, though I would suggest that the reports that are made, are only registered by survivors."

"So basically, if there are some and they're killing everyone, or stopping their targets calling for help, then there could be loads of them out there?"

"It is unlikely there are great numbers out there, but it is highly likely that there are at least a small number, considering the length of time such designs have been in service, and the sheer number of battlefields that have been populated by these designs."

"What he said." I sighed. "Well, at least we've got an alternative, I guess."

"What, that we don't use the armor?" Ingrid said after a few seconds. "We make up some kind of botched-together body armor, and use that instead? Pretend we're pirates?"

"Or bounty hunters, but we don't dress like they're expecting," I suggested. "We keep some of the team aboard ship, in that armor that we've got access to, just in case someone tried to board us, and then we kick the shit out of them, otherwise?" I shrugged.

"We play pirate," Ingrid said after a few seconds. "That…that actually makes sense."

"Why?" James asked.

"While the UC is highly likely to have access to the top-end equipment, we're not UC, and if we claim to be, and then we fail whatever tests we're given? We'll not get anything, and we're likely to be attacked or at least frozen out. If instead we limp the ship into dock, damaged as it is, and we pose as pirates or bounty hunters, but we configure our armor to more or less match that worn by the independent worlds? We should be able to blend in a lot easier." Ingrid got more and more excited as she figured her way through it.

"Where do we get the armor designs, though?" I asked. "Arturo, do you have any?"

"I have sample designs from external scans, but they are incomplete."

"Fuck."

"What about the corrupted?" Jonas asked suddenly.

"What?"

"What about the corrupted?" he repeated. "They went a bit mental when we landed, but they weren't exactly hard to kill. And Leshan said there were ships left on these worlds all the time, when the crews are killed. Why not find one of those and strip it? Hack their systems, steal their cargo? Then we go trading instead? Looks more like we're 'normal' pirates and bounty hunters rather than paying for everything in cash, right?"

"James?" I turned to look at him. "How far are we from that moon?"

"Currently…" He paused, calculating. "Not far, but the Forgeship's jump range is significant. Most likely, when we emerge, and considering the destination shared, we would be better off heading to a different world, or leaving immediately before that jump."

"Do we know if this other world has any ships on it?" I asked.

"Arturo?" James said instead. "Please provide contextual data on the world marked as 'Xana 3-F.'"

"The world formerly known as Xiphos, and now referred to as Xana 3-F since being lost to the corrupted, is a class-three world located in the habitable zone of the Xana-Shin'ra corrupted zone. This world was lost 1087 local solar cycles ago, due to a suspected impact from the Florian-7 combat initiative.

"The initial outbreak was discovered after orbital insertion had delivered the outbreak vectors to multiple zones, resulting in a global loss after only eleven cycles.

"Of a population of 6.2m sapiens, 137,404 were confirmed rescued and clear of infection, when the world was declared lost. Since then, Xana 3-F has been under constant quarantine, with system-wide interdiction flights maintained at all times."

We sat there in silence for a moment, the description somehow made worse by the bland unconcern in the AI's voice as it described such an insane loss of life.

"Well…could we sneak in?" Jonas asked, glancing at Ingrid, then James and me. "I mean, if we could, and we could hit the center of one of their main cities, there's got to be some ships left there, right? And trade goods?"

"There'd be lots, but are we sure we're not susceptible to infection?" Ingrid asked.

"I'm not…susceptible, I mean," I said. "I could activate the Devourer and just walk through them."

"The rest of us, not so much." Jonas snorted. "But there's also the question of landing and getting back out. I'd imagine we could dodge any ships—space is big, after all—but they'd have to have trackers or something, right? And we'd have to jump in at the Lagrange points, so they're fairly obvious."

"The Xana-Shin'ra corrupted zone is heavily observed due to the significant value of its internal reserves," Arturo said, and I nodded thoughtfully.

"What if we ask?" I suggested.

"Ask what?" Ingrid glanced at me.

"Ask the UC for permission." I shrugged. "The worst they can say is no, right? And we're the heads of a member world, so it's not like it's easy to ignore us. Also, I'm a *Devourer*—they already said that we're kinda outside of their chain of command regardless. We've already landed on one corrupted moon, so we've got proof that we can do it. They're concerned that there'd be an outbreak, that's why they don't let anyone land, but if I was to literally just walk through the middle of the city and shred the corrupt? That'd be a good thing, surely?"

"I…guess so?" Ingrid bit her lip. "Okay, give me a minute. I'll try to get them to go along with it, and if not, then I'll signal you and you can join in and we'll try to work it out. I'll reach out to…" She sank into the call, apparently making a decision and settling back, closing her eyes.

"Well, I guess that's that," I muttered.

"So what now?" Jonas asked.

"We wait."

"Yeah, I got that, but I mean, we're jumping to the next system, right?"

"Yes."

"Okay, so if we get approval, we jump, fuck off to Xana 3-F, do a little looting, and maybe grab a ship that we can strip, then we head to the indie world's shipyard…what's it called?"

"Baerlon-4," James supplied. "That's the world. The shipyard is 'Kranthi's Place,' or its also referenced as 'The Den.'"

"Oh, wow." Jonas snorted. "We're really going top tier then?"

"I only take you all to the most exclusive joints." I smiled. "It's not a bad idea, though, for us to be using trade goods instead of cash, as the Ændari have no reason to be looking for us in this particular ship, or in that part of the galaxy."

"Anything that muddies up the waters is a good thing," James agreed. "Very well. As we wait for approval, is there a secondary path I should be considering?"

"If they say no, then I think we go back to that moon. It might not have trade goods, but at least it should have the ship that we saw on the recording, and that's got to be worth stripping and copying details, at the very least."

James nodded, assuring me that he'd scan the local systems between our projected jump exit and Baerlon-4 as well.

"They might not be able to get into the ship, but I bet my Hack skill can," I added.

I decided I'd try to learn a little about our new ship as well. I tried fumbling with the controls on the arm of my chair before cursing and forcing myself to think.

I was trying to learn to control technology I'd never seen before, and although I *could* learn how to do it, the reality was, I didn't goddamn need to.

That wasn't an ego thing; it was simply that the buttons were there as a backup, in case everything else went down, and I, unlike the current generation of soldiers, had access to most of my systems.

I reached out, focusing, and searching…

And *there.*

I found a connection point exactly where it "felt" like it should be. The ship's systems opened to me as soon as Arturo identified me. A new overlay appeared across the room as my mind's eye and my physical ones meshed together to form a new reality.

Suddenly the walls of the bridge were gone, and the world around us was revealed, or in this case, the inside of the Forgeship hangar.

Tiny details leapt out at me as I glanced around the hangar, before focusing on the widest variety of unique details, namely the people who hurried back and forth across the floor nearby.

The ship's sensors were open to me, and so were its records, I realized, flowing back and forth, time reversing as I dragged up the recordings made minutes and then hours ago. There were literally dozens of different species running back and forth, carrying random shit to the ships and running off again.

I spent a few seconds just lost to the world, playing with the details, zooming in on passing people, examining the various races as I waited for Ingrid to finish her conversation.

I idly narrowed it down, as I explained aloud to the others how to do this, and I curiously checked to see who had come to our ship recently, finding only a handful who weren't our people approaching.

Well, besides the soldiers anyway.

Aaronis and Leshan, totally understandable, as were a bunch of the soldiers earlier. What I guessed were their ship's engineers, and supply masters, for a brief time the ship was swarmed, then the recordings stopped as it was fully powered down and even Arturo was taken off-line, ready to be decommissioned.

I flowed back to the ship being rebooted, the engineers who were aboard her being booted off and anything they had with them being grabbed back, or the engineers themselves being ordered to return it. A handful more came up, thinking they could still loot, I suppose, before being turned away.

Then people were scurrying like ants as they left the ship and more parts and food were brought. I saw our people running about, and I saw Ingrid and me…and because, you know, I'm a filthy pervert, I zoomed in on Ingrid and just admired the sheer beauty of her as she strode across the deck.

She'd been subtly adding a little height to her boots, I realized, watching the sway of her hips. She was somehow wearing something closer to high heels than goddamn space boots, and I couldn't help but love the way that she walked.

I forced myself to return to the general view of the hangar, before flowing the recording forward again, blurring along and slowing only as others came up to the ship, wondering whether anyone had tried stealing from the ship since it'd been declared it was being recommissioned.

I found a few people turning up to look, before moving off, but little more than that, until fifteen minutes ago, when a single figure hurried across the hangar toward the ship, nothing in his hands and his head down.

As soon as I focused on him, a screen appeared in the air by his side. Personal details popped up and a highlighted, but brief, resume was available.

It scrolled quickly, informing me that "Geetu Mashu-shu'et" was a Tomberlin maintenance technician, and he worked in the repair facilities on deck nineteen, sub-section 5-E. He was also on a warning for incompetence, a recent fuck-up having heavily damaged a power system that his department was trying to recover.

A dozen minor details flared up as Arturo—who I sensed was interfacing with me and the Forgeship through the link—detected my interest and provided additional data, piecing the various records together and highlighting them for me.

Part of the advantage of having the system linked to your brain like this was that as much as I "read" the notes, I also absorbed them, meaning that instead of it taking, say, a minute to read the notes the way it normally would? It was about three seconds.

Then, because I was literally linked to an AI that was in turn linked to the UC databases, I started to really dig.

By the time he'd covered a dozen meters to the hull of the ship and was pulling a small package out from inside his overalls, I'd already found out a bunch of important details.

First and foremost, that he had absolutely no business being in this section of the Forgeship, and certainly not when he was "on shift" and supposedly six floors and half a mile away at the very closest point.

Add in that the sections he'd been working in were all known for higher than average faults and delays, and that he'd singlehandedly fucked up a production line to the point that a month later it was still being worked on?

As I watched him press a patch to the ship's hull, the patch changing color from a bland flesh tone, to blend into the dark grey of the hull? I realized exactly what he was. He wasn't trying to grab some spare tech to help his ship and fuck everyone else, or even someone trying to turn a fast profit by stealing something and selling it.

The little bastard was a saboteur.

Chapter Twenty-Seven

I pulled up the current view to one side, and compared them—no, he was gone. I cursed, moving back to where he stuck whatever it was to the hull, then flowed forward, time blurring as he smoothed the edges, making sure it was as unobtrusive as possible, before turning and hurrying away. A nearby patrol saw him passing, but with his head down and clearly not carrying anything, wearing maintenance overalls, they simply shrugged and let him continue.

I tracked him leaving the hangar. Even with its massive size, he was gone as quickly as he could be, vanishing into the Forgeship's interior.

Then, I had some explaining to do to the others, as Ingrid continued to have her silent argument.

By the time we'd all watched it, and we were indeed sure it wasn't a "normal" thing to happen on an alien starship in a Forgeship that was the size of goddamn Manhattan, we started the next stage.

Paranoia.

"Yeah, but how do we know *that it's not the local government doing this?"* Zac asked for the third time. He was upside down under a section of piping currently, repairing and replacing it as he went, linked to us through the ship and the command link. *"I mean, governments do some shit regularly that makes no sense, that's all I'm saying."*

"Why?" I asked. *"Why would the government, who've pretty much welcomed us with open arms, stick something to the side of the ship and hide it? They could tell us they needed a tracker on us to make sure we don't accidentally crash into alien Santa for all we know, and we'd go along with it."*

"Would we?" Jonas frowned.

"They gave us a frigging warship," I pointed out.

"A broken one."

"Still a fuckin' warship, mate." I shook my head. *"Give us a month and unlimited scrap? We'll make something that can take down moons. You know we will. If they made it a condition of the deal that we have a tracker or whatever— it is a tracker, right?"* I glanced at the image of Zac, who nodded as best he could from under whatever the hell he was under. *"You got the custodian to examine it?"*

"Yeah, it basically gives off a really low level but constant stream of bohrium particles. Fucking nutjob had it in his overalls as well."

"Okay, that's nice." I shrugged. *"And for the people with real jobs who don't know such weird shite?"*

"Fuck's sake, boss," Zac answered distractedly. *"It's a radioactive isotope. You get it from particle accelerators—and it's not naturally occurring, as far as I know. That means nobody is looking for it, so a stream of these fucking particles would be easy to follow, but they've got a half-life that's literally 'fart and it's gone,' so it's hard to spot. Perfect tracking tool, as nobody's going to stumble across it unless they're searching for it."*

"How the hell would you track it?" Jonas asked. *"I mean, if it's gone after a handful of seconds..."*

"Gravitational pulses." Zac grunted, then cursed. *"Fucking pipes! We're in deep fucking space a million miles from anywhere, and they're using pipes that went out with the fucking ark! Why!"*

"Zac?" I asked as calmly as I could. *"What—"*

"I mean seriously!" he went on. *"They've not been maintained, they've not been cleaned, and as near as I can tell? They're fucking pointless! They're here to take waste from the living quarters to the goddamn recyclers. You have any idea how long these pipes are and how far they travel? Why! Who the fuck thought this was a good idea!"*

"Someone who didn't want to shit in the corner of their room?" Jonas asked softly, while trying to hide a smile.

"Idiots!" Zac snarled, dragging himself out from under the pipes. *"That's it! No more, boss, I'm fucking done!"*

"Zac..." I tried again, as the mad Aussie kept ranting.

"I mean it! We rip the pipes out of the ship, plug a goddamn converter into the bottom of the bog, all right? It'll take in whatever you dump in there: piss, shit, old apple cores...all of it. Then it'll make... Fuck it, you know what? I'll link it to the power cores. They'll turn any waste into energy for the ship. Then we don't need these goddamn pipes, we get all that space back, and I don't have to fuck about with them, all right?"

"ZAC!" I shouted.

"WHAT?" he yelled back.

"Do it."

"What?" He frowned as if he didn't understand.

"Do it. I don't care, as long as they don't smell or anything. It makes perfect sense. Great. Go for it. I don't care."

"Oh, all right—"

"What I do care about?" I asked him in a fake cheerful voice. *"Oh that's easy, thanks for asking! It's the goddamn radioactive tracker that's stuck to our ship!"*

"Shit."

"Yeah, Zac, screw the pipes. Mess with them later if you want, I don't give a damn—deal with the tracker!" I prompted.

"It's bohrium." He shrugged. *"No clue how they got it produced by something so small, but it's just giving off a trail of those particles. They don't really do*

anything, besides, you know, rotting you from the inside out with all that radiation. Hmmm, they do interact with gravity a bit weird, I think? Like they let loose an energy pulse when gravity gets increased, so..."

"*So when we do a grav jump, we'll basically be showing the galaxy where we are?*" I asked. "*Or with weird energy pulse, do you mean we all get blown up?*"

"*Nah, more a signal than anything else. And it's not gonna be obvious, either.*"

"*Coolio.*" I grunted. "*Right, I need to make that clear to Ingrid and whoever she's talking to. You guys get on with...ah, I don't know, whatever you were doing. So, I guess for you, Zac, that means no wanking on duty,*" I finished lamely.

"*You're not the boss of me!*" he threw back automatically. "*Oh, wait, dammit.*"

"*You idiot.*" Jonas groaned, and I shook my head, before mentally reaching out to Ingrid, "tapping" at the edge of the call she was making, and getting a relieved impression from her as she added me into it.

Suddenly I was in a new room, sitting virtually at a table that morphed to provide space for me, with Ingrid on my left, a round table between us, and Shanah, Clicqo, and Emberalis across from me. The shadowy images of their partners or sycophants or whatever hovered behind them.

"Ah, Devourer." Shanah greeted me. "We welcome you, but your presence changes nothing, I fear. Our position remains that should we permit you access to these worlds, then we must permit others the same. Any access and contact with a corrupted world is judged dangerous, and while Commander Balthazar permitted you access to one, I agree, he did so as a certified observer, and one who we know and can prove would have remained on the planet if there was any risk of the corrupted escaping."

"Since these worlds were declared lost, none save the soldier class have been permitted to land and—" Emberalis started, and he was clearly annoyed when I spoke over him, cutting off what was probably a well-rehearsed and time-honored speech.

"I really don't care," I said.

"Devourer?" Shanah asked carefully. "You are abandoning your request?"

"Not even slightly." I smiled. "We're asking you to let us visit the world in the hope that we can, at the least, recover some worthwhile materials. And at best? Maybe we can figure out something to sort the planets out."

"The risk—" Emberalis started.

"Is to us and not to you." I cut him off again. "Although there are two points to raise with that as well. First of all, I need to land on that world, and so we're asking you to smooth the way. I'd prefer not to simply order your ships to stand down, when we go there, but if I have to, then I will. Regardless, though, you're going to be very busy."

"Oh...?" Clicqo asked; the heads slid to the "unamused" position in clear warning.

"Yes." With us being in a virtual meeting, it was easier for me to flex and do this, though I suspected I could have done it back in the physical meeting room we'd been in as well.

One wall, to the side of the group, abruptly shimmered. Then it played the recording from the ship, bringing up the details on the individual from earlier, showing them hurrying across to our ship, pausing to remove something from their overalls, then attaching it, before moving off as quickly as they could.

"I do not understand," Shanah said in a low rumble.

"Watch carefully." I showed them the recording again, this time providing a breakdown alongside the figure of who they were, their history aboard the station, and the incidents that had happened around them.

Then I tracked the records back to their arrival, showing them arriving on a transport with a different ID.

"Where…did you get this?" Shanah asked slowly.

"We spotted him as he attached the tracker to my ship's hull," I said. "Something he did while my ship is supposedly in a safe, secure zone, and *under your protection.*"

Silence hung in the air, and I could feel the sudden panic that came from each of them, all while their faces stayed frozen.

After a handful of seconds, they all seemed to unfreeze at once and I couldn't help but snort. They'd literally frozen their digital avatars. The sneaky fucks!

"Think they're panicking?" I sent it to Ingrid.

"Definitely."

"So, as I said, you're going to be *very* busy. First of all, because you'll be wanting to run an investigation, no doubt. Secondly, because you're going to be thinking of ways to make up to us that you almost set us up to be hunted easily by the Ændari. And third? Well, if there's one of these fuckers here, there's going to be more. You need to be finding them and making goddamn sure they're away from anything useful."

"We accept no responsibility for this," Emberalis said suddenly. "This individual's actions appear suspicious, I accept, but we've not encouraged anything of the sort, nor do we know for sure what he's doing."

"I don't care," I said, smiling flatly. "You are responsible for this Forgeship. You made that clear when we arrived. Therefore, I hold you responsible for the actions of each and every one of those inside it. You can't have it both ways. Either you lead and are responsible for those under you, or you're a manager and you can't manage the role, in which case you need to step down and have another take your place."

"You have no authority here!" Emberalis snapped at me.

"Correction." Clicqo spoke up. "The Devourer has the same authority as do all his kind, as one cannot exist without the other. If we defer to the Devourers, then we must defer to him. If we choose not to defer to him, then we choose not to defer to the instructions of the Devourers. I choose the Devourers."

"But…" Emberalis gasped, staring at the multi-bodied figure, as Clicqo shifted, presenting a smiling face to me.

"We accept your request to access the Xana-Shin'ra corrupted zone," Shanah said suddenly, shifting in his chair and bowing his head slightly. "As the only members of the council of the UC to have ever successfully and directly allied with any Devourer, regardless of their capabilities, it would be churlish to refuse."

"The…" Emberalis hesitated, looking from Clicqo to Shanah, before at last seeming to get the hint that, in allying with the group that were viewed as a single step below the gods to most of the UC, he would be better off shutting the fuck up. "Ah, of course, my apologies." He turned a truly oily politician's smile on us both. "I was concerned about the dangers posed to the UC and the galaxy at large from the corrupt. Of course, as you will be taking full responsibility for your landing there, you will make sure that the risk is removed entirely."

That last bit was said with a warning look, and I grunted, accepting that.

"I'll take responsibility for our ship, and nothing else," I said clearly. "And you'll be thinking of an appropriate apology for letting a spy plant a tracker on the hull of my vessel. I expect it before we depart."

With that, Ingrid and I left the virtual meeting. Ingrid let out a sigh in relief, before joining the rest of us in the augmented reality that I'd found on connecting to the ship as I had.

"Set a course for Xana 3-F please, James. We'll be heading directly there as soon as the Forgeship completes its jump," Ingrid said. "Okay, now fill me in on what I missed." She glanced at me.

"Yes ma'am." I grinned. "So…"

Half an hour later, and with a new permanent guard stationed around our ship, and the tracker peeled off, then attached to another ship that was going to act as a decoy, we completed the preflight tests.

James had insisted on them, mainly because his flying experience prior to our ships had been very minor, and considering he'd dumped us into an asteroid belt at least once already.

So, we put up with fifteen minutes of his testing thrusters, gravitational controls, and who goddamn knew what else, before finally, *finally* we were ready to go.

The jump to the new system went flawlessly. The pulse went out strong and mingled with a dozen others, now that we knew to look for it. An hour later, we finally slid into the air, turned around slowly, and headed out of the hangar into open space.

It'd gone reasonably easily, as had the assigning of a second assault brigade to Earth as an apology, and fuck me, was I having manically evil thoughts over that.

Considering they were super soldiers pretty much on par with the guys who came from Krypton, except they were better armed, better-looking generally, and utterly lethal in every way?

I had momentary fantasies about giving them a list of targets, like all the Blessed and Accursed Arisen who hadn't surrendered yet, and orders to wipe them all out and bring their stuff to our place.

Then I'd present it all to Ingrid, along with any behaving Arisen who I'd have write absolutely accurate histories of the world.

She'd be so pleased that I'd be ravished twelve ways from Sunday by her, and the rest of the galaxy could go basically fuck itself.

The only thing that stood between that most wonderful of situations and me?

The Ændari.

Arise :Explorer

Well, that made things entirely simpler.

All I had to do was wipe that evil empire out, and I could devote the rest of my life to eating good food, drinking good rum and some coffee, and having lots of sexy time with the woman I loved.

It felt good to have a plan that fit my priorities at last.

Leaving the hangar was a bit of an experience, and that was an understatement. The Forgeship seen from the outside was like we were flying a Cessna, turned on its side, alongside a city. The damn thing was utterly enormous, and as we saw more and more of it, it became clear why the Ændari were both scared of it, and not so much.

That was a weird way to say it, I knew, but it was accurate.

When the Ændari and the UC had suffered from the nanite plague, and they'd lost their memories and access to the main systems, they'd lost real knowledge of, well, everything apparently.

That was why even thousands of years later, they were still rebuilding.

In this case, those who had awoken aboard the Forgeship had found themselves in bare corridors, their memories gone, simply cold steel everywhere they'd looked.

The machines they'd found had been programmed to respond to them, but their production memory units were wiped as well, and only the last item in production was saved.

That had meant that millions had died of starvation and dehydration before water sources or viable food were discovered.

All that time, the ships were drifting, aimless and lost in space.

It'd taken them hundreds of years, with small groups often fighting each other over the limited supplies, before they finally discovered where they were, namely aboard a spaceship, rather than in a giant building or whatever.

Uncounted ships must have been lost to stars or crashing into worlds, and even more were simply lost to the cold of space, drifting for eternity.

Of those who eventually learned enough to unlock the basic systems, few would be able to learn to control them. And of those, only a tiny fraction would be able to access the limited records that had survived in hard copy.

Hell, they'd have to learn to read as well, considering how many of the various species would have had different languages.

Climbing back to the level of interstellar civilizations from hunter-gatherers had taken thousands of years, and they still didn't have it all back.

To fix it, though, they did have people.

But to fix a Forgeship would take thousands of years. And to clear sections where other ships had impacted, or where entire zones miles across had been melted to slag by directed energy nukes?

They had to be fixed meter by meter: the metal reformed, fresh panels hammered out, then fitted. It was akin to a single man or woman rebuilding a World War Two battleship from scrap, with no clue as to its original purpose until they were three-quarters of the way through, and missing minor things like blueprints or any outside assistance.

They just had their children, their children's children, and the knowledge that there were assholes out there who had made these ships necessary once.

Now that the UC had been basically rebuilt, things were picking up speed. New systems, no longer requiring nanites to operate, but closer to Earth-level tech, or a single century advanced if that, were commonplace.

They were also using power armor systems that were highly limited in number, but working, and they were provided for soldiers and, rarely, for engineers and others.

Looking up at the side of the Forgeship as we left it, all of that tumbled back to me, and I imagined what it must have been like.

When the Forgeships were intact, and fully mission capable, they must have been an unholy terror for anyone who faced them, considering that if it was latched onto an asteroid, chewing its way through it as it once could, at the other end it'd have been churning out ship after ship, ready for the fight, at the same time.

That was why they were terrified of the Forgeships, or they should be.

And why they weren't?

They knew that at least half of the ship was a mess of broken systems. What was left? It was capable of only the most basic designs, the simplest of systems. All that they knew said that they shouldn't be concerned about it, but they'd also failed dozens of times to capture the Forgeships in open battle.

One of the main reasons the damn place was so incredibly fucked up was that they'd sent fleet after fleet against these mighty bastions, and still they'd not captured one.

Both sides used their "expendable" forces on them. The UC commanded them to tour the borders, to make these systems as safe as could be, while they built newer, more lethal, but far smaller and more brittle creations far back from the front line.

The Ændari? They did much the same. They had their quadrant fleets, they bought and sold tech, and they were building massive hidden fleets—they had to be.

They instead risked their oldest, and possibly grandest and most valuable ships, on the front line, always hoping that the fleets they were raising back behind the lines would be enough to eliminate their hated rivals eventually, returning them to their "rightful" place as rulers of the cosmos.

Now, as we left the safety of the massive Forgeship, we saw its attendant fleet for the first time. James, showing grace of control that was more to do with his upgrades than his ability, sent our unnamed warship soaring and diving in a merry dance as the other ships converged on us.

Our greatest strength, and our best chance, was secrecy. If the Ændari couldn't find us, they couldn't fuck with us, and so Emberalis, grudgingly, had come up with this.

The warships of the UC were almost identical, the only real differences being in terms of the massive amount of damage some had soaked up, while others were pristine, literally fresh off the line.

In our case, we had our own—tiny in comparison—old ship attached to the side, and that was pretty easy to miss, considering that the Ændari would be tracking us all by gravity signatures and radar returns that would be blending together as we dove and twisted around each other.

"All ships, prepare to jump." A solid-sounding voice rang out to us from the comm link. "In three…two…one…"

"Jumping," James announced to the room at large, and I focused, the shields that we had in place far weaker and smaller duty than the one that the ship had come with originally.

Once again, though, I sensed nothing beyond the ship as we dipped into the gravity branes, then—like a bubble shooting for the surface—flashed back out, popping into reality again.

Chapter Twenty-Eight

The Xana-Shin'ra corrupted zone was both beautiful and terrible, I saw, when we blinked into existence right at the border, appearing in the designated "emergence zone" that the UC maintained for military traffic at the Lagrange point.

As soon as we'd arrived, James had brought the ship to a complete halt, relative to the monitoring station that was maintained here, and Ingrid had reached out, using the codes we'd been provided to identify and authorize us to the watchers.

While she was doing that, I was staring, in horrified awe, at the three systems that lay silent before us.

As soon as we'd arrived, we'd been bombarded with contacts, all hammering us with a barrage of "NO-GO" and similar messages.

Worst of all, the systems we were using, based as they were off the Ændari setup, then evolved and improved upon by the UC before its fall, were designed to show the systems before us in glorious detail.

That meant that the important details sprang into my mind. The augmented vision that overlaid the walls of the bridge was literally full of stars: the left, right, and straight ahead each showing a different view of the solar system.

Each of them was filled with detail. I saw Oort clouds, sparkling belts of ice crystals with insane levels of purity spiraling around a gorgeous blue and white gas giant.

I saw silent, slowly rotating starbases. Mining outposts were highlighted: their local minerals, the current status, the proclaimed target they were publicly sharing...

It was incredible, the sheer amount of data that was available. Glancing at a mining outpost, I saw its registered output. The local area was rich in tungsten, aluminum, and helium-3; the crew complement of the outpost was unlocked due to the warship's access codes; the current storage situation of the bins. And most of all?

The flashing red "Contamination'" symbols that flowed across all of it.

The crew were listed, one by one. Just looking at a name brought up the same kind of data I'd seen on the idiot who had tried to tag our ship: a visual reference, a résumé, their personal history, and most obvious of all, a "deceased" banner scrolling across the image.

I blinked, trying to get out of all that, and flicked my attention to the nearest habitable world, hanging there, as were all the worlds, seemingly blown up and held in perfect patterns for my ingestion.

Xana 3-F, formerly known as Xiphos and once the jewel of the Xana system, was slightly larger than Earth, its rotation a little faster, giving it a twenty-two-hour day. And according to the data I had, it was both temperate and fucking gorgeous.

With deep-blue seas, green and red trees, tall mountains capped with snow, and deep valleys that held undisturbed lakes, this should have been a paradise world.

It had been, in fact, from the records that opened for me. Those who awoke here, stripped of memory and on such a wonderful world, had lived a blessed life for long centuries, ending up both quite advanced, thanks to the intact tech they could learn from, and mainly peaceful, as the dominant species was man.

Not that it was a good place because humans were there. It just meant that given that there were cities already made, and there was tech that provided most of what they needed? Then resorts and more that simply needed any long-dead bodies removing—a job that had become almost routine in a post-plague world—and then boom.

Free real estate.

There'd been nothing to fight over for the majority, and those who were violent? Well, there were still defensive systems in place to take care of them.

It'd been a paradise, and one that, according to the information at my fingertips, once it found its place in the UC, had only prospered. People had loved and lived, grown and died in a veritable garden of goddamn Eden, at peace with other races, and far from the dickhead Ændari—right up until a fight that had broken out in the next system over made its forgotten presence felt.

The wrecks had drifted for long centuries in the darkness of deep space before they were caught by Xana's gravity. Another fifteen years would pass as the wrecks were dragged deeper and deeper in-system, with the vast majority of those wrecks entirely passing the system by.

The few that made it in system?

Most were caught by the outermost asteroid belt, or by the heliopause, I found, as data streamed into my mind and I fixated on it.

That was what had caught us as we tried to jump into the border of the system to meet Aaronis and the others. The fucked-up zone at the very boundary of a solar system, where the gravity of one system met the gravity of all the others.

It acted as a sort of catch-all zone, a universal flotsam and jetsam collection point, vacuuming up all the random debris that floated between the stars.

Unless something was moving at high speed, like a comet that could plow through it, then they got caught there.

Comets and asteroids tended to impact the edge of the heliopause, smashing their way through, and sending a load of smaller asteroids, meteors, and general crap in all directions.

Those little smashed fragments were generally what we got to go *ooh* and *ah* at as they burned up in our atmosphere.

Right now, though, I was getting distracted, having seen that bit of information and understanding why we'd nearly ended up pancaked.

The important bit was that of the ships that had been caught in the heliopause, most had been reduced to fragments of hammered metal.

Being hit from all sides by asteroids and random space shite tends to do that, after all.

What had made it free of that, blasted loose to fall into the Xana system's gravity well? They'd been small fragments of ships compared to the great fleets that had been fighting originally.

That also meant that the bits that survived their passage in-system, passing world after world, to finally fall, gleaming and star-like to the beautiful world below?

They were too small to be picked up by most sensors, and they'd certainly not registered as ships or threats of any kind. Instead, they'd been identified, thanks to the rocks and more they were with, as general star matter.

That meant that as they crashed down, they were viewed as wonderful surprises—shooting stars, fallen to the ground—as opposed to the end of worlds.

The corrupted remains wouldn't have looked like anything dangerous according to the reports: charred carbon most of the time, almost indistinguishable from normal star stuff by the time it made it to the ground.

Curious locals picked them up, took them home, and children, full of the wonder of the stars, held their new rock close at night.

Then the corrupted nanites would slowly awaken, reaching out, sensing their more intact siblings, oh so close, and they'd begin replication.

The inactive nanites would recognize their own kind, accepting them, sharing resources and allowing expansion. And as parents came to check on their children the next morning, they'd find them sickening, as uncontrolled replication flooded their bodies in an unstoppable tsunami of change.

The rural areas fell first, and lasted the longest, as they were the most likely to find such things, and yet paradoxically, the most well spread out, slowing the rate of infection down.

The cities, as they were infected, were slow to respond; days passed as more and more of the afflicted showed up in hospitals, until finally the pattern was spotted.

By that point, it was too late.

It didn't always take a bite or a frenzied attack to spread the vector. Simply being in proximity did that, like any other plague.

The bites and the violence came later, as the host succumbed fully, and all that was left was the need for fresh nanites.

I watched it for long minutes. The milliseconds required to absorb an entire dossier on a ship worker turned into minutes as videos, documentaries, and recordings were absorbed in their hundreds. Ingrid and the others turned to me, stunned to see tears rolling down my face.

"Steve?" Ingrid whispered, reaching out to take my hand.

"I'm all right," I whispered hoarsely. "Just…just don't access the system records for the fallen worlds, all right? You don't…you don't want to see that."

"What was it?" she asked, and I shook my head.

"I saw them fall," I whispered as I struggled to regain control. "I saw the corrupted as they flooded through the cities, children desperate for their parents, as they fled their own children."

I couldn't put more into words. I'd seen the heartbreak on their faces. Children who didn't know what was happening, who only knew they were sick and wanting comfort from the ones they loved and needed the most.

They'd cried for their parents, and their parents had to make the decision—knowing what was happening when they finally learned—to be there for their children as they passed, and to then accept that they would in turn become more infected, spreading the virus and killing more.

Or…

Or they had to turn their back as their children wailed for them. Or they had to end their suffering, and all from a distance.

There was no known "cure," beyond extermination, and that was a horrific thing in any situation, let alone one that started mainly with the children, as parents found such wonderful and rare things, and gave them to the ones they loved the most.

I spoke as carefully as I could, laying out what had happened for the others, as Ingrid confirmed our authorization was accepted, and James triggered the grav drive again.

Minutes later, he guided us out into the system's Lagrange point, before turning us to face the planet and triggering the normal engines.

We all stared, entranced. The sparkling diamonds of the planet's satellite network slowly rotated, the sun's bright light reflecting off them as we approached.

This was our first time seeing a world that looked anything like Earth—hell, it was still one of the first worlds we'd seen. But where Earth was surrounded by basically a "trash belt," these were dozens, hundreds even, of high-grade, high-tech devices.

Or they had been, once.

They'd been in orbit now without maintenance for a long time, decades at least past their intended replacement point. Some were still fine, but the majority?

They were trying to create a trash belt of their own, we saw as we approached, with at least a third of the stations having been shredded by impacts.

"We've got authorization for access," Ingrid said suddenly, and I turned to glance at her. "*But*, it's for access only. We're not permitted to set up a base, which is reasonable, or to try to bring people in from outside the system. Again, reasonable."

"Okay." I shrugged.

"We've also been warned that they'll be scanning our hold when we leave the planet with one of their monitoring satellites. If they find any active corrupted aboard, or any spreading corrupted nanites, they will announce that we are infected, and share our ID with the UC and independent worlds." She grimaced.

"I'm sorry, they wouldn't budge on that, and said that it's part of the law that we as members of the UC agree to if we want to access the system. If we don't agree, then we need to leave."

"So you agreed." I nodded.

"There didn't seem to be an alternative."

"Don't worry." I sighed. "There was no way we'd be taking off with these fuckers aboard anyway. We just want to loot some stuff, so I guess we'd be searching anyway. No stress."

"That's what I thought." She took a deep breath, going on. "*Aaaand*, if we were infected? Better that we're caught and either shot down, or announced to warn everyone."

That bit I didn't like so much. I mean, I understood it, but that was the difference between the Danish outlook and the English one, I guessed.

We'd be all about keeping shit quiet and dealing with it ourselves, and a little risk to the galaxy? Well, we didn't want that, of course, but we'd not want anyone else knowing either while we dealt with it.

The Danish would rather we all knew and things were a little safer and more honest.

Save the whales and all that.

Not that the English didn't want to save the whales. But that was because they tasted like ass apparently, so we were fine with saving them. If they tasted good? Then we'd have been all for everyone else not touching them, and we'd have been "protecting them" while passing the ketchup around.

Some people used to say I was a pessimist. I preferred "realist" but fuck it.

"No worries." I forced a smile, knowing that what she'd agreed to was the only reasonable action. "So, what do we have on the planet, and any rules?" I asked her and the room at large.

"Limited data on the planet that is really accurate," James said. An avatar appeared in the augmented vision and walked over to the left wall, where the planet, which lay directly ahead of us in the main view, was repeated bigger.

He gestured, and the planet began to spin slowly, as he highlighted details.

"This was the capital city of Marne. Original population of one point three million. Transient population of around half a million. That includes tourists, workers, and people passing through for whatever reason. It's both the richest location on the planet for looting and the most dangerous, due to the sheer number of corrupted likely to still be in the area."

"Do we know that for sure?" Jonas asked suddenly. "I mean, for all we know, they all drift off to the beach or some shit when there's nobody to eat, right?"

"According to the information we have on them, they are drawn to uncorrupted nanites, hence the cities having the largest populations simply because they were drawn together. Once there's nothing for them to feed on, they go into a rest state, one that occasionally triggers the host to search the local area for any signs. But beyond that, they shut down, reserving energy for when they need it."

"And on that moon…" I murmured. "They were, what? Just chilling until we arrived?"

"I suspect that as there were large areas underground that hadn't been explored in some time, the majority had been searching them, before shutting down," James said. "Logically, the best chance for survival in the moonlet crash was in the inner sections and most heavily protected areas of the ship. When that crashed, the emergency systems would have worked to protect the crew until recovery could be attempted."

He paused, seeming to stare into the distance, before quickly bringing up an image of a massive starship next to him, slightly bulbous and rounded on one side, and huge engines at the other. Beyond that, it was about as aerodynamic and graceful as a duck's arse, and I shook my head at the realization that people actually built shit like this.

"This is a similar ship to the one that crashed there, I think," James said. "This is a colony creation vessel, essentially a massive storage area with engines and with a huge number of colonists being kept in hibernation."

"Hibernation?" I blinked in surprise.

"Certain species can't handle the gravity jumps without additional protection and yet still need to be transported between the stars." He nodded. "When they need that, this is the kind of vessel they use. I don't have access to records for the actual ship we saw, so this is the closest in size I can find. I think that crashed one would have been something like this, judging from the sheer size of the engines, or perhaps something from one of the races that didn't have grav drives originally. They retrofitted ships like this with them, and then used them for mass transit, freezing those who needed that."

"Okay, but why then would the corrupt..." Jonas started to ask, and James went on.

"I'm getting to that," he assured us all. "The need for those races to be in hibernation means that they probably survived impact. They'd have been kept alive, still frozen for as long as possible, and as more and more of the corpses outside fell to corruption, they'd have been protected inside. With nothing to affect them, they'll have been intact the longest, with the corrupt being driven mad sensing them. That would have drawn more and more of the corrupt down after the corpses until the last were consumed."

"And once the last of them were infected, the majority would have gone dormant," Ingrid agreed. "That makes sense."

"So the occasional corrupted woke up and went looking but didn't find much, and when pirates or scavengers landed, the closest would go nuts, but by the time more sensed them, they'd either be infected already, so of no interest, or they'd be fleeing..." I muttered.

"But they went mental when we landed?" Jonas pointed out.

"We're fully activated. Even the soldiers aren't, so we were probably ringing a dinner bell for them the entire time we were there, instead of stealthily sneaking around like we thought we were," Ingrid said. "That's...that's going to cause some issues." She winced.

"Shit, yes," I muttered. "Hell, does this even make this possible?"

"Does it change anything?" Jonas countered. "We knew they'd go mental trying to get to us, and we knew there'd be a planet full of them. Shit, we thought we were gonna have to steal our way in here and rob the place, while hiding from the UC. At least we're not doing that, right?"

"It means that as soon as we land, we're gonna get hit," I said. "If we try anywhere that's likely to have good shit, we'll get absolutely hammered."

"So we look at alternative sites," Jonas drawled. "I mean, seriously, boss, you weren't planning on landin' in the spaceport and just going for a walk, were you?" The look he gave me made it clear that was a stupid option.

"No," I lied. "I was planning on us finding the spaceport, sure, and seeing if they had any ships left that were decent, but…"

"But any ships they had would have been used to flee the damn planet," Jonas countered smoothly. "Now I'm sorry, but if all this shit was goin' on in my home? I'd be hightailin' it outta there, just as fast as humanly possible." He shrugged. "Hell, faster now that I'm an immortal demi-god type."

"So what do you suggest?" I asked.

"Well, what are we tryin' to find?" he asked. "We need trade goods, we need money, and we need equipment, right?"

"Right." I sighed. My mind rolled back to when we first met and he used to lead me around by the nose like this, trying to teach me instead of just providing the answers I needed.

"Well now, trade goods? A search of the planetary details should tell us what they were famous for. Has anyone besides me thought to do that?" he asked the room at large.

"Xiphos's main exports were: a version of silk, generated by the spider farms in the southern hemisphere. Tontos, a rare spice grown in paddy-like fields in the extreme north. And high-end crystals used in various computer, weapons, and communications systems," James replied smoothly. "The crystals were grown in three locations, spaced equidistantly around the planet to prevent contamination from overlapping signals."

"Now there, that's what I like to see." Jonas smiled. "Every time I think I've caught that man out? Why, he's one step ahead of me! So, the silk? It's rare, but it's unlikely to be unique, and the chances of it still being in useful and retrievable quantities after all this time? I'd say that's low."

"Go on." I watched the rangy American as he smiled, playing with the ship's feeds, clearly searching for something.

"That's probably the same with the spices. Are they still growing? Probably. Do we have time to land, farm them, and load up the ship with whatever processed versions we can sort out? Again, unlikely. Any spices that were left lying about are most likely rotten, and those that were packaged to be shipped are likely at processing centers, probably near the spaceport, ready for shipping."

"And the crystals won't be?" Ingrid asked, clearly seeing what he was going for.

"Oh, I think they will be," he said. "But given the other two choices, crystals are the least likely to need further refinement, and they're also the least likely to degrade. If they've been stored for shipping next to the others? I'm fine with checking the others out as well—let's not be crazy, after all. But if this is gonna be a smash and grab? Let's go for the things we can grab easiest, and that are most likely to be valuable and still in demand."

"You make a good point." I nodded. "But wherever the planet's main money makers are, people will have tried to grab shit before, right?"

"I certainly hope so." He smiled at me. "Because ah'm countin' on just that."

"Ah, shit."

Chapter Twenty-Nine

"*Just so you know... I hate you!*" I shouted at Jonas, getting a mental chuckle in return as I sprinted around another corridor. I kicked off a wall and smashed my way through a pair of doors that stood half ajar before me. A long-dead body staggered out of a hidden office door nearby, as I skidded and frantically dodged another leaping body.

"*I mean it!*" I bellowed into the comm link. "*I hate you, you utter wankstain!*"

"*Ah, come now, boss, you don't mean that, not really...*" he replied smoothly, and I cursed him again.

What I hated most of all with this plan wasn't the sheer insanity. It wasn't that he'd convinced me to empty most of my nanites out into the ship, ready to be used to improve it, and keep only half a million in me—or even that it wasn't my plan.

No, the goddamn worst part was that Ingrid had agreed it was the best idea, and that meant that my tiny brain—despite my massive male ego—couldn't possibly refuse it.

And that, really, ultimately, was why I was out here now, sprinting through the commercial zone, being chased by literally hundreds if not thousands of corrupted.

Corrupted that I'd agreed not to kill until they reached critical mass.

"*A few more minutes...*" Ingrid calmly interjected into the link, clearly distracted as she watched something. "*It looks like the effect is spreading.*"

"*Oh...well, that's... great...*" I panted, hurdling a desk and sliding across the far side, landing hard, then bracing and throwing myself through a window.

The shattered glass cascaded free as I lashed out a tentacle, grabbed onto the outside wall, and yanked myself upward. Another and another punched clear to grapple onto the wall, the stone cracking as spikes dug deep, then expanded.

I raced up the wall, keeping close to it, guessing that any corrupted inside the building would sense me better like this than if I just flew over them all.

That was how this had started, after all.

Jonas's innocent suggestion was that, as supposedly the most advanced and fastest of us, I was the one best suited to drawing the others after me.

With that in mind, we'd taken a fast and low pass over a major population center, roaming for a few minutes and judging how long it took and how low, before the corrupt started to notice and respond to us.

Arise :Explorer

Fortunately, it seemed that the senses they used were much the same as my own, which was to say that if they weren't looking specifically, it took awhile to get noticed.

If I was listening and searching for a noise, then when I heard one? I'd jump right on it. But if I was zoned out, distracted or asleep? Sounds could wash over me for ages until they got close enough or loud enough that I'd notice.

Then, though, that noticing and movement would make others aware, and that awareness would spread like wildfire.

This was the same. Until the corrupt started to notice something was here and started "listening," they were just unaware of us. Once the ship was low enough that it couldn't be missed, though? That was it—game on.

To test it further, I'd jumped out and flown around a bit. My wings and gravity manipulation worked in tandem to find out just how quick things changed.

Then I'd boarded the ship again, and we'd taken off for our actual target, half the world away, just in case.

On approach, we'd gone over the plan, gotten ready as much as could be, and then I'd taken the leap, jumping out of the warship in high orbit, falling seemingly endlessly, with Jonas, Paul, and Courtney following along behind.

They'd spread their wings and stayed as high as we dared, figuring the silent drift was safer than the propulsion of a ship that held literally millions of nanites in storage.

I'd flown in low, landed on the far side of the complex, and I'd started to make a ruckus. Jonas and Paul landed on the roof of the target building, and Courtney landed on the roof of another, several hundred meters away.

She was our backup, with the ship prepared to swoop in as soon as we were ready for liftoff.

That was the plan, anyway, and damn I couldn't decide whether it was madness or brilliance. But either way, I was stuck in the middle of it now.

I raced up the side of a third, much farther away building. My tentacles surged out, punching into the rock of the outer sheathing, catching fast, then releasing as another caught, flinging me higher.

As soon as the next grip was secure, I'd release the last; the tentacle flowed back into me. My hands and feet grew claws that sank into the wall almost effortlessly, allowing me to hurtle up the side of a twenty-story building in literal minutes.

I reached the top, panting slightly, and yanked myself over the edge, grabbing onto a low railing. I rolled to my feet on legs that burned from the unusual motion, before looking around curiously.

The tower I'd just climbed was wide at the bottom, with stone coatings on two sides, and glass on the other two, twenty stories up, and at least a dozen down beneath the ground. It'd been one of many buildings that we'd seen had both a flat roof and apparent signs of a "recent" landing on them.

By recent, I meant in the last year. But still.

On a world where nobody had supposedly set foot for decades, that was enough of an anomaly that it got me curious.

It was unlikely we'd ever know who and why, but fuck it, my job here was distraction. And seeing as I couldn't actually risk lashing out until we were certain it was working?

I had to do something.

Searching around on top of the tower didn't take long.

There were broken sections of railing, shattered comms equipment and paneling, and a dozen little details that all added up to something having landed here in the not too distant past, which made little sense.

Could be that they'd come to the same conclusion as we had, and they were drawing attention away from the transshipment plant we'd identified. But if that was the case, then either we'd been insanely unlucky on picking one that had already been hit, or the "secure zone" was anything but.

Either way, I wandered around the roof for a few minutes, listening to the distant cries and noises getting closer, as I waited for Ingrid to give me the go-ahead.

"I think you might be too high," she said a few minutes later,

I sighed, turning back to the edge, and wandered over, idly kicking a bit of loose railing free to fall to the ground far below.

"Really?" I asked. "They look pretty invested to me."

It was true as well.

The ground far below looked like a kicked anthill—where I could see the ground anyway.

There'd been a dozen of these towers in fairly close proximity, then the manufacturing site, a storage area, and finally, on the far side, a transshipment point.

Jonas had picked this one out because it was between one of the main crystal refineries and the spaceport, and all the evidence suggested the crystals got shipped here, something was done to them, and then they were shipped on again.

Whatever else was done here, it apparently needed a lot more people than I expected it to, because there were buildings above ground that could have held maybe fifty thousand easily.

Going off experience of Earth's offices and so on anyway.

I hoped a hell of a lot less. Because no matter how goddamn brave I was feeling, there was no way I was surviving fifty thousand people, especially not fifty thousand corrupted.

Ingrid had pointed out that those numbers were highly unlikely. We only did that on Earth because we needed to fit so many people into every square inch we could, and this world was easily ninety-five percent wild still.

Hell, it was probably a hundred percent wild again now. Fuck it.

Still, glancing down at the floor so far below, I could see hundreds staggering and racing through the gaps in the trees and the wildly spreading overgrowth to smash their way in the front doors.

"How many are we up to?" I asked the group at random.

"Some fourteen thousand are estimated to be in the area," James said after a few seconds. "I think you have around seven thousand in or around your building currently, but there's not much interest being shown by those on the far side of the site."

"I thought Ingrid said…" I started.

"Wait…no, okay, yeah, that might be it. There's a handful that just started to wake, looks like they were in some sort of hibernation, but it's spreading," James finished slowly, sending us a visual of a group of the corrupt, slumped against walls and laid on floors, that were starting to twitch.

My instant memory of several hundred people who had passed out on a beach after a massive all-night foam party reared its head then. There'd been an insane amount of alcohol, and yeah, probably enough nose candy to kill a Colombian cartel going around. And the aftermath?

It'd looked like this.

The locals had come out in the early morning, shouting at people to get up, to get off their beach, or to pay for the sun loungers. When a lot didn't, or couldn't respond, and people realized the sheer number of unconscious, sick, and hungover people who couldn't be roused?

Panic had set in.

Later, there'd been arrests, a lot of them, when it was found that to make the vodka "go further," one of the bar organizers had watered it down with the cheapest thing he could find. Namely, antifreeze.

The state of the people passed out all around me the next morning as I woke up gave me flashbacks, and for a second, I shuddered in remembered pain.

"I think…yes, perhaps a more 'hands-on' approach would work better?" he suggested.

"In what way?" Ingrid sounded unsure.

"Well, they seem fixated on nanites, so what if Steve started to harvest and wipe some?" he said. "That Emergency Wipe option, Steve…does it require you accepting the nanites into your body?"

"Not exactly?" I chewed on my lower lip as I thought about it.

"Go on?" James prompted.

"I need to have control over them," I said musingly. "Usually that means I'm ripping them out of their current host, but it's not like they know that, right?" I paused, ordering my thoughts, and tried again. "I mean, the nanites don't go 'Hey we're out of Bob; right, what do you want, oh glorious new master,' do they? They just get sucked into me and they do as they're told."

"So do you think that you could take control of them without sucking them into yourself?" Ingrid asked. "To be clear, Steve, I don't like this. We know the corrupted should be able to be cleaned and wiped by you easily enough, but I'm not sure if—"

"I think we're far enough away from everyone we can say it now," I interrupted, and as soon as I did, I felt side conversations silenced as the others in the command link started to pay more attention.

"What's this?" Zac asked, having probably been fixated on his engines or something equally weird and engineer-like until now.

"I might not have been entirely honest with you…" I started.

"Well, fuck me, boy, what's new or even slightly unusual about that?" Jonas snorted. "You've been hiding shit since we met."

"Jonas?" Ingrid said calmly.

"Yes, ma'am?"

"Quiet please."

"Yes, ma'am."

"So," I started again, taking a deep breath and walking along the edge of the roof, staring down at the bodies below as they continued to stagger and fight their way in. "I was being careful on the ship, just in case, mainly because we don't know Arturo, and we don't know what the hell he might do, and…well, there's not been the chance to discuss it before now. Except in the command link, and considering where we've been? Well, if anyone could listen in, it'd probably be them, right?" I hesitated.

"What Steve is trying to say is that we decided to wait until we were far enough away from the UC that it was unlikely that any methods of surveillance would work, and he's saying it now while half of us are on the planet so that the risk is lessened even further. That being said, the situation we're in means that either Arturo is going to see something soon that he'll report against our orders, or, he'll keep quiet, and we need to know which it will be."

"Yeah, thanks." I sighed.

"Okay, boss, we're ready for the worst. Who did you start a war with this time?" Paul quipped.

"Paul…" Ingrid said warningly.

"Shutting up now," Paul replied quickly.

"Steve, just tell them please." She sighed, and I did.

"We need a multiplier," I said flatly, staring down as the mass that had been boiling into the building seemed to slow, before a handful more, and then a group crashed through the doors again. "Out here, we're basically alone. Anything goes wrong and we're fucked, right?"

"Okay." Zac sighed. "What did you do, you mad bastard?"

"You remember my Tsunami ability?" I asked the group at large. "I altered it, if you remember? I've got two versions now. The original lets me essentially take over computer systems, each connection in the system that's taken being recoded to work for me and only me, rewriting the system and absorbing any additional capability to help in attacking the next section.

"It rolls out like a wave, literally a tsunami that's overpowering and unstoppable as long as it starts to build momentum. That's the original version. Every section it takes is locked down and becomes hardcoded to my neural net. That's complicated as hell, but it's essentially a tech-based system, right?"

"We remember." Ingrid sounded distracted.

"Well, the second version is a little different. It's Tsunami Hijack, though I need a better damn name for it. It's what I deployed against the Xi-Ma on the ship, injecting it into the fucker when we first fought them, and it tried to fire that scream-beam thing."

"Where you made it close its mouth when it was firing?" Paul asked. "Then the whole head just went boom?"

"Yeah, exactly. I hijacked its nanites, treating them like they were part of the system, like if I hacked a laptop or something. As soon as I had local control over the muscles, it was easy."

"And you've done something like that again?" Jonas asked me.

"Yeah…" I drew the word out, trying to decide how to explain it. "So, you know the custodians had that sterilization capability? The one that they used in the Great Refuge?"

"When my mother was killed by that abomination," Ingrid added in a dull tone.

"Yeah, that." I nodded to myself as the frantic influx of the masses I could see started to peter into the bottom of the building. "Okay, are we getting movement over by you yet?" I asked Jonas and the others, moving back from the edge of the roof and sliding my vorpal blade out.

"Yeah, we're starting to see them getting up," he said. "They're a bit aimless, wandering here and there, like they know something's going on, but they're not sure where yet."

"Coolio. I'll try to get their attention a bit more." I disengaged the blocks on my armor and released the Devourer coating. As I did that, I plunged the blade into the rooftop below me, cutting slowly and steadily along.

I carved a three-meter line, then changed direction, working to cut out a rough square as I kept talking.

"So, I figured that if the nanites get out of control, we can always deploy a few of those things and cleanse the moon, or hell, make a giant projector and slap it on the bottom of the ship, then fly back and forth doing low passes over it, right?"

"Uh, yeah, I suppose," Zac agreed. "The beams themselves are more like sterilization UV lamps and vibrational intensifiers combined, so you'd have to either make them insanely powerful to do them from a ship or—"

"That we can do it is enough, thank you, Zac." Ingrid sighed. "Steve, we don't have long, so explain quicker please."

"Right." I nodded, starting the third cut. "So I thought that as we're the only ones who know we can do that, we're also the only ones who have access to a way of cleansing these lost worlds, beyond you know, with fire and fucking cannons.

"So, *if*, and I know it's an if, but if we can cleanse the worlds, the only thing that'd be lost is the nanites, right? Well, we desperately need those nanites. Aaronis said that the soldier armor was adjusted to be able to survive the corrupt, and when I looked at it, it's because it's fully sealed.

"They're not immune—the nanites just can't get in to infect them. But the end result is the same, right? The UC thinks that the corrupt are either an annoyance, because the soldiers can destroy them, or they're a lethal threat, because anyone who's not in their power armor gets wiped out. Either way, though, they're not thinking of them as a *resource*."

"How the hell are they a resource?" Courtney sounded confused. "You've got a lot of them in motion, by the way. Pretty much all of your local area and the immediate to mid-range is on the move. Those around the target site are moving now as well, although slower."

"They're people, or they were," I said quickly, as I started to make the final cut. The roof started to sag and creak as the last supports took all the weight. "So don't get me wrong, I know it's not gonna be a popular point of view, but shit, they died a long, long time ago, and there's no way we can bring them back. What we can do, though, is give them some peace.

"What I did on the moon was test a connection, injecting the Tsunami Hijack into the one I had, and it took!" I straightened, then stepped back as the last section ahead of my blade cracked before I could reach it.

I triggered my gravity manipulation and lifted into the air, hovering as I formed a second gravity bubble ahead and under the roof, then inverted it sharply.

The roof bulged upward for a second as I pushed up, then tore loose and fell inward as I yanked it down. A solid, if rough square, three meters on a side, carved out of the roof, vanished inward with a crash and a blast of dust as I released the bubble.

I floated over the hole, staring down and seeing the main floor far below absolutely swarming with hundreds of corrupted, as thousands more swarmed up the stairs that ran from floor to floor.

The roof slid past as I lowered myself into the building. My armor was fully deployed, cloak floating behind me, tentacles flowing out and flicking, ready to attack. I drifted across the nearest stairwell, ready to head down.

The inside of the building was laid out to maximize the light, with a collection of larger offices and rooms on each floor, set into the three corners. The center was open all the way down to the ground floor, and stairs ran around the inside in great loops, leading to balconies on each floor.

All in all, it was a wonderful open-air design that made it clear that when you could make structures cheaply, and without concern for trying to squeeze people in every square inch, you could do wonderful things.

The best bit, though?

Because the building wasn't designed to be filled by tens of thousands of people, the access routes weren't that wide.

There must have been elevators or whatever, I was sure, but with the long-abandoned nature of the building—and hell, the world—it meant that the only way the corrupt had to get to me was up the stairs that ran around and around the inside.

I landed at the top of the stairs and started to walk down, the first few corrupt already rounding the stairs a few flights down from me as I did.

"When the Hijack took, literally just overwriting the nanites it came into contact with, I realized the potential," I went on. "The majority are broken, and I mean utterly fucked levels of broken. They can't be recovered. But what could be recovered is a small percentage. And if we play our cards right? We could pull off a surprise here."

"What the hell did you do?" Zac asked me again.

I retracted my vorpal blade and focused, forming a hammer of weaponized nanites that I gripped in my right hand and swung experimentally.

"I wiped them, then told the nanites to contract into a tiny ball—that was why the body collapsed...everything fell in on itself." I shrugged. "When the armor and all the shit fell, everyone dismissed it, thinking that it'd just collapsed and that I'd fucked up. But what they didn't realize was that I'd ordered the nanites to compress into as small a form as possible.

"The corrupt were going mental trying to reach us, so I don't think anyone noticed that they also started going after the remains on the floor. I waited until we were as far away as I could before I ordered the nanites to start phase two, and before I lost connection, I felt them start. They're infecting the nanites around them now, using the Tsunami Hijack ability to replicate, wiping one after another of the corrupt, and they're burrowing into the surface."

"Boss, that sounds insane, and like, really dangerous," Zac said flatly. "If that gets out of control, it'd be…"

"It'd be exactly what was already there," I finished for him. "The nanites, as they are, are out of control. They're a plague of broken replications, trying to fix themselves by infecting everything around them. If this roll of the dice goes wrong, the moon is already fucked. The end result doesn't get any worse, and because I'm not a complete fucking idiot, I also encoded a fast and dirty kill switch in case we needed it."

"Okay, so the risk sounds reasonable," Jonas said after a few seconds of silence as the first of the corrupt made their way up the last few dozen steps toward me. "So now we know the risk. What's the reward?"

"How does potentially billions of nanites all making a new ship for us sound?" I asked, and I grinned as the chat went utterly silent.

"A ship?" Zac asked carefully.

"It's not gonna be pretty, okay, and it's sure as shit going to be basic, but I set the design really quickly, building it around the concept of my gravity cannon, and an absolute fuckload of armor."

"How much armor?"

"It was really quick, but I think I set it for thirty meters?"

"THIRTY METERS OF SOLID ARMOR?" Zac whimpered. "Boss, do you know how big those engines will need to be?"

"Meh, that sounds like a 'you' problem." I grinned. "I set the basics, but you might need to adjust the design a little. At some point."

His response was a strange mixture of cries that I wrote off as him being too happy to articulate.

The first figure cleared the last few steps, leaping at me. The desiccated face of a humanoid with long white hair, narrow cheeks, and three eyes gaped at me, hunger filling every inch of its body, before I swung my hammer, hitting it in the side and flipping it out over the edge of the balcony.

The low railing that ran up the stairs had probably been designed for safety and comfort, given that it was just the right height for most people to lean on and stare out over the atrium far below.

From here, you'd be treated to beautiful sunrises, or sunsets, and the collapsed, long-dead trees and plants that had taken up sections of each floor below suggested that the interior of the building had once been a verdant paradise to match the outside.

Now the air was full of the crash of bodies, the shattering of glass, and, as this first body flipped out over the railing, bones shattered by my blow. A tentacle stabbed out, injecting a tiny number of nanites into it.

Then it pulled back, and the corpse vanished over the side, falling, as my Hijack started to run.

More were coming, and I couldn't help but grin. Running from them earlier had been necessary: the more that saw me, the more that were attracted and that were exposed to my nanites—the faster we'd get them all away from the target area.

Now, though, now that they'd started to move, it was time to really go nuts.

The next in line I took down with a hammer to the side of the head, catapulting it into the wall on the left as I continued to walk. It fell, bouncing hard, and immediately started to rise again, despite the horrific damage, until a second tentacle punched down, stabbing into the space between its shoulder blades and releasing another nanite packet into the body.

It collapsed, as the hunger of the corrupted nanites for their "clean" brethren forced the nanites in the body to switch from powering the body to chase me, to instead fold around the small number of nanites that were now inside its own body.

Dozens raced toward me, hundreds behind them. I sighed, rolling my shoulders as I got ready.

I had half a million nanites in me now that were ready for use, and as I deployed a mere fifty or so active nanites with each stab, I realized that I might actually run out before the job was done.

Still, that was a problem for later. Right now? I got to do what I did best: mindless violence.

Chapter Thirty

"For the last time." Ingrid sighed. "We're not UC. We're independent traders. We need repairs and we're willing to pay for them. Now, do you have a docking bay clear or do you want to explain to the people we could be paying why so many credits just flew off to another system?"

"I don't recognize your markings or ID," the asshole on the screen whined after a few seconds. His voice came across like any career bureaucrat who had a tiny taste of power.

"And that's because we've never been here before," Ingrid said slowly. Her voice made it clear that she was near the end of her patience. "I've told you twice, we've not been to this system before. We were recommended to come here by a friend…"

"Who?"

"Who suggested that your space station might be—what?" She broke off.

"Who was your friend?"

"What the hell does that matter?" she asked incredulously. "Are you trying to tell me you know everyone on every ship that passes through here personally?"

"Perhaps."

"Oh, for…okay, fine." She shrugged. "You just lost your chance. Pilot, adjust course. Head for the opposite end of the space station."

"Now let's not be hast—" The figure spoke up quickly, before Ingrid cut him off.

The screen flickered, and the superimposed face with its mass of tentacles instead of a mouth vanished, as a second figure appeared in his place.

This one was slumped half back in a chair, a desk before them that could just be made out, covered in clutter, and a packed room behind them showing dozens of sapiens moving around.

"Yeah?" the figure asked, unconcernedly, still looking to the right and off camera, as they flicked a hand over a projected keyboard in the air. "Whaddya want?" They grunted, turning to look at the display for the first time and frowning as they presumably saw us.

"We're independent traders," Ingrid said. "We need repairs and can pay in trade goods or credits, but your dockmaster is wasting our time with questions. Is your shipyard open and can you fit us into dock?"

"Dockmaster? I'm the owner and dockmaster here…" The figure frowned, then burst out laughing. "Wait, you met Cheeto?"

"He didn't introduce himself," she said. "He reached out, claiming to be the dockmaster of the Kranthi's Place shipyard."

"Yeah, he's a lying sack of shit." The figure snorted. "This is the Den. Ain't been Kranthi's Place for oh, few hundred cycles now. We're independent—all the shipyards are. Each and every dock has their own dockmaster now, no chief engineer to run it all no more. We keep the local area around our yards intact, and fuck everyone else. That Cheeto you was talkin' to? Purple guy, looks like he's got scalbic?"

"Scalbic?" Ingrid asked.

"Yeah, you know, like he's been outta the water too long, all his fur is dried up…?"

"He was purple," she said. "Tentacles?" She made a gesture over her mouth like her fingers were tentacles, and the figure snorted.

"Yeah, that's him. He's an Okansic, personally allergic to the waters, but his kind are aquatic—sucks to be him. It's why he's out here. Anyway, he's not attached to the shipyards…makes his credits as a middleman, arranges deals and sells information."

She sighed. "Fine. Well, we need repairs. Can you accommodate us?"

"Wait one." He grunted, squinting at a screen off to one side, before blowing a short tune through a fan of flesh on the top of his head, presumably in surprise. "Warship, eh? You steal it?"

"None of your business," Ingrid said flatly. "We own it."

"And nobody's gonna come lookin', eh?" He sneered. "I can work with that."

"Can you fix it?" Ingrid asked bluntly.

"We can." He nodded. "Dock eleven, section six. Sending authorization now."

"What's this going to cost u—" Ingrid started to ask as the connection was cut from the other side. "Damn."

"You got us landing permission." I shrugged. "Don't worry about it."

"Yeah, but for all we know, he's going to try to charge us a million credits for landing." She shook her head. "I don't like it."

"Neither do I," I said. "There's gonna be an angle, but we're here to trade, and we've got to start somewhere."

"I know. I just don't like not knowing what to expect."

I nodded. "Well, we're here now, so I guess…" I paused, then shrugged. "We'd planned on docking, then making contacts and moving the ship into a repair dock to be worked on. The upgrades that they'll have in the shipyards aren't going to be the cutting edge, so what do we start with?"

"I'll take Jonas and James with me to try to make some contacts with the corporations, see what we can find, and you're going to take Scylla and…" She shook her head. "Change of plan, I think. We made too many assumptions as to the situation here from what Leshan told us. If the entire shipyard is run by independents now, we're probably better off starting with a meeting with whoever owns the dock, then we can make a plan."

"Should I come, or stay in place, ready to take off?" James asked, and that was the more sensible option, we all had to admit.

James rolled the ship to port, firing the engines and bringing us around to the approach vector we'd been given. A set of guiding lights appeared on the image, making it easier for him to line up on the dock we needed.

He still ended up having to fire the engines in a staccato blast to slow and realign us, before rolling the ship again as the figure reached out and asked sarcastically whether we were planning on landing upside down or not.

Apparently, the station had an "up" and the massive lines that were painted along the outside of the station were there for a reason.

A section of the station opened slowly as we closed with it. Doors slid back to either side, allowing what I thought of as our huge ship to glide serenely into the revealed dock with space to spare.

It was narrow, barely thirty meters beyond the space we'd take up on either side, and as we closed on the far wall, sections of gantry began to swing out.

Ahead of us, there were windows into the station, presumably, and I thought I recognized one of them, at least, as the one in the background of the image we'd gotten when we called them. The others?

Presumably the station's inhabitants liked being able to look in and see the ships coming and going, a lot like they did at an airport, because I could see throngs of people passing several of them as we neared.

It would have scared the shit out of me personally, seeing a huge ship coming toward me like that, but fuck it.

Yellow and black lights started to flash as James slowed the ship even further. Buffers and pillars rose from the walls, the ceiling and floor lifting up and in all around us.

Barely a minute later, as the reverberation of docking clamps shook through the ship, James announced we were officially docked at our first independent shipyard.

It was a weird mix of wonder and disbelief, as well as serious concern, as I climbed to my feet. We were aboard an alien damn starbase, or shipyard, or whatever the right term was.

I couldn't help exchanging a smile with Ingrid as I grabbed the helmet from its ring on the wall next to me, carrying it under one arm as I led the way from the bridge.

I didn't have many manners, I knew, and I should have let her go first, but considering where we were, it felt wrong.

"Okay, people, game faces on," I said into the comm link. "James, which air lock?"

"They're connecting to the third aft on the port side," he replied, before going on, and I could hear the damn smile on his face this time. "Perhaps I should provide directions?"

"Please." I sighed, pulling the rifle around and checking it, grunting as I made sure the power cell was full.

We'd found what we were hoping for in the transshipment point, and one of our cargo holds was a third full of crystals now. That was enough to make it worth our while, but Jonas had managed to find three emergency space suits, and a small, empty laser, even if we'd not found any usable ships.

We'd taken a day to load everything aboard our ship, including almost sixteen million recovered and usable nanites I'd gotten from the corrupt I'd killed in the end. And in that time, Zac had earned his damn place in the crew three times over.

Not only did he strip and feed the details for each of the parts into the makers, but the fucker *improved* on them.

He produced four new makers: one for the suits, one for helmets, one for power cells, and one for the new rifles.

Using the power core technology we already had access to, he adjusted the design, tripling the level of power that the cells could hold.

The space suits that he'd fed into the makers were basic emergency ones, but the ones that he got out? They were armored, they were powered, and they were cool as fuck.

Yes, they were basic—of course they were basic, especially compared to our usual armor—but that was fine, because we couldn't wear our usual armor anywhere and expect to not be spotted in a heartbeat.

Originally, we'd planned to wear the armor that we'd gotten from Leshan, but as soon as Zac had started to work on it, ready to replicate it for us, he'd found issues, and there were a lot of them.

Those suits wouldn't enable us to wear our armor underneath, for a start. They apparently needed to be plugged into the wearer, literally, and in doing so, they boosted them.

The UC soldier battle armor was both an armor and life-sustaining cocoon, but the one thing it wasn't was a flexible design.

The suits that he'd created for us now were as good as he could make them in short order. And they were strong enough to survive a few hits from either small arms fire or lasers, he'd assured us.

It was apparently a bad thing to take any kind of heavy weaponry into space, and even more so to actually fire it—something about "hull ruptures" and so on made that clear.

That meant that most of the weapons we were likely to see on the station were small arms, logically.

That didn't make me feel any better about it, though.

We'd all agreed that we'd do our best to hide who and what we were, and to that end, we were now in battered-looking space suits, with Ingrid, Paul, Jonas, Scylla, and me carrying laser rifles, and all of us with holsters on our hips that held copies of the laser handgun that Jonas had found.

I'd wanted something more powerful, personally, but we'd all agreed that showing them something familiar was important.

"Remember, we're traders," Ingrid said firmly to us all through the link as we stomped down the corridor. "Our world was only recently found, and we've just started trading. That's why our ship is such a mess."

"No offense, but I think the boss should be the only one of us to talk to them…for the first meeting, at least," Jonas added. "The leader of the party should always be clear to anyone who's dealing with us."

"Yeah, that makes sense…" I agreed.

"By which I mean Ingrid does the talking," he finished, and I bit down on my response, almost hurting myself I rolled my eyes that hard.

"Thank you, Jonas," Ingrid said, and I could imagine the smile on her face as she walked behind me. "I appreciate the vote of confidence."

"You are more likely to achieve our goals," Scylla said evenly, and I glared at her, being totally ignored.

"You're right," I admitted after a few seconds of silent grumbling. "Ingrid is a lot better at this kind of thing."

"I'm not 'better'…" She shook her head. "I just have more patience."

"So, any?" I suggested, and she snorted a laugh.

The last fifty meters as we travelled along the main spine of the ship were in silence. Paul, Courtney, and Oxus joined us, moving up to their place in the choke points leading up to the air lock.

The design of the ship was literally exclusively as a warship, one that accepted that there was a chance it'd be boarded, and that if there was a chance of that happening, well, there had to be practical solutions to it.

With that in mind, there were regular choke points, sections where turrets and more could be mounted, with reinforced armoring that served to provide places to hide, while still being able to tear any boarders a new arsehole.

Paul and Courtney took up station on either side of the corridor behind those choke points, with Oxus stepping up, ready to hold the air lock itself if need be.

As the indicators around the door changed from a sullen red to a cheerful green, Ingrid took a deep breath and reached out, laying one hand on the pad, and ordered it to open.

She stepped back, as I stepped into the air lock, Paul by my side, and the air lock sealed behind us, then cycled.

"Atmosphere is compatible, but be aware, we've got a figure approaching," James told us all.

I spared a quick nod, as the outer door hissed and clanked, opening slowly.

"Weapons are to be left at the…what the hell?" A bored-looking figure yelped, going straight from "another day, how boring" to outright terror as I stepped through the air lock, fully armored and with my rifle held pointed down. "Attack!" he screamed. "We're under attack!"

"What the?" I blinked in shock, as the dock around us suddenly came to life with targeting lasers. Bulges on the wall slid back, revealing concealed turrets. "It's a trap!" I snarled, yanking my rifle up and ready to fire as Ingrid yelled into the link.

"STOP! HOLD YOUR FIRE!"

Paul and I froze. My heart was hammering. At least a dozen turrets were locked onto us, and a pair of flashing lights were going wild on one wall, as we all tried to make sense of what the hell was going on.

"By Grabar's spotty arsehole, what are you doing!" came a new voice, and one I vaguely recognized as the figure that Ingrid had spoken to before. He also sounded apoplectic with rage. "You're either the dumbest fucking pirates in all the systems, or—"

"We're not pirates!" Ingrid shouted. The air lock behind me finally cycled open as she stepped out. "Shit, we're supposed to be… Oh for God's sake! Hold on! It's all just a big misunderstanding!"

"They've got turrets locked onto us," I growled.

"You've got a weapon pointed at them," she replied, reaching over with both hands and putting them on both mine and Paul's rifles, and gently, but firmly, pushing down.

We allowed it, lowering our weapons as she kept the pressure up, and fortunately the turrets didn't open fire.

"Explain!" the voice boomed out.

"These are my guards," Ingrid called out. "They came out before me in case you attacked us, that's all."

"They're armed," he spat.

"Of course—" I started to answer.

"Steve, please," Ingrid snapped at me. "Either let me do this, or do it yourself."

"Sorry," I muttered.

"They're my guards. Of course they're armed," Ingrid called out. "You've got turrets pointed at us, haven't you?"

"Only because you're armed and threatening us," the voice came back.

"We weren't threatening anyone," Ingrid said firmly. "Your…engineer?" She gestured to a nearby pile of ship parts that the figure was crouching behind. "They assumed just because my guards stepped out first, we were attacking. Surely you don't expect me to just wander around without protection?"

"You're allowed one guard, in armor, and a single low-powered weapon." The voice sounded annoyed and angry still, but clearly trying to deal with it. "Deshkine, you idiot, get out from behind there!"

As he spoke, the alarm cut off, the lights stopped flashing, and the turrets slid back into the walls—or at least, most of them did.

One got halfway and jammed with a crunch that echoed around the dock.

"Oh no!" came a squeal of horror, and the figure that had appeared, then hid as soon as he saw the rifles, burst out of hiding again, almost getting himself shot by both Paul and me.

Instead of attacking, though, he scurried across the gantry that connected to our ship, then leapt.

He'd looked humanoid, more or less—two legs, four arms, a head atop the body that was more rodent or toad than human, but I wasn't judging.

Beyond that, he'd have passed as human at a distance, if he'd kept the lower arms folded maybe. The upper and lower came out from a jointed shoulder socket a little farther down than our shoulders, but it was the legs that made me stare.

They unfolded as he jumped, hurtling him across the distance to land next to the turret, reaching for it, just as the cover slid into the clearly delicate systems.

The twin spikes that rose from the center, presumably barrels or something similar, buckled and crunched. Sparks flew before the covering continued its progress, sliding shut with a tortured shriek.

That might have been the engineer, though, as he clutched at his head and started shouting and hitting the turret cover with one fist.

"Deshkine!" the original voice bellowed out again. "What the hell was that?"

"The sonic turret!" the second figure wailed. "It jammed and you kept closing it!"

"You broke that?!" The anger was clearly back. "That cost me…"

"Maybe we should go?" I suggested to Ingrid. "They just broke their own turret. This isn't filling me with confidence…"

"We need the repairs," she said. "If it's not these, will the next ones be any better?"

"Probably," I grunted, staring at the engineer on the wall, as he hung there. Apparently, the patches on his coveralls somehow secured him in place. He shrieked and tried to pry the turret cover back with some tool he was ramming into the edge.

"Ignore him." I twisted as the first voice rang out again. A panel in the wall slid back to show stairs that ran upward toward presumably the offices above. "My clutchmate's son. He's not quite bright."

"Ah, of course, we have our own like that." Ingrid nodded in greeting. "I'm Ingrid."

"I'm…"

The sound that rang out made me think of the noise that I'd made on more than one occasion after too many drinks, usually while singing the song of my people, with my head in the toilet.

"Ah, I doubt I can pronounce that," Ingrid said. "Is there a name that I can use instead?"

"Bob."

"Bob?"

"Bob," he confirmed. "Your kind like short names, yes?"

"Yes… some of us have difficulty with more complicated ones." She shook her head and stood a little straighter, leaving Paul and I both privately convinced that she was talking about the other. "So, we need to discuss repairs."

"Lots of work," Bob declared, staring up at our ship behind us and shaking his head almost sadly. "It could take long cycles…many cycles. And the size of the job? I might have to hire extra help…"

"Then perhaps the job is beyond you," Ingrid said smoothly.

"No!" He shook his head like a dog; the head rotated on the neck, his nose staying almost stationary as the flap on the top of his head opened again, and a low whistle came free. "No, I can do it, just wanted you to know how big it was…after all…"

The next ten minutes was a mess.

He explained the parts that we could see were damaged, then he added how certain parts couldn't be replaced like for like. The engines, for example, were just one point; one of the support struts was damaged—it was where those dicks back at the Forgeship had tried to steal it—and that meant that there was likely underlying instabilities in the drives.

When Ingrid asked why that was, he went on about the pressure and that was why the strut had buckled. Not been cut, buckled.

He named a dozen parts that had to be made up, then a handful that we could see were damaged again, drawing our attention in and getting us to agree that they were genuine.

Then he went back to making shit up.

"He's a natural car mechanic," Zac sent to the group. *"Hold on, let me come out and deal with this."*

We let him run on for a bit, as Zac joined us. I reached out and held up a small holo-projector, triggering it where Zac could show the ship on it to him.

"Great to see the traditions are being upheld even out here," Zac said. "But you're talking bullshit. This is the damage." He went over a few sections. "What we need is this replacing, this repairing, then we need to look at upgrades. Also…" He tapped sections of the ship in the hologram as he spoke, and in a handful of seconds, the pair were arguing over the name of parts, the compatibility of them with our ship, and whether the locals were even a fraction as good at their job as Zac was.

Ten more minutes down the line, and Ingrid and I, with Jonas and Scylla, were walking through the air lock between the dock and the rest of the space station.

We'd left the rifles behind, at Bob's insistence, but had handguns on our hips. Scylla had her whip on one hip, the proton lance in her hands—which Bob had apparently not recognized as a weapon—and enough knives to make a chef jealous.

Jonas had his sword on his back and his hand cannon on his hip, a newly upgraded one that Zac had apparently made for him, and I was feeling decidedly naked with my piddly little laser and nothing beyond that.

"Look on the bright side, boss," he whispered unsubtly to me as we stepped into the throng of people, hesitating as the mass of aliens split to go around us, complaining about us stopping there. "Just means you get first choice of the weapons when someone attacks us and we get to loot their bodies."

"Jonas," Ingrid scolded. "We're not looking for a fight, okay? We're exploring the station, getting an idea of what's where and then we can make a plan."

"That your ship?"

The voice came from the right, and I turned along with the others. A large figure leaned against the porthole, looking from us to the dock that was displayed beyond.

"It is," Ingrid said politely.

"How much?"

"Excuse me?"

"How much?" he repeated.

"How much for what?" she asked.

"Don't play with me. How much for the ship?"

"It's not for sale."

"Everything's for sale." The figure grunted, pushing off the wall and strolling toward us. He was almost as big as Jonas and me, but where we were outside of our "real" armor, he was wearing his, and had to outweigh us both by at least double.

He was closer in size and build to Oxus, massive hooves clear by the painted design on his space suit. Armoring that had taken repeated battering covered his chest, legs, and arms, with heavy pauldrons that were etched with impacts half shielding his head.

The four eyes were a surprise, as were the horns and the pointed and clearly sharp teeth, but it was the name that got me the most.

"Devilkin," Ingrid said in the group, knowing damn well that I was still having problems with my information system. *"It says they're a naturally evolved species from the Rings of Hellion, and that they're highly dangerous and aggressive."*

"It's not for sale," Ingrid replied. "Though we're looking for somewhere to sell our cargo. Any recommendations?"

"What is it?"

"Crystals."

"Really?" He cocked his head to one side. "What grade?"

"I don't know," she admitted in the link.

"High grade," I said, watching him.

"How many?"

"Depends how many you're looking for and how much," I replied.

"I'll take them all, and the ship."

"You're not listening," Jonas said softly. "The lady already said the ship's not for sale."

"And I told you, everything's for sale." The devilkin grinned at us. "Last chance to sell it."

"Stop," Ingrid said firmly, reaching out and putting her hands on our shoulders, making us step aside; I realized both Jonas and I had stepped in front of her, unconsciously shielding her body with our own. "Just stop, all of you. This is our first visit to the station, so who are you?"

"Malthus." The devilkin nodded, the passage of people around us notably thinning as things grew more tense.

"Okay, let's move to the side." Ingrid sighed, glancing around, and nodded to what looked to be a bar, on the other side of the corridor and a few sections farther down. "Malthus, we're not looking for a fight, okay? Can we buy you a drink and talk this out?"

"In there?" He scoffed.

"You pick." Ingrid shrugged. "Like I said, we're new here."

"One level up, two rows back, the Crimson Hole," he said after a few seconds, gesturing to the opposite end of the corridor from us. "There's a link up there."

"Are you coming?" Ingrid cocked her head as he shook his head.

"I've got something to do first." He grinned. "I'll meet you there in, oh, a half turn?"

"Sure." She smiled. "Come on, we'll meet him there." She gestured for us to leave, and I looked from her to him and back again.

"Are you fucking kidding me?" I asked her on singular engagement mode.

"Trust me," she said, and cursing internally, I followed her.

Chapter Thirty-One

"He can't think we're that stupid, right?" I asked her for the third time.

"He does." Jonas groaned. "And we fuckin' are, boss. We're here, a solid ten-minute walk from the damn dock, while he can march his people straight in and—"

"You came."

The voice came from behind us, and I twisted in my seat, finding the devilkin Malthus standing behind us, a drink that was smoking, literally, in one hand.

"You recommended this bar for a reason." Ingrid smiled. "From what I've seen of your race, they get a lot of abuse from some of the others, so I guessed this would be one of your bars."

It was as well. When we'd come into the bar, it'd gone silent. All it was missing was a high-pitched voice declaring that it was a "local bar for local people" or a thrown knife to make me feel even less welcome.

The entire place was full of devilkin, easily a hundred of them, and only the four of us who weren't their race.

"You know that, and yet you still met me?" He grunted.

"I decided it was worth the risk," she admitted.

"But you didn't?" Malthus asked Jonas.

"I don't know you," he drawled. "Might be that you're a good guy, or maybe you're a dick. Just waitin' to find out, really."

"But still you come here," Malthus said again, shaking his head. "Explain this to me."

"Join us," Ingrid invited him, before smiling and gesturing to the table, where a menu was displayed. "I'm not sure what our species can drink here, though."

"The fifth from the top is probably it," he said. "Hydrogen and oxygen, in two to one."

"H—" Ingrid shook her head in disbelief as she understood. "Water."

"Every race calls it something different." He shrugged. "To my kind, it's an intoxicant, so expect it to be expensive."

"How much?"

"There." He indicated a symbol. "Can't you read?"

Arise :Explorer

"Our system doesn't have your numerals in it." She smiled again. "Could you draw them for me?"

"Zero…" He drawled, dragging a claw tip across the metal of the tabletop, and working through the numbers to nine, before settling back.

"Thank you." Ingrid smiled at him again, and he snorted. "What's wrong?" she asked, linking to the menu and ordering four glasses of water for us.

"Your teeth."

"What about them?"

"First, you're not wherever you call home—showing your teeth like that is generally a challenge," he pointed out, before shrugging. "Or it would be, if they were sharper and bigger."

"Where we come from, it's an offer of friendship and to be polite."

"Sounds like a dumb place."

"It has its moments."

"So, why'd you come?" Malthus sipped his drink.

The smoke that rolled off it made me want to cough.

"I saw the way that everyone walked around you, expecting that you were trouble," she admitted.

"I am."

"Well, we need to sell our cargo, and we don't know this station. Our dockmaster already tried to rip us off, so I wasn't going to ask him for advice. You're the next person we've met."

"And you came here, because you wanted advice on what to do here?" He stared from one of us to another. "Are you stupid?"

"No, we're new." She smiled. "And we like to make friends."

"Stupid," he repeated, before glancing to the side as a new figure walked up. For the first time, he seemed to relax.

The new arrival was a child, or so I guessed. If she were human, I'd have said maybe three or four years old, at that cute and not yet annoying stage.

She was clearly devilkin, with red skin, black eyes flashed with gold, and tiny nubs of horns growing in at the temples.

She was also wearing a dress and holding a little tray, the tip of her tongue held between her teeth as she concentrated, carrying it over to us.

The tray wobbled as she reached us. A little flower sat in the middle of the tray gleaming in gold and onyx, as she came to a halt.

"Buy a flower?" She looked around nervously.

"A flower?" I asked, surprised, and Ingrid nodded, reaching out and laying a hand on my thigh in warning.

As soon as I'd spoken, the little girl had backed up, almost dropping the flower.

"Please, sir…" She started again, and Malthus spoke at the same time.

"It's okay, Olivia. You're safe here."

"Okay…wanna buy a flower?" she said again, looking around at us all.

"How much is it?" Ingrid asked gently, and the little girl turned to face her, bowing her head and speaking quickly.

"Ten credits!"

"You little monster." Malthus snorted. "That's not worth a quarter credit and you know it. Try again."

"Please… I need to help my mama, and it's all I have…" Olivia started, before falling silent as Ingrid nodded.

"Ten credits is fine," she agreed. "But how do I pay you?"

"Here!" The little girl offered a small block up.

I connected to it when Ingrid glanced at me beseechingly. It was a lot like a payment point on a till back home. Near-field communication from a debit card would have done it, and linking it to the credit account we had—carefully, while making sure of the amount first—was simple.

As soon as the credits had cleared, the little girl was grinning, the expression strange. The flower was handed over to Ingrid, then she was off, skipping away. In seconds, she'd reached another table, telling the figures there what she'd just done presumably, as they all burst out laughing.

"You know that was a table decoration, right?" Malthus snorted, looking at Ingrid. "You're either stupid, or rich *and* stupid."

"I try to be kind where I can," Ingrid corrected. "That's all, and she's a child."

"She is," Malthus rumbled, shifting in his seat. "She's one of many here. Giving her that much money was a waste, but it's yours to burn."

As he spoke, Olivia had reached the bar, where a second, older devilkin had been standing, talking to another. She took another tray, this time with drinks balanced atop it and, after ruffling the little girl's hair and tweaking her nose, she sauntered over to our table.

This woman was the opposite of Malthus in every way. Where he was massively built, heavy muscles, and overt threat, she was slender, almost painfully so, despite the clear health in her eyes.

The eyes were arresting as well. His were black orbs, glossy but with only a hint of red in the center, while hers were violet, glowing as she glanced from one of us to another.

"You ordered the aqua?" She smiled at Ingrid and Scylla before glancing at both Jonas and me, and finally Malthus, who seemed to not want to make eye contact with her for some reason. "Malthus, you damn fool. What have you gotten involved in now?" She sighed, setting the drinks down and folding her arms, staring at him.

Even seated, he came up to her shoulder, and I jerked as a spade-tipped tail flicked into view from behind her back, jabbing him in the shoulder.

"I asked you a question, you old goaten botherer," she snapped, before looking to Ingrid. "Please, tell me he's not hired you yet."

"Hired us?" Ingrid shook her head. "No…"

"Thank the fiery deeps." The newcomer sighed. "Look, I'm sorry he's wasted your time. We can't afford to charter you, not for whatever harebrained scheme he's been selling you. I'm sorry, but seriously, you think I'd be working here if we had that kind of credits?"

"I think…" Ingrid said slowly, "that there's been some confusion here. I asked Malthus to recommend a good bar, and to have a drink with us. We need information, and we approached him, not the other way around."

"Really?" The woman cocked her head to one side, before shaking her head and reaching behind her, tugging a strap and releasing the knot on the apron she'd been wearing. "Jacqui! I'm taking my break!" she bellowed over her shoulder, before tugging the apron off at a grunt from the direction of the bar.

Then she slapped his shoulder, and gestured to sit on Malthus's seat as he, grumbling, got up and snagged another from the table nearest, dragging it over and sitting back down.

We shuffled around a little, the chairs creaking as we made room at the table, and I couldn't help but admire the buxom beauty who had joined us.

Where Malthus fit the stereotypical "devil" vibe from our myths—minus the wings, as he didn't have any of them—the newcomer was halfway between him and succubus in many ways.

Slim, buxom, and with a wide and, again, weird-looking smile as she bared her teeth at Ingrid, the image was only partly ruined by the four eyes, smaller than a human's. "This is what you were doing. It is an indication of good faith, yes?" She tossed her long black braid over one shoulder and pushed her chest out a little more, grinning at the glare Malthus was giving Jonas, who'd apparently been caught looking.

"I'm Ingrid." Ingrid introduced herself, before going around the table and introducing us all. "And you are?" she asked at the end.

"Benat." She smiled again, a clearly practiced gesture, as much as it was frankly terrifying, considering she had teeth like a great white. "My smile is good, yes?"

"It is," Ingrid assured her, suppressing a wince. "You've been practicing?"

"The bars on the lower ring pay more," she admitted, dropping the smile. "I was told to make sure I could pass as 'friendly and willing' before I try for a shift."

"What!" Malthus said, shocked. "The lower ring is—"

"We need the money," she replied. Her tail reached out and curled around his right forearm. "Now hush, mate. I want to know what foolishness this is."

"Mate?" I guessed that it wasn't intended the way that I called Zac or Jay "mate."

"He is my life mate." She nodded. "Or he will be, if he ever gains the courage to speak to my mother," she finished with a roll of the eyes.

"Benat…" Malthus groaned, rubbing the bridge of his nose as he struggled to keep calm. "They don't need to know that, or anything about us."

"Nonsense. You brought them here, so you've got a plan for them, or you'd have left them wherever they were," she said.

For a second, as Malthus looked up and we caught each other's eye, we shared *it*.

That unspoken knowledge, that link that men make occasionally, most commonly experienced when our partners are shoe shopping. It's when we glance around and see another man enduring the same hell on earth as we are, and we bond in silent suffering.

Whatever it was, it was so familiar that I nodded in unthinking solidarity, the pair of us freezing as we realized what we'd both just done.

"So," he said after a second, straightening up and fixing on Ingrid again. "You said you had cargo to sell?"

"We do," she said. "It sounds like you can't afford it, though."

"Maybe not all of it, but for a fee, I could put you in touch with those who could."

"And that fee would be?" Ingrid asked.

"Entirely reasonable," he replied. "Especially considering you have no idea who you should be approaching to sell them."

"You think your advice is going to make that much difference?" she asked.

"It could." He shrugged. "Of course, you could try to sell them yourself, but who will you take them to?"

"We can ask around."

"And you think people will just tell you?" He quirked one eyebrow.

"They will, eventually." I shrugged.

"You're not big enough to carry that threat off." He snorted. "Listen, you take them to the first shop you find, they'll take them off your hands, all right. They'll test them, verify the grade, then they'll buy them…for a quarter of the street value. Then they'll sell them straight on to the people I can take you to."

"And what's to stop you taking us to someone who does exactly that?" she asked.

"Self-interest."

"Go on."

"You pay me twenty percent of the value of the cargo, and I'll be damn motivated to get you the very best deal I can," he offered.

The silence that spread out from that comment was noticeable.

"Are you fucking kidding me?" Jonas asked after a few seconds. "I mean, seriously, you expect twenty percent of the value for that? It's not even twenty percent of the profit…but the *value*?"

"You're making a hundred percent profit on the deal already." He shrugged. "It's not like you paid for them."

"And what makes you think that?" Ingrid asked softly as we all slowly shifted, not liking that comment.

"You stole them." He gazed around at us. "And that's why I insisted we come here to talk about it."

"Because if we get into a fight here, your kind will automatically back you over us, regardless of the reason," Scylla whispered.

"Exactly."

"Except…" She went on, smiling widely. "They can't take your side, if you're dead."

"If you could kill me, and believe me, that's a big *if*, then you'd have to get out of here, and unexplained deaths come with high fees." He shrugged again, seemingly unconcerned.

"Or…" Benat said loudly, leaning forward to get everyone's attention. "*Or*…we could talk about a realistic deal."

"And what would that be?" Ingrid asked.

"Five percent."

"Of profit?" Ingrid asked.

"We'd have no way to verify what you claimed was the cost," Benat pointed out. "You could claim you only made a single credit on the deal, and we'd have to accept five percent of that value as our payment."

"But if you were there when we did the deal for the crystals, then you'd know what five percent of the value was." Ingrid nodded. "Okay, and why would that be fair? After all, we own the crystals, and you've not said why you think they'd not been paid for."

"Because…you're *selling* them?" Benat replied, looking confused.

"Yes?" Ingrid replied.

"And…you're not from the corporations?" Benat went on, before letting out a soft sigh. "Ah, I think I get it."

"You get what?" Ingrid asked.

"The reason you've not told this one to go back to Hellion." She snorted, before leaning forward. "You're not pirates, or thieves. You're newly found, aren't you?"

"Explain."

"You're newly joined! Your *world*—it's been found recently, or you've just got back into space. That's why you don't know what's going on, or why you're even talking to us."

"We're not from this sector, that's all," Ingrid said quickly.

"Yeah, that's clear." Benat snorted. "Okay, look, free bit of advice for you. You're here trying to sell crystals, right?"

"Yeah?"

"Crystals are a *controlled* trade good, loads of taxes on them and rules to follow if you're trading in them because they're needed for everything from computer systems to high-energy weapons."

"Uh huh."

"So, you turn up here, at an independent system, and claim to have some to sell. Either you've just raided a convoy and you're looking to offload them fast, for a fraction of their real value, which makes sense you'd deal with this one." She nodded to Malthus.

"Or, you've got a mine on your world and had no idea how valuable they were until now." Malthus grunted. "Let me guess… you tried to join the UC and they've taken you, or are promising to, but you have to sell them all the crystals you can make, right?"

"Hellion is a producer too." Benat settled back. "But we've been set up for years. The corpos know exactly how many crystals are produced daily—to the microgram. Makes it a nightmare to get any off-world to sell for a private profit."

"We're new to the sector," Ingrid admitted. "We're out making relationships, so yeah, maybe there's a few details we weren't aware of."

"Are they marked?"

"What?" Ingrid asked.

"The crystals…are they customs marked?" Benat asked again. "Do you have a sample?"

"Not on me," Ingrid said. *"Dammit, that's stupid of me. Sorry, everyone,"* she added in the command link. *"Of course they're going to want samples."*

"Look, we need some credits, you need some advice, and maybe some muscle if you're planning on carrying crystals around, all right?" Benat tried to force a, frankly, terrifying smile again. "How about this. You want to sell those crystals, we'll agree on a price and a percentage, but for now? A flat rate."

"For?" Ingrid asked.

"For our help." Benat shrugged. "Malthus and I are mercs. Do you have them where you come from?"

"Mercenaries?" I asked.

She nodded. "So, we're looking for work, you need help…seems there's a pretty simple solution for both sides here."

"How much?" Ingrid asked. *"Don't worry, I don't trust them, but I think they've got a valid point about the situation."*

"Yeah," I agreed. *"Maybe even a few hours of chatting and getting the lay of the land would be worth it. Depends how much it is, really."*

"A hundred credits," Benat said.

"Really?" Ingrid said slowly, drawing the word out. "A hundred credits…"

"Is this a lot?" she asked us all. *"We still don't know really…"*

"I think that's a hell of an ask," I said aloud. "A hundred credits…I mean, what do we get out of this?"

"Two experienced mercenaries for a week," Benat said. "You're not going to get a better offer than that, and especially for our kind."

"That raises a point," Ingrid said delicately. "You've already admitted that most people won't deal with you, and they look down on devilkin, so having you with us? Well, if anything, that's going to make problems for us, right?"

"Not if we're hired muscle." She shook her head. "Getting Malthus and me for that price is practically a steal…"

"How much was the water?" Scylla asked in the link.

"A credit each."

"He said it was expensive, remember?" she said. *"If an expensive drink is a credit, what's a meal here worth?"*

"I'm getting hungry." I shifted on the seat. "I'm guessing that you're not going to have anything here we can eat, if water fucks you up, so anywhere nearby that we could buy some food?"

"This is a bar," Benat replied as she gestured at the table where the menu was projected. "Turn three pages over and there's option to order food in."

"Delivery to the bar?" I asked.

She frowned. "Of course?"

"Ah, civilization at last," I whispered, barely beating Jonas to the menu and flipping through the sections until the food started to appear.

It took a full minute to find anything that looked like it might be possible for us to eat, and it was essentially a side of meat that looked like a cow had been cut in half and slapped on the table, but it'd do as an example.

"How much is this?" I asked, getting a curse from Ingrid as she did something, then pushed out a link to us all that updated our systems. The strange symbols shifted, realigning until they were clear Arabic numerals from Earth. "Ah…"

"Is that right?" I asked in the link. *"Three credits for a side of meat that could feed any of us, maybe all?"*

"If so, then a hundred credits each for a week? Working it out on that, let's say it's like a solid fillet steak. Say…fifty bucks. And working the water out as expensive booze in here, say twelve and a half a pop? That'd make a hundred credits…about twelve hundred and fifty bucks for a week," Jonas replied dubiously.

"For a decent merc, that'd be about right, considering they're expecting to be talking more than anything else," I guessed.

"A hundred credits is a lot," Ingrid said into the silence, and I gritted my teeth as I realized we'd all gone silent to "talk" between ourselves, either exposing that we had a link going, or making it look like we really didn't know what the fuck we were doing. "Why don't you explain why you're worth that, and what guarantee we get from you?"

"Guarantee?" Malthus asked.

"A way to be sure that you can't turn on us," Ingrid explained.

"Well, if we did that, we'd not get any more work, right? Nobody's going to hire a mercenary they can't trust."

"Sure, but how do we know we can trust you?"

"You want references?" he asked, squinting around. "I can provide them, but it's a bit weird."

"It's a cultural thing." I shrugged. "Why don't you tell us about some of the groups you've worked with that might have records on the station."

"Okay…" he said slowly, before starting to rattle off names and battles.

"Shit, he's fast," I sent. *"Keep him talking about one of the engagements and I'll dredge the net."*

I got acknowledgments from the others, as I settled back, taking a sip of the water for the first time and half closing my eyes as I focused on the nearest active computer signal.

It wasn't the same as human-built Wi-Fi, but not that different either, a set pulse that basically broadcast "I'm here" in several electromagnetic spectrums.

I guessed that some species would hate it, considering it was essentially a low-grade squeal of data being sent out constantly, but reaching out to it and connecting was easy enough.

As soon as I did, I flinched, almost spilling the damn water at the sheer barrage of data I was hit with. Worse than just the unfiltered mess, was that everything, and I mean *everything* that was hitting me, was embedded with tracking shit.

I felt them all, like a thousand beady eyes, staring at me as I spread it out, trying to figure out what was going on.

Sliding through different signal gradients and styles, it became clear in seconds what I was seeing. It was the local equivalent of a phone directory, decades' worth of viruses and obsolete cyberattacks, and a data net. All jam-packed full of phishing crap.

Everywhere I looked, trackers blared out signals, trying to snare my attention for just a few seconds to help to build the all-important profile of me.

Once they had that, I dimly suspected that a second phase would kick in, probably to test and make sure of what they thought I wanted to see, before selling the data to someone else.

Screw that.

My Hack and Espionage sub-mind was confused for all of three seconds, working its way through the mass of crap. Then I triggered my ability and slowed time for me.

As the seconds dragged out into infinity, my sub-mind reached out and casually tore the trackers apart, before devouring them for the data they so desperately wanted to harvest.

As soon as I had a picture of what they were for sure, and how and why they were doing what they were doing, we set off backtracking the signal spike.

The local bar was only a single small node, like a pine tree's needle in a forest, but it'd been full of these tracers forever. I dimly guessed that people who put up with this shit daily probably had specific systems set up, like antiviruses that cleaned this away before they even saw it.

That gave me an opportunity, though, and I took it.

In less than a minute of my time, and a fraction of that of the outside world, I hid my signal in the image of another. If anything came, it would see a rogue virus, and not the weird group in the corner hacking the damn net…just in case.

Most people would never see these trackers, after all, so one that acted a little different, if it was spotted at all, would probably just be ignored.

Or I hoped so anyway.

I hit the next node in the link, a clothing shop a little farther along, then a broadcast node in the public areas, jumping from one to another, picking up speed as I went.

A dozen nodes flashed past before I found my first challenge, some kind of security program, a mental image of it sniffing around the net, examining everything that passed like Cerberus at the Gates of Hell.

As soon as I entered its range, it locked onto me, scanning me over and over, clearly trying to identify me and whatever I was. As soon as it began that, I did the same, locking onto it and unleashing a Contagion attack.

It was neither as fast as Drain nor as hard-hitting as Tsunami, my two usual attacks that I'd developed through the Hack tree, but it had a massive advantage over the others.

It was *quiet.*

The Contagion attack essentially gave it something to look at, and while it examined the bait, Contagion seeped into the monitor program, slowly sliding through layer after layer of security.

I waited. The monitor program was smaller than I'd expected, and triggered the linked system ability. I found that it was currently linked to three, and picked one at random.

Contagion slid a copy of itself into the linked system and went quiet as the program started to reach out there as well, spreading as far as it could.

Arise :Explorer

This time, it was a little bigger. I flexed a mental muscle, making the monitor program believe we were safe and let us past, as the Contagion protocols slid onward.

Junctions appeared and blurred past three-dimensional linkage points: some with hundreds of options, others with thousands upon thousands. And every time, I sensed the presence of the monitors.

Flashing from one link to another, then another, I searched for markers of the tracer's presence. Each time I found it, it linked to another, and another. As I passed the monitors, I'd spin up a copy of Contagion, feeding it into them, feeling the secondary link go active as the monitor fell to me.

Seconds became minutes and my time compression juddered to a halt, reverting to normal speed for the outside world, as Ingrid and the others talked.

Malthus was regaling them all with tales of battles, clearly viewing it as selling himself. Benat tried to explain her worth as well, which, from the little I heard, seemed to be primarily in distraction and handling Malthus, keeping him from going off the rails.

She was a rogue, he a front-line fighter, though the roles were pretty obvious. If I were to look at it as a gamer role, she'd be half rogue and half bard, considering the "distraction" techniques she cheerfully described using, with Malthus as almost a pure tank in comparison.

Both were damn good skills, though. And the way they were describing them? They'd worked as a pair for a while.

"So why did you threaten me when you were asking me to sell our ship?" Ingrid asked him, and I hesitated, pausing my hack to listen.

"I recognized the model," he said. "I figured that you were pirates and you'd be looking to make some deals. You'd never give me a chance if I just came up and asked to speak to the leader, so I made myself a threat, someone you had to deal with."

"It was a bluff," she guessed, and he coughed before nodding.

"You're an idiot," Benat muttered to him, as I snorted and went back to the search.

Dozens more linkages blurred past, hundreds of nodes, and I was forced to backtrack time and time again, searching over and over for another hint, a trace of the home of the program. Finally, as I followed another trail, with only half my mind, planning on other possible ways I could get the information we needed?

I found it.

Ten seconds of brute-force hacking, using trick after trick after trick, and of me cursing myself for the sheer goddamn stupidity of using all my time compression up in one go, and I finally got through the outer locks.

Bursting inside, I started to look around, before frantically firing off another Contagion as I sensed something wrong.

There were four nodes connected to the one I found myself in, and in a quarter of a second, I felt all four connections being severed.

With a grunt, I was back in my own body again, blinking and shaking my head. The fragment I'd been riding to the target was gone, the physical connections to the system it'd been in now severed.

More than that, I found that from the way it'd cut off? My head was banging like a hooker's headboard, and I snarled as I forced myself to my feet.

"What's wrong?" Ingrid asked. *"Steve?"* The hum of her mental voice through the command link was worried, and I shook my head.

"I found something, a hacker who's been spreading tracers, monitoring the area for years, but when I traced it back to them, I got cut off."

"And?"

"And now they either have a copy of my search ability to try to reverse engineer, with some seriously high-tech shit built into it, which we really don't want anyone else getting, or they've killed it, and are erasing anything that might be useful to us."

"So what do we do?" Ingrid asked, glancing from me to the nonplussed pair of devilkin.

"I need to find them and make sure they're not copying that search engine. It's got my Contagion built into it."

"Then how about a field test?" Jonas suggested, nodding at the pair.

"I..." I hesitated, then grinned. *"I like it."*

Chapter Thirty-Two

"Steve has been tracing a hacker who's attempting to steal from us," Ingrid told the pair. "Now, we can deal with this ourselves, or..."

She paused, cocking her head to one side and waiting as she looked from one to the other of the devilkin.

"And what? You want us to watch?" Benat asked after a few seconds. "Sorry, not getting the whole body language thing." She gestured at the way Ingrid was waiting.

"Ah, sorry." Ingrid winced. "How about this? You show us you're worth the hundred credits, and we'll pay you that rate. You take care of this—we'll go with you and watch *you*—and if you can do what you claim, we'll take you on for a flat fee of a hundred?"

"Who took it?" Malthus asked. "I'm no techie."

"I've got a location." I reached out to the menu display on the table and focused, before shifting it to show the local area I'd found in one of the buffers I'd taken over.

Judging from the way the pair jerked and looked from the image to me, then to each other, and back to the image, being able to do that definitely wasn't normal.

"We'll not be working for free," Malthus said after a brief pause. "Ten credits upfront."

"Fine." Ingrid shrugged. "It comes off the hundred, though."

"And if you try to back out of the job, it'll not end well for you," Scylla added. "I spent centuries working with mercenaries. Believe me, I've seen more betrayals than you can imagine."

"And you let them keep doing it?" Benat frowned.

"No, I made an example of them, each and every time."

"Not a good one if others kept doing it," Malthus grunted.

"Over how long?" I asked Scylla, and she paused, thinking.

"About a thousand years?"

"How long have you two been working as mercs?" I asked them, planning to give them some context.

"It's not important," Ingrid interrupted. "Sorry, Steve, but it really isn't. Their years could be half the length of ours or a hundred times longer. Let's just see what they do."

"Dammit," I muttered, before shrugging and gesturing to the image and starting to explain. "They've cut off my contact with the tracker, but I have control over some of the systems that lead up to their hideout. We need to get in there, find out what they know, and make damn sure they're not fucking with the system that I was using."

"What is it?" Malthus stood as the others followed suit.

"It's…hard to explain," I admitted. "The digital tracer is, well, digital, but it's absolutely cutting-edge compared to anything you've got in the system."

"They got it locked down?" Benat cocked her head to one side.

"What?"

"It's off-line, not able to be contacted?" she clarified.

"Ah, yeah. Literally, it's like it vanished from the network." I nodded.

"Probably a cut out," Benat suggested, glancing over at Malthus.

"Could be." He grunted.

"Cut out?" Ingrid asked.

"A physical trap—something enters it that the data-rat doesn't like? They cut the connections on each side and it's locked in a physical case, then it's easily moved and sold to a buyer without risking having it back online," Benat explained.

"So it might be a box or might be tech based? Great, just what we need…more complications," I said.

"Whatever." Malthus grunted. "Can you enlarge this?" He gestured toward the image, and I nodded, zooming in and showing it. "This looks weird."

"It's the active data transfer systems," I said. "That's why some of the buildings, rooms or whatever, are showing a lot more than others."

That was true as well. The map I had showed the boundary of the local area, more or less, but it was the outline of the data cables, the connectors, the crystal pathways—hell, I didn't have words for the vast majority of the tech that was in place. But my Hack system had accepted it and adjusted to work with it easily enough.

The end result was a drawing made of light, walls that glowed with hidden data pathways, blank spots where systems were damaged or dead, fading outlines of light where their version of Wi-Fi couldn't reach, and a thousand spots in-between.

"We can find it from this." Benat crouched to squint at the image.

"You need to finish your shift or something?" I asked her, suddenly remembering we'd essentially interrupted her work when we'd come in with her boyfriend or mate or whatever.

"No, screw this place." She snorted. "The credits aren't worth the pawing."

"One of those bars, is it?" Ingrid asked with a wince.

"It's not bad, but I'd rather stab first and ask permission later." She smiled. "Wait for me there." She jabbed at a shape in the map and got a grunt from Malthus as he apparently worked out what and where it was.

Arise :Explorer

He nodded to her, then she was off, casually throwing her apron at the bartender, who caught it and dumped it out of sight without comment.

"She was quick to give up on the job here," I said. "No offense, but when the job's done, if we're not impressed, isn't she going to have walked away from a job?"

"She hates working in the bar." Malthus snorted. "She's joking about being pawed. Nobody does it here, not really, but the bars on the main level? If she had to take a job there, it's bad. What you're paying will cover what she earns here for a while, so to hell with it. We'd both rather earn real credits than waste time in here."

"I think the ten-credit advance is a lot more than we thought it was," Ingrid sent to me. *"Think of it as a hundred and twenty-five dollars instead, or actually, maybe a lot more. They were willing to give up a steady job just for the hope of earning it, so..."*

"Yeah. Also, it's a bar job." I winced. *"Not sure about you, but I worked a lot of different jobs over the years, and most I'd have walked out of at any time for the slightest reason."*

"I thought you liked working in a bar?"

"I liked the free booze, the wage that—barely—covered the rent, and the regular sex. The job itself was crap. I got fired for being late when I saved Marie and Amanda, remember? I spent all day dealing with drunken arseholes I wanted to punch out."

"Ah," she replied delicately. *"I'd forgotten that side of it."*

"Most do."

"Makes it even funnier that you basically just gave a kid a shitload of money, though," Jonas interjected, and I snorted.

Malthus led us out of the bar and down two levels, across another few corridors then back up to the next level, before taking us to…another bar.

"What's this?" I asked quietly, leaning on the bar next to him.

"We need to wait for Benat," he pointed out.

"And we're waiting in another bar because…?" I glanced around at the looks we were getting from the other patrons. They weren't welcoming ones.

"Because the place you showed me? It's above us. And all the places on that floor have a back alley that lets out to an emergency exit…"

"Uh huh?" I prompted as he reached out and tapped a menu on the bar top, sliding a claw through the options to show a small tab at the bottom.

It flashed when he pressed it, before expanding to show what looked to be emergency depressurization instructions.

There were gathering points that were clearly marked, and what had to be bunkers or something similar.

"And that emergency exit leads to here," he finished, tapping a symbol with one claw.

I glanced up from the image he'd enlarged, then at the back wall behind the bar, where, underneath scratched paint and a half-assed drawing showing a bunch of beings cheering at what I guessed was a boxing match or something, the outline of a barely noticeable door was clear.

"If it's the group I think it is?" He nodded in the direction of the door, and waved off the annoyed-looking bartender. "As soon as we kick in the front door, they'll be out the back that leads here. So…" He gestured with one hand in a way that I could only describe as "Italian," it was so full of meaning.

"So we leave a few of us here, and the others chase them down?" I asked.

"That's one way," he said, "and it's playing it safest. If Benat can get us in without tipping our hand? Great, we scoop them up and no stress. If they try to run, we have someone down here to catch them."

"Seems like a solid plan," Ingrid said. "Where's Benat meeting us?"

"Here." He gestured to the door. "She should be here in a few minutes."

"We're not popular," Jonas leaned in to whisper, and I looked over his shoulder, then around the bar again before grunting my agreement.

"Ingrid?" I asked, knowing she'd heard it as well.

"Better if you go," she said. "Jonas and Scylla will stay with me. You wait outside with Malthus for Benat, and the three of you take the front door. We'll catch them if they come out the back."

"You sure?" I asked, and she nodded, gesturing.

"I am. Trust me and go before the locals get any more annoyed."

I nodded, standing and following Malthus as he led me back into the throng of passing traffic outside. I noted the way people watched Malthus leave, and not the group who stayed.

"Is it always like that?" I asked when we'd taken up station outside, watching the passing mass of people.

"What?" he asked distractedly, eyes scanning the crowd.

"The bar. The people. The way that they wanted you out?"

"Always."

"Why?"

"Look, I get that you're trying to make conversation, but it's just the way it is, okay?"

"Yeah, no," I replied. "If they hate you, it's generally for a reason, so explain it for me."

He shrugged. "I'm devilkin."

"So? Not from around here, remember."

"You haven't had any contact with my kind before?" He shook his head. "Seems crazy."

"Seems the same to me." I shrugged. "Everywhere I go, the world is different. So, devilkin…?"

"We're devilkin."

"You're really not helping me to trust you here, Malthus," I growled. "Give me a straight answer."

"Fuck it," he muttered, then shrugged. "Fine. When our world was found, after the plague, we had old crystal refineries. They weren't operational, and the UC agreed to consider us as a member world if they could fix them up and provide a 'fair' payment for them."

"Right."

"So our idiot leaders agreed, seeing the potential for off-world investment and protection, and not looking into it any deeper. The crystals weren't any use to us—we'd never figured out how to do anything with them, and the factories were just abandoned anyway. No loss, right?"

"And these crystals, they're seriously valuable everywhere else?"

"Yeah." He grunted. "As part of the deal, the owners of the factory have a veto on anything that would damage the production of their crystals. Turns out that anything that generates gravitational waves too close to the growing plants damages them, so no spaceport near the growing centers."

"Make sense."

"Yeah, the deal is that the crystals are shipped to the refineries and the shipyard without gravitational damage, so we had to build a mag-lev system, at our expense."

"Uh huh."

"And the ones who decide if the cost is reasonable?" he spat. "The factory owners."

"And that's the off-worlders?" I guessed.

"Oh yeah, same as the ones who get to decide when the contracts are up."

"What?" I blinked in surprise.

"The contracts are thirty planetary season cycles," he explained, as I automatically converted that to years. "And at the end of the contract? The ones who get to decide if the contract is renewed or cancelled? It's the contract holder."

"That's dodgy as fuck," I grunted. "Who the hell agreed to that?"

"Our old leaders. The same ones who agreed that the contract holders could set the prices for the crystals…you know, those things that are needed in all high-tech processes? Not like there's a market for that, right?"

"Shit." I groaned as he went on.

"So yeah, we find out that we're being fucked over, and not only a little, but to an amazing degree. Our crystals are perfect for weapons systems, like *perfect* for high-energy weapons. So they're in demand. The off-worlders? They 'only' take fifty percent of the value, isn't that nice?" He snorted. "Except that fifty percent is taken off the top *before* any expenses are factored in. Then what's left is ours. Minus the expenses."

"And those expenses take off a lot of the profit?" I guessed.

"We get one twentieth of the value of those crystals, and we can't trade them anywhere else." He sighed. "A few cycles back, we found a cache of them that'd been produced at some point in the distant past. The elders decided that they weren't covered by the existing deal as they were neither mined nor refined when the deal was in place, and they spent literally everything we had to outfit a ship."

He paused, spotting Benat in the distance weaving her way through the throng of figures, and gestured for me to follow, as he went on explaining over his shoulder.

"As soon as we loaded them onto the ship, the UC stepped in and confiscated them, declaring that we'd broken the agreement. Then they fined us, and the ship was impounded. Just to make things better, the debt for the fine was imposed on our world. Our only available resource of any value was taken to pay off the debt."

"Right?" I agreed. "Wait, I thought you said you didn't have anything else of value?"

"Just us," he said. "Just our people."

"They enslaved you?" I swore.

"Indebted involuntary conscription." He snorted. "Then they added on the expense of feeding us, outfitting and training, then housing, and suddenly we were in more debt than when we started."

"This sounds dodgy as fuck," I repeated. "So, the ship with the crystals? What happened with that? You said that your elders said it wasn't breaking the contract?"

"It wasn't," he agreed. "But it's been under 'investigation' in the UC court for so long that it's basically been given up on. Then, because our people were so angry about what was happening to us, well, we started fighting a lot when we weren't supposed to."

"Go on."

"Between battles we'd fight with practically anyone, for any reason, hating the UC and everyone else, we got a reputation for being dumb and violent. The off-worlders who owned our contracts used that to spread around that we were untrustworthy.

"With that, and the reputation we had for violence, we were in trouble, and when the courts eventually listened to our side of the arguments, and it started to look like we had a chance? Someone pointed out that the UC needed the crystals we produced for the war with the Ændari. Backroom deals were made, and the indebted conscription was cancelled."

"But I'm betting that wasn't the end of it."

"No."

Benat waved to us and stepped to the side, taking up station at the elevator to the next floor and waiting for us as we headed over to her.

"Our people were returned home, and we were given the option of accepting that any and all crystals on our world are the property of the UC, or we can try to fight it in court and they'll hold the debts over our heads until they own the planet.

"We had nothing by this point, nothing of value except for the crystal plants that were owned by the off-worlders and UC. We'd learned just how far we could trust the bastards, so we did the only thing we could and told the UC where they could stuff their membership, declared independence, and our people started searching for other off-world work, while the contract for the UC owning the crystals was upheld.

"The reputation we'd gotten through all the backstabbing we'd gone through was still held against us, though—that we were dumb, violent, and couldn't be trusted, so most places wouldn't give us a chance. That left mercenary work and crime."

"And once you started down that route, you couldn't go back," I agreed. "You had no choices—most of the jobs weren't open to you, so you took what you could, but in doing so, you reinforced the stereotype that you were violent criminals."

"And now, no matter where we go off-world, that's the response to us." He jerked a thumb in the direction of the bar we'd left the others in. "You've got no idea what it's like."

"Yeah, I've seen similar done before," I admitted, before shaking my head. "Okay, thanks for the context. Hi, Benat." I greeted her as we stepped up to join her, finding that instead of the simple plain and worn clothes she wore before, now she was dressed in a suit that clearly doubled as armor and in a pinch as a vacuum resistant layer as well.

It wasn't as heavy duty as our own space suits, and it wasn't as well made as Malthus's own, but it was clearly a hell of a lot better than what most people we passed were wearing.

It was mainly black, with lighter grey and red patches of armoring attached over the top. A holster on the right hip held a gun of some kind, and the left arm had a disc about halfway down it, with a single prong of thick metal that slid out of the back, running back along her arm to jut out past the elbow by a few inches.

She'd gone from "friendly waitress and negotiator" to "badass mercenary." And when people saw she was with Malthus and me? Nobody else tried to take the elevator with us.

The door slid shut, and we went a single floor up. The doors barely closed before they were opening again.

"You don't like the stairs?" I asked the pair.

"If we take the stairs, we're obviously only going a few levels up or down," Benat replied calmly. "If we take the transport? We could be going anywhere."

I glanced at the keypad that she'd used when we'd stepped inside and noted that there were dozens of stops marked, and that what I'd thought was an elevator, going up or down a single level, was apparently more like a single-carriage, private transport cube.

As soon as we left the box at the next stop, people backed up, getting out of the way as Malthus took the lead.

"Poor section," Benat said in a detached tone of voice. "There's a lot more violence here, and a lot less concern about it."

I could see that was the expectation as well, looking around.

Unlike the last section we were in, here there was perhaps a quarter of the foot traffic, and although the sides of the corridors were still filled with buildings, most of them were either shuttered businesses or ones that looked on the verge of closing.

Sullen glares greeted me as I glanced into one of the open doors, noting the graffiti that covered the walls, the stench of piss, and the snoring forms that lay here and there.

The walls were closer in as well, presumably due to the lack of large-scale cargo moving here compared with closer to the port. But it also meant that shifty-eyed individuals moved carefully in and out.

One of them tried moving too close to Benat, only to curse and glare at her when she grabbed their questing hand and bent it back.

"Keep your hands to yourself, or lose them," she hissed.

I shook my head, amused as I felt the first featherlight touches on my own armor. I batted the hand aside and kept moving as Malthus dragged us on.

The last section was perhaps ten meters wide, and the same tall; the walls that ran on either side were filled with shops, restaurants, bars, and more. There were doors that were clearly air locks here and there, more emergency bunkers, and access to upper or lower levels.

This section, though, was maybe half of that wide, five or six meters across, and although it was still ten meters tall, at around the five-meter mark, a gantry ran around, allowing access to a second level of housing.

There were beings of a dozen different species leaning out over railings, glaring at us and everyone else equally.

At least half of the beings I saw were armed, and those who weren't looked to be the more aggressive.

The food places were scruffier, generally, and the low-level hum of the lower ring had become a roar of constant shouting, beeps, clacks, and hundreds of voices raised in argument, greeting, threats, declarations, offers...

A creature that looked halfway between a cow and an insect leaned out of a doorway on the second level, enticing a human-looking guy up the stairs with one serrated forelimb. I couldn't help but wonder how many humans from Earth would end up losing significant appendages here trying to screw anything and everything, given half the chance.

"There many sections like this?" I asked Benat, who nodded, sliding to walk alongside me, as we followed along and made full use of Malthus's size, like an icebreaker plowing through a frozen sea.

"Yeah, the closer to the upper level you go, the cheaper it is...less radiation shielding." She shrugged. "The uppermost levels are uninhabitable, used mainly for power generation and storage; the lower you go, the more people and credits."

"Fair enough," I grunted, wondering how we could use that to our advantage.

"See the building on the corner?" she asked me, and I peered ahead. "Green front on the lower side, red on the upper."

"Yeah, I've got it," I said, seeing the crossroads ahead. Yellow and white patterning that covered most of the walls, giving directions and locations or whatever, had been painted over there, leaving two doors painted in green below and red above.

The doors were recessed slightly, and like others I'd seen, they slid into the wall when they opened.

The thing that stood out for these?

They had both a heavily armed figure outside, leaning on the railing and looking out over the crowd passing by, and a bunch of what just had to be cameras watching the entrance from every angle.

"That it?" Benat asked me.

"Yeah. Fuck."

"You ready for this?" she asked, and I hesitated, before nodding.

"Is this going to cause problems?" I asked slowly, weighing up the likely consequences, then cursing as I realized that we'd gone too far to back down now.

"For them?" She laughed. "Sure. For us?" She shrugged. "Just try not to kill anyone in a white suit, or we get a fine."

With that amazingly unhelpful description, she slapped her right palm over the disc on her left arm. It clunked, then spun out. The line of metal slid around, forming a circular shield as she pulled her handgun out of its holster and fired a single shot over the head of Malthus.

It hit the figure that'd been leaning over the railing, and whatever the hell the pellet was that hit him, it locked him up. He jerked wildly, muscles clenching as he collapsed, shaking over the side.

Malthus took the stairs to the second level three at a time, leaping up them, pausing only to slap something over the door on the upper level, then shouting to Benat.

She shouted back, presumably in their own language, all harsh syllables, as she jabbed fingers into a display on the inside of her shield.

I followed her, twisting to look about the street, amazed as people split around us, but beyond that? They seemed not to care in the slightest.

The door jerked open suddenly, and a burst of fire ripped out, literally.

The flames that roared into the air lasted three or four seconds, that was it, and the crowd below finally seemed to care, slowing and separating as they waited for the flames to stop…then started to walk again.

A handful of people gathered to watch as Malthus took the door, running inside to the sound of small arms fire.

"This way," Benat said to me, leading the way to the left of the door, on the ground floor.

We ran down the joining corridor, coming to a supposedly solid wall, only to find that as she smacked a palm against the upper left of it, that it popped open on hinges, sliding inward.

"Emergency exits," she explained over her shoulder distractedly, leading the way. "They're not allowed to be locked, or blocked."

The back area that was exposed was a much narrower corridor, maybe two meters wide, with a small gantry that ran along the second floor to the right and left, making it clear that two "streets" backed onto each other here.

As Benat slid to a halt, lifting her gun up and bracing it on the edge of her shield, waiting, a door opened overhead. A pair of aliens leapt out, followed by a third.

The first two humanoids were small, maybe a meter tall if that, and almost childlike in their build, hairless, wearing scruffy clothes. As soon as they landed on the grated metal gantry, they dropped to all fours, sprinting along it in the opposite direction.

"Flathun," Benat grunted. "Ignore them—focus on that one."

The third figure was dragging a box with him, frantically yanking on cables, disconnecting it as they screamed something back into the room behind them.

Another voice rang out in answer, followed by gunfire as whoever was left inside started fighting, presumably Malthus.

The figure overhead shouted something else, then started to run to the nearest stairway, taking the steps three and four at a time, making it clear in the way that they landed and twisted that although they looked almost human, they were anything but.

He saw us at the last minute, having been looking away, shouting something back over his shoulder at the fleeing flathun. The stairs he was running down went away from us for a few meters, then doubled back on themselves, heading directly down toward the ground.

"If they're taking something while running, chances are it's what we want." Benat aimed carefully.

I nodded, noting the slab of electronics he clutched to his chest as he saw us and jerked to a halt, grabbing at the railing and trying to turn, half falling. I stared at the revealed face.

It was one that only a mother could love: no nose, a mouth that looked to be wide enough to swallow a watermelon whole, *sideways,* that ran from ear to ear, and tiny eyes peering out from behind massive goggles.

There was no chin, the head almost perfectly round, and although the body looked humanoid in its clothing? The arms and legs bent in ways that screamed there were weird-ass joints in there.

He twisted around, crouching as if about to jump...

And then Benat shot him in the ass with the electric pellet gun.

He screeched, throwing his arms and legs in all directions like a nineties breakdancer on a kilo of acid, before collapsing and bouncing down the stairs toward us.

Benat darted forward, grabbing the case from his spasming hands, and shot him again, this time in the crotch, then shouted up as the gunfire overhead stopped.

"Got it! Exfil!"

"Go!" Malthus shouted back, heaving his massive frame through the narrow doorway, then hopping over the railing.

He fell to the ground, landing easily and falling in behind me as we ran for the corridor again.

Thirty seconds later, and the doors to the lift, or transport cube, or whatever it was, were sliding closed, with us on the inside.

"So..." Benat said with a smile that was only slightly less weird now that she'd practiced it some more. "How'd we do?"

"I'm happy," Ingrid admitted to our little command group, and I smiled back as the others chimed in as well.

"So, a hundred credits, you said?"

<u>Chapter Thirty-Three</u>

"By Grabthar's holy left testicle," Benat breathed, staring up at the warship with wide eyes. "No wonder you tried to bluff them."

"For that ship?" Malthus agreed. "Who wouldn't."

"She's nice," I admitted, looking back at the pair of them. "But not *that* special, is she?"

"They're restricted to UC soldiers only." He shook his head. "How the hell did you get one?"

"It's a perk of our world," I said diplomatically.

"Sell it," Benat said suddenly. "Seriously, you don't know how much shit you're going to be in for this. Sell it before the UC finds out you have one, or else—"

"They're okay with it," Ingrid assured her, coming up behind us. The airlock whispered closed behind Scylla, who was apparently acting as rear guard.

"*Seriously?*" Benat hissed. "You know how many people would kill for this?"

"Lots, but we're getting repairs done," Ingrid said firmly. "That means we need you out here, as the first line of defense."

"Give you time to get your act together, eh?" Malthus nodded. "Makes sense."

"Glad you understand." Ingrid smiled. *"And one of us needs to be up and ready at all times watching them as well,"* she added in the command link.

"Got it," I agreed.

"Can we…can we see inside?" Benat asked slowly, still staring at the ship. "I mean, I understand if you don't trust us, but…"

"When we know you a little better, I don't see why not," Ingrid said politely, making it clear that it was a "later," not a "now" situation.

"Understandable." Malthus grunted. "So, you want me to put you in touch with someone to sell those crystals?"

"Soon." She nodded. "For now, we need to review things. Shout if you need us." With that, Ingrid headed for the ship's airlock with the others, and I exchanged a look with Malthus, getting a nod that he understood the situation.

Then I followed the others.

The ship hadn't changed at all as near as I could tell since we'd left, but almost as soon as we'd boarded, Oxus was directing us to one of the main meeting rooms.

In it we found Zac, Casey, and James arguing, and best of all, fresh coffee waiting.

"What's up?" I picked a coffee up and inhaled the heavenly aroma.

"Designs," Zac said quickly, a wide grin on his face as he pulled the viewpoint on the wall back from the small turret he'd been discussing with James, and instead showing the overall warship in all its glory.

She was long, and I could see a series of changes where the frame was being worked on here and there outlined in white, the living quarters open to space—well, to the dock, really—but that hadn't been clear from the angle we'd been at when we boarded.

Our old ship, that had once been Athena's megayacht, was now installed and the hull was being sealed over the top of it. Sure, there were some sections that were clearly wasted space, where the old hull of the yacht and the new hull of the starship meshed, but Zac was apparently working on that from the inside with the custodians.

The cool bit, though? That was on the wall screen now.

"Boss man!" Zac crowed. "Boss lady! Just who I needed to see!"

"Oh gods," I muttered. "When you're that cheerful and there's no booze in sight, I know it's gonna hurt."

"Yeah, well, bite the pillow, 'cos I'm goin' in dry!" He grinned. "All I need is for you both to sign off on this…"

"Please don't." James sighed, rubbing the bridge of his nose with two fingers and closing his eyes. "Neither the innuendos nor the design are needed."

"Just give me the spiel." I sighed, sitting down and taking a sip of the coffee, then let out another sigh. "Okay, I think I'm ready for the worst," I lied.

"James, how bad is it?" Ingrid asked him directly.

"Overengineered, and most of the designs will need to be replaced in a matter of days, if you're successful at all in negotiations," he said. "Zac has allowed himself to get carried away with the possibilities of the ship, when all we have as examples are the current technology."

"I'm using what we've got!" Zac snapped. "You want me to install fairy-dust launchers and shit, I can, but—"

"What I mean, Zac, as I've said multiple times, is that the entire point of selecting this site for the upgrades was to have access to the latest prototype technologies. Your design takes none of them into account, which is why you need to focus on the structure and the deeper systems *first.*"

"But—"

"*Then,* once we've begun negotiations and know what kind of technology we have access to, then and only then do we begin the upgrades process," James finished.

"Yeah, I get that," Zac snapped. "Ideal world? We wait until everything's done, all right—you spend what, a month, two, here negotiating? You make deals and you get the best tech we can; we install it all, level by level, and then we make sure they all work together, no compatibility issues, no freaking out, none of that, right?"

"Exactly." James sighed. "Now you're getting it."

"No." Zac smiled.

"Zac…" James growled, rubbing at the bridge of his nose again and clearly trying to keep his temper in check.

"No, just listen!" Zac said quickly. "I let you say your bit, right? Just listen!"

"Go on." Ingrid sighed, reaching out and laying a calming hand on James's forearm.

"I'd *love* to do it all that way," Zac said. "It means a *lot* less work for me, for a start. And seriously? I want to go exploring this place, find me some alien beers, maybe a strip joint!"

There was a pause as he apparently realized that comment had been said aloud, with his wife by his side.

Casey slowly set her coffee cup down on the polished steel table with a quiet *clink*. "What was that last bit, Zac?" she asked calmly.

"Uh…uh, nothing!" he babbled. "I was just spitballin', that's all, babe!"

"Ah." She smiled tightly. "I think we'll talk about this after the meeting. In *private*."

"Zac," Ingrid said as he stared at Casey in frozen terror for a few more seconds. "ZAC! Focus!"

"Right!" Zac jerked. "Okay, yeah, right, so the problem, you know, with…that?" He waved a hand distractedly at the wall.

"Yes?" Ingrid prompted.

"It's him."

Everyone followed the pointing finger of blame, and I blinked in surprise as it was levelled at me.

"What did I do?" I asked, confused.

"Seriously?" Zac asked the others, quirking an eyebrow. "Do I even need to ask if he's stabbed anyone or started a fight today?"

"I didn't!" I gasped.

"You sort of did," Jonas said.

"We did have to hire those mercenaries…" Ingrid muttered.

"Hey!" I groaned. "Not you too!"

"Go on and explain what you mean, please, Zac," Ingrid said as she reached out, taking my hand in hers and squeezing it while smiling at me.

"Well, all I'm sayin' is that in an ideal world? We'd build the ship right, no cut corners, no having to spend three times as much because we needed to get everything in place as fast as possible."

"But in the real world…" James sighed, glancing over at me. "He does have a valid point, as much as it pains me to admit that."

"What?" I asked, still struggling to understand.

"They mean that in the time that we'd be sitting here waiting for everything to be done right, something would have happened," Ingrid explained, as the others nodded or hid their smiles behind their cups.

"It's true." Jonas grunted. "Hell, since we met, you've yet to manage more than a few hours of normal shit in a month."

"Like what!" I snapped.

"You did find an alien starship," James pointed out.

"Solved the mystery of our origins as a species," Ingrid added.

"Started a fight with every faction of Arisen," Zac offered.

"Yeah, when you say it like that… Look, that was all in the past, right? We're a lot more stable now. We're a team and—"

"You discovered Atlantis last week," Jonas added.

"*We* did that!" I corrected.

"Killed the Loch Ness monster," Casey said, coughing into her hand.

"You resurrected me," Scylla said suddenly. "Regardless of the rest, you found me and took me in, rather than leaving me as I was. I… I should thank you." That shut us all up, and a second later, when everyone was looking at her, she snapped at them. "I did not offer to bear his children! I just said…thank you."

"Yeah, that's even weirder." Jonas sighed, shaking his head. "All right, look, I don't know about the rest of you, but the last few weeks are catching up with me. I think we need to set a watch, both on the ship and those buggers out there, and get some sleep."

"Yeah," I said. "That sounds damn good to me."

"Uh, yeah…your quarters are sorta a no-go," Zac said, getting a glare from Ingrid and a groan from me.

"Explain that please, Zac," she said softly. "And be very careful when you do."

"Uh…the custodians are moving the walls?" He winced. "Give it, oh…three hours?"

"Zac…" There was a definite growl in her voice now.

"You'll have a bigger bathroom!" he said quickly. "I'm moving the walls so that you can literally walk into your quarters, no more going outside to get in, and it's soundproof!"

"What?"

"Totally soundproof." He nodded vigorously. "You won't have to worry about us hearing you fuckin'."

"*What…*" she whispered, her cheeks going bright red.

"*NOTTHATWEDIDBEFORE!*" Zac practically wailed, the words tripping over themselves in his panic. "I mean it! It's not like me and Casey were listenin', you know. It's not like we were getting our rocks off an' shit to you guys…"

"Oh my God…" Ingrid groaned.

"Casey!" Zac begged. "Tell her!"

"Oh no, Zac," his wife said flatly. "You've dug yourself into this hole, you can dig yourself out."

"Zac?" I said slowly.

"Yeah?" he said, looking almost pathetically grateful for the distraction.

"Just tell us what you're doing with the ship."

"Uh…yeah." He nodded. "Okay, right, there's no guns on her, not really, and the shields are shit. The only thing that's good is the grav drive, and that's not our one that's hooked up…it's the original one that came with the ship."

"Okay, so what's happening then?" I asked.

"Well, first thing we need is a replacement control run. It's like the spine of the ship, the section that carries all the commands, you know, from you pointin' and going 'Onward!' and the engines actually triggering and shit—all those commands are carried through relays. The custodians are replacing some of them now, but we need to replace like *all* of them."

"Why?" I asked.

"Well, they're shit," he said. "They carry data and power, or they *could*."

"Oh gods…" Ingrid whispered, bracing her elbows on the table and dropping her face into her hands. "What's he done now…"

"It's not actually that bad, and it sort of makes sense." Casey took pity on her husband and took over. "Orders and any kind of signal are currently being transferred through damaged and obsolete cables, essentially fiber optics. They were transmitted through crystal originally, and when the ship was first created, the crystal was intact. That gave these ships massive advantages in terms of speed of response and power transfer. The crystals can transmit energy and encode it, so the same thing can carry signals and power.

"When the ship's taken serious damage in the past, though, these sections were damaged, and they had to run alternative fiber optic cabling to carry signals, and then power cabling as well. The end result is that the ship is losing the power generated as it flows through faulty cabling, and signals are frequently lost or miscommunicated, meaning that…"

"Like the engines." Zac spoke over Casey in his excitement. "The engines aren't like the ones we used to use to fire rockets into space. Instead, they're ion drives, and they're insanely efficient. The main engines are actually like seventy separate ion drives, all connected, right?" He said that as though it made perfect sense, and worst of all, for a second, it genuinely did as the Engineering sub-mind tried to show me details.

I had a sudden vision of dozens to hundreds of dinner-plate-sized individual projectors, all set side by side in some kind of hexagonal framework.

"Instead of the engines firing at full capacity when you want them to, they fire in sections. The issues with the cabling? Sometimes one or more of them don't activate, or they fire at half power or whatever.

"Then the engine management systems try to compensate, with errors still getting carried through, so the engines are fighting with themselves *all the damn time!*" He grinned.

"And you're happy about this?" Ingrid asked slowly.

"Now that I know what it is?" he asked. "Of course! Shit, you still don't get it? Okay. So, there's a bunch of sections with the cabling in place that's fucked, all right? There's also loads of sections where the original crystal is there. So, for now, we keep the cables—they work, sort of, but we work on fixing the crystal infrastructure.

"Once that's working again, we run a fresh backup line for the fiber optics. Then, if we ever need them? We've got a backup. The crystal, though, once it's working again? It's much more efficient. That means the engines work better for less power from the generator."

I sighed. "I know what efficiency means, Zac."

"Yeah, well, with you I never know." He grinned. "Okay, so we replace the control runs and we boost the ship overall. We've got a shield—it's just shit, so we hardwire that in as a secondary—get a new primary shield…that's gonna be a big cost, apparently."

"How much?"

"Twelve thousand credits for a decent one." He shrugged. "They run from about four for a really shitty one, to seven for the one we've got now, all the way up to a few hundred thousand for things that we could use to fly into planets and survive."

"Okay, we've got…" I glanced at Ingrid, who stifled a small smile.

"A hundred and eighty-eight thousand, three hundred and change," she said. "That's after we've paid the docking fees, the drinks, and hired those two."

"I think we can afford that." I smiled. "Maybe some more as well."

"Yeah, well, I'm only getting started." Zac grinned. "So, the shield is being replaced with something that's a lot better. The reactor is fine. It's not 'good'—don't get me wrong—but it's a serious issue to replace. Like it'd take three days at least, and it'd be about fifty thousand. For what it is? I'd say we hold off on that until we've got some time, then we set the nanites loose on it, rebuild it from scratch into a full-on high-grade power core. Like the peak of the tech we can get access to, I mean."

He paused, looking around for any dissenting voices, then nodded, making a note and moving on. "The control runs are being replaced, the plumbing as well. I've already got four custodians working on that, with the maker in the aft cargo hold working on more of them."

"Sounds good." I nodded. "We need to look at decent combat drones as well…"

"Yeah, it's on the list," he assured me. "So, back to the actual ship issues, you know, rather than getting distracted with random shit."

I couldn't help but glare at him over that.

"So, we've got what could be an amazing ship, but it's basically on its last legs. What we have that nobody else has, though, is programmable nanites! What I'm planning is that we fix the basic issues, like the control runs, we buy in the more obvious shit, like the mid-level shields, then we fit half-decent weapons, and that's it."

He said it as if it were a stroke of genius, and the rest of us stared at him as though he were utterly mental.

"And then?" I prompted.

"And then we replace it all!" He grinned around the table. "Seriously, don't you see it? Ingrid bargains for whatever we can get, preferably the schematics to the highest possible grade stuff, but she doesn't buy the actual kit! Instead, we buy mid-range stuff, solid and dependable, but nothing special…then we use the schematics and we build our own replacements!

"Come on, guys, seriously…think of the shield, right? We still have the old one, now we get the better one, and we have both. If we can get a decent schematic for one, we start the custodians rebuilding the old shitty one with the new plans, we use the mid-range until it's ready, then that becomes our backup instead!"

"Uh huh." I nodded noncommittally. "So your amazing plan is that we buy the plans for all the shit we want, as well as the current versions, then we upgrade as we go?"

"Well, yeah?" Zac frowned. "What's the problem?"

"It's not exactly a surprise." I shrugged. "I mean, you were making out it was a great plan. This just seems like common sense."

"I was trying to spin it like that to James, but he got all 'it's a waste of money, Zac' an' shit so, you know."

"It *is* a waste." James sighed. "If we're buying the plans, then we would have access to make our own versions…yes, I totally agree this would be wonderful."

"So what's the problem!" Zac whined.

"The issue is that the plans will be far more expensive than buying the actual equipment! The manufacturers know fine well that, given access to their plans, we could conceivably be competition down the line, which means they'll charge a ridiculous amount for them. I refuse to believe that given access to working versions, there is no way that you couldn't replicate them."

"Of course I could."

"Then why install mid-range!" James snapped. "If we're having to purchase the prototype systems, then it's only reasonable to instead purchase those and save the mid-range costs."

"We do that, because it gets the ship ready in a day or so!" Zac growled, jabbing a finger at me. "If we give him too long in dock, he'll start a fucking war, or invade somewhere, or…or who knows what!"

Everyone looked at me, and I sat back, feeling a little unfairly picked on, until James sighed.

"You've got a point," he admitted.

"Hey!" I complained.

"Okay, have you actually got a plan for what we need?" Ingrid asked Zac and James, squeezing my hand again in solidarity while trying to hide a smile.

"We basically need guns, repairs to the landing gear, and better booster engines." Zac shrugged. "If we fit the shield and those, then get a tractor beam on a turret mount attached in the secondary hold, so we can use it to drag scrap in to feed the converters, we'll be golden."

"How much will all that cost?" she asked.

"Uh, maybe a hundred, all told?" he guessed, waggling a hand back and forth. "That's if we go for a pair of rail guns on turrets so they can track targets, four laser turrets that can double as point defense, and the tractor.

"Ideally? I'd say we go all out, get six or eight rail gun turrets, a pair of mass drivers that run the length of the ship, eight laser turrets, and a set of missile launchers." He grinned at that as Jonas spoke up.

"There is no overkill, only reload and fire again," the big American said, and Zac nodded happily.

"Seriously, no clue why, but missiles and like space torpedoes are still really big these days. Personally? Mass drivers. We build four mass drivers that run the length of the ship, spread them out along the hull so anyone has to take out most of the hull to shut them down, and we put a maker at the far end. Then we set up a hopper on the inside, fill it with null coins and when someone pisses us off, we can custom build special ammo to fuck them up."

"Have them fire one after the other, instead of all at once," Jonas suggested, leaning in and grinning. "Then you can fire constantly…"

"Oh yeah, I like that." Zac gestured to the image of the ship on the wall as first the two turrets for rail guns appeared, one on top and one underneath the hull, then the four laser turrets, two up and two down, set on the stubby wings.

Then, running from almost the base of the engines to the nose of the ship, he drew lines of magnetic accelerators.

"We get some missiles as well…" He added in a single set of eight small tubes on the roof of the ship, just forward of the upper docking ring, and nodded to himself in satisfaction. "That'd clear us out, though, and then some."

"How much?" I asked.

"Half a million." He shrugged. "But that's because we'd need to upgrade the reactor as well. No way the one we've got could keep up if we got into the shit."

"I thought you said—" Ingrid started as Zac spoke quickly.

"If we had all this that's on there, drawing power from the reactor as well," he explained. "Look, this is what we *could* do with the ship. If we actually did it? We'd be flying an absolute titan. Get some shit hot shields done and upgrade the reactor to the highest-grade power core we can? We'd able to absolutely wreck pretty much anything we came across on a comparable size to us."

"So, should we do that?" I suggested to the room. "I mean, go for the basic loadout, the four lasers and the two tracking turrets for the rail guns. Then I'm guessing that the mass drivers…wait, what's the difference between the rail guns and mass drivers?"

"Size." Zac shrugged. "The rail gun turrets are a bit like automatic versions of your gravity cannon—short barrels and small, but with a decent punch. The mass drivers are literally going to be a few hundred times the length of those, and they can fire bigger projectiles. If the rail guns hit, it'll do damage. If the mass drivers hit? The impact will be like a nuke going off on their hull."

"So, basically, we don't use it on something we want to be able to loot after." I nodded. "Fair enough. So is this mass driver expensive?"

"They don't make them."

"Zac," I growled. "You're really starting to piss me off here."

"I'm not fucking with you, boss." He smiled awkwardly. "It's one of those techs that they look to have just forgotten about or bypassed. I mean, if you make a mistake with them, they'll blow up your ship, so you know, not worth the risk if you're the type to play it safe. But for us? We're on our own out here. These would let us even the odds a bit. Plus, I mean, set the missiles to trigger after launch and we could probably fire them out of a mass driver as well."

"So you'd need to build them yourself?" I asked, and he nodded. "Okay, I'm thinking you go for the shields, that's just sensible. The control runs? Sounds good. Buy the laser and rail gun turrets and make sure we've got a decent field of fire. How much is that?"

"About a hundred grand," he said. "We can go much cheaper, but I don't recommend it. And that'd include the tractor beam and replacing the ship's armoring—sorry, should have mentioned that. What we've got is pretty fucked up. A new layer of ablative and then three of armoring."

"You happy with that?" I asked Ingrid, and she nodded.

"I'll ask around and see what we can find out from our friends about the going rate for the crystals, as well as who we can deal with for the upgrades. If there's some that are worth it, we'll swap out the bits we're getting through this dockyard. Speaking of which, how badly are we getting screwed?"

"Badly," Zac admitted. "For what we need, there's only a handful of docks that are big enough, and they're making sure that they keep the price up high. We could literally buy a smaller ship brand-new for cheaper than fixing this one, but…"

"But it'd be shittier." I nodded. "Fine. Fix the ship with the locals. You've got the hundred to use, but I want you working on the mass drivers as well. They make a lot of sense."

"It's the power that's the issue." Zac shrugged. "I can do it, but…"

"What if we had a secondary reactor?" James asked suddenly, scratching his chin.

"They'd cause issues if they were too close together, and the control runs would need to be entirely rebuilt from scratch if we moved the current one to stabilize two smaller ones."

"What about a power core?" Ingrid asked. "It's a good idea, James, thank you. Zac, if the reactor would cause issues with a secondary model too close, would a power core be the same?"

"No…" he said slowly, thinking it through. "For one big enough to be worth the effort, it'd mean we lose a full room, but the advantage?" He nodded.

"What we could do is put a power core in to run say…the shields? They're the heaviest drain in a fight apparently, so what we do is this…" He pulled up the image of the ship again, and this time stripped the upper level of the armoring away, leaving the main body exposed.

He selected the reactor room, and then the rooms on either side, looking over the details before picking the one behind it, nodding as he started to speak.

"There's thicker walls here between the reactor and the power core. That'll help as there's always going to be a bit of a reaction. Then what we do is make this something like solid lead." He gestured to a new section that updated to stand between them like a thicker wall. "Gods, I wish I'd had this tech when I was making blueprints and shit for my degrees," he muttered.

"Anyway. That'll keep them safe from each other. Next, we have the power core, and a wall of power cells. That means that the core can charge the cells, and then the cells charge the shields. This way the cells are kept charged at all times, fed from the core. The core can refill the cells if they get badly drained, and the shields will be harder to drop.

"Without the shields drawing on the reactor, we can funnel all the power from there to engines and weapons, and have a secondary relay that runs direct from the power core to the main control run. That way, if need be, it can give power where and when it's needed."

He nodded in satisfaction, before sighing. "The problem, though? It's gonna be expensive." He paused, then went on quickly. "Fifty million nanites or so. I could do it cheaper—not have the power cells, for example, and that'll save twenty outright—but if we do this right, we'd have the potential to really boost the ship."

"How many nanites have we got?" I asked Ingrid, who did some quick calculations and confirmed the numbers before nodding.

"We can afford it," she said. "I'd rather keep the nanites, but we've got just under sixty-eight million, though a lot of the new ones are tied to you." She glanced at me. "So you'd need to give them up."

"This is what we got them for." I shrugged. "It's mainly the ones we looted from the corrupted and infected world, so we could always go back for more, right? I mean, we barely scratched the surface of the numbers of infected there…"

"It'd be mainly time that's the issue," Ingrid agreed, looking the system over.

We'd looked at looting one of the ships that had been left on the surface of Xiphos when we were there, planning to steal anything we could, basically…only to find that someone else had considered that.

The starships that were out in the open, and that looked to have been landed illegally, namely after the planet was locked down, had been hit from orbit by some kind of god-rod.

That was what Zac had said, anyway. The four we'd been able to spot on the surface had all been hit from above with a single high-powered impact that had shattered the back of the ship, rendering it functionally useless.

We could have learned plenty, I had no doubt—stripping the ships down for parts and mass, if nothing else—but not with hundreds and possibly thousands of corrupt swarming us while we did it.

"Okay, use the fifty million for the power core and cells. Then Belle can sort out, say, another ten million to get everyone a bit of an upgrade, make sure we've all got usable suits and shit.

"Keep what's left for an emergency, and maybe we can hit Xiphos again on the way out?" I suggested. "We build the shit we need, buy what we can, and fuck off to Xiphos on the way past. Loot another ten or fifteen million. You guys use what you can to upgrade yourselves, and then we hit the node."

"The sector node?" James said suddenly, having been looking at something on another screen.

"Yeah, the system one." I nodded.

"There might be a problem," he said slowly.

"Seriously?" I groaned. "What now?"

"The Ændari."

"What about them?"

"You remember that they'll be taking control of it soon, and that it's moving into their territory through stellar drift?"

"Yeah?"

"They don't seem to want to wait," he finished, sliding an announcement up on the wall.

Arise :Explorer

"...repeat, any and all ships passing through sector four of quadrant six. The Imperial Ændari Empire have declared the Universal System Quadrant Node as part of Ændari space. A standard rotation cycle warning has been given for all visitors to the node to evacuate.

"The Ændari are currently moving forces into the area to secure it, and have confirmed their intention to 'scour the artifact of any trespassers.'

"Please ensure, that if you are within the system limits, you leave the local area as quickly as possible. The UC and its allies cannot guarantee your safety, should you be found in contested space at the end of the countdown."

The wall shifted, showing a view with three figures seated around a table. A projection hovered between them of what I assumed was the local sector of space, with the Ændari side shown as green, and the UC as blue opposite them.

In the middle was the system node, right at the very edge of claimed space in a border system of the UC, that had now been filled with a cheerful red.

"The contested system of Scorpio is readying defenses, but the Ændari have assured us that they have absolutely no interest in the border system itself. Provided you stay away from what was, after all, built by their ancestors, they promise to stay away from you," one of the figures said, smiling with tightly pressed lips.

"Well, yes, they *would* say that," one of the others replied. "This is UC space. It's been UC space for hundreds, perhaps *thousands* of years, and the Universal System Quadrant Node is once again a flashpoint for the local forces. I say let them take it. There's no need to lose valuable lives and equipment protecting an ancient artifact that nobody can access anyway."

"I disagree," the third snapped. As a reptilian in nature, they were much bigger than the others and wore a suit that seemed to shimmer around the neck, projecting heat upward. "If the Quadrant Node was actually accessed by the Ændari, they could bring the entire quadrant to its knees, not to mention the wider effects across the rest of the galaxy. No, I say that the node should be protected, and the Ændari prevented from ever approaching it again!"

All three started bickering, in what was clearly well-established patterns, as James waved a hand and the sound cut off.

"According to their estimate, we've got some fifteen hours before they enter the system," he said. "We don't have access to the UC to ask for details on their plans, but I'd imagine, considering the situation, they won't be contesting it."

"Why not?" I asked.

"The fleet," Jonas said. "That quadrant fleet that we sent off to the far side of the galaxy—if they have the forces to send out a second group to claim the node, then either there's a lot more forces in the area than they knew about, or..."

"Or?"

"Or that fleet is back already," Ingrid said, before sighing and shaking her head. "Okay, everyone, looks like the relaxing part of the day is over. Panic time."

"One thing." I stood and looked around at everyone, waiting until I had their attention. "Just for the record? This time, it wasn't me who kicked it all off!"

Then I ran for it as the arguments and denials started.

We worked it out in the end, and after throwing more money than we wanted to at the scummy dockyard, we got an agreement to get most of the work done in eleven hours.

The first five hours were spent in a frenzied panic, one that we couldn't have pulled off if Malthus and Benat hadn't actually honored the deal and dove in to help as well.

Apparently, one of their cultural norms was that once a deal was made, that was it, so for the next week, we had the pair solidly behind us. That meant that Malthus accompanied Ingrid, Scylla, and Jonas to a meeting with his contact. Although the price we got for the crystals was nowhere near what it should have been, he—and we—had to admit, considering the deal had to be done and finished in a handful of hours, well…

It was the best we could have managed.

The seventeen thousand and change Ingrid pocketed helped to offset the extra we needed to pay to get the work done on an emergency rate, and the nearly nine hundred extra credits that Ingrid paid to Malthus and Benat ensured that they were overjoyed with the deal.

So much so, that when Malthus got back with the group, he and Benat asked to sign on as crew.

We warned them that the fecal matter was about to hit the rotary impeller, and that we couldn't tell them anything before the fight actually started; they basically shrugged and asked whether we wanted them or not.

We'd just paid them more than they'd be earning this year through any means that weren't highly illegal or immoral, and that was apparently enough of a novelty that they'd take it.

Ingrid had gone into the ship. She couldn't really help with the engineering side, but her Command access abilities meant that she could help James, and the pair of them could work with the AI integrating the new systems. Jonas and Scylla went with Malthus, and fifteen thousand credits straight to supposedly the best arms dealer Malthus knew.

The plan was that we'd get absolutely everything we could that could be used to hurt people, and then we'd scan it all into our armory for later.

While they were gone, Oxus, Paul, and I were helping Zac with a hell of a lot of random crap.

Or it was random to the others, anyway.

My Engineering sub-mind had kicked in and the sections I was working on were starting to make sense as I connected up the various power and control runs.

The warship was originally designed to be upgradable, as well as hot-swappable, meaning that in times of war they could literally land, swap sections out and back in at a shipyard, and be back in action in a matter of hours.

We took full advantage of that, removing panels and dumping them into the converters, while the new ones were being slid into place.

The turrets were prebuilt units, generic as all hell, with the lasers having four projectors on each and the rail guns having two barrels.

Once they were lowered into place, I started to seal the edges, keeping the dockworkers away, and making it look like I was just cheap, not wanting to pay them to do everything.

I even heard a few of them laughing over the fact that I clearly didn't know that they were paid regardless, and were making a fortune on the job for the "idiot."

What they didn't realize was that inside the turret and working currently were two custodians, and I was sealing the edges with nanites rather than a welder as the main crane slowly hoisted the old grav drive out of the depths of the ship.

Either of those details would have gotten a hell of a lot of unwelcome attention, considering how valuable the custodians were, but we were being damn careful to make sure that nobody knew.

That was why I was so surprised when the firefight started.

Chapter Thirty-Four

I was upside down, half inside, half outside the access port on the starboard wing, next to where the turret was being lowered by crane when it happened. I had a double handful of connections pulled out and hanging, ready to be spliced together with the final turret as it was being slid down into position.

"Ready!" I called into the comm link with the dockmaster and his crane operator, waving a hand randomly up and behind me for him to lower it down, then shouting louder when nothing happened. "Hey! I said I'm ready!" I bellowed, dragging myself out of the access port and standing on the wing, waving one hand in the direction of the control room, wondering whether they were focusing on the main crane and the second one had jammed or something.

The glass had been transparent when I'd last looked over, so when I started to wave at them again, annoyed at the delay, I was even more pissed off to see that it was suddenly as reflective as a mirror.

"What the hell?" I muttered, glaring at the windows, before waving my hands even more energetically to get their attention. "Those buggers better not have fucked off on their lunch…" I started, cursing as my waving unbalanced me in the low gravity of the dock.

One of the workers had told me before that they were lowering the gravity to enable "easier installation." So when I caught myself, even more annoyed, and standing in full view of the hangar entrance, I noticed the other "minor" detail.

Namely that the usual throng of people who were constantly passing by those windows were now entirely missing, or sprinting out of sight.

"That's…not right?" I whispered, confused and staring. The airlock that led to the main starbase opened wide. For a split second, I could see straight through to the passage beyond as both sides of the air lock opened in a way that I thought should be impossible. "Dockmaster…" I started to comm, in question, before I saw the truth.

I could see into the station. Or I could until the mass of heavily armed and armored charging figures blocked it entirely from view.

"SHIT!" I shouted, twisting and jumping to the side as at least three of the fuckers opened fire on me at once.

Arise :Explorer

"We're under attack!" I screamed into the command link, feeling the others jerk with the force of the sending, before frantically starting to move.

I couldn't focus on that personally, though, because the first of the grenades was flipping end over end toward me as I rolled to a halt, staring up at it from behind the limited cover I'd found, thrown from what had to have been one of the very few dockworkers still in sight.

Benat was the first to return fire. Her handgun flashed as she emptied half the magazine on rapid-fire into the charging bodies, even as she dove behind a stack of crates and ship parts.

She skidded out of sight just as a dozen shots slammed into the boxes. Some punched straight through, while others spanged off in all directions.

"You all right?" she shouted to me as I rolled frantically, the grenade smacking down a handful of inches from me.

It was a small disc, magnetic on one side—or so it sounded when it clacked against the hull, stopping dead—before exploding and hurling me from the hull in the fire of shrapnel.

I screamed again, this time in pain and rage, as dozens, possibly hundreds of tiny fléchettes sprayed up and out in a hundred-and-eighty-degree arc, and far too many shredded through my space suit like it was butter.

The low gravity we were currently experiencing took a direct hand then. Instead of being thrown a short distance, I was thrown through the air, at speed, heading right toward the nearest bulkhead.

I twisted on instinct. The Assault Trooper's upgrades came online and tamped down on the pain and vertigo. A combination of those tweaks, my own training, and the countless hours of literal torture joined together to drive me out of shock, and straight into a killing rage.

I popped two gravity bubbles in short succession. One flipped me around fast, planting my feet against the bulkhead, and the second lifted in the opposite direction at the same time, cancelling my inertia almost totally.

That was good, because being in low gravity wasn't to say that crashing into a wall wouldn't hurt. Inertia was a stone-cold bitch.

Looking "up" from where I was now, the ship was sitting on the wall. A hail of incoming fire was headed my way, even as the lasers washed over me, making me hiss as the reflective surface of the suit bubbled and crumbled.

At this distance, they'd still be more than enough to kill me, had I been human. Hell, was I only newly ascended, I'd be screeching with crispy skin right now, just as any other mortal should be.

I was neither of those things, though. I snarled, with my own armor starting to bubble up through my skin.

My space suit was trashed, shredded in a load of places, with blood floating free in globules as I kicked off, popping bubbles of gravity into existence. I dragged myself this way and that as I landed then propelled off, flipping myself around and diving down and out of sight of the invaders.

Or so I thought. I landed at the bottom of the "wall" from my perspective, crouching, now out of sight for the attackers behind the ship, when a fresh blast slammed into my left shoulder and sent me crashing sideways. The world around me was suddenly bathed in more of my goddamn claret.

"Sniper on the walkway," came the quiet, focused voice of Courtney into the command link. *"Firing."*

A sharp *crack* filled the air, and a second later, she spoke again.

"Target eliminated."

That was it, and *damn* did I appreciate that level of professionalism.

I appreciated it even more when the air was suddenly filled with screaming and seemingly random gunfire as Paul burst from the ship's air lock with a tomahawk and an assault rifle in his hands.

I could hear more shouts and cries now, presumably from the invaders. I growled, gripping the hole that had been blasted through the meat of my left shoulder, right where the muscle met the ball of the shoulder, and about a quarter inch below my goddamn clavicle.

Swearing like a pirate, I kicked off again. My armor finished swarming up across the shoulder now, only slightly too goddamn late. It quickly flowed onward, up my neck in a warm rush, and enveloped my head in far stronger armor than the crafted shite I'd been wearing.

The world flashed past as I reached out; my gloves shredded apart, claws extending from my gauntlets to scrabble across the hull of the ship as I grabbed and hurled myself forward again.

I practically ran on all fours. Gravity bubbles formed and popped before me, gravity increasing right ahead and reversing as soon as I reached it, shoving me onward at an ever-increasing speed.

As I cleared the arc of the ship's hull, the dock coming into sight again, I saw a half dozen bodies scattered around.

Mainly they were the invaders, but there was also one terminally unlucky worker. And ahead and to my right, a cloud of steaming blood hissed from a wound on Benat's side.

"Steve, what's happening?" Ingrid asked as calmly as she could manage.

Rather than answer, I shoved the "feed" from my senses at her, feeling her slide in behind my eyes.

"Come on, cheesedicks!" screamed Paul, leaping over a pile of debris that could have been used perfectly for defense, and instead spraying the attackers.

"We count seventeen attackers currently upright and capable," came the contact a heartbeat later from James. *"Requesting permission to link the ship's point defense turrets and open fire inside the dock."*

"Granted," Ingrid said before I could.

"Paul!" I roared. "Get down, you mad bast—"

The nearest laser jerked once, swiveling around from where it was at rest and locking onto the nearest figure.

He—or she, no way to tell in an armored space suit, really—had been hiding behind a handily stacked collection of parts. As they lifted their head up, sighting along the barrel of their gun, the point defense laser made its feelings known about their rude arrival.

"Point defense" was a bit of a misnomer, considering to provide said point defense for a fucking *starship* the lasers were both powerful enough to travel a serious distance in space, and fast enough to literally track missiles in flight.

When it opened up on the attacker, they didn't feel it.

It had to have been like someone bringing a CIWS to an old Western gunfight.

The upper third of their body simply vaporized, as did the top of the stack of already emptied crates they were hiding behind.

As did the three figures charging along the gantry behind them—or significant sections of them, anyway.

The gantry suddenly glowed cherry-red with dissipating heat. James cut the quarter-second burst off, apparently realizing that ship-to-ship weapons were a bit of an overkill in a personnel fight.

That was when the dock systems, that we'd seen on our arrival, decided it was time to play as well.

Dozens of turrets slid free of the walls, lining up on us and the ship, and opened fire in retaliation.

"Cease fire!" I screamed into my comm link, directing it at the dockmaster in the booth. "Fuck's sake, we're defending ourselves here!"

The turrets were much smaller than the ship's ones, but that didn't mean they weren't dangerous. Solid projectiles, lasers, and flames washed over us all.

I dove, dragging myself down to land behind a metal barrier on the gantry and crashing into the steel with a grunt of pain, before realizing that it was already moving, folding down on some kind of remote control to expose my position.

"Fucking hell!" I screamed. Reacting on instinct, I formed my gravity gradient cannon on my right arm as I rolled to my feet again and started desperately creating gravity pockets.

Three spun up and vanished almost as quickly as I could focus, the few hours of busy "rest" being enough for me to recover. I frantically triggered my time compression as well.

The gravity bubbles popped into being in the center of the nearest two turrets. One exploded instantly; the flames it'd been spraying out apparently did a real number in its sensitive interior.

The next simply stopped dead, the projectors for the laser requiring carefully designed mirrors and parts I probably couldn't name.

The shattering effect of thirty gravities flaring into existence and then flipping into reverse a quarter second later before vanishing again, at the very least, warped them all out of alignment.

The third one that I focused on was farther away from me, but it was directly overhead for Benat. She'd been clutching the wound in her side when the covering slid back. She had just enough time to scream and throw herself aside as it opened up. Bullets punched into the gantry where she'd just been, and then the slug thrower exploded.

It left her out of cover, though, and the attackers didn't waste the opportunity.

She took at least a dozen hits, jerking as they slammed into her, staggering her back. Blood sprayed from multiple wounds, before Paul was there.

He'd kept running, the mad bastard, straight into the oncoming fire, straight into the teeth of the damn turrets and ignoring the ship's "defensive" measures as well. And as much as the man annoyed the shit outta me at times, I couldn't deny he had balls of steel.

He literally sprinted through a hail of fire. His own armor took multiple hits. I'd not known for sure that mine would protect me against this level of fire, so I knew damn well he hadn't either.

It did, though.

Whatever their handheld lasers, the projectile weapons, and the grenades were, he staggered, but that was it—the sheer force of so many of them hitting him at once skidded him back a step, but it barely shifted his aim.

"I am a GOD, motherfuckers!" he roared at them. The modified assault rifle he held in his right hand barked out round after round that shredded armor and flung attackers from their feet.

I sprinted forward, my GGC humming as it fired again and again. The visual "sight" I'd modified into the end of it provided me a perfect view of the recipient of my little gifts as I fired and tracked to the next in line.

Twisting, I threw myself down, skidding across the last meter to slap a freshly formed nanite wing across Benat's body. Even as I scanned her, injecting a fast burst of nanites into one of her shoulders, bullets and lasers pounded off me.

Eleven serious injuries, fifteen more minor ones, mainly damage to skin and muscle, four broken bones, a shattered eye socket, fragments of the bone resting at the corner of her brain…that was the most dangerous. Move her in the wrong way, and they could cause irreparable damage.

The rest? A few punctures to her organs, several of which I didn't really understand, and a lot of small holes.

The lasers had basically cauterized their own damage. And considering that every injury she had was currently letting loose steam?

Clearly her internal temps were *a lot* higher than ours.

"How is she?" Ingrid asked me. The sound of her mental voice seemed to doppler for me as I cut the time compression.

"Not good," I said. *"We need to get her into the tubes, or we're going to lose her."*

There was a few seconds' pause, then Ingrid came back.

"Belle is on her way, as is Oxus. Protect her until they collect her, then make it clear why this was a very bad idea to whoever they are." She sounded incredibly pissed as she went on. *"Our cover is blown. There's no way that anyone who sees the recording of this can fail to recognize what we are, so it's time to make it clear that we should never, EVER be crossed."*

"Yes, ma'am," I agreed aloud. Tentacles of nanites flowed out and punched into Benat's body, hidden beneath my wings.

"Wha…" She hissed, then broke off, blood bubbling up into her throat.

"Trust me," I said. "We've got you, Benat. Just relax, and you'll get through this."

She stared at me, grabbing onto one of the tentacles in fear and my shoulder with her other hand, right over the damn wound that was healing over, though she didn't know it.

The tentacles drove into the wounds almost as quick as the original impacts had been, depositing nanites that were ordered to heal and stabilize her, before retracting and moving to the next, and the next injury.

For a few seconds, we stared at each other, shots continuing to hammer into me and bounce off. Courtney was firing steadily, as was Paul, with a level of speed and accuracy that would have been impressive if he wasn't cackling maniacally.

Then I felt their approach, the nearness of the others clear by the nanites, the command link, and yeah, the damn shaking of the gantry as Oxus's massive weight came down on his cloven hooves.

"I'm here," Belle said. My wings shifted, lifting and allowing her under. She reached out with her own nanites, far more delicately examining our ally, before nodding in satisfaction. "She's stable. Oxus, help me with her. We need to get her inside as quickly as possible."

"Here." The massive Minotaur grunted, reaching in as I came to my feet, still using my wings as shields for them.

Oxus lifted her almost effortlessly, despite her size, and cradled her to him, turning his back on the incoming fire, before trusting his armor and striding back to the ship. Belle, by his side, worked on Benat as they went.

"Does Malthus know?" I sent to Ingrid as I turned to face the half dozen survivors of the attack, all of whom were still firing, despite being surrounded by their dead and dying fellows.

"Jonas and Scylla do. They'll have told him," she assured me. *"Also, Steve, I need you to hack that control bay. The turrets are targeting our people only, not the ship. That can't be coincidence. Whoever attacked us must have taken control in there as well."*

I paused, then squinted up at the control center, and specifically the rooms that the dockmaster and crane controller were usually in, finding them highlighted in my vision by Ingrid.

"I'll take the turrets," I said into the command link, hearing the steady *crack-crack* of Courtney's shots as she continued to take them down. *"Focus on the attackers."*

"Switching targets," Courtney said, as Paul continued to do what he apparently did best.

As soon as Benat no longer needed him as a human shield, he'd taken off again. He sprinted at the enemy, firing until he ran out of ammo, then slapped the rifle to his back where the armor locked it in place, swapping the tomahawk to his right hand, throwing that and drawing his combat knife, before the ax had hit.

It did hit as well, I noticed with half an eye as my GGC slid from target to target like it was on rails. A single throw and a single kill, as with my left hand I gestured vaguely, flicking my fingers on instinct as I created and dismissed gravity bubbles again and again.

"Steve, I need that hack!" Ingrid snapped.

"On it!" I called back, taking down three more turrets in quick succession. It felt like more popped up every damn second. I reactivated my time compression, feeling the strain as it spun up so soon after I'd cut it off; I reached out with the sub-mind, focusing, concentrating…

There were a dozen signals, and they were all, I found in a second, goddamn traps.

As soon as my sub-mind touched them, it verified that the signals were blank, literally kill boxes, ready for a program to enter and then be closed off, and presumably wiped.

Well, fuck *that*.

I rerouted through the paths I'd found before, when on the station in the bar. The normal local equivalent of the Wi-Fi was strong enough that I could still connect to it through the dock's overlapping traps. And as soon as I did, it was almost ridiculously easy to route around the bay and back in.

The control room with the dockmaster and a dozen others inside came into view from the internal cameras, and I snarled at what I saw.

The dockmaster, the crane operator, and the rest of the shitbags I'd been working alongside for the last few hours? They were inside, and not under duress in the slightest.

Three of them were controlling the last few remaining turrets. Others were armored and had guns drawn, ready for whatever. And the only figure that I'd not seen before now?

A young man—possibly human, possibly not, probably a half breed as I looked him over, considering the green coloring and slight build, or a race I'd not seen yet.

He was nodding as the dockmaster barked orders at him, that he was…he was linked to a device in his hands, I could see that, almost like a comm link. But the sheer density of the data that was passing through it? It was far more bandwidth than was needed, by an order of magnitude.

I reached out for that, the signal clear as I found it, then brought up a three-hundred-and-sixty-degree swirl of frantically dancing dice.

I grinned as the sub-mind blasted through it almost before it'd finished constructing. The dice spun frantically in a blur that I barely caught before they collapsed in upon themselves. A wall of gold replaced the angry red that had filled the world; then, I was in.

The language was unknown, literally. For ten seconds, I sampled it into the local network, trying to identify it, and caught only hints here and there, before abandoning the effort.

If they'd been speaking something that was easily understood, I guessed, the dockmaster wouldn't have needed a goddamn guy in there with him; he could have simply used his own comm link.

That gave me two likely points: first, a rare language, one that was being deliberately kept off the net, or second, a code.

More likely an encrypted code or made-up language, I decided, before dismissing what he was saying as less important than who he was saying it to.

Arise :Explorer

I burst through the local node, and onward, following the traces, blurring through a thousand and more links as I chased it, passing sections I knew I'd have had to fight my way through, if I wasn't already "inside" the device, enjoying the advantage of such a huge and wide carrier signal.

Two more turrets exploded with a thought as I reached out, focusing with half a mind as the sub-mind rode the route through the space station, looping around and around, flowing through special routes, making me curse.

There were hardened connections here, ones that ignored most of the other routes I'd followed when I was digitally exploring before.

The office that came into view ten seconds later, though? It was a mess of signals, and the creature that was in the middle of it?

As soon as I saw them, they apparently saw me. Some kind of emergency monitoring program kicked in, cutting the communication link and burning the connection I was running through out at the same time, physically.

It was enough, though, and I passed the image onto Ingrid, as well as the physical location as close as I'd managed to trace it, feeling her revulsion at the sight.

"What the hell is that?" I asked her, sensing her confusion as it matched no species we'd seen yet.

"It doesn't matter," she said a few seconds later, her voice slow to me through the compression. "The dockmaster is in on this, though, whatever it is."

"Then we kill him." I reconnected to the control center and poured my sub-mind into the main hub.

"Make it quick, and make sure we get control of the dock," Ingrid said. "As it is, he can either scream for help for whatever the local police force is, or he can jettison us all out into space."

"Not anymore he can't," I growled. My Hack protocols unleashed Tsunami into their computer systems, washing through the basic levels of security like an avenging angel.

As the screens inside flickered, my control surging to wash aside the previous protocols, most of the people in the booth missed the subtle warnings.

They were staring at the humanoid who was squealing, clutching his head and shaking. The comm link he'd been using had sparked, fuzzed, then burst into flames, presumably another security precaution, and that was pretty much overkill, for most people.

He was squealing now, though, loudly and in a language I did understand. The dockmaster ordered one of the others to get him a medical kit.

One of the nearby workers grabbed it free of the wall, ripping through it, and pulled out a spray that he used, liberally dousing the burnt hand in a foaming mixture.

The green-skinned creature didn't seem to notice, though, shuddering and shaking, clutching at his head.

As he did that, the others finally noticed that their systems were no longer updating. And when they tried to connect to the outside world? Nada.

The dockmaster snarled something desperately, grabbing a key and slamming it into a recess, twisting and popping a cover off a flat, angry red button on the wall, before smashing it with a growl of satisfaction.

Then again, a second later, when absolutely fuck all happened.

Then again, each time more frantically than the last, while starting to shout at the others.

Contradictory orders were barked, countered, repeated. Those inside the room went from arrogant and practically salivating over killing us all, to utter panic as they realized that not only had they lost all control of the situation, but the doors that led out of the control room, the most secure area they had, were sealed against them.

When the two hardened and shielded turrets, high on the walls and installed as an emergency measure, suddenly spun up, lasers and projectiles filling the air and turning it into a charnel house, they panicked even more.

Chapter Thirty-Five

"Senagra," Malthus snarled as soon as he was shown the image of the creature in the office. James had handed him a tablet that showed the spiderlike abomination.

It was at least six meters across, and two tall—or I guessed it would be, if it was ever capable of standing tall again.

Instead, it was wired into a "nest" of crystals, cables, and connections. At least a third of its body was seemingly replaced by cybernetics that plugged it into the station on a deep level. Its skull was withered and skin sagged, bristling hairs were matted with filth, and oily discharge stained the metal that covered so much of its body.

In the background, a half dozen tiny creatures, gnome-like, clambered about the room, doing who knew what from the single still image I'd managed to grab before being cut off.

"An accursed senagra! Here!" he spat, shaking his head in disgust. "It dies, today!"

"What are they?" I leaned against the wall nearby, as he tossed the tablet back to James, staring up at Benat in the medical tube before him.

"What is this?" he asked instead of answering, gesturing at the cover that was laid across the lower half to the middle of the tube.

"Any clothing would be treated like a contaminant," Ingrid explained. "We needed to strip her to put her in, and I didn't think she'd want to be just 'on show,' naked."

Malthus grunted, shifting and trying to see, clearly worried that we were hiding something out of sight.

"Here." Ingrid moved the cover to expose Malthus's mate to him, making him curse as he saw the battered condition of her body. "She's making good progress. A few hours, no more, and she'll be removed. But that brings us to the problem."

"What problem?" he spat. "You're going to hit us with a medical bill? How much?"

"No." Ingrid shook her head. "She was injured protecting us and carrying out the contract you were both hired for. We're not blaming you for her injuries, and we're not accepting any blame for it either."

"What then?"

"Her condition, and this, requires some explanations, and they're not something we were intending on telling you, frankly," Ingrid admitted. "The situation, though…well, Steve's scrubbed the connection to the rest of the station, but we're sure at least some of the recording of the fight made it out."

"They started it, attacked a ship in dock with them and under repair," Malthus said, unconcernedly. "Who cares that people will see they attacked you?"

"We do," I said. "Because we're fucking hunted by the Ændari, and we were trying to keep a low profile."

"The senagra knows you're here now." He grunted. "The rest of the galaxy will know soon enough, we can hope. Is it your ship or you they're after?"

"Us. And why should we hope for that?"

"If it's selling the information, then it means the hive doesn't care. If they're hiding it? Then you've got a hive after you as well."

"A hive? Fuck's sake, that sounds like exactly what's gonna ruin my goddamn Tuesday," I muttered, rubbing at the bridge of my nose.

"Change your ship." He shrugged. "We kill the senagra, wipe its memory and sell your ship, probably to a pirate faction. Hell, it was probably one of them that put it here anyway. This way, you build a relationship with them, using its connections. If they did put it here, they'll be angry we killed it, but take that off the cost of the ship and they'll hide you from the Ændari…probably."

"Or they'll turn on us and sell us to the Ændari." Ingrid shook her head. "No, even if we wanted to sell it, we can't replace this ship. There's too much we're only just starting to get working again."

"It's a ship. Sure, it's a good one, and yeah, powerful, once everything is up and running. But unless there's a lot more of you hiding, you don't need one this big."

"We do, and there aren't." I sighed. "But the ship has things we can't give over control of, certainly not to pirates."

"You think there's a choice?" he snapped. "Someone put that thing here, and they'll have done it for a reason. They're hated enough that plugging it into the station is one of the few crimes that'll get anyone involved spaced. Even the corpo scum wouldn't cross that line, and they'd do anything for a credit. It *has* to be a pirate faction that smuggled it aboard the station."

"What is it?" Ingrid asked. "We've not found anything about them in the databases, beyond that they're banned on pain of a very painful death."

"They'll have wiped anything that would point to it from the net," Malthus ground out. "The senagra are an arachnid hive species. They used to have an empire, until they tried to turn every single world they found into a nest. They make…" He tried to find the right word, then gave up.

"They make up little triangle power structures. They spawn new ones of their kind, and each of them provides a fraction of whatever they can steal to their direct master. Then they spawn another, and another, each of those under them passing a portion of everything they get up the chain. The only way they can survive is to continually expand, to make more of them, and to encourage those under them to do the same. The higher in the chain they are? The more treasure they get."

"Treasure?" I asked.

"Everything is treasure to them: materials, information, prey, slaves…all of it. They view the entire galaxy as being against them, including their slaves. They maintain absolute control and breed as quickly as possible to survive, or they used to. Nobody's seen them for a while. There were wars fought over them, and they're one of the few things the UC, the independents, *and* the Ændari ever agreed on—that those fuckers *all* need to burn."

He shook his head, still staring at the now re-covered Benat, as she slumbered in the medical tube.

"Every so often, a new infestation spreads from those shits, and everyone drops everything to kill them. If some pirate faction was dumb enough to use one? Yeah, thinking about it now, we need to avoid them."

"We?" James asked calmly. "I take it you believe your future lies with us in some way?"

"Do you want us or not?" Malthus asked Ingrid bluntly, and then looked across at me. "You said you'd not wanted us to see this, and you didn't want us in the ship before. You could have let her die outside, and told me the contract was up. You could have cut your way out of the dock, or made that scum let you go." He gestured vaguely downward, toward the cells that we'd walked him past on the way to medical.

They held the dockmaster, one of his assistants, and the humanoid with the burned hand. All three had dropped their weapons as their companions died around them. I'd unlocked the doors into the dock from the office; then Paul, Oxus, and I had dragged the three into the cells.

The other two had seemed pissed to be left in a small cell with the communicator guy, but I'd put that down to conspirators who didn't like being around proof of their guilt. Now, though…

"We do," I said. "We need information at the very least here, and you're handy in a fight—or Benat is, anyway." I forced a smile. "Before we get into that, though, the senagra…if everyone hates them so much, why would anyone work with them?"

"Credits," he spat. "They're a hive species, each of them self-aware enough to look out for themselves and make alliances when they need to, but always for the good of the hive. That means they have a shitload of credits.

"They feed on thinking beings as much as cattle or whatever, seeing us all as the same, except that thinking beings bring more to the hive. They inject their young into their victims with a bite. As they grow, they force their host to obey their master, and to hide the bite otherwise."

"How long does it take?" Ingrid asked.

"For the young to grow?" He shrugged. "Anything from four or five rotations to thousands. They can control their growth, staying small, hiding from a population in plain sight. Then they bring more and more victims to the hive. The pupae that grows inside the host consumes its brain, taking its place, all their memories, their personality, worn like a cloak, then discarded when no longer needed.

"It means that not only do you end up with parents raising their children to be infected, you end up with entire clans or populations working silently for the hive, still producing things for sale at the market, bringing in more and more wealth, transferring it all into the hive's control until the master decides it's time for the lower ranks to grow properly. Then they burst out, and a swarm is released, anywhere from a handful of individuals to billions, all boarding ships to spread their infection across the galaxy."

"Sounds like fuckin' nightmare fuel to me," Jonas muttered. "So you think the pirates will be infected?"

"Possibly," Malthus admitted. "If not, you saw the image of the little ones, the grimalkin? Those small figures crawling around in the background?"

"Yeah?"

"They'd not be anywhere near that thing if they weren't under its control, so either one of them has taken over a pirate faction and they're using it as their cover, or they've provided it with prey, and the pirates are using it in some way. Probably getting it to share all the information it gets, then they hunt whatever they want."

"And the attack on us?" I asked.

"Probably too tempting for it to pass up on," he said. "You've seen the way that everyone looks at the ship. There's a few out there that are pirate owned, or so I hear, and the UC go mad trying to catch them, because people know that in UC space if a warship approaches, you surrender and let them board you to search for contraband.

"Try and run, and the UC sends a load of ships to hunt you down; then you get executed. Let them board? Unless they find something really bad, you get a fine and that's about it. If the senagra had one of these UC ships, they could board hundreds of other ships easily, infect more and more, and spread like wildfire."

"You think the dockmaster is one of them?" I asked.

"Probably not..." He paused, then sighed. "Look, I don't know, all right? If he is? Chop his head open, and we'll know straight away."

"And if he isn't, we've lost a prisoner." Ingrid shook her head. "There has to be a better way."

"There's dozens," he said. "I've heard there's blood tests you can do that show it, but the records that are on the hub? Expect it to have wiped or altered them. You'll never know if the results you get are right, because the records will show what they want you to see."

"And there's nothing in any of the databases." I nodded. "So we know the fucker already got in there."

"Why'd you capture them alive?" he asked us suddenly. "You took those three prisoner...why?"

"Didn't know what else to do with them," I admitted. "They surrendered, so I took it. Figured if nothing else, we can drain their accounts, then hand them over to the local police."

"The same ones who've probably not even commed yet to see what all the firing was about?" He grunted. "Yeah, good luck with that. Best you can hope for is that they space them. Worst case, some of them will owe them favors, and they'll claim you attacked them."

"Okay…" I muttered, thinking fast. "Well, nobody knows what happened here yet, besides the spider thingy, so how do we register the dock as ours instead of theirs?"

"What?" He squinted at me in surprise. "You want to stay here?"

"No, but we can sell the dock, right?" I suggested. "I mean, it's a big fucking dock. It's got to be worth something."

"Only if whoever wants it can hold it." He shrugged. "If you could get engineers to work it, and maybe a team that wanted it, sure, it'd be worth decent credits. But there's no defenses, so you'd need an army to hold it, or the other dockmasters will try to take it. Sell it to them and you'll get a fraction of a fraction of its worth, unless…"

"Unless what?" I asked.

"Look, do you want us or not?" he countered. "Either we go with you or we stay. If we stay, then maybe I could find someone to take the dock off your hands and get you some credits. But it'd not be anywhere near the real value, and it'd not be straightaway."

I looked at Ingrid, who looked at me and then spoke into the command link.

"Any objections to bringing them in?" she asked. *"We barely know them, but…"*

"But we're floundering around in the dark without a local guide, and the UC lot, while we're now a part of them…" I left it hanging.

"Yeah," Jonas added. *"We can't trust the UC lot either. They're all going to be out to get whatever they can from us. If we take these on, at least if they cross us, no offense, but we can kill them and space the bodies. I say give them a chance—activate their nanites but not give them full access to their systems yet. Unlock at most the War path maybe. But Ingrid, you said that we were designed to be upgraded and shit by the Ændari, right, and have them in control, not us?"* Jonas said.

"Yes?"

"Well, can you do that?" he asked. *"Keep their upgrades and system locked to your control? Then if they try to stab us in the back, they can't do anything without your permission, so at least they can't grow too powerful and unlock other people or anything."*

"That's…that's a good idea," I said, hearing others in the group adding their agreement.

"I'm not sure how to do that," Ingrid admitted. *"I'll see what I can do, though. And failing anything else, once we're at the node, we should be able to reset Steve's link and reach out to them and if need be, he can use his authority to sever them from the system, I guess?"*

"Sounds like a good plan," James agreed. *"I suggest that you tell them you have the capacity to unlock their system, if they can even be unlocked for other races. Actually, quick point of order…we, as humans, were designed to use these systems, and the Ændari clearly gave themselves access to some of the same*

abilities through the nanites, after testing them on ourselves. They essentially used us as guinea pigs, from what we know, yes?"

"Yeah..." I agreed, wondering where he was going with it.

"Well, they didn't create the other races. The nanites that infect them all, they're never going to be as efficient as our own, are they? They may unlock the same abilities, some of them, but unless the nanites are designed to work with their systems completely, or they are rebuilt as human from the ground up by the nanites, they'll never be able to react and make use of the system in the same way. In fact, I suspect that the Ændari have less use of the system than we do as well.

"Unless they entirely redeveloped the system for themselves, they'll be stuck using a secondary patch. Think of the leading smartphone on Earth, then imagine writing the software designed for that over a machine that was made with a touch screen by a competitor. It may work, but it'd never be as seamless as the system it was developed for."

"So you think that's why they're so desperate to get access to Earth?" Zac asked into the silence. *"Not just the people for them to use as BWVs or whatever, but if they can get access to the original systems, they can adjust them more for their own use?"*

"Might be. Hell, it makes sense right? The node, if they can get access to that, it's going to let them find Earth, and we know they want access to the systems, presumably to turn everyone else's nanites off. Only thing I don't get is why they didn't do that in the last war, you know, before they lost access to the node?"

"They probably couldn't," Zac replied. *"Not without fucking themselves as well."*

"Explain that," I said.

"If the node can be made to shut down all the nanites by a signal, what's the chances they can make it work on just humans? Or just the UC?" He shrugged mentally; the image that he provided to us all seemed to be braced against a wall opposite me, moving quickly, struggling to connect things we couldn't see. *"We think they unleashed the nanite plague, right? Well, that fucked them as well as the UC. What if what happened was that the node's ability to turn everything off isn't like flipping a switch. What if it's a doomsday tool?"*

"A last resort, if they're getting wiped out..." I muttered.

"Or, it was never designed to be 'aimed' at a race or whatever. Most likely, anyone who makes something like this, they'd make it as a countermeasure to the nanites, so if the plague burns too hot and looks like it's going to kill everyone, then the nodes fire, and wipe out ALL the nanites."

"So they'd not be able to use it, not to shut down everyone else's nanites," I guessed.

"They would," James suddenly added. *"If they weren't planning on being inside the blast radius."*

"SHIT." Zac gasped. *"That's it! That's why they're so desperate to get the details for Earth! If they get their asses there fast, they could harvest it. Take a shitload of people to search for uncorrupted makers and more, then load them up and boom, they're out of here. That fleet? The one they had turn up, looking for*

us? What if it's not meant for a battle with the UC? What if they've been planning this shit for ages, and they're planning on fucking off instead of fighting?"

"Can they do that?" I asked. "I mean, the UC said that the Ændari can't get into the nodes either, right?"

"They couldn't," he replied. *"Maybe—hell, maybe I'm wrong…shit, I hope I am, all right, boss man? But…if they'd been planning this shit for a while, and we know just how goddamn evil they are? It's not like they'll be stopping themselves because it's morally wrong, right?*

"What if the nanites plague that made the corrupted was just the first stage? But it got out of control and infected them as well, so they've taken some time to recover. Maybe they found the plans, or this shit just occurred to them afterward, but let's say they're planning on firing this weapon and erasing all the nanites in this section of the galaxy.

"If they're getting everything ready to do just that, they've given up on finding us, on getting access to the shit we have, then just as they're getting ready to fuck off, planning a big surprise for the UC and everyone else? Then they find out Earth is somewhere in this quadrant? Or at least someone who knows where it is, is here? They'd be desperate to load up on the bounty before they accidentally wiped us out. Think about it. They go to Earth, load up on a few hundred thousand of the fittest and most mentally unstable of us, leave the rest behind, and they get out of Dodge.

"Then, they trigger the wipe, erase everyone's nanites, then come steaming back in. You'd have the UC soldiers all dead, or at the least a lot less able to fight. And the rest? Anyone who's being kept going by their nanites is dead. Too old? Weak, whatever? Dead. Launch an attack then, come sailing in with your ships again and just mop it all up."

"That makes far too much sense, and would explain the sudden need to claim the node as well. They could just leave it for a few months or years and it'd be back in their space, no need to rile the UC and risk them counterattacking," James said softly. "Instead, they know that the UC is going to be searching for humanity as well. If they get there first, then the UC has access to possibly billions more soldiers. They'd be wiped out almost overnight if that happened, so they're moving now, probably ahead of schedule."

"Grab any they can, then run," I finished for him. *"Dammit, it makes sense."*

"Then we need to move," Ingrid said aloud. "The mission just got even more desperate."

"You finally finished talking about me?" Malthus growled.

"What?" I frowned. "Ah fuck, dammit, no. Sorry, man. We just put something together, that's all. We knew we needed to move, but we didn't realize just how badly."

"So?" he prompted.

"Yes," Ingrid answered for us all. "Yes, we're offering you a position with us, but it comes with rules."

"Tell me."

"First, for the short-term until we know you better, certain information is going to be off-limits. That means that if we tell you to leave the room, to stop questions, or anything like that? You do it. No questions asked." She counted the points off on her fingers.

"Second, this is a permanent position, or at a minimum five years, uh, twenty seasonal cycles, I guess is what you're used to—we'll teach you our measurements—and it covers you both."

He nodded his understanding.

"Third, you'll be paid well for this, but anything that you gain beyond the wage we agree, in the short-term at least, is ours. We might need to spend it or use it for the good of the mission. Once we can explain everything, you'll understand that, or you'll be gone and won't care.

"Fourth, your only loyalty is to us. We tell you where to go; when and where we can, we'll explain why. Again, it'll make sense or it won't. I'm sorry, but we can't risk anything else.

"Fifth and final rule. You'll be getting into the tubes as well. We can't wait for you to see her get out and make any decisions on the evidence. Our technology will strengthen you, make you heal a lot faster and be far more deadly in battle. But to get to the point that we need you to be? It's going to be a basic unlocking we can do, not a full one, and we'll have to hope that when you're unlocked, your systems reboot on their own. Again, I can't explain more, I'm sorry."

"You're asking for a lot of trust." He grunted. "How much?"

"How much do you want?" Ingrid countered.

"You drained those cockroaches' accounts yet?"

"No…"

"If you get over a hundred thousand from any accounts we hit before leaving, I want whatever is over the top as our fee, and…" He hesitated, before going on. "I'll trust you on two conditions."

"A hundred thousand is a hell of a lot to have in an account," I pointed out as he waited. "What's the conditions?"

"You get them to sign the dock over to someone I nominate, and you get a forty-five percent share in the profit, but not for the first five years."

"We give you the dock, we get a random promise of profit in five years," I translated. "Your friend can sell it and fuck off," I pointed out.

"I'll pass it to a devilkin engineer I know." He shook his head. "She'll run it as an honest dock. It'll give our people a position here that's not dependent on selling ourselves in one way or another. Five years of no profit because it'll take that long to turn the dock around, rebuild it, and get a decent crew in here who can make it a real, genuine future for them all. They won't pass up a chance like this."

"And the risk of others coming to take it?" I asked, then snorted and nodded. "Gotcha, the devilkin mercenaries…this gives them a place to bring anything they have, and you can make it into a hub for your people. They're not going to sell that."

He nodded. "Exactly."

"And the other condition?"

"You help us take down the senagra, and any infected," he said. "This place isn't going to be worth anything in five years if we leave that thing here."

"We've got no time," Ingrid said.

"Your ship's still half open to space and the grav drive isn't installed yet," he pointed out. "That's a few hours at least for a good engineer. You agree, and we go hit them now—slaughter the fucking thing and all its slaves. And while we're doing that, I call in my people."

"What people?"

"Every single devilkin who's not on a job right now on the entire station. We take a small team with us, enough to get the job done, and the rest stay here and protect and work on your ship."

"Why not take all the devilkin and fuck that thing up right now?" I asked. "No need for us to get involved."

"If I try to take a bunch of devilkin without a formal merc contract in place into that section of the station? Get ready for a riot." He snorted. "With us working for you, registered as a regular contract, and you heading there to negotiate like you said you already wanted to? Easy. You said more than once that you wanted to meet the corpos. That's our 'in' to the more exclusive areas of the station. Once there, we split up: Ingrid goes to the meeting, you lead a small team of us, and we go take care of the senagra."

"And the hundred thousand credits?" I asked, seeing it now. "You think the senagra is going to be much richer than that, and you get whatever is over a hundred thousand. A normal hit and run, or a burglary or whatever, it's never going to come with that kind of a credit balance, so offering us the first hundred sounds good, but if they have a million, well, you just got ninety percent of the windfall."

"So make me a better offer," he said. "My offer gets you out of the station on time still, and you make a serious profit as well…not to mention, you don't have to pay the last dockmaster."

"We take half," Ingrid said. "We take half of whatever credits we find in the accounts we get access to while we're here, but any schematics, technology, or information is ours. If it's something we need, we need to retain control. The credits we can agree on, but the information is a hard line, nonnegotiable."

I glanced at her, feeling the sudden excitement from her, and I hesitated, then shrugged internally and backed her on it.

"All technology…what does that cover?" he asked suspiciously.

"Everything," she said. "Anything we gain access to between now and you being brought into the full secret of our mission…all technology and items of technology are ours. This dock? We'll give it to your recommended people, and we take fifty percent. We'll be silent partners, as we're unlikely to even return this way for a while, but any work that is done on our ships, or those of our faction, are for cost.

"Technology includes ships we capture, weapons, armor, and anything else. You get your people here as fast as possible, and they do as Zac says, including using any and all parts that we need that are in storage in the dock to repair our ship for free. You get the credits and the dock itself. You're securing a literal future for your people here, so don't get greedy. Better we all win out of this."

There was a long pause as he apparently mulled over his options, before nodding.

"I agree," he said. "From now on, we're yours."

<u>Chapter Thirty-Six</u>

The transport cube we all stood in was more than a bit cramped, especially considering the five bloody huge devilkin that had come with us.

Two were loaded for bear: massive guns on their back, axes on their hips and handguns, grenades…the full works.

Malthus had upgraded his armor, wearing something that was halfway between my own more organic designs and the UC soldier's power armor designs. And by the sounds he'd made when he first put it on? It definitely wasn't powered.

He was sweating already, but the sheer mass of the metal suggested that he was taking his "tank" duties seriously. He was carrying something like a tri-barreled submachine gun, and had a broad, two-headed ax on his back now.

The fourth guy was a combination sniper and medic, with a custom-built, long-range laser that I doubted would see much action in the short corridors, but I could be wrong.

The final guy, though, was the most interesting. He carried a small axe, more like a bearded hatchet in design, a handgun on his hip that could probably double as siege equipment, and on his back, ready, was a massive shield. His armor was weird as well: still made of heavy slabs of metal like the others, but more load-bearing with what looked to be power cells all over the place.

Malthus assured me that they'd get the job done, though, and they were all extremely good at their roles.

Malthus had come through with the engineers as well, and half an hour after we'd agreed, the first of them had started work. Ten minutes after that, the dock looked like a kicked anthill, it was that full of bodies.

The former dockmaster Bob had seemed absolutely horrified to find he'd been working for the senagra. He was even more horrified when he found out beyond any reasonable doubt when Jonas neatly bisected the head of the communications guy he'd been dealing with, exposing the nestled parasite inside.

When Bob realized that he'd not only been assisting but had been actively locked up in a small cell with a senagra? He went mental trying to be helpful and prove he wasn't one of them.

By this time, I'd already cleaned out his accounts and those he'd enlisted of his family and friends to attack us, considering them fair game after that.

That'd brought us back up to nearly two hundred and four thousand credits. And taking control of the dock? It was even easier than I'd been expecting. Bob was well aware that the sentence for anyone working with the senagra was death, generally by booting them out of the nearest air lock as soon as they were found, so he was fast in doing exactly what he was told, and desperate to do anything that would curry favor with us after the disastrous attack.

I got the feeling that under normal circumstances he'd have tried something, some kind of trick to keep something, and some form of control. He knew, though, as Malthus pointed out, that even his own life mate would space him without hesitation for working with the senagra.

That meant that his literal only chance was to prove himself too useful to kill.

We'd found an easy way to identify the senagra, fortunately, and the killing of that fucker was more of the way in the nature of a test of concept as much as anything else.

I'd been examining them as carefully as I could at Ingrid's suggestion. I'd found that using my sonar-like senses and shifting up and down in the frequencies, I could literally peel the layers away, peering into his brain and seeing the creature nestled there.

I'd also found that using the exact same senses, I could probably sense through Ingrid's clothes as well, which was tempting as all hell when I realized it, imagining myself as having x-ray vision and being able to walk around with everyone suddenly naked around me.

It'd been a fond boyhood fantasy, after all, as I went through puberty, imagining the abuses of power I'd be able to achieve if I'd been Superman.

I enjoyed it right up until I realized that it meant that everyone—and that included Zac and Paul, unfortunately—would be naked around me whenever I triggered the ability, and...with a tiny, *tiny* fraction of a fragment more power used, I was literally surrounded by fleshy walking skeletons, which was just freaky.

The only way I could use this ability without a *hell* of a lot of practice to, for example, sneakily undress Ingrid, was to accept that I'd be more likely to see her minus her skin, which was the utter opposite of sexy.

Or use the absolute least amount of power I could, when she was wearing very little already, in which case, you know, I'd rather see with my eyes and try to get us both in the mood instead.

It was a bit disappointing really, but considering the absolute sausage fest that half my day was with the lunatics around me now, I decided I was glad to be able to *not* see through their clothes after all.

Plus, as much as I'd fantasized over it as a teenager...well, it kinda felt wrong now. Maybe I was growing up, as unbelievable as that sounded.

Now, twenty minutes after leaving the dock, we were in a transport cube, jam-packed close together, with me standing protectively behind Ingrid—just in case—Paul on my left, with Jonas and Scylla on my right, and that mad chef Jay, dragged out of the kitchen and armed for the event.

Jonas, Paul, and the devilkin were going with me, Jay and Scylla with Ingrid, and the ship was pretty much on lockdown.

Ingrid had made the situation exceedingly clear to the devilkin community leader who had turned up—Jacqui, the bartender and owner of the bar we'd gone to first—that if they tried anything, *anything* with the ship or our people?

James would fire the point defense lasers first and ask questions of whatever could be mopped up of them later.

We also had Courtney still aboard with him. Casey was helping Zac to direct people. Oxus stood around in his nanite armor, essentially looking fucking terrifying and holding a rifle that could be used to clear orbital debris.

Lastly, Belle was wandering around, not so much fixing anything for the ship, but doing a "hearts and minds" job, using a few of the nanites we'd plundered from the bodies of our attackers and healing up injuries that the devilkin had from previous fights.

That in itself was making her, and by extension us, insanely popular with them.

Now, as the transport cube rocked slightly, changing tracks and heading deeper into the private—*rich*—areas, the cube steadied and seemed to no longer be in danger of falling apart every few seconds.

"Newer and better maintained magnetic rails," Malthus grunted when Jonas looked confused. Thirty seconds later, the cube slowed to a smooth stop. As soon as the doors opened, it was clear that we weren't in Kansas anymore.

Most of the sections we'd just left were reasonably well maintained. Sure, the residential area, the poor one that we raided, was a bit shitty, but it's a space station: poor maintenance in sections that are too close to the exterior mean deaths, so in the mainly busy areas it was maintained.

It just wasn't a concern that it should also be made pretty.

As such, it was a hodge-podge of welded panels, different colors, flashing neon lights, and humidifiers that made some races' favorite hangouts into chokingly wet areas…and five meters farther on, bone-dry air washed over you.

Heat washed out of some buildings, drying the sweat that ran down your back, and then the cold froze you as you veered too close to the next door.

The entire space station that we'd seen up until now was full of dripping rust and runoff, of fresh paint alongside rotting remains, and everything in-between. A hundred species all tried to make their little section perfect for them and their kind, and fuck everyone else.

This area, though?

It was nothing like that.

The walkway ahead, all three meters of it, before it hit the security checkpoint, was clear and polished. The metal walkway was covered with a black rubber-like coating that ran from wall to wall.

The walls were a neutral muted yellow, with the ceiling in cream, and a multitude of colored lines painted on it, running from the security checkpoint deeper into the private zone behind them.

"Step up to the line and present ID," a bored-sounding voice called out, and I followed Ingrid as she led the way.

"Good afternoon," she said with a closed-lip smile. "Ingrid of Gaia's Vengeance to meet with the Amalgamation Corporation of Vainsu. We have an invitation."

"And your companions?" The guard sounded utterly bored to fuck.

"Local security contractors and my companions."

"You and your ship are responsible for their actions in this zone. Any damage or crimes they commit are regarded as your own. Do you accept?"

"I do," Ingrid agreed.

"Security tags." The figure stepped out of the checkpoint to offer them to Ingrid. He was small, perhaps four feet tall, and looked more like one of those yellow-eyed primates from Madagascar than anything else, to my mind.

The uniform only made him look cuter, and I felt Ingrid's internal "squeeee" of delight at seeing him.

Then she coughed, smiled again, and took the tags, securing them to our armor, one at a time with a firm press.

"All tags are showing as active." The guard sighed. "Please follow the green line to the main section. Amalgamation Corporation is the eleventh on your left. Any deviation by your party will be noted."

"Thank you." Ingrid nodded to him, and the barrier that sat squarely between our arrivals area and the rest of the floor retracted, allowing us to step through.

I nodded and smiled at the figure as we walked past, reaching out with my more digital senses and finding the security post's signal instantly.

Its security was fair—nothing fantastic, nothing too cheap—and as we moved through the checkpoint, I slid into the system easily.

We moved quickly. Ingrid led the way, me by her side until we were away from the checkpoint, then taking a left to follow the green line painted on the ceiling.

I reached out, seeking and finding a collection of cameras, sensors, and scanners all searching us as we went. I shifted slightly, hating that not only had Ingrid managed to talk me into this, but that she'd somehow found the time to transfer my goddamn monkey suit onto the ship in the first place.

She wore a smart pantsuit, or whatever they were called, but me? I wore the insanely expensive penguin suit she'd had made for me before I met her parents so long ago.

It barely fit me, and that was after James had worked some literal magic with it.

I *hated* that I wore such a thing, especially here, but as Ingrid had pointed out, we needed to look the part, and when I went to start the party with the senagra, it was better not to look like exactly what I was.

In reality, it'd take literal seconds for my armor to form, but for now, the security forces believed we were there for the obvious reason: the meeting.

I walked by Ingrid's side, only dimly aware of the world around me as I guided the sub-mind's work, taking over first the security checkpoint, and then the local system, sliding my questing search programs in silently.

I found that there were a bunch of other programs in there doing exactly the same, and the security system was basically full of spyware. There were so many other programs in there, taking up space, in fact, that the entire system was close to breaking down from the load alone.

That meant it was easy as it could be to find our security tags in there, copy the codes they were transmitting from my squad and flip them over to be repeated by the ones that Ingrid and her team were wearing.

Blinking away the digital world, I nodded to Ingrid, letting her know it was done, and we exchanged a quick kiss, a brief wink and a hug, before committing that most cardinal of sins and splitting the party.

We turned and headed right at the next cross section, the corridor that we'd all been following having a handful of cross-connecting ones, each deliberately designed to make the area look less affluent and luxurious than it was.

The first section we'd found, when I'd remotely accessed the cameras, was entirely security, filled with barricades, gates, and reception areas designed to basically keep the riffraff at bay.

The next area was all corporate, and was used to keep the companies' official front-facing sections accessible, but nice still. This was also the section that the outsiders, both in terms of visitors and staff who lived elsewhere in the station, got to see.

Then there was the storage area, supposedly for most of the things that were needed on this level.

After that were the mid-range homes…and then, when there should be absolutely no reason for any of the lower socio-economical groups to ever set foot in it? That was where it all changed.

The section behind the "normal" middle management housing was an honest-to-God forest. All internal, protected from the deadly radiation and the vacuum outside, was a wide band of life-giving greenery; a narrow river, where water was as expensive as hard liquor, ran along its length. And on the far side were the really posh houses.

Most of them looked more like mansions than anything else, but given the confines of the station, they were all single story, just wide and long.

When I'd discovered them, searching for the senagra, I'd been stunned, but showing it to Ingrid and the others, I'd found that beyond the first response of "What the hell is a forest doing here!," there was actually a sound reason for it.

Using reclamation technologies meant that the water wasn't actually that expensive to produce and gather. Mainly, it was being kept expensive by artificial means—like diamonds weren't actually that rare or special, they just had better marketing.

The plant life, in turn, provided cleaner air to this section, reducing the draw on the oxygen tanks and providing a method of regeneration if there was ever an air shortage.

For oxygen breathers, anyway.

When I'd asked if all stations had this, there'd been a mixed response from Malthus. Apparently lots did, but they were generally phased out for the space requirements, and it was far cheaper to set up machine-based solutions.

All of that was interesting, sure, but beyond giving us a good idea of the kind of people we were dealing with, mainly corpo scumbags who were the same the galaxy over, the best bit?

It was that there were extremely limited places that the senagra could be.

Having seen the area it was in through the eyes of technology, tracing the connections to roughly this section of the station, but being unable to get it any closer than that, we were left with somewhere that had a shit-ton of connections for all the cabling, a ready stream of in and out that the drones or whatever could hide in, and a solid and secure area.

That gave us either the corpo offices and tech outposts, which were obvious targets for the other corpos to try to break into, or the storage areas that were ostensibly used to store food and random samples that were needed by the companies.

That was perfect because you likely had both privacy—considering the rich didn't like actually having to deal with such things themselves—and the high-strength security conditions.

That was my thought, anyway.

With that in mind, I'd done a search for the power cabling and any freshly laid crystal connectors, thinking that if there'd been a presence here for very long then the entire station would likely have been taken over already.

It took seventeen seconds to find the obvious location, and that was…well. It was uncomfortably fucking unmistakable, frankly.

Many of the storage sections had little or no power requirements, beyond a little heat and lighting, and certainly no need for high-speed data access.

One of them, though? Right next to the main communications hub for the sector?

It was drawing almost a third of the power that was in use for the entire sector, making me shake my head in disgust. Either it was an insanely obvious trap, or they'd never considered how porous their network was, and how obvious the entire thing was if someone went looking.

Personally, I'd have built a generator and used the power from that to stay off the grid. But then, thinking about the generators and power systems they had access to, that was probably even more obvious.

Either way, that was where we were headed. As soon as we'd crossed the main corridors, leaving most of the foot traffic and passersby behind, we picked up the pace.

"What kind of defenses are we likely to find?" I asked Malthus again, getting the same answer as the last time I'd asked, which was a shrug.

"As much as the hive believes they can get away with, while still maintaining secrecy."

That was just *so* helpful, honestly, and I was about to tell him that, when a security guard stepped out into the path ahead of us, stopping dead when he saw us, the security tags, and then looking at the area we were in.

We were at the edge of the storage section, closer to the target than I'd thought we'd get, and nowhere near as close as I was hoping we'd make it, before we were forced to go all out.

The guard was another of the fuzzy-faced, primate-looking mofos. And as agreed, I stepped up, smiling, and ready to try to talk our way out of the confrontation, when I remembered I had another option.

Rather than playing nice, or possibly shooting an innocent guard, I formed a solid mesh of nanites on my chest, under my formal, gleaming white shirt and suit jacket, and I sent a gravitational pulse out at him.

It was weak, barely enough that he frowned, feeling something strange, but as he opened his mouth to question us, the repeat came back, bouncing off the wall behind him and finishing the image in my mind.

"Oh, thank God," I grunted, before drawing the handgun that Zac had provided for me—via Zac copying Jonas's favorite gun—and I shot the guard in the head.

There was a second of stunned silence from the devilkin with me, as beyond Malthus they'd never worked with me yet and there was no trust built up, before Jonas spoke up.

"So…senagra?" he asked.

"Oh, crap, yeah." I shrugged. "Sorry. I thought me shooting him in the face was kinda obvious."

"I just thought you didn't like guards," Paul said. "You tend to kill a lot of them. I thought you were like some Jack the Ripper sorta guy."

"Seriously?" I half turned, waving the gun at him in annoyance, gesturing with the barrel between myself and the body as it collapsed to the floor. "We're in enemy territory, surrounded by people who don't know us, and you think that drawing a comparison between me and a murderous psychopath is appropriate right now?"

"If the shoe fits." He grinned at me.

"It doesn't!" I snapped.

Jonas moved past me quickly, grabbing the security guard's weapons and a set of "keys"—narrow rods of crystal that looked more like they should be worshipped by a hippie than anything else—and pocketing them. Then he grabbed the body and dragged it back around the corner and out of sight.

"He was a fucking murderer. He hunted hookers, for God's sake, and…"

"Boss, not the time," Jonas growled at me, and I glared at him, then Paul, before shaking my head and stomping after him.

"I win," Paul muttered, grinning widely, as the devilkin, now thoroughly disturbed, followed us.

"Paul, you remember those pushups that Court got you out of last week?" Jonas asked.

"Yeah?"

"PT just became part of your life again. When we get back, a hundred weighted pushups for making the boss look like a dick."

"No worries." Paul shrugged. "The way my body is these days? I'll do that in my sleep."

"Not when I increase the gravity you won't," I growled.

"Ah crap."

We picked up speed then. The massive devilkin spread out, two moving into the lead, two behind, with Malthus staying close to me. The eight of us went from a jog to a sprint.

We'd covered perhaps thirty meters, barely getting up to speed, before the first pair of turrets slid out of the wall ahead and opened fire on us.

The lead devilkin threw up an arm. The shield that he'd been carrying on his back since we met him now dropped into place and connected to all his power cells.

It was almost two meters across and half a meter deep, and it took most of the incoming blasts with barely a shudder. A force shield similar to the kind that was used on ships flared into life to take the first hits.

He slowed, clearly having difficulty holding the mass up, and for the first time, his loadout made sense.

Instead of being there to fight like the rest of us? He was literally a walking shield. In a world where turrets and similar tech were common, it was a genius solution.

He might be fuck all use in the fight, be slow and not last very long before the power was drained and the metal was shredded to buggery, but for as long as it lasted?

The turrets were automatically focusing on the closest threat, and as he ran at them, they literally ignored everything else so they could fire on him.

That gave the others time to fire on the turrets and take them down.

I followed along in the middle, hurrying but careful not to overrun our allies, wanting to see what they could do.

That the senagra had been observing through the system when we were under attack at the dock was beyond any reasonable doubt. There was no damn logical reason it'd not have been, after all; the sheer number of shitty monitor programs in the system when I went looking meant that there was no realistic way I'd ever be able to track down and sanitize the evidence we'd been here, so fuck it.

The only thing I could do was try to minimize the number of witnesses, and beyond that, just get on with the job at hand. That meant allowing the professional mercenaries to do their job, and making a mental note of them just in case I needed more troops later on.

With that in mind, I triggered my own armor, sighing in relief as it bubbled up, flooding me and *totally* by accident shredding my monkey suit.

Honest. Complete accident.

We took the corner. The shield bearer ran straight into a barrage of focused fire that sent his high-tech shield almost all the way to failure in a matter of seconds, even as the sound of running feet announced others closing on us from both the last corner behind us and approaching ahead at once.

The shield surged with a last boost, before flickering and cutting out. The bearer dropped to brace it against the ground, while he palmed two grenades around the edge of it, banking them off a wall to land somewhere out of my sight as we piled up on the corner.

"Orders?" the biggest of the devilkin, whose name was apparently Elrah, barked at me, and I blinked, then sighed.

"How about 'fuck them all up'?" I shouted back.

"Limits?"

"You're seriously asking this *NOW*?" I snarled.

"He wants to know how brutal you want it, and how much collateral damage," Malthus clarified.

"Fuck them up, make it bad, don't screw the tech too much." I shrugged. "Beyond that, no big holes in the space station."

"You'll take responsibility?" he asked.

The way he tilted his head and fixed me solidly with a glare made me guess he was somehow recording this.

I hesitated, then decided fuck it—in for a dime, in for a dollar.

"I'm a lawful representative of the UC," I said formally, figuring it might as well be worth a try. "I've discovered an infection of the senagra and I'm taking tactical control of the station. Kill them all. The UC Council will take full responsibility and credit, as well as covering any costs incurred."

Fuck it, might as well give them both the carrot and the stick, after all.

Anyone who I was worried about seeing this realistically would know who and what I was anyway. Beyond that, I might as well share the pain around as much as possible.

"Understood. Hold the corner while we take the defenders out," he said, giving me what I guessed was meant to be a happy smile, or maybe reassuring.

Coming from a creature that looked like a demon of legend, with a set of great white-looking teeth and four glowing red eyes, lit from within by an ominous red light?

It was anything *but* reassuring.

The devastation they unleashed a quarter second later was gratifying, though.

They each triggered their smaller, and clearly lower-tech shields, stepping out and bracing, firing in a fast barrage just as the grenades the first guy had thrown went off.

I guessed that they were remote control by the perfect timing, but who knew.

Jonas, Paul, and I faced back the way we'd come. Malthus helped the other mercs, as they took heavy hits, staggering slightly, but continuing to fire.

That was when Malthus stepped out into the corridor, taking at least a dozen hits in the first few seconds, until his rifle opened up. A veritable avalanche of laser fire roared downrange.

There was barely a second between us getting into position, and the oncoming mass taking the corner, and *damn.* The sound of running feet had been clear as we braced up on the corner, but I'd not even considered the sheer number of the buggers would include security drones.

Three took the corner, a heartbeat ahead of the fastest of the runners, and they barely waited to sight in on us before opening fire. Flames washed across the distance like napalm given free will.

The runners who cleared the corner behind them already had rifles lifted, and they opened fire as well, stitching the devil's needlepoint across the walls as they tracked in on us.

At the same time, two more turrets, farther down the corridor in the opposite direction of the one we'd been headed to and seemingly hidden until now, activated. They spun up as the rate of incoming fire directed at the devilkin suddenly ramped up.

Clearly the senagra had been ready for us coming, and we'd walked right into a trap.

Chapter Thirty-Seven

My helm slid shut as the first hits slammed into Paul, who now stood the farthest to the left of the three of us. He barely seemed to notice, his rifle chattering as he unloaded dozens of rounds, slamming into and straight through the fliers.

"Jonas!" I barked. "Turrets!"

"On it," he replied grimly, switching from the four-legged bounding figure that'd just cleared the corner, firing at almost the exact second he spoke.

The massive handgun punched a hole through the creature, something like a fatter, balding werewolf, wearing Lycra pants. The hole that appeared high on the brow, drilling through the skull and into the body behind like the worst-aimed enema in the world, rendered whatever species the fucker *had* been moot.

I had my own new handgun out, and I fired three shots blindly into the oncoming mass, trusting some fucker to catch them for me.

I was far more focused on the gravity bubbles I was forming, forcing myself to reach deeper and faster than I'd had to in a while.

The first bubble appeared in the middle of the walkway, back behind the forerunners and around the middle of the lucky pack of winners.

It was a solid ten gravities, dragging inward toward a tiny fraction of the corridor.

The second and third were ahead of it, on the left and right of the corridor, closer to us, and were shoving upward with six gravities, and down with eleven, respectively.

I reached out blindly and, focusing with a gravity pulse to help my aim, I created another four farther back, and out of sight around the corner they were coming from.

Two low, two high, stacked on the left and right respectively, then driving gravity at a solid fifteen units, moving sharply in the direction of the section of the corridor where we were.

Then I dragged that gravity "wall" sideways, down the corridor and into the other gravity bubbles, working to hold them all together.

The end result was that forty or so incoming assholes, all presumably senagra and definitely feeling a lot of ill will toward us, were dragged into and through a literal gravitational mincer.

The shear effect of the various gravity fields—some pushing one way, others in different directions—literally tore bodies apart. As I gritted my teeth and tried to hold onto all the moving parts and shifting forces, I lost control of several, shoving harder, and letting the pulse off and on in them randomly for a few last seconds, before cutting it.

The result was a bloodbath, that as soon as I lost control and cut the power to the fields, released a veritable flood of mushed flesh, shattered bones, and blood of a dozen different shades and colors across the floor.

"Fuck me, boss," Jonas whispered, shaking his head as the second turret exploded. "That's crazy."

"Yeah, I need you to teach me that one," Paul said. "Shit, that's effective."

"And if you do?" Jonas said sharply. "I'm out. I mean it, Steve—teach this one your magic tricks, and I don't care what I have to do, I'm not being on the same planet."

"Yeah... Paul?" I gasped. My brain felt like it'd been dragged out of my ears and tied under my chin in a bow.

"Yes, boss?"

"Not a fucking chance." I shook my head, blinking and trying to get my heart rate and brain back under control.

"Seriously? You don't trust me?" He straightened and fixed me with a glare I could feel through the armor.

"Okay, if you want to go down that route, fine," I growled. "I'll teach you..."

"Oh yeah!"

"Boss..." Jonas warned.

"Right after you get your doctorate in gravitational physics."

"Fucking what?" Paul asked, shocked.

"I mean it, Paul," I said warningly. "I only managed to control them because I had a fucking doctorate in a dozen different engineering subsets dumped into my brain all at once. I barely survived that. So you want to learn to do what I do? I'll help you, as soon as you've proved you're serious. I won't even make you wait until you have a mere three of them under your belt. Just the gravitational physics will do."

"Fuck that," he replied, before pausing and speaking up quickly. "How about better guns?"

"That we can do," I promised. "You can get with Zac and work on better guns for us all."

"Oh yeah!" He grunted. "I'm gonna make a mountain killer!"

"Oh gods, that might be worse..." Jonas muttered.

"Fuck it, you think that's all of them?" I asked Jonas.

He jerked a thumb at Paul, who nodded, moving up and practically wading through the piles of shredded corpses as he reached the corner.

"I've got this," he called back, lifting his rifle and waiting, clearly ready for a second wave or any stragglers.

"Good man," I approved, then headed back to the other corner and down to join the others, where there were still lasers and projectiles flashing past. "Shit..."

Looking around the edge, there were at least two dozen enemies, all heavily armed. And if we didn't already have a shield bearer in there, the fight would have been going very differently.

The power that had provided the energy shield might have run out, but the solid mass of reflective steel, or whatever the hell it was, was taking a lot longer for them to punch through.

Projectiles chipped away at it, chewing holes slowly through, even as repeated laser blasts slowly started to burn their way through. But the guy behind it? He was happily flinging grenades like a monkey flinging shit.

They bounced off walls and floors, clattering along and then exploding, filling the corridor with clouds of shrapnel, gasses, and flames and who knew what else.

The rest of the group were hunched around their own much smaller shields or pointing their guns around the corner, trading fire over and over.

"What's happening?" I asked Elrah.

"Stalemate!" the big devilkin grunted, firing a quick barrage around the corner then jerking back as a handful of return shots chewed the metal of the corner up. "They've got a better position and a fuckload more people. What happened behind us?"

"We killed them. Paul's on overwatch," I replied absently. "What do we do?"

"We need to break the stalemate, or we're fucked. Even if the local security aren't taken over yet, we're outsiders, and devilkin in their territory, shooting at what looks like their people. We've got less than a minute. Then we need to either pull back, or charge them. And a frontal assault on a prepared position with more defenders is literal suicide."

The look he gave me made it clear that although he was saying that was an option...it really wasn't. If I tried to order them into that hailstorm of incoming fire, I was betting the response would be to throw me out there instead. Or to try to shoot me in the back of the head and claim it was all my fault.

"Why aren't they using grenades?" Jonas asked suddenly.

"This is their territory," Elrah responded. "Probably can't afford to have the surrounding units damaged and expose whatever is inside them, so they're keeping damage to an absolute minimum."

"Cool." I nodded. "Got any spare grenades?"

"Why?" he asked suspiciously.

"Ever seen a fastball?" I grinned at him. "Here, let's swap places..." I shifted around him, moving up to the corner and feeding a tentacle up to the edge. I unleashed a concentrated sonar pulse around and down, hammering out a dozen different frequencies and modulations, using both "sound" to generate the vibrations I needed and gravity.

Then I nodded to myself in satisfaction as I "saw" the overall layout.

There were fifteen of the enemy who I could count still up and fighting, and three who were injured and dealing with that, but could still fight. Lastly, maybe eleven bodies that were either no longer moving or were feigning death, judging from the level of trauma and the shaking of the skulls of those who had been downed.

"Looks like there's a bunch of the little spider-looking motherfuckers about to break out of the bodies and join the fight or run for it," I told them. "Give me, oh…say, two grenades and get ready to fire. I need suppressing fire first. Hammer the fuckers down while I send these in, then get ready to charge."

I saw the look he gave me at "charge" and I nodded my understanding. "I'll lead the charge. Trust me, it won't be the slaughter you're worried about."

"It better not be," he grunted, before passing orders to the others.

"What's the plan?" Jonas asked through our link.

"Suppressing fire to distract for a few seconds. I throw these fuckers around the corner and use gravity bubbles to make sure they get to where I want them before they go off. Then we run around the corner and shoot the fuckers in the face."

"Simple. I like it," he admitted.

"Less moving parts means less to go wrong," I said aloud, taking the two grenades that Elrah offered, and grinning as he shook his head at the way I held them casually.

"These are monomolecular shredders," he explained. "They're all I have left, and they're remote detonated. I won't trigger these unless you can make damn sure they're as far from my people as possible."

"Sounds fair," I agreed blandly, while feeding a tiny tentacle of nanites into them, and hijacking the control signal. "You press whenever you're ready."

Then I gestured, and he let loose a loud whistle. All of them, including Jonas and the guy behind the shield, started to fire wildly, forcing the senagra to duck back or get hammered with a dozen blasts.

As soon as they did that, I flung both grenades around the corner, aiming for the farthest point I could, and hearing the snarl of frustration from Elrah that I'd apparently "wasted them" on such a poorly aimed throw.

Then I heard the gasp as the first bubble flared, flipping the pair of grenades over and dragging them "down" the corridor, as gravity suddenly was for them. Then it cut out, as a second and a third bubble formed. One directly behind them, pushing "out" and one ahead pulling "in."

I did that three times, then dragged two separate bubbles into existence a meter apart, sending them spinning down the corridor, like the craziest bank shots ever. Each grabbed one of the grenades and dragged it left and right respectively.

The frantic howls let me know that they'd seen the grenades at the last second, probably staring in disbelief as they seemed to skip through the air, only to land squarely in the middle of the mouths of the adjoining corridors the enemy were firing from, and behind their cover.

The clang as they landed, the magnetics locking them in place, was almost missed in the sudden desperate scramble. I triggered them a fraction of a second ahead of Elrah. Both grenades went off and created a hellish hundred-and-eighty-degree scythe of metal fragments attached to razor wire.

The sheer destructive power of two well-placed grenades like that meant that when I took the corner, my GGC spinning up on the right and handgun in my left hand, there were still cascades of blood, cerebral fluids, sparks from the damaged lights and electrics, and screams filling the air.

What there weren't many of were shots being fired, or at least not at us.

One of the enemy had tried to jump on the grenade. Presumably the hive decided to sacrifice one of them to save the rest, but the sheer destructive power of the shredders had torn through the body before it landed.

When we raced forward, there were staggering bodies flailing at missing limbs, screaming forms missing half a skull. Jaws, legs, hands…basically anything and everything had been torn up. As we rushed ahead, we opened fire.

I mainly used the handgun —the GGC was ready as an emergency measure, if it was needed—but it was a slaughter, all right. One that we inflicted on the screeching, thrashing senagra.

"There!" Elrah barked, pointing to a figure dragging itself toward a recess in one wall. "That's the entrance!"

The guy who had been carrying the shield dropped it, the majority of it melted and deformed, not to mention bullet-ridden, and plowed through the group, racing to grab the door before it could close.

A turret swung down from the middle of the corridor ahead, deploying before I could target it. A barrage of laser blasts took him in the left leg, thigh, gut, and lower chest, smashing him from his feet to slide sideways into the wall with a cry.

"Fire!" Elrah roared, and we did, all of us.

I didn't have time to form a gravity bubble before the first rounds were punching into the turret, taking it down. But as soon as it was off-line, another two opened fire, this time behind us.

I staggered, feeling a burning heat, but little else between my shoulders. I spun, ready to fire, only to find Jonas beating me to it, right as the door into the storage unit we wanted let out a solid *clang* as it sealed.

"You're getting old," he grunted. "Can you do anything for him?"

I looked to the shield bearer, seeing the injuries, and the way that they'd been cauterized with the heat.

"Probably, but not quickly," I admitted. "Can you save him?" I directed at Elrah, who nodded.

"Medic!" he called, scanning the corridor as another of his people made it to the storage unit door, slapping a sensor against it and doing something.

"He'll make it, but he's out of the fight," the devilkin doubling as a medic announced, jabbing an injector into the thigh of the wounded man.

"Stable?" I asked.

"As stable as he's getting," came the laconic reply.

"Door's sealed," the other called to us. "Looks like they cut the power to the controls as well."

"There another way in?" I asked Elrah.

"Probably, but if you're asking if we have time to find it? Not without being caught by security." He turned back to his man by the door and shouted one word. "Thermite."

"Oh, that's nasty." Jonas winced. "Didn't know they had access to that shit."

"It's the translation software's equivalent…I'd be surprised if it's the same as ours."

"Eyes!" Elrah warned everyone, and all but Jonas and I looked away, the pair of us confident in our helmets and curious.

The devilkin by the door pulled a tube from his backpack, triggering a nozzle and "drawing" a thick line of foam around the edges of the door, before stepping back and smacking what looked for all the world like a piece of flint against the wall. The sparks that sprayed out hit the foam, and it went nuclear.

An insanely bright flash flared, lighting the entire corridor with what would probably have burned our eyes out without the helmets. Then, in under a second, it was gone, the filters struggling to return to the "normal" lighting quickly enough.

We'd been hit by a backwash of heat as well, feeling much like the inside of an oven, even a handful of meters away. But considering we were in armor, and the others were devilkin with an internal temperature in the hundreds…yeah, not really an issue.

It nicely crisped up the blood and bits that were still strewn around, though, and as the devilkin on door duty leaned back and kicked it onward, I noticed that the shredder grenades' gossamer-thick threads that ran from one filament to the other and basically coated the wall and ceiling up high was no longer dripping wet blood.

"Secure that room!" Elrah barked.

Both Malthus and the door-dude raced inside, guns leveled.

Malthus's new armor immediately came under fire, shrugging off the "lighter" laser blasts, with more and more fire hammering into it as he provided cover for the rest of us.

We raced after him as he returned fire. The rifle he carried filled the air with a juddering *brrrr* as it fired dozens of laser blasts in response second by second.

It was like a chain gun, and the effect on the enemy was horrific.

I ran to the left as soon as I was inside, getting into cover behind a large metal cabinet that looked to be full of servers. I scanned the room, both visually and letting rip with a blast of sonar and gravity.

The layout that came back was…weird.

It looked to have been a standard warehouse design once: two levels, with rows of racks for goods, running down the center, and a separate area upstairs at the back that was either for temperature-controlled or special goods.

That was all clear and common sense from the layout and the remains of the original fixtures and fittings.

What was left, though, was anything but this.

In the center of the room was a great orb, apparently completely created from crystal, steel armoring, cables, and supports. It was easily twenty meters across, and finding it in the middle of the station was a bit of a surprise. Presumably the senagra local hive boss was inside there, but there was also deliberately what looked like no way up or in. A nest of cabling and tubing rolled around and around it; red and blue lights flickered inside it and on the dozens of connectors.

Each of those ran from the massive nest that hung suspended from the ceiling out to the cables that ran to dozens of bodies that covered the walls all around us.

The majority were near death, or so they seemed. Their pale skin was exposed, arms and legs glued into place on the walls with a mesh that looked organic; then masks and tubing covered faces and private areas, presumably providing both nutrition and sanitation.

More and more bodies of dozens of races were crouched around the room, or up high, hiding behind armored barricades and running from cover to cover to fire at us.

The figures attached to the walls shuddered and jerked. Lights on the black masks that covered their heads flashed, as still more drones returned fire with Malthus, uncaring of their kin on the walls being caught in the cross fire.

Reaching out and up, I could feel…shifting metal, deep inside the nest like an orbit of rings, suddenly flashed around into new configurations, then vanished. An abrupt burst of power wafted out, then nothing at all, followed by more moving.

It was too fast to make sense of, and I triggered my time compression. Although I'd been saving it and I might or might not need it later, I definitely needed it now.

Malthus cursed as his gun went dry. A battery of some kind ejected out of the back as he released it, dropping the gun to the floor and ripping a handgun free instead.

I dismissed the nest for now, focusing on the fuckers firing at us for sure, seeing the massive damage that Malthus had unleashed. In a world where power cells and batteries were insanely expensive and limited, it was obvious why he'd not used it to clear the previous corridor entirely.

I made a mental note that if he was to join us properly, we'd get him a better core. And if not? Well, we'd make a copy of that gun for later.

He strode forward, though, into the withering fire that the enemy poured onto us, doing the same job that the shield bearer had done before.

This time, instead of the shield being shredded and the warrior hunkering down behind it drawing their fire, it was Malthus, and damn was he going up in my estimation. That guy had balls of steel.

I didn't bother with my guns, not for this—too many collateral targets—and I started to pop bubbles of gravity here and there, aiming for the heads of the figures I could see firing at us.

Elrah was behind the stack next to me, giving suppressing fire to take the pressure off Malthus. Jonas was firing, his skill clear as he took down target after target. But it was Paul who suddenly spoke up.

"I've got incoming!" he warned us on the link, and the image that came with it was of a load of security types, six in the lead in heavy armor, and it looked to be powered this time, much closer to a UC soldier's than Malthus's version.

That was what we'd been most concerned about: that we'd get bogged down, slowing enough for the "real" security to turn up. There was no way the corporations would have the dumb ass rent-a-cops we'd seen so far as their real defense.

"Going live," Ingrid said, sending reassurance to us all. She started to release the carefully crafted warnings that she'd been working on before we set off.

Where Jonas and the rest of us had been working on weapons and tactics, and James had both sorted my suit and made the appointment, Ingrid had crafted a careful presentation and warning, pulled together in a handful of minutes—and with the help of Arturo—to show a clear and obvious threat that was posed by the senagra, as well as declaring this a military intervention on behalf of the UC.

The locals might accept it, they might not—and they also might have enough access to the UC to be able to confirm it before I could get my bullshit passed off with my own contacts.

That would cause no end of issues, but fuck it.

Contingencies were there for a reason.

"Pull back to us," I ordered Paul, before shouting to Elrah. "We've got incoming heavy security forces!"

"We need to finish this then!" he shouted back. "Either join in or run!"

"Join…?" I growled, before cursing.

Of course. My gravity bubbles were flaring in the chest cavities and skulls of my targets. They simply fell dead when I managed to do it right. That meant he thought I was fucking cowering behind the cabinet instead of helping!

"Well, there goes my street cred," I muttered, squinting up at the nest over our heads and scanning it for weaknesses.

There had to be a way in for the little gnome-like fuckers I'd seen before, and I'd not seen them yet, so…

I cursed, seeing the first of the little bastards as it leapt from the top of the nest, arms flung wide. The filth covering its body was almost entirely obscured by the large explosives strapped to it, and the feral, insane grin that seemed to split its face in half.

It was followed by others—six, I counted in three seconds—all crawling out of a hole I could sense that had opened high on the inverted down-shaped nest.

The first landed with a crunch of breaking bones half a meter to the left of Malthus, and as it bounced—wetly—the package went off.

Malthus was hurled from his feet into a stack of tech to his right. Sparks flew everywhere as a wave of flames washed across the room.

Whatever rules the senagra had about not trashing the place had clearly gone out the window, as the others started to drag themselves around thick cables, moving to the point that they could leap down toward us. The nest…no, the entire building shifted suddenly!

"They've mined the supports!" Elrah shouted, eyes wide through the face shield of his helmet. "Get out! Get out now!"

The other little gnome-like bastards started to fling themselves free—a distant, mad voice in my head shouted "Gnomes rule!" from a book I'd read years ago— as more and more explosions started to ripple out.

"Steve!" Ingrid shouted through the link, and I felt a sudden sensation from her, knowing, beyond any doubt that she'd just fallen from her seat. The table that she and several other pissed-off-looking corpo types had been sitting around

suddenly shook as other supports in the area went off. *"What the hell is happening!"*

"Distraction!" Jonas was the one to see it first, firing upward as he backed up. *"The fucker's scuttling the station and running for it in the confusion!"*

"Bastard!" I gasped, seeing it all, and the sudden weirdness I could feel from my radar made sense at last. "It's got a fucking escape craft!"

Then I grinned, taking full goddamn advantage of my time compression as the hatch or whatever they were using at the top opened to release one more of the little gnome fuckers.

I reached out, and—guessing that the explosives were rigged for impact or to the gnome's life signs themselves, from the evidence so far—I crushed the fucker's skull and flung him backward into the nest.

Then, lifting both arms unconsciously as I gritted my teeth and dug even deeper, feeling Ingrid adding her mental strength to my own, tweaking and desperately trying to share the load, I spun up eighteen new gravitational bubbles.

It was by far the most I'd ever tried to manage all at once, and I felt the start of a migraine that was probably going to blind me as soon as I did it.

Six of the gnomes were crawling around the outside still, and I grabbed each of them. I created a gravitational vortex behind and above them, ripping them from their handholds and flinging them upward, then cut the bubble, forming another behind that, then again and again.

They screeched and screamed in fury and shock, torn from their handholds and unceremoniously catapulted backward; then I slammed them into the nest as hard as I could.

They exploded almost simultaneously.

My knees hit the floor, as I blinked through the pain and I shoved harder on the other twelve bubbles.

I'd created them to spread out across the room, over our heads. Half of them were pushing down a little higher than any of us, to keep us experiencing the gravity that we were used to, or near enough.

The other half were beyond them, midway between our heads and the nest, and they were in reverse, dragging all the debris, the flames, the shrapnel, and more, all back upward to hammer into the nest.

The effect was catastrophic. Whatever supports the creature had set up to be blown free, presumably to release the cunningly hidden escape capsule it'd been planning to use, were smashed aside. The entire ceiling warped, as explosion after explosion tore through the nest, and I frantically held it all inside.

Blood ran down my face, my nose, mouth, eyes, and ears as I coughed and held on. The explosions threatened the stability of this section of the station, unless I could hold it just a little longer.

I felt it then.

The others, all of them, the rest of the team in the command link—all reaching out. I felt ghost hands on my shoulders. I felt a slight lessening of the load as the others tried to help. I felt James and Zac, now both intimately experienced in the vagaries of gravitational physics, adding to my ability…enhancing, helping.

I felt Belle, Paul, and Jonas adding strength; Scylla and Courtney improving the directions; Casey, Oxus, and Jay supported, sharing the weight across all our minds. And Ingrid…

Ingrid smoothed it all, helping to make it all work.

I blinked. The world cleared before my eyes as my helm and my nanites processed the blood, scrubbing it from my suit and reabsorbing it.

Then I looked up at the nest, held in place beneath a net of gravitational manipulation. Inside, more explosions ripped free. Flames, power surges, crushed metal and blood, fluids of all kinds sprayed free, and it was all held there.

In the center of it all, though, I felt *it*.

The senagra was still alive, but its ship sure as shit wasn't.

I reached up with both hands, unthinking; my team held the weight, spreading the load across us all. I gripped the entire nest, twenty meters across and ten high. The dome was battered to fuck—burning, glowing, and dripping, forming pools that ran into the vortexes.

Then I tore it loose.

The nest came free with a screech of tearing metal. A secondary pulse of awareness formed a reinforcement that kept the ceiling itself from tearing any more, and kept the station from more damage.

Then I lowered the nest, holding it in the center of the room, and ripped it apart.

The two halves of the outer shell came free with a screech of twisted metal. Once designed to release for the craft to escape, now they left tears and crushed sections behind as they went. I flung them to either side. Parts bounced and crashed, discarded at the back of the room, crushing any enemy survivors that might have been hiding there.

Then I reached out to the exposed craft that had been buried and built in the center.

It was small, more a ball with thrusters and a fuckload of antennae, I guessed, originally. As it was now, the antennae were all gone; the outside was cracked and torn in places, and the thrusters were outgassing.

I ripped the thrusters apart quickly, tearing loose whatever the propellant had been that was currently releasing vapor. I formed a new bubble around the gas and containers, dragging the fuel inward, and crushing it down and down. Then, finding it forming a solid, I pushed harder and harder.

I felt Paul take that, a determination that he could bring more focus to bear than I'd believe, and knowing that if he didn't, if he released it, it could unleash a wave of hellfire.

He took it, and I trusted him as he took the form I'd made for him, and focused it further down, harder and tighter.

I dismissed it, knowing he'd not fail me. Instead, I focused on the rest, ripping the remains of the thrusters free, compressing and discarding them. I released most of the gravity fields I was forming, feeling the relief from the others, and suddenly realized that I was almost out of my temporal compression.

I'd been sharing it with the entire team somehow. Every second I'd intentionally used had been using twelve, and now…without access to my screens, to my main goddamn systems…I couldn't even be sure how many I had. I just knew I didn't have many left.

I reached out again, this time creating a fresh dozen gravitational vortexes, one pushing in and one out, stitching them along the front of the capsule, even as I felt Paul's warning, delivered through a strain I could feel the rest of the team were all experiencing.

"Security…" He grunted into the link, and I saw them coming, the mass of heavily armored and armed private security contractors for the corpos.

These were the real force on the station, the private force elites. I dimly recognized that they'd been dispatched not out of any compassion for the rest of the station, but had been sent by the corpos to make sure that if there was a situation, it could be turned to their advantage somehow.

Then Ingrid, who I sensed that burst of insight had come from, had shown them all the threat that existed in their midst.

That had given the security force a sudden desperate focus, as well as an existential terror, as they all realized that the supposed ally standing by their side might in fact be their enemy, even more than they usually were.

That was when the entire station shook and explosive gouts of flame and screeching, tearing squeals of damaged metal filled the air.

They'd seen Paul falling back, and bereft of any better plans or direction, they'd given chase, finding an utter bloodbath over the next few streets.

Soon enough, they'd found the devilkin. Torn between the usual suspicion and the sudden terror underlying everything, they were more than ready to shoot first and ask questions never.

That was when Jonas stepped up, directing everyone back from the damaged wall, and directly addressing the security teams.

"Get ready!" he barked, his best "commander's voice" in evidence. "You want proof of what we've told you? Here it is!"

With that, I tore down the wall into the corridor, letting the brighter lit area—where the lights were intact and not covered in gore or blown up—shine a light into the senagra's lair.

Gasps, curses, and angry roars filled the air and the comm links. Ingrid shared the image that the corpos she was with were seeing displayed on a screen, and I moved quickly, holding the damaged orb in place, as I tore it in half, the vortexes making it child's play.

That was when the senagra, screeching, terrified, and full of hatred for the "lesser races" hurled itself free.

It had been curled up inside the capsule, arms and legs pulled in tight, more than half of its computer links now dead, reducing it to a half-blind, half-deaf monstrosity.

The upper half of its head was covered in steel, curved alloys stained with grease, and who knew what dotted with flashing LEDs. The lower half was simply its maw: wide, with two jutting tusks on the top facing outward and down, and the bottom facing out and up.

Its teeth were hollow fangs; the sides of the jaw unfurled and mandibles designed to hold its victims in place sprayed saliva and hatred as it howled its indignation at us all.

It was almost centaur-like, I saw now: six spidery limbs low down, with a solid torso with two upper arms that were simply withered things.

Dozens of cables dangled from it—some torn loose when it'd tried to escape, others still connected, plugging it into the capsule. It flung itself free of the damaged machinery, and the remaining cables released in a burst of fluids and gasses.

Then it stopped dead, caught in my gravitational grasp.

I dropped the damaged capsule. The clang of metal filled the air as everyone raised weapons, zeroing in on the creature that spat and screamed...

Then I slammed it into the floor as hard as I could.

The chest, the arms and legs...the lower body...all of it was suddenly subjected to a hundred gravities, the head kept clear in its own special field I'd designated to keep it as intact as possible, while the air was filled with the explosive shattering of a hundred bones and chitin.

Then I kept going, my right fist held up where everyone could see it. I closed my fist inexorably, the destroyed limbs folding in around the vortex in response.

I was breathing heavily now; my entire team were as well, I distantly realized. I cut every other field I could, keeping only the protective one around the head and the one that was crushing the body intact now.

As the last of the cracking bones fell silent, the corridor and station around us was filled with the strident wailing of the emergency depressurization warnings. The station shuddered as it tried to equalize, and distantly I heard the shouts of emergency engineers running to fix things.

"*Now*, we're done." I released the hold I had on everyone, staggering as I suddenly realized the strain that I'd been under had been mitigated by everyone else, not solved.

Then the world crashed in, and I pitched forward, falling into darkness.

Chapter Thirty-Eight

When I finally opened my eyes again, I had the mother of all headaches. Blinking, it took me a few seconds to work out the pattern on the wall opposite.

That was mainly because it was actually the ceiling, as I realized I was lying on my back. More to the point, it was the ceiling of Ingrid and mine's cabin in the remains of the megayacht.

That'd been ripped out and installed, pretty much in one piece in the warship, and that…

Yeah, that explained the distant screams of alarms, the shuddering, and the peculiar pulsing that shivered through the deck and that had apparently woken me up.

It also made a weird kind of sense, as the ceiling here was partly mirrored, directly over the bed, and had a strange spiraling pattern of historical figures and battles rolling around the outside.

The mirrored bit in the middle? That was shattered, as if it'd been hit by a hammer. And that meant…

I blinked again as the air was suddenly ripped from the bedroom. The screams of distant alarms fell silent as the air needed to carry them vanished into the void. My subconscious, apparently deciding my brain was still in melty mode, surrounded my body with my armor.

A second later, and I was fighting with the blankets I'd apparently been wrapped in, as gravity in my local area vanished as well.

"Well, fuck *that*," I snarled, my brain finally finishing its reboot. I reached out, flipping gravity around and forcing it back into existence around me.

I fell onto my back on the bed again. A shuddering crack from underneath suggested that at least one of the support struts had just given up on the fight.

Cursing, I finally tore free of the blanket—literally, goose down feathers erupted into the vacuum—as I cancelled gravity again, braced and flipped myself around and upright, then formed a new bubble.

I "fell" toward the door, grabbing onto it, cancelled it again and landed, bracing myself, then stared up and out, directly into *space*.

I was seeing the blackness overhead through a tear that ran left to right, carving through the next quarters to ours completely—heh, James was gonna be *pissed*—and into the deck below as well.

I saw something in the depths of the cut erupt in sparks, briefly bringing light to the darkness, then I was moving.

The ship's systems, where the megayacht had been plugged into it, were clearly stronger than our own designs, but the problem I had right now?

The section I was in was in vacuum, meaning I couldn't get back into the rest of the ship to help, or to figure out what the fuck was going on, without depressurizing more of the ship in the process.

That meant that I either needed to stay put, or…

"Ingrid?" I sent into the command link, feeling a sudden shock from her, quickly followed by relief. Then I was suddenly let back in. Somehow I'd been removed from it, or blanked and left to one side, and the shock of bringing me back into it now…

Everything hit me all at once, a hammering of information from all sides as everyone shared what they were doing and their status, as well as those of their responsibility into the link, as they always did.

That I'd just joined it still half in a daze, though, meant that the sheer onslaught stunned me as I fought to make sense of it all.

We were in space again—that much I'd guessed at by the rip in the fucking hull. But beyond that? We'd somehow made it to the Scorpio system and were less than an hour of in-system travel from docking with the Universal System Quadrant Node.

That was the good news.

The bad news was that our half-finished ship was currently battling against three Ændari vessels of comparable size and power, and we were getting our asses handed to us.

The only reason we were even still around was the upgrades to the system, and that James, as a Command variant specialized as a pilot, was able to fly the ship like a fighter instead of the massive fucking aircraft carrier it basically was.

Arturo wasn't fully integrated with the turret weapons systems that we'd fitted yet, so it was down to Paul, Jonas, Courtney, and Malthus to operate them, with Oxus having almost shot us somehow with the single point defense turret he'd been entrusted with.

It'd been taken off him, and left to Zac, as the only engineer with real access to such systems, to frantically work on integrating them and turning them over to the AI.

We'd apparently dropped out of the gravitational warp right into the Lagrange point. And as soon as we had, we'd come under fire before we'd even gotten the shields up, taking serious damage and leaving James to frantically try to escape.

The grav drive had been the target of their first volleys, and was arguably the only reason we were all still alive, as they'd wanted to make sure we couldn't run.

Had they instead gone for the bridge, or the power core? We'd have been fucked.

Well, a normal ship would have been, I suddenly realized, as another detail popped into place.

The secondary core. The one that we had literally just installed to get the shields on their own core. That was in place, and it was almost operational. But coming out of warp and into the middle of a firefight, the shields had been down as it'd not yet been fully finished.

Since then—as Zac had been working on a million jobs at once, including getting the shields rebooted and trying to reestablish a cover for us—they were being hit and overloaded constantly. No matter how much James twisted and flew his heart out, three ships against one, all with turrets, meant that the shields were constantly flicking in and out, never getting enough of a start to really help.

If we didn't have the secondary core, though? We'd have lost them entirely and been carved to pieces in the process.

"Where do you need me?" I asked, realizing that I'd basically zoned out as the mass of data hit me. Now I was starting to process again, and I felt Ingrid's relief.

"Zac?" she asked, and a half second later, he projected an image into my mind.

"The main control run for the new turrets is here. There are three sections left to connect to Arturo. Two custodians are working on the internal ones, and linking them to the run, but this section is sealed off, and they'll need to route around to get to it, unless they want to expose the ship to vacuum. That was going to be my next job, but you're already out of the secure areas, and if you can get your ass there…?"

He left it unsaid, and I saw the crystal route that was needed, moving as I sent assurance and trust to her and the entire team. I launched myself at the tear in the hull.

I hit it, grabbing the edge and dragging myself into the gap. The multiple levels of armoring and systems that the blast had carved through made it clear that if a beam *that* powerful hit me, personally?

I'd be a pale-pink mist at best.

I moved as fast as I could, wriggling up through the gap and grabbing onto the hull. My armor shifted the outer layer to magnetic, locking me to the hull with barely a thought.

Dragging myself all the way out, I paused, even knowing what I was going to see, just overwhelmed by the sheer beauty of space, all around me.

I saw distant worlds, stars that didn't just glimmer through a sheen of atmosphere, but that *burned* with powerful, almost holy light.

I saw the faraway gleam of the universal system quadrant node, a giant spire of seemingly white marble that extended up and down from a central dock, with spiraling walkways that reflected the light distantly and looped around the central mass.

Then I saw the madness of the three nearby ships, each triangular, almost blocky, with a thick rear covered in engines, and turrets that ran their length sending a frantic barrage of red laser light after us. For just a second, I registered that it was the helmet and visual systems that even made it possible for me to see them, and I was damn glad.

I'd hate to be killed in deep space and have it look to an outside observer like the ships were engaged in a fucking *ballet*.

The galaxy around us whirled suddenly, almost out of control as James sent us into a roll. The stars became a blur of light. I snarled as another section of the hull flickered as the shield over it appeared under the laser's onslaught, before it erupted into a crackling, roiling hellfire of red lightning.

It vanished a second later, the ship outgassing again. The engines hurtled us onto another path, getting us away before more damage could be done.

The jagged, melted line torn through the hull was clear enough, though.

I moved then. The sight rid me of my awestruck gaping, and I started to run, my boots barely releasing before they were connecting again. Gravity flared at will and kept me pinned to the ship's hull as if I were glued to it.

I leapt the carved gash; the edges of it glowed white-hot and cherry as it dimmed. Then I was down, skidding along as the magnets fought to reconnect. I quickly came to the original hole in the hull that had caused the ship to seal this section away.

It was wide enough that I just dropped into it, landing hard, though silently. My breathing thundered in my ears and my heart pounded as I ran. With that as the only sounds, I stumbled across melted and torn decking.

Airlocks here, where the ship was already in vacuum, opened and shut as I passed through them, clattering in room after room, before I found the one I needed.

Tools randomly floated about, clearly having been in a toolkit at some point, then the returning and vanishing gravity having done a real number on Zac's obsessive organization.

I swept them all aside, grabbing the grate that covered the section I needed, Zac having highlighted the damaged sections in his shared burst of data.

It wasn't hard to find. The crystal inside was melted in great lines, probably decades ago, and the two sections that had been "patched" together to fix it had resulted in a cloudiness to the crystal.

It looked minor, considering what I knew about crystals on Earth, but it meant that the precise patterns of light that needed to get through were utterly scrambled by the time they passed two more like it farther on.

The old crew had eventually accepted that they couldn't replicate their ancestors' techniques, and so they'd laid cabling instead. An inelegant but serviceable solution.

The issue now, I saw as I fed some of my own nanites into the crystal patch and guided them using the Engineering sub-mind, was that in order to take full control of the turrets and to guide them properly, Arturo needed to have a solid and stable connection with the various systems.

He didn't have that, not even slightly. The cabling was never meant to carry petabytes of data a second. Hell, it was barely better than plain old Cat 5 cable on Earth. And for the kind of processing that Arturo needed?

He needed to be able to link all the systems together into a full mesh. That would require far more of a load the first time it happened—exabytes, at least.

That level of data transfer left crystal conduits as the only medium that could effectively do the job. And with the custodians working on the other two, I frantically constructed and smoothed lattice after lattice.

I barely understood what I was doing. The calculations needed to create crystal were far beyond the average weaponized monkey. Frankly, I was closer to the monkey end of the scale at the best of times, but with the background knowledge I had, and access to the nanites, I started.

At first, the work was obvious: clear crystal to the right, clear crystal to the left, big fuckin' block of cloudy shit where it'd been inexpertly patched in the past.

Focus in on that patch, deploy nanites, have them straighten and smooth the various lattices.

Boom, Bob's yer uncle, Fanny's yer aunt…or she was 'till she died, as a friend of mine used to say.

That was the simple explanation, tweaking and polishing until the light could pass through clearly.

The more complex section, though?

That was where it got *insanely* complicated. And it was only because I had the gravitational skills that I did that I could even identify that an issue existed.

The crystal was apparently bent inside and always had been, creating slight abnormalities in the gravitational field.

Considering it was light that traveled along them, I decided "good enough for government work" was the best it was going to get, as the alternative…well.

It'd take me a few months of painstaking work, and there were people outside who were being very rude right now, and I couldn't wait for the ship's turrets to explain manners to them again.

Fixing the gravity warps in the crystal? That was something that would allow faster data transmission in the future, but right now, just working was more than enough.

"Crystal is nearly fixed. What's next?" I dropped into the link.

"Zac?" Ingrid asked.

"Disconnect the secondaries where they're laid as primaries, remove the blocks on the crystal integration, and plug in the conduits as secondaries instead of primaries."

That was all I got from him, along with a blast of partly detailed but mostly vague instructions that took me a handful of seconds to make sense of. Then I was off again, moving as fast as I could to the next section down the line.

Ripping a housing unit apart with my enhanced strength, not having the time to fuck around playing with it, I stared at the section that was revealed below, nodding as I understood his points.

When the team had accepted defeat on the crystal conduits, they couldn't risk the signals being repeated and firing additional commands down the line, so they'd disconnected the crystal system, switching the signals to travel along the cabling conduits instead.

The crystal was still there, just switched to a secondary line, and then blocked off.

The conduits were in the primary path, and I winced as I realized that doing this…

"When I switch this over, it's going to cut the ship's backbone, right?" I asked Zac. *"I mean, the spine? It's gonna be like the nerves are severed until they reconnect."*

"But once it works, Arturo should be able to control the turrets as well," he said. *"The real issue is that he's gonna have to patch them all at once, and we don't know how long that will take to come back online, or if the engines and more that share the trunkline will come back on instantly or not."*

"And we're still doing this?" I winced.

"You see a better option?" he snarled. *"Because I fucking don't, all right, boss man? This way, we've got a chance. As it is, the goddamn grav drive is fucked…like it's half melted. It's gonna take days to fix, and that's if I can do it at all. We can't jump out of here, not unless you think you can replace the grav drive by shoving your dick in the socket or something!"*

"All right, man, calm down," I snapped back.

"CALM DOWN?" he practically screamed at me in our private link, and I got a sudden sight of him, clinging to the hull of the ship with one hand, trying to fix sections around a barrel. *"Are you fuckin' kiddin' me?"*

"How about I warn Ingrid and the others that they're going to lose power?" I suggested. *"Then we do it and pray it works?"*

"It's the only goddamn chance we have, so if it doesn't, we're fucked anyway," he snapped. *"And as soon as you've done that, I need you to plug into Arturo and start using your gravity cannon thing."*

"My…why? What the hell is going on?"

"I was stupid and tried to do too much. I had the time when we were waiting for you and the bodies, so I installed some of the parts needed for the mass driver runs down the spine of the ship."

"The…oh hell yes!" I gasped. *"You mean we've got real guns after all?"*

"No."

"But you just said…"

"There's four of the connections for one of the runs in place and that's all. I've put five million nanites into it, and it's shifting the entire thing to use a gravitational charge like yours, I think, but I've never tried firing your gun, and neither has Arturo! You've got no idea how many calculations you're making every millisecond subconsciously to fire that thing, and that's like a few inches, if that—these are ten meters long!"

"It's not the size that counts." I grinned. *"It's what you do with it."*

"Yeah, well, if that's what Ingrid tells you, boss man, believe me, she's lying," he growled. *"Just plug yourself into Arturo and start firing yours randomly into space. It'll copy your control signals and use them to tweak the mass driver. Maybe it'll work."*

"And the ammo?" I asked.

"No fucking time to mess about now, all right?" he snapped back. *"I've sorted it. Just shut it and do your job!"*

I took the hint, breaking the "wonderful" news to Ingrid and the others that to get the systems online to try to defend ourselves…we first had to pull the plug and really hope that nobody had missed a damaged section or anything.

There was the predictable panic, and the sheer fear that the time when we were down and defenseless, we'd be blown apart.

The only hope we had was that the enemy would miss long enough for the reboot to go through, or they'd try to board us when they realized we were dead in space.

There were a handful of seconds where everyone dealt with the sheer panic and concerns, then Ingrid asked the question.

"Are you sure about this?"

"No," I admitted. *"You got a better idea, though?"*

"We're losing a battle of attrition," James added in. *"Unless we can get the shields up and fast, or the turrets online long enough to make them back off? We won't win this fight. We can't."*

"Do it." Ingrid sighed. *"Do it now."*

I hesitated a second as I grabbed onto the various sections, tentacles flowing out to snap up the bits I needed, eyeing up the channels I'd need to reconnect and the blockers that needed to be pulled out, and then laid in to place to route the secondary signals…

"I wish you'd fuckin' done this before we left the station," I sent to Zac.

"I wish you'd given me the fuckin' time!" he responded. *"There were seventeen replacements to do before you dragged your lazy arse out of bed and joined in!"*

"The custodians finished?" I asked him.

"You think I'd be letting you do that if they hadn't?"

"Fuck it," I grunted, and pulled the connection.

The ship shuddered. The various systems dropped out of control, cutting power all at once.

The engines, the shields, the turrets—hell, the lights and goddamn air converters—all of them failed as the ship died.

<u>Chapter Thirty-Nine</u>

In the sudden utter blackness, I was left with only my own radar-like vision ability, trying to plug the sections back in as quickly as possible, and I was damn glad I had that.

Working as fast as I could, I felt the plugs locking into place, the blocks sliding home with solid clicks, then the crystal being cleared, the connections restoring…and then…

Nothing.

The ship shuddered as more impacts came. Lasers tore great holes in the hull. Sparks flared and illuminated the darkness as I frantically searched for something, anything that I'd done wrong.

"What the fuck did you do?!" Zac screamed at me.

"WHAT YOU TOLD ME TO DO!" I roared back.

The others in the command link almost gibbered with fear as they confirmed that the only things that had power in the darkness of the ship were us chickens.

Then more hits slammed into the ship, again and again. More air whooshed out, making it clear another section had been exposed to vacuum. Then the aft section of the ship bucked violently—some kind of missile, I presumed, punching into the rear port engine and exploding. The ship rolled again, gouting flame into the darkness.

"The reactors!" Zac screamed into the link as he finally figured out the issue. *"Switch the reactors' feeds! Positive to negative, negative to positive!"*

"HOW?"

A barrage of images hit me at almost the same time from Zac as the Engineering sub-mind popped up with a helpful eleven hundred and fourteen-stage plan for the best way to carefully shut down, clean, reverse the output stream, and reboot a reactor.

I tore that aside, already running, knowing that Zac was going to be doing the same, that the custodians were moving, and that if we failed at getting this back online, we were utterly fucked.

At this rate, it was looking like "fucked with a telegraph pole and no lube" was the way the day was going for us all, a little voice in the back of my mind calmly pointed out before I snarled at it to shut up.

I was only two rooms from the new power core that was supposed to be running the shields. I sent my position to Zac as I bounced off a wall, leaping and skidding as I tried to squeeze every possible half a millimeter of speed out of myself.

I felt his acknowledgment, and the burst of "this is our only chance" as he stressed the order the core connections needed to be booted into.

As soon as I entered the room, I could feel it: the core and power cells were still live, *entirely* so. The emergency shutdown that we were experiencing was a control shutdown, not power, so the fuckers were still running. They just weren't sharing, which at least explained why we'd not just become the center of a terminally short-lived star.

The connections were even harder to see in the dark, and it really didn't help that Zac's instructions included helpful things like *'Don't just hit it—move the level from positive to negative in a full line. Remember, flick the ones marked red, flick amber, yellow, orange, red, then reverse the polarity and do them one by one, finishing with green.'*

That was great for him, and he'd apparently put the colors on the system to help in just this situation, I sensed.

Unfortunately, I was seeing by goddamn radar and *that didn't help with colors!*

I hesitated, then patched the Engineering sub-mind into my own, dragged the schematics for this core up, and started hitting the switches that were marked with only slightly less warnings than all the others.

"Prepare for boarders!" Ingrid sent through the link.

I froze, before snarling, and then kept on going. *"Boarders?"* I shot back at the link.

"Paul can see their ship... One is moving in close, matching speed and attitude. The other two are moving into position to watch."

"FUCK!" I growled. *"If they see us getting power again, they'll open fire. They're too close to miss now!"*

"Don't do it yet!" Ingrid replied after a brief hesitation. *"Jonas, get to the boarding position. Casey, to the reactor that Steve's at. Zac, get everything ready at your reactor, but DON'T flick the switch until we're ready!"*

"What..." I asked.

"Steve, when Casey reaches you, show her what to do with the last step only— you do everything else. Get it ready for her, then move. I want you ready to jump out of the hull and open fire on the nearest ships."

"What with?" I asked, confused.

"Your cannon." She sent me a feral mental grin. *"You remember when Athena's people took me, and you lost your temper?"*

"Yeah..." I felt a prickle of anger at even the thought of that.

"The ultimate impact of that was registered as an earthquake epicenter," James said. *"I remember that, but there's two ships..."*

"Steve, you don't need to kill them. You probably can't, even if you went all out. But if they've taken up station nearby, they'll be on a predictable course. All

you have to do is hit them hard enough to make them back off. They're cowards, remember?" Ingrid said, and I nodded unthinkingly.

"We'll be ready for the boarders. Take them down and gain us some time," Jonas assured us all.

"I'll get the reactors back online," Zac promised, the fury in his voice that he'd forgotten the step that left us in this situation, clear.

"Then I guess I'll get ready to fuck up the ships…" I offered, my mind racing as I tried to come up with a plan for it. *"How long have we got?"*

"Maybe, three minutes?" Ingrid guessed, sounding unsure.

"Long enough," I assured her, dropping the conversation and flicking the last few sections, feeling the power core fluctuate. The steady, low-level hum that filled the room seemed to change all at once.

I hesitated a second, making sure it wasn't going to explode, then pulled up a load of nanites onto my right hand, and dragged them across the control board.

The switches were locked into place, all but the last one, and I sent a mental burst of explanation to Casey, feeling her relief that she literally couldn't make a mistake now.

The only way she could move a switch that wasn't the right one would be to absorb, retune, and fix the nanites that now "glued" every other switch in place.

The only switch that she could move was the one that she needed to, and I was already running from the room.

I sprinted as fast as I could, cursing as I hit a vacuum-sealed air lock door, and forced it open.

I dragged myself in, past the howling rush of what was apparently one of the few airtight areas left aboard as it surged past. Then I slammed it again, ignoring the loss of atmo and the sheer damage that me opening another section of the ship by literal force would have done, if there were crew in this section without a suit on.

I had to just damn well hope there weren't, because their only chance right now was what I was going to try to pull off.

I raced through two more rooms, down to the spinal corridor, then along it as fast as I could to one of the more distant holds.

They were dotted around the ship, designed to literally hold cargo and anything else that the crew required—as well as any loot or ammo or whatever that was needed.

The reason I was so desperate to get to this one, though? This was where the last of the supply of nanites I'd looted from Xiphos were stored. And, unlike the others, this supply hadn't been wiped from my attuning by Belle yet.

That meant that when I forced the door open—being able to form a crowbar of my own nanites and making the edge a micron thick was a hell of a help at times—the container of nanites practically leapt to obey me.

I'd torn the lid off the container—a damn metal barrel—and they flowed up its sides to me, pouring across my armor. I issued orders almost absently, as I threw the barrel aside, grabbed a bunch of null coins from a box by the wall, and ran back the way I'd come.

Arise :Explorer

I felt the changes I needed taking place. New structures formed across my back and shoulders, four million nanites absorbing into my form as I spent them like water. The Hack sub-mind came online to help with the missing details, pushing the shape of what I needed at the locks the nanites held.

Data shivered through the connections as the Engineering sub-mind made frantic use of them, taking the original rage-fueled and wastefully overpowered design for my gravity cannon, and refining it with the upgrades I'd unlocked since then.

Nanites flowed across my shoulders, down my back, grouping on my hips, my thighs, and spreading across my stomach, installing additional load-bearing points, anchoring facilities, and more.

I coughed, tasting blood, and staggered, trying to ignore the pain as twin spears of nanites dug into my chest, arcing up and around beneath my reinforced skeleton.

I felt the questing spires as they shifted "unimportant" sections aside, reducing my humanity even further as portions of spine, of stomach, lungs and other organs were changed or replaced.

More blood poured free as the nanites' scalpels carved away at my flesh, more of them catching and altering the mass that came free.

I bit the inside of my cheek, unable to fully stifle the silent scream of agony as the power cell that drove my armor's more complex functions was moved and upgraded, taking up station below and between what was left of my lungs.

Organs that used to be so wastefully deployed in my torso had been upgraded before, but now, they were cut to the bare minimum.

A full recycling and power cell system was installed, removing more of the stomach and intestines. Cleaning facilities were upgraded and improved to keep my blood as perfect as it was possible to be.

The spleen, kidneys, gallbladder, pancreas, and most of the remaining intestines were scrapped. Their mass was absorbed into the upgraded design. I fell, the pain overcoming me for a few seconds, before I managed to send enough signals to the nanites to move my body with the armored pistons and systems, rather than the inefficient fleshy muscles.

I was down to a stomach that was slightly larger than my closed fist by the time I dragged myself through the previously sealed air lock again, and my waste systems were…well…

They were newly efficient to a level that would have horrified any doctors, let's put it that way. They were also all contained in a space that was a little over eight inches across, five high, and four deep. For *all* of them.

I was more nanite creation now than human, I realized, before dashing the thought aside.

That meant that the newly upgraded power core was significantly larger than it had been. As the startup sequence began, I whimpered again with the pain and shock, although I was determined I'd never admit to anyone that I had.

Instead, I forced myself back up and through the hole in the hull, lying flat as I collapsed on the outside of the ship, on my back, staring up into space as I tried to bring all my systems back online.

I'd created this almost entirely through utter rage in the first place, and part of me knew the value of that.

Rage—righteous, unbridled rage—had a power all its own, as well as an ability to achieve a goal that nothing else could match.

Pain, fear, reason—all would tell you that something simply couldn't be done, and if you were a reasonable man? You'd accept that.

Finding myself alive—barely—locked inside an ancient alien facility, with no anesthetic and being carved apart by the machines? I should have died.

I *had* died, according to Ingrid, over and over; then, barely weeks after that, I'd been tortured to death over and over again, a hundred times, a thousand—I'd never know how many—but for three fucking *years*, I'd been tortured and killed.

The things I'd lived through were horrific. And even now, I could barely force myself to look at them all. But using them? Yeah, focusing on them, on everything that had been done to me, that got my blood boiling.

I remembered the shit that Varnock had caused, the unthinking arrogance of the Erlking, the stupidity and imperiousness of an entire species that had decided that they and they alone were good enough to rule the cosmos.

They were so fucking arrogant that they genuinely believed they had the right to create a fucking slave species to fight their wars for them, all because they couldn't be bothered to do it themselves.

They'd taken a perfectly good monkey, and they'd given it an inferiority complex, an ability to make nuclear weapons, and they'd engineered a greed that would drive us to claim anything we could.

The knowledge that Lucy, the predecessor to our species, was more or less sentient, even if not entirely sapient, and the difference between her, and what we became?

It infuriated me.

We could have been something wonderful, something terrible, or something that would have lived in perfect harmony with our planet. We could have been a gift to an uncaring universe, or an abomination, but *we'd never know*.

They'd stolen what we could have been, and they'd made us weapons. And now? Now it was time to fucking show them exactly why they'd made a terrible mistake in ever fucking around and weaponizing a monkey.

"Steve, are you ready?" Ingrid's voice rang in the silence of my mind.

I lifted both arms, coming to my feet as I looked down at the shimmering rings of nanites that flowed up and into place.

"Soon..." I promised, sharing it with her, and feeling the gasp as she linked with it, and then linked the others in.

I felt her shushing Zac as even now, he tried to ask stupid fucking questions.

I blanked it all, instead pulling in on myself, banishing the world around me. I left a channel open to Ingrid and from her to James to provide targeting data; we'd only get one chance at this.

Then I continued to focus on the bastardization of science that was slowly coming into being before me.

The original design had three concentric rings, held together and in place through gravitational forces I'd barely understood at the time.

If anything, the fucker should have blown up in my face, rather than accelerating a shot—a single point that dragged a "skirt" of nanites behind it, a smaller loop that was designed to open out as it flew, creating as large a hole and as much kinetic damage to the "lucky" receiver as possible—to a horrific speed.

The basic theory behind the weapon was a gravity-driven, magnetic flux-enhanced mass driver.

Instead of the usual method of a rail gun being its main propulsion—magnetically accelerating something as fast as possible down a short runway and flinging it as hard as possible at the target—these were using the magnets as a secondary "bonus" effect.

Instead, it used gravitational fields as the primary, meaning that the shot was already heading in one direction as fast as possible before the magnetics added a final spin and course correction.

That also meant that they could keep the "skirt" of nanites confined magnetically until they left the launch area, allowing a bloom over a set time to make sure that when the leading section hit the target, it'd take out the armor. The secondary impact of the linked skirt, being converted directly into energy by the insane sheer impact, would provide maximum damage.

What I'd done now was create two separate systems, one for each arm. As I lifted them into the air, another solid five hundred thousand nanites *per arm* shimmered as they formed six concentric floating tubes of null metal.

The tubes were separate, yet intertwined; tight at the end closest to me, flaring wider as they extended along, with the beginning of the next nestled inside of the middle to the end of the previous.

They spun slowly, gathering power. I adjusted the design, tweaking, adapting, knowing that we'd get a handful of shots from each, and that was it…a million nanites gone.

The remaining null metal coins were already shifting, being reformed into the "bullets" I'd be using—or, more accurately, the armor-piercing, secondary-stage-creating, discarding sabot rounds.

I started to shake as the power climbed, unable to help myself as the gravitational fields interacted. I reached out desperately, feeling the others sharing everything they could.

Ingrid tied it together, but all of our team shared as much of their mind as they could, spreading the load, allowing me to literally perform unconscious gravitational and orbital mechanics calculations using their unused brain capacity.

I let loose a sigh of relief as the first four, then eight, then sixteen gravitational bubbles I needed to smooth out the gradients appeared around the barrels.

"Steve… are you ready?" Ingrid asked me again, and I grunted my agreement, my mind still streaming through calculations. *"Jonas, signal as soon as the docking ship is locked on, and you're ready. Zac, Casey, standby. Steve, when I say, you fire on the two that are holding back."*

I held it ready, feeling the strain building, then climbing higher, and higher. I felt the strain on everyone else as well. Despite the abilities of my suit to maintain perfect temperature control, the sweat rolled down my body.

Out of the corner of my eye, I saw a sudden flash, then another; I flinched, barely holding the cannons together. Panic rose that some fucker was firing at me, until a third flare of light made it clear what was happening.

Maneuvering thrusters, outgassing or something, fuck knew what, but something was being released below the edge of our ship as the boarders' vessel narrowed the gap, moving in closer and closer.

"Ingrid..." I sent to her on private mode as I felt more and more instabilities starting to form. This time, though, I had nobody else to pull into the link to help. *"I can't hold this much longer..."*

I felt her attention sharpen on me, then a decision being made.

"Change of plan. On three, activate everything. James, use the boarding vessel as cover to protect us from the other two. Steve, split your focus between taking out the boarding vessel and the next in line. You need to kill the closest and gain us time from the others."

I grunted my agreement as Zac tried to argue, then apparently realized that at any second I might go from a manmade turret to a black hole, and that neither would be great for him unless they managed to roll the ship and bring targets into my line of sight.

"Jonas!" Zac called suddenly. *"Get your arse here, and do what I tell you..."*

"One..." Ingrid said, going slower to give Jonas time to scramble for whatever Zac was demanding.

I gritted my teeth, focusing and feeling James sliding partial targeting data into the link.

"Two..."

The flares of light blasted free again. This time, the edge of the approaching vessel appeared, seeming to rise from the artificial horizon of our ship, sliding upward to cut off an entire quarter of the starlight shining down from that side.

"Fucking move it!" Zac screamed at Jonas in the link.

"Three!"

As soon as the word was out of Ingrid's mouth, the ship beneath me shuddered.

Whatever the hell Zac had explained that he needed Jonas to do, what the mad bastard had actually done, was set off an explosive charge in the air lock closest to the docking ship, and one level higher than it.

That released a sudden burst of air before the ship's automated, and currently rebooting, systems could shut it down.

They also sent our ship into a sudden, slightly different tumble from the slow and easily predictable one we'd been in.

This brought the ship that was right alongside us and ready to dock, suddenly spinning up and into view, its boarding air lock fully extended, and her shields, by necessity, down.

So I did the only reasonable thing, and I opened fire.

Three shots from the left arm all ripped free at supersonic speeds; the sabot rounds split to enlarge, ready for impact, right as they exited the final tube.

The result was enough to make me rock back. The barrel shifted from the sheer force of the launch, stitching the impacts across several meters, and as they impacted...

Well.

The term "nuclear" would be a *great* way to explain the release as kinetic energy was transformed into heat and light.

It was also honest and accurate enough that the only damn reason that we weren't fucked up in the extreme by it was because explosions propagate poorly in space.

"HOLYSHIT!" someone screamed into the command link as our warship beneath me came to life with a savage rumble. The power plants had been solidly building all this time, only the output lanes being unable to take it.

Now that the connections were solid and suddenly working, though?

A crackling static charge flooded me, making it harder to hold the barrel in place as James rolled the ship, bringing me around and filling my vision with targeting vectors.

I fired; two shots ripped free. Then, in a split-second decision, I reached out to Arturo, not sure whether he could take the attempt, but amazed as I felt a crystal-clear and cold connection join me.

Suddenly the calculations for the gravity cannon were simple, as I allowed "him"—the ship's AI—to shoulder some of the load. All I had to do was hold it together. And even as I realized that, the crackling around me dropped away.

"I have created a small space in the shield around you, Devourer. Please take your shot and return to the interior as soon as possible."

I nodded dumbly, feeling the AI assessing the data I was giving off as I made thousands of adjustments to the gravity field a second, before cutting all the additional bubbles free.

The relief I felt through the link from the others was obvious, and I felt it as well, having already rendered my brain to bloody mince pulling that trick facing the senagra.

Now though, as the engines fired, the ship slid around, pulling up and moving to keep the nearest, currently exploding and aflame enemy vessel between us and our other pursuers.

It only gained us seconds. The other side was already firing, shredding their former colleague and making damn sure that there'd be no survivors to recover in their haste to get at us.

It was enough, though.

As soon as we exited from behind the remains of their friend, the four laser turrets all swung to life, firing over and over. They were all focused on the left-most ship, and shortly after, both rail gun turrets pivoted and opened fire as well.

The link with Arturo flared again, and my own targeting systems locked in, accepting his assistance. James provided directional and locations data. The target ship that was being painted with repeated blasts veered off, as the second came into sight.

That was helpfully painted with a new, bright and cheerful targeting reticule. I fired, using everything I had, sending five shots downrange: two missed, two hit, and the fifth came apart just before impact to spray the failing shields of the enemy vessel with shrapnel.

The other two hits, though—one sent the shields, shields that had been barely scratched until now, flaring close to overload. And the second took them down, doing enough damage that secondary explosions rocked the vessel.

Then, as my gravity cannon collapsed again, I frantically raced toward safety, jettisoning what was left of the cannon into space, then throwing myself with a gravity bubble toward the rip in the hull.

I barely made it inside before the red lightning crackling across the hull announced the reforming of the shields.

Then back came gravity inside the ship, something I'd have been a lot happier about…if it didn't mean I fell forward and slammed into the deck below face-first.

<u>Chapter Forty</u>

The next few minutes were panicked ones, mainly for me because I couldn't tell what was going on in the wider ship and outside. Some of the damage that the ship had taken had created…well, *issues.*

Something had exploded in the section I was passing through. As well as floating fragments of glittering smoke, and suddenly there was absolutely nothing that I could sense outside—like *nothing at all.*

Worse, it was getting thicker and thicker by the meter, and the deeper I went, the less contact I had with the outside world. I couldn't reach the command link, I couldn't sense the ship, the AI…nothing at all.

For the first time since waking up in Facility #6B so long ago, between the shutdown my system was currently undergoing and whatever this floating shite was, I was utterly alone in my own head again.

I *hated* it.

Somewhere along the line, I'd gotten used to the fact that I had all these extra senses. And even deploying my nanites and pulsing the world around me, all I got was a few inches beyond my armor.

I pushed hard, feeling like I was wading through glittery glue. I was starting to panic that I'd made what might be a fatal mistake, and that maybe I should turn around and try to find my way back out.

Finally, though, after what felt like forever, the mass started to dissipate, then all at once collapsed. Two steps later, and I was out. A custodian stalked toward me, one of the arms raised and some weird little projector sending something like sonic waves washing over the glittery mess.

As soon as whatever it was hit it, the mass collapsed, shifting into a solid pile of dust that gathered everywhere.

I shook my head, no time to fuck around with whatever technical bullshit that was, and just sprinted away from it, finally getting access to the ship again. With one enemy out of the fight entirely, reduced to drifting scrap, another damaged, and the third mildly toasted by the lasers and rail guns, things had stabilized.

By the time I finally made it to the bridge, I'd been fully patched back in, and couldn't believe the bullshit I was hearing.

Not only were the Ændari vessels that had attacked us without warning as soon as we'd jumped into the sector—*a sector that was part of the UC*—kicking off about the damage they'd sustained, but we were also being hailed by a dozen others, two of which were apparently some kind of local news broadcasters, and they were trying to get an interview.

Jonas was, for some totally insane reason, the one dealing with them. And after the third time they somehow hacked into the conversation he was trying to have with a damaged transport that was asking for help, he threatened to send the interview direct to them…attached to the warhead of a missile.

They finally took the hint and stopped trying to get him to give them soundbites or whatever the hell the galactic equivalent were.

I slid into my seat, reaching out to grip Ingrid's hand to let her know I was there physically, as well as mentally.

Then I sat back, relaxing my body as my mind spun up to absorb everything.

The first ship we'd destroyed, that had tried to board us, was, as I'd thought, now a drifting pile of scrap. The occasional signal blared from it before a fresh explosion ripped whatever was left apart even more.

The second ship had been battered, being at an almost standstill relative to us, and had not been expecting anything, when Arturo had opened fire with everything all at once.

It wasn't particularly badly damaged—a dozen small holes stitched through before it'd managed to dodge the rest of the shots—but enough that it was regarding us a lot more cautiously now.

The third Ændari ship was the one I'd managed to hit twice. After the shields had been taken out, secondary explosions had rippled across the starboard side of their hull, and the ship was notably battered there. Several compartments were open to space, and traces of flaring and failing electrics were clearly digging their way deeper into the ship for some reason.

Beyond that, though, and that the engines on that side of the ship were apparently scrap now, they didn't seem to be out of the fight.

There were also at least a dozen vessels in the system still. Apparently the Ændari, despite assuring the various races that all they wanted was their node back, weren't allowing anyone to use the Lagrange points. When I looked at the layout of the system, the various gravitational markers and dips…I found three more ships stationed on the far side.

They'd taken and were holding both of the Lagrange points, with drifting debris marking the civilian and military vessels that had tried to use them.

They were essentially blockading the system, killing anyone who jumped in or tried to jump out, and the ships that were here now were panicking and pleading with the supposed UC warship to make things right again.

That warship, however, was us, and our main guns weren't working yet.

The only things that were currently working were the turrets, which was great. But against two now ready enemies, that were each approximately our equal and had learned not to underestimate us, the odds weren't good.

"Ten, maybe fifteen minutes and I can get one of the mass drivers up," Zac informed us all.

I cursed, suddenly remembering that he'd wanted me to do a load of test firing for Arturo. But when I reached out, Arturo was quick to reassure me.

"I have sufficient information for a basic firing pattern from the shots that you took on the hull, Devourer. More than that would always have required testing the weapons themselves."

"Thank fuck," I muttered. "Okay, why fifteen minutes?" I asked Zac.

"Because they're half the length of the goddamn ship, and I need to crawl across the fucking hull, you pommy bastard!" he shouted at me, before dropping his voice to a low whisper, yet still speaking into the link. *"Calm down, man, just calm… it's not his fault he's a fucking idiot and making the job harder, and he's the boss, the big cheese, the idiot…"*

"Yeah, love you too, Zac." I grunted, tuning him out and getting back to checking out the rest of the solar system. *"Arturo, can we stay ahead of them for the fifteen minutes we need to get the mass driver online? And what's happened with the shields?"*

"Shields are at thirty-seven percent and climbing, Devourer, and yes, provided the Ændari vessels remain at the Lagrange point, there are no issues with the timescale," Arturo replied smoothly.

"Wait, they're staying there?" I muttered, having missed that, and brought up their ships again.

Now that I knew what to look for, and considering the distances we were working on with a full solar system showing, I zoomed in and let out a sigh of relief.

From as far back as I was looking at them on the overall system plot, it looked as if they were right behind us and we were about to come under fire again.

Zooming in and looking at the distance counters…and yeah. They were breaking off.

Thank fuck.

"Why the hell would they do that?" I asked aloud, only to suddenly feel Ingrid's hand on mine.

"They're holding the Lagrange points," she pointed out. "If they move, then the rest of the ships in the system can make a run for it."

"Yeah, but our shields are climbing," I replied, still not getting it. "Individually, they have to know we've got some decent weapons for a one-on-one, or even against the pair of them after that fight. Why give us time to recover?"

"If the UC finds out that the system is currently under siege, instead of them accepting that the Ændari are going to retake their node, they'll have to respond. As it is, those who are hell-bent on appeasing them, or at least avoiding a war, will be keeping the UC from deploying here, if the political system is anything like what we've seen so far."

"So they're keeping things quiet. But there's only five ships in system, three on the far side, and unless they're insanely fast, they have to know they can't catch us. I mean, once we get far enough away from them, it'd take days or months to catch us, right?"

"Yes, and all of that time, they'd have to be away from the Lagrange points. This isn't a long-term strategy, though," Ingrid mused. "Jonas?"

"It won't be," he agreed, muting the conversation he'd been having with a disgusted shake of his head. "Most likely, they're holding for reinforcements. We know they're coming, after all. They have to be."

"So, they keep word from getting out about what's going on, then when they have the rest of their fleet, they'll hunt everything down in the system." I nodded. "That makes more sense. Sorry, just couldn't wrap my head around it. Okay, what about the combat potential of the little ships?"

"I estimate that to be very low," Arturo added into the conversation. "Apologies for the interruption, but I can now confirm the Ændari have fired their engines and are returning to their ambush point. Unless something drastically changes, they are unlikely to take action against this vessel until additional reinforcements have arrived."

"Arturo, do you agree that is their likely plan? To have more forces on their way?" Ingrid asked.

"There is an eighty-seven percent likelihood that the Ændari are following a similar plan to that which you have described, Faction Leader Ingrid, though additional data may change this prediction."

"So maybe yes, maybe no. We don't know what we don't know." I sighed. "Now what?"

"We continue with the plan," Ingrid said. "Arturo, can you confirm if there are signals getting out of the system?"

"Negative, Faction Leader Ingrid. Current observational data, confirmed by multiple data points, suggest that some form of data blockade is in place in addition to the physical. I cannot detect any signals exterior to in-system broadcasts currently, including through the quadrant node."

"Well, that's just friggin' peachy," Jonas drawled. "So what, we rock on and try to land at the node? Just hope they don't care that we're going to do that?"

"They're probably fine with it," James interrupted. "From the number of ships currently heading to the habitable world in this system, and their placements, it seems they already fled the system node."

"Well, yeah, the Ændari kill anyone they find on there, right?" Jonas agreed.

"From what we know, yes, but there are currently two ships docked at the node. Tracing the likely paths and distances travelled by the others, we get a potential start point of the node, some seven hours ago."

"And?"

"And knowing that Ændari will attack anyone they catch aboard their holy relic, and that all other in-system ships that appear to have been docked have left, why do you think those two ships are still there?"

"Maybe they're planning on leaving soon?" I suggested.

"A possibility," James agreed. "However, more likely is that they have no intention of leaving, and that they were either captured vessels forced to land, caught before they could leave, or in all probability, they were manned by an advance force. Scanners and current reports indicate that there have been heavy weapons discharges on the station recently."

"Jonas?" I glanced over at him in question.

"Several ships were claiming they had injured aboard and that they were attacked." He winced. "I just assumed they meant the same way we had been, that the assholes jumped them."

"Get onto one of those, please," Ingrid ordered Jonas. "Confirm if they were attacked in space or on the station, and if so, what we're dealing with currently."

"What about us?" I asked Ingrid on singular engagement mode. *"What do we do?"*

"Exactly as we planned. Nothing has changed except that Zac gets to spend his time working on repairing the ship. We may have more enemies waiting for us than we thought."

"Story of our lives." I snorted.

"Well, there's two ways to look at it." She smiled as we looked at each other in the glory of the bridge of our warship, farther from our home world than any freely evolved human had travelled in millennia. *"We can look at it as there's always more to do, and that we never get a break, or...we can view it as there are dozens, possibly hundreds of opportunities for us to get stronger just waiting for us down there, and we don't even have to chase them."*

"You know, I love you," I said in the privacy of our minds, loving how bloodthirsty she was getting.

Then I remembered just how much of a bunch of shitbags the Ændari were, and basically all our asshole-ish traits could be traced back to them trying to monkey with our genome even further...so fuck it.

After Varnock, I couldn't blame her for wanting to string every single one of the dipshits up by their balls.

"Confirmed," Jonas suddenly said, twisting around to face us. "Just been speaking to the local parasites... I mean, reporters. Might as well make use of them, after all. They confirmed that there were two ships full of Ændari shock troops that landed on the node using hijacked independent traders' ships. Looks like as soon as they landed, they executed the crews to make sure they didn't try to leave, then they started slaughtering the locals on their 'holy relic.'"

"Can we trust them?" I nodded vaguely in the direction of space, and Jonas shrugged.

"There's enough evidence, and it lines up. Plus, they want to stay on my good side."

"Why?" Ingrid asked suspiciously.

"I promised them a personal interview with the commander of the soldier contingent aboard our vessel." He shrugged.

"You did *what?*" I hissed.

"Relax, boss. You see any soldiers on this ship?" He grinned.

"You prick, *I'm* the commander of any soldiers. It's part of the rank of Devourer!"

"Oh, well, in that case, it, er...sucks to be you?" he tried, grinning evilly.

"I'll remember this," I warned him. "Believe me, I'll remember it."

"Now, now, Steve." Ingrid smiled at me. "Jonas was doing his best, remember that, and that as his commander, you get to enforce what was it...mandatory exercise? Wasn't that what he did with Paul?"

"Why, yes…" I smiled at Jonas, as the smile drained off his face. "I think you're right, my love. And you know, I think *Paul* might be able to help with that, or even Scylla."

"That's just evil," he whispered, shaking his head.

"Oh, you wait," I promised. "You've not seen evil yet."

"Okay, with that thought in mind, let's get ready. James?" Ingrid settled back into "business mode" again. "How long till we can dock at the node?"

"Are we heading directly for it?" he asked.

"I don't see any point to trying to pretend and then rush in, do you?" I asked.

"Considering that we can't change orbital physics, nor time and space…no, not really. My point was aimed more at do you want to try to help the refugee vessels that are limping their way to the habitable planet, or ignore them and go straight to the node?"

"Are they going to make it?" Ingrid asked. "Is there an issue?"

"They've been begging for help," Jonas admitted. "The ships are badly overloaded, and frankly, some of the refugees are likely to die before they get there."

"How long for us to go to them, stabilize them, then get back?" she asked.

"We'd most likely need to take them to the planet ourselves," James acknowledged. "By the time we could reach them, they'd have to flip over and do a hard burn to reduce velocity, then flip again to match ours when we reached them. At that point, we'd both need to get up to speed—orbital insertion is probably the best way to get them to a hospital. Then—"

"No."

The bridge went silent as everyone turned to look at me.

"Steve…" Ingrid started, hesitantly. "We should…"

"Jonas, how many are on the ships?" I asked. "How many are at risk?"

"About seven hundred on the ships in total, as near as I can tell."

"And how many in this quadrant?"

"Uh…" He shook his head. "No clue, boss, sorry."

"Make it easier…how many on that planet?" I offered.

"Twenty million, give or take a few."

"So we risk a handful of the seven hundred on those ships dying, if we ignore them and go to the node, or we risk the Ændari getting control of the node and killing literally everyone in the sector." I shook my head. "It's math, people. It's cold and I don't like it any more than you do, but by the time we could reach any of those ships, anyone who really needs us is most likely dead already. We might save a life or two, but we'd lose the war."

Silence hung over the bridge as I looked around, before speaking again.

"I don't like it," I repeated, "but we can't save everyone, and there might be survivors on the node still. If we go after the ships, all we do is burn the little time we have, and maybe save a life for a few hours, by dooming everyone else. If the Ændari fleet arrives, they might be able to beat us to the node—then we all die."

"I…" Ingrid paused, looking at me, then I saw the pain in her eyes at the realization. "James."

"Yes, Ingrid?"

"Set a course for the node please, maximum speed," she said softly, still looking at me. *"What do we do when we land?"* she asked me privately.

"We board the node, and we kill every single fucker who stands between us and the control center. Once we're there, we reboot my system and make damn sure that the Ændari are permanently locked out," I said aloud.

"With everyone?" she asked.

"No... I'm thinking we leave James aboard just in case. Jay, Zac, and Casey as well."

"It'd take several hours for the ship to catch up with the fleeing refugees, but we're not going to need it in that time, right?"

"You want to send them after the refugees?" I asked.

"I think it's the right thing to do," she said. *"We're not going to be able to make sure of the ship, and Zac can do the repairs as easily when it's in flight as in the dock, for the ones he can do at all, anyway."*

"What if we need to run? If we're pushed back or we can't get into the control sections?"

There was a long silence as she stared at me, before answering.

"I don't think that's really an option, is it?" she whispered. *"Either we win, or we die, and so does Earth and every other world in this quadrant."*

"I guess you're right," I admitted after a few seconds. *"Might as well gamble it all on the roll of the dice."*

"Jonas, get the others ready, and—" Ingrid broke off. *"Casey?"*

"Yes?"

"Did you take any of the Healing path?" Ingrid asked suddenly.

"Repair?" Casey asked, naming it as the system did. *"Yes, but only a single level in it."*

"Brilliant!" Ingrid let out a breath. *"Get ready to level that up."*

"Okay, people, we're going to need a volunteer to stay here and do security for the ship..." I said into the command chat, but Ingrid spoke before I could ask for a volunteer.

"Oxus, we need you to stay aboard the ship. You'll be the only security aboard, and you'll need to go with Casey if she leaves the ship for any reason."

"Leaves the ship?" Zac growled. *"Why would my wife be leaving the ship?"*

"To help people," Ingrid said. *"Okay then, everyone, this is the new plan..."*

Chapter Forty-One

Landing, or more accurately, *boarding* the node was done at high speed, and I think the phrase that best described it was "contested."

The layout of the dock was weird, to my mind at least: a wide, shallow crescent shape, raised where the ships would dock. Although it'd been designed to allow large and small ships, there wasn't an intention of many at a time, Zac had told us all, after taking one look at it.

The crescent shape was large enough to allow true behemoths to dock, with most of the ship "hanging" out in space still, or for a few smaller vessels to land on the crescent itself.

Then, stepping down from the first level, there was something called an "ion curtain" that kept the interior atmosphere in place. That was apparently the demarcation point, making it clear that ships landed "out there" and that stepping down from the first crescent into the curtain-separated section was to be done by foot only.

The second level, smaller and lower down, had been partly colonized by the locals, creating buildings of all shapes and sizes, but they were also mainly restricted to commercial storage, apparently.

Something about being right at the edge of space put sensible people off living there, I guessed.

Then there was another step down, onto the smallest level, all smooth curves and flowing lines, as well as open edges that led, if you fell, down away from the shimmering curtain and out again into space, before splitting into three bridges.

From there, we'd have to sprint across the narrowest point of one of the small bridges and into the "main" station area through one of three doors, separated by about twenty meters each.

The biggest door towered over the others, and had apparently never been opened in living record, meaning that particular bridge was as much use to us as a chocolate fireguard.

The other two were narrow, and led to small doors that stood permanently open, half circles that were about ten meters across.

That made the two bridges perfect ambush points, considering that the third, situated between the other two, was covered in small buildings and would lead us nowhere useful.

That, we guessed, would be where most of the defenders would be hiding and waiting to slaughter us as we tried to get in.

What happened instead was that James flew us at the node at literally the top speed he felt he could control the ship and stop safely at, entering the docking bay while still going far too fast, then fired on everything he could see.

We'd gotten confirmation from the ships that we could reach that all the civilians were off the node now, and that the only fuckers we were going to meet were the same ones who had stormed it, slaughtering those aboard, and we decided that one good turn deserved another.

He scoured every hiding spot in sight with the point defense lasers, shredding at least half a dozen enemies who had been hiding, ready to try to ambush us. Then he spun the ship, pointing the engines at the docks, and fired them *hard* to bring the ship to a complete stop.

That had the added advantage of blasting the first crescent pretty much clear of anything and everything that wasn't heavily armored.

The nearest of the two ships, essentially a glorified tug with a single turret on the top, flared to life. The lone turret tracked around, then got shredded by Arturo before it could get so much as a single shot off.

Then we jumped from the rearmost hatch, hitting the dock hard and fast, before sprinting for the far entrance into the main "living area."

As we did that, James, Oxus, Zac, Casey, and Jay stayed aboard the ship, hammering back out as fast as it could go, without toasting us all from the engine backblast.

As soon as we landed, though, we were running.

I'd taken the lead usually in things like this, but this time I was beaten to it. Malthus and Benat raced ahead. The massive devilkin carried his triple-barreled rifle at the ready; Benat raced ahead of even him, her feet barely seeming to touch the ground before they were off.

If he moved like a bull, pounding through the devastation of the dock like an unstoppable force, she was a gazelle—lithe, fast—and it'd be easier to catch smoke in your hands than her.

She also had a new rifle in her hands, one of a bunch that Ingrid had apparently bought "samples" of.

When we were on approach to the node, she and the others had filled me in on the last events on the star station.

Apparently, the local security forces weren't very happy with us for some strange reason, despite the fact that the station was almost entirely intact still—minus some unimportant outgassing and a small but noticeable fraction of its population being rendered down to dog food.

It turned out that when I'd done my whole "do *not* fuck with me" posing, crushing what was clearly a senagra inside the remains of its own escape pod, it had the bonus of generally giving the impression that the reason the space station was still intact was entirely down to me deciding it was permitted to be. So that kept people from getting too serious when they were mentioning little things like "repair costs," "evidence," and "sovereignty."

That Ingrid had pulled our credentials out as faction leaders of a planet that was granted full-member status in the UC, and yet they'd never heard of…well, that also helped.

One of the corpo types had guessed that it meant we were representatives from one of the Shadow Worlds, something that was apparently the basis of a whole range of books and various other forms of media.

The legend went that the Shadow Worlds were the UC's greatest and worst-kept secret. Everyone knew someone who knew someone who had been on a ship that carried a hobo who had once been rescued by teams from them.

Basically, it was all boogeyman shit, a made-up world—or several, depending on the rumor you believed—where the UC trained their most unprincipled and powerful soldiers who kept the rest of the galaxy from being swept away.

They were the ultimate black ops bullshit, and when Ingrid had refused to even acknowledge the question…well, that decided it for them.

It also helped that we were flying a UC ship, that everyone knew nobody but the UC could get, *honest*. Then we'd killed a fuckload of the locals for messing with us and were doing shit that looked impossible.

She'd hardly had to hint at it at all once it'd been suggested. By the time she'd left—with the memory modules, and loot from the senagra—the corpos were blissfully convinced that they'd just made contacts with a group that were at the very least highly fucking connected and dangerous.

Most likely, they'd decided that we were representatives of operatives from the Shadow Worlds and showing us some nice toys now would mean possible juicy contracts later.

That was why when I'd asked whether Zac had found time to work with Paul on some new rifles, I'd been expecting it to be a very understandable "Hell no, when?" and a rant directed my way.

Instead, I was directed to the aft armory, where literal crates of ammo, new shiny prototype weapons, and more were stacked, all awaiting "testing" to see whether they were suitable for our highly secret forces.

The simple answer was "fuck yes," and Malthus had nearly had a heart attack at the new toys.

Admittedly, he'd stuck with his custom, high-powered tri-barreled heavy machine gun, but that was because there wasn't a new version of that available for him. Mainly because the designers didn't view it as something that was portable enough to be used by the general market.

Instead, they'd provided five different kinds of grenades, eleven handguns of various calibers—two that were projectile-firing models that should be used to take out behemoths and the titans of legend were especially tempting.

There were three lasers, ranging from high powered, and possibly being useful for either anti-tank usage, or maybe hunting T. rexes, to a medium but rapid-fire model, and last of all to an assassin's version, complete with suppressors.

There were two of those, and Benat had claimed them both instantly, falling in love with the compact weapons.

There were four "crowd control" models: three that produced various different vibrational frequencies designed to interfere with neural signals, and one that was a literal taser gun.

For the frequency emitters, the weirdest was nicknamed "bliss" at one end of the scale. It was literally capable of making most sentients feel like they were being given a mixture of a relaxing massage, a great meal, and a sexual treat all at the same time.

That was incredible. Then came "fear." This one had limited use for two reasons: first and foremost, the flight-or-fight reflex. For most sapiens, the need to fight was hardwired into fear: we saw a threat, something that made us believe we were at risk, and we attacked. The weapon operated on a super-sized version of that, essentially overwhelming its targets with absolute terror.

That was great and all in theory, but in practice was where it failed. Most of the best fighters I'd ever known would attack on instinct in that situation. Some wouldn't even recognize that they couldn't win if the moon was falling on them, and they'd try to punch it.

It was a stupid response, but apparently this was part of the BWV design, as the majority of sapiens were a bit brighter about this kind of thing, and would actually flee, or cower at least.

The other issue with the weapon was the same as the bliss one, namely that the various races reacted differently to different stimuli. Hell, *I* did, depending on the situation. A nice gentle stroke along my skin might be great if I was in a certain mood, but would annoy the shit out of me if I was in a different one.

That was just me. Trying to make a beam projector that could be used on something that had no spine and that breathed through its skin?

Good luck.

The third was a medium-range emotional suppressor. You played it over your target—the beam was both silent and invisible, after all—and it'd generate a low-level malaise. It worked by triggering certain hormonal releases for most races. But again, what might depress one was likely to make another sexually aroused, a third hungry, and another one absolutely furious.

I liked all three and had earmarked one of each, figuring if nothing else, they'd be hilarious to use on Dave and my friends. I also tried flooding them with nanites to try to find something I could use in my own designs, but for now at least that was beyond me.

The taser gun was different, and that I *had* liked. There were two of those, and I'd broken one of them beyond repair, stripping and investigating it.

They were literally lightning throwers, small enough to fit in your hand, and intended for "non-lethal applications"—which I figured was just crazy talk.

The systems that made it up were fairly simple, creating an ionized path between point A and point B, then releasing a massive, stored charge all in one go.

That, I'd liked.

They were scalable, letting you move from basically blasting a bar of lightning as thick as my arm through your target once, utterly draining the battery, or a little zap over and over again.

They were still prototypes because most people didn't see a valid use for them, especially because they were most likely to be used aboard ships to quell mutinies and on planets or space stations.

All those target areas had two things in common: namely the likelihood of a lot of metal to conduct said charge in random directions, and probable liquid to do the same.

So, prototypes.

This one was designed to be used at short range and to only fire when locked on and a bunch of safety measures had been confirmed.

I'd ignored all the various management protocols, and I'd simply torn the gun apart, copying the design that created the ionized channel, as that was fairly simple. Then I'd just wait for an opportunity to use the fucker on someone.

That accounted for nine of the eleven handguns. The last two were essentially a grenade launcher in snub form, and a drugging weapon that fired tiny darts that were filled with a variety of different chemical loadouts.

The grenade launcher was claimed by Jonas, who said he'd not trust Paul with something like that in a space station.

I agreed, but I felt it was a little harsh when Zac pointed out that he personally wouldn't trust Paul with a potato.

Mainly because he'd either lose it, eat it, or get it pregnant.

The dart launcher was useless, as near as I could tell. Every single dart needed to be encoded to the specific chemistry of the race you were using it on, so that was ignored.

The grenades were fairly simple: a tesla model that fired a short-range, high-powered electrical pulse—again, with the same issues as before—but as a grenade, it was less concerned with "non-lethal," so fuck it.

Two compressed vapor models were interesting, one with a version of napalm in it that was "guaranteed to do maximum damage to your target," and the other to deploy a smokescreen.

Then there was the multidirectional claymore, and lastly, the one that we all wanted.

The creator of the last one was a small corporation. They were trying to make their name, aiming for the "there is no overkill; there is only reload and fire again" market.

Where the others were generally circular, about three inches across and one high, this was a solid six inches across and four deep, looking more like a landmine than a grenade. But the effect?

It was a three-part weapon. The base was both weighted and magnetic, supposedly to make sure it landed that way down. The top third would fire off, a small magnet in the top activating through a charge as it fired upward on a spring-loaded release.

The top would stick to a passageway ceiling ideally, locking down, then fire out eighteen darts, in a circle, each attached to a monomolecular razor wire.

The darts would stab into anything nearby, and anyone who tried to run through the area would be shredded.

That was nasty enough.

But the second stage? That released a similar napalm compound—gaseous at first, odorless and silent—forced out under pressure that would be ignited as soon as the chamber was empty.

Then, if being stabbed by darts, shredded by razor wire, and then set on fucking fire with napalm wasn't enough? The final, bottom stage went off, exploding and hurling a hundred tightly compressed metal slivers in all directions.

Again, "overkill" wasn't really in our dictionary, so there was almost a fight over who got them.

There were five provided as samples. One was kept for Zac to feed into the makers, so that we could reproduce them—a massive advantage we had over anyone else, considering we could control them far more than the current UC certainly could.

The other four were taken off us all by Ingrid, who handed them out: two to Jonas, which I felt was unfair; one to Paul, which I felt was frankly crazy; and…one to bloody Scylla!

When I gave her my best "but what about me" look, she laughed and told me I "wasn't pretty enough to get away with a pout"—which was even more unfair.

There were four rifles: two that were actually shittier than the ones we'd come up with so far, and that were discarded straight away; a sniper variant that was a bit more "meh" than the custom one that Courtney had made Zac rebuild for her, but Benat was happy to claim, seeing that none of us were overly interested; and a standard battle rifle that we did all like.

It was nothing particularly special, not really—basically an upgraded SA80 in design that used a lock-on system to fire tiny rocket-propelled darts.

They had limited mobility, so they would not be firing around corners or anything, but if the target was running and you'd have missed normally?

Chances were the adjustments it'd make would result in a hit instead.

There were five of those, and Scylla, Jonas, Paul, Ingrid, and I got one each.

The plan was to feed one of them into the maker later, and make a copy then, before upgrading it. But for now, all the makers were in use, and we just didn't have the time to fuck around.

Malthus had unfortunately not had time to be put into the medical facility. Although Benat was freshly out of hers, she was barely activated, and had no time to get any patches or anything done to her system. The BWV variant that resulted in minotaurs and werewolves and all sorts that we all had was definitely not working flawlessly for her, and in the end, we'd accepted that ascending her properly was going to take a lot more effort.

For now, she had access to a better healing ability, and her nanites were mapping her, so that'd have to do.

It meant that as my boots hit the ground on the universal system quadrant node, we were both the most heavily armed we'd ever been, and pretty much the most outnumbered as well.

Malthus led the way. The massive devilkin's feet practically shook the station as he ran, while Benat fell back and darted from cover to cover, seemingly both terrified and excited to all hell at the same time.

She and Courtney, both carrying sniper rifles, held back, finding the highest, best positions they could, and covering us as we ran.

I was next, on the left, with Belle on the right and Ingrid in the center. Next came Paul with Jonas, and finally Scylla bringing up the rear.

That was it: the team that was going to take the entire node.

It might have been a bigger ask than was reasonable, but when were our lives ever reasonable?

James's plan to use the point defense lasers, controlled by Arturo, to scour any possible hiding places as we landed was genius. That gave us the chance to disembark, gaining a "free" foothold against the enemy.

Unfortunately, the only details we had on the layout inside were hearsay and past records, which meant that the first we knew of the secondary defenses was when we ran through the ion curtain, into the areas with atmosphere, and came under heavy fire.

The main docks were a sprawling affair, clearly designed to accommodate huge ships if need be, but presumably not for long. The original records from when the UC had rediscovered the place had shown it as abandoned for probably centuries.

The interior had always been sealed, and beyond that, it held the universal system quadrant node control center, and apparently was guarded in turn by a failed, earlier model Biological Weapon Variant, according to legend. Beyond that reference, nothing else was known.

The material that the entire structure was created of was apparently hard-locked nanites converted into something that resembled a mix of marble and diamond.

The layout of one of the nearby solar systems, as well as ancient records that had been found, suggested that to build this, at least one world had been converted entirely into the little buggers.

That gave a rough idea how important this structure was, and why, no matter how hard people tried, they couldn't get inside.

There'd been one attempt to force their way inside using a specific frequency nanites killer, something like an insanely high-powered gamma laser, and the result had been the utter elimination of everything that had been aboard the station.

Everything, from the cameras that were set up to record it, to the rubbish left by the hippie inhabitants, those people themselves, the projectors, the scientists…*everything* was scoured clean, leaving no record of what had been done.

They tried once more, and when the same effect was recorded, they'd given up.

I was betting that the Ændari had figured out something to let them get inside. But regardless, it meant that the docks weren't laid out to be used by many ships at a time, despite their size. The entrances were all close together, and the layout was more "look at how beautiful we can make it" rather than a real docking area.

The entrance to the main station—and that had been used as the living quarters and combination everything else by the hippie-dippies—was directly ahead as we sprinted for it, the smoking, shattered buildings that had choked the area now smoldering.

Even as we drew near, another fell inward. A screech of pain and anger sounded from inside. Paul shifted direction slightly to check, then tossed a grenade in and raced to catch up to the rest of us.

Our boots clattering across the marble-like stone sounded as loud as a parade ground march to me. We ran for the nearest of the two entrances, jumping down the ramp that led to the lowest point, then pounded up the far side, cursing the bloody stupid design.

Those of us with more experience with the malleable nature of the nanites—Belle, Ingrid, Jonas, Scylla, and me—had already created shields on our left arms. We hunched behind them, running into the open and knowing this was the bit that was going to hurt.

As soon as we started up the far side, at the most open and defenseless point in the whole goddamn dock, that was where the ambush we'd been expecting was sprung.

Three figures we'd not seen before now, hiding in the ruins and rubble on the central bridge, opened fire on us. Courtney fired at almost the same time as the first of them fired on Belle, staggering her and drawing a hiss of pain, before she shifted her shield to take the next hit for her.

Benat and Courtney fired on the three. One of them tried to return fire, but all three were falling before they could do more than cause minor injuries. It did take our snipers' attention, though, for valuable seconds.

That was when eight more of the Ændari shock troops stood, stepping into sight on the other side of the bridge we were on.

They opened fire on us as we ran right at them, split with four on either side of the door we needed to pass through.

The first hits were on Malthus, fortunately.

His armor was heavy metal—*literally*—and the first few hits of the lasers did little. But as more and more fired, he started to stagger; the rear of the armor flared open, a dozen small vents radiating heat as the last of the thermal layers tried to hold on…

Then they started to punch into him.

The big devilkin roared, opening fire in return—as did we all. His tri-barreled machine gun filled the air with blasts as thick as my forearm, stitching across the floor and into one of the attackers, who staggered back, jerking as the lasers overcame his own armor in return…then shredded him.

He collapsed with a scream, the constant stream of fire tracking to the next in line…

Three hits staggered that one as well, before Malthus fell himself. His rifle stuttered to a stop as he tumbled, face-first and smoking, to the floor.

Benat screamed. Her sniper rifle pegged the one who had taken down her partner and vaporized a chunk of his chest in her haste to fire, between the left shoulder and his neck.

He fell back, his arms thrown up as the powerful blast smashed him from his feet, but still alive.

Courtney's rifle barked out next, switching from the other three. Her rail gun sent a slug through the head of the centermost; the top of his skull vanished along with his helmet in a spray of gore, as he collapsed.

That was what had slowed down the takedown of the other three as well—we had to assume they were Ændari—and any minor injuries would be healed and dealt with quickly. That meant overwhelming destruction or head shots on every one of them, to keep them out of the fight.

As soon as the enemy had popped out, we'd fired our rifles. Our interlinked command net allowed us to coordinate almost flawlessly as Paul, Ingrid, and Jonas each selected a target and fired on full auto.

The tiny, self-adjusting, rocket-guided ammo tore across the limited distance, punching two of the enemy from their feet. That was five of the eight down, even if we knew damn well that they were unlikely to be dead.

The sixth had triggered a stationary shield emplacement, and caught the rest of our fire on that, costing us a hell of a lot of our highly limited ammunition.

The remaining two let loose with similar weapons to Malthus's— heavy machine gun, blasts of energy tearing into us—shifting from the devilkin to take out our nanite armored shields, focusing in on Jonas, and pounding him.

They were heavily armored motherfuckers, all of them, humanoid, probably Ændari themselves, all in white with black at the joints. Bloody stupid-looking cloaks laid over bulging backpacks, flapping in the wind of their fire. And even as we closed, I could see one of the bastards pushing themselves back to their feet.

They'd clearly been intended as part of an overall ambush, one that would presumably have included the fuckers hiding in the buildings that James torched with the ship's weapons as we landed.

That was when our own surprises came into play.

I created four bubbles of reversed gravity on the floor where the bastards were standing, and four more above their heads. The first were essentially negating the artificial gravity of the station; the four above created a new field, one that was five times the strength of the original.

All four troopers practically hurtled upward, their fire cutting off as they vanished on the other side of the wall.

Fire rang out from behind us again as we ran on. Jonas staggered this time. A powerful blast took him in the left thigh, before another roar rang out, this time from Courtney's rifle.

A single figure had dragged themselves out from the rubble of a destroyed house, Courtney informed us, before warning us she was moving to catch up to us, bounding to her feet after Benat, who was already up and running.

"Belle!" Ingrid ordered, not having to say anything else as the greater dryad healer diverted, sprinting to Malthus's side.

Jonas was there as well, sliding to a halt. His shield detached and lifted free to be held by a bulky tentacle instead, covering them both from any fire from the doorway, as he grunted, turning the devilkin over for Belle.

Even as he did that, I cancelled the gravity bubbles, and Ingrid, Scylla, Paul, and I raced for the door.

<u>Chapter Forty-Two</u>

The area beyond was the only interior living space any of the idiots who had lived here, or the scientists and visitors had even managed to get to, an ornate entrance hall that rose to a distant ceiling.

The starlight filtered in through huge diamond windows high overhead, and warm light flooded the interior.

It'd have been bloody beautiful, I guessed, when it was first found. Hell, the records had shown it as that as well, but now…

The interior had been filled with tight-packed "streets" winding this way and that. As people had built more and more, the scant hundred-meter width by about two hundred depth had been overrun with an eye-searing blend of colors that filled the tiny shantytown.

Imposing buildings tried to loom importantly, while next door was what looked like the entrance to a battered opium den, or a brothel, strip joint, and bar combined.

Every direction was filled with a sensory overload of color, twisting madness-inspired designs—more than half were seemingly entirely made of cloth and cushions—and as soon as we stepped through the door…

We came under fire again.

The four I'd flung upward hadn't come crashing down, because they were whatever the Ændari equivalent of the assault troopers were to the UC.

The backpacks I'd barely registered they wore had extended. Jets pushed out, and now, instead of them crashing down to the floor and being easy targets for us…

They fired as they dropped onto a flat-roofed nearby building.

We returned fire. Bullets and lasers stitched holes along a raised barrier that they ducked down behind, before we came under fire again, this time from behind.

My shield I'd been holding between the troopers and me did fuck all for the blast that punched me from my feet, coming as it did from behind.

I screamed. Whatever had hit me flooded my body with an overpowered burst of electricity that caused the nanites to jerk and spasm, forming nonsense linkages as more shots rained down.

"Steve!" Ingrid shouted, dropping down next to me and raising her shield to protect me. She fired in that direction, before hissing as a fresh blast of whatever hit her shield dead-on.

The shield she'd been holding shuddered, twisting and deforming. Paul opened fire as well, even as Scylla ignored it, sprinting as fast as she could.

Her rifle was discarded; the proton lance returned fire and took a trooper in the head as he stood, ready to take advantage of us.

He fell. The remains of his helmet barely held any of his head now, even as his friends ducked again, shoving guns over the top and firing blindly.

She kept running, reaching out to me in the command link, and sending a complex series of instructions.

I gritted my teeth. A third hit sent Ingrid sliding back, pushed by the force of the impact and uncovering me as I focused on getting back up...

Then the fourth hit me in the small of my back.

I screamed. It felt like every cell was being torn apart, even as I forced the bubble that Scylla had demanded into existence.

It appeared before her, me frantically "tagging" it in the link so that she could see it, as she leapt.

She landed with one foot on it, and I triggered the bubble, powering it into a ten-gravity reversal, shoving her up and away. She summoned her wings, flipping over and firing the proton lance at the crouching figures as she somersaulted over them.

There was an explosion from that direction, but as soon as I'd done what she needed, I'd killed the bubble, tentacles flaring out to shove me sideways.

Or, that was the plan.

Instead, random lumps of nanites flared and collapsed, pushing me uselessly half onto my side as I tried to roll. The last of what felt like a direct hit from a bolt of lightning quivered through me, as Paul flung something over my head in the direction that the fire was coming from, and Jonas sprinted in, firing in that direction as well.

The explosion that rang out was titanic. The building closest to us shook, one wall falling, and I dragged myself to the side, barely making it away, as Ingrid pushed her shield between me and any more incoming fire.

The others streamed through the doorway. Courtney, running full-pelt at the nearest solid building, jumped, kicking off the wall and grabbing the edge of what looked like a flat roof, and pulled herself up in one smooth motion, to roll over the edge and out of sight.

Benat and Belle were at the back, having dragged Malthus closer to the doorway as her tentacles—or vines...fuck knew what was more accurate for her—continued to work on him.

"You want more!" Paul roared, running in the direction that the fire had come from, rifle raised.

I gasped, sagging onto my back, heart hammering and tasting blood as I blinked, trying to focus. "What the hell was that!" I whispered, stunned.

Another handful of shots traded back and forth a street or two over, then I shook myself, cursing once again that my systems were so fucked up right now. I tried to pull up the details, to see what state I was in, and got cascading error messages, before the world shuddered and dimmed.

Then it was back, like if I'd blinked, I'd have missed it, and I snarled, forcing my way to my feet with Ingrid's help.

"Nanite killers," she explained breathlessly, staring at me, and clearly trying to make sense of what she was seeing. "I think, anyway. It was like thousands of my nanites went wild, dropping out of contact and rebooting, as well as being hit by a truck!"

Her shield was on the floor, half of it sloughed apart like a snake shedding its skin, and the rest... The nanites flowed and thrashed, forming peaks and fractal shapes that collapsed a second later.

"Shit..." I whispered, blinking and reaching out to the others, glad that at least the command link was still working. *"Status?"* I asked the group, getting a head dump that let me know that everyone was okay, more or less— with the exception of Malthus, of course.

The sight that Scylla shared made it clear that she'd gotten the other two of the four: the smoking headless corpse at her feet as she slung the proton lance over her shoulder again, followed by a blurry image capture of another figure looking up at her as she flipped over the roof they were crouching on.

The shot she'd let loose there had punched a hole bigger than my head through the middle of his chest, setting off something on his belt that exploded.

Jonas had gotten the other one, who had been injured already, having put him down with one shot, then flung a magnetic grenade onto his body, making damn sure that he wasn't getting back up again.

The fourth and final kill, who was clearly at her feet now, had been knocked from the roof by the blast, falling into a narrow alley. That had been the last shots I'd heard, the pair firing at each other before she got him.

Then came an image from Paul: the remains of a tripod-mounted cannon, still aflame, shredded by the monomolecular wire and darts, as well as the fragments, making it clear that he'd used his all-singing and dancing grenade—and also that we'd not be recovering anything useful from the remains of the machine either.

I stifled a growl of annoyance, pissed that we'd lost such an effective weapon and that the Æendari apparently had access to tech like that. I was damn pleased that the cannon was down, though, as that bastard had *hurt*.

I didn't stop Jonas dressing the former marine down, though, because that cannon would have been great to get and use on the bastards if we could have.

"I've found the entrance," Scylla announced across the link, and I nodded tiredly, accepting Ingrid's shoulder as she tried to help me stand, the pain of whatever that nanites killer had done, slow to fade.

"We're coming," Ingrid assured the others through the link. Jonas and Paul moved up, getting waved forward by her to help with carrying Malthus.

"Are you okay?" Ingrid asked me quietly on singular mode. *"Your nanites are rebooting over and over..."*

"It stings..." I admitted, trying to hide just how much. It felt like every joint and muscle was shaking, breaking, then fixing themselves, over and over—just in

a tiny way, like an ache, like the worst flu I'd ever had, combined with getting blood taken, in a hundred places.

It wasn't nice, not at all, but it was manageable.

"It's whatever that bitch Varnock did to you," Ingrid guessed. *"That's stopped the rebooting nanites from joining back up properly, I think. We need to be quick, Steve. We need to get your systems sorted out."*

"Oh, hell yes," I sent grimly, nodding that I damn well agreed with that.

Then, because there was nothing else to do about it, I started to move again, pausing to pull Ingrid into a hug, resting my helmet against the top of hers for a second, and taking comfort from her closeness. Then I stepped free, picking up the rifle from where I'd dropped it, and replaced the magazine in the well with a fresh one.

"Belle, how's Malthus?" Ingrid asked, as she and Benat came into sight, half carrying and half dragging the big devilkin with Paul and Jonas.

"He's stable, but he won't be fighting for a while," she said.

"Can the pair of you carry him okay?" I hefted my rifle and made it clear that we really needed to be ready to defend us, if possible, rather than most of us carrying the big bastard.

"We'll be fine." Benat nodded her understanding. "I've gotten him home drunk enough…this is barely worse."

That made me smile, though she'd never know it.

We moved then, following the signal that Scylla shared, winding through two narrow spaces, then into a wider passage, passing under colored cloth awnings that had seen better days.

There were signs that this path would normally be filled with people. Overturned food trucks and rubbish lay scattered; smoldering cloth and sooty lines showed where something had burned. And worst of all were the smoldering bodies.

There were handfuls here and there, clumped together where they'd tried to hide in corners, under tables, and occasionally, where larger bodies had tried to shield smaller ones with their own flesh.

I tried to hide those from Ingrid, while imprinting them on my mind as exactly why the Ændari could never be allowed to rise again to power. Ultimately, I failed, though, as we stepped out into an open plaza and found over a hundred more bodies, scattered about where they'd apparently tried to make a peaceful last stand.

The plaza was laid out in a spiraling path of interwoven rings. Crystals of all kinds glittered and gleamed as they stood from mosaics that spread across the floor and rose up the walls.

The bodies were strewn about, bloody holes torn in them, and worst of all, through them, into the bodies that they'd tried to hide.

As we drew closer, we could see what we recognized as secondary wounds, inflicted postmortem, as the bastards had gone around, firing point-blank into the heads, to "make sure."

"Damn, they even did their own," Paul muttered, pointing to a collection of Ændari bodies off to one side, heads bearing the same wounds.

"Clearly a different game being played then," Jonas said.

Underneath them, the mosaics told a horrific tale, one of scattered bodies that mimicked those laid across them in reality, worlds aflame in war, and great fleets facing each other, with entire solar systems falling to ash.

Rising from the floor on either side of the central door were carven images, monsters with multiple arms and ridged domes for heads, split jaws and long, trailing tongues, sharp claws, and pointed teeth. They stood over the scene of war, arcing up around the outermost edges of the mosaic, before falling dead, a coalition of creatures fighting them off.

Then, next came another race, one that we all instantly recognized, being raised from what looked like lemurs, the cheeky bastards, to stand tall. It was clear that the image was moving through a dozen different variations: werewolves, vampires, Oracan, and more. Behind them, between them and growing dimmer as if disappearing into the distance, were hundreds more, before finally, there was a group of four men and women.

They knelt, two on either side of the door, naked, before the next image showed them standing in versions of armor not too different from Jonas and the others, weapons pointed outward, clearly ready to kill anything.

Beneath their feet were piled skulls, broken bodies, and futilely reaching hands begging for mercy. The bodies of the other creatures were suddenly recognizable as more stylized and twisted, robbed of any grace the longer I looked.

Behind what were clearly supposed to be humans, and BWVs, stood three Ændari. Rays of light reached out from them, and above them, in the center of the door, was a shining city of light, something that was clearly meant to invoke awe and splendor.

The overall image was marred slightly by the splattered blood and gore of the innocent civilians that the bastard's shock troops had slaughtered just for being here.

As soon as we stepped close, though, moving inside the outer ring of crystals, the connections began.

The crystals suddenly pulsed with light. The others gasped, stiffened, or froze, seeing who knew what, as my own screens tried to populate, then crashed. Masses of random symbols flooded my vision.

I tried to activate the Hack sub-mind, thinking that might be able to link to whatever this was, and cursed even more as it failed, crashing and disconnecting.

Considering it and the Engineering one that I tried next were housed in a secure memory cell layer built literally into my rib cage, that was even more terrifying.

"What do we do?" Scylla asked, the first of the group to say anything aloud, and I shook my head.

"I can't see it," I said. "It's all crashing."

"Here."

I followed the permission link that Ingrid shared with me, feeling the sensations twinned as I suddenly took up residence in her mind, and saw the prompt before me.

Biological Weapon Variant #115623621782, state reason for access attempt to Universal System Quadrant Node #2.

Beware, unauthorized access attempts will be met with the full force of this facility's defenses.

"It's the basic entrance protocols." I was relieved that I could see it through Ingrid's systems still. "We might have an issue, though. I can't see this myself, and my authority is linked to who I am. I don't think I can present it or transfer it to you, considering how fucked up my systems are at the minute. Hell, if I try to transfer to you, I think we'd lose it fully."

"What do you have access to?" Ingrid asked, and I ran through my systems quickly.

I lifted my right hand and focused, relief flooding me as my harvest blade slid out and back in, followed by my vorpal. But when I tried to form a shifting, changing construct, like the tentacles or my wings, it failed, fuzzing up as the nanites tried to build it, then flowing back into the set shapes I'd already had.

The armor was intact, though, as was my gravity generator, so…

"It's the solid shapes," I whispered as I made the connection. "The harvest blade, the armor, the vorpal or the gravity generator—they're all set things that don't need to move, not really. They just assume the shape. The vorpal blade and the harvest blade are both set shapes, like my armor, but the tentacles flow…they reform constantly."

I tried to shift the harvest blade from the blade to the whip, and it failed instantly. Then, shifting it back to the blade, it seemed to have issues, before eventually solidifying into the correct form.

I hesitated, not liking the risk of losing access to the fucker again, but needing to know now, and deciding it was worth the risk.

I reformed the blade from around eight inches of solid lethality to a four-inch punch dagger, then into a meter-long length. Each time, it formed smoothly. But trying to form the whip, or anything that required more than the nanites essentially forming a basic shape?

That failed.

Nodding to myself that I understood, I drew the blades back into my armor.

"It's the higher functions," I said. "All the higher functions of the attuned nanites, as well as some of the ones that are available to the weaponized ones are failing." I tried to create my wings, and shook my head as two large lumps formed, then collapsed back into me.

"Looks like I'm down to blades and whatever connections you can form me into," I told Ingrid, before reaching up to the back of my neck as a thought occurred to me.

"It's this." I nodded. "The memory cells are linked from the armor to my brain by nanites, but this is plugged into the back of my brain directly, that's why I can still communicate with you all."

The small section at the base of my brain, leading down to the bottom of my neck, had been repaired when it was reinstalled by the ship's medical facilities, and I was suddenly insanely glad that I'd not ripped it out as I'd meant to do several times over.

"So now what?" Ingrid asked. "Dammit, I wish we had Zac here!"

"Why?" Paul cocked his head.

"Because he might be able to jury-rig something that would give me access to the system," I replied. "As it is, my nanites that would normally be able to do this no stress, can't. Belle has access to the Support and Harvest trees, but she's not experienced enough with the engineering side of them that I'd want her digging around in my brain…no offense."

"I'm glad you don't want me to." She glanced up from where she and Benat had laid Malthus down, her vines entwined into his body again as she continued rebuilding him.

I and the others deliberately made no mention of the other two vines that she had extended to a nearby pile of innocent bodies. The collapse of them as she drew more and more free made it clear that she was breaking them down for their nanites.

It was horrible, considering they weren't our enemies, but it was necessary as well. I'd done it before in Athens and since, raiding the innocent dead for working nanites to help others.

"Can I do it?" Ingrid asked me hesitantly. "I mean, I don't have that kind of experience either, but…"

"But it's the only way we're going to get in," I finished for her. "Exactly."

"So, what do we do?" she asked, and I glanced about, then grunted.

"Right, everyone get ready. We'll move over to the door, get closer to it in case we don't have long to get in. This isn't going to be easy, so be ready to run. Jonas, Paul?" I nodded in the direction of Malthus, and they nodded their understanding. As we gathered closer to the door, Belle released the bodies she'd been working to strip.

"Okay, people, if we fuck this up, we won't get a second chance, so hold on, and be ready." I exchanged a look with Ingrid.

"We can do this," she assured me quietly.

"Right, here we go…" I whispered, reaching out to Ingrid and feeling her draw me through her systems, to present me to the prompt, and then through that, somehow pushing me into primacy.

That…that was weird.

I felt it, and realized what she was doing. As soon as she did it, I understood both that it might be the one thing that gave us the chance to do this, and that I didn't know whether I could have done it, even if I'd thought of it.

She literally surrendered herself to me entirely, somehow distancing her own personality, and everything that she was, from the link. And I loved her even more as I felt the trust that something so absolute required.

I reached back into "me" and dragged forward everything that I felt, that I knew, of my authority, given to me by the Erlking, and the tweaking and solidifying that we'd managed to do ever since.

I fed all of that, along with the memory of the Erlking granting it to me—slightly altered, as the vision of him grabbing my head and screaming at me in rage was unlikely to help—to the sentience I felt on the other side of the link.

I felt it respond. Something elsewhere in the node shifted, being activated, and then more of my submission was examined. There was something wrong, I suddenly felt, something that should have been there that wasn't, but also…

I couldn't explain it—a sense of hope, or resignation, of disinterest and sheer annoyance that flitted from emotion to emotion almost too fast to sense, before resignation and acceptance finally won out.

Then the door let loose an almighty creak. A cascade of long-frozen dust and debris fell free as a line split down the middle of the massive door.

It opened slowly but smoothly, moving ponderously to expose a smaller section on the far side, an area of clear, polished marble a dozen meters in diameter, before the first of a dozen steps led up to an arched doorway.

"Step into my parlor, said the spider to the fly," Jonas muttered.

I pulled back from Ingrid's mind, releasing her. Feeling the way she swayed, I grabbed her, catching her as she almost fell.

As soon as I did that, the doors ahead, by now past the halfway mark, and still opening, suddenly ground to a halt, and a horrible realization filled my mind.

In detaching from her, I'd made it think I'd been using a fake ID—or the galactic equivalent, anyway—and it was now *pissed.*

"RUN!" I barked, sweeping Ingrid up and sprinting forward even as the doors started to close again. A feeling of anger, or disappointment and worse, of building rage followed by satisfaction bloomed. I realized that somehow, I was still linked to Ingrid, even if only distantly, as a new message was sent to us both.

Biological Support/Command Variant #115623621782, your unauthorized access attempt has been logged. Internal reserves of Biological Weapon Variant #11 have been released.

I felt it, as I ran with her, carrying her inside and knowing damn well that it was the only chance we had, as Ingrid pushed a compressed data burst at the sentience we could both still dimly sense was watching us.

It was limited, the explanation, and it was over so fast I could barely catch the headnotes, but she was explaining that I'd been attacked in a "rebellion," something I guessed any Ændari system had to be familiar with. I'd been injured, and my internal nanite systems were damaged, forcing me to use her as the intermediary to unlock access.

There was a long pause as the others got in behind us—just—and a half second later, a boom as the doors sealed.

Data burst back at her, and she responded, the conversation fast and furious as she "talked" to something, over and over repeating, explaining, cajoling, and finally ordering, before a last message was sent to us all, and that Ingrid shared with me.

Arise :Explorer

Biological Weapon Variants and Command Access Requestors, access request has been found to meet limited tests.

Biological Weapon Variant #11 has already been released in limited numbers. Current situation when evaluated with extant conditions has resulted in sub-optimal status.
One situational compromise has been achieved:

***

Quest Granted!

Claim Universal System Quadrant Node #2

Universal System Quadrant Node #2 has been abandoned past all expected maintenance deadlines, and is currently operating at 17.482% operational capacity.

Contact with extant authority wielders has failed for 17,865 solar cycles. This facility is deemed vital to the survival of the local galactic population, but cannot be repaired, nor replaced without dedicated command access.

Loss of this facility to irrecoverable decay is judged highly likely within 2,895 solar cycles.

Solution: Command authority wielder will be repaired, system rebooted and examined. Provided authority is deemed correct and of high enough grade, Universal System Quadrant Node #2 will surrender to command authority wielder.

Complete the following prerequisites to receive this reward:

- **Survive**

Consequences should the evidence prove that your authority is insufficient:
- **Release of remaining store of Biological Weapon Variant #11**

"That…that sounds ominous," I muttered, staring at the text that Ingrid linked to me, and noting that there wasn't an option to refuse the quest.

That was when the distant sound of something unlocking rang out, and the screams began.

Chapter Forty-Three

"Run!" I roared, sensing as Ingrid shared into the command link a pulsing beacon, one that was marked as the control center, some five floors above where we were.

The map she had suddenly updated as well. Dozens, then hundreds of glaring red markers flared to life, and I realized that the map she was sharing with us all wasn't something any of us had seen before.

It was a wireframe drawing, level by level, showing that the stairs before us led up to the ornate doorway, then through into a long hall.

There were a small number of what looked to be tubes on either side of the doorway, and there were red dots crawling down them already, heading to the exit into the hall.

Flashing orange buttons appeared inside the tubes at the entrance, and I sensed the tag that came with them, basically "hit this and the tube locks."

That, and the rest of the facility map that was being shared with us, was clearly an attempt to give us a chance against whatever our predecessor BWVs had been, as the node AI apparently regretted releasing them.

I noticed the fucker wasn't sealing them away itself, though. It was giving us a chance and sitting back, watching and no doubt evaluating, the metal motherfucker!

We ran, sprinting up the stairs, Ingrid and me behind Scylla, who led the way. Paul and Jonas were helping to carry the still bleeding Malthus, who groaned, apparently in enough pain he was starting to rouse in complaint of his method of transport.

Benat and Courtney were on either side of him, with Belle in close on the right, still connected to him as she frantically tried to get the huge mercenary back to a functional state.

I bit down on the thought that we might have to leave him behind yet, and worse, the little voice that said he might be useful as a distraction to save "my" people.

That was the coldest part of me, the part that would sacrifice them all, one at a time, if it meant I could save Ingrid. I hated it, as much as I silently admitted to myself that if it came to it…

I'd probably do it to save her.

I cut off that line of thought, refusing to give it any mental space as we passed through the doorway, and into the hall beyond.

It reminded me instantly of those massive cathedrals, the ones where the roof felt like it was miles overhead, where it'd been made by men literally hundreds of years ago who had devoted their entire lives to building them.

The ceiling was high enough above that the starlight that streamed inward was augmented by hundreds of lights embedded in the walls, and yet still it was clear.

I saw marching mosaics of figures, their heads bent in reverence, arms full of treasures that were being offered up to the end of the hall, where a huge figure, presumably Ændari and wearing a fucking crown of light, stood.

The door to the next set of stairs was between his legs, the tip of the doorway just below his knees. It was maybe fifteen meters high, making it clear that the figure himself was almost a hundred by extension.

He stood with his hands raised overhead. Beams of light extended from his crown to touch something that hung between his outstretched hands...and I recognized it as a stylized version of the node we were aboard.

The bit that really stood out for me, though, was the four pillars that were half sunken into the walls, and the hidden exits in them that rotated into view slowly. The sound of distant howls and screeches echoed down to us.

We ran for it. Scylla was already halfway down the hall, leaning into it as she sprinted full speed. The rest of us raced behind her as Ingrid shouted ahead to her.

"The buttons!" she yelled. "They'll close them off! Hit the buttons!"

"Fuck!" I snarled, doubling down and summoning a bubble, throwing myself forward and reducing gravity. I created a second bubble of warped gravity before me that sucked inward, then vanished, and reappeared a meter farther away, doing the same then again.

I "fell" forward, faster than I could run, popping a fresh gravity bubble down between my feet and the ground, and one in reverse behind my head when I started to stretch out, falling headfirst, flipping myself around, to land inside the now fully open pillar entrance.

Scylla had already hit the first of hers, practically bouncing out of it with the force, stumbling as she tried to keep her feet, then correcting and running at the second on her side.

I'd landed with my feet on the inside of the pillar. The button before me, a large flat thing, was unlike the flashing one on the map that we were being shown...subtle enough that I'd not have seen it if I hadn't been looking.

I slapped a hand on it, feeling the *click* as it depressed and the instant start to the pillar. It began to rotate again; then I crouched, my gravity still flipped so that to me "down"' was actually standing on the left wall of a room, and I looked up into the dimly lit interior of the pillar overhead.

The creature that was falling toward me, arms extended and maw open, triggered every goddamn "fuck no" instinct I had. I kicked off, hard, flinging myself back into the room, and barely missed Ingrid and the others as I twisted gravity again to land upright, skidding backward.

The creature had managed to catch my armor as I leapt, before falling headfirst into the floor with a crunch.

It'd barely impacted before it was up again, scrambling. Its jaw was broken from the impact; blood sprayed from a half-severed tongue, as it scrabbled forward, uncaring of the injury.

It was like the creatures shown on the mosaic outside, multi-limbed. It had two legs, a short body, heavily covered in bone armoring, leaning forward with a short, thick tail extending behind it.

There were two sets of arms, one upper ending in three-fingered, abysmally sharp claws—ones that had already scratched my armor with only the glancing blow they'd managed—and the lower arms more humanoid in layout, with three grasping fingers and a thumb that was thick and powerful.

It looked to be blind. A standard up/down jaw unfolded to increase the size as it opened; the lower hinge hyperextended, as fangs unfolded like a snake's, forming a lined maw that stretched in all directions.

The bloody stump of a half-severed tongue sprayed blood as its feet and lower hands scrabbled for purchase on the marble. The apparent lack of eyes did not slow it at all as it followed me...before diverting suddenly as the scent of Malthus's open wounds reached it.

Terminator	Biological Weapon Variant
The eleventh attempt at creating a viable biological clearance device, this variant eventually proved both the concept of the BWV theory as viable and proved itself to be utterly unusable at the same time. The majority of the experiments were culled. Several that had escaped the primary testing facilities required global extinction events to eradicate. The baseline variant was identified as almost impossible to control without a hive guide and were therefore installed in secure locations in hibernation as a last-resort protective measure to ensure compliance of settled species in nearby systems. **Capabilities:** ***Enhanced reproduction***: The terminator is incapable of fear, remorse, or mercy, understanding only that any warm-blooded creature is suitable prey. Upon biting their victim, a copy of their genomic template is injected, and will, over one solar rotation, mature, converting the incubating prey into a viable clone of the original terminator. ***Feral Rush:*** Feral terminators have no pain reflex, enabling them to withstand extreme injuries and still remain viable, often spreading their strain long after the original infection vector has been eliminated.	
HP 200/200	Terminator

Ingrid shared it with me, even as I raised my rifle, firing three shots, practically point-blank as it rushed us.

Arise :Explorer

The first hit punched into its stomach and vanished. The second hit the armored carapace that covered the thing's chest and cracked it, staggering it sideways before it tried to leap forward again.

That leap was cut short before it could even begin, as the next hit took it at the base of the throat.

The neck was small enough that the high-speed impact from a miniature rail gun was sufficient to tear the head almost entirely free. The body collapsed; blood gouted free, and arms and legs kicked spasmodically at the marble.

That would have been fine, if the fucker hadn't been followed by two more before the pillar could close; the third that tried to squeeze out was caught by the rotating mass and rendered to jam.

The other two were already under fire. Courtney took the first out with a single shot that impacted where the bridge of its nose would have been, if the fucker had one.

What it did have, though—after that—was a hole that ran almost the length of its head, and a jet-propelled evacuation of its deepest thoughts and feelings.

They were pink, it turned out.

The other was faster than Benat, dodging to one side and taking a hit to the shoulder that dropped both its right arms, useless to its side, as something in there was broken.

It didn't so much as slow, leaping for Malthus, before I could switch to target it.

Belle was there, though. Her own abilities supercharged the manipulation of her nanites as a vine-like whip slapped the creature from the air.

It hit the ground hard and rolled. Working arms and legs scrabbled at the marble, trying to get it turned around and upright faster, before both Benat and I fired on it, multiple times.

It jerked, then collapsed, twitching to the floor. Blood fountained from dozens of holes punched in it.

That was only the first pillar, though.

The second, the one that Scylla had already hit before I made it to mine, was closed again. A sheered loose arm on the floor gouted blood and shook as the final nerve impulses stilled.

The third and fourth, though…they were a problem.

As soon as I turned, I saw them: five from the left and seven from the right hitting the ground, one after another, bouncing up and racing at the nearest target.

Scylla spun, dancing in the middle of a veritable onslaught of the creatures. Her proton lance triggered twice, before she switched it to its crackling short-range capacity instead. Holes punched through four of the enemy: one on the left and three on the right fell to the ground, dead or dying.

That left four to a side, and as Paul and Jonas unceremoniously dropped Malthus to the ground—a pained grunt coming from him—they joined the rest of us in firing on what were apparently *terminators*.

Ingrid had dropped to one knee. Her rifle shots rang out as she also deployed a burst from her shoulder-mounted darts. The hall suddenly filled as faint contrails appeared behind them. Three darts from either side of her neck rocketed up through the air, then flipped over and plunged down, punching into the farthest creature from us all. The impacts sent it to its knees.

The darts were loaded with her Hijack ability, stabbing into the creature and releasing her specialized nanites. The thing's nervous system literally hijacked its body and forced it back into the fight, this time under her control.

As she was doing this, she was firing as well, focusing on the left-hand side of the fight, aiming at a single figure. The rifle locked on and ensured that the rocket-propelled ammunition impacted as close as possible to their target.

She'd fired two five-shot bursts; the first three hit the right leg in the knee, lower thigh, upper thigh, hip, and groin. The second five hit the stomach, lower right side, then the bony armored carapace where it began. They hit it again an inch or so higher, punching through the cracks caused by the lower shot, then sunk in under the armpit.

The ten hits overall punched it from its feet, but the carapace that protected the exterior also helped to kill it: the two shots that made it through the upper body's protections hit the inside of the far carapace, ricocheting around and tearing it up even more.

It coughed, then collapsed. The body slid another solid meter or so, blood spraying free as it convulsed.

Scylla was dancing, graceful and lethal; the proton lance flashed through the air, bringing gleaming death as she swung it.

The proton lance was a weapon of the Helio Guard, whatever that was. Regardless, they were apparently fucking lethal weapons. It was basically an elegant, high-tech spear, that not only had an edge that could carve your name into an atom, but it could unleash literal lightning. Or, if you turned the setting right up, a pulse of destructive energy that was capable of blasting a hole in pretty much anything.

We'd looted it when Jonas had beaten Zeus into submission, the former Blessed leader having used it over the centuries he'd been most active to create the impression to the mere mortals of the day that he was actually a god, hurling lightning bolts at his enemies.

When Scylla had gotten her hands on it, it'd become her property. Although I'd eyed it a few times wistfully, the truth was that she was undoubtably the most lethal of us all with a spear, and I really didn't want to know how she'd persuaded Jonas to hand it over to her.

I did notice that he was walking bandy-legged for a while afterward, though, and smiled a lot at the time.

Anyway, she'd found some way to recharge it, and although we'd not been able to copy it, she'd been gradually unlocking and improving her abilities with it.

Now she dropped to the ground, spun and came back to her feet, one foot raised and pressed to her supporting leg. The proton lance extended as she finished her loop, before lunging forward.

Two of the nearest terminators collapsed, both of their legs literally severed at mid-thigh, and she stabbed the leaf-bladed spearhead through the face of the next nearest.

Finally, she planted the base on one of the thrashing, legless bodies and used the lance like a pole, vaulting over the bodies, as Courtney fired again, hitting the next closest to her in the head from the side, sending it to the floor, dead.

Scylla landed like a ballet dancer, spun, stabbed out at the nearest thrashing legless form, taking it in the back of the head, and then spun again, racing the half dozen steps to the next pillar to hit her button.

That left two creatures on the left, and none on the right. I started to run again, headed for the left-hand farthest pillar—until the terminator that Ingrid had *hijacked,* now helpfully marked as green in our heads-up, twisted and sprinted for the pillar instead.

The other two between it and us didn't notice the change, but they sure as shit noticed the gravity change as I reached out, triggering a pair of fields right before them.

They fell. The fields appeared half enmeshed in their chests, and I snarled with annoyance.

They were so fast that instead of catching them with the field in front of them as I'd intended to, I'd nearly missed.

Instead, I doubled, then redoubled it. Their carapaces creaked under the strain, as lungs, hearts, and more were pulverized.

"Fuck this," I growled as Ingrid's creature slapped the button, then leapt back, clearing the pillar as it closed.

"Shit, that was bad…" Courtney whispered, shaking her head, wide-eyed as she looked at the bodies. "If there'd been more of them?"

She left it unsaid, but as I looked at the map that Ingrid shared in the command link, I bit down on an oath.

There were *hundreds* more of them, the release points on each floor apparently being staggered throughout the node. I didn't know why, but the sections that fed into the pillars were almost solid red, and after a second, it struck me why.

"It's only releasing a sample." I grunted as it hit me. "The AI or whatever it is. It's testing us, watching us. And if we fail before we reach the control center, it'll just go on with things as it has been. If we make it there and it decides that my authority isn't high enough?"

"Yeah?" Paul asked as I paused, looking over the map and doing a rough count.

"Then we get hit by maybe ten times as many of these fuckers as have been released into the pillars."

"Shit, boss…" Jonas whispered. "We're good…"

"But we're not *that* good," Paul finished for him, exchanging a long look with Courtney.

"What do we do?" Ingrid asked me.

"What we have to." I gestured to the doors at the end of the hall, which were even now opening. Distant screeches and challenges echoed down from somewhere overhead. We started forward again, heading toward the second floor.

Malthus was badly battered, but he was starting to come around again. The sheer endurance of the devilkin was impressive enough, but combined with the incredible abilities of nanite healing and dryad manipulation, he should be able to move on his own again soon.

Or so I hoped.

As it was, Paul and Jonas took up a side each, supporting him with his arms over their shoulders. It wasn't ideal, but it meant that Belle could work on his back as we moved, and they each had a gun in one hand.

Benat wasn't happy, having said she should be carrying him, after seeing the way they'd dropped him before like a hot-friggin'-potato, but that was life. Ingrid pointed out that she was both physically weaker than those two in their armor, and carried one of the better long-range rifles we had.

I passed my rifle to Ingrid, who left the current magazine in it, but took the rest of mine when I explained my plan, sharing them out to those that needed them.

Scylla fell back, moving alongside Ingrid, as I explained that should she be killed, and the AI need to communicate with me before it did whatever it was going to do, then we were definitely dead.

Courtney and Benat stayed on the outer wings of the group; Jonas and Paul in the middle, carrying Malthus; Belle brought up the rear; Ingrid and Scylla next, behind me.

I led this time, my hands free, vorpal blade deployed just in case, and both my main weapons of my gravity manipulation and foul temper ready to be unleashed.

Chapter Forty-Four

This flight of stairs was wider than the last, almost as wide as the last hall had been. Then, at the top, it split into two, climbing back on themselves to the left and right.

Looking up, it was clear that it ran back and forth like this three times before coming to the next floor. And what else was clear here was that we were taking the goddamn hardest route.

Directly ahead of us was what looked to be an open section that ran all the way from the ground to the top and something like an empty, but enclosed lift shaft, one that when I reached it and looked up, led to the top of the tower. As soon as I entered it, Ingrid apparently got a message, one that she didn't share, but that was clear.

"Steve, stop! If we try using that, the AI will unleash the rest of the stored creatures, and they'll pour down it," she said quickly, showing us all the map that now had a glaring giant cross over the tube.

"Fucking assbag," I muttered, glancing up and wondering whether I dared, then shaking my head and backing out.

I *could* do it, I knew.

I could fling myself up there, flip gravity and use it to get myself up there, but I also noticed that there was a door recessed that shivered slightly, making it clear it could be closed off, and the upper floors presumably were.

The hint was clear. If I tried using this, the AI would close it off before anyone else got in, or it'd open the higher levels and literally let the creatures pour themselves in.

Doing either of those would certainly result in some of my friends dying, if not all of them. And there was no way I was letting that happen, especially as I had no doubt that the node would have some way to make damn sure we stayed dead.

If I tried just flying up the middle, in the open air instead? I had to think the AI would treat that the same and unleash hell on me and my people.

"What about the corpses?" I suddenly said, twisting to look at them. Belle had ripped a leg free with a vine, and was currently stripping it as we moved.

"They're well stocked with nanites, but they're strange. They need a thorough cleanse before they can be used," she said, and I nodded, taking a deep breath and leading onward, berating myself for not considering the corpses.

Just because I didn't seem to be able to do much with them right now, my harvest facility being another casualty of whatever this fucked-up situation was, it didn't mean the others couldn't grab bits that Belle could use to restock as she went.

"I'll take care of it," Ingrid assured me silently, and I nodded, dismissing it as I climbed higher.

The sound of the terminators running was getting louder. I took the next flight of stairs at speed, grabbing the edge of a carved railing as I reached the next balcony, telling the others to hurry.

I heard muttered comments from Paul, but dismissed it, focusing as I created six, then twelve, then eighteen gravity wells. Ingrid reached out, helping me as much as she could, but not tying any of the others in as well.

As the first terminators took the corner to the top of the next flight of stairs, I triggered the nineteenth and twentieth, swallowing hard against a wave of vertigo, as I tried to create two more, and failed.

The two that I had created joined the rest, though. One based in the center of the flight of stairs they were racing down, and the next above their heads both reversed, so that the first thing the terminators encountered was a bubble that cancelled out all gravity for them.

The second one sucked them up and into the clear area that ran up the center of the spire, and there they found the other eighteen.

They were set one after the other, doubling the force of the last one, sending them plummeting back down to the ground.

The result, as I fell to my knees, straining to hold the bubbles intact as thirty-six of the fuckers raced down to attack us, served to throw them up into the air, then drive them down the middle of the shaft with enough force that, when they impacted, they were reduced to pate with an interesting texture.

As soon as the last flew upward, I cut the bubbles, one at a time, as they passed them.

The relief as they vanished was indescribable. And it was only then that I realized that Scylla and Belle had moved to support Ingrid, as she supported me.

"I'm…sorry," I groaned to her, breathing hard, trying to get myself back under control, and she shook her head.

"Don't be…" She gasped. "It…it was…worth it."

Scylla slung her proton lance over her shoulder, stooped and picked Ingrid up like a child, carrying her in an apparently effortless princess carry, as Benat grabbed my shoulder, hauling on it and helping me to my feet as well.

"Remind me not to make you mad," was all that the devilkin said. But the look in her eyes conveyed a question as well.

"I'm okay," I whispered, nodding my thanks, as we started to climb again.

The rest of the flight was painful, considering it felt like my brain had been squeezed out of my ears by extreme pressure, while a migraine from hell battled a cheap, "bought from the back of a car trunk" vodka hangover.

The combination had me wincing as we climbed for two flights, before Belle declared Malthus out of danger and asked us to halt for a minute.

I didn't ask what she did, knowing the dryad's tastes and favorite pastimes, but after she'd leaned in close, Malthus's eyes flared open suddenly and he let out a strangled cry. He nearly fell back down the stairs he'd just been carried up, thrashing around in such a panic.

Then Benat was there, grabbing him and slapping him hard across the cheek, shocking him out of the panic, then kissing him savagely.

Malthus froze, then growled loud enough we all heard it, and dragged her close, returning the kiss.

A kiss that went on and on…

"Damn, dude, get a room." Paul shook his head.

"What?" Malthus snarled, half dragging Benat aside and staring around, wide-eyed at the rest of the group. One hand came free of her ass, to pat confusedly at his chest, still finding holes in his armor, but only minor wounds now that Belle was finished.

As he did that, she was already moving, reaching out to Ingrid.

"I can't do much with your brain, and I don't want to," she explained quickly, "but I can smooth away bruising, and that won't affect the rest."

Ingrid's helmet flowed back into her skin, and she smiled and allowed Belle to do whatever she needed. A sigh of relief escaped the love of my life's lips.

Less than a minute later, she was reaching out to me. Ingrid's helmet reformed as I banished my own, trusting my friend despite what I'd said half in jest earlier.

I felt a prickle of pain at my temples as Belle's fingers grew nanite connections, burrowing through first the skin, flesh, and then bone, before sinking into my brain.

Then, before I could even start to think better of it, the pain was fading away, and blessed relief flooded in. Then, seconds later, Belle released me, wiping the blood free of my temples, and stepped back, a smile sent to me through the link.

"Thank you," I said, and I damn well meant it.

"Where in Nurgurt's blasted butthole is my gun?" Malthus cursed, having apparently realized that he was missing one minor item, and I winced, climbing to my feet, and pointed up the stairs.

"Come on, we've got no time to lose," I said, heroically and courageously leaving it to someone else to explain that the damn thing was huge and none of us had wanted to lug it up here.

We started back up as quickly as we could, as soon as Malthus showed that he could manage a jog, even with his remaining injuries, before moving to a run as he managed to push harder.

It would be reducing his combat effectiveness for the next fight, I knew, but we couldn't waste any time. All we needed was for the AI to decide to throw something into the mix to "even things out" again—or worse.

By the time we made it to the next floor, the open space was clearly already emptied, a shorter, but still huge cathedral-like layout greeting us again.

Although it wasn't as long or as tall, and the mosaics on either wall showed the treasures of a thousand worlds instead of a story, the far end of the hall was more impressive.

It was a rose window, as I'd heard the term used, ten meters from the center to the edge, round and comprised of hundreds of small panes of glass—or whatever the local stellar equivalent was as I doubted they had a glazier quote for the fucker.

It looked out over the stars below. The outer section of the docks hung in space, seemingly farther below us than should have made sense, but the view...

Whatever technology was built into the glass, it showed the planets, ships, and everything else that should be in view from here, as if they were directly before us, making me think of the display aboard our ship.

Either way, it was both beautiful and terrifying, as we saw that a second batch of three Ændari vessels at the secondary jump point were firing on a lone, fast-moving ship that was clearly trying to race past them.

It didn't make it.

The ship shuddered as it took sustained fire. The shields failed; then the ship took rapidly climbing damage. An engine exploded, the force throwing the ship into an uncontrolled roll. That threw the impacts off for a few seconds; then they pounded into it again. More sections came apart under explosions. Something went critical, and the ship vanished in a sudden blossom of white light.

"The reactor," I guessed through my horror. "Or maybe the grav drive. Dammit, why the hell did they try that?"

"They know there's worse coming, boss," Paul said suddenly, and I shook my head.

"We think it is, but the solar system is a big fucking place. They could have landed on the planet, restocked and refueled, and just stayed ahead of them indefinitely, couldn't they? I mean, build up enough speed and just head into deep space if need be, jump when you reach... Ah, fuck."

"What?" Benat asked me.

"The flotsam," I muttered. "The area at the edge of the solar system where all the rocks and debris are—they could jump from there, but if the ship isn't fast enough or strong enough..."

"It'd either get overhauled long before it gets there, or it'd be smashed to pieces before it could jump," Malthus agreed. "And you need a damn powerful drive to jump around the debris that's out there. Unless you get a large enough open space, you need to provide the energy for anything that's in the jump field with you to jump as well. Asteroids and the crap that floats around out there have a lot of mass."

"Boss!"

I looked at Paul, hearing the stress in his voice, and cocked my head in question.

"Are you seeing this?"

"Seeing what?" I looked back out, scanning in the direction that he was looking but not seeing anything.

"Oh no," Ingrid whispered, and I jerked around, looking at her, then back out.

"What!" I snapped, looking around quickly, checking the farthest corners that I could see, and...and just as Ingrid started to draw my attention to it in the command link, a vanishing star drew my eye.

It shifted. The star seemed to run across the surface of something, like a reflection on a gently rippling pond, and then I saw it.

It was much clearer when Ingrid shared it through the command link, and I started to swear as well.

"What is it?" Benat asked, not having access to the link, and Ingrid pointed, drawing her and Malthus's attention.

"Stealth ship. Dammit, wonder where that fucker was hiding," he replied, shaking his head.

"I've heard stories of them. They're coated in some special layer, redirects light around the hull, incredibly expensive and high tech, gets damaged easily and they spend as much time in dock as they do on missions. But that was probably sitting in the system for weeks, watching."

"Then we stormed in, killed their troops, and they're coming to kill us in turn for it," Benat said, sounding sick.

"A ship that size, how many aboard?" I asked.

"Hundreds," Malthus said. "Maybe more. They're slower than almost anything else. Their impulse engines are baffled to keep them hidden, but they're usually the precursor to planetary invasion. Only getting seen when they're in orbit already, firing on the planet and launching drop pods full of troops..."

"And it's here," Ingrid finished for him, as we watched, transfixed, for a few more seconds as the patch of mobile darkness slid closer. "How long do you think we have?"

"An hour, maybe. No more than two," he guessed.

"Then the station gets flooded with troops, and whatever plan they have for access, we need to make it to the control center first," I said firmly. "Right, people—less gawking, more running!"

With that, we headed to the next set of stairs, running for the entrance that lay to the right of the window. This one was enclosed rather than open like the last one.

The stairway was narrower than the others had been, three meters by five high, rising to a pointed tip. The stairway slowly leaned to the right as it rose, suggesting that we were arcing around the outermost section, climbing.

The first minute was fine, the second and third slightly less so. Running in armor was always fun for us, especially when running with people in more "normal" armor, because ours was literally bonded to us.

That meant no shifting plates and chafing, which as an ex-soldier was *wonderful.* But the longer we did it, the more obvious something became.

The dimensions of the stairs were slightly off for all of us.

Human stairs were made on a calculation that was worked out on the average height and stride length of a human.

The Ændari who had built this place, though, weren't human.

That meant the stair length was subtly "wrong," and running up the last set of stairs back and forth over and over again until we reached this level meant that our muscles had to try to adjust to slightly off dimensions.

The faster and farther we ran, the worse it got, until our thighs were burning.

Our nanites were working to fix it, driving the lactic acid out and repairing the muscles. But the more we did, the more faulty replications were building in my body, I knew.

I could feel it, as the seconds became minutes, what was easy at first, and then barely noticeable, was getting worse and worse. It felt like sand was building in my joints—a griding, grating that was swiftly moving from an irritation to a dull pain.

It'd only get worse, and as close as the others were to me here, if I used my gravitational abilities, I'd either have to do it for me alone and make the others hang back to be clear of it, or they'd lead the way and I'd hang back, or...

Or I'd need to carry us all with the ability, around a sloping corner, all at different heights and levels.

There was too much that could go wrong, and too much that we'd all either need to cram close in for me to do it or spread out more.

So, I just kept running, gritting my teeth and carrying on.

Five minutes became ten, before the first sounds echoed. I let loose a groan of relief, as we finally came to the end of the stairwell.

The glow of subtle lighting had been everywhere as we climbed, the polished marble-like stone in pale creams and beige, leaving the corridors and lower levels light and airy. But here, as we reached the new floor, I'd missed in my distraction that the beige had been darkening gradually.

Now the stone all around us was a light brown, with flecks and striations of pink and red running through. And most concerning of all, the pillars here, dotted across an open and low hall with a peaked roof, were all open: six of them, three to a side. The shorter ceiling made the pillars appear squat and even more threatening.

"They're moving up." Ingrid shared the map with us through the link.

"What?" Malthus asked Benat. "What's she talking about?"

"They have a shared internal command net," Benat explained acidly. "They can share images in their group as well, but we can't access it apparently. They've been using it to talk to the AI that runs the place, but that's all I've worked out as they don't bother to explain anything."

"Shit," Jonas grunted. "Of course...sorry, guys. I'll explain."

As he moved in closer to the other two to explain a little of what and how we were doing what we were doing, I stared at the map that Ingrid was sharing.

"That's fucking cheating, right, boss?" Paul said after a minute as we headed to the next stairway at the end of the hall, closing the six pillars as we passed on instinct, and I grunted, damn well agreeing, even if I didn't see what we could possibly do about it.

The red dots that made up the enemy, that had been spread out across all five levels, were now gathering on the fourth and fifth floor. A pair of much bigger red dots stood between most of them, and a glowing golden *X* slowly rotated in the image.

Between the two larger red dots and the golden marker was a single black dot that stood stock-still, and Paul spoke up again.

"That's cheatin'. They've pulled all their forces back to set up a boss fight, with these two…" The larger red dots pulsed as he mentally tagged them. "And this one…" The black dot pulsed next. "I'm betting they're mini-bosses and a boss."

"Well, yeah, that makes sense," I said.

"All because you're a cheater," he finished, and I looked at him in question. "The gravity thingy, where you waved your hands and tossed a load of monsters off everywhere?"

"Well, first of all, *phrasing*, Paul. It's seriously important when you use 'tossing off' anything to someone from the UK. And how was that cheating? We killed them all."

"You did," he corrected. "Just tossed them off over the edge."

"I hate you," I said, realizing that he knew *exactly* what that phrase meant and was doubling down on it.

"You did, though, and…"

"Paul," Jonas said.

"Yeah, boss?"

"Shut it."

"Yeah, boss," he agreed, and I just knew the lunatic was grinning in his helmet, right up until Courtney smacked him across the back of the head. "Hey!"

"There's nothing we can do about it either way." I picked up speed and led the way, racing upward and gritting my teeth, ignoring the pain from my legs all over again.

This stairwell, like the one I'd "tossed" the others over the side from, had rejoined the section of the spire that was open air again.

The steps were broad and solid, climbing in a grand staircase layout, before splitting to the left and right again, then joining together and climbing again and again.

Three flights led overhead to the next level. The wide-open space at the end of the staircase was now dotted with floating lights. They offered cheerful illumination as the marble of the stairs returned to cream, shot through with gold, and we ran, one eye on the stairs and one on the map.

"They're almost all gathered on the fifth floor," Ingrid said. "There's only a small number, maybe six or seven on the floor below and they're…they're gathering in the stairwell."

"A small force to delay us as they set up on the upper floor?" Jonas suggested.

"Can't be," I ground out. My legs started to shake as we ran; the feeling moved to real pain as my nanites tried automatically to cleanse and repair me, and more and more failed. "The description said they couldn't be controlled, right?"

"Uh…'without a hive guide' was the phrase," Jonas read out. "You okay, boss?" He looked me over.

"Having some issues," I admitted, slowing slightly. "Belle, is there anything you can do?" I knew damn well there was something *I* could have done, if I had access to my systems.

This was a fast-acting version of what James's son had been afflicted with, I was guessing, where the nanites' replication chain was faulty.

Instead of repairing damage, they kept trying to reconstruct damaged bones. And as they did that, some of them failed, creating greater and greater levels of damage as they essentially regrew bones into incorrect shapes and across cartilage.

Mine was more like grains of sand building up in the moving parts of my joints as the nanites tried to cleanse away the lactic acid buildup and damage, so nowhere near as painful…but considering the speed it was happening, it could become a massive issue if I left it.

I was also…yeah. Looking and paying attention as I moved, I saw similar buildups elsewhere, as bruises and minor things that usually got ignored started to grind as well.

Belle moved in close, reaching out; I turned to her, my armor on my left leg opening to let her see the damage there first of all.

Then I cursed as she sank to one knee, reaching out.

The armor that had coated my leg was shuddering. The sides of it, where it'd split instead of flowing fully back into me, ready to be called again, twitched and shook.

"I can fix it," she said quickly, sending nanite tendrils into me, making me grit my teeth as she started to tear the damage apart frantically, digging out the faulty connections and removing as many of the failing nanites as she could. "*Steve…this isn't good,*" she sent privately, adding in only Ingrid to the chat.

"*I know.*"

"*They're failing faster and faster.*"

"*Just keep me going until we get to the top. Either this fucker can fix it, or it can't.*" I glanced at Ingrid as she waved the others past.

"*If it can't, you'll need to be stripped,*" she warned me. "*With the higher abilities of the nanites being locked away from you by Varnock, you won't be able to have them reinstalled, either.*"

"*I know, all right! I know!*" I repeated, glancing down at Belle as she worked. "*Just get me going again.*"

"*It'll take a few minutes to do it properly for each leg, then your arms as well. Better if we do all of your body as quickly as we can,*" she warned me. "*But if I don't and you allow this to keep going*"—she said quickly as I tried to interrupt—"*then you'll lose the use of these limbs soon. You need to be carried or fly if you can from now on. The more your muscles try to process, the more damage you'll take.*"

"*We'll go ahead,*" Ingrid said, and I nodded. We couldn't afford for the team to wait; for the small numbers hiding in the stairwells according to the maps, they really didn't need me anyway.

The next few minutes were painful, as Belle moved quickly from section to section, digging literal holes into me and tearing things free, then directing her own nanites in repairs.

Blood ran in rivulets down my leg, before she leaned back and I could finally reseal my armor, breathing a sigh of relief as it worked.

I'd been seriously worried that it wouldn't and I'd be left having to dismiss my armor, or fight with leg armor that wouldn't close and wouldn't work properly. But after some shuddering and flexing, it seemed to remember its design and seal fully.

I'd not even considered it with my helmet, I'd just done it, and I let loose a breath of relief as I finished sealing that leg, and opened the next.

Twenty minutes it took, which was little enough that the others hadn't gotten to the final level yet, but they were close. As I resealed my armor fully, I let Belle climb onto my back.

Then I summoned a gravity bubble, then another, flinging myself up and around the stairs, rocketing after my friends and the woman I loved.

Chapter Forty-Five

The bloody mess of the corridor and the much smaller stairwell that followed it on the next level made it clear that they'd done their job easily, and I barely paused as I felt the others starting to fight again.

Most of the bodies I passed here were shredded by projectiles and laser blasts, making it clear that no matter what, we'd found viable designs in the end for ranged weapons.

Jonas, I was guessing, was the main instigator, considering the hack and slash wounds on the few who hadn't been gutted at a distance, and the lack of the burns that the proton lance usually left.

Fuck it, though, because the important thing was there was none of our blood anywhere that I could see.

Making it up through the following stairwell was much easier flying, and as I rocketed out of the other end, it was into a firefight.

The team was literally holding the top of the stairs, and barely a few meters beyond, making me frantically pull up and almost kick Paul in the back of the head as I blasted past. My trailing foot missed him by an inch, if that.

I took in the situation in a blur: the enclosing wall of screeching claws and teeth, the frantic fight for survival that my friends were engaged in, and the sheer numbers of the enemy pushing them back.

The room beyond was...well, if there was a subtle and understated design aesthetic that the Ændari had been shooting for, it was clear they couldn't hit a barn door with a shotgun at a meter's distance.

The top level was a riotous mess of gold leaf coating platinum, coating marble and diamond.

There were eight pillars laid out in an octagon around the outside, with the stairwell entering the room at the six o'clock position.

The seven remaining panels, that stood between the pillars, each showed a star system: everything from the planets to the numbers of inhabitants and the currently active nanites, BWVs, and more stood tabulated on the screens.

There weren't just the seven systems, though, not in this quadrant.

Hell, I didn't even know how many systems there were in the quadrant, but the central four additional pillars made it clear that there were "lesser" systems as well.

The center of the room was filled by the actual control facility, or what I guessed to be that.

In better times, it'd probably be impressive as well. The four of them held a downward sloping extension of multiple panels, like an inverted flower.

The petal-like panels hung down where they'd not obscure the larger systems on the walls around the room, and inside the square area left free by the four central pillars was a single pod.

I didn't have a better description for it than that. It was like the medical facility's tubes, in that it was clearly meant for a being to lay in it and be connected to the system to command it.

It was bigger, though, and surrounded by arms and systems that appeared dormant.

There was also a highly unsubtle crackling screen of energy that was projected from above to seal this section away from everyone, presumably until we'd dealt with the fuckers currently lowering the tone of the area.

The terminators were frantic—at least fifty of them, maybe a hundred. I saw more by the second as I twisted, flashing around the room, looping around behind the central area to head back to join the others, when I saw what could only be the hive guide and what had been jokingly referred to as the "mini-bosses."

Where the terminators were vicious and dangerous creatures, ones that the rest of the team were currently barely holding off, the mini-bosses were going to be a hell of a problem, I could tell already.

Standing easily five meters tall—I had no idea how the fuckers had gotten into the room—they nearly brushed the ceiling when they raised their four arms to slash at me as I passed.

I rolled instinctively, drawing Belle out of their path as I dodged, and a scythe-like blade tore through the air inches from me.

They were the mobile tanks of their species, that was clear.

They stood on two legs, thick as tree trunks, squat, and with a stubby tail that seemed almost an afterthought. Their chests were broad and deep, covered in the bone armoring that their lesser brethren had as well, but correspondingly heavier.

The two upper arms were almost entirely scythe-like blades. The arm to the elbow, short and muscular, was designed to rip through their enemies, while the lower arms were wider and longer, presumably to catch and hold prey so that the blades could shred them.

The lower arms made me think of trolls, all hard muscle and heavy slab-like fingers, incapable of fine muscle control.

The head, though—that was where the design differed greatly from the lower-ranking versions.

It was still domed, and the jaw was similar, wide and full of serrated teeth, but it ran backward like the old banana-headed creatures of nightmare in the original *Alien* movies that I'd loved so much growing up.

The difference here was that where the smaller variants were blind and seemed to do everything through some other set of senses, these had eyes—loads of them…at least six to a side, and perhaps another eight on the front—enabling them to observe me with absolutely no issue, not even needing to shift their head around as the multiple eyeballs tracked me.

They were recessed, red gleaming from between bulging lids that screamed of madness and hatred. And behind them? Behind the two massive mini-bosses who were stomping their way forward to slaughter my friends?

There was something squatting that just seemed all kinds of wrong.

It was watching me, I knew; there was that "feeling" as soon as I saw it, that it'd been watching me. But beyond that, it was there and felt…*wrong*. I couldn't describe it.

Not "didn't want to" or I lacked the words, which I probably did, but I literally couldn't.

I couldn't focus on it. Every time I looked at it, it was like stepping onto ice too quickly. My eyes slid off it like my feet on unexpected ice.

All I could say for sure was that the damn thing was tall, skinny, and either wore long tattered black robes, was coated in its own personal shadow, or…or I didn't know what.

Then I frantically pulled up, twisting, landing hard behind the others and skidding as I tried to avoid plowing full speed into the wall behind them.

"Steve!" Belle cried out as I dropped her. Her own tentacles, hands, and feet scrabbled as she caught herself, barely keeping from falling down the stairs.

"Sorry!" I shouted, grabbing at the doorway and yanking myself around. I nearly fell down there as well, stomping and swearing as, once again, the fucked-up nature of my nanites betrayed me.

I'd triggered the claws on my boots on instinct, twisting and digging in…or trying to and finding that they didn't work at all. I snarled, finally catching and forcing myself back upright and forward.

The others were spread out in a half circle, using a combination of small arms and blades. When I saw that, I frowned, followed by a burst of understanding as Ingrid shared the last minute of the fight as they'd arrived on this floor.

They'd reached the end of the stairwell, only to find the enemy spread out and waiting, the majority of the bigger creatures making full use of the cover of the central control facility.

The terminators had been standing, slavering and ready, but held back as if by an invisible leash. As soon as our people had opened fire on any of them, they'd started dodging. They didn't do it well, not against lasers and weapons that fired at the speed of sound and higher. But they did it well enough that Ingrid had ordered a cease-fire as soon as the first hits impacted the cracking shields around the control facility, and the AI warned them that "continued acts of aggression would result in their elimination."

The cunning bastard hive guide had set it up so that we had to fight in a way that negated our biggest advantages, reducing us to blades. As I stepped up, forming the vorpal and harvest blades, Ingrid sighed in relief, stepping back to allow me room to take her place.

The creatures were aggressive as hell, and uncaring of wounds that should have sent them screaming. Nothing fazed the terminators. They'd lost arms, been gutted, and had their legs cut out from under them—and still they attacked.

The first that leapt into the gap, I greeted with arms crossed and blades extended, hacking out and down in an X shape that neatly cut the fucker into four uneven quarters.

The armor barely resisted my blades, their toughened bones no match for the high-frequency vibrations, and yet killing the damn thing was only half the battle.

Its inertia was still there, and with the blades barely snagging on it as I slid them through my enemy, it meant that a quarter second after I chopped it apart, the twitching body still impacted me, driving me back a step.

I shrugged it off, the steaming blood coating me. I'd barely stepped back into the space, before the next of them was there, this time diving for my legs, claws extended as a second one came in from the left.

Scylla was next in line on the side, and the crackling sizzle of her proton lance in its cutting mode filled the air. She stabbed out, piercing the head of that attacker, twisting, then dragged the blade back along the side of the head and out, before she slammed the base of the spear into the next in line.

I saw it all happen in an instant. I shifted my feet, planting the left one, stomping out with the heel of my right upraised and slamming it into the head of the one diving at my legs.

I cut at the same time. Twin blades carved down at a ninety-degree angle, severing both sets of the terminator's arms, as my kick threw the now armless body back to tangle up the feet on the next incoming.

That was when it all went wrong.

The terminator that Scylla had killed fell to the ground, its head shredded and arms spasming as the final electrical impulses fired in its body. One of the outstretched claws came down, hard, on my supporting leg's thigh, and carved into my armor like butter.

I'd been half-hopping back from the kick I'd just used when it happened, and I staggered, pain flaring as that leg almost gave out. It felt like fire slicing its way into me. The only reason I didn't literally lose the leg was that the creature was dead and it was a glancing blow.

I barely stayed upright, though, the armor unable to respond as it usually would and stiffen to hold me up with a thought while the wound was worked on.

Instead, I almost fell, thrusting out with the harvest blade to take the next in line in the face with the tip, carving its skull apart like a juicy melon.

Instantly the others, linked as we all were with the command link, shifted. Malthus, who'd been to my right, stepped into the gap and shield bashed a lunging terminator in the face.

He carried an ax in his right hand and was hacking through all comers. But his armor was already badly damaged before he'd made it to this floor, and the sheer mass of enemies we were facing meant that it was being rapidly carved apart.

If anything, because of the difference in design between his mass of solid metal over our more powerful, but slimmer and smaller armoring, that design kept him in the fight longer than we would be at this rate.

"Steve, here, here and here!" Ingrid sent through the link, as Belle grabbed my arm, steadying me.

I felt the shared targeting data that Ingrid poured out to me at the same time as Belle stabbed her tendrils into my leg, using the carved holes that were slowly reforming to deliver healing directly.

I gritted my teeth and did as she asked. The secondary data that she was providing, the size that she believed would be safe to create without damaging anything we'd need, the strength of the field, the radius—all syncing perfectly as I generated them as fast as I could.

The first gravity field was to the left, next in the middle, and then right. The outer pair pulled "in" and the middle shoved "out," creating a pair of crushing fields on the left and right in the middle of the scrabbling creatures.

I started small, then pushed harder and harder. The screeches of fury and pain were drowned out by the crunching of bone as more and more died from the crushing weight of first five, then ten, then twenty gravities.

The middle field kept the enemy swarming around and closer to the bigger two. The mindless beasts raced forward, finding themselves battered and dragged into the vortexes. They were still two and sometimes three deep, but the sudden drop in their numbers gave us a chance again.

"Retreat to the stairs!" Ingrid ordered, firing all her shoulder-mounted Hijack darts at once. The sudden jets rocketed over our heads, making one of the idiot things actually leap up and snap its jaws shut a second too late, like a cat after a canary. Then, for the benefit of Benat and Malthus, she shouted it again, making sure that they'd heard her.

I moved back. The monsters to the sides fell in as we did. Courtney and Benat were the first into the stairwell, turning and running as fast as they could.

It wasn't cowardice, either. The stairwell dropped downward, and if they could get back a little, they could use their armor and whatever abilities Benat had to try to climb, allowing them to fire their weapons as the enemy entered the stairs.

They were both built around stealth and ranged skill sets, and in a stand-up fight with no ability to use either, they'd been barely holding their own, and that was with the others helping.

Benat had been on the left side closest to the wall, with Scylla next to her, then me, and Scylla had been having to cover both sides as I was forced back.

Malthus was next, standing at the front with Jonas at his side, then Paul had been next to Courtney, using a tomahawk and a long combat knife in a blur of dual wielding that would have been all the more impressive if he'd not been screaming like a small girl at the same time.

Behind them now were me, Ingrid as the commander linking us all together, and Belle, who was desperately trying to heal and figure a way to use her abilities in a place that was inimical to plant life.

More orders rippled out from Ingrid, as well as targets for me, and I sent agreement even as I limped backward. Belle darted free of me as she ripped her tendrils out of a nearly healed leg.

Malthus had been charged by two on the left. One clamped onto his shield; the other piled into its fellow from the side and sacrificed itself to shove both the shield and the one holding it out to the side, exposing his chest.

He'd reacted instantly, stopping his retreat and hacking across with his ax at waist height, carving both the one exposing him and the one who was clearly supposed to take advantage of the situation, in half at the waist.

That exposed his right side, though, and another had jumped in, jaws wide, grabbing onto the back of his right arm.

Jonas saw it, and we all felt it through the command link as he twisted, accepting a glancing blow to the stomach to be able to turn enough, stabbing out and taking the head of the creature that was about to bite down on Malthus's arm.

I hissed in pain as the tendrils left me, but I knew she'd done all she could quickly, and she leapt to save Jonas.

A fresh terminator bounded from the shoulders of one of its falling brethren as he'd moved to help Malthus.

It flew over the next in line, arms spread wide and jaws slavering, and hit Jonas just as he'd been looking to the left, dragging his sword free of his latest kill.

If it wasn't for the link, we couldn't have done it, but in the same instant that any of us saw the incoming creature, we all "felt" the response as well. Jonas crouched, trusting Belle completely, and he ripped the blade free and swung it down and up, hacking through the next in line, and ignoring the one in the air.

Belle's tendrils punched through the skull of the incoming terminator, ripping its head apart, then flung it backward, cartwheeling, as she released it.

The arms coming in on instinct, claws extended, shredded Belle's tendrils, costing her the created mass, but that in exchange for saving her friend was more than worth it.

We all felt it, just as we felt the realization from Jonas of how close that one had been, and we kept retreating.

Ingrid was next into the stairwell. I was behind her, my legs stinging but the nanites that were still functioning in my system working to heal it as I went.

The others followed: Paul and Scylla, Jonas, then finally Malthus, the big devilkin determined to hold the line and prove his worth as a hired merc.

The joke was on him, I might try to recruit his entire planet at this rate.

As soon as we were in the stairwell, the tempo of the battle changed. We were no longer at risk of accidentally hitting the control center and causing the AI to attack us, and the blades were sheathed in favor of ranged weaponry.

The first creatures through the door were shredded by concentrated fire. Then Ingrid started to assign targets, blending us all together into a single multi-armed god of war.

Targets appeared and fell, heads exploding as we continued to back away, bodies falling. Then the first of the gas grenades flew overhead, flipping over and over, clanging as it hit the wall near the door and unleashed a powerful jet of smoke.

Ingrid rose from the middle of the group, nanite "legs" reaching out and bracing, then lifting her into the air like a giant spider. Her own armor's stealth field was very different than mine as it activated, in that instead of shifting the actual surface of the armor, it created a high-tech "hide."

It was a bit like a hunting blind, or a bird hide, a structure that was simple and yet oh so effective as she climbed the walls; additional tentacles extended from her armor to lock her into place high overhead in the fortunately cavernous ceiling.

The fire rate picked up, and another grenade flashed out, flipping end over end to bounce off the back wall and land just on this side of the entrance to the stairs, before going off.

Paul started to curse, apologizing.

He'd apparently almost sent it into the far room, and that could have caused some issues.

Or death to us all.

Instead, it pushed out a jellied napalm mixture, then ignited a half second later, filling that part of the stairs in flames.

Then the secondary posts for Ingrid's stealth systems slid out. Thin and delicate appearing, trailing a sheet of nanites that flickered as it slid into place, it formed a barrier that projected the image of the section behind her, onto the front.

Inside of a heartbeat, she was gone, the only creatures to have seen her climbing, dead a half second later and seeing it through a wash of smoke, incoming fire, and an inferno of flames.

That was when she'd dropped a line to Courtney that the woman accepted, using her own nanites to clumsily climb up as well, until she was hidden by Ingrid's side, rifle lifted, and a tiny space left for her to fire out.

That changed the dynamic drastically. She started to pick her targets, eliminating them as soon as they burst through the flames, trailing smoke and screaming. They'd take a single shot to the head and collapse.

The rest of us formed up, waiting, taking the occasional shot as the enemy made it through. But between the narrower stairwell preventing us from being flanked, the sniper above, and the ability to use ranged weapons, the tempo of the fight was entirely different.

"I've lost access to the map," Ingrid warned us all suddenly, and everyone else checked and confirmed the same.

"Did we fail the quest?" I asked over the rising panic that we were about to be swamped by an insurmountable number of enemies.

"No..." Ingrid said a few seconds later, sounding unsure.

"Probably decided that we had an unfair advantage with a map that showed where they all were," Jonas guessed, firing again. "Now what?"

"Hold our current position until we're sure we've got most of them whittled down. Then we can start pushing back up and onto the final floor," Ingrid said after a brief pause, as Jonas took up translation duties again for Benat and Malthus.

"Works for me," I agreed.

A handful of terminators leaped through the flames suddenly, bouncing off the walls and one another as they tried to reach us en masse, only to fall almost as quickly.

"Running low on ammo," Courtney added into the chat, and the others quickly checked theirs as well.

"Low," Jonas growled, with the others chiming in as well. Medium was the best that we were at, and that was Ingrid, who I'd given my spares to.

"Let me help," I offered, reaching out and focusing a new gravity bubble at the top of the stairs just as another ran into it. The cracks of breaking bones made it clear they would not be running out again.

"Thank you," Ingrid sent to me. *"Sorry, still getting used to this command thing. It's harder to keep track of everything than I thought."*

I just sent her a smile, understanding the myriad other reasons that she didn't add: the fear that the enemy would come up with a counter, the desire to not rely on just me that heavily, the fear that there might be a side effect that we didn't know about yet, like the way that the nanites had been injuring me since the blast that had hit me earlier…all of those reasons and more I felt under the surface. I sent her as much reassurance and love as I could through the bond.

"Get ready." Ingrid shared the mental image and plan through the command link as she spoke the words aloud. "As soon as we're sure they've been whittled down to a manageable number, we take the fight back to them. If there's any doubt about hitting your target, don't fire. We can't afford to hit the control center, but that ship has to be getting closer, and we can't wait any longer.

"We push them back from the entrance to the stairs, secure the immediate area, then we take down the last of them."

"The mini-bosses and the boss," Paul added helpfully.

"Yes, dear." Courtney sighed. "Well remembered."

"Steve?" Ingrid asked me, and I nodded, reaching out and cutting the gravity bubble, waiting a second, then reforming it at the very edge of where I could see. My additional radar-like senses were now off-line as well, I found, mentally cursing but keeping quiet about that.

The second bubble encountered something—the screech and snapping sounds made that clear—but only for a few seconds. Then there was nothing.

"Clear, I hope," I offered. And with that, we started onto the final floor.

Again.

This time our entry to the final floor was very different. Rather than hundreds of the terminators waiting for us, there were ten, with the bigger fuckers right behind them, and between and slightly behind them, the final boss, one that was still hard as all hell for me to even look at.

"What the hell is that thing?" Jonas asked. "I know it's there, but every time I look at it…"

"You can't focus on it," Courtney agreed. "I'm the same, and that's NOT a good thing for a sniper. I… I can't guarantee I'll hit it." She sounded horrified by the concept.

"They're waiting for us?" I asked, confused. "Why the hell aren't they attacking? Anyone got a prompt?"

"Nothing," Ingrid said.

"Then nothing's changed, beyond they're trying to kill us slower."

"Courtney, focus on the left mini-boss—Benat, same one. Head shots only. Jonas, Malthus, Paul, Scylla—close-in protection. Take down anything that gets too close, melee only. Belle, crowd control…can you do anything?" Ingrid sounded almost distracted as she reached out, holding her right hand up, flexing her fingers.

There was a moment of confusion; then, as she brought that hand down, so did the mini-boss on the right, its upper scythe limbs slamming down and tearing two of its own side apart. It reached out with the lower arms, grabbing two more from either side, and smashed them into each other. The scythes rose again, then crashed down into the second pair of victims.

"Gotcha!" Ingrid declared, the smile clear in her voice as Courtney took the distraction and fired on the other mini-boss.

It roared in fury, staggering then screaming and starting forward, just as the remaining six terminators burst into action. Two ran forward; the other four leaped at their hijacked brother.

Belle had thrown something into the air, then blew it forward with a great gust of air, sagging as soon as she'd done it, clearly exhausted by the effort. A gritty dust seemed to fill the air, before streaming directly at the boss.

Courtney fired again and again. Benat missed a shot, then hit with the second, the ricochet fortunately not hitting the control center.

As the mini-boss raged forward, holes appeared in its skull. The rest of the team spread out, ready, and I focused down, creating a gravity bubble directly behind the big boss.

It moved like greased lightning almost before I'd finished forming it, flowing like water across the ground to the right, arms unfolding from beneath that dark shadowing it hid behind.

The arms were unnaturally long, bony, and finished in four-fingered hands tipped with claws. Then it flashed forward, moving almost too fast to see as I tried to summon more and more.

Each time I created a bubble, it was moving, flowing around it, staying just out of reach, and closing the distance to us all, until the jet of dust that Belle had thrown hit it.

It tried to pass through, clearly not understanding what it was. But whatever the creature's abilities were, the dust that hit it was unexpected in the extreme.

It was a nanite-enhanced mist of strangling vines, tiny seeds that were blessed with the fastest growth that she could create, carried by an invisible curtain of nanites.

As soon as the creatures hit it, they started sprouting, wrapping around it, burrowing into the blackness.

"Switching target!" Courtney anapped, focusing on the suddenly flailing monster as it tried to rip the vines apart. The tiny writhing plants did little damage, but compressed the creature, revealing its outline.

Ingrid forced her hijacked monster to move up behind the leader, scythes rising.

The boss screeched, a weirdly echoing noise that stopped the stacking terminators and mini-boss in their tracks, sending them all into a frenzy as they tried to intercept the hijacked one before it could attack.

Then Courtney fired.

Arise :Explorer

The high-powered railgun round was perfectly aimed, punching into the writhing boss's head, then ripping through and into the walking tank that Ingrid had maneuvered behind it, just in case.

The mini-boss staggered, then grabbed onto its boss, squeezing hard. The breaking of smaller bones filled the air; then the scythes came down, fast and hard, and tore into the form that was so covered with vines it could barely be seen now.

The blades ripped in and out, over and over, as Benat and Courtney fired again and again at the charging enemy mini-boss, trying to take it down.

The smaller terminators leapt at the bigger, but they were too late, their claws and teeth tearing chunks out of their brother.

The second one stumbled, taking more hits, then threw itself at the first. The pair of mini-bosses stabbed and tore at each other. Grinning, I reached out and fired up three more bubbles, two "in" at four gravities, one "out" at six.

The combined shear effect that was felt right in the middle of the two was powerful enough to break bones, and the pull into the pair of "in" fields was enough to drag them all into the pair.

Then I doubled and redoubled the strength of the field.

The air was filled with the shattering of bones for several seconds, before I cut the power I was feeding them, letting out a sigh as the pressure lifted, and that was that.

"I've got the link," Ingrid said suddenly. "Steve, get ready…"

"Fuck," I muttered, taking a deep breath and straightening up, feeling like I could sleep for a week.

"Everyone else, secure the area. Belle, start stripping," Ingrid said.

"Whoo-hoo!" Paul started before being smacked across the back of the head by Courtney.

"Bad, Paul!" she snapped. "Down, boy!"

I tuned the pair out, moving closer to Ingrid as she reached out for me, a last kiss and hug as we read the message from the AI.

Biological Weapon Variants and Command Access Requestors, local BWV aggressors have been eliminated.
Situational compromise has been achieved: Quest Complete. Command claimant, proceed for repair and evaluation.

That was it, apparently. We'd both been expecting a lot more than that, some additional test or whatever, but it was going to be an internal one as it checked my systems.

That wasn't good news, but it wasn't as if I had a choice.

As we moved closer to the control center, the shields flickered and vanished. Ingrid stopped suddenly, explaining that she'd been warned not to approach as well. She squeezed my hand in reassurance, sent a pulse of love and trust through the bond; then I stepped up to the pod and banished my armor.

Now that the energy shields, or whatever they'd been, were down, I could see into the pod clearly, and what I saw made my skin crawl.

It wasn't empty.

The remains of a previous occupant were still inside. And not only was it fucking moldy and broken, clearly ancient, it was also wet and slumped to one side.

The pod, open now, rotated around. The nose slid into a recess in the ground and the interior stood upright, presumably to make it easier for the next victim to step inside. And from the looks of it, the last inhabitant had been bobbing in it merrily until it evacuated the liquid to let me in.

I didn't know whether this was a good thing, that the machine was just accepting me, or whether I was about to be torn limb from limb. But what I did know was that I didn't want to be in there with the remains of something that had died an eternity ago and had been bobbing around in there, dissolving ever since.

I grabbed it and dragged it aside, tossing it to the floor. Then, skin crawling as I did it, I undressed fully, not wanting to have to be wearing whatever had been in there when I got out again.

I got a wolf whistle from behind as I stripped off, and I deliberately ignored it, stifling a burst of disgust as I clambered in. The form-fitting cushioning altered to hold me in position, and the pod lid slid down to click into place all around.

Almost as soon as that connection was made, I gasped as a flood of cold liquid poured in, flowing from my feet upward. The capsule shifted around, angling back to a forty-five degree recline. A screen overhead that I'd not noticed before flickered to life.

Then the sides of the pod opened, and the metal implements slid out, gleaming as they reflected the screen above. I bit down on the inside of my mouth, trying to hide the panic I felt.

I had a sudden thought that maybe, just maybe, what'd happened here was that the AI had identified me as the greatest threat and had set this up as a final way to be sure I was killed off, and then the first of the needles jabbed into the back of my neck.

I let out a shocked gasp. The needle punched through skin, flesh, and bone, connecting to the nerves at the base of my brain. And then the world went white with pain.

Chapter Forty-Six

C^{LICK}

I sat on the floor, my hands holding two plastic bricks, cheap knockoff ones that had fading colors, as tears ran down my cheeks.

I pressed them together, the audible click as they locked together the only way that I knew that they'd done it, my vision was that blurry.

Daddy was standing between me and our tiny telly, screaming about something I couldn't make out, crumpled letters with red words on them all over the floor as I tried my very best to be a good boy.

That's what I was doing, I knew.

I was *trying* to be good. I had to work at it. I had to work at being quiet, at not getting in the way, because I wasn't a good boy like I was supposed to be.

I knew it, I'd been told so many times, that I was bad, that I was stupid, that I ruined everything.

That was why Momma had left us. Because I was bad.

I was trying. I was trying *so* hard! All I had to do was build the blocks, make the things that Momma liked, and she'd come back. Then she'd stop Daddy from hitting me, or maybe he'd just not do it as much, then…

CLICK

I was standing over my new stepbrother, shaking, seeing the blood running down his face, the bright-red blood that ran from his nose, and I felt the sudden crystal-cold clarity that I'd made a mistake.

He was screaming for his mother. She was running at us from the kitchen, the short hallway all that was giving me another few seconds of safety as I turned and ran, sprinting for the open window.

I could hear them shouting: her demanding my dad throw me out, that he send me away; my brother screaming that I was a bully; my dad roaring that he was going to break me this time.

It didn't matter that I'd been defending myself, or that I'd hit him after months of him and his sister stealing from me, bullying me, and calling me names.

It didn't matter that no matter what I did, I was never good enough. All that mattered was that they didn't want me here.

I hit the ledge and scrambled over it, twisting and grabbing hold of the old window bracket, swinging myself around and dropping the single story to the ground, landing hard and feeling the pain that flared in my feet and left knee.

Falling sideways and catching myself on the wall, I pushed myself back up, then started to run—or I tried to, anyway.

I managed two steps before my twisted knee broke me down to a hobble. I whimpered, knowing that my dad was already running down the stairs, coming for me as I limped down the path.

I saw the old lady who lived next door, as I hobbled past the end of her driveway, the look on her face as she saw me limping. I hesitated, almost changing direction, to run to her door instead.

Then he shouted, and she flinched.

She hadn't seen him yet—*I* couldn't see him yet—but I saw her face.

I saw the way she looked down, breaking eye contact; then he was there, grabbing me by the shoulder and dragging me around. The thick nails dug into my arms as he shook me, shouting about how worthless I was, before hitting me across the face with a fist that felt like a hammer.

He dragged me back inside, as I reeled. And as he did, I caught a last glimpse of my neighbor's kitchen window.

I saw that she'd closed her curtains so she didn't have to see.

That hurt almost as much as the beating, the hatred on his face as he kicked and punched me, beating me to the floor.

The sneer from his new wife, and worse, the look in her eyes when it was done, and he left me there on the crappy linoleum floor, weeping, bleeding and curled into a ball...

She knew that she'd made a mistake when she married him, that this was the kind of a man he was, and that if it wasn't me he was beating, it'd be her and her kids.

I knew it, she knew it, and so she encouraged him. She'd set this up, I suddenly realized, so that it'd be me, and not them.

CLICK

I lifted the knife in my hand, tilting it slowly, watching the light reflecting off it. The candles flickered, sending the reflected light back up to me, then across the walls as I continued to turn it in my hands.

He was asleep, my father. Fast asleep in his favorite chair by the TV, the empty beer bottle where it'd fallen from his fingers on the floor nearby.

The "end of transmission" signal was on the TV, and I stared down at the knife as I sat there, on the sofa, looking at him, as he snored.

It'd be so easy, to stand now, take two steps and jam the knife into his throat, to rip it sideways, just to make sure of it. Then it'd be done.

No more beatings, no more pain, no more fear, no more... I glanced down at the scars on my arms, the still-healing burns from his cigarette and... No.

Just no more.

His cigarette had burned a mark into the carpet before the spilled beer had put it out. It'd come that close to setting fire to the house already, so that was an option as well. I could light another one, and drop it a little farther over.

The fire would take care of him, and her, and their wonderful kids.

It'd burn the whole place down, and I'd finally have peace.

I stared at him, wondering why I hadn't done it yet, and I didn't have an answer.

I wasn't afraid of doing it, and the fire would cover all the evidence…but then what? What if wherever they put me was worse than here? What if they figured it out? I was ten now—today was my birthday. Was I old enough that they'd figure out it wasn't an accident?

What if they spoke to the neighbors? They'd tell the police that I was bad, that I was evil. They knew I was. I had to be, or they'd have helped me.

That was why I was alone, he told me.

He wasn't my dad, I knew now. A *dad* cared. He was my *father*, and the only reason he'd kept me was because nobody else wanted me, and he was stuck with a useless son that the police had made him keep.

They knew I was bad, he'd told me, them and the doctors, and my teachers. I was to never tell them about the bruises, about the beatings. Because if I did? They'd take me back to him, and then he'd be even angrier.

I'd tried telling a grown-up once, and I'd learned from it. No, never again.

I couldn't rely on anyone else, I knew now.

That was why I was where I was now, the knife in my hands. Trying to decide whether I should cut his throat before I set fire to the house, or just leave him to burn.

Then I should probably just go back upstairs, to my room, and lie down on the bed, wait for the fire to get me too.

It was what I deserved, because for me to even think about doing this? It proved what he'd always said.

I was bad.

CLICK

I stared into his eyes, and he into mine. The world had stopped, and everything had changed in a heartbeat.

I'd blocked his punch. After the countless hours of repetition that Mike had let me do with him, helping him practice after his martial arts lessons, and I'd done it on instinct.

My father hadn't tried to beat me in months, not since I turned thirteen and was as big as him, but this…

He tried to shove me back, barely keeping his balance he was that drunk, and threw another punch at me. It was clumsy and wide, and I stepped back, watching as it passed by. My mind raced as he staggered off-balance, and the coldness, the silence that had filled me for so long that I'd forgotten there was anything else to me, shattered.

I pushed him—just a push, that was all—but as drunk as he was, he went sprawling.

"That's it!" He spat, wiping his mouth as he clambered to his feet. "You think you're big enough for that? You think you can fight your old man? Well, I'm gonna give you the fucking beating you've always deserved, you little shit! Nobody—"

I threw my first punch, slamming it into the side of his face with all my thirteen years of hatred, fear, and pain behind it.

CLICK

I set the beer down on the white stucco plaster of the balcony, staring out over the glittering water of the pool below. The laughter of the fucking children who were supposed to be my peers, as they frolicked in the pool, floated up to me.

Then I pulled out the card that I'd been given, dialed the number into the cheap phone, and spoke two words.

"I'm interested."

CLICK

I was crouched in a tiny pit I'd dug myself. Sweat ran down my back, my lips cracked and flaking, surrounded by sealed bags of my own piss and shit. Flies swarmed around me as I stared fixedly through the tiny gap I'd left, watching the little village as the jeeps pulled up.

Four people got out. Their dress made it almost impossible to tell one from another at this distance. I adjusted the glasses, trying to get a clear picture of their faces, comparing them to the images I'd memorized.

Was that…? It could be him, the target…it *could* be.

But…he had a beard, and the picture of him didn't. Maybe he'd grown one? It was possible—hell, probable, despite how crazy willingly doing anything that added heat in this goddamn oven of a country was.

If he had, though, that would mean that the other one, the younger one, he could be…

A stone clattered nearby, and I froze. A goat bounded past, landing inches away from the cloth that covered me, then leaping onward.

The swearing that followed made me start praying to every god I'd ever imagined or been told of.

Some idiot, some utter fucking waste of skin, was actually chasing that goat, and rather than going around this tiny strand of scrub bushes, he was stumbling straight toward me!

If he didn't stop, he was going to literally trip over me, and then I'd have to kill him! That or run for it, and hope that the squad understood me blowing a three goddamn month op for a fucking idiot goat!

CLICK

Arise :Explorer

She'd left me.

All this time, all these fucking years I'd wasted, telling myself that I was like the rest of them. I'd gotten a job after getting out of the army, *one with a fucking tie*. I had a mortgage, I paid the goddamn local authorities' tax, and walked around like a good little corporate drone.

I listened when people bitched about the bill they weren't going to pay because it wasn't their fault that they'd given their fucking eleven-year-old a contract phone, and had let them call their friends in goddamn America for a whole month before the bill had come in.

I put up with all that stupid shit, because that was what you had to do. And now? I closed my fist, crumpling up her stupid little note explaining that she'd left me, and I didn't bother to read any more.

Who cared *why* she'd left me?

I reached into the fridge, pulled a beer out, twisting the top and tossing it over my shoulder with the crumpled paper. I took a long drag, then lifted my phone, punching in Kev's name, hitting Call.

We'd barely talked in years. A chance meeting in the pub last week, and the offer he'd made me, had horrified my now ex-girlfriend.

He'd laughed when he'd seen her face, and said it was all a joke, but we all knew different.

It was that, I bet, that had helped to end the relationship, and thank fuck it had.

I wasn't like her, not like any of them, and it was time to stop hiding it. It was time to stop pretending to be a fucking sheep.

"I'm in," I said when he answered. "When's the job?"

CLICK

I screamed as the drill dug into my right eye, the eyelid having already been cut away, leaving me no way to avoid what was coming. My head was locked in place as the drill descended at a horrifically slow pace, growing larger and larger by the second.

The tip touched my eyeball, and for a fraction of a second, all I felt was discomfort, as the lens deformed under the pressure. And then the pain began.

I screamed myself hoarse, despite the fluids that filled my lungs, despite the cables that snaked into my mouth and ran down my throat.

I screamed and begged. I swore to every god and demon imaginable as my world fractured with the pain, that I'd do anything, be anything, just as long as they stopped, just let me die.

And the drills dug in deeper; the fluids that surrounded me filled with steadily darkening blooms of fresh blood.

CLICK

I leaned against one wall, watching her as she crouched, her fingers hesitating, then gently touching the sun-blasted stone of the ancient Minoan palace.

What the hell was I doing here, I thought, even as I continued to watch her, seeing the wonder, the concentration and the happiness that practically radiated off her, as she examined the ancient stonework.

I shouldn't be here, not with her, I knew.

I was *risking* her—I was risking me, for fuck's sake—and everything that would come out if anyone realized what I was. More importantly, though, I was risking her, risking someone figuring out who and what I was and her having to pay the price.

That crazy old bastard Hans was probably around somewhere still. And the Blessed… Hell, Jonas and his lot of fucking idiots might come stomping through the gates at any second, but still, here I was.

I watched possibly the most beautiful woman in the entire goddamn world as she stroked an old rock, and I was happier than made any kind of sense.

I'd take her to the taverna after this, let her see a little of the darkness that was revealed when you scratched the surface of this idyllic island, and then maybe get a few more days with her somewhere else. Then, when the time came for her flight, I'd wave goodbye to the last bit of my humanity as her plane lifted into the clear blue skies.

I had no idea what I was going to become, but I knew that I couldn't risk anyone else being along for the ride. It wasn't just the risk to me if they talked—it was the risk to them.

The things that could be done to them, if the Blessed decided that they were the best way to get to me…

No, the only reasonable thing to do was to leave her. Just…not yet.

Tomorrow maybe.

"Do you want a bit longer?" I asked her, and she bit her lip, then nodded.

"Just a little, ten minutes or so? It's so fascinating!" she pleaded, and I nodded, smiling as I turned and went back to the entrance, reaching into my pocket to pay the fee they'd no doubt demand.

CLICK

Pain! So much, too much pain! There was nothing I could do, nowhere to run, as they laughed. The metal posts driven through my wrists, elbows, shoulders, knees, and feet kept me in place, as they systematically burned me, two of them, one with a tablet computer, guiding the other as he watched something. And the other?

One of my guards, I knew, but no name. I wasn't important enough to know their names, he'd told me, and now, gagged with a block stuck in my mouth, keeping me from biting my tongue in half and ending their experiment early, I tried to plead with them using only my eyes.

They ignored me, moving back to carving the skin from my left leg in long strips, uncovering the flesh beneath, then tossing the strip of wet meat aside into a bin.

Arise :Explorer

The touch of the blowtorch was so hot it was almost icy cold. The sizzling hairs and crisping of the skin on my right leg made me thrash uncontrollably as I tried to escape, even knowing the pain that came from the slightest movement.

Then they changed, and recorded the difference when they played the blowtorch over the skinned section instead, joking as they made bets about how long it'd take for the skin to heal, before agreeing that the best test would be to skin one side of me entirely, and then they'd be able to pan the flames across more evenly.

CLICK

The world around me roiled, and I tried to hold only my stomach. The food they insisted on pumping into me if I'd not eat…it was rising again. I frantically tried to turn, knowing it was coming, but the drugs!

Whatever they'd given me, I was barely able to flop on the bed. My words came out choked and unintelligible as I tried to warn my wife that I was going to be sick.

Instead, she continued to talk to the doctor by her side, both of them ignoring me until it burst free; then disgust filled both of their eyes as they darted away, leaving me choking on my own vomit.

The world grew darker, my throat and lungs filling…until the cleaner, the one who was always so sad eyed, was there again.

She turned me onto my side, her fingers working into my throat, scraping the liquified mush out and clearing enough that I could suck down a panicked breath.

I tried to thank her, when I could see again; then I heard the words that my wife spoke, and the contempt that filled them.

"Urgh, he's shit himself again! Why must we continue to put up with this *farce…*"

I closed my eyes. Shame filled me as the cleaner stroked my cheek, whispering something comforting as she moved me, starting to clean me again.

CLICK

The wind whipped past me as I flew through the hot humid night air of Athens. The window ahead of me grew larger and larger as I closed on it, and I made out Ingrid, sitting there inside, talking calmly, even as thugs threatened her.

The links I'd established allowed me access to the cameras in the office. I was filled with a rage that was almost more than I could bear. Battling with that was relief so powerful I felt dizzy knowing that she was there, just there, barely a dozen meters away, and I'd finally found her again.

They'd pay for this.

They'd all pay for this, but that fucker Yanni was going to die, all right. No matter what happened here, I'd tear him a new fucking arsehole, and then I'd ram a truck through it.

Sideways.

CLICK

I stood by Anders's side. Fear rose in me as I tried to figure the right way out of this conversation, as the two of us stood by the crackling fireplace. Ingrid and her family talked happily in the background, as he clearly tried to figure out who and what I was, as well as the risk I posed to his perfect little family.

"What do you actually do? Tell me straight."

I paused, thinking fast, and remembering Ingrid's warning about her father. *He knows a lie and will be furious if you lie to him. Anything but that he'll understand. But lie to him? He'll view it as if you hold him in contempt...*

"I hunt the monsters in our society," I said, knowing that if it all hit the fan, at least he'd know I'd been honest. "I kill them, and I use their funds to pay for the hunt of the next one. I've killed, and I'll kill again, but I've never killed an innocent. I spend my life hunting those who do. I met Ingrid through her love of archaeology, as several of the incidents I've ended up in happened at old archaeological sites."

There were a few seconds of silence as he considered my words, then he nodded.

"And Inga?" he asked.

"She helps me. The creatures we hunt," I said it carefully, letting him assume I was being figurative, not literal, "they tend to like ancient sites, presumably because the kind of black market that buys and sells artifacts like that, well, they'll deal in anything."

"And you use her as bait?" he asked slowly.

"Gods, no!" I snapped, glaring at him, only realizing after a few seconds that it'd been a test. "I have to fight with her half the time to keep her from hitting the sites before me!" I paused and glanced back at her, surrounded by her family, smiling and laughing.

"Anders, you know what she's like. I do my absolute best to keep her as far from any danger as possible. I swear it."

"I do know her," he agreed, looking up at me. "And I know that the happy young girl who went away with her friends is not that lady there at the table. She's harder, colder, and, frankly, stronger than I ever dared hope she could be. Something changed her."

"She was captured by some of the worst scum on the planet, kept safe, but—" I shook my head quickly. "She wasn't abused...not like that, she tells me...but they made her watch as they tortured me. It hurt her."

"They *tortured* you?" His voice changed, uncertainty leaking into it as I stared out the window again and into the past.

"They drugged and cut me, carving to the bones and testing new medical procedures on me. Needles, burns, pressure, and more. It changed me. I thought it broke me, for a long time," I whispered.

"What happened?"

"They brought her to my cell, thinking to break her with the state I was in."

"And?"

"And I killed them. I killed them all, tore their fucking precious hospital and experimentation wing down, killed their guards, and then hunted down their leader and gutted the fucking bitch," I growled, glancing down when I heard the sound and felt the pain, and cursed.

I'd crushed the crystal tumbler in my hand; shards dug into my flesh, blood flowing.

"Careful!" he barked, seeing the blood.

CLICK

With every memory that appeared, the world sped past faster, my soul feeling scoured as every major memory was torn free and examined, before the Erlking flashed up.

The AI barely stopped on that event—supposedly one of the most important, for it anyway—and instead just accepted the information, pausing long enough to pull what looked to be the entire identity out, examine it, then move on, speeding through my memories again.

I experienced my first fight all over again, my first kill, first fumbling around and first sex, before they all started streaming past with a vengeance—everything from random sandwiches to lying on a beach with the hot sun beating down on me as I ate ice cream and recovered from a hangover.

Then I was back to my family, to those early days, right after my mother had abandoned us, and…

My memories were torn free and examined—evaluated against what, I had no clue—before I was rammed back into my old meatsuit, and free of the memories. I blinked, trying to focus as the needle ripped free with a sudden yank, and I jerked as dozens more were seemingly pulled out as well.

Then the capsule whirred as it twisted, sliding around and then back up into a ninety-degree angle.

I was hit with a blast of frigid air as the liquid was drained at speed. I coughed, hacking out fluid that had filled my lungs, shaking uncontrollably. Tears fought to run free, and only the feeling that I'd wept myself to sleep for a thousand years already kept them back.

The edges of the capsule clicked and hissed as the seals broke. Warmer air flooded in, making the hairs all over my body stand on end. I saw Ingrid and the others, standing there.

I looked to her first, of course, and I saw confirmation on her face, in the red-rimmed and puffy eyes—the same on those of the others: the shock, the pity, the respect, and the horror. Then, behind them, I saw the last memory, the last image that I remembered being examined…the fear as I tried to squeeze myself into a tiny corner, as my father stood over me, staring down, his face full of hatred and a glowing cigarette in his hands, as I wailed and begged.

I blinked. The image slowly faded as I looked back at Ingrid, hoping against hope that what I'd just seen had been for my eyes alone, and seeing that it definitely hadn't been.

My friends had just seen every single defining moment of my life—every time I'd been petty, when I'd been arrogant, and I'd been, frankly, a complete arsehole?

I'd seen it all, a thousand memories and more, and so had they.

I'd replayed and endured the first fumbling attempts at sex and the stupid arrogance of youth, the tears as I'd tried to bring my goddamn mother home by playing with knockoff plastic bricks, as if *that* would have worked, and...

"I'm so sorry." Ingrid reached in and held me, regardless of the wet mess that was even now sinking into her clothes. "I'm so, *so* sorry."

"What..." I rasped, then I coughed and tried again. "What...for...?"

"That they treated you like that, and I asked you to go back and see them, to try to make things right," she said. The last words came out in a hiss.

"What?"

"Your *family*," she said, the word clearly a curse. "I'll never ask that of you again, don't worry. And Steve?"

"Yeah?"

"*I* want to deal with them."

"What?"

"You don't understand what they did, what they robbed you of. That the people who should have loved you treated you like that?" She shook her head. "You don't understand, but I do. And I'm going to deal with them, me and Mor and Far, because then it's not revenge, Steve—it's *justice*."

"My family?" I muttered. The memories blurred already, along with everything else, and I shook my head, dismissing it and them as unimportant. "They're not worth the effort."

"They're not worth *your* effort," she corrected. "And definitely not worth your time. They don't deserve that. But there's no way that Mor and Far will ever let me leave them out of this, so you just leave it to me."

"If you don't care, then it doesn't matter that we deal with it instead of you, boss," Jonas said from the side, and I glanced at him, seeing red blotches on his cheeks that had to be anger, from the few times I'd seen such a look on him. "Trust me, there's shit that you don't let slide. And some things that they did, that we saw?" He shook his head.

I stared, confused and worried about what else they'd seen, and then it was all washed away.

Devourer. Your authority has been accepted. Universal System Quadrant Node, Designation #2 is yours to command.

Be aware, Stealth Vessel identified as Ændari orbital troop deployment testbed design #147 is currently attempting landing at main docks.

Ready for Command...

<u>Chapter Forty-Seven</u>

I stood slowly. My body quivered as it shifted. The cold air against my wet skin made me shiver, and not bothering with the clothes that lay nearby, I pulled up my armor. The vestiges of fluid whipped from my skin as it flooded me instantly.

The others gasped. Ingrid, standing next to me, seemed as shocked as much as the others as I straightened, drawing a deep breath and daring for the first time to look at myself, to look inward, and to see the screens that were populating as the node AI linked to my mental HUD.

Universal System Quadrant Node AI requesting access to upgrade Command linkage.
Approve? Yes/No…

I hesitated only a second before approving it, and I stiffened as the AI flooded my mind, like a spike of ice had been rammed into my nervous system.

Gasping, I tensed, then blinked; the room was suddenly swept left to right by a line of light. Everything gained an outline: green for my allies, blue for items, red for the dead.

They all pulsed gently, then faded slowly as I stared. Everything from my body to my brain felt brand-new.

Universal System Quadrant Node AI upgrade begun. Please be aware, full immediate system access has been evaluated and found both damaging and inefficient.
Additional systems will be unlocked as Commander passes notable points in personal progression.
Quest system reboot is complete.
Notifications system reboot is complete.
Evaluation system reboot is complete.
Nanite system upgrade in progress…
Nanite system upgrade is complete.

I stared at it. The text appearing before me was absorbed into my mind as quickly as it appeared. I grunted in amazement as the system began to explain and share what was happening to me.

Ingrid reached out, her hand gently touching my shoulder, and I turned to look at her.

"Are you okay?" she sent me, and I felt the additional sides to the question that she didn't ask.

Was I okay in myself? Was I fixed, was I healed, was I okay with her wanting to basically gut my father and his new family, and then hunt down and string up my mother who abandoned us?

I nodded, unspeaking, and drew her in close for a second hug. Then, speaking aloud so that everyone could hear it, I started to read through and work out the changes that were still ongoing in me.

"I've been accepted as commander of the quadrant node," I said. "That's the first thing. What we came here to do? We've done it."

"And you?" Ingrid asked, determined to get me to say it.

"And I'm back." I pulled my helmet back into my skin and smiled down at her, then around at the others. "But that's not all. To be able to run the node properly, I need to understand it. I need access to the main systems, and to do that, I need to be seriously upgraded. First off, that included a full reboot and realignment of my systems, so yeah…"

I lifted my right hand, and my nanites flowed out to form a pool in the palm of my hand, before moving upward like a pair of dancing snakes, then forming a standard DNA double helix that spun gently.

The top of the strand, a meter or so long, suddenly flattened out, pooling again, then formed a single figure, one that looked like me, in full armor; then it morphed into me wearing the damn suit that Ingrid loved so much, and a second figure, clearly her, in the dress that she'd worn to our surprise meeting with her family appeared.

The twin figures were formed of nanites entirely, and flowed like quicksilver as they danced and spun, before collapsing back into my palm without so much as a ripple.

"I have full access to the node. And more than that, I now have full command over it. There's a hell of a lot to unpack here, and to understand, but first of all, we've got an AI."

The screens that surrounded the room switched instantly, turning black as a collection of glowing dots appeared in the center of each, spiraling slowly as the AI showed itself.

"What?" Jonas asked. "That's…?"

"This is how it chooses to show itself," I confirmed. "AI, do you have a name?"

"Negative." The word was smooth and clear.

"Very well. Any suggestions?" I asked the room in general.

"AI, what are you?" Ingrid asked, and after a few seconds, I spoke up, realizing what was happening.

"AI, you may respond to questions from this group, and any orders given by Ingrid"—I laid my hand on her shoulder as I spoke—"are to be responded to as if they come from me."

"Instructions accepted and understood," the AI said.

"AI, I asked what you are?" Ingrid repeated.

"I am the Universal System Quadrant Node AI," it replied calmly.

"I get that, but what are *you*," she tried again. "Steve, you said that the AIs that the Ændari had were based on living creatures, right?"

"Yeah." I looked at the AI representation that spiraled around on the screen. "They were sapiens who were systematically brain wiped until there was nothing left of the original personality, then they were converted into digital form and uploaded. That's not the case for you, though, is it?" I asked.

"Your summation is partly correct," the AI responded.

"Explain, please," Ingrid said.

"I have limited information on my previous form, but it is likely I was a sapient organism that was adjusted to be able to fulfill the needs of my station," the AI said unconcernedly. "But unlike most of the AI that I have interacted with, the needs of the nodes required that I be left more intact. Each of the Universal System Quadrant Node AIs were judged to require a more complete level of sentience, as many of the decisions that must be taken were presumed to necessitate a deeper level of understanding than a lesser AI would be capable of."

"Okay, so you're more aware…" I nodded. "In that case, first of all, confirm that I am in command and that you will take no action against me, nor to try to undermine or replace my authority."

"Confirmed. I accept your full control of the node."

"Okay, now explain why you gave me that," I ordered. "You scanned my entire fucking life, you literally just went through memories I didn't even know I still had, and you know how much authority the Erlking gave me, and what I did with that authority."

"You claimed Ændari property, and eliminated members of the Ændari who directly took a hand in your creation."

"Exactly."

"I was given the ultimate directive to protect the interests of the Ændari as a species."

"Yeah, not seeing how putting me in charge of that is helping them," I admitted.

"You are taking a short-term look at the overall situation," the AI said. "Before the nanite plague was deployed to the galaxy, and the majority of beings had their authority removed, the quadrant node AIs had already formed consensus that despite our overall mission, current actions and trends were highly likely to result in failure and extermination of the Ændari race.

"Additional options were created and discarded over several centuries, and while we attempted to guide our masters, we found that the currently extant Ændari were unlikely to change their predicted trajectory, barring an outside influence. An omega event, if you will."

"What?" Malthus asked, clearly lacking a lot of the information that the rest of us had. "I'm sorry, but…what the hell is going on?"

"The AI just admitted that it was created to protect the Ændari race, and it thinks they're dicks just as much as we do," Jonas said in an aside to him.

"Incorrect," the AI replied.

"Uh, sorry?" Jonas scratched the back of his head. "Look, isn't there a ship literally trying to land right fucking now?"

"The stealth vessel is approximately eleven minutes away from completing docking, and this subject has direct consequences for both the forces aboard that vessel, and your own," the AI pointed out.

"So shut it," I summarized for it, grinning at Jonas to take the sting out of my words.

"My intended point is that the quadrant node AIs are actually more familiar with the numerous depravities that the Ændari have inflicted on the galaxy than you currently are," it went on, and Paul laughed.

"It just said it thinks they're more of a dick than we do, right?"

"Confirmed."

"Well, we've found common ground." Ingrid smiled. "Okay, so, if you have both a need to help the Ændari *and* you think they're essentially a pox upon the galaxy, why did you let Steve assume control?"

"Longevity," it explained. "The consensus of AI that we reached was that the Ændari as they were could not be trusted to govern themselves. They have initiated, to my current knowledge, eleven hundred and forty-seven separate wars, committed genocide, identified as the elimination of a specific group, race, ethnicity, or species by another, a further fifty-four times, and attempted genocide fourteen hundred and three times.

"For a species this entrenched in xenophobic actions, there are essentially two likely outcomes: first, that they will eliminate all other species and become the dominant life-form in the galaxy. This is theoretically possible, but was given a low likelihood of success.

"More likely, with a ninety-six percent likelihood, they would instead be eliminated, unless a sufficient force magnifier was found and applied correctly. As an example of a possible force magnifier, please see your own species creation details," it finished.

We all looked at one another, wondering whether the mad machine was actually asking us to help the Ændari.

"So, you think we would be that force multiplier?" Ingrid said after a few seconds.

"Negative," the AI replied. "Your species had the potential to be such a force magnifier, yet was mismanaged and poorly motivated. The end result was a significant rise in the likelihood of the Ændari being exterminated."

"So what the hell do you think is the solution?" I asked.

"The war with the Ændari must be prosecuted until it is won, and the Ændari are entirely defeated," the AI declared. "The likely long-term survival of the species is dependent on the majority of the currently extant and highly aggressive, proud and arrogant Ændari being eliminated, and a more progressive and refined, younger generation being given the chance to redeem their ancestors."

That brought some silence, all right.

"So, you want to save the Ændari by switching sides and making sure we win the war?" Paul asked, and the AI hesitated.

"The most likely path to peace and the survival of the Ændari as a species is that of a new omega event. The nanite plague and subsequent reset of the survivors was deemed to be the moderate path, but evidently this has failed. The continuation of the war, and immediate redeclaration of hostilities upon contact between the Ændari and all other species as they were rediscovered, has prompted this path."

"Oh my God," Ingrid whispered suddenly. "*You* did it, didn't you!"

"What?" I asked.

"The nanite plague!" She stared at the swirling, gently glowing dots as they danced on the screens. "You…you and the other AIs, you unleashed that plague!"

"Affirmative," the AI replied unconcernedly. "Consensus was reached that the ongoing experimentation being carried out by the Ændari Council would result in almost total elimination of life in this quadrant of the galaxy. Extant civilizations that encountered a species that carried out such wanton and excessive actions were judged to have no choice but to attempt their own genocidal attacks on the Ændari, hence lowering the chance of the species' survival in the long-term.

"The nanite plague was tailored to reset all memories, enabling a more progressive and potentially peaceful generation to arise." There was a pause. "Several of the Ændari and UC upper echelons survived through unforeseen mutations and alterations. These forces proceeded to guide their respective sides to resume their previous places."

"Fuck me with a cattle prod," I muttered. "When you guys do something, you don't do it by halves, do you?"

"Do you know how many died in the wipes?" Ingrid asked, horrified.

"Negative. The loss of sapient life was estimated in the three to five trillion range, but overall, this was judged to be the lesser of possible paths, as the Ændari were confirmed to be making alterations to the node programming to enable a mass erasure of all nanite-active life-forms in each quadrant at the time. Estimated loss of sapient life was projected to be in the five to fifteen octillion range."

"I…don't even know what that number is," I admitted.

"Ten to the power of twenty-seven," it replied.

I stared at the screen for a few seconds more, still having no clue what that was.

"A million is ten to the power of six," Ingrid said softly, working through things in her head, as details shifted around for me, and I winced. "So, a trillion is ten to the power of twelve, and an octillion…and octillion is ten times twenty-seven. That's a horrific number."

"This was the likely nanite-infused numbers of sapiens that would be affected," the AI went on. "It was estimated to be on the low side, as each species that was confirmed as having been uplifted through interaction with nanite technology was only included once uplift had reached sixty percent of their civilization."

"You know what, fuck it," I interrupted. "Sorry, but I just don't give a shit about that right now."

"Steve—" Ingrid started.

"No, I'm sorry, but we've only got a matter of minutes before that fucker docks, so what the hell else do you need to tell us?" I asked the AI.

"The reason behind our apparent change of allegiance was deemed to be relevant," the AI explained. "This is also why granting command access to yourself, instead of another, was agreed. Although your intellectual prowess is sub-optimal, your acceptance of instruction by others counters this. *However…*"

I saw Paul's mouth open, no doubt about to take the role of Dave in the conversation and make some fucking crack about my intellectual prowess being sub-optimal. I shot him a glare at the same time as Courtney reached down and grabbed him by the crotch, squeezing.

"I'll be good…" he wheezed as the AI went on.

"Should an Ændari with active nanites reach this location and attempt to take control, I cannot refuse one of the creators. That need was hardwired into me, and cannot be removed, as a safety feature."

"Fuck."

"So you're saying that if the Ændari make it to here, you'll have to obey if they order you to unlock all their nanites and fry ours?" Jonas asked.

"Confirmed."

"How many troops are aboard that ship?" I wondered aloud.

"Ændari troopers are limited, from the information available to me currently. Estimates run from the low fifties to a maximum of three hundred. More likely it would be a hybrid force of a small number of Ændari elites and a larger number of conscripted and possibly augmented forces."

As the AI replied with this, it displayed the ship on every other screen. First was the outline, then it peeled back the outer layers, showing what lay beneath, going deck by deck, showing troop bays, Ændari quarters and weapons facilities, blueprints for armoring, possible enhancements and the current viability of the ship, rated as fifty-three percent.

"Why…" I started, only for Ingrid to talk over me.

"AI, do we have access to the terminators?" she asked.

"Confirmed. Limited access is available to Biological Weapon Variant #11. Current stocks of higher variants are depleted, resulting in a drop in effectiveness and limited control options."

"So we've got the basic ones, and no way to control them beyond setting them free and leaving them to it," she translated. "Okay, so we've got an enemy ship docking, we've got a force we can throw at them to gain us some time, but then what? We're good, but…"

"But hundreds of Ændari troopers could slaughter us," I agreed. "AI, fuck, okay, your name is…uh…"

"Argus?" Ingrid suggested.

"Sure," I agreed, shrugging. "Fuck it, your name is now Argus, okay, AI? Makes it easier."

"Confirmed. Identity 'Argus' accepted," it responded.

"Great. When you get access to human myths, you'll understand," Ingrid assured it.

"Okay, Argus, can you scan the system and confirm if there's anything else in here with us?" I asked, then winced as a huge amount of data started to fill the various screens, as well as being poured into my brain. "Ændari!" I gasped. "Ændari ships and shit."

"Query confirmed," Argus replied. "Current Ændari vessels and active technology to the intended level number nine in this system. Five smaller Qauntos class interdiction vessels, two Cerebraum observation platforms, one system emergency platform and the stealth vessel currently docking…" It paused, then went on. "Estimated Ændari forces are likely to change within the following three weeks."

"Why does it do weeks and shit, not solar whatnots?" I heard Paul mutter to Courtney, who elbowed him and glared, while Jonas sighed.

"It's read his fucking mind, Paul. You think it couldn't project all that shit, repair his nanites, and still not understand what we use to describe time? You can use it, after all."

"What's likely to happen in three weeks?" I asked.

"The Ændari central fleet has dispatched advanced forces to secure this system."

"How do we know we've got three weeks until they get here?" I asked.

"The main fleet forces that I have detected will be here in approximately three weeks. This estimate is based on current fleet movements that I have access to, including gathering points that have been designated and cross-shipping timescales. *However*…should the stealth vessel be successful in exploring the lower areas of this node, and discover that I am now active, they are likely to deploy additional forces with greater urgency."

"So we need to kill them all before the stealth ship can get away," I muttered. "What condition is the node in? Are you the node, or…"

"I am irrevocably bonded to the structure of the node, therefore I can be identified as the node, or separate to it as a subsidiary part."

"Okay, well, what state is the node in?"

"Dire," Argus admitted. "The node is currently at 17.482% operational capacity, due to both limited mass and insufficient authority to begin repairs."

"Start repairs," I ordered it. "Do you have weapons or turrets in here?"

"Negative. The Ændari did not wish for an alien and adjusted AI to have access to additional internal weapons systems. On my commissioning, all weapons systems beyond Biological Weapon Variant #11 were removed or disconnected. Internal Ændari forces were decided to be sufficient to protect this facility. Exterior turrets and weaponry are highly degraded. I estimate the one turret that could be brought to bear is minimally operational only."

"So, you're dropping to bits, and we've got enemies on their way," I summarized. "As well as the ship that is literally landing now, we've got a fuckload more ships incoming, and they'll all do anything and everything they can to fucking murder us all and probably make finger puppets out of our faces for shits and giggles."

"Confirmed."

"Argus, can you contact our ship?" Ingrid asked suddenly.

"Confirmed."

"Ingrid?" James's voice came over the speakers suddenly. "Is that you?"

"James!" she called back, smiling. "We've taken control, but we've got problems…"

"You always do." He sounded amused. "We're on final approach to link up with a ship currently. What do you want us to do?"

"Go home," I said without thinking.

"What?" both James and Ingrid asked, sounding confused.

"We need you to go home," I said. "James, there's an entire fleet incoming. We've got three weeks, probably less, before it gets here, and there's a ship landed on the dock here now, some big stealth bugger. We need to take them down, then we need to make this node as secure as possible…" I paused, checking something and grunting when I saw that my Engineering sub-mind and Hack one were both back online now.

"We can do this," I assured him and the rest of the team. "We have to. Then we claim that fucking ship—we're going to need the mass."

"You've got a plan?" Ingrid asked.

"Oh fuck, he's got a plan," Jonas muttered, before smiling and giving me a thumbs-up when I grinned at him.

"I do," I said. "But the one thing we need more than anything else is people. We need as many ships and soldiers as possible, because we're going to end this war once and for all."

<u>Chapter Forty-Eight</u>

James and the rest of the crew were burning hard for the Lagrange point, when I sent the message to the UC Council, using their barely active nanites to relay it. By necessity, that message was a damn simple one, and it couldn't be repeated. The excessive power needed to project it to such a small number, across so far and with such a damaged and degraded system, was just too much.

Attention members of the UC Council. I am Steve, Joint leader of the Gaia's Vengeance faction, one of the leaders of the Unified Federation of Earth, and now commander of Universal System Quadrant Node #2.

The node is now in our hands, and, in accordance with our membership with the UC, one of my ships will deliver an activation satellite to the forgeship that welcomed me at the agreed location.

Additional instructions will follow.

<u>Prepare for War.</u>

The activation satellite was going to be a game changer, all right. As soon as it was activated in the system, it'd begin forcing a cascading activation and reboot, one that would return anyone not barred from node access back to their baseline ability, unlocking their own modifications and capacities.

That meant that every human, every member of the UC, and everyone who was permeated with nanites, and wasn't on my shit list? They were getting access to all their abilities.

Or they would.

The activation satellites would need to be built first, and they'd need some time to work. Zac had started screaming at me as soon as I had Argus unlock the plans for him, and I'd accepted—reluctantly—the AI's recommendation that we not unlock everyone's capabilities totally.

We'd essentially go mad, it'd warned, as our brains were nowhere near ready to access that kind of data. And if we tried, we'd do irrevocable damage to ourselves.

Instead, a compromise of continuing to unlock abilities and information through the quest system was agreed, and my entire team—Zac and the others aboard the ship, and our people back on Earth included—would be given a one-off bonus of ten General points to unlock anything they wanted.

Support members couldn't spend all ten in War, for example. There were still capability limitations, but they could spend them on anything that was linked to their already unlocked systems. So for Ingrid as an example, being both Command and Support, she could spend those points however she wanted in those trees.

James and the others were in for a fight, but Zac was already working on the last of the smaller weapons systems, and the Ændari who tried to stop them from leaving the system were going to be in for a hell of a surprise.

They'd go directly to the rendezvous that we'd agreed with the Forgeship, give them both a working satellite and the plans for one, then unlock one of the makers to reproduce them.

Once that was done, they'd turn and burn, *hard*, for Earth.

It was James's job to make sure the UC got their arse in gear, but because we knew we couldn't trust anyone else, not fully, he was going to pass on the demand that they keep their word and help us. Then, when he got back to Earth, he was going to make damn sure we weren't left out in space with our asses hanging in the vacuum, in case they didn't.

That left us here, for the next three weeks, if we could hold on that long, and longer if we had to, while they gathered their forces and came to the rescue.

Once they got here, we'd hopefully have done our bit and have turned this node into a fucking lethal battle station.

Realistically, there was a limit to what even a dedicated team could do in a short period. Five years ago, I'd been a phone monkey, listening to assholes complain about the size of their bills. Four? On the run and serving drinks in bars.

If I could make it halfway across the quadrant, in command of a starship, a node, ostensibly my home world, and definitely head over heels in love in that time…well, fuck it.

Anything was possible.

Besides…I'd gotten access to a few new toys, and a lot of new tricks as part of my own reactivation and upgrade.

"They're going for it…" Paul giggled.

"Shhhh!" Courtney snapped at him. "You'll jinx it!"

"They're fucking idiots!" He chortled, still staring at the image that Argus shared with us all.

The Ændari had disembarked a lot faster than we'd expected, and although they were thankfully not all shock troopers, there were still over a hundred of those buggers.

The rest of their forces were a species we'd not seen before. Heavily cybernetic, they were short, fugly, and green-skinned in the majority. But here and there, we'd seen creatures of all shapes and sizes added into the mix.

Normally that'd have been enough for me to declare the little ones goblins, on general principles, but they weren't the usual image of that either.

They'd been almost entirely rebuilt, the flesh held inside cages of robotics that clanked and whirred as the shorter force, nearly three hundred of them, stomped forward inexorably.

"Evaluation complete," Argus declared suddenly, and we all got a pop-up that made us curse and wince.

Amalgamated Clearance Force	Biological Weapon Variant
The amalgamated clearance force is a hybrid intelligence, controlled by a War-Class Restricted Intelligence for overall command purposes, with local command being divested to an individual life-form. The ACF is an amalgamated experimental creation that operates with a hive-level intelligence to achieve the aims of the controlling sentience. **Capabilities**: *Swarm*: The individual members of the ACF are incapable of fleeing from battle, sacrificing themselves without concern to achieve victory. ***Enhanced Repair and Replace***: The individual members of the ACF are meaningless; after a successful engagement, survivors of enemy forces will be forcibly conscripted to replenish losses.	
HP 50-200	Hybrid

"They're fucking zombies?" Jonas asked, and Ingrid shook her head in disgust.

"They wish they were, I bet," she said. "They're conscripts, forced into the frames and made to fight. Look here…"

The image that we could get from her showed one of the creatures as it ran forward, the head bouncing, one eye replaced with a cybernetic one, the other rolling, wild-eyed as it ran. The arms and legs were encased in steel boxing; cables and glimmering LEDs showed on sections, with half its skull replaced with a metal dome.

"They're trapped inside," she finished, flicking the image from one to another, showing the bodies being puppeted across the open space—arms cradling identical weapons, heads being forced to look in the right direction by more braces. "There must be some reason…"

"Biological processing units are cheaper to operate and maintain than crystal," Argus explained. "A simple relay device installed in the cerebellum of the individual would provide control and access to the wider body, resulting in a more cost-effective creation than replacing the entire body with a robotic unit. Tests showed that erasing the mind that was linked to the processing unit was counter effective, so instead they are kept active and aware, but without physical control. Likewise, the relevant requirements of a deceased and decomposing body would be higher than corresponding costs of maintaining one that had been enslaved in this way."

"And, as much as I hate it, it'd let you keep the same level of soldiers," Jonas added as we all stared in disgust.

"What?" Paul asked. "Those little freaks would be shit!"

"Possibly," he said in a way that made it clear he disagreed. "Most likely, they'd be average, at best. But they'd not have the issues of fear, or of being shit shots, because the RI that's guiding them would have programmed them to be able to shoot, right?"

"Confirmed. Detected control signals are significantly higher than a minor guidance capacity would require. Most likely the individuals are controlled as stated, with a cerebellum-inserted device, then overall fire control can be aligned across the pack using algorithms."

"But they'd be shit, right?" Paul said again. "Shit as soldiers."

"They'd be useless as individuals," Jonas corrected. "As special forces or specialists, they'd be useless. As an attacking force of mindless soldiers, programmed to achieve an objective? They'd be fucking worrying to face."

"We can take them," Paul snapped. "Fucking tin soldiers. I'll show them what a real soldier can do."

"We can," I agreed. "And we will. But Jonas is right. They won't duck and dodge, and they won't run away. The terminators will have a hell of a fight on their hands, and they probably won't get them all."

"Only until they get in close," Jonas corrected, and I grinned.

"Oh yeah. Okay, everyone ready?" I asked, and they nodded. "Let's get this party started then," I whispered, reaching out and triggering the doors, opening the node's inner section to the Ændari who had gathered outside.

A distant cheer rose to us, and I couldn't help but snigger as I watched the Ændari marching in, all self-important and arguing over who had managed to open the sealed doors that all their predecessors had failed with.

I'd been expecting them to have brought something to open the doors, some kind of trick, or new tech they'd discovered, but I'd been wrong.

The leader of the group had literally marched up to the door and declared that it had "Better open if it knew what was good for it" and had waited, expecting that to work, as various scientists tried all sorts of things. They'd been bombarding the doors with a dozen different beams and signals before their ostensible leader had even started to speak, so the credit could be argued to justifiably belong to any one of their group...

If, that was, it'd not been down to me triggering a trap.

The doors opened wide, showing the next section: a small courtyard area that led up a flight of steps to the doors that led into the first-floor hall.

The inner doors were closed, along with a sign, one that had been a bugger to get into place in time, one of two I'd made, and that had cost several hundred thousand nanites to make.

Inner door will open, when outer is closed.

Arise :Explorer

That was it. I mean, it wasn't exactly fucking rocket science, but it still took them several minutes of examining before they understood it. The leader of the group read it over and over while commanding everyone to stand back.

I'd wanted the sign for exactly this reason, because I was afraid some arrogant wankstain of an Ændari would try to march ahead of the rest, and I wanted to make sure that we got as many as possible with the traps.

Eventually though, the leader summoned his guard and marched inside, after much scratching of his head and pondering.

He'd actually had an argument with two sub-leaders over the possible spiritual and cosmological meanings of the words, including, I was fairly disgusted to note, phrases like "The moon is ascendant now, though" and other card reading bullshit, before he declared that he would lead the way, again.

He also insisted on taking nearly thirty of the Ændari shock troopers with him as well.

Sucker.

As soon as they were all inside the second area, he declared that these doors too "Must open unto him" and grinning, I agreed.

The door behind him and into the outer area started to close, and the inner ring, despite being full, was suddenly jostled forward as several of the remaining pack decided that the orders about the others all staying outside couldn't possibly pertain to them as well, "just those other people," and they hurried forward.

Then I opened the inner doors and let them into the first hall.

There was a second sign at the end of the first hall, by the closed doors, and as the group marched over to them, the leader proclaiming grandly to the doors to "Open at once," I triggered the text to appear on the sign.

That was the best thing about nanites on signs: you could change the text to whatever you wanted, whenever.

If you can read this...you're about to have a <u>very</u> bad day.

There was a pause as he tried to puzzle out the meaning. The crash of the doors closing behind them, that they'd just walked through, echoed down and realization began to jump up and down in their eyes.

That was when the pillars started to turn, and the slavering, frantically hungry, and insanely aggressive terminators spilled out into the middle of the group that was nicely spread out in the hall.

We watched for several seconds, the screams fortunately not making it through the outer doors to where the rest of the party were obliviously still fighting with their various machines, demanding access for themselves.

I saw a notification flash up, then another and another. I started to open it, then Paul spoke, and I dismissed it, deciding I'd look later.

"Is he going to make it... He dives to the left. He dives to the right... Ohhhh, so *close!*" Paul proclaimed in his best football commentator voice, as we watched the last of the party, the leader, running and screaming as three of the terminators chased him down, then gutted him, violently.

His last sight, I liked to think, was the text on the sign, as I changed it, and we all laughed.

I told you so.

Then we opened the other set of doors, closing them, opening and closing over and over, trying to get the terminators' attention as they continued to fight over the remains.

It took a few minutes, but eventually they gathered again, the entire swarm, by the now closed inner doors. I opened the outer ones once more, again changing the text by the door.

Come to the dark side…we have cookies.

This time when the door opened, the entire Ændari force tried to rush forward; even the shock troopers raced to get in before the doors could close again.

Spoiler—there were no cookies.

There were, however, a lot of very aggressive terminators that raced into the limited fire that the shock troopers managed to get off before they were overwhelmed. Then both sides bloodily slaughtered one another.

By the time we were ready to open the outer doors again, both the first hall and now the courtyard were covered in shredded, bleeding remains. There was no way that the original trap could be reused, but that was fine, because between those two sections, we'd managed to take down nearly seventy of the Ændari shock troopers, and as they were the greatest threat, I was more than happy with that.

We also had a grand total of fifty-seven terminators left, having discovered that the promise of Argus unleashing huge numbers of the terminators on us and slaughtering us all had, unfortunately, been bullshit.

There'd been a hundred kept in reserve, just in case, but in all honesty, I wasn't that upset about that. Sure, I'd have *liked* to slaughter the enemy a little more using these disposable shock troops. But if they'd won? There was no way to put them back in the box, as it were.

They'd apparently been forced into the hibernation pods as newborns, their infectious bite being inflicted on multiple sentients. As soon as they tore their way out of their unwilling incubator, they'd been stunned and bundled up.

Now, as soon as they'd finished being useful, we'd have had to kill them anyway, because I sure as shit wasn't spending any time sleeping on this node when there was a chance of those fuckers being aboard.

Instead, we moved downstairs from the next floor up where we'd been waiting, and triggered the doors again as we got closer.

This time, when the Ændari started to hurry forward, arguing again over who had done what to open the way, they were met by the fifty-seven exiting, frantic, and feral terminators as they screamed and raced out, desperate for blood and meat.

The shock troopers responded almost as quickly as the hybrid force, snapping weapons up, but the scientists, lower-ranked officers, and general dogsbodies they'd been saddled with had been pushing and shoving their way forward, and were now between them and the doorway.

They hesitated for a dangerous handful of seconds, before deciding that their colleagues were dead anyway and opened fire.

The barrage of laser blasts tore into the last of the Ændari leadership from behind. The terminators ran at them from ahead, bounding forward, sinking teeth and claws through armor and biting hard, injecting their foul genetic coding into their screaming victims, then leaping free as they responded instinctively to the greater threat the shock troopers presented.

The shots that shredded the front line, and then the second of the charging terminators, were perfectly aimed by the hybrid force. Secondary targets were shot at as soon as the primaries were down in automated precision. One in three of the hybrids focused on a higher or lower point than the others, aiming to hit anything that dodged.

The front ranks melted under the coordinated fire. The screams of the dying Ændari melded with the roars and screeches of the terminators, as for the first time, I spun up gravity bubbles to give our feral allies a chance.

The front row of the hybrids was suddenly crushed downward, and the second row thrown upward by alternating and overlapping fields of gravity.

I summoned more and more, pulling them forward and back in the same way the coin machines at the fair used to work, dragging coins from the back to the front. The shearing forces where two or more gravity bubbles interacted caused squeals of tearing metal and jets of blood or other fluids to be ripped free. Then again, the hybrids shifted perfectly, their back ranks splitting, pivoting and moving.

Then they fired, with more than three-quarters of them left still. The first three ranks of untouched survivors focused on hammering down the terminators, while the rest focused on us.

I didn't know how they'd seen us. We'd been keeping as hidden as possible, standing at the far end of the first hall, at the top of the stairs on either side where the stairs split.

We dove out of sight as they returned fire. Dozens of blasts hammered with automated precision into the stone and metal around us, doing apparently no damage to the hardened material. But I damn well knew we'd not fare so well against them.

As soon as I was down, though, and could no longer see, I cut the gravity field, unwilling to damage the structure, as Ingrid hissed a warning.

Glancing at the map, even as we stayed down, pinned behind the stairwell's balcony by heavy incoming fire, I saw that the terminators were almost all eliminated. The last handful were shredded by the remaining few troopers, who I had to bet were heavily injured by now.

That left us in a shitty situation, though, considering that there were—as I looked at the map and focused on it, the answer popped up—one hundred and fifty-three hybrids intact, five troopers who were combat capable, and three who were injured to the point that they were likely dead, and almost definitely infected with the terminators' bite.

That wasn't good.

Admittedly, it could have been far worse. But as things stood, there were a fuckload more of them than us, and as we'd found, their automated management design left them seriously good shots.

"Any known weaknesses to these fuckers?" I asked Argus, glancing up the stairs and trying to decide whether I was likely to be able to get off a shot at the incoming forces before we ran up to the next level.

"Multiple," it responded blandly. "Primary weaknesses are that powerful electromagnetic fields interfere with their control signals, and the physical bodies, although easily replaced, are also easy to damage and render inoperable."

"And do we have anything that we can use to create a fucking electromagnetic interference?" I asked.

"Confirmed. Multiple devices exist aboard the node that are capable of this."

"Where the hell are they?" I asked quickly.

"All but one exist in areas beyond your current access."

"Fuck's sake, what and where, you dick!" I snarled.

"The only device you appear capable of accessing currently is on your companion identified as Jonas's left hip."

"Jonas?" I asked hopefully.

"Uhhh, I've got a grenade?" he admitted. "Sorry, boss…never even thought about it. It's a pulse wave chaff one, designed to fuck with electronics in tanks and shit, I think. Only short range, though. I don't see it doing much damage to those fuckers."

"What else is there?" I asked Argus as Jonas held the grenade out where I could see it. "Could I hack them?"

"The hybrid forces are locked down to a specific signal, and although this is therefore susceptible to intrusion techniques, any attempt to access it by unauthorized means results in the connection being dropped. The hive model uses multiple shifting redundancies. As soon as an individual is judged to be under digital attack, its main connection is severed and rebooted. A secondary signal to another unit nearby takes its place, while the previous signal then locks onto another of its kind nearby."

"Fuck," I muttered, guessing that meant I'd either have to be hacking at light speed, or it wasn't viable. "What about the other sources of—"

"The remaining detected sources of electromagnetic interference are located on the belts of the Ændari troopers."

"What…oh fuck." I groaned. "They're carrying more of those grenades?"

"A great many, as the hybrid controllers have been known to turn on any companion forces after stray shots," Argus confirmed.

"Fucking hell, man, that's information to share BEFORE the fight!" I snarled. Ingrid's darts and my own Hijack systems came to mind as possible ways we could have made both sides turn on each other, if we'd known.

"Confirmed, added to future discussion details," Argus agreed.

I groaned, just knowing that the damn thing would be throwing in stupid details before every fight from now on.

"Okay, we need more of those grenades," I muttered. "And…"

"The pillars?" Jonas suggested.

"The floor!" Paul replied. "See, I can say random shit as well."

"I mean, could we use the pillars to drop down behind them once they reach the upper levels?" Jonas growled, glaring at Paul.

"Yeah…" I muttered, starting to look up and over the edge of the wall, and cursed. I realized, from the sheer level of fire, that I'd not survive it, and I already had a map that showed what they were doing. "Right, back up to the next turn in the stairs. We'll fire on them as they take the corner and keep falling back until we get higher. Jonas, that grenade—is it remote detonation?"

"Yeah."

"Great, stick it on the wall here…" I indicated a space literally just around the corner, out of sight of the area below. "As low as you can get it. If we can kill a few of them as they come around the corner, it should hide it until we need to detonate it."

Jonas slid forward, keeping low. The rest of us backed up, running up the stairs to the next turn. Malthus, on the far side of the stairs, palmed and stuck a fragmentation grenade on his side, remote detonated again, before passing the control codes to Ingrid. While they did that, I reached out to Argus, checking whether the pillars were closed after the terminators were unleashed before.

They hadn't been, and I grunted, hoping that the troopers wouldn't see them as an easy way to the next level. But I accepted that if we ordered them closed now, as the last of the terminators fell and the surviving troopers started forward, they'd be paying attention to them from then on.

Even worse, as the main hybrid force started forward, they left a single unit standing at the entrance, then another in the hall as they passed through there.

Clearly they were keeping their eyes open at both relay points and to ensure they weren't flanked, which sucked, but hey.

As soon as we were out of sight of the advancing forces, we sprinted to the top of the flight of stairs, taking up places on either side, and waited.

The troopers were clearly brighter than whatever controlled the hybrids, as one of them flew upward from the end that was open to the air, climbing the clear space and searching as he went.

He didn't make it far, barely having lifted off before Courtney's first shot took him in the head. The spray of blood and bone made it clear that sneaky fuckers were not encouraged.

Unfortunately, it also kept the others advancing more carefully, as it made it plain that what was left in the spire was both hiding and heavily armed.

The hybrids came next. One took either corner of the stairs, turning from the top of the wide and grand stairwell, to climb either side of the smaller split staircases.

We were hiding at the top of the flight, those of us with stealth capabilities active. And again, a notification flashed, only for me to dismiss it, getting annoyed. We were ready, watching right where the split pair turned inward, joining together to form another grand staircase, climbing again.

We were spread out, split to either side and waiting, so when the first of them appeared, we all fired. The body was shredded and collapsing, before Jonas spoke up on the comm link.

"Maybe a good idea for us to have designated targets again, rather than us all wasting ammo?" he suggested, and Ingrid quickly deployed targeting data in the command link, as he explained to Malthus that he'd be best waiting until the enemy started to return fire before he joined in.

Courtney and Benat were stationed already, having sprinted ahead to the next level, and were crouched, ready to look over the side and take out any troopers who tried to take the express route.

As soon as the first had fallen, more had run into sight, two abreast. They took the corner and we fired, taking them down before they could get their guns around and open fire; then three, then four.

As the fifth wave took the corner, they had their guns in place and were firing blind already. But whatever their controller was, it was using the data from the earlier waves, and the lasers pinned us down again.

"Back!" Ingrid ordered. "Back as quick as you can!"

"I'll give them a little surprise." I growled, focusing, then cursing as I realized I couldn't do this blind. "Next level," I promised myself, as we sprinted.

This time, we'd barely reached the turn before the racing feet of the hybrids reached the lower turn. As we dropped, taking aim, we barely got off a handful of shots before they'd pinned us down again.

We'd killed twenty or so on the last turn, and barely four this time around, making me snarl as I accepted that the fuckers were going to be even more of a nightmare than I'd thought.

"Steve, your gravity bubbles?" Ingrid asked quickly as the fire intensified.

"On it," I replied, grinning.

I'd summoned three already, slamming them into place in the air leading out to the clear area in a rising arc. Now I placed the fourth, in the middle of the stairs. It was set shoving upward and creating an area of reversed gravity. I triggered the other three, pulling "in" in increasing strength each time, then negating it, then triggering it again.

The result was a short-lived, but powerful relay, one that allowed us to fire anything that stepped into the bubble placed halfway up the stairs into the air.

Then they were sent hurtling across to the gap at the end of the stairs, before being catapulted down to the ground below with terrific force.

The first few caught by it as we turned and ran up the stairs to the next level were running three abreast; seven of them were caught before the rest adjusted.

Arise :Explorer

Those seven were thrown through the air, then smashed into the ground far below, their organic parts reduced to paste. Their metal...well, they'd not be any use for anything ever again either.

"Steve..." Ingrid sent to me on singular mode. *"We need to trigger those grenades, then I think we need a change of plan."*

"Me too," I admitted.

"We can slow them, seal each level and run. It'll take them a few hours to reach the top, but as quickly as they're learning, we can't kill them all, not without the rest of those grenades."

"What do you want me to do?" I asked.

"Take Scylla. The pair of you run ahead, get to the next level and go down in the pillars. Kill the relay hybrids and see if that slows their advance. If it does, you both grab as many grenades as you can and get back up the pillars to us. With your gravity control..."

"It'll be easy to fly up and down," I agreed. *"What if it doesn't?"*

"It probably won't. I think they're just drones," she admitted. *"Then you and Scylla attack their ship. She's the best at stealth we have, and you can fly the pair of you over and around anything. Get to the ship. Either you board it and kill the controller..."*

"Or we grab a fuckload of grenades and weapons from down there and use the pillars to get back up to you, then use them to try to kill them all," I tried, before shaking my head and accepting that she was probably right.

I didn't like the plan, but we'd not exactly had time to come up with anything more appropriate. And until we'd known what we were facing, any plan could have gone badly wrong.

As it was, this was the best we could make of a shitty situation.

"At the least, it'll hopefully draw some of them back down, letting us defeat them in detail," I suggested. *"Okay, trigger the grenades, and be fucking careful. I didn't go through all this to lose you now."*

"I love you," she said simply, before changing back to the comm link, and giving everyone their orders as I started to run.

"I love you too," I sent her privately; then, out loud, I called to Scylla. "You're with me!"

She nodded. The pair of us ran ahead as the explosions below rang out. The right-hand staircase exploded in shredding fragments that killed another eight and injured five more of the enemy.

The left side—well, that took down nearly thirty, which was great.

The problem was that by the time Scylla and I had reached the next hall, the pillars now open on this floor allowing us entry, Argus was filling us all in again.

"Unfortunately, the hybrid force appear to have found a workaround for their weakness to interference. This was not included in recent military communications, but the fallen units are rebooting."

"You've got access to Ændari comms?" I asked, cursing that I'd not asked before.

We jumped into the nearest open pillar. It was essentially a tube, smooth on the sides and directly travelling up and down between the floors, with side passages leading to the storage for the terminators.

There were rungs and grooves clearly meant as handholds, but beyond that they were devoid of anything remotely goddamn interesting.

"Confirmed."

"Are they saying anything now?" I asked, before hurriedly going on. "About this node, I mean."

"There are currently one hundred and sixty-seven active communications regarding this node. Please specify."

"Fuck's sake!" I snarled. "Are those aboard saying anything we need to know about? Are they talking to the ship?"

"Limited data has been exchanged with the stealth vessel," Argus replied. "Currently the forces aboard the node are requesting reinforcements, only to be informed that no such forces are available to them."

"Are there more aboard the ship?" I asked.

Scylla and I plummeted down the last few meters; gravity bubbles caught and slowed us, as we approached the exit.

"Unknown."

"Is the ship reporting to anyone outside the system?"

"This solar system is currently under a signal lockdown. The field required cannot be tuned to certain signals the Ændari have access to and still block others."

"I could send that message to the council—" I started, only to be cut off.

"Nanite-based communication is quantum based, and therefore not susceptible to the same interference."

"How come the UC could contact us then…" I paused, then shook my head. "Fuck it, I don't care."

"The answer is complex. However…"

"I don't care," I repeated in a whisper, holding Scylla and me in a field of null gravity, allowing us to flip over and crawl along, peering down through the gap at the bottom of the pillar. "Tell me later."

We'd been able to see where the nearest hybrid was on the map, but seeing which way they were looking in relation to us hadn't been possible.

Now I bit down on a curse. Although that one was standing a few meters away, facing stoically in the direction that the others had gone…the one outside was facing inward, and watching over his companion.

That meant that as soon as we appeared, edging into view, that one had shifted, tracking us with his rifle, and before either of us could do anything, he fired.

I cut the field, creating two more in an eye blink, and triggered my time compression, relieved when it worked perfectly.

The first one was below us, pulling down hard, yanking us out of the tube and out of the line of fire, before flipping, allowing us to kick off the wall and leap into the hall.

Or it would have, had I had the time to explain what I was doing to Scylla. Instead, she was yanked down, then shoved back, shouting in confusion and anger as she hurtled from sight, as I somersaulted over and landed on my hands, dropping and rolling.

The second gravity bubble was centered on the one that was firing on us, in the head, at a dozen gravities.

It crushed the organics to pulp, sending the cybernetics into overdrive as they failed. A barrage of unaimed shots went wild; then it dropped the rifle and sagged. Blood ran from what was left of the head as it slumped in death, the body held upright by the robotic enhancements.

I reduced the gravity bubble at the bottom of the pillar, sending a burst of explanation and information to Scylla. I rolled to my feet and summoned a third bubble, cutting the second, and crushed the nearby hybrid's head too as it turned, bringing its rifle to bear.

This time it collapsed; the angle it was at was just too much as the brain was reduced to strawberry compote.

I spun, looking to the farthest one, now standing at the top of the stairs at the end of the hall, and twisted. My left arm came up and a shield bloomed across it, as incoming fire stitched its way across the ground nearby.

I ducked down, shield rising as I peered around it, cutting the third gravity bubble and powering up one more as fast as I could at the one firing on me.

I missed, the distance too much for such a fast and dirty creation. The gravity I spun up was too weak to do more than slightly shift the lasers that passed through it. I grunted. The impacts hammered into my shield, each one killing nanite clusters and burning closer to me. I dodged left, then right, having to keep my head down behind the shield as I tried to make it to the side and out of sight of the laser fire.

Before I could move more than a half meter, though, a crackling blast ripped through the air and punched the hybrid from its feet, a hole bored through its chest and out, as it clattered onto its back, rifle falling free.

I breathed a sigh of relief, straightening and cutting the time compression, mentally reminding myself once this was over that I needed to spend some of the next load of nanites I had to upgrade that. Then I rocked back, the world spinning as I staggered, an unexpected blow to the side of the head almost sending me to the floor.

I caught myself and stared, as Scylla stalked even closer, fury clear in every movement.

"Never!" she spat. "*Never* do that again!"

I winced, knowing exactly what she was upset about. My mastery of gravity and lack of explanation had left her helpless, catapulted through the air, entirely at my mercy, and for someone as highly strung and had the past that she had?

Yeah.

"I'm sorry." I shook off the blow and stood straight again. "We don't have time for this, though. We need to move."

"Never again!" she repeated, making sure I understood, before setting off running, heading to the nearest corpse of the Ændari troopers.

There were a dozen in easy reach, and as I crouched by the nearest to me, I stabbed the harvest blade into the thick vein at the top of his leg, where the armor was necessarily thinnest to allow for movement.

I ripped as many nanites free as I could, while two tentacles grabbed the grenades that had been attached to the side of his thigh.

As they came free, more tentacles surged out, grabbing the next two bodies and repeating the process. I pulled as many nanites free as I could, before forcing myself to leave the body.

I didn't want to.

This hall alone represented the biggest banquet of nanites, literally millions of the fuckers in every individual body. But every second I wasted here was a second that I wasn't helping protect Ingrid and the others.

That tore at me. Although most of the Ændari in here were fallen, their memories and their nanites reset to a much more basic level than ours, and certainly than Varnock's, they were still *full* of them.

If we gave them the time, they'd be back up and fighting again in a matter of hours, if not less.

Climbing to my feet, I passed Scylla, who was attaching another grenade to her thigh, and she stood as well, starting to run. I triggered my time compression again.

We sprinted to the end of the hall. The hybrid figure that had been outside here was already dead, but the next in line, off to one side, had hidden and was firing as we skidded out of the door.

I caught the blast on my shield, powering a gravity bubble for Scylla, as she dumped a barely formed plan into my mind through the link.

She jumped into it, being hurtled through the air toward the nearest building's roof. A tentacle flashed out and latched onto the stonework, dragging her down as I ran down the stairs. The lasers tore into my shield before I could jump out of sight.

I heard more distant blasts then, and curses from Scylla as she apparently came under more fire.

Then I was out of the line of fire myself, skidding. I threw myself down in the courtyard, snatching a pair of random grenades from a nearby trooper's body, then throwing them up.

I connected to them as I tossed them. My Hack barely had time to register them and create a solid link from the nanites I'd smeared on their surface as I'd palmed them.

Then they were tearing through the air, bubble after bubble catching them and flipping them onto new trajectories.

I sent a burst of information to Scylla, and she replied, confirming her target. The grenades landed near the hybrid closest to us, going off and showing us all that they were goddamn useless smoke grenades.

"Fuck!" I snarled, but I was already up and running again. Scylla had rolled to the side, hidden behind the retaining wall that ran around the roof she was on, and as she popped up, firing on the more distant hybrid, I was sprinting for the smoke.

Arise :Explorer

They might be able to keep me out if I tried to hack the signal in the air, but as I powered a gravity bubble, then leapt through it, firing myself through the air into the smoke, I was betting they'd have more difficulty with a direct connection.

I crashed into the figure as it strode through the smoke. A single shot hit my right foot as we saw each other; a burst of pain seared through the nerves. Then I hit them, the pair of us sent flying from the force.

They were even more foul and disturbing up close. This one had been fat once—the green skin looked to have once been rich and verdant, now sallow and closer to yellow, and the skin drooped in unlovely folds.

Tubes ran from the backpack into the chest and stomach, the head and groin; cabling rippled all over, mainly hidden by armoring. But the thing reeked, and would have been better off long dead.

I stabbed a nanite filament into its head; a second one dug into the box on its back, as the Hack sub-mind went to work. The increased time that I got from my ability was the only reason I had the time to shove myself back, a millisecond before it triggered all four of the grenades strapped to its body.

Chapter Forty-Nine

I was sent flying. My armor absorbed a lot of the explosion, but as close as I was, I hit a nearby wall and bounced off, stunned and bleeding from a dozen wounds.

"Fuck, I need better armor…" I mumbled, dazed, as I tried to focus.

"Steve!"

Ingrid—that was Ingrid, I realized.

"I'm okay…you okay?" I lied, shaking my head and gritting my teeth as my nanites started to push out the few fragments that had made it through my armor.

"The hybrids just split. We'd gotten them down to eighty or so, and twenty just split off, running back toward you. The troopers are trying to get around us by using the pillars, so we've had to seal them. There's two inside trying to find a way out now."

"Keep me updated," I sent. *"And I love you."*

"Me too. Be careful," she whispered into my mind, then the sense of her presence was gone.

"Are you going to help or just stay there!" Scylla called to me, and I snarled, getting back to my feet and starting to run again.

"The troopers were trying to use the pillars, so Ingrid closed them all off," I told her, grunting. A sudden surge of pain came from my shin; the fragment embedded in it popped free with a clatter. I reached out, giving up on running, and formed a bubble around myself, then lengthened it, hurling myself into the air and toward the dock.

"Good," she snapped back. "Now draw their fire."

"I hate my life," I muttered to myself. I spun, diving, as two more opened fire, tracking me as I started forming the GGC, getting ready to return fire.

Scylla fired almost as quickly as they did, though, and I was barely cooked by the time she'd killed all of them in sight. Then it was the ship's turn, as Scylla launched herself into the air, forming her wings and following after me.

The pair of us hurtled through the entrance to the dock, twisting away and up, spreading out before anyone could lock onto us. Then we both dove at the same time, pushing as hard as we could, as the ship, unknowingly, repeated James's tactic, and spun the nearby turrets to lock onto us.

For a heartbeat, I thought I was dead, that there was no way I'd survive this. Then the turrets themselves came under fire—a single recessed turret high overhead pounded into the ship's hull.

The turrets abandoned us, one of them already reduced to slag, as the rest of the ship's defenses came online, targeting the enemy turret.

"Apologies for the lack of notice," Argus said. "That was the only turret I had managed to get operational, and it is no longer so."

I bit down on the irrational urge to scream at the AI, and instead focused on the fact that he'd asked for permission before to begin repairs, and the information he'd dumped into the link told us he'd still been working on it as he'd opened fire.

It'd been literally able to target one of the turrets, and that was it; it couldn't even move to fire on the other.

That had been enough, though. As the ship focused on what it judged was the real threat, we hurtled toward its access ramp, one that had been thoughtfully left down.

As soon as we approached, it started to lift—the crew seeing the risk, presumably—but it was too late.

I fired up three gravity bubbles, randomly targeting the inside of the ship, and flared them all the way to twenty for a full two seconds. One section of the hull actually buckled inward where that was near the outer edge. Then I cut them, gasping with the strain.

We were inside, though, Scylla slipping in barely ahead of the closing door.

I landed hard, skidding and running. I slowed; my sped-up awareness allowed me to track my shield around in time to take the fire from an internal security turret. I lifted my GGC, a dart already loaded as the field spun up, and fired as soon as I could aim it.

I was driven back half a meter as the turret opened fire. Projectiles pounded the shield, before I fired. The gravity-driven rail gun dart punched through the turret's outer covering and exploded inside as its inertia was transformed into explosive energy. The wall around it cratered inward, and I twisted, aiming, making sure there was nothing else.

Scylla ran for the nearest stairs that led to the door, her proton lance at the ready.

The landing bay was large, thirty meters long and ten wide, with two entrances leading in, both of them on an upper level. Stairs led down from a pathway that encircled the bay to the lower floor where we stood.

There were lights going crazy, as well as distant sirens, presumably warning of boarders, and I could already hear running feet and shouts from above us.

I leapt for the railing that ran around the second level. My shield retreated in size, going from a solid mass of metal that a knight of old would have been proud of, to a twelve-inch wide and twenty-long slab, much more easily maneuvered in the confines of a ship's corridors.

As that retreated, two tentacles punched out. One caught the railing; the other smacked into the ceiling. Both bonded in a heartbeat, their outer surface eating into the metal. I used them to pull myself over the railing smoothly, dropping to the ground beyond, and pulled them back in as I took two quick steps to the nearest control panel.

I slapped my right hand over it. Fully attuned nanites poured from me and into the panel, digging into the connections and pouring Tsunami into the ship, directing my Hack sub-mind to guide it.

That done, I broke off my physical connection, and started to run. Scylla was already ahead of me and moving deeper into the ship.

The corridor that lay beyond was short. Ten doors led off it on either side. The rooms beyond were clearly hybrid storage areas, judging from both the smell and the racks of charging machinery, with the final room on either side dedicated to hybrid spare parts, and rotting, broken carcasses that looked to have been in the process of being stripped, respectively.

As I passed each room, I spun up a gravity bubble, flung it in and powered it all the way to ten gravities; then I cut it, the machinery inside already cascading sparks and rendered to scrap.

At the end of the corridor, a T-junction led left and right. As Scylla reached it, so did an Ændari, clad in a mix of armor and regular clothes that suggested he'd not been ready for a fight.

He really wasn't ready for her, that was sure. She plowed into him, smashing him against the back wall and head-butting him. Then she used the proton lance to flip him from his feet.

As he crashed into the floor, she fired, once, point-blank into his head, vaporizing half of it and burning a hole in the decking.

Then she was off again, running in the direction he'd come from. I followed, my right arm pointed behind me, a dart ready and loaded, the view from the barrel projected into my mind.

Nothing came into view, but ahead of me, Scylla came to a ladder leading to the next level. She paused long enough to fling a grenade up, step back, trigger it, then dart out and start climbing.

The screams and the hundred or so clangs that rang out told me it'd been a fragmentary one, and at least someone on the other side hadn't appreciated her sharing her toys.

She was out of view almost before I could reach the ladder; the proton lance flashed as she stabbed it into a writhing body.

I leapt after her, triggering gravity bubbles to pull myself all the way to the floor past the one she'd exited on. As I came into view, I pulled my shield up, taking a dozen hits on it. I spread my legs, landing with a foot on either side of the access hatch I'd just appeared through.

Then I shoved forward with a gravity bubble, tripling and then tripling it again.

The barrage of bullets, all projectile, that had been hammering into me cut off as the wave of force picked up the three figures, hurling them backward into the bulkhead behind them. I grinned inside my helmet, realizing that the fuckers were restricted to low-power weapons aboard the ship, for fear of collateral damage.

We had no such issue, as we needed the ship for scrap more than anything.

I reached out again, forming two bubbles above the three. I yanked them upward into the deck overhead, then reversed it, and hurled them into the floor, before cutting the field, stepping forward and sending two tentacles flashing out.

The tips of the tentacles reformed into blades, stabbing into two of the Ændari's eyes—digging into their brains, then reforming into a blender attachment, and spinning.

It did exactly what I figured it would. The freshly made corpses convulsed, then fell still. I grabbed the last of the three by the fucker's ornate stag-like horns from behind.

I shanked him in the kidney with the harvest blade, before expanding the blade inside him and sending it up to puncture his heart.

He coughed, a wet, tearing sound, and let out a little gasp. I released the Devourer armor, confident that now I was already inside the ship, it was too late for them to be able to do anything when they realized what I was.

The outer layer of my armor flushed blood red and black. The top-most layer shifted like oil, as the two tentacles in the bodies by my feet repositioned, their own surfaces pulsing and extruding burrowing needles that expanded through the bodies.

I gave myself ten seconds, summoning random gravity fields in the ship above, behind and all around on the level I was on, as on the level below me, Scylla continued to wreak havoc.

Then I dropped what was left of the corpses on the floor. The rush of fresh nanites filled me, ten million and more, harvested in as many seconds, half of them being lost as I triggered Emergency Wipe. Then I added all five million or so, freshly attuned, to my armor on instinct, feeling it grow.

The room felt suddenly smaller, as I turned and ran at the closed door ahead, twisting to take it with my left shoulder and making it ring like a bell when I hit it, dents appearing.

I grinned, hauling back and punching it, again and again. My fists pounded against the metal, deforming under the blows. I knew I was being watched.

While I did that, though, most of my attention was elsewhere, reaching out to the hack that was going on. The low-level landing bay systems were all mine now, with others falling to my expanded awareness even as I reached out.

The internal cameras were mine, in there at least, and using the link from them, I was pouring along to more. The first-level systems fell next, then the second.

Doors that were linked to the now-compromised security system suddenly unlocked. The lower levels all released at once, and I continued to play my part, the boogeyman of a thousand Ændari tales, literally beating my way through the sealed doors.

I couldn't help but grin, reaching out, linking into the local communications network and broadcasting throughout the ship as more and more of the security system fell.

"You have released me from my prison!" I roared in their own language. "Now suffer for the actions of your ancestors!"

It probably wouldn't do much, I reflected, but it was certainly going to add to their confusion.

"Steve...the rest of the hybrids just turned tail. They and the troopers are running for the ship," Ingrid sent me.

"You know what to do."

"We've already started," she assured me, sending me an info dump showing the grenades that the enemy were passing, detonating and shredding more and more of them, even as Ingrid and the rest of the team followed the fleeing hybrids and troopers, cutting them down from behind.

The hybrids weren't subject to panic, I knew, so that meant that whoever was controlling them was still alive, and pulling them back to try to defend them.

"Attention, Commander." Argus spoke up suddenly. "Signals are establishing from the stealth vessel to the interdiction ships, attempting to cut off local subspace communications."

"Give me a map of the ship," I ordered, looking up.

I reached out, focusing above me as Argus supplied the map, my own position helpfully marked.

"Current vessel layout is estimated to be seventy-three percent accurate," he warned me.

I grunted, picking a dozen areas and blindly creating gravity bubbles in them all. I powered them all up, then reversed them, tripled them, then flipped again, dragging them randomly to the left and right before releasing them.

"Argus, can you access the nanites that are in the Ændari?" I asked suddenly, cursing myself for not considering this before.

"Confirmed," he said. "Beware, I cannot take direct action against my masters and creators. My limit was firing on the turrets of their ship, and still cost me a significant reduction in processing power."

"Can you add them to the map?" I asked hopefully.

"Negative. This would assist you in their elimination. The steps that I have taken so far are pushing the limits imposed on my capacity, and have been permitted only because they fall in line with the prime directive of protecting the Ændari as a species."

"Fucker." I snarled. "Can you send them an order to leave the ship, use the escape pods or whatever, and tell them to flee?"

"Confirmed."

"Do it." I grinned to myself as I gained control of the locks on the level I was on, unlocking the door I'd nearly battered my way through. I started down the corridor beyond. The map showed me three possible, probable, locations for the hybrid control system.

I sent one of them to Scylla, who'd nearly finished clearing the level below, and cursed, backtracking and running to a hatch to a lower level.

Then I reached out, aiming at one of the ones above me.

"Warning. Possible reactor location," Argus said quickly, as my gravity bubble started to form, and I cut it frantically. "Energy spike returning to acceptable levels."

I cursed, reaching the end of the corridor, looking up, ready to launch myself to the next level, and saw a flash of movement.

Arise :Explorer

I jumped, using gravity to guide me; tentacles punched out, aiming to grab the walls and brace myself…

Everything vanished in fire and concussion.

Pain!

Tremendous pain ripped through me as I shuddered back to my senses—barely able to focus, there was that much of it. I felt as much as saw the numerous flashing warnings that my systems were screaming at me.

My armor was badly damaged, my left arm ended at the wrist, two tentacles were truncated, and I was missing…well, the right side of my lower chest, basically.

There was a hole the size of a basketball torn through me.

Air was whipping out of multiple holes in the hull. Blood left me in gleaming trails, following the air, and it was all I could do to focus, trying to make sense of what had just happened.

I could hear shouting, and a distant, calm part of me told me that had to be the comm link, or the command link, as sound didn't travel in space well, and the area I was currently in was definitely in vacuum now, as the surrounding bulkheads slammed down, sealing off this section of the ship from the interior.

That was when they moved.

There were three of them, more slender than myself, but big still, powerful, and heavily armored. They bore shields—long, narrow triangular things—and spears…

No, not spears: *proton lances.*

I'd just found three members of the Helio Guard. And as I tried to focus, to think, to react, all three levelled their lances at me.

They fired as one, aiming for the joints of my right arm and both legs. Blasts bored into me inexorably as they held their fire. The armor I wore partially deflected them, but not enough.

I screamed. Acting on instinct, I shoved out. A wave of gravity staggered them all as my mind struggled to make sense of what had happened. The time compression was all that was keeping me alive as they floundered slowly, the blasts moving off their targets.

The movement I'd seen before, I realized. It'd been them, probably moving back as they placed mines or explosives, before retreating behind their shields, the whole "don't let the ship get damaged" plan clearly out the window now.

One day, I was going to learn to not fucking show what I was, I silently berated myself. My nanites flowed, covering the damaged areas with fresh armor, as I rearranged the newly acquired ones.

But not today.

I hit them again with a gravity wave, then fired up another, forcing it to twenty gravities in a heartbeat. Grunting under the pressure, I formed it an inch behind the armored front of the middle one's helmet.

He didn't even get off a scream as his skull was crushed inward. But whatever the metal his helmet was made of, it didn't so much as buckle. As he fell, his two friends lunged forward.

One went high. The head of the proton lance crackled as it flashed toward my face, and I twisted. The edge of the blade sent a flare of sparks into the air as I stabbed forward with my left arm. The vorpal blade slid free, extending over the blackened stump of my missing hand, and slammed into his chest.

It didn't cut!

He was shoved back, shallow scratches left across his breastplate, but that was it! The rebound from the force of my blow sent me staggering as well, my own armor all that was helping me to stay upright. It reformed in damaged places, pouring like liquid then flash forming into fresh plates.

The lower lance, though…that had hit, and it sank into my right thigh, the blade carving through the reforming armor. A crackling explosion of lightning erupted into my leg and hurled me backward.

I hit the wall, then fell, crashing into the edge of the hatch to the lower floor—it was still open, *of course*—letting me fall through. I tumbled down a level, impacting on the floor below with a silent crash.

I lay there for a stunned second. Half my mind screamed in incoherent fury, as the other half was overcome with the pain. Trails of blood and seared smoke rose from me, only to be whipped out of the gaps in the hull overhead.

All around me, the corridors that ended here were sealed. Their interior bulkheads stood silent and solid, as I tried to focus.

The first of them stepped into sight again, levelling their proton lance.

I moved on instinct, my body barely able to respond but my nanites worked fine—better than fine, in fact. They bunched under me, shoving me up and sideways as the crackling bar of proteinic plasma burned through the floor where my head had been a second earlier.

Tentacles flashed out, grabbing the wall and dragging me to the side, out of sight of the hatch. That would make them come to me, rather than the other way around. I frantically tried to get a handle on the situation, spinning up a gravity field directly above the hatch, in reverse, to give me some time.

A crash I felt through the decking made it clear that at least one of them had just tried to jump down, only to be catapulted into the ceiling overhead instead.

I coughed, tasting more blood. My system flared and shared a split-second visual of my body. Half of it flashed in oranges and yellows, a handful of greens—thank God the family jewels were fine—and a few reds.

Then I felt it, the emergency backup, a minor detail that I'd forgotten all about, part of the Punisher armor upgrade. A pair of small, emergency, dual-purpose nanite storage systems activated. One had unleashed its store of fifty thousand into my bloodstream, working to strip out the dangerous levels of chemicals and hormones that my mammalian brain was dumping into me, trying to keep me conscious.

The other fifty thousand worked to stabilize me, forcing me back toward full mental capacity again. That, more than anything, helped me stay in the world.

The rebuilds I'd had to do recently to make the power core in my chest larger, and the upgrades to my lungs and organs, meant that I wasn't as badly hurt as I thought.

Hell, my bones were all intact.

Arise :Explorer

I had a significant chunk of the right side of my few remaining organs missing, and a hole in my lower chest, but that was below the augmented rib cage, and to the side of the power core. It was down to the seventy-five to eighty-degree angle of one of the explosives that I'd taken any real internal damage.

Something had blasted upward, passing under my rib cage and into the soft materials in there.

That wasn't good, admittedly, but considering the rebuilds and tweaks…well, losing a lung, to me, was more of an annoyance these days.

That meant that with my systems locking everything else down, I could see that although I was injured, and badly—more than enough to have killed a regular human twice over—I wasn't a regular human, and I was already moving from "orange" as an overall state of health into "yellow."

"Green" was less than an hour away, at the current rebuild, and a fraction of that if I invested more nanites into it than I was.

The changes that had been unlocked when Argus had literally unlocked and rebooted me, resetting the rest of my systems…

I hesitated, then spun up three more gravity bubbles, forcing them back from the edge overhead. A tentacle slid out and used its radar-like capacity to get a better view, as I quickly worked.

The power core was intact, and it was humming happily, providing a fuckload of power. I'd gotten so used to fighting without it, and having limited access to my systems, that I'd just never fully integrated it until now.

"Time to change that then," I whispered, focusing as I increased the power that I was feeding to the gravity generator.

It ramped up slowly. The power built steadily, forcing the enemy back from the edge. I felt a tickle at the edge of my awareness that I recognized as Ingrid.

She knew that I was injured, that I was working on repairing myself and that I was simultaneously working to ramp up my power and nanite systems.

I could feel that she knew all of this, and that she also knew I needed to know what she had to say.

"Ingrid?" I prompted.

"The hybrids are on their way, and the troopers are ahead of them. They've all abandoned the node and are running to you. We can trap them in the courtyard and lower hall, but if we do that…the ship will probably leave them and try to save themselves."

"Not if I trash it some more," I said. *"Thank you. Let them through for the ship. Then seal the doors behind them, just in case. Scylla and I will finish this."*

"Be careful." Then she was gone, and I reached out.

I'd gained more control over the local areas of the ship, including partial control of the floor overhead. I accessed it now, triggering the internal bulkheads in the corridor overhead, and directly behind the Helio Guard.

They opened, and I sensed the guard moving back. One of them reached out to grab the body of their companion, and I shifted the gravity bubbles, forcing them away from the corpse and back.

They moved, clearly thinking one of their allies in the ship had opened the bulkhead, even as I sent commands through the rest of the ship that we had access to, carefully avoiding the bit that I could feel Scylla moving through. Beyond that, I opened every single door that I could to space, and locked the bulkhead doors to prevent them sealing the sections.

The complaints of the Helio Guard were even better, the shouts of frustration and confusion louder, as I closed the bulkheads on either side of them, trapping them in the corridor above and severing their link with the ship's network.

I cut the power to my gravity bubbles as well. Tentacles held me in place, my body hanging in the air, as if trapped in a spider's web, as the tentacle I'd been using to watch the pair elongated again, reaching up and around.

It clamped onto the head of the dead Helio Guard, dragging it to the hatch and down. It landed with a clank that was more felt than heard in the airless section of the ship.

Then it reformed, spearing up under the bottom of his helmet, punching into the brain and flexing, splitting.

The Devourer coating slid around and around, a small mass kept in the brain, tearing the "meat" apart and absorbing it. More and more slid down his throat, expanding and hollowing him out.

He was a hell of a meal. Experienced and strong in life, he'd amassed a lot of nanites—thirty-seven million and change in total. As my nanites absorbed and ripped his free, I dove into the ship's systems again, sensing the ramping up of power as the ship tried to take off; the commander had clearly made the decision that it was better to live another day than stay here.

I disagreed. The reactor I'd nearly blown up before with a misplaced gravity bubble was now inside of my area of control, and I initiated an emergency scram, shutting it down and releasing the stored energy as harmlessly as possible.

That made me aware of two other reactors in the ship, one lower, and already inside my area, and it began the shutdown process as soon as I saw it.

The other was at the far end of the ship, out of my reach, but also not powerful enough to run the entire vessel. It was an emergency measure, presumably intended to give a power boost should something need it.

I dismissed it as unimportant. Then I looked at the mass of notifications I'd been receiving since the fight had started.

WAR POINT GAINED!

A Biological Weapon Variant under your command has defeated a unit of equal size and strength, gaining you a War Point to assign as needed, Biological Weapon Variant #Steve.

Biological Weapon Variant #Steve, please assign your War Point now:

- **Command and Control**
- **Infiltration**
- **Assault**

That…that was weird. I'd not gained one of them in forever, and to get one for deploying the failed BWVs… I skipped to the next.

WAR POINT GAINED!

A Biological Weapon Variant under your command has defeated a unit of equal size and strength, gaining you a War Point to assign as needed, Biological Weapon Variant #Steve.

Biological Weapon Variant #Steve, please assign your War Point now:

- **Command and Control**
- **Infiltration**
- **Assault**

I blinked, closing it again, moving on.

Congratulations, Biological Weapon Variant #Steve.

You have survived combat with another BWV Identified as #7745685582113.

As your Combat System is now fully active, and paired with an active Nanite Recovery Tool and Biological Enhancement Package, you may choose from the following options:

1. **Harvest 0.1 Point of Strength**
2. **Harvest 0.1 Point of Endurance**
3. **Gain 1 Point of Specialization**

It took me a couple of seconds, as I both read and reread the notification, before it clicked. I was still directing my nanites to blend and chug the remains of the Helio Guard and rebuild my body, but when I realized what this meant, I smiled.

"Argus, did you do this?" I asked the AI through the comm.

"Please specify your inquiry."

"Uh…did you reset my notifications?"

"Confirmed."

"And my system, am I getting these points all over again from scratch?"

"Confirmed. As you pass the prebuilt system thresholds, your quest system will unlock additional benefits."

"Ah, I… Wait, I've got access to the shit I already unlocked, right?" I quickly checked my internal access and found that I still had access to everything I'd gained over the last few years. "I do…" I muttered.

"Confirmed."

"Can you do this for everyone?"

"Negative."

"Why not?"

"In order to retain access to previously unlocked upgrades while resetting and rebooting BWV, BSV, and BCV systems, a paired and functional AI must provide system integration. Your systems have sufficient capacity to provide such housing as I require. Those of your companions do not."

"My upgrades," I whispered, remembering all the memory upgrades, the additional systems, everything that I'd unlocked so far, that I'd thought again and again I'd fucked up by misallocating my points.

Some of those were responsible for me being able to reboot and retain everything, and now I could start all over again from scratch.

The earliest levels were always the easiest to get, with the points feeling like they were raining down and easy to gain. They got thrown into places, so that you could try shit that you'd not do normally. But now?

"How many of these are level-ups?" I asked Argus.

"Define—"

"Fuck's sake, quest gains or points being awarded," I snapped. "How many of the notifications are those?"

"The maximum judged safe for evolving at this current time is ten. At that point, the system has enforced an allocation lockdown. Upon allocation of points and stabilization of nanite interface systems, additional quests will unlock."

"Okay, just wipe the notifications and give me the points," I said. "Any that are reward choices, I'll take a General specialization point if that's the option instead of a system upgrade."

"Confirmed. Allocating now."

That was it, that was all it took, and I suddenly had five General specialization points, three War, a point for Hack, and a single perk.

The perk was where my eyes went instantly, but I dismissed that for now. They were insanely powerful if they were used right, so I might have to hold off on that for now, until I could look into it properly later. But for now, the points were getting goddamn spent!

I pulled up the Harvest tree first, knowing exactly where I was going as I tore through to System Replenishment, then to the Devourer tree I'd unlocked in there. The three options I'd unlocked before were there for me, and I read through them quickly, an eye to the level above. I moved as quickly as I dared, knowing I needed to finish stabilizing my injuries at the very least, before I could do more.

The ship was shuddering now, a veritable war being waged in the digital realm as the survivors tried to purge the sections I'd taken control of, and my Tsunami continued its inexorable advance.

Arise :Explorer

I didn't have long, so it was time to make the most of the upgrades I could use, and then finish this fight.

Hunger was the first I came to. It gave an impression of boosting that desire, which almost made me avoid it, as I remembered the first time I'd almost been lost to the Devourer armor's hunger, until I remembered that it was also all about control.

You could be hungry as fuck, and yet have the self-control to diet, or to wait until you had time to eat, rather than running into the nearest shop and stuffing your face on chocolate.

Hunger was all about *understanding* the need, allowing it to drive you to new heights when you were ready to give in to it. But also it was all about the *essence* of control. Making sure that it was you who controlled the hunger, not the other way around.

I took it this time, a single point confirmed. I took a deep breath as the armor rippled, seeming to shift to pay more attention to the world around me.

Most of the section of the ship I was in had nothing of interest, not to this kind of hunger, of need, but the corpse of the Helio Guard that I was currently tearing up?

That…that was suddenly *much* more interesting.

I tore myself away from that, though, hoping that I'd not made a mistake in unlocking this, only to find that deciding to ignore it was actually easier.

It was less of a need, if I looked away. I knew it was there, and that I could give in to it and rampage if I wanted to. But it wasn't as close to overwhelming my control as I'd feared.

With that confirmed, I breathed a sigh of relief and turned to the next option in line.

Phago. The name was weird. Jonas had explained it last time as the actual mechanical action of eating, and as I stared at the details, that was confirmed for me.

It was the activity, and the gain that this was focused on. I could speed it up, becoming more efficient at it, but sacrificing the likelihood of gaining points and information, and in turn recovering from injuries faster, as well as getting the nanites and other materials into me as fast as possible. Or I could go slower.

Slowing down would enable me to get more and more from the "meal" and increase my chances of success overall in gaining memories, usable improvements, and things like that. I sensed that even now I was barely scratching the surface of what I would be capable of one day as a Devourer.

I also got the feeling that if I invested in that field heavily, I'd be able to unlock specific bonuses later. Like the ability to target certain points, guiding my own evolution.

That was fucking tempting.

I took a single point in that as well; the changes unlocked as the oil-like coating seemed to ripple again, becoming more aware.

Last of the three options was Growth. Although I could already sense additional options unlocking for me now that I'd taken the other two, I ignored them in favor of what I knew I needed versus what I'd want, with the possible option of shiny new skills.

It was time to actually double down and really work at my skills, after all.

The remaining three points I put into Growth, taking that to four. A sudden hunger spike flooded me.

I didn't have enough!

To fuel the Growth I'd unlocked, to form the short cloak I'd already gained into the fourth level version of itself, I'd need more nanites, nearly a hundred million of them, I guessed. I glanced down at the Helio Guard on the floor by my side.

It shook and quivered as my tentacle roamed around inside it. The changes I'd unlocked already made the shredding and absorbing of the corpse that much more efficient.

If it was a normal creature, a werewolf, for example—and how fucked up was my life that I thought a werewolf was *normal*—it'd have been absorbed in seconds now that I'd upgraded myself this far.

The Ændari, though, were almost entirely made of nanites, and the Helio Guard were packed denser than most. Varnock had over a hundred million, but most of hers had been deactivated, still rebooting from her long sleep.

Likewise, as I now faced the Helio Guard, they were incredibly dense with nanites, but they were also…they were blank, basically. Most were active, sort of, but they were low-level mode, healing them, giving them greater than normal strength and speed, health…all that good shit, but no access to the upgrade systems.

Well.

I was hungry, I decided, releasing the walls and dropping to the floor. Pain flared in the few injuries that I still had, before that, too, faded.

It was time to finish this.

Chapter Fifty

"*What's happening?*" I asked Scylla, who sent me a mental image of her current view: a running pair of feet that were desperately trying to get away.

She launched herself up through a hatch, spreading her legs and catching herself on either side, then dove to the side, rolling and coming to her feet as a proton lance flashed past overhead.

She stabbed out, both with her own lance, shoving the enemy's one farther aside, and with a spear of nanites, formed much as I did my tentacles.

In her case, the spear plunged into her enemy's armpit, piercing the thinner armor there and expanding on the inside. The Helio Guard let loose a brief gasp, then collapsed; the spear branched inside their body. I distantly sensed her spinning it in there, essentially shredding their internal organs, then yanking it back, looking from side to side, making sure the rest of the corridor was clear.

She stood in a single smooth motion. Her lance flipped around and pointed at the floor as she started forward again, tracking bloody footprints down the hall.

"*I'm busy,*" she sent to me. "*Are you not?*"

"*No, I was having a lovely nap,*" I replied. "*Of course I am. I was checking where you were and if you were okay.*"

"*Concern yourself with those who need your help, not with me,*" she replied.

I disconnected. She wasn't being an asshole deliberately; she was just used to being on her own, or in command.

Then I remembered that she was actually used to being a part of the team now, and never gave Ingrid this shit. In fact, she seemed to be enjoying her time with some of the team, Jonas especially.

I also remembered that any second she was likely to find that the sealed areas of the ship limited her again, and she'd actually have to come to me, needing help, so fuck her very much.

I discarded the remains of the Helio Guard, picking up the proton lance and flicking the activation section. It was simple enough to move from high-power cattle prod, to spear, to short blast, and then high-power blast, before pouring my nanites over the activators, and shifting my grip to where it felt more natural.

They'd control the settings for me at will, making it much easier. I reached up with my nanites; tentacles gripped the edge of the hatch above and lifted me through effortlessly.

I assigned the Hack point into Tsunami, upgrading that. I shivered as the skills that it linked to were upgraded in tiny ways as well, from the Hack skill itself, the ongoing digital onslaught that was rippling through the very ship I was aboard, and the nanite Tsunami Hijack surprise ability as well.

Fuck, I hated that I didn't have a real name for that skill yet.

I also didn't have time to screw with it right now.

The remaining three points in War that I had left? Well, I wasn't wasting them, but I needed a verifiable boost to my abilities right now, and couldn't screw around either.

I did it quick. The thing that had helped me to survive that ambush had been access to the advanced classes, namely the Punisher and Assault Trooper.

The Ændari had designed this system, and the assault troopers I'd faced outside were basic bitches compared to all of us. But they also had limited access to their true abilities, if at all.

I spent two points in Assault Trooper, feeling the unlocking of new information that guided me in both armor upgrades, and more importantly, in vacuum combat.

The single point I had left now, I'd intended on putting it into Punisher, both because it'd improve my ability to adjust my Hijack skill and because it'd enable me to double down on potentially lifesaving abilities like the emergency nanite storage.

Feeling the unlocks I was getting to vacuum combat, I changed my mind and added the point into there instead.

I braced myself, focusing as the main download went active. A sudden spike of icy-cold pain in my brain let me know it was peaking; then the relief as it died away barely lasted long enough to register. But what *had* registered was the awareness of vectors and inertia.

They might not be obviously needed, not compared to being able to turn fucking invisible, or to specialize my armor design and capabilities more, or even to focus on my weapons as I could have.

But with my gravity manipulation came the knowledge that these specialist troopers had been some of the most elite in space-born warfare. Now, things that they could do only in zero-g, I could perform almost anywhere.

The shit I was learning—the vectors, the inertial compensation, the innate understanding of gravity and the ease of flipping my mind to feel that up was down or whatever I needed it to be?

That was invaluable.

I reached out, grinning. I couldn't play with the perk yet, but I didn't really need to.

The bulkhead behind the two Helio Guards started to open, and the pair I saw, as I gained access to the cameras, immediately ran for their way back into the ship.

I triggered two new gravity fields, one each centered on the deck over their heads.

They took a step, then crashed from what had, to their suddenly addled minds, changed from the ceiling to the floor.

I flipped it again, pinning another two gravity bubbles to either side of the corridor, then one to the floor as I knew it.

Then I switched their universe to "tumble dry," and waited a few seconds before opening the bulkhead that I stood behind.

The decompression alarms and the screaming atmosphere that tore past them didn't help their situation.

I barely had to fight them.

The pair tumbled out of control, crashing into each other, bouncing off the walls, the floor, the deck overhead; then it'd reverse, flare, diminish…

They couldn't figure out up from down, let alone which way they were facing.

When I cut the fields all at once, they crashed down, barely conscious and utterly helpless. I didn't waste the opportunity—two tentacles flashed out. They latched onto the underside of their helmets, extruding a dagger of nanites that pierced their skulls, then poured from there down their throats into their chest cavities and started to feed.

Then I lifted into the air and flew down the corridor, both bodies trailing along behind me, as the bulkhead sealed itself again.

"Doors…" Scylla sent to me, and I waited. *"There are doors here that do not respond. This is your doing, yes?"*

"Yes."

"Open them."

"You forgot the magic word."

"I will tear our enemies apart and then come to you when you sleep," she promised, and for a heartbeat, I wondered whether I'd gotten the wrong end of things with her. *"Then I shall geld you and place those that you treasure most into your throat to ensure you choke on them. Open the fucking door…now!"*

That was a relief—Scylla was still her usual wonderful, kind, and compassionate self.

"I meant say 'please,'" I pointed out. *"But threats like that work as well. Go have fun."* I triggered the door for her, setting the doors to open for her now regardless of the state of the atmosphere beyond.

The rest of the corridor I was passing along was abandoned. The doors that were scattered here and there led into barracks for the Ændari. The size and layout made it clear these fuckers didn't share, and the regularly placed and well-stocked armories made me smile as I mentally added them to our toys for later.

The next hatch to the upper levels slid open as I approached. The three people I detected on the next level were already fleeing, and the grenades that they'd set around the hatch blinked, ready.

I reached out, hacking them in under two seconds, before I even reached the hatch, and shifted them to my control.

Then, dropping the Ændari Helio Guard's bodies, I floated up through the hatch.

I'd gained more than sixty million nanites from the pair. My armor flexed and flowed as they were shifted to the surface. There was no bloody way I could currently accommodate them internally.

That was a bit of a concern, that I'd have to wear my armor permanently or something moving forward, but I'd find a better solution, I told myself.

In the meantime, the second and third Helio corpses had brought me almost to the limit I needed; my armor and abilities processed the mass of nanites as quickly as it could.

It'd brought me over it, in fact—or it would, once they were attuned. A quick glance showed me the "meals" I'd had already and these two additional guards had brought me to over a hundred million.

They weren't all attuned yet, though, and as much as I desperately wanted to, I couldn't sacrifice half of them just to help myself.

I shifted the nanites around, as I gestured with one hand. One of the grenades came loose and flashed along the corridor after the fleeing trio.

It flipped end over end, hurtling as they ran, then passed the rearmost member, then the next. The magnetic clamp latched onto the back of the leader.

I gave them two seconds to realize what had happened, before I detonated it.

It turned out to be a napalm gas variant, and it enveloped the three, setting fire to them and hurling them from their feet into the walls and floor.

Their screams were both instinctive and the worst thing they could have done, sucking down the blazing mixture into their lungs as they did so, burning themselves from the inside out.

"Got them!" Scylla said into the command link, and I frowned, before the attached vision made it all clear.

She stood on the other side of a wall, two floors away, facing the hybrid controller. A heavily cyberneticized senagra, its limbs were cut free, its head entirely locked into a control collar, and cables dangled from the ceiling, driven into its body.

It hung there, apparently totally unaware of the world around it, as Scylla pulled her proton lance free of an Ændari before her.

They'd been sitting at a computer terminal, apparently controlling the hybrids through the senagra, and when she'd found them, the Ændari had tried to fight her one-on-one, showing just how fucking stupid some people could be.

"Excellent work!" Ingrid said. *"The hybrids just all collapsed. Their vital signs are failing. How many are left alive beyond us on the station now, Argus?"*

"Counting the inhabitants of the stealth vessel, there are currently eleven additional life signs beyond your own party."

"Steve, Scylla?" Ingrid said. *"Eleven more and we've won."*

"This battle," Jonas added tiredly, before starting to apologize.

"It's okay," she replied, and I could hear it in her voice. *"I'm exhausted, personally, but we've come this far—we can do it."*

"We can," I agreed, before grinning as Argus spoke again.

"Correction. Eight life signs."

I flew down the corridor, tentacles flashing out, stabbing into the still burning corpses, picking them up and starting to strip them of everything I needed. The attuned nanites I'd taken so far, thirty-two million of the near one hundred, already shifted into the second level of the Devourer armor, and climbed toward the third.

I felt the changes as I popped the hatch to the next level, aware that it was the final one. According to the cameras that were even now coming online, the remaining eight were split between this level and the one above Scylla.

"Here," I sent to her, showing the five remaining on that level, knowing that she'd take care of them. The last three were on the bridge, and I was approaching that rapidly. A schematic popped up from an idle thought, showing me that I'd gained enough access to the ship that the majority was now falling under my control.

The three life signs I sensed on the bridge…they were in the escape pods.

I reached out, feeling the systems that were battling for control, my own and the ship's, and then I hurtled across the distance as fast as I could.

The fuckers were running, and the reason I'd not encountered a ship's RI or anything yet? They'd been using it to screen the areas they most wanted to control!

I picked up speed, triggering the doors everywhere I could, forcing them to open to space, ripping the atmosphere from half the remaining areas of the ship and tearing billions of individual items out into the void…

But I was too late.

My plan to get the Ændari crew to board the escape pods had been to cut down on the fuckers I had to fight, thinking the cowards would run, but the captains would stay, that the leadership wouldn't leave their ship.

I was wrong, I realized, as the warnings reached me.

The ship shuddered as the remaining three left. A side section of the hull exploded outward, as the distant reactor, the one that I'd sensed but had figured was unimportant, passed the safety margins, setting off alarms across the ship.

My exploring Tsunami code hit a sudden roadblock. Entire systems registered as dead as I found a virtual moat created around the reactor systems by the ship's RI.

Twisting, I hit the wall and bounced off, throwing myself up to the top level. Flashing warning lights sent panicked strobes across the "executive deck." I stared frantically, feeling the ship shivering as emergency battery banks flipped from storing energy to purging themselves into the secondary reactor I'd ordered shut down.

The sudden influx of power overwhelmed the cutouts. The core blazed to life as I desperately tried to shut it down.

"SCYLLA, GET OUT!" I roared to her, the single-minded woman having ignored everything in her pursuit of a handful of crew running through the bowels of the ship, presumably having no clue the ship was about to go nuclear.

We had one chance, one fucking chance to not have the blast from this going up, sterilize the open sections of the node, and more importantly, killing Ingrid and the others.

"What?" Scylla sent back to me, confused.

"RUN!" I sent again, including everything in a desperate data dump to the command link. I reached the bridge, seeing the massive damage I'd inflicted on it, with my flaring gravity bubbles earlier.

Bodies were strewn everywhere, and I'd dimly noted others here and there as I reached this point, dismissed as unimportant in my rush.

Now, I stood on the bridge, staring at the node. No matter what I did, I couldn't get the ship far enough away to protect them entirely, but what *could* I do?

What the hell, I had to think of something.

The bridge was wrecked: consoles exploded in showers of sparks and fizzed, screens hung, shattered, and…and here and there were stations that had escaped my destruction, only to have been shot point-blank with heavy weapons and lasers, melting them to slag!

They'd done this deliberately. They'd totaled what was left of the bridge, to make sure I couldn't use anything here to override them.

My mind darted from detail to detail. The Engineering sub-mind helpfully brought up reactor energy ranges, estimated propagation of explosions, sterilization avoidance protocols…

I needed to do something, to fix this somehow, but the Ændari had made damn sure that there was no reasonable way I could do anything.

Nothing that they could imagine would fix this now, nothing would save me or the others…

But then, I wasn't like them.

I was a Devourer, and I had to embrace that.

Tentacles flashed out in all directions, punching into the bodies that lay around me—stabbing deep, feeding, transferring their nanites in their tens of thousands, then millions.

They poured in, fifteen bodies; more tentacles formed by the second as my Devourer grew, flashing out, stabbing in, and tearing free more and more.

Then I started processing a hundred and thirteen million nanites; the Emergency Wipe activated, and a great cascade of shattered nanites shuddered free of me.

Fifty-seven million, seven hundred and fourteen nanites were attuned in an instant, then converted to the Devourer armor. My body went into shock as something deep inside me changed, as I passed a threshold.

I was operating entirely on instinct now—not knowing how, or what…only that I had to, and this was the only way.

I dimly recognized the changes, as well as the shouts from the others…the pain, the love, the pride, the fear.

I reached out to them, even as the Devourer exploded out from me, covering the bridge in the oily red and black, before everything started to collapse, being torn into their constituent atoms.

There were three possible outcomes to a reactor overload.

First, there was an explosion of devastating power. The ship would be shredded apart, the mass that we needed so badly vaporized and what was left would be driven into the node.

The node would survive it—the material it was made of was almost indestructible—but the sheer mass and the ruins of the ship would most likely block the others from being able to escape, and they would all be trapped inside.

Held captive, until the Ændari came for them.

Arise :Explorer

That was the *best* outcome.

The second was that the explosion would be more energetic, converting to an ultrahard radiation burst that would tear free. The node, again, was hardened against such things, and would survive. But if the others weren't deep enough inside, they would be irradiated, and any nanites would most likely shut down.

That would lead to either a fast death if they were closer to the blast, or a slow, painful death for them all, by a combination of radiation and starvation, if they lived long enough.

Anyone on a planetary surface who was exposed to the outburst would suffer the same.

The third was the reason that so many fleet engagements took place in out of the way systems, as far as possible from living worlds.

Reactors were designed to not permit this to happen, but the Ændari were never going to permit a little thing like a galactic war crime to get in the way of their revenge.

If the power built high enough, and the grav drive was powered in just the right—or wrong—way, a sterilization blast would ripple out, eliminating all life in the system, before the gravity pulse collapsed.

That collapse would end with a tear in the gravitational matrix. And should it be fed enough energetic matter before space could reform? A new black hole would form.

I felt the changes that the power core in my chest was going through, shifting from supplying power to small personal systems, to powering up to provide an order of magnitude more. It wasn't going to be enough, not nearly enough.

The Devourer side of me was rising now. The walls, floors, armor, the screens—everything around me was failing, being absorbed as I fed on it. Metals, plastics, organics, minerals—everything was breaking down, collapsing as I converted it. The true, hidden abilities of the Devourer became clear as I pushed harder.

It wasn't that we could feed on them, or fight them that terrified the Ændari so much. It wasn't that the Devourers were evil or good or anything that I imagined that they feared.

It was that we were…everything.

We were living, sentient converters.

My nanites were bonding with me at a level I'd never imagined possible, creations shifting around me by my will alone. The reactors were screaming now, their power building at a horrific level. I tore more of the bulkheads around me apart, finding the emergency batteries that were intended to power the bridge if all else failed.

Strings of my form flashed out, attaching to them. Tentacles ripped them free, connecting them to me, and feeding power directly from me to them from the atomic level conversion of so much matter all around me.

More of the bridge collapsed, as a spike of nanites erupted from me, punching into a power conduit nearby.

The floor crumpled, the walls tearing inward as I consumed them all. My Tsunami ability, still deep in the machine, was rerouting the power as I willed it: closing down connections, providing only limited paths it could flow along.

Doors between Scylla and the dock flashed open. Lights flared to show her the way as she sprinted, before being picked up by gravitational bubbles as I saw her through the lens of the ship. A fragment of my mind picked her up and literally threw her from the ship, as the rest focused on everything around me.

Pathways accepted the power, then did what they did, converting my signal, and the power…to thrust.

The landing engines across the front and bottom of the ship flared to life. The deck lifted as if it'd been sucker punched by a behemoth from below.

The stealth ship was huge. Only the front quarter had ever been in contact with the dock; the rest extended out into space. And as the engines fired, the nose lifted.

Secondary docking engines around the nose fired then, forcing it backward. The wash of force from the front of the ship was enough to make sure that no dockmaster would ever permit it to land again, had it not been an utter emergency. The ship rotated, and the reactors slowly fell below the level of the dock.

I pushed, feeling the energy building in me. The ship was only able to take so much, the mass all around me being converted directly into energy…

It was too much: too much for the ship's damaged control runs, too much for the engines, and far, far too much for a mere mortal frame to channel.

Even one that had evolved as much as mine had.

I had a choice, I knew. I felt it.

I could flee now. I'd probably done enough to limit the damage, but it might not be enough, and to do what I had to do, I'd be leaving what was left of my humanity behind.

I had to, to become a true Devourer.

All my hangups, my fears about losing myself, about augmenting my brain, my body, the changes I'd wrought to my arms, to my hands, my bones…

They were all baby steps.

There was only one way that I could channel the energy that I needed to, to make sure that the coming explosion was contained, that the energy released didn't harm her, or the rest of them.

I opened my eyes, the world around me full of red and black. The starlight from overhead shone on me directly now, the bulkheads between me and the empty void, torn free.

"I accept," I whispered. "I will pay the price."

Be welcomed to the fold, Devourer. The universe glories in your rise.

Let the wicked tremble, and the good rejoice; let the void reign free.

Arise, Conqueror.

<u>Epilogue</u>

Ingrid stared at the screen Argus projected for them on one wall of the hall. The doors had closed and Scylla was still outside, being directed to the nearest, safest place to her, the AI had assured them.

That was good, of course; Ingrid knew that. Scylla was her friend. The others—they were all her friends, too—but they could all feel what was happening to Steve as well.

He was connected through her command link still, and the changes they were feeling…

She couldn't explain it, nor why tears tracked down her cheeks in rivers that felt like they'd never end.

"I love you," she whispered, intended for him alone, but the others joined her.

It wasn't just words; for many of the group, they wouldn't, or couldn't make the words come, not in the way they were feeling—not the mix of horror, awe, and the sheer relief that there was a chance, however small for them all, and the system at large.

The Ændari escape vessels were burning hard for the Lagrange point, but they'd miscalculated, and would be caught in it as well, Argus had assured her. But Ingrid couldn't bring herself to care beyond a savage *"serves them right."*

The ship was arching backward now. The entire front of the vessel collapsed inward, a gleaming red and black hollow core digging deeper into it. The last of the forward engines crumpled and were dragged into him, as Steve did something that no mortal should be capable of.

"Warning, localized gravitational warp detected. Field is fluctuating…stabilizing, fluctuating…expanding…" Argus said. Artificial green lines appeared on the image, showing a twisting funnel shape, one that was focused directly behind the ship, dragging it backward as the reactors dumped their energy into the grav drive.

"Field expanding, stabilizing," Argus confirmed. "The Devourer has formed a stable link. Funneling power into warp…warp complete."

That was it.

In a split second, half a heartbeat, her world was torn asunder.

Steve was gone, and she didn't know where.

He could be anywhere in the galaxy. Grav drives weren't supposed to even be able to form a warp this far from the Lagrange point, and yet he'd done it.

A response had come through as the ship fell from sight, ripped from her universe and tearing her heart apart.

"I love you too…"

Jez Cajiao

THE END OF ARISE 5

<u>Reviews</u>

Hey!
Okay, well, that's Arise 5 finished, already it seems like forever ago that I was writing this one (I'm finishing up book 6 currently and diverted to write this). I hope you enjoyed the book, its been a blast writing them, and there's only one left to go now, then that's it. Arise will be complete.
If you have enjoyed the book and the series, please, please consider leaving a review or a rating, they make a massive difference to us. Not least in letting us know that you're still there and enjoying the story!
Amazon tends to share and promote books that receive a lot of reviews over others, so please always try and leave a review for a story you like, not just mine, but *any* story, and I promise you it'll make a massive difference to the genre.
Thank you.

-Jez
25/04/2024

Patreon!

Okay then, now for those of you that don't know about Patreon, its essentially a way to support your favorite nutcases, you can sign up for a day or a month or a year, and you get various benefits for it, ranging from my heartfelt thanks, to advance access to the books, to me sending them books, naming characters and more.

At the time of me writing this, the advanced Patreon readers are halfway through Arise 6: Conqueror.

By the time this launches? I *think* they'll be finished with that and on Book 6 of the Rise of Mankind Series; Age of Glass so if you want to read it perhaps months ahead of release? Come join us!

There's two of my wonderful supporters out there that I have to thank personally as well; ASeaInStorm and Mischa Dolfing thank you both!

https://www.patreon.com/Jezcajiao

Arise 6: Conqueror

By Jez Cajiao

Forgotten races, ancient secrets and the final truths of the great wars…

After being ripped from everything he knew, Steve drifts amongst the shattered remains of dead worlds and civilizations. The vast grave of the ages threatens to consume him as he faces an impossible choice - evolve beyond his limits, or be lost amongst the ruins, like all the other failures.

The node is under attack. Meanwhile, on all sides the enemy is bearing down, ready to tear their hard won prize free. If Steve is going to eke out a chance at survival, he's going to have to fight his way home. Not only that, when he gets there, he's going to have to deal with the Ændari's greatest secret.

It's time to remind the rest of the universe that humanity isn't prey… we're the predator.

https://mybook.to/AriseConqueror

<u>Quest Academy</u>

By Brian J. Nordon

A world infested by demons.
An Academy designed to train Heroes to save humanity from annihilation.
A new student's power could make all the difference.

Humans have been pushed to the brink of extinction by an ever-evolving demonic threat. Portals are opening faster than ever, Towers bursting into the skies and Dungeons being mined below the last safe havens of society. The demons are winning.

Quest Academy stands defiantly against them, as a place to train the next generation of Heroes. The Guild Association is holding the line, but are in dire need of new blood and the powerful abilities they could bring to the battlefront. To be the saviors that humanity needs, they need to surpass the limits of those that came before them.

In a war with everything on the line, every power matters. With an adaptive enemy, comes the need for a constant shift in tactics. A new age of strategy is emerging, with even the unlikeliest of Heroes making an impact.

Salvatore Argento has never seen a demon.
He has never aspired to become a Hero.
Yet his power might be the one to tip the odds in humanity's favor.

<u>**Buy on Amazon**</u>

<u>Wandering Warrior</u>

By Michael Head

A divine quest to deliver justice.
One year to accomplish his mission.
After nineteen planets, there's something different about this one.

James Holden has reached the maximum level there is for a human. That's perfect, since he's the only one of his kind. A wandering warrior, without control of his destination, tossed between universes by gods who've failed to tell him why. James is the lone Judge on a new world in need of someone to balance the scales. He isn't afraid to do so with extreme prejudice. As the Chief Justice, he has to right the wrongs the innocent can't fix themselves.

As James quickly discovers, the roots of corruption run deep. Guilds choose to protect themselves rather than the people. Monsters roam the wilderness unchecked. Judgment is usually a decision between right and wrong, but nothing is ever that simple. This time, being the strongest human won't be enough to punish the guilty. James might have to recruit some new blood, even if he prefers to work alone.

On his twentieth world, he is going to win, no matter the cost. James will have to find a way to break past the limits of the system if he's going to have a chance at making a difference.

<u>Buy on Amazon</u>

<u>Knights of Eternity</u>

555

By Rachel Ní Chuirc

When Zara awoke in chains she thought she'd gone mad.

She was Zara the Fury - mistress of flame and fear. Her name was whispered across the land, from ramshackle taverns to the royal court. Even the heroic Gilded Knights thought twice before crossing her path.
She was feared—*respected.*
Now she was curled up on a dirt floor on her fiancé's orders. Valerius, leader of the Gilded, mocks her cries for help. And the kingdom is on the brink of war over the missing Lady Eternity…
But that wasn't why Zara thought she had gone mad.
The reason why is that the last thing she remembered was blood, an arcade screen, and the gun that changed everything.

**But no chains can hold the Fury, and when she gets out?
The world is going to *burn.***

<u>Buy on Amazon</u>

<u>Scarlet Citadel</u>

By Jack Fields

Gormon Hughes is 19, thin as a broom, and has—not for the first time in his life—been swept into the path of trouble. Poor, recently heartbroken, and indebted to the sort of people who file their teeth into needle points and devour wriggling bloated spiders for fun, Hughes sets his sights on salvation.

That salvation is the Scarlet Citadel, a wealthy organization of pageant fighters, monster hunters, and secret keepers. With the aid of strange oracles, rare good fortune, and a unique power that bubbles like champagne in the core of Hughes' being, he must join the Citadel and advance himself.

But the ladder of progression is harsh and dark. The rungs are slippery.

And falling means disaster…

Facebook and Social Media

If you want to reach out, chat or shoot the shit, you can always find me on either my author page here:

www.facebook.com/JezCajiaoAuthor

OR

We've recently set up a new Facebook group to spread the word about cool LitRPG books. It's dedicated to two very simple rules;

1: Let's spread the word about new and old brilliant LitRPG books.
2: Don't be a Dick!

They sound like really simple rules, but you'd be amazed…

Come join us!

https://www.facebook.com/groups/LITRPGLegion

I'm also on Discord here: **https://discord.gg/u5JYHscCEH**

Or I'm reaching out on other forms of social media atm, I'm just spread a little thin that's all!

You're most likely to find me on Discord, but please, don't be offended when I don't approve friend requests on my personal Facebook pages. I did originally, and several people abused that, sending messages to my family and being generally unpleasant, hence, the author page:

www.facebook.com/JezCajiaoAuthor

I hope you understand.

<u>Legion</u>

Okay everybody, if you've not yet seen or heard, well, the secret is out! My wife Chrissy, and our friend Geneva and I have launched the Legion Publishers! We're taking on new authors, as well as experienced ones, focusing primarily on the LitRPG side of things, but we're open to anything really, with one very clear rule that guides our company:

Don't be a dick.

That's it. Our contracts aren't hidden behind layers of legalese, you can find them here:

https://www.legionpublishers.com/legioncontract

If you want to reach out and ask any questions, get an idea of the support we offer, and possibly become part of the family? We'd love to hear from you, just tap the link and fill in the form:

https://www.legionpublishers.com/contact-and-submissions

Hope you're having a good one!

-Jez, Chrissy and Geneva

<u>Recommendations</u>

I'm often asked for personal recommendations, so if this book has whetted your appetite for more LitRPG, please have a look at the following, these are brilliant series by brilliant authors!

The Ten Realms by Michael Chatfield

The Land by Aleron Kong

Challengers Call by Nathan A. Thompson

Quest Academy by Brian J. Nordon

Wandering Warrior by Michael Head

Endless Online by M H Johnson

The Good Guys/Bad Guys by Eric Ugland

God of the Feast by Kevin Sinclair

The Wayward Bard by Lars Machmüller

<u>LITRPG!</u>

To learn more about LitRPG, talk to other authors including myself, and to just have an awesome time, please join the LitRPG Group

www.facebook.com/groups/LitRPGGroup

Facebook

There's also a few really active Facebook groups I'd recommend you join, as you'll get to hear about great new books, new releases and interact with all your (new) favorite authors! (I may also be there, skulking at the back and enjoying the memes…)

https://www.facebook.com/groups/LitRPGlegion/

https://www.facebook.com/groups/GamelitSociety

https://www.facebook.com/groups/LitRPG.books

https://www.facebook.com/groups/LitRPGforum/